Save

My

Soul

K. S. HAIGWOOD

Save My Soul
By K. S. Haigwood

Published by K. S. Haigwood

Copyright © 2012 by K.S. Haigwood

For Riley: May your dreams always come true. I love you.

Acknowledgements:

With immense gratitude to Riley, my daughter, who gives me the inspiration and imagination I need for my books in every minute of every day. To my readers, never forget you are the reason I write. I couldn't do this without you. To Ella, my editor, friend for all needs, and chosen sister; there aren't enough good words in the dictionary or enough time in my life to explain my gratitude. To Patti, my cover designer, book trailer designer and my friend, it's amazing how you can make a cover exactly how I envision it. To Ella and Patti, that big pond will not keep me away forever. To all my writer friends, you know who you are; a writer is truly the only one who can understand another writer. Thank you so much for your encouragement and guidance in this extremely scary, but amazing self-publishing world. Every bit of advice was noted and appreciated. You made it easy for me. To my sisters, Stacey and Penny, growing up was an adventure and you both molded me into what I've become today. Thank you for the love, and the encouragement you gave me to keep following my dreams until I found them. To my Momma and Daddy, thank you for teaching me that if I want something bad enough I have to go out and get it myself, that something deserved is something earned. I would like to thank the voices. You all have taught me so much over the past two years. I know at times it gets crowded in my head, but you all know you will get a turn to tell your story. I'm in this for the long haul. And last, but certainly not least, I would like to thank God, my writing and all the things I'm grateful for in my life I'm sure I would not have if I didn't follow you and accept you as my savior. Thank you for my gift. I shall not waste it.

Chapter One

"We're losing her, Dr. Chamberlain!"

I could hear a faint beeping but could not, for the life of me, figure out what I was supposed to do. It seemed like I was supposed to do something, at least try to do something. I didn't know why I was here, or even where *here* was for that matter. Moreover, why was there a woman telling a doctor that they were losing someone. It couldn't be me...could it?

"Shit! Come on, Kendra. You are not dying on my operating table," a male voice said, clearly ignoring the woman. It was a deep voice, a rather nice voice actually. Evidently, the very insistent doctor, who was obviously trying to save my life, had no plans of letting me meet my maker anytime soon.

There wasn't any pain. It was as if I was dreaming and could only hear the noises around me. I couldn't see anything except darkness, but still didn't know what I needed to do.

I tried to open my eyes, but it was as if my eyelids had been sewn shut. They were so heavy, and just the thought of prying them apart was too exhausting to consider. What the hell was going on? What had happened to me?

The woman, apparently a nurse or another assisting doctor, spoke again. "I can't get her to stabilize doctor; she has too many injuries. She is bleeding from every appendage of her body, and there is no telling how much blood she lost before the ambulance brought her in. If we don't get the wounds closed soon, she's going to bleed out and we will lose her."

I heard a loud noise as if a heavy object had slammed into a wall. I jumped. Well, I'm sure my body didn't move, but it scared the hell out of me nonetheless. The doctor spoke again in a rather unkind tone of voice. I had a hunch he was the culprit who had thrown the object. "Just do your damn job, Sherri! It isn't your call whether she dies or not. It's mine!" I could just imagine him pointing at his chest with an angry scowl on his face. "Do what you were trained to do, or get the fuck out of my O.R.!" I was guessing that it would be God who made the decision if I died on the doctor's table, but if Dr. Chamberlain wanted to play the part, I would let him if it meant I could open my eyes again.

"Yes, Doctor," Sherri whispered, then evidently went back to work on fixing my injuries, because she didn't say anything after that, and he didn't tell her to leave again.

I heard soft beeps. I presumed it was coming from the heart monitoring machine. Then the sound suddenly changed from beeps to one continuous drone. From watching years and years of hospital series and movies on television, I realized exactly what path I was heading down. It looked as though the determined doctor wasn't going to get a say about it.

Flatline.

I felt strangely calm at the realization that I was dying, and that bothered me a little. I mean, shouldn't I be panicking or something? What confused me the most was that I was still here, still hanging out in my body. Shouldn't I be walking toward a bright, white light right about now? There was nothing. I was stuck in complete darkness, listening to the people around me try to bring me back.

"Give me the damn defibrillator. Turn it to one-twenty. Shoot her up with atropine. Mason, get in here and fix these bleeders. Sherri, get the hell out of the way!" He was barking orders at the staff, and from the sound of small metal instruments, they were doing whatever the hell he was telling them to do.

"Adam, I was fixing…" Sherri pleaded, but he didn't let her finish the thought, let alone get the words out of her mouth.

"It wasn't a request. Get the hell out of my operating room, and if you ever address me by my first name while we are on the clock, it will be the last time you scrub in with me. Get out!" I heard a door open then close gently, but none of the other nurses had stopped working on me throughout the whole shouting match. Well, it wasn't exactly a shouting match; "Adam" was doing all the shouting. It seemed to me that there may be something a little more personal than work going on between Sherri and the doctor.

"Clear…" another voice said, and I heard my body jerk on the operating table. Eerie, but true, don't ask me to explain it; I've only been dead once. It was really troubling me that I couldn't see or feel anything. At least one of my senses had not been taken away from me yet. I could hear just fine, but the rest of my senses were…pretty much nonexistent. I couldn't even smell, not that I wanted to. I hadn't ever been in an operating room but I was sure the room smelled sterile and of iodine, with that faint hint of old and new blood, that metallic coppery smell that you never seem to forget exactly what it is.

I could only imagine what I looked like. And again the question, "What the hell had happened to me?" I couldn't remember what I'd been doing all day, or even last week for that matter.

I heard a single beep, and then another before I flat lined again.

"Damn it! Shit!" I heard Adam take a deep breath in then let it out slowly. "Again…do it again at one-eighty. I'm not going to lose her. Debbie, call up and get another bag of blood, no…make that two, AB Negative, STAT! And get more fluids."

"Yes, Doctor." I could tell by the urgency in Debbie's voice that she was not about to question Dr. Adam.

"Clear…" Again I heard my body jerk then settle back on the table with a thump.

Beep…........Beep…Beep…........Beep…Beep…Beep…Beep…Beep

"You got her back, doc," Mason said.

I could hear more shuffling around, more metal instruments being used on my body, but the most important noise I heard was the sigh of relief from Dr. Adam Chamberlain. I swear I could feel the tension leaving his shoulders as I heard him pull the gloves from his hands. I heard a faint sound of metal squeaking and assumed he was throwing his used gloves in a hazardous material waste container.

"Did you find all the bleeders, Mason?" the doctor asked.

"Sure did, doc." I could hear the smile in his voice from where I was laid out on the table.

"Get her sewed up nice and pretty for me. Put her on I.V. antibiotics. Give her the blood and fluids, and have a nurse, not an aid, a nurse, sit in the room with her. If they have to piss, they better have a relief. She's not to be left alone for even a minute. Do you understand?"

I didn't hear an answer from Mason, so I guess he nodded in agreement with the doctor, because I didn't hear any yelling either.

"Keep her on the ventilator until I say otherwise. I'll check on her in a bit." I heard the door softly open then close. Adam was gone, and for some reason I felt lonely.

I was happy I guess, but something still didn't feel right with my newly righted body. I still couldn't feel anything, or smell, or open my eyes. I'm sure they had given me some powerful shit to anesthetize me so I wouldn't wake up, but I was awake...sort of.

The speed of the beeping began to rapidly increase, and I could hear something that sounded like flapping, or loud thumping.

"Shit, she's seizing. Get Dr. Chamberlain back in here. STAT!" I heard the door open then a woman shouted down the hall. I couldn't see or feel what Mason was doing to me, but I knew he was close to my face. I could hear his frantic breathing and whispered curses.

What was so ironic was that I hadn't prayed yet. I guessed I needed to, but I wasn't worried for some reason. I didn't know if I was in shock or if I was actually this calm. Maybe it was because I was somehow sure that Dr. Adam Chamberlain would be my savior. Or would he be? I was almost positive the words seizure and stabilized wouldn't be written side-by-side on my chart. Something was definitely wrong again.

I heard the door quickly open and then fresh gloves being snapped into place on wrists. "What have we got?" the doctor said, and he was a lot closer than I thought he would be. His voice was so close that I knew I would be able to smell his aftershave or cologne if my sense of smell hadn't flown the coop. I had the strongest urge to inhale the scent of him, but after trying, I realized it wasn't possible.

One thing was for sure, I didn't feel alone with him so near.

"I don't get it..." Mason said, with a little confusion in his voice. "Five seconds after you walked out, her vitals went crazy, and she started seizing. Then you come back in and speak, and everything goes back to normal, as if nothing ever happened. Hell, her vitals are better than mine right now. You're a god, man."

"You're joking, right? Mason, I have nine hours left of my shift, and I haven't slept in over twenty-two hours. I really don't think God would put himself in my shoes. Besides, he's only a figment of everyone's imagination, something someone made up to explain why we are all here. No one really knows why we're here. And no, I don't think she started seizing because I walked out, then stopped when I came back in and spoke aloud to you." I was a little disappointed to learn this tidbit of information about my doctor, but I wouldn't be the one to judge him come judgment day, so he wasn't my problem. I only needed him to patch me up.

"I swear, Adam," he lowered his voice a little. "She was seizing when you walked through the door, and she stopped the second you spoke."

Adam sighed. "Does she have a history of epilepsy or seizers?"

"Nope," I could hear the grin in Mason's voice. He was really enjoying the hell out of this. "She gets annual check-ups, and she is hardly ever sick, sick enough to see a doctor, anyway. She may not have gone to a doctor for the stomach bug or snotty nose, but there's nothing in her medical record about epilepsy or any other conditions."

I was nodding to myself, and to no one else evidently, about everything Mason was saying about my medical history. I was actually getting a little bored with their small talk about me. I'm not epileptic; move on to the next thing. There was no way my body reacted that way just because he had walked out of the room. Mason was crazy to even think that. I am a very independent woman with a strong career and extreme hobbies. I have a friend with benefits but never really let myself get too attached to men. I don't have time for a person in my life with issues, and all men seem to have issues.

"Fine," Adam sighed. "Has anyone been able to locate a friend or relative of hers? I can go down and let them know that she is stable for now and that we will have someone with her the whole time she is in S.I.C.U." It sounded as if he blew air out through puffed out cheeks. "I can't believe she fell to the bottom of Dead Man's Cliff, and is alive with no fractures. I know she was wearing the little helmet that almost no one uses while rappelling, but I never dreamed they would be so effective from such a serious height."

So, that's what I'd been doing. The events of the day slammed into my frontal lobe, but I was still lacking the memory of the accident.

"A few guys and another girl were asking about her earlier. They had blood all over them, and looked to be dressed like our famous daredevil here. It hasn't been that long ago, they may still be here."

The door opened again, then something that sounded like a gurney, or a bed on wheels, was placed to the right side of my body. A short moment later I heard Mason, "On three. One…Two…Three"

"You got it this time, Mase?" Adam said with laughter in his voice. He had such a good laugh. I hated that he was leaving me here with the nurses, but if I really had the episode a few minutes earlier because I missed him, then I had to try extra hard to keep my emotions in check.

Chapter Two

I could hear the wheels squeaking beneath me as I was being transported from the O.R. to the recovery room. I could even hear the blood and fluid bags that were swinging above my head and to the left a little. It is amazing how well your hearing increases when you lose all of your other senses.

The noises stopped, and I had come to the conclusion that I was in recovery. My assumption was confirmed when a whistling nurse walked near to me. The whistling abruptly stopped. "She lived?"

Mason chuckled. "Dr. Chamberlain operated on her, of course she lived. He hasn't lost a patient yet. He wanted her to stay here in recovery until she wakes up, then we'll move her to S.I.C.U. He said that she has to have someone with her every second. You want the job?"

"Hell no. I don't want to sit and stare at a half dead girl my whole shift."

He laughed again. "You couldn't do it anyway. He said it couldn't be an aide."

The girl laughed a little. "If it could be an aide, you know that he would force me to do it. You know he doesn't like me."

He chuckled. "Adam doesn't like anybody. You know that."

"Well, he doesn't seem to have a problem with you. But then again, it is kind of difficult to dislike someone that looks as good as you do in scrubs. See you around, Mase."

It sounded to me like there was a little flirting in her tone, but who was I to judge? Maybe she liked Mason, and just maybe he liked her back.

"You won't if I can help it," Mason muttered. Evidently the girl was gone, but maybe still in hearing range, because it was almost a whisper. Maybe he didn't like her.

"I'm going to be right here beside you until you wake up, Kendra. And I'm gonna need for you to wake up pretty soon, because I have a date in two hours." I heard buttons snapping beside my left ear, and figured whoever had dressed me in a hospital gown hadn't taken the time to finish dressing me. "There you go." I heard him yawn, and then heard buttons being pushed on a machine, probably my blood, fluid and antibiotics, then the low hum of a blood pressure machine. I couldn't feel it on my arm, but I was sure my blood pressure was being taken.

"Your vitals are good. There is nothing wrong with you but the obvious, so you need to wake up now." I heard Mason sit in a chair to the left side of my bed. He yawned again.

I really would wake up if I could. I had been trying to get control of my body for the last hour. I wondered if I was in a coma, and if this was how comatose patients felt, like they're trapped in an empty shell with nothing but their hearing. It was maddening.

After a short time, I could hear soft snoring coming from Mason, and I wondered how pissed my doctor would be if he walked around the corner and caught him napping when he was supposed to be watching me. The doctor seemed pretty insistent that I be watched carefully.

Well, alone with only my thoughts again.

"You aren't alone, Kendra."

I jumped. Well, my body didn't; I couldn't move, remember? There was a voice in my head that wasn't mine. It was a man's voice.

"Who's there?" I said back to the voice. Great, now I was talking back to the voices in my head. Who is crazy now? It was worth a shot; I needed some answers.

The man laughed.

Another man's voice in my head said, *"Don't freak her out, Coen.*

She's probably scared to death as it is." Yeah, freaked out was one of the things I was beginning to be. I'd always wondered what went on in the mind of a schizophrenic, but I didn't actually want to become one to find out. Great, I was crazy.

"*There is no way to not freak her out about this, Rhyan,*" voice one said. I had names for the personalities in my head, and they were both men, so they were going to have issues. This was just fan-freaking-tastic.

"*Maybe if you just introduced us instead of making her think she has gone crazy...*"

"*Guys, guys, I'm right here, and crazy isn't the worst thing that has happened to me today.*" I guess if I was going to talk to the voices in my head, they could keep me company until Dr. Adam caught Mason sleeping. Even I was looking forward to hearing him get chewed out. But it was mainly because I wanted to hear the doctor's voice again.

What was wrong with me? I had never in my life obsessed or ogled over a guy before, and I didn't like doing it now.

"*Yes, we know about your unfortunate accident; that's why we're here. We came to get you,*" Coen said.

I couldn't have heard him right. I was going to need a little more explanation than that. "*I'm sorry. I don't think I understand what you are saying. Where, exactly, will you be taking me?*" I so did not want to hear the answer, but I wasn't sure I was going to get a choice. I was almost positive that I couldn't make them leave.

"*We're here to take you to heaven, Kendra,*" Rhyan said.

I was beginning to like Rhyan less and less. "*No, I don't think so. You see, Dr. Chamberlain fixed me and I'm all better now. They're just waiting for me to wake up. Then I will heal and go home. Back to my job. Back to my dog, Hercules. Back to my life.*" The thought of my miniature Chihuahua at home made me want to cry. Who was going to take care of him if I let Rhyan and Coen take me? I couldn't let them. I had too much left to do with my life. Hell, I was only twenty-nine and hadn't even considered marriage yet. I didn't have any children yet, wasn't sure I wanted any, but I wanted the option.

"The thing is, Kendra, you aren't going to wake up," Rhyan said.

"Well, there is one way..." Coen said.

"No, Coen, I was sent here to get her, and she is going back with me," Rhyan said.

I spoke only to Coen. I didn't like how Rhyan was so definite, but Coen clearly had another option. I wanted to hear it. *"What? Tell me, Coen. What can I do to stay here? What can I do to live again?"*

Rhyan tried to speak again, but somehow Coen muted his voice so I could barely hear him shouting at me.

"I have been Adam Chamberlain's guardian angel for the last thirty-two years. Rhyan has been yours. You have listened to Rhyan, or your conscience, should I say, in your twenty-nine years here on Earth. Adam has a lost soul. He is a disbeliever and I need someone's assistance to help him find his way back to the good side. I was the reason you could hear in the operating room. I wanted you to understand what a God complex our young Adam has before you made the decision to take or reject my offer. If you can help me, I promise you will have your life back."

I was quiet for a few moments. I didn't know what to say, but I knew I had to try. *"What do I have to do?"* I couldn't see Coen, but I could have sworn he was smiling.

"I can only give you until next Friday, Kendra, but I have faith in you. You have a very kind heart, and a competitive mind. It's simple; all you have to do is lead him in the right direction."

"Which direction is that?" I asked.

"He has to believe in God, Kendra. We are not allowed to mess with free will, and his mind is so closed off that he no longer hears me. I only have one week to get him on the right path before they give me to someone else. Adam will no longer have a conscience. No one to tell him what is right, or what is wrong. He will truly be lost then."

"How do I do that, Coen? I was raised believing there is a God and that I am saved. How do you make someone believe, who has never believed?" I could hear him smiling again. I didn't know how I was able to sense his emotions, but I could. I wasn't going to question it further.

"Oh, he has believed before, Kendra. The thing about a conscience is that it's split in two halves; the good and the bad. I'm the good half, and I must warn you now, you will meet the bad half before your week is up. He has a lot more influence over Adam than I do. I would say Murry has about ninety percent to my ten percent. It will be hard, but if you want to live, I know you can do it and save the both of you."

"But how..." I knew my mind's voice cracked, because for the first time in a long time, I felt helpless.

"Perhaps the young doctor needs to remember how it feels to love again."

Chapter Three

I opened my eyes to no pain at all. I could feel my body, but I didn't hurt anywhere. Let's hear it for miracles! I didn't know how Coen had done it, but I was definitely going to give him a big kiss when I met him for real. There was an oxygen mask on my face and an I.V. in my left arm. I had little round white patches on my chest and back, and something was clipped onto my right index finger. You would think by looking at me that I was dying or something.

I took the mask off and sat up. I looked to my left and saw that drool was dripping out of Mason's mouth. His head was bent in an awkward position. How could anybody sleep like that?

I knew one way to get him on his feet. I slipped my finger out of the plastic device, and the machine went from beeping steadily to flatline. Just as I had thought, he jumped to his feet before his eyes were even fully open.

He stared at me as if I had an extra nose.

This was fun. I wondered momentarily how the doctor would react the first time he saw me awake.

"Hi, Mason," I said cheerfully, then looked down at the I.V. still stuck in my arm. "Will you help me take off these sticky things? I could really use a shower. I'm still all dirty from the accident."

Mason rubbed his face frantically with both his hands, then ran them through his semi-short brown hair. He had very pretty smoky blue, almost gray, eyes. I could tell immediately why the nurse's aide had been interested.

"Are you just going to stare at me, or help me take this stuff off?" I asked as I yanked off two of the little white patches, simultaneously. It hurt, but then again, I figured it would. I started to grab two more, but he grabbed my hands and shook his head without taking his wide eyes away from mine. He hit a few buttons on the heart monitoring machine, and the solid beep went silent.

"Stop..." he said, as if there wasn't another word in his vocabulary.

I turned my head to the side and smiled up at him.

"You died...twice. You should be in pain. You shouldn't even be off the ventilator yet, but I went on instinct that you didn't need it. You do, however, need oxygen and blood and antibiotics." He was talking like he was trying to convince himself more than he was me.

I nodded in agreement so he wouldn't think he had gone crazy. There needed to be only one crazy person in this room, and that was yours truly. "Yes, Mason, but as you can see, I am already healed."

He looked away from my face for the first time to look at my arms. There were no scars, or even any scratches for that matter. His eyes grew wider, and he slowly backed away from me.

"How? I sewed you up myself. You should still have stitches." He rubbed his eyes again. "I'm still asleep, I have to be."

I was getting absolutely nowhere with him, and I suddenly didn't want to know how Dr. Chamberlain would react to my miracle recovery. He was good, but he wasn't that good. I just hoped he knew that, or my shoes were bigger than I was going to be able to fill. I ripped two more of the sticky things off my chest and watched Mason as he picked up the phone without taking his eyes from me.

"Dr. Chamberlain to recovery, STAT...Dr. Chamberlain to recovery, STAT."

I finished ripping the little stickers off my chest and then began to work on the tape around my I.V.

"Look, you have got to stop. At least wait for Dr. Chamberlain to get here. I'll get in trouble if I let you do all this." His eyes were pleading with me, and I felt bad that he didn't understand, so I stopped trying to remove the I.V. needle from my arm. "How do you know my name? I forgot my name badge this morning, and I'm sure I haven't met you before." He smiled, sheepishly. "I think I would have remembered."

I thought for a moment, and then decided the truth would set everything straight. "Well, you may need to sit back down, and if I'm going to tell you the truth, you have to promise to try and understand. Otherwise, I will tell Adam that you fell asleep while you were supposed to be watching me." I gave him my most serious face, and I guess it worked, because he sat in the chair to the left of me, the one he'd been sleeping in.

"I promise to try and understand," he choked out.

I heard a loud bang, and both our gazes shot to the recovery room door where a man ran in with five nurses close at his back. They looked like a S.W.A.T. team in scrubs, ready to take down anything in their path. The man in front was wearing navy blue scrubs; they fit him a little too well. He was about five-ten with broad shoulders that had, "I hit the gym regularly" written all over them. He wasn't too muscular, but he was clearly in shape. Every inch of him was lean and defined. I had to focus on my breathing. He had black hair, cut neat, with eyes so dark brown I wouldn't have been able to swear if they were dark brown or black. I could see the coldness in his eyes, and knew then what Coen had put me up against. This was my doctor, our Adam that I had to fix, or I died again in a week and he could possibly lose his soul forever.

His eyes widened in amazement, and his lips parted ever so slightly. I had a strange urge to touch those lips with my own. I shook my head to clear the thought then smiled at him. "Hello, Adam." His lips opened a little more as if he were about to speak, or maybe he was in shock. Then he closed his mouth and just stared at me.

"Kendra was just about to explain how she is already healed, and also how she knows who we are," Mason said nervously.

Dr. Chamberlain licked his lips uneasily as he stared at me. "She was, was she?" His voice was just like I remembered it. It may have had a little nervous quiver, but it was still beautiful to me.

I nodded at him, glanced at the nurses, then moved my gaze back to meet those dark eyes of his again. "If you don't mind, Adam, I would really like to get the rest of this stuff off me and take a shower. Then we can talk more about this in private. I would prefer only you, but I told Mason I would try to explain, and I will keep my word. So, only you and Mason if you don't mind."

Adam stood there and finally blinked at me. He turned to the nurse on his left. "Debbie, will you please help Ms. Larkin to a shower and help her get cleaned up." Mason began to unravel the tape around the I.V., and the petite older woman to Adam's left came to my right side and began removing the sticky patches from my back.

When everything was removed from my body except for my hospital gown, Mason rolled a wheel chair to my bed. I just looked at it and raised an eyebrow at him. I threw the sheet off my legs and set my feet on the floor. Everyone looked on edge, as if they would all jump to catch me if I fell.

Mason took my left arm and looked at me. "I know you think you can do it, but until I hear how this is all possible, let me escort you for my benefit."

I nodded as I smiled up at him. He wasn't that much taller than me. He had me beat by a few inches maybe, and I was five-six. Mason was handsome in a high school baseball guy sort of way. You knew he played sports by the way his upper body was built, and by the way he walked and stood. He still looked like a kid to me, but I was twenty-nine, so a kid to me was twenty-eight and under.

I looked at Adam. He was still in shock, and I didn't think he looked like a kid at all. If I ever swooned, I would have been swooning right then. I wanted it to be him escorting me to the shower so I could catch a whiff of the cologne or aftershave he was wearing to see if it smelled as good as my imagination had let on earlier, but he had only blinked once that I had noticed. I had better let Mason, or I may be the one holding up the good doctor, instead of the other way around.

"I'm going to need clothes," I whispered to Mason as we walked toward the double doors of the recovery room. I was a little embarrassed asking him for such things, but it wasn't as if I had planned to go pin wheeling down a rocky cliff face, landing myself in the trauma center.

He laughed a little then looked behind him at the other gawkers. "Any of you ladies have a change of clothes you are willing to part with for a little while?"

A very pretty nurse with short brown hair stepped up. The look on her face wasn't of amazement or shock like the others. She looked upset about something, and I could tell she was trying to hide it behind that fake smile of hers. "I'm about the only one close to your size. Follow me to the women's locker room, and I'll give you what I have."

I noticed the voice instantly. It was Sherri, the girl Adam had shouted at and kicked out of his operating room. I nodded in agreement then Mason and I followed her through the door.

"Bring her to my office when she's finished with her shower, Mason," Adam said from behind us. I had to turn and look at him. The urge was too strong not to. Yep, he was still perfect with that confused look on his face and that cold look in his eyes. I took a quick mental picture so I could compare it to the one I would take after I took that coldness out of his eyes. I had one week, one week to make him believe in God. God help me.

Chapter Four

Sherri handed me a pair of black scrubs from her locker. "I don't have an extra pair of panties, and I'm sure my extra bra wouldn't fit you." She looked at my chest and I looked at hers. She couldn't have been any bigger than a "B cup" and I was a solid "D." I could go without any panties, but I very much disliked going without a bra.

I smiled. "Was my bra totally ruined in the accident?"

She nodded without looking at me. "Adam, I mean, Dr. Chamberlain, cut it off you before the operation began." She seemed to look at me for the first time, and realization crossed through her eyes. "You don't have a scratch on you." She absentmindedly ran her fingers down my arm. I didn't pull back. It wasn't like she was coming on to me or anything, but for the first time, I saw amazement in her light brown eyes. "You aren't going to tell us how this happened, are you?"

I nodded, a little embarrassed that Adam had seen me naked. "I will tell Adam and Mason, but I don't expect them to believe me. Hell, I wouldn't believe it if it hadn't personally happened to me. I'm not a freak or some immortal creature that can magically heal my wounds by wishing it so. Stuff like this just doesn't happen." I lowered my gaze from her eyes and looked at my bare, unpolished toenails. "It was just a miracle, I guess."

She was silent for only a moment before she spoke again. "The showers are through there. We all keep it stocked with the items you will need to get clean. Help yourself. I'll be out in the hall with Mason. You look capable of washing your own body." I could tell she was irritated with me for not sharing the reason for my rapid recovery, but I didn't want everyone to know. It was truly a miracle what Coen had done, and I didn't want to be caught up in the lights of camera crews for the next week. I had a mission to complete.

As I walked away from her to the showers, I heard the door open and close behind me. The shower room was large and didn't have stalls. That was fine, I was alone. There were ten shower heads, four on the left, four on the right, and two on the narrower wall in front of me. I laid my scrubs on a dry bench outside of the shower room and went to the nearest shower head that was stocked with shampoo, conditioner and body wash. I took the hospital gown off and let it fall to the floor before I stepped up and turned the spray on. The water pressure was perfect. I stood for a moment with my eyes closed, soaking in all the heat from the water.

How was I supposed to make someone believe in God? Coen said that Adam had believed before. What had happened to change his mind? I didn't know, and I wasn't going to find out until I talked to him face-to-face. I quickly washed my hair and body then used one of the white towels I found folded on the bench to dry off.

I dressed quickly and wrapped my long, dark brown hair in the towel I had used to dry my body. I walked barefoot to the door and opened it to about twenty people standing in the hall. Mason moved swiftly to me, put his arm around my shoulder and pushed through the crowd of onlookers. There were shouts from a few of the nurses, but I was too stunned to understand what they were saying.

Mason got me in an elevator and hit the fourth floor button. He sighed and rubbed his eyes again as he leaned back against the elevator wall.

"I thought you had a date?" I said.

He slowly opened his eyes and looked at me like I was crazy. "What are you?"

I smiled. "I'm just a girl who's getting a second chance."

The elevator dinged, letting us know we had arrived at our

destination. The doors opened and Mason walked out without waiting on me. I followed him. We didn't have to go far. A brown and white nameplate by the third door on the right read, "Dr. Adam Chamberlain, M.D." Mason walked in, and I followed. He shut the door behind me and locked it. I turned around, giving him a confused look.

He shrugged. "It's for your safety. You're building up quite a fan base here at the hospital and they all want to know how you healed so quickly."

I nodded at him then looked back at the desk. Adam was sitting behind it with his face in his hands and his elbows propped on the solid wood. There wasn't any one particular thing that made him handsome. He had a nice body, nice eyes, nice hair, and a nice symmetrical shape to his face, but nothing stood out and screamed beautiful. Everything that was nice about his body worked together to make him beautiful.

He removed his hands from his face and motioned for me to sit in one of the two chairs in front of his desk. I did, and Mason took the other. I was suddenly aware that I wasn't wearing a bra, so I crossed my arms over my chest.

Adam sighed. "Where would you like to begin, Ms. Larkin?"

"Call me Kendra, please."

He nodded once. "Fine…Where would you like to begin, Kendra?"

I took in a deep breath and let it out slowly. "I could hear you talking the whole time you were operating on me."

Adam and Mason both sat up a little straighter in their chairs. "You are telling me that you heard everything that happened in the operating room? Could you feel anything?"

I shook my head and lowered my gaze. "No, I couldn't feel or see anything." I waited a moment then continued. "I heard you arguing with Sherri. I heard when I died…twice, and how persistent you were to save my life. I heard Mason, and other nurses, trying to stop me from bleeding to death. I remember hearing my body flap against the table when I was seizing. I heard you and Mason talking about my medical history, and then he sewed me up and took me to recovery." I glanced at Mason. I wouldn't get him in trouble by telling Adam that he fell asleep in recovery. That would just be mean.

"Wait…you are telling me that you heard everything, even when you flatlined?" Adam said.

"Yes, I, uh, was still in my body and could hear everything, even when I was…dead." I took in a breath and let it out. I could feel a lump in my throat, and my eyes were burning as if I were about to cry. I was alive, what did I have to cry about?

"How?" Adam and Mason both said together.

I didn't know whether to tell him the truth now, or a little at a time over the next seven days. I thought it better to wait a while. I needed answers from him myself. "May I ask you a personal question?"

Adam looked at Mason, then back to me. "I may or may not answer it, but you can ask whatever you like, Kendra."

I smiled at him and he smiled back. He had beautiful teeth, very white and straight. I wondered briefly if he had ever had braces on those pearly whites; I'd needed them when I was younger. "What happened in your life that made you stop believing there's a God?"

Adam lost his smile and stared at me for a moment as though I had just lost every marble I'd ever possessed, then he shook his head slowly. "That's a little too personal, Ms. Larkin. I don't see how answering your question will lead to any answers to the questions we have about your remarkable recovery, so any questions pertaining to my private life or beliefs, are not now, or ever will be any of your concern." He looked away from me and moved a paperweight to a small stack of files on his desk. After a few moments of uncomfortable silence he finally sighed and looked back at me. "You told us that you would explain this…" he motioned to my undamaged body with his hand, "Phenomenon. I'd appreciate it if you'd get to that; I need to make my rounds."

I was getting angry. My face was turning red. I could feel the heat rushing up my neck, into my cheeks. Why did he have to be so damn difficult? He wanted personal answers from me, and I asked just one about him, and he wouldn't play fair. I jumped up, forgetting all about not having a bra on, but at the moment I didn't give a shit. I only had one week to help Coen get this jerk on the path to good. "Why should I tell you anything? You wouldn't believe me if I told you!"

He looked surprised at my outburst, or maybe it was the fact that my breasts were so very obviously unleashed, because his eyes wondered there for a moment before meeting my gaze again. "Why would you think that? I haven't acted like I didn't believe anything else you've told me. The fact that you were able to hear when you were dead is pretty farfetched, but I believe you, Kendra. Otherwise, you wouldn't have been able to tell me what happened in the operating room earlier. I don't think Mason relayed any information to you. He seems as bewildered as I am."

I'd had enough. He might have very well thought I was crazy, but how else could I explain healing this quickly? I didn't have a choice. I had to tell him the truth. "Fine...You have a guardian angel and a guardian demon. Coen is your guardian angel, and he's giving me one week to get your life on the right path. The only reason I lived today is so I can save your ass, or rather your soul. I hear you've never lost a patient."

Disbelief was written all over his face, but he responded to me without calling the psych ward for a straight jacket. "I've been a surgeon for six years without losing anyone, that's correct."

"Well, I can promise you in one week's time, if you don't change your way of thinking, you'll lose one...me." I pointed to my chest and a tear fell on my hand. I hadn't noticed that I was crying until that moment. Oh well, the damage was done. I sat back in the chair and Mason handed me a tissue.

"So, you're saying that you made a deal with my uh...guardian angel? That he's the one that healed you, and is letting you stay alive for...what was it, another week?" Adam said, but there was something in his voice and in his eyes that told me that no matter what answer I gave him, he wouldn't believe it.

I dabbed my tears with the tissue and blew my nose. "Yes," I whispered around the lump in my throat.

"It's the only possible explanation, Adam. She couldn't have healed so quickly and so thoroughly through natural processes." I'd regretted Mason being in the room while I talked to Adam until that moment. Maybe he could help me with my mission.

Adam looked dumbfounded at Mason. He rolled his eyes and sighed. "Don't tell me you're buying this bullshit."

That was it. I had to get away from Adam for a little while. I turned and started for the door.

"You can't leave, Ms. Larkin. We still have to do tests on you to make sure there is nothing physically wrong before you can be discharged. I think you need to be mentally checked out as well."

I turned and thrust my arms out where he could see them, then pointed to my face. "Does it look like there is anything wrong with me?" I looked at Mason. "How many stitches did it take to close me up, Mason?" He lowered his head. I could tell he believed me, or wanted to, but he didn't have a clue as how to help me with Dr. Chamberlain. I was beginning to like Mason more and more.

"I will sign myself out, and there isn't a damn thing you can do about it." I turned then opened the door. Mason ran after me.

"I'll make sure you don't have any trouble getting out of here," Mason said as I hit the elevator button with a shaking hand.

"Mason! Get back in here!" Adam shouted from his office, but Mason didn't turn around. The doors opened and he entered the elevator with me. Guess he wasn't too worried about losing his job.

"I believe you, Kendra. It's amazing and unbelievable, but I believe you," he said, and I broke down. He pulled me to him, wrapped his arms around me, and let me cry. He made shushing noises and rubbed my back. He didn't say it would all be all right, because he couldn't have known if it would. But he believed me. That had to count for something.

Chapter Five

The elevator doors opened to the ground floor. Mason walked me to the reception desk. "I need to sign a form that doesn't hold the hospital responsible if I leave and something goes wrong with me. I've got to get out of here." The receptionist's mouth fell open and she shot a questioning glance at Mason. He closed his eyes and nodded to her. She looked back at me with her mouth still wide open, then handed me a sheet of paper with writing on it. There was a signature line at the bottom with a date line beside it. I signed and dated the form, then handed it back to her. I started to turn and leave, but she finally spoke.

"Uh...Ms. Larkin," the receptionist said.

I turned back to her and she finished her sentence. "You have friends and family members in waiting room number three. It's the only waiting room we have that's big enough to hold them all."

I had completely forgotten that the friends who had been rappelling with me were the ones who had brought me in. They must have called my parents and half the state by now. Shit! I just wanted to go home and cuddle with Hercules. It had been a long day already and the sun was still out. I sighed. "Where's the waiting room?"

"I'll take her," Mason said, and then he grabbed my hand and began to walk away from the receptionist's desk. I pulled my hand free; he let go without turning to look back at me. I could follow him just fine. I didn't need to be attached to him.

He stopped at a door and opened it. He was standing in front of me, so I couldn't see who was in the room. There was a lot of noise, but soon everything went silent.

"Is she okay, doctor? Please, tell me my baby is okay." It was my mom's voice, and I could tell she was frantic. I started to move around Mason, but he moved so I couldn't. What the hell?

"I have good news everybody. Kendra is going to be just fine."

"Well, when can we see her?" My dad asked.

"Right now." I could hear the smile in Mason's voice. He opened the door a little wider and stepped inside so the entire room could see me. I recognized everyone, and I was surprised by the number of friends and family that had showed up. Dear God, there were a lot of people. There had to be sixty or seventy people in the semi-small room. There were people sitting on the floor and standing up against the wall. Word travels fast.

"Kendra!" My mom screamed. She hurled herself across the room and engulfed my body with her smaller, more petite, frame. I was suddenly smothered in hands and arms. Through all the chaos, I could hear Mason's light snickering. I looked and found him out in the hall. For some reason, I wanted to be out there with him instead of in this room with all my loved ones. I felt claustrophobic and I wanted to escape. I guess he could see my discomfort, because he stepped back in the room and spoke again.

"Now, let's all calm down. Kendra has been through a lot today, and I'm sure she needs a little rest."

Rest...yeah. A little rest was exactly what I needed. Like until sometime next year...if I lived that long.

Slowly, the hands and arms started to fall away from me. Thank God. I instantly felt better. I don't know what had come over me, but I needed Mason near me. It may have been because he had been by my side for the last couple of hours, but I needed to touch him in order to feel completely relaxed. I reached for him and he touched my hand. I laced my fingers with his and he drew me away from the crowd and into him. What was wrong with me?

He brushed my cheek with his hand, and I looked up at him. The touch was so tender, and tenderness was something I wasn't used to. I avoided it most of the time, but for some reason I needed him near me; I wanted his tenderness. I felt as if I would drown if he didn't keep my head above water.

I had been staring at his beautiful gray eyes. His eyes were the type that would seem to change color based on the shirt he was wearing. If he wore blue or bright colors, I was sure his eyes would appear blue. If he wore gray or dark colors, I was sure they would appear gray. He was wearing deep hunter green scrubs and his eyes were light gray with a dark blue ring around the iris. I couldn't look away from him, but I didn't want to.

"Kendra." I heard Aven's voice, and I looked toward him without pulling away from Mason's embrace. Aven was one of my best friends, and it just so happened that he had been with me this morning when I fell. He was also a friend with benefits, and for those of you who aren't up to date on the terminology, it means that we have sex with each other. We date other people, but having a friend with benefits means we don't have to sleep with the people we date, hence not adding anymore notches to our headboards, and if you don't know what that means, well…it doesn't matter anyway.

Aven dated other people and I dated other people, but I don't think either if us had ever seen the other with another person. He honestly looked hurt, or maybe he had just been worried about me, but he wasn't happy. He held out his hand and I went to him. I knew he was worried, they all had been. By avoiding them, I was acting like a selfish bitch just so I could comfort myself, and I was somehow okay with that.

I hugged him back and he kissed my forehead. He usually kissed the top of my head, but my hair was still wrapped up in a towel. I pulled back and he kissed my lips. That was crossing the line. I may be twenty-nine, but my parents were in the room, for Christ's sake. Only a couple of our friends knew how close Aven and I were, and I didn't want anyone else to know. I especially didn't want Mason to know. He was standing right where I had left him, staring at me with absolutely no expression.

I pushed against Aven's chest with my hand and backed up. I gave him the "you've gone too far" look, and he let me go. "I want to go home."

"Okay, I'll take you home," Aven said, and tried to pull me back to him.

I resisted, and he stopped smiling. "I want to go home alone, Aven."

He put his hand over his mouth then rubbed his chin. "I thought I'd lost you, Kendra. We all thought you were gone, and here you are without a scratch on you, and cuddled up with a nurse that you've never even met before today. That's not like you."

He was right. It wasn't like me, but then again, I hadn't been myself since I'd died. "Look, I'm just tired, and Mason helped save my life today." I looked at Mason. He knew the truth; Coen had saved my life, but I didn't want to tell anyone else what had happened. I didn't have the energy. "I would like to go home and get some rest. I will turn my phone back on when I get up tomorrow. I just need to be alone for a while."

My mom and dad hugged me again. "Okay, honey, we're just glad you're all right."

"I'm fine, Mom. I'm really fine." I didn't have the heart to tell her that I may be putting her through this again in a week, with no miracle to save me then. I wanted to hold her tight and never let her go, but on the other hand, I wanted to be alone, completely alone with only my dog for company.

She let me go, and I hugged each and every person in the room. My best friend, Kobhye, cried the hardest because she thought the accident was her fault.

Mason was still standing in the hall as I followed the last person out of the waiting room. I'd sent everyone on their way, promising I would turn my phone back on by nine the following morning. Aven was the hardest to get rid of. He kept insisting to give me a ride home. I knew how that would go. He would ask ten million questions then try to get in my pants, in my case, scrubs, as soon as we got to my house. I didn't want that tonight. I really wanted to be held and that was it, but Aven wasn't the type. He didn't even like to cuddle after sex. Neither did I, but that was beside the point. Hercules was a cuddler, and he was the only male I needed in my bed.

Mason and I were standing alone in the hall. "So, are you going to call a cab?" he said with a smirk.

I knew what he was doing. He'd heard me turn everyone down that had offered me a ride home, and he was the only one who offered me another option. He wanted to offer to give me a ride too, but he was going to let me choose, cab or him. "Yeah, I guess I am."

"I don't care to drop you off on my way home if you need a ride. I'm leaving now. It'll probably take the cab twenty-five minutes to get here. By then, you could already be in bed. Besides, how're you going to pay for cab fare? I doubt Sherri left any money in those," he nodded to my attire.

Damn, he had me there. I could always tell the cabbie to wait while I ran into my house to get money, but Mason was right, the cab could take a while to get here. Damn. I sighed. "I guess you're right. Are you sure you don't mind? I don't want to have to explain to anyone else what happened to me today."

He smiled a smile that made my heart skip a beat.

I really needed to figure out what I was going to do about Dr. Chamberlain, but right now all I wanted was to go home. "C'mon, Kendra, I'll take you home."

I followed him, but he led me past the front exit doors. He took note of my confusion and smiled. "The employees have a different parking lot than the visitors."

"Oh," I said, then he stopped and scanned his card through a black box on the wall.

"I had to clock out." So, that was the reason for the little black box. I didn't miss those days of punching in and out of work.

We got in a service elevator and Mason hit a button with a "G" on it. I thought we were already on the ground floor, so I assumed it must have meant garage. All I knew was that I was finally getting out of there. The door opened to a big underground garage and Mason led me to his truck. It was a nice truck, black and shiny and all chromed out. It had four-wheel drive and a tall lift kit on it. He used the keyless entry to unlock the doors, then opened up the passenger side for me. I guess he knew better than to try and help me up, or maybe he just wanted to laugh to himself as I struggled. To his amazement, I didn't have a bit of trouble. Evidently, he must have forgotten about my extreme hobbies, or maybe he just wanted to see me in action. The last thought made me giggle involuntarily, but Mason only smiled as he shut my door.

He got in on the driver's side and buckled his seatbelt. Mine was already fastened. Safety first. Although I doubted I had to worry about dying...until Friday. I had two guardian angels watching over me now.

"Where to?" Mason said as he pulled out of the garage and came to a stop at the stop sign.

"480 Oakwood Rd. It's to the west and out of town a few miles," he nodded as if going that far out of his way didn't bother him at all. I was guessing it was out of his way, he may very well have lived out west also.

We rode for a while. I was daydreaming and trying to come up with a solution to my problem when I remembered one of Mason's. "I thought you had a date tonight."

He smiled so big that I thought it was going to split his face in two halves.

"What?" I said.

"I never had a date." When I still looked confused, he continued, "Brittney, the little nurse's aide, was listening and she has a crush on me." I just looked at him, and he frowned. "And the feeling isn't mutual, so I was trying to let her know I am interested in someone else without hurting her feelings if she ever did get up the courage to ask me out."

"Oh...so, there is a girlfriend or someone that you're interested in?"

He looked at me, then back at the road. He cleared his throat a little as he looked out his driver's side window. "Maybe," he said and fixed his eyes back to the road without looking at me again. I stared at him a moment, there was a hint of a smile on his face. I didn't put too much thought into it. Evidently he wasn't going to say anything more on the subject.

I remembered then that Adam wasn't the only one in the operating room when they stripped me of everything but my pride. Mason had seen me naked as well. Crap. I closed my eyes and gritted my teeth. I know, it's a nasty habit that can crack your teeth, and I'll end up with TMJ syndrome. I've heard it all, don't waste your breath.

We were getting close to my road and I asked Mason to slow down. I pointed out where to turn, and he complied. "It's the third house on the right." He pulled in the driveway and cut the engine.

"Nice house," he said, and I smiled.

It was a nice house. Actually, I'd purchased four acres out in the middle of nowhere and designed my own twenty-two hundred square foot house, then had it built. There were only two bedrooms, a guest room and my own, and all of the rooms were big and spacious.

"Wanna see it? That is, if you're not in any hurry to be anywhere else."

Mason smiled. "I don't have anywhere else to be."

Chapter Six

"Great." I opened my door and instead of climbing down, I just hopped out. I'd had my fill of climbing down things for the day.

I put my hand above my eyes to shield them from the setting sun. This was my favorite part of the day. It had the best light for working in my studio. Mason walked up beside me and I led him to the door. I could hear my baby barking as I walked in. Hercules was jumping up and down on his little back legs when I opened the door. He sniffed the air then caught a glimpse of Mason. He did his usual growling at the male stranger.

"He won't hurt you; he's just protective and jealous whenever another male is around. The only man he likes is my dad." I picked Hercules up and he showered me with kisses, almost as if he wanted to make it perfectly clear to Mason that I was his.

He laughed a little. "Oh, okay, because I was just about to be afraid."

I gave him a sour look then smiled. "His name is Hercules."

His brow shot up and he laughed involuntarily. "I think he has the personality for the name, but I believe he's somewhat lacking in the body department."

I set Hercules down and he ran right for Mason's leg, tugging on the material if his scrubs with his little teeth. He was really self-conscious about his size. "Hercules, no!" I shouted, but Mason had already picked my miniature Chihuahua up in one hand and was eyeing the little dog.

Hercules growled at first then began to whine. Mason ran his hand over the little dog's gray fur, and Hercules licked his lips and quieted down. Mason nuzzled him at his shoulder and Hercules began giving

Mason kisses on his chin and neck.

"Oh my God! He has never reacted like that to a man before. How did you do that?" I asked, bewildered.

Mason smiled and set Hercules gently down on his paws. The little dog looked up at him and whined, then sat back on his haunches and stared up at Mason. "I have an affinity for animals. You only have to prove which of you is the more dominant. Looks like I won this time, or I would be lying on the floor licking his face." He smiled and I smiled back. You had to love a person with a good sense of humor. Like! You had to like a person with a sense of humor.

I shook my head at the slip of my inner vocabulary and waved for him to follow me. I showed him every room except for one.

"You have an amazing home. I'm stuck in a small apartment; heavy metal music blaring through one wall, classical through another, and the man below me thinks that I'm the one making all the noise. This," he looked all around the room and nodded. "Is perfect."

My face lit up. "Well, thank you. I designed it. There's one more room I haven't shown you yet. I was saving it for last."

I walked to a set of French doors, looking back over my shoulder at his expectant expression, and opened them to reveal my favorite room. It was also where I made my living. There was nowhere else in the world I felt more comfortable.

Mason came up beside me and I watched him as he took it all in. Props, cameras, backgrounds and closets filled the 650 square foot room. The windows were all different shapes and sizes; some of them were extremely unusual. I had this room built especially for my work needs. This was my photography studio, and I had been named the best in the city and one of the best in the state by a few magazines and newspapers. I enjoyed my work, and truly felt I had a gift for capturing an image at just the right moment.

I could tell by the look on his face that he was impressed with the room, and for some reason I was dying to take shots of him. "Would you mind if I took a few shots of you? It won't take long. You can see how I do, what I do." He smiled and I took that as a yes. I took his hand in mine and pulled him with me to one of my massive wooden armoires. I opened it to show it was full of adult male clothing. I looked at him a moment and decided his shirt size would be a large because of the extra broadness of his shoulders and the bulk of his biceps. I looked back at the shirts and chose a bright royal blue cashmere sweater; I wanted to see just how blue I could make those eyes of his. It was summer, and very hot outside, but in the cozy coolness of my air-conditioned house, a photo could lie and get away with it.

"Here, put this on." I pointed to a large screen that he could change behind, but he either didn't see me point or he didn't care. He pulled his uniform shirt over his head and let it fall to the floor. My God, he was perfect. I almost changed my mind about the sweater to put him in something a little clingier, but he took the sweater out of my hand and pulled it over his head. Damn.

"I uh, um…yeah." I didn't have a single solid sentence in my head, and couldn't remember the last time a man had affected me this way. I closed my eyes and thought to myself; work, work, work. I even counted to ten before opening them again. I was focused now. I looked at that gorgeous smile, then up to his eyes. I was right; his eyes were almost as blue as the sky on a cloudless winters' morning.

I walked away from him to one of my more unique windows. It was large and the wood trim around the glass was unstained and all natural. "Sit here and I'll be right back." I glanced through my backdrops and found the one I wanted. It was mostly gray with a little green at the bottom and a few black lines in the middle. All together the backdrop looked distorted, but for what I was going to use it for I wouldn't need clarity. I went for the door in my studio room that would lead me outside and found the window I was working with. I had mounted bars above each window that I used to hang backdrops from. The sun was still fairly bright and that wasn't what I wanted for his background. I put the backdrop in place and put my side walls on each side so the sun wouldn't shine through and ruin the effect. The daylight coming in from the top and bottom would give just the right amount of natural light that I needed.

I turned a knob above the window, and water began to trickle and dance down the glass. If you want a rainy day on a sunny day, you need to have a little imagination.

I walked back in and saw that my subject had an amazed look on his face. "That is awesome, Kendra." I smiled but continued to set up equipment around him that I would need for this particular photograph. I lowered all the shades in the room. It was dark, except for the dim lights that were spotlighting Mason. There was just enough light to make everything gray except for that bright royal blue sweater and those blue eyes of his.

I positioned him so that he was looking out the window. It looked as though he was looking out on a dark rainy day. The green portion at the bottom of the backdrop appeared to be green grass, and the black lines streaked vertically here and there looked to be trees in the winter, leafless and dormant. But from my view behind the camera...I saw magic.

I took several shots then told him that he could change and leave the sweater on the table by the closet. Instead of going behind the screen, he pulled the cashmere over his head and took slow special care in folding it perfectly, then picked his uniform shirt up off of the floor. He paused and looked at me.

I still had my camera in my hand and I was ogling at him. He smiled. "You want to take some shots of me like this?" he asked as he raised an eyebrow.

I couldn't speak. I couldn't breathe. He had caught me fantasizing about him and I was at a loss for words. The truth was, I really did want to take a photo of him like that, but how do you tell someone "yes" to a question like that without getting embarrassed. My main focus in photography was landscapes, weddings and taking pictures of school kids. Nudes were not my forte'. Well, I actually didn't know if they were or not, I couldn't get past my discomfort to try it. I turned my eyes away from him and lied, "No…you can get dressed now. I apologize for staring."

I could feel him walking toward me, like a predator creeping toward their prey in the woods before it pounces. I closed my eyes. I knew they would betray me if I kept them open. I felt his fingers brush my cheek and stop at my chin. He turned my head back to face him but I stubbornly kept my eyelids firmly shut.

"Look at me," he whispered.

I couldn't do this. I had just met him for Christ's sake. I couldn't let him kiss me. I just couldn't.

"Open your eyes, Kendra," he whispered again, and I couldn't fight it any longer. I did as he requested. I opened my eyes.

The look on his face was so serious. He tilted my head up a little further and bent and placed a gentle kiss on my cheek. That was all, just a light kiss with those amazing lips of his.

He moved back from me and smiled. "Make sure you turn your phone on by nine a.m. Being your nurse, I feel obligated to call and check on you."

He pulled the shirt over his head, then turned and left my studio.

Chapter Seven

I felt strangely alone, even with Hercules staring up at me. It was time for him to eat, and when that time of day came, he followed me around until I put food in his bowl.

I went to the pantry, filled his bowl and set it down for him. I leaned on the kitchen island and watched Mason drive away as the last rays of sunlight expired. I didn't have a clue what to do about Adam. Something would come to me. It had to; my life depended on it. On the other hand, I didn't have a clue what to do about Mason either. He was nice, very attractive, and he clearly affected me in ways that Aven never had.

I remembered the photos I had taken of Mason and quickly ran to my studio. I picked my camera up off the table and went into my darkroom. I flipped on the amber and red light. I couldn't wait to see the outcome of the photos. I knew I had caught the perfect angle on a couple of the shots. Some photographers used digital, and sometimes I did too, but it relaxed me to develop film the old fashioned way.

I filled three different trays with the chemicals I would need to develop the photos; developer in the first tray, acidic bath wash to stop the developing process in the second tray, and the last tray I filled with the fixer chemical, which would allow me to turn the lights back on and look at the finished masterpieces after I hung them up to dry. After filling the trays, I unloaded the film from my Canon and placed it in the enlarger. There were about fifteen other photos on the film that I hadn't gotten around to developing yet, but I decided to do them later. I had an itch to see the ones I'd taken of Mason.

I placed a 3x5 piece of photo paper on the easel and moved the film toward the end where his shots would be. I froze. I stared dumbfounded at the blank place where that amazing body should've been. I took the film out again and held it up to the red light. All of them were close-up and far-away shots of landscapes. I lowered the film and shook my head. I knew I had used that camera. It couldn't be a bad roll of film; there were other shots on it. I was going to be pissed if there was something wrong with my camera.

I left the darkroom and grabbed a new roll of film from my storage cabinet. I quickly loaded it, and then took a few pictures of the scene where Mason had been sitting. It didn't have to be perfect; I didn't really have a subject. I just wanted to know what the hell had happened to those shots.

I ran back through my darkroom door and secured myself inside. I unloaded the new film and held it up to the red light. The shots were there, all five of them.

What the hell? I shook my head in disgust. For some reason, I really wanted a picture of him. I wanted to look at his face. The mental picture I had of him was fading far too quickly.

Maybe, for the first time in my life, I was trying to get attached to someone. I wouldn't have the chance if I didn't make a believer out of Adam. I moaned, and turned the red and amber light off on the way out of the darkroom.

I got my pj's out that I would wear to bed and started my bath water. I had left the towel I had used at the hospital in Mason's truck. He promised he would return it for me. I hadn't even had a brush to detangle my hair, so I was having a bad hair day on top of everything else that had happened. That was the least of my worries, but I still didn't feel clean. I lit the candles around the big tub and turned the lights out.

I eased into the water to soak my sore muscles. It looked as though Coen had not cured everything that had been wrong with me. I would have paid him the same as I did my massage therapist, more even. I sipped my White Zen and relaxed.

I heard a loud pop and my eyes shot open to see a man I didn't know standing in my bathroom staring at me. I let out a scream that would wake the dead. He laughed and lowered the lid of the toilet seat to sit down.

"Who are you, and why the hell are you in my bathroom with me while I'm naked!?" I said as I quickly grabbed a towel to cover myself.

The man rolled his eyes and shook his head. He was attractive for an older guy. He wasn't old, but he was way older than me, mid forties maybe. What the hell was he doing here sitting on my toilet seat? Pervert maybe?

"Have you made any progress?" As soon as I heard his voice, I knew he had to be Coen.

"Coen?" he nodded once and I continued. "Well, no, not exactly. He thinks I'm a fruitcake." He turned his head to the side and gave me a puzzled look. I rolled my eyes. "He thinks I'm crazy. I mean, what would you think if I told you that I'd talked to your guardian angel and he sent me to give you a message? Wouldn't you think that would be a little strange?"

He shook his head, with the confused look still on his handsome face. "No, I wouldn't think that strange at all, Kendra. I talk to my guardian angel nearly every day. If she needed you to give me a message, I believe she would ask you to."

I sighed and then slumped down in the tub even further, getting my dry towel all wet. "Well, it's not easy for me to explain to someone I've never met, if he doesn't start believing in God within the next week, I am going to die. Do you have any suggestions?" I huffed.

He shrugged. "Maybe if you concentrated on Adam instead of letting the young Mason woo you, you might find the answers for yourself."

That pissed me off, but he was right. It still pissed me off though. Nobody wants their mistakes shoved back in their face. "Mason was nice to me, Adam wasn't, Coen."

"My child, I never said that it would be easy, only that it would be worth it." He looked thoughtful for a moment. "I think God said that at one time or another. Anyway, your life is at risk, my dear. Do you solve your problem now, and spend time with young Mason later, or be with him now for only six more days?"

Damn, I just realized I didn't even have an entire week; I only had six days left. It didn't matter anyway. Either I was going to figure it out, or I wasn't. End of story.

"I'm thinking that maybe Mason can help me with Adam. I mean, he believes me, and I think he and Adam are pretty close friends."

"The fewer people involved, the better off you will be, Kendra."

I frowned. "What the hell does that mean?"

He didn't smile; he actually looked concerned. "You have your guardian demon that you struggle with everyday. Now you will have Adam's to deal with, and he's very strong. The more control you let them have over you, the stronger they will get, and the weaker you will become. Murry has almost total control over young Adam, and if you want young Mason in the game, his guardian demon will be added too. You want my advice? Worry about young Mason when you are sure that you will live."

He was right again, but I didn't like how he kept putting young before their names. They were older than me and I didn't consider myself young. That being said, if he had been my guardian angel, I would have listened to him.

He smiled, there was a loud pop again, and he was gone. Had he heard me thinking?

"Well...I don't guess angels think it rude to leave without saying goodbye," I said. Hercules only turned his head to the side as if he didn't have a clue what I'd said. He hadn't even barked at Coen. Had he even seen him, or was I really going crazy?

I really did need to stop talking to myself though. I talk to myself, sometimes I answer myself, and I see and talk to angels. Yep, I don't need a psychiatrist to tell me I'm crazy, I already know.

Somehow, the bath just wasn't doing it for me anymore. I rung the water out of the towel I was supposed to dry off with then laid it on the edge of the bathtub. I had to tiptoe, soaking wet, to the shelf that held the dry ones. Oh well. Why did I expect my luck to change?

I swiftly dried off and put on my pj's. I still had uber tangles in my hair, but I was too tired to care about it tonight. I had unplugged my house phone when I was showing Mason around, but had only put my cell phone on silent. I plugged it in to charge and saw that I had missed seventeen calls. I wasn't surprised, but had no urge to talk to anyone. I crawled beneath the covers of my queen size bed and took only a few breaths before sleep pulled me under.

My dreams were hardly ever clear or defined. I dream in color. Most people don't, but the majority of the time I can't see the faces of the people in my dreams, only a slideshow of different scenes. Those dreams have given me some great ideas for my career. My dream that night was different, but somehow the same. I could tell it was a dream, but it rode that fine line where it almost seemed real.

The reason I knew it was a dream was because I was watching myself. Not like watching myself in a mirror, but rather like I was looking at a home movie. The Kendra in the dream was angry and crying. The other reason I knew it was a dream was because I couldn't see the guy's face she was screaming at. His body was a little fuzzy, and I couldn't distinguish his physique from any other well-built man.

The me in my dream was lying on a cot or a small bed, and he was towering over her while I watched from a corner of the small dark room. I could see and hear myself shouting and crying at the man, but he seemed just as angry and scared as she was. He was making jerky movements and shouting back at her, but I couldn't make out what either of them were fighting about. There were a few times when I thought he was going to hit her, but he refrained. He finally ended up sitting in a chair facing away from me with his head in his hands and his elbows propped on his knees. He looked upset, not angry, but sad or scared. I realized then that she was tied to the bed, and had blood all over her. I concentrated on the man in the chair. His head lifted like he'd just noticed I was there.

He stood, ignoring the Kendra on the bed, and held out his hand to me. I didn't want to, but the urge to touch him was almost too much to ignore. I was afraid. I was afraid he would hurt us. She screamed for me to "Run, get out!" He began walking toward me, and I to him. His face came into focus a bit the closer we got to each other, but I still couldn't tell if I knew him or not. I wanted to know him. I wanted to know everything about him. I didn't know what had changed my mind about him, or chased away my fear, but I didn't care. I had to touch him.

"No, Kendra! It's a trick. Wake up! Wake up now, Kendra!" the Kendra on the cot screamed at me. I stopped, and so did the man. We both turned to look at her. She pleaded with her eyes, and I got a little more control of myself. I remembered that I'd been scared of the man. I was afraid he would hurt us.

My face filled with doubt as I looked back at the unknown man, and I took a step back.

The man held out his hand to me. "No, Kendra. Don't listen to her lies. You want me, I know you do."

The voice was distorted so I still couldn't tell who it belonged to.

He took another step forward, and I took one backwards step equal to his.

"Kendra, wake up. Just wake up and he can't hurt us." she pleaded from the cot. My gaze shot back to her. "Just wake up." she cried.

Out of the corner of my eye, I caught sight of the man running toward me.

"Wake up!" she shouted, and this time I listened to her.

I shot straight up in my bed and looked around me. I was shaking and scared. That was a first for me. I enjoyed living alone and didn't mind sleeping by myself. I had the urge to sit upright in the center of my bed with my teddy bear. It was like childhood all over again. I knew there was a boogieman under my bed, and I knew if I put a foot on the floor that he would grab a hold of my ankle and pull me under like the creepy clown in Poltergeist.

I grabbed my cell off my bed side table. It was 7:28 a.m. I wanted to talk to Mason, but I didn't know his last name to look him up in the book. I didn't even know if he had a landline, but he was probably already at work anyway. I didn't want to tell anyone else what was going on with me. It was too much to explain and I didn't have time.

Coen would know what to do. "Coen!"

I waited a moment then heard a loud pop, then another. Coen and another man stood at the foot of my bed. The other man was very good looking. He looked to be in his early thirties, and he was wearing a scowl on his face. He looked upset, but I didn't summon him, so why did he come?

Coen smiled at me. "Kendra, I would like to introduce you to Rhyan, your guardian angel. I figured with the recent activity that you would need a little more firepower on your side."

I was confused. What recent activity? He couldn't be talking about my nightmare; it had only been a dream. I looked back at Rhyan, but he wouldn't meet my gaze. He looked a little nervous about being around me, but he didn't look so upset anymore. "What recent activity are you talking about?"

Coen frowned. "You almost let him get control over you. I should have warned you better. Murry knows you are trying to save young Adam, and he almost took control of you."

The nightmare had been real? "Are you talking about my nightmare?"

Both of the men nodded. "That I am, young Kendra. It wasn't only a nightmare. Angels and demons are allowed to enter the dreams of humans, but we aren't allowed to mess with their freewill. You would have to choose on your own, but Adam's guardian demon is very powerful and influential. He will make you want to join with him, and when you do, he will win the souls of both you and young Adam.

What the hell did he just say? "What the hell did you just say?"

Rhyan looked angry again. "I told you this would happen, Coen! I knew you wouldn't tell her everything she needed to know before she agreed to your deal. If I lose her soul, I will hold you personally responsible and have you reprimanded."

Chapter Eight

He couldn't be serious. So, this was why Rhyan had been trying to intercede yesterday, and why he was so clearly angry today. If I didn't complete my mission, then I wouldn't only lose my life, I would lose my soul as well. I stared at Coen in disbelief. "You tricked me? I bargained with you, not the devil. My soul shouldn't be up for grabs, Coen." The more I talked the more pissed I got, and I cry when I'm pissed. I felt the hot tears streaming down my face and I ignored them.

"It is the price for such a gamble. I thought you were aware. I apologize for not informing you better."

I threw the bed cover off my legs and started for him. "The price!? It's the price *I* have to pay?" I pointed at my chest. "Well, if a soul is the price, I think it should be yours that we are gambling with. You are the one who has failed to keep Adam on the right path. Tell me something, did you cause my accident?" Rhyan's head turned swiftly, and there was a look of shear horror on his face as he stared at the other angel. Coen didn't flinch. I continued pressing for answers. "I think you did and then made your option of me helping you sound easier and better than dying and going to heaven. You knew I wouldn't turn you down. Am I right?"

Rhyan stepped a foot closer to the angel. "You know I'll be able to tell if you lie to her, Coen."

Coen dropped his head and clenched his jaw. He waited a full twenty seconds before responding to either of us. "I had nothing to do with your accident."

"Liar!" Rhyan shouted almost before Coen finished his sentence, then hurled himself at the other angel and they both tumbled to the floor. Rhyan was straddling Coen's chest and had both hands around the other angel's throat. I didn't know what to do, so I backed up to the wall. I couldn't call the cops and say, "Oh, hey, yeah, my guardian angel and another angel are duking it out on my bedroom floor. One of them tried to kill me yesterday, and he will be the cause of me dying, for good, in six days. Can you send someone out to break up the fight for me, please?" Yeah, that would so not be happening.

"What would you do if Patrick had her soul in the palm of his hand, and they only gave you a week to get her back?" Coen said, after taking three solid blows to the face.

Rhyan got to his feet quicker than I would have thought possible. He looked down at Coen with a kind of sadness on his face. "I wouldn't have risked another human's soul for mine, Coen. I would have suffered greatly, but what you've done is unforgivable. You know the consequences of your actions."

Coen closed his eyes in defeat. "My brother, I thought with the feelings you have for her that you would understand."

My jaw dropped, and Rhyan slowly raised his head to meet my eyes. He wasn't holding Coen down any longer, but he didn't really have to, Coen was smart enough to stay on the floor. Our eyes met and we stared at each other for the longest time. He finally looked down at Coen, then bent and placed his hand on the angel's chest. There was a loud pop, and then both of the angels were gone.

I guess angels just don't believe in good-byes.

Chapter Nine

I showered quickly then took Hercules out for his morning run. Well, he was running, I was jogging. A dog that small just can't keep up with me if I'm at a full out run. I had to do something to clear my head and help me think. My morning jog usually helped me organize my day a little better. If I missed a day, everything fell apart. So, off we ran.

I reluctantly turned on my cell phone, and set it so I could talk through my ear bud if anyone called. I would be breathless and winded, but if anyone called and wanted to talk to me for the next hour; that was how it had to be. I'd skipped the previous day's run to go rappelling with my friends, and look where that had landed me.

"Come on Hercules." We kicked it up a notch from our usual warm-up trot to my full out jog. Hercules used to struggle to keep up with me only jogging, but he realized that if he couldn't keep up, I would leave him at home and go running on my own. He was getting better. I'd considered getting a bigger dog for the days I want a good hard run, but Hercules is so possessive of me, it would have been a shot to his ego.

My cell phone went off. First one of the day, and I had a feeling that it was going to be a very long day. I glanced at the name before I hit my ear bud to receive the call. "Hello, Mom." I said a little winded.

"My God, Kendra! What on earth are you doing? No, wait; don't tell me, I don't want to know. How are you, honey?" My mother sounded anxious, but I had to smile. She must have thought I was having sex. Now, why would I answer the phone if I was having sex? If it were good sex, there wouldn't be a chance in hell, but I admit I have answered a call a time or two. It kind of ruined the mood, but the times that I had, the mood wasn't really there for me to begin with. But I would never, in a million years, answer a call from my mom or dad in the middle of a sexual act of any kind, not even kissing. I wouldn't be able to hide the embarrassment in my voice.

"I'm just taking Hercules out for his run, Mom, and I am fine."

"We were so worried about you yesterday. I can't believe your friends would tell us that you were close to dying, when there was clearly nothing major wrong with you."

"I know. It was just a misunderstanding. They thought something was wrong, don't blame them." My phone beeped, letting me know I had another call waiting. "Mom, I have another call coming in. Can I call you later?"

"Yes, honey, we're just so glad that you're all right. I'm sure your phone will be ringing all day. We love you."

"I love you and dad too. I'll call you later. Bye."

"Bye, baby."

I glanced at my phone, but didn't recognize the number. It was local, but I usually didn't answer to anyone I didn't have programmed into my phone. Calls like that went through my landline, they were mostly business, but my cell phone was private.

I went ahead and tapped my ear bud. "This is Kendra Larkin."

"Ms. Larkin, my name is Cal Hanner of the Independent. I would like to ask you a few questions if you don't mind."

Great. There was a leak somewhere, and that leak had given my personal cell phone number to the press. "Actually, Mr. Hanner, I do mind." I hit the button on my ear bud and ended the call.

My phone immediately rang again. I was ready to be angry when I hit my earpiece, but the voice that came through made me smile instead. "Good morning, Kendra. How's my favorite patient?"

"Well, I'm fine. Thank you for asking, Mason."

"I need to do a follow-up on you, you know, vitals and stuff, to make sure everything checks out all right. Do you mind if I drop by your house, say around six-thirty tonight?" He sounded a little nervous, but I didn't know what he was doing besides talking with me, so I had no clue why.

"Actually, I was going to run into town later and try my luck at Dr. Chamberlain again. I could look you up for a vitals check then if you want."

He laughed lightly. "Well, that would be fine, if that's what you want to do. I was just trying to get up the nerve to ask you out tonight. I was using that excuse to come by and pick you up. I know you are fine or you wouldn't be exercising right now."

I looked immediately to my left, then my right. Could he see me? Was he hiding somewhere watching me? "Where are you?"

"I'm at the hospital. I could hear your labored breathing. I didn't figure you were lying in bed taking it easy like the doctor ordered."

I smiled. "Actually, the only thing the doctor ordered was for me not to leave the hospital. He didn't say anything about jogging or any other type of strenuous activities. Hercules needed a run, and I felt good enough to take him."

Mason laughed. "So...can I pick you up at six-thirty?"

I'd completely forgotten that he'd asked me out. Coen may be the cause of all of this, but some of the things he'd said made sense. What would one little date hurt, though?

"Kendra?" Mason said.

"I'm here, and yes...six-thirty will be fine Mason."

I could almost hear him smile through the phone. "Great! I'll see you then. Good-bye, Kendra."

"Bye, Mason." I hit my earpiece with a smile.

I rounded the halfway mark of my jog. Hercules was panting heavily, but we weren't stopping and he knew it.

I heard a loud pop and ran smack dab into Rhyan. Couldn't he see where he was going to appear? He caught me, but I was going too fast to help him balance. We went down on the hard pavement and he broke my fall.

"What in the hell are you doing?" Hercules was whining as I got to my feet. He didn't get tangled up with us, but I knew he was worried if I was hurt or not.

Rhyan stood up and brushed off his clothes. He was wearing a short sleeve polo shirt with khaki shorts and flip-flops. He looked nice, really nice, but that didn't explain him popping up in front of me where I could run over him.

"I don't think the date tonight is a very good idea, Kendra. You have things to take care of, and I don't think getting distracted is the best option for you right now. Besides, I can't find Mason's guardian angel. I don't know what type of person he is."

"He believes me, Rhyan, and he's the only person I can talk to about all of this." I said.

"That isn't true. You can talk to me," he said and dropped his head to stare at his feet.

I looked at him a little closer. Did he really have feelings for me? I didn't know him, but he had known me my whole life. Imagine the things he'd seen. I sighed, "What happened with Coen?"

He spoke without looking at me. "He's confined and waiting for a hearing." He looked up at me then. "What he did was inexcusable, but it won't change the outcome. I begged for them to release you from this deal, but they will not. You have to get Adam's soul back. You made the deal, Kendra."

I looked shocked, I know I did. "I didn't know what I was agreeing to, Rhyan."

He nodded with unshed tears in his eyes. "I know...I know."

Chapter Ten

Rhyan had popped out of sight before I had a chance to say anything else. I guess he didn't want me to see him cry. I wouldn't have held it against him. I wanted to cry myself.

I didn't have time for Hercules' short legs to try and keep up, so I gathered him up in my arms and ran as fast as I could back to the house.

There was a dark cloud moving in and I felt the first sprinkle of rain just before running through my door. I had to take a quick shower; I couldn't talk to Adam smelling like sweat. I jumped in the shower before the water was completely warm and made a loud girly exclamation. I looked at my dog sitting on the tile staring up at me. He seemed to be smiling. "That wasn't funny, Hercules." He licked his lips and curled up on the ceramic tile.

I was in a hurry, but I took the time to shampoo and condition my hair. I couldn't put it off any longer. I finished up and quickly got ready. I did take the time to apply a little makeup and fix my long hair. I felt like I was running out of time, but I have learned that men are more apt to talk to a woman who looks professional or pretty, than one who looks like she just crawled out of bed. Better to be easy on the eyes in any situation involving a man.

I knew that Rhyan and Coen were right about me staying away from Mason until all of this blew over, but I felt a strong pull toward Mason. It would be rude to break the date with him. I sighed. I had to break the date with him. I would tell him that, mentally, I had way too much going on this week. If he couldn't understand that, then he wasn't right for me anyway.

I looked in the mirror one last time. I wasn't beautiful, but I could turn a few heads. I'd always had a good complexion; I was one of the lucky ones throughout my adolescence. I had bright green eyes that were now expertly applied with eye makeup. My sister was a consultant for Mary Kay, and she gave me free samples and makeup how-to's all the time. I was five-six, and I wasn't too thin. I had an athletic build with runner's legs and got compliments on my body all the time, so I didn't think I looked too shabby.

My cell phone rang, and I answered it without looking, which I normally didn't do. "Hey babe, how're you feeling?" Aven said through the line. I closed my eyes and clenched my jaw. I so did not want to talk to him right now.

"I feel all right, Mason. I mean, Aven. I took Hercules out for a run…"

"Wait, what did you just call me?" I had hoped he hadn't caught that, but I guess he had. Well shit. It wasn't like we were in a monogamous relationship or anything.

"I'm sorry, Aven. Mason, the nurse from the hospital, called me a little earlier and wants me to come in for a checkup. I still have that conversation on my mind, and I'm actually about to leave right now."

"Oh, well in that case, I'll drive you. I have a few errands to run and I would really like to hear what he has to say." I'd just bet he would. I rolled my eyes.

"No. I don't have time to waste in town. I have a client showing up at twelve-thirty. He promised he would be quick so I could get back home in time." I said then held my breath.

"Oh, okay." I could tell he was disappointed, but I didn't say anything. "Will you call me as soon as you get back home? I really would like to know how this miracle happened. I held your limp, beat-up body in my arms all the way to the emergency room yesterday. I thought you were gone and it made me realize a lot of things about us. I'd like to talk more in-depth about all of this with you tonight over dinner."

Did I just get asked out twice in one day, and both times before ten a.m.? "I would love to, but my week is all booked up. I'll be working until ten or eleven o'clock all week. These juniors are all wanting their Senior pictures done this week and next. Call me next Sunday and we can reschedule. I'll be busy, but I think I can squeeze you in somewhere."

"Yeah, okay, Kendra. Whenever you find time for me, I'll be around somewhere. Call me."

"No, Aven..." I pleaded, but I was talking to myself. He'd hung up on me.

"Dammit!" I didn't want to upset anyone, but Aven was probably the first of many this week. I sighed then opened and closed the door behind me.

I got in my Land Rover and drove to the hospital. I turned the radio up as loud as I could stand it and sang along with Theory Of A Deadman. He had a bad, bad girlfriend. It had a good beat, and I knew most of the words. The ones I didn't know, I made up as I went along. No one was here to criticize my singing anyway. Well, maybe Coen and Rhyan could hear me, but they weren't complaining.

It didn't take long to get to the city. Like with any city, you had to travel during off hours or you got stuck in traffic. Ten o'clock in the morning wasn't too bad a time to travel. I only hoped I could make it back out before noon.

I used the parking garage where Mason's truck had been parked yesterday. There wasn't a sign that told me I couldn't. I pulled in and found a spot somewhat close to the elevator. I got out, locked my doors and headed for the elevator.

I heard someone whistle, but I didn't turn around. If it was meant for me, I didn't have time to be flattered.

I pushed the button and heard the whistle again, a little closer to me this time. I was really starting to get creeped out, so I hit the button three more times, trying not to look obvious that I was a scared shitless. I had thought I was the only one in the very poorly lit garage.

The doors finally opened and I forced myself to walk slowly into the box. I didn't look back out as I pushed the button for the fourth floor.

"Hey, Kendra, hold the door!" Mason shouted from the garage. I caught the doors just before they closed.

He rolled a wheelchair into the elevator and hit the button for the second floor then smiled at me.

My heart was still up in my throat, and I knew my face had to be beet red. "You scared me. I thought you..."

"You thought I was an evil monster whistling at you in a dark garage?" Mason said with a grin.

I had to laugh then. "Yeah...yeah, I guess I did." I looked at the wheelchair, then back up at his face. God, he was so good looking. "What are you doing down here?"

He looked at the wheelchair and made it do a little wheelie. "I was taking a patient to his vehicle. He was discharged a few minutes ago, and unlike you, he didn't refuse the wheelchair exit. It's standard protocol for the patient to be wheeled out in one of these and helped into their vehicle. I think it's frivolous, but if a patient refuses and they fall and get hurt, they can sue us."

The elevator dinged, and we both looked up as the doors opened. "I think Adam is in surgery right now. If he isn't in his office, come back to this floor and ask for me. I really do need to check you out. If the surgery goes all right, he shouldn't be much longer.

I nodded and the doors closed. Damn. There went my chance of getting out of the city by noon. It was only about fifteen miles to my house from here, but driving fifteen miles in rush hour traffic could take up to an hour and a half. I might as well take my time and wait until traffic slowed back down at one-thirty. I did not want to spend three and a half hours in a hospital that I had been in such a hurry to get out of yesterday. This is what I get for telling Aven I have a client coming at twelve-thirty, when I actually don't. Karma's a bitch.

I went up to the fourth floor, and sure enough, Mason had been right. Adam wasn't in his office. His door was open, so I peeked in. I wasn't going to touch anything. I only needed to find something personal of his that I could relate to. It's easier to talk to someone if you at least know a little bit about them.

I stood in the center of his 12 x 15 room and looked around. There were very few pictures on his desk and absolutely none on the wall. There was a painting on the wall behind his desk, in between the only two windows in the room. It was a landscape. I didn't recognize the print, but it was good if you asked me.

I looked again at the pictures on his desk. There were three, all candid shots. There was one with a little boy and a teenage girl. The boy looked like a miniature Adam, so I assumed it was him when he was around ten. The girl in the shot looked a whole lot like Adam as well, and I assumed she was probably Adam's sister. In the second photo, there was a man and woman. The man had his arm around the woman in a loving embrace; must be their parents. The last photo was of all of them together. Adam was sitting on his dad's right shoulder with a baseball raised to the sky. His mom, sister and dad were all smiling up at him.

I wondered if he'd won the game or if he had caught a foul ball or homerun ball at a minor or major league game. I smiled. They all looked so happy.

I did notice something though. There were no recent pictures of his family in the room. Had they all died except for Adam? Was that his reason for turning against God?

"Excuse me," Adam said. I couldn't help it; I jumped and screamed like a girl. He didn't smile, he just looked annoyed. You're not supposed to be on this floor unless you are accompanied by a member of the staff, or a doctor asks for you to come." He looked around, then back to me. "I don't see anybody else, and I'm positive that I didn't call you, Ms. Larkin."

I closed my eyes and counted to five, there was no time for ten. "I came to apologize for my outburst, and me storming out of here yesterday. I can now see how that all must have sounded to you, Adam."

He walked to his chair behind the desk and sat down. He didn't look at me; his gaze went to the third picture, the one where he was holding the baseball.

"Did you win the game, or catch a fly ball?" He didn't look at me, but he did answer me. It was a start.

"My little league team won All Stars in 1991. I was twelve years old, and I hit the home run that won the game."

"Your family looks really proud of you." I said, and he tensed.

"Why are you really here, Ms. Larkin?" He stood and walked slowly around to me. I didn't know what he was going to do, but I did know I didn't want to be sitting down when he did it.

I didn't back up after I stood. I didn't want to show weakness. I may have been shaking in my shoes, but I wasn't going to let him know it.

He looked angry, but somehow I didn't think he was angry with me. I looked away from him. "I'm sorry for wasting your time, Dr. Chamberlain. I'm supposed to meet with Mason so he can look me over and make sure there's nothing wrong with me. I will see you again in six days."

I started for the door of his office and he spoke.

"Why six days?" he asked me.

I stopped, but I didn't turn around. I just answered his question. "Because six days is how long I have before I die and we both lose our souls. See you Friday." I said, then walked out the door.

Chapter Eleven

I had every intention of seeing him before my six days were up, but I was hoping he would come to me first. I didn't really even have six whole days, more like five and a half. I stepped off the elevator onto the second floor. There was a nurse's station about twenty-five feet from the elevator. How convenient. There were two nurses, cackling like hens with their eggs about to hatch, behind the big counter. I really hated to interrupt, but I was going to.

I cleared my throat. "Excuse me…"

They both immediately fell silent and gave me harmless, helpful smiles. "Can I help you?" one of the brunettes asked me.

"Yes, maybe you can. I was looking for Mason." I said.

They gave each other a funny look then looked back at me. The other brunette spoke this time. "Is he a patient or staff?"

I raised an eyebrow. Of course, a "Mason" could be either one. "Staff."

They gave each other another quick glance, then turned back to me again. The brunette that answered this time didn't look so happy with me being here. Actually, neither of them did. "We don't know of any Mason that works in this hospital."

Oh, really? Huh. I could play this game too. "Well, I do, and Adam sent me to get him from the second floor." One of the girls looked surprised, the other confused.

The girl that had looked surprised responded back. "Adam who?" she asked, and I could tell she was a little nervous about what would come out of my mouth next.

I smiled sweetly, with a little menace behind it. "Adam Chamberlain," I said and watched closely as her expression changed from snotty to frantic.

She swiftly picked up the phone receiver and hit a button on the phone. "Mason Carter, come to the second floor, station one, please." She hung up the phone, but didn't look at me when she spoke. "He'll be here in a minute. You can wait in the waiting room over there." She pointed to her left and I turned to look at the small waiting room. There were four chairs lined up against one of the walls, with a drink and snack machine across from them.

"No, I think I'll be fine right here," I said.

"I'm just trying to make sure you're comfortable." Man, what kind of asshole was Adam?

A pair of hands reached around and covered my eyes from behind. "Guess who?"

I smiled and turned around. Mason didn't back up, so he was standing all up in my personal space, but with the attitude I had gotten from the nurses behind the desk, I wasn't going to show that I cared.

"How was your talk with Dr. Chamberlain?" I moved my eyes toward the nurses so only he could see and then looked back at him. He smiled and gave them his attention. "Danielle, Ashley...you girls staying out of trouble today?"

They giggled like they were high school Freshman girls, and the hottest guy in the Senior class had just flirted with them. I rolled my eyes. Mason gave them both a cunning look, then laced his fingers with mine and led me down the hall.

"They weren't too hard on you, were they?" Mason said before he pulled me into a room. It wasn't a patient's room, it was smaller. It had a small cot, some medical equipment and that was it.

"Typical bitches," I whispered.

"What?" Mason grinned at me.

I shook my head. "Nothing." I looked around and found a stool with wheels on it. I started to sit down.

Mason shook his head and pointed at the cot. "Shoes and socks off."

I gave him one of my best looks; one that plainly asked a person, "Really?"

He shrugged. "I could have you strip down and put one of these on." He held up a hospital gown, complete with missing backside. I hopped up on the cot without another word and slipped my shoes and socks off.

He got something out of a drawer that looked like a small metal gavel. One end was pointy and made of metal, and the other end was rubber. He took my foot gently in his hand, and with the other hand he ran the pointy end from heel to toe. I shrieked and almost fell off the cot, but he caught me. He was laughing as he helped me sit back up straight and then did the same to the other foot. My reaction wasn't as bad that time because I knew what was coming.

He used the rubber end of the contraption to check my reflexes. "You're good. You can put those back on, and then I'll check your vitals." He wrote on a chart as I put my socks and shoes back on.

"Is that my chart?" I asked. He nodded then laid it down. He picked up the blood pressure cuff and placed it gently around my arm. I was looking at him the whole time, but he was focusing on his task. He had to be really good at his job to not get distracted by a woman he had a date with tonight.

Oh shit, I'd forgotten I had to cancel. He was so distracting. I looked up at him. He had to be a decent person if he was a nurse, right? He cared about people. It wasn't my fault that Rhyan couldn't find his guardian angel. He or she may be on vacation for all I knew. I knew I needed to cancel, but I just really, really didn't want to.

He had me breathe in and out several times while he listened with his stethoscope. He placed it on my back and listened to my lungs, then moved it to my chest and had me breathe deeply again. My heart was beating normally at first, then I thought about him with his shirt off the day before and it went into overdrive.

He looked at my face and gave me a strange look. "Are you all right?"

I nodded and turned my head, a little embarrassed. "I was only thinking."

He smiled and put the stethoscope around his neck. "I would like to be in your head and know what you're thinking right now."

"I'm sure you would." I said a little flirtatiously. He was already in my space so I leaned a little closer. He seemed to realize what I wanted him to do, but he backed up and wrote something in my chart instead of meeting me in the middle. Well. That had been the first move I'd ever made on a guy that had backfired.

"So, did you get anything accomplished with Adam?"

I huffed. "He makes me so angry. I swear I could bite through metal nails if I had any."

He chuckled. "It went that well, huh? He kind of has that effect on people until you get to know him." He seemed to realize that I wasn't in a joking mood. His expression changed to concern and he rolled the stool over to the cot and sat down. "Look, don't get discouraged. We'll think of something."

I hopped down from the cot. "I don't have time to get to know him. I only have six days left."

He slowly blinked. "Do you really think you only have six days left?"

My eyes grew wide. "I thought you believed me."

He grabbed my hand. "I do...I do, Kendra. It's just a lot to take in. I don't see why God would take your life over this though. Do you understand what I'm saying?"

I nodded. "It wasn't God I made the deal with. It was Coen, and he tricked me. Not only will I die in six days, well, actually five and a half, but I'll lose my soul, too."

"Well, it sounds like Coen may have made a deal with the Devil instead of God." He stood and hugged me. "We'll get this figured out.

I'll kick Adam's ass myself if I have to."

I laughed through tears, and nodded.

"I'll see you tonight, and I won't leave until we come up with something." He tilted my head up by my chin. "Okay?"

I knew I should break the date, but I couldn't do it. He was going to help me find a way to convince Adam I was telling the truth. I nodded my head and smiled. "I'll see you tonight."

Chapter Twelve

Mason walked me, past the two cackling nurses, to the elevator. Of course they shut up the moment they saw us. I looked at my watch when we stopped at the elevator. It was 11:45 a.m. Damn, there was no way I'd be able to get out of here and out of the city in fifteen minutes. Truth be known, the traffic was already at a standstill.

Mason picked up on my agitation and he smiled. "You aren't going to get out of the city in time, are you?"

I shook my head. "It doesn't look like it."

He lifted my hand that he was still holding and kissed my knuckles. I wanted more than that, but if that was all I could have right now, so be it. What the hell was wrong with me? I'd never acted this way before. "I'll see you at 6:30."

I hesitated and he caught it. I spoke before he could. "I don't know how tonight will go between us Mason, but with everything that's going on right now with Adam, and my imminent death," I shrugged. "I have a lot of work to do in the next couple of weeks, senior pictures and a few other things. I just think after tonight, we need to wait until after I find out if I am going to live or not. Now is not the time for me to get distracted."

He ran the back of his fingers along my cheek. "You're so beautiful."

I smiled as I blushed. "You're distracting me, Mason."

"Not on purpose." He leaned in to smell of my hair. "Mmmm, I think that you're the one distracting me."

I was having trouble breathing. I couldn't think straight with him standing this close to me. He smelled so good. I think he was wearing Pleasures. Aven wore it sometimes. It was one of my favorites. I threw his line back at him. "Not on purpose."

I heard him breathe a soft laugh. "I'll see you tonight and we'll get the Adam thing resolved. Then I can distract you all I want, deal?"

I nodded. I definitely wanted to be distracted by him when this all blew over. The elevator dinged and I pulled away from him. When the doors opened, Adam was standing there looking at us.

He nodded at Mason. "Mason,"

Mason nodded back and flashed those pearly whites. "Dr. Chamberlain,"

Adam looked back at me and sighed. "I'd like to finish our conversation if that's all right with you, Ms. Larkin." I heard shuffling and I looked back at the nurse's desk. The two brunettes were no longer cackling hens. They were running around like chickens with their heads cut off. I rolled my eyes and looked back at Adam. I was still irritated with him, but at least he was willing to talk to me.

I looked back at Mason and he let go of my hand. "You want me to go with you?"

"No, I think I can handle him all by myself." I said as I stepped into the elevator beside Adam.

"I had no doubts, Kendra." He smiled and the doors closed, shutting me inside the small box with the guy who was in total control of my fate.

Chapter Thirteen

We didn't go back up to the fourth floor like I thought that we would. He had hit the "G" button in the elevator, and the doors opened to the garage.

I expected to walk up to a Corvette or Porsche, they seemed like the kind of vehicle a doctor would drive, but he surprised me when he unlocked a bright red 1967 Ford Shelby Mustang GT500. I may be a photographer, but cars have always been something I've taken an interest in.

I let out a low whistle, and he looked up at me. There was still no smile on his face. Man, he was going to be hard to save. I thought as he unlocked my door from the inside. I got in. I wasn't worried about him killing me and hauling my body off to bury it in the woods somewhere. Mason and two other nurses had seen me leave with him. I really didn't think I could count on the hens, but I was counting on Mason.

"So…where're you taking me during lunch rush hour? You do know that it will take us forever to get there, and then get back." He didn't respond so I looked at my watch. It was straight up twelve o'clock.

He pulled out of the garage and took a right. He turned left down an alley and then turned right again at the end. We were close to the older part of the city now, and traffic wasn't nearly as bad here. He continued in that direction, and soon we were completely out of town, heading north.

The radio was off, and I couldn't hear anything but the soft purring of the big engine. He wanted to finish the conversation, but he wasn't talking at all, just driving. Maybe I should start. "So…where are you taking me?" I asked again. A few moments passed and he didn't say anything. I slumped back in my seat and looked out the window.

About fifteen miles north of the city, he turned down a gravel road. He did just as I expected he would do, the car was doing only a little more than idling. At least he took care of what he had. I could see a big hill and a long line of trees up ahead.

We finally reached the top of the hill and, before my eyes was one of the biggest graveyards that I'd ever seen. I knew then that my assumption must've been correct about his family being dead. Crap! How was I supposed to deal with this? I'd never lost anyone close to me. I even still had both sets of grandparents. The only thing I had ever really lost was my gold fish when I was seven. I hadn't taken it well, so I didn't get another pet again until I found Hercules. Actually, I should say Hercules found me. He showed up at my front door when he was no older than six or seven weeks old. I didn't know how he got there, but it was love at first sight.

I spoke in my head and hoped he was listening. *"Rhyan, help me. How do I deal with this? What should I tell him?"* I didn't get a response, but I really wasn't expecting one. They were counting on me to do this. If they could have done it, it would have already been done by now, and I wouldn't be fearing for my life.

Adam stopped the car in the middle of the cemetery and killed the engine. He opened his door and got out. He stood there a moment, then bent at the waist and glared in at me. "Are you coming?"

I glared back at him for a moment, then opened my door and got out. It was hot already, and there were very few shade trees nearby.

He walked, and I followed him. We didn't have to go far before he stopped and looked down. I didn't want to look down, but I did. There were three beautiful tombstones, one big one and two smaller ones. The largest had two names on it; Daniel Lee Chamberlain and Sylvia Ann Chamberlain. The dates they were born were different, but the dates that they were laid to rest were the same. It read at the bottom: In Loving

Memory a Husband and Father a Wife and Mother.

The stone beside that one was a single, and the date of rest was the same as her parents. Heather Lynn Chamberlain's name was written in stone. "An angel taken too soon," her stone read. She had been only seventeen on the day or night that she and her parents perished.

I felt him watching me, waiting to see some kind of reaction. What did he want to see? I finally moved on to the last headstone. I don't know what I expected, but it wasn't this. I guess I expected Adam's plot to be bought and paid for, with his name and birth date carved, but missing the final letters and numbers that would let a passer-by know when the man in the ground had died. It wasn't what I expected at all, and I knew it must have been showing on my face.

I stared at the stone for a long time. Now I understood why Adam wouldn't want to believe. How, if there was a God, could he take a thirteen-year-old boy's whole family away from him? I had always heard that God wouldn't put more on you than you could stand. How strong would a child have to be to endure this kind of misery? I stared down at the last tombstone. I realized I was sobbing, and knew then that I had been doing it for a while. Benjamin Lee Chamberlain was the name on the third headstone. I hadn't expected this because I didn't see any pictures of another sibling on Adam's desk. Then I read the date through my tears. Adam's baby brother had only been two days old.

"Oh my God," I sobbed around the lump in my throat, and then fell to my knees. I still believed in God, and I knew that he wasn't the cause of this obvious accident. But how would a thirteen-year-old boy feel about everything he loved being ripped from his life? He was a big brother for only two days. Had he even gotten to hold him?

I looked up at Adam through my tears.

"I don't want your sympathy," he said quietly.

What else did I have to give him?

"How…" I took a breath. I didn't want to know, but for some reason I had to know. "How did it happen?"

He stepped closer to me, bent down and held out his hand. I looked at it for only a moment before I took it. After I got to my feet, he immediately let go. He took a few deep breaths, and I knew that he was going to tell me. Maybe he was going to tell me all along, and that was why he brought me out here. Or maybe he thought that he wouldn't have to tell me because he thought I wouldn't want to know. Who knew, but he'd clearly made the decision to tell me.

"I was at baseball practice when it happened. My mom and the baby had to stay in the hospital for forty-eight hours before they could come home. Heather was staying at home with me, so dad could stay at the hospital with them. She was a good sister. She didn't raise hell or do drugs like some of the other teenagers her age. She had a boyfriend, Kevin, who played catch with me. I still run in to him from time to time." He paused for a while, I guess so he would get the words right. It had probably been awhile since he'd told anyone this story, if he ever had.

"I had practice after school, and Heather went to the Hospital to pick up Dad, Mom and Ben. My best friend's mom was giving me a ride home so Heather wouldn't have to come back and get me. Practice was over around four, and when I got home, the front door was open. Jacob was spending the night so he was with me, but it didn't make it any easier to see."

I covered my mouth with my hand as I stared wide-eyed at him.

"They had walked in on a burglar." He shook his head. "Who the hell robs a house at four in the afternoon?" He was looking at me, but it was clear that he didn't want me to answer. To my relief, he continued. I didn't have an answer for him. "The guy shot my mom, dad and sister. I don't guess he had the heart to shoot Ben because he didn't. I guess my mom was trying to protect him from the burglar, I don't know. I didn't even know that Ben was in the house because I was in shock. Jacob called the police, and when they got there, I heard one of them shouting that there was a baby under my mom."

"I came out of my daze and ran back in the house to get my brother. He was blue and they were trying to administer infant C.P.R., but I knew it was too late. He'd smothered to death."

I touched his hand and he let me. "God didn't do that, Adam."

"There is no God!" He shouted at me and tried to pull his hand free, but I squeezed tighter. "What do you want from me, huh? You want me to believe in Him again?" he pointed to the sky. "I can't do that Kendra!"

"What do you have to lose by believing? It's obvious you hate everything. There is a huge hole in your heart waiting to be filled, and you won't let it happen. You have a great job, a nice car, nice clothes, and I'm sure you have a nice house too, but no matter how much you buy, you will never be able to fill that hole."

He stared at me. He was considerably calmer, but the heat in his eyes was starting to flare again. "Love," he sighed. "Is that what you mean?"

I nodded. "You can love again."

"So He can rip it away from me!" he shouted, then turned his head so I couldn't see his face. I assumed there were tears in his eyes, threatening to betray him. How could I fix this?

"Do you honestly believe that?" I asked.

He stepped closer to me. He was way into my personal space. He looked me in the eyes, and it was like I could see through his, to his soul. It staggered me a little, because the feeling was so strange. I pulled myself together and concentrated on what I was looking at. It was his soul. It was battered, but it wasn't completely lost. I wondered if this was a new gift Coen or Rhyan had given me when I was brought back. "Do you honestly believe you'll die in six days?" he said, pulling me out of my concentration.

I looked down. "You know I do, or I wouldn't be trying so hard to get you to believe."

He laughed and I looked back up at him. "Is that all it will take to save your life? Fine, I'll say it." He raised his face up to the sky and shouted. "I believe!" He looked back at me. "Is that good enough?" I knew it wouldn't be, because I didn't believe it.

I heard the familiar loud pop. Rhyan was sitting on a tombstone about twenty feet behind Adam. He was shaking his head from side-to-side. Dammit.

Adam turned and looked at where my attention was focused then turned back to me. "Will that do? Will you live now?" He must not have been able to see Rhyan.

I didn't know how to explain to Adam that my guardian angel was sitting behind him, so I didn't try. I shook my head. "You didn't mean it, so no."

He pointed to his chest as he yelled at me. "I'm not ever going to mean it, Kendra!"

I pursed my lips together. Anger wouldn't help me any, but being nice wasn't getting the job done. I truly felt bad that he'd lost his family, but I wasn't a shrink and wasn't qualified for this job. "Well then," I blew out my breath in frustration. "I guess I will die in five and a half days."

He was calmer, but he still wasn't stable. "Look, if you die on Friday, there's nothing I can do to stop it unless operating will help."

My eyes pleaded with him. "Don't you see, Adam? You're the only one who can keep it from happening." He shook his head and sighed, then turned and walked back to his car.

Chapter Fourteen

The silence was almost painful on the way back to the hospital. Again, we missed any real traffic, and I was thankful for that. I didn't want to be cooped up in this car with him any longer than I had to be. He pulled into the garage and parked in front of my Land Rover. I didn't ask how he knew which vehicle was mine. I didn't care.

My hand went for the handle and he spoke softly. "The thing you've got going on with Mason…It's a good thing Kendra. He's a good guy. If you are right about all of this dying stuff, I'll hate myself when it happens. I know it will hurt him to lose you. He really likes you."

Of course he was worried about his friend's feelings, but it was my life that was on the line, and he didn't give two shits about that. "You're the only one who can prevent that from happening to me."

He shook his head. "I'm going home. I wasn't even supposed to work today, but there was a trauma case, and they called me in. I saved the boy's life," He looked at me then. "And I will save yours on Friday."

I got out of the car, and then looked back at him through the open door. "Only if you're praying before then." I shut the door and walked to my Land Rover. Adam drove off, leaving me alone in the dark garage.

I screamed when I opened the door. Adam had already left, so I wasn't afraid of catching anyone's attention, not that it would have mattered. I was alone in the garage, except for Rhyan, who was sitting in my passenger seat. I guess locked doors couldn't keep out the holy. I just prayed they could keep out the unholy.

"What are you doing here…and why didn't you help me out with

Adam earlier?" I said as I sat behind the wheel, buckled up and started the engine.

"I'm here to talk now, and before...I'm not allowed to interfere. I can only give you advice, not him." I looked at him. He looked so sad.

"You look depressed, Rhyan. What can I do to help?" I already felt like a rubber band that had been stretched to its limit, but he'd been helping me, silently, for years, and I felt I needed to return the favor.

He shook his head. "The damage is already done. Either way, I'm going to lose you."

"Look, this thing isn't over. We haven't lost yet, Rhyan." I said.

He shook his head again as he looked back at me. "I have."

I gave him a questioning look, and he explained in further detail. I would wish later that I hadn't encouraged him to, but let's hear it for adding more problems to my list.

"Either way this turns out, I have lost you, Kendra. I was so excited when you died yesterday. I know that sounds harsh, but that meant that I could actually be with you." He looked away from me. "Coen stepped in and ruined it for us."

I know I looked confused, because I was, very much so. "What are you talking about?"

"I'm your guardian angel, not your soulmate. I want to be your soulmate. I've always wanted to be. Coen caused your accident before you met yours, so I had a chance and that made me very happy. Then he made you an offer you couldn't refuse. I don't blame you for wanting to live, but now I lose you either way."

"Either way, what are you talking about?" I understood that he was in love with me, just as I had suspected after running into him that morning during my jog. I knew that Friday I could lose my life and with it, my soul. But I didn't get the rest of what he was saying.

"If you succeed, I will have still lost you." He stared at me, and I could tell he was really heartbroken. I hadn't done it intentionally. "You've met your soulmate now, and even if you beat this...you will never be mine." he said quietly.

So Mason was my soulmate. That was why I was so attracted to him. I felt bad, because I was happy about that, while Rhyan sat there looking like a sad puppy. He shook his head in shame and grimaced, and I turned my head to the side and looked at him quizzically. Could he read minds? He nodded after that last thought.

"Shit! I've got to really watch what I'm thinking when you're around."

"I can hear your thoughts even when I'm not around you. Your thoughts run parallel to my own." He paused for a moment, then he spoke again. "Mason isn't your soulmate, Kendra. He never will be; don't try to force it. I told you to break the date with him. He is only a distraction for you."

I was shocked. Then who the hell was? I had only met two guys since the accident. Mason and Ad…no. No!

Rhyan nodded. "I don't like it anymore than you do. If you succeed by Friday, then I have to watch the two of you live happily ever after, forever."

"Adam cannot be my soulmate. There has to be a misunderstanding somewhere." I had an idea. "There are people all over the world who live their lives and never meet their soulmate. I'll just choose to not be with mine. I may end up divorced, or alone, but I won't have to live with that arrogant asshole."

"Freewill is a powerful thing, and you do have that choice, but you won't choose that path. I could only be so lucky for you to not choose to be with him. I might have another chance to be with you."

I didn't know what to say to that. I was hoping it would be a long time before I died again, and maybe when I did, I could be with Rhyan. I didn't see anything wrong with that. His face lit up like a Christmas tree. "Stop, Rhyan. My thoughts are very personal to me."

He turned his head away from me, but I could see that he was still smiling. "I can't tune your thoughts out, but I'll try and keep my expressions from being so obvious."

I exhaled loudly, making it clear I was annoyed. There wasn't really anything I could do about it. I had to get back to solving my problem. "So, I have until Friday sometime to help Adam. What do you suggest?"

He frowned again and shook his head. "I was happy a minute ago. Not because I think that you will ever be with me, but because you considered it. It's nice to know that you would, if you could."

"Of course I would. What are you talking about, now?" I said.

"I know it can never happen. The only way to help Adam is to make him love you. It's impossible to truly love someone without believing that there is a God who made that person just for you. Now that you've seen the reason for him not believing, do you think he would take it lightly if you didn't return his feelings? If you make him love and make him believe, then walked away, he would be worse off than he is now."

I nodded. I was trying to understand. "So, how do you make someone love who doesn't know how to love?"

He turned away from me again and continued to look out the window. "You have already looked into his soul, Kendra. Try looking into his heart."

Damn. I hated riddles.

Chapter Fifteen

Rhyan popped back to wherever it was he popped to when he popped, and left me alone. I knew he could still hear my thoughts, and I wasn't thrilled with that tidbit of information.

The drive back to my house passed in a blur. I was concentrating so hard on my thoughts, that I couldn't remember the drive at all. That could have landed me back in the hospital before my time was supposed to be up. I really needed to start paying closer attention, especially when I could get someone else killed.

I unlocked my door and picked up a very hyper Hercules. He showered me with kisses until I set him down to check the answering machine. I had missed four calls since I'd left. I pushed the button to listen as I made my way to the fridge for a late lunch. Leftover meatloaf and creamed potatoes sounded good, so I took those containers out as the first message began. It was Kobhye, and she was uber-worried about me, and wanted me to call her back ASAP. I put a good-sized portion of meatloaf and potatoes on a paper plate, put it in the microwave, set the timer and licked the fork as the second message began. It was Aven apologizing for hanging up on me this morning. He still wanted to know what Mason had said about my check-up. Call him ASAP. I rolled my eyes as I put the leftovers back in the fridge. The third was from Mason. He was checking up on me and making sure Adam hadn't murdered me and thrown me in a ditch somewhere. He didn't ask for me to call him back ASAP, but he did say that he would see me tonight. I didn't think he was actually worried that Adam had cut me up and buried me in little pieces.

The forth call surprised me. It was from Adam. The microwave dinged and I ignored it. I walked closer to the answering machine so I wouldn't miss anything he had to say. "Kendra, this is Adam. Look, I'm sorry I was such a jerk to you earlier. I shouldn't have taken you to the cemetery. I already have plans for tonight, but I would really like to make it up to you. Say, tomorrow for lunch at Cavernous. It's at the corner of Wilkes and Vine. It wouldn't be a date. I only want to make up for being such an asshole. You don't have to call me back. I'll reserve a table for two for noon. If you accept my apology, then you can show up. Again…I'm sorry, and that isn't something I say often."

I stared at the machine for a long time. I played his message back four times. There was sincerity in his voice, and I could only hope that meant I was making progress. He said it wasn't a date, but when one person calls another and asks them to lunch, it's a date. I had dates with my daddy all the time. Oh well, he could look at it however he wanted. Either way, it meant that I would have a chance to work on him a little more. I was running short on time and hadn't made much progress. I smiled. I was actually looking forward to seeing him tomorrow.

I ate, cleaned the house up a little, finished the laundry and got ready for my date with Mason. I was applying lip gloss when I heard his truck door shut outside. I hurried through the house and opened the door before he had a chance to knock. He had his raised hand in a fist and was about to put knuckles to wood. He smiled and his eyes made their way slowly down and back up my body again. I was wearing one of my favorite dresses. It was red and cut above the knee, and I knew I looked hot in it.

He let out a low whistle, the very same one that I had let out when I'd seen Adam's car. Mason got a more appreciative reaction than what Adam gave me. I couldn't worry about Adam tonight. I was going to have one night of fun with Mason, then stick to my rule of not seeing him again until all of this blew over. I hoped it would go that smoothly.

He held out a single, perfect red rose. I smiled as I took it and opened the door further, inviting him inside.

Hercules ran up to him and stood on his hind legs until Mason picked the little dog up in his arms. I stared at them. "It still amazes me how you can do that." He only smiled and watched as I found a vase and added a little water. I put the rose in and grabbed my purse. "Are you ready?"

"Yeah, we'll be a little early. I was counting on having to wait another thirty minutes for you to get ready."

I smiled. "I'm punctual."

He smiled back. "I noticed."

He set Hercules down then walked out the door. I locked up and he walked me to his truck. He even opened my door for me. Not that I needed him to. I think that traditional stuff is way overrated.

Seether was playing when he started the truck, and he lowered it to a level that we could talk over if we wanted to. It appeared he had good taste in music and he was very considerate. Why couldn't he be my soulmate? Maybe Rhyan was wrong.

"I'm not wrong, Kendra." Rhyan's voice said in my head.

I rolled my eyes and he laughed. I spoke back to him only in my mind. I didn't want Mason to think I was crazy. *"May I have this one night, Rhyan? I'll jump back on the soul saving train tomorrow morning, I promise."*

I waited a few seconds for a response, and I finally got one. *"Very well, I will not interrupt your evening again. Have a good night."*

I smiled to myself. *"Thank you."*

"Uh-huh, anytime." I knew he was still watching and listening, but I was confident that he wouldn't barge in on my thoughts again unless I needed him.

"Where are you taking me?" I said as I looked over at Mason.

He smiled. "The Framont."

My eyes widened with eagerness. "Did you already have reservations that you placed, like, a month ago?"

He laughed and shook his head. "No, the manager is one of my friends. He pulled some strings for me."

The Framont was a very classy restaurant that I had only been to once before. That occasion had also been a first date. The restaurant was very elegant and nice, but my date had not been. Maybe I could enjoy it this time. It was a good thing that I dressed for the occasion. I looked over at Mason. He too was dressed to eat at The Framont. He looked nice in his black slacks and bright blue button up, complete with a red tie. He had a back blazer lying in the seat between us. It wasn't a "casual clothing" type of establishment.

"I'm impressed."

He moved his hand to mine, and we laced our fingers together. His smile broadened. "That's what I was hoping for."

When we got to the restaurant, the parking lot was full. Mason drove around back and pulled his big truck up beside a black Tahoe that was just as chromed out and jacked up as Mason's was.

"Are we eating in the kitchen, too?"

He laughed. "No, but parking out here is better than driving around waiting for someone to leave or walking a half mile." He pointed to the Tahoe. "That's Nathan's vehicle. He would expect me to park back here."

Good, so there was no chance of Mason's Truck getting towed for parking where he shouldn't.

He came around to my side and opened the door for me. He held out his hand to help me down. I wasn't going to refuse it. A truck this tall and high heels was not a good combination. I stumbled when my feet hit the ground and fell into him. He caught and steadied me, then breathed in the smell of my hair and perfume along my neckline.

I was getting distracted again, but I didn't care. I had this night, this one night when I didn't have to care.

He found my hand with his and tugged. "C'mon, if we don't go in, I'm afraid I'll have to kiss you."

The idea didn't sound so bad to me, but whatever. He led me to the front of the building, then to the back of the line. It wasn't a long line and the weather was nice, so I was fine.

"I may be able to swing a table for two, but going straight to the front of the line well," he squinted his eyes and sucked air in through his teeth. "Nathan isn't that good of a friend. I would have to be tall, tan, blonde and have different plumbing equipment in order to get right in."

I laughed. "I didn't expect another miracle this week. This is fine, Mason. I'm still impressed."

He bent and kissed me on the cheek, then whispered in my ear. "Good, when I start disappointing you, let me know."

I smiled. "Believe me, you will know."

Chapter Sixteen

The line started moving and he pulled away from me. The way he affected me made me feel light headed, and I was beginning to enjoy the feeling. I only had to stay alive until Saturday, and then I could be with him again.

"Mason Carter, party of two." Mason told the host.

"Right this way, Sir." he said, and we followed him to our table.

I was following Mason while looking around the beautiful restaurant when he suddenly stopped in front of me. I heard him talking before I came up beside him to see who he had stopped to talk to.

"Sherri, you are a vision as always." I saw Mason kiss the hand of the nurse I had met at the hospital, then my eyes moved to her date. I felt my face flush all of a sudden, and had to look away quickly.

"Adam." Mason said as he shook hands with my doctor and the guy I had a date with tomorrow. Adam may have been shaking hands with Mason, but his eyes were looking at me. I didn't want to be rude so I looked back at him. For some reason, his eyes looked more brown than black. It may have been the lighting, but they were beautiful.

I forced myself to look away from him to his date. I smiled and extended my hand to her.

"Kendra, I can't believe it was only yesterday that we were bringing you back to life. You look stunning in that dress."

"Thank you, Sherri…" I started to compliment her on her earrings, but Adam interrupted, and I turned back to him.

"Mason was telling me earlier this evening about what a talented photographer you are. I'd like to see some of your work sometime. The hospital could use some new landscape portraits. I thought maybe black and white photos would look good on some of the walls."

"I'd be glad to show you what I have whenever you get spare time, Dr. Chamberlain." Better to keep it formal. "I know you're very busy. I have some photos featured on my website. You are free to look at it anytime."

I thought Adam was about to speak again, but Mason beat him to it. "We should let the two of you get back to your meal." He looked at me. "We're holding up the host, Kendra." I nodded, and then we said our goodbyes.

The host was waiting for us four tables away. He was standing behind the chair I would be sitting in. It would put Adam directly in my line of sight, and I would be directly in his. Great. I thought about asking Mason to switch with me, but I was a big girl; I could handle it.

I sat down and placed the napkin in my lap. Mason thanked the host and then sat down across from me.

"So, it looks as though Dr. Chamberlain has done a one-eighty. Now I'm the one who is impressed. I didn't think he would hurt you today, but I had no idea how good of a job you would do on him." He was smiling but his voice wasn't. There was something there in his tone that let me know that he wasn't very happy about the job I had done on Adam.

"Actually, he was a jerk today, but he called and left an apology on my machine. I'm meeting him tomorrow for lunch to accept his apology."

Mason stiffened. "You have a date with Adam tomorrow?"

"I'm meeting him for lunch." Just then, the waiter walked up with a bottle of wine, so I didn't have to go into further detail. Not that there was any more to tell, but Mason was looking at me like I'd done something wrong. "Yes please," I said to the waiter who was holding a bottle of Chardonnay, and I held my glass out to him.

Mason looked up at him. "Leave the bottle and give us a minute," he said, shortly.

Had I done something wrong? The waiter left, and Mason cleared his throat. I looked up at him and gave him the straightest face I could manage.

"Kendra, I like you. I like you a lot."

"I like you, too," I said, and left it at that. At that moment, I wasn't sure I liked him "a lot." I didn't handle jealousy well.

He cleared his throat again. "Do you think it's a good idea to date my best friend while you're dating me?"

Okay, so he was upset. A new problem to add to my list. Just perfect. "First of all, Mason, it isn't a date, it's only lunch. Second, I think I'm a big girl, and I can choose to date whomever I like. I have less than six days to make Adam a better person, and I can't do that if I'm not around him, now can I? To answer your question, yes, I think it is a very good idea to date your best friend, given my current situation. If you want to take yourself out of the equation, that's completely up to you."

He filled my glass, then his own. He didn't say anything right away, so I picked up my menu. I glanced around the side of it and looked four tables over. Adam was looking right at me, so I quickly looked back at the menu. "What's good here?" I asked, but my mind wasn't on food. I was wondering if Adam had just witnessed Mason and I having an argument about him.

"I've only tried the salmon and the grilled shrimp. They were both excellent."

The waiter came back to our table and recited a list of specials that weren't on the menu. I told him I'd like a salad with house dressing, and the six-ounce filet cooked medium rare with steamed veggies as my entrée. Mason placed his order and we were again alone, and I no longer had a menu to hide behind.

He cleared his throat again. Was he coming down with something, or was it just a nasty habit? "You're right, Kendra. I've just never been as interested in someone as I am in you, and the thought of sharing you with anyone else...it just caught me off guard, that's all. I wasn't prepared to hear that, and I'm sorry." he smiled, causing me to smile back. Smiles are contagious.

Our salads showed up, and I felt someone staring at me. You ever get that feeling? I knew who it was before I even looked up. I didn't for a minute; I waited until Mason was distracted with his own food before glancing up. As soon as I got the chance, I took it. He was looking at me again, and this time I didn't look away. He was alone at his table, but I saw Sherri coming back from the ladies' room. He saw her too, but kept his eyes locked with mine.

Mason was staring at me when I looked back, so I tried to play it off. I was supposed to be focusing on Adam this week anyway, and Mason knew that. He had even offered to help me come up with solutions for my problem with Adam. "I think he's trying to figure out if I'm crazy or not. He keeps staring at me."

"You're a very beautiful woman. Why wouldn't he stare?" Mason said.

"He isn't looking at any of the other women in here, including his date."

"Maybe he isn't interested in any of the other women in here, including his date." Mason said shortly.

"It's very uncomfortable talking about someone while they are looking at me. Can we talk about something else?"

"I would be more than happy to not talk about another man on our date. What would you like to talk about?"

Great, he was still angry. "Maybe we can talk about the photos I took of you yesterday. I tried to develop them, but they weren't on the film that was in the camera I used. The other shots I'd taken last week were on it, but yours weren't."

Mason shrugged. "You have that happen a lot?"

I shook my head. "Never."

"I'm not a photographer, Kendra. I don't know anything about developing."

Oh well. I hadn't gotten answers to any of my questions, but I'd managed to change the subject. "How long have you been a nurse?" I asked after the waiter sat our entrée's in front of us. Mine looked really good, and I realized that I was more interested in eating, than talking to my date. I glanced up again at Adam, but he hadn't been looking at me until the moment I glanced at him. I looked away. I didn't want to get back on the subject of Adam again.

"Twelve years."

My fork stopped half way to my mouth. There was no possible way he could have been a nurse for twelve years. "How old are you?"

He laughed. "Thirty-five. Why?"

My jaw dropped. He looked younger than me. I recovered and shrugged nonchalantly. "I figured that you were younger than I was, that's all."

"And how old are you?" he asked, still clearly amused. He had to already know; he had my medical records.

"Don't you know that it's rude to ask a lady's age?" I said with an eyebrow raised.

"I figured I'd ask. If you don't want to tell me, then you don't have to."

He was clever. "I'm twenty-nine."

"See, and I thought you were older than me."

My jaw dropped again and he burst out laughing. "God, the look on your face, I was only joking. You look younger than your age. I was guessing twenty-seven, which would make you the youngest woman I've ever dated. I usually date women a little older than me."

"Cougars?" I said.

He laughed. "No, I prefer women my age or a couple years older. A lot of women under thirty-five are still too immature."

I lowered my eyes to my plate and cut a piece of steak with my knife.

"Yeah, well, most men under fifty are too immature for me."

"Where do I rate?"

I shrugged as I put the food in my mouth. "I don't know yet."

I caught movement out of the corner of my eye and looked up. Adam was walking up to our table with Sherri behind him. Mason and I both stood up.

"We just wanted to wish the two of you a good night." I shook Sherri's hand again, but when Adam took mine, our eyes locked, and he gave my hand a little squeeze before raising it and kissing my knuckles. "Will I see you tomorrow for lunch?" Sherri shot him a questioning look. He didn't seem to notice, but I did.

I didn't know if he really wanted an answer, or if he was trying to piss off his date, or mine. I didn't want to be in the middle of a fight, but if there was going to be one, it would be his fight. I would gladly back out of the way. What if I hadn't checked my answering machine? Would he have gone into detail like he had over the machine, or would he have just asked me to check my machine when I got home? "I'll be there at noon."

He nodded then turned back to Mason. "See you in the morning, Mase." They walked off, and we sat back down. All of a sudden, I wasn't hungry anymore, and I wanted to go home. I figured Mason would be in a bad mood the rest of the night because of how Adam had acted toward me.

I took another bite then focused mainly on my Chardonnay.

"Would anyone care for dessert?" the waiter asked. I shook my head.

"No, but you can bring me the check." Mason said.

The waiter hesitated. "Was everything good, Sir?"

"Everything was great. Check please." Mason said.

The waiter glanced at me nervously then scurried off.

"Why are you being such a jerk?"

The waiter came back with the check and laid it on the table by Mason, then he started to walk off. "Wait." Mason said calmly, then put a hundred and fifty dollars in the ticket book without even looking at the bill. He handed it back to the waiter. "Have a good night."

"You too, Sir," he looked at me and nodded. "Ma'am," I nodded back and stood when Mason did.

Chapter Seventeen

We rode back to my house in silence, making it the second time that it happened to me in one day. He'd even turned the radio off. I thought about calling him a jerk, but I really didn't feel like walking. We were about two miles from my house and I couldn't stand it any longer. "You knew I was meeting Adam tomorrow for lunch. Why are you so upset?" I said as I looked out the window.

He didn't answer for a while. He'd already pulled up my drive and shut off the engine before he did respond. He took in a deep breath through his nose, then let it out through puffed out cheeks. "I'm not upset with you. I'm pissed off at Adam. He was on a date with Sherri, and you and I were on a date. If I had suggested that her and I go somewhere and leave the two of you alone, he would have been delighted with the idea. He hardly took his eyes off you the whole time we were there."

I didn't want to tell him what Rhyan had said about Adam being my soulmate. I thought I would try asking him for advice first. "What do you think I'm supposed to do about it? Stay away from him and just wait for the inevitable to happen on Friday?"

"What do you plan on doing with him?" Mason asked, meeting my gaze.

"Whatever I have to do to stay alive."

"And what exactly would that be?"

I looked away from him. Dammit, I didn't want to tell him. *"Tell him, Kendra,"* Rhyan said in my mind.

"You tell him, Rhyan. Show your ass and tell him yourself," I said a

little angrily.

"You know I cannot do that. I'm sorry, but you have to end this with him. He is only a distraction, and not a good one." Fine. I knew that he was right. How the hell did my life get so damn complicated?

"Coen made your life complicated." he said.

"I wasn't talking to you, I was talking to myself."

"Don't do that, people will think you're crazy." I could hear the smile in his voice, and I knew he had tried to make a joke to cheer me up, but it didn't work.

"Maybe I am." I said out loud.

"What?" Mason said.

I sighed. "Sorry, I was having a conversation with my guardian angel."

His eyes got wide like he didn't believe me. "And just what did your guardian angel have to say?"

"He wants me to tell you the truth. He wants me to tell you what I have to do about Adam, but I don't think I have the energy for this fight any longer. I'm going to bed." I got out of the truck, being careful not to break my neck on the long trip down. I heard his door shut, then my gravel driveway under his shoes as he walked around the truck to me.

I looked up at him. He had calmed down, but I knew if I told him what I had to do, he would be angry all over again, or he would tell Adam what my intentions were. I didn't need him causing any more problems than I already had. I didn't figure Adam would enjoy being told that I was going to try and make him fall in love with me so I could stay alive.

"I think you may be right on that one, Kendra. Don't tell him, just get rid of him." Rhyan said.

Mason didn't say anything; he just took my hand in his and walked me to my front porch swing. I sat down on one end, and he sat in the middle so our hands could still be joined.

"What is it, Kendra. What do you have to do to Adam?"

"Do you like me, Mason?" I asked.

"Yes," he said, sounding a little leery.

"Do you like me a lot?" I asked again.

"Yes, Kendra, I like you a lot. What's this all about?" There was a hint of nervousness in his voice now.

"Then you don't want to know. I'll tell you, but it won't be tonight. Drop it, please." I pleaded with the eyes I gave my daddy when I wanted something. To my amazement, it worked on Mason as well, because he nodded.

"Tell me you aren't going to hurt him physically, and I'll let it go," he said.

"I swear I will not physically hurt Adam."

He nodded again. "All right then, consider the matter officially dropped."

Even after Adam had pissed him off earlier, Mason was still worried about the welfare of his friend.

"He told me today that what me and you had going on, was a good thing. He said you were a good guy." I said.

"Why did he act that way tonight toward you if he wanted us to be together?" He didn't want me to be with Mason. Adam wanted to be with me. He just didn't know it yet.

I shrugged. "Maybe he was trying to piss off Sherri so she would leave him alone, and he thought you would know what he was doing."

"You may be right. He's been trying to get rid of her for a while now. She wants something serious, and he never will."

I yawned. "I think I'm going to head in and get ready for bed. It's been a long two days." Mason stood and then helped me to my feet. He looked at me for a moment, then placed a gentle kiss on my cheek.

"I'm sorry it wasn't a great date. Can I call you tomorrow?"

"I may be busy, but if I miss your call, I'll call you back. I'm doing senior pictures all this week and next." He smiled and nodded, then walked back to his truck.

It was the same line I had told Aven, but it was actually true. I was booked solid, starting at nine in the morning. I had a three-hour break from eleven till two, but the rest of that week and the next, I was betting on no sleep. That was, if I made it to the next week.

I took my heels off and let them dangle from my fingers as I watched Mason drive away.

I sighed. Two days down, five to go, and praying for another miracle.

Chapter Eighteen

I woke up on Monday morning surprisingly bright-eyed and bushy-tailed as my daddy would say. No bad dreams, hal-le-lu-jah. I quickly showered and carefully applied my makeup. I had to get ready before my first appointment showed up, just in case my last appointment made me run in to my midday break. I had to meet with Adam for lunch, because I'd already told him I would be there. The smart thing to do would be to cancel all of my appointments for the week. I did actually die, twice, the day before yesterday. No one really expected me to work this week, but if I didn't do it, the kids would go somewhere else, and that would be bad for business.

My first client showed up about fifteen minutes early. If all three did that, I wouldn't have to worry about being late for lunch. She was very easy, and my camera loved her. She had a pretty smile and eyes that shined.

Sometimes a photographer gets people that, no matter what the hell you do with them, it just isn't going to work. That's where my unique skill comes in handy. I can make the un-photogenic look photogenic. Don't ask me how; everyone has their secrets.

I was done with my first appointment in record time, and as she was pulling out of my drive, my second appointment was pulling in.

This client was a guy, and guys were always easy. They don't care where you put them or how you arrange them. I can put them in a field, on the road, or in front of a backdrop, and say "smile", and that's what they do. Most of the guys like the more serious shots where they don't have to smile at all; that's fine with me too.

It didn't take long to finish him up, and he was out the door. I checked my watch. It was ten o'clock. I fixed myself a cup of coffee. By the time it was cool enough to drink without scalding my tongue, my last appointment of the morning rang my door bell.

I've always heard that bad things happen in threes. I guess good things only happen in twos. I opened the door, and the girl was a mess. Evidently, she didn't have a sister or even a mother, by the looks of her. She was wearing mismatched clothes, her foundation was four shades too dark for her skin tone, her eyeliner was too heavy, her hair was in a ponytail, and she had bright blue eye shadow on. What the hell had happened to this girl, a train wreck? A friend or even a teacher should have helped this girl out.

I looked at the hopeless case and a light bulb came on above my head. She was about my size, and her skin tone was almost the same as mine. I looked at my watch again. 10:10 a.m. Well, at least she was early.

I grabbed the girl's arm and pulled her through the house to my bathroom. "Get in the shower and scrub all that stuff off your face. Wash and condition your hair. I'm going to try and find you some things of mine to wear." She didn't argue with me. I didn't know if it was because I sounded angry, or maybe she wanted someone to help her.

I found three outfits for her to wear. They were some of my best clothes, but the girl wouldn't have them on for very long. I opened the door enough to get my arm through, and I hung the hangers with the clothes, on a hook inside the door.

"Put one of these outfits on when you get out," I looked at my watch again. "And hurry. If we aren't finished by 11:25 we'll have to end our session early." I didn't mean to sound rude, but damn.

The door opened, and the girl still looked bad, but she had potential. I had her sit on a stool I keep in the bathroom. I use it when I don't want to stand up to get ready. No joke, I am lazy sometimes. I finished removing her mascara and eyeliner, she looked like a raccoon. She already looked 99% better than she had when I opened my front door.

I told her that her foundation was too dark. Then I told her to make sure it matched her skin tone in the future, or she shouldn't wear any at all. I applied my foundation to her face while she watched in the mirror. Someone had to teach her. I dusted her with loose powder then gave her a precision line on the tops of her lids with my eyeliner. I explained everything I was doing, and showed her how to put it on herself. We went through blushes, eye shadows, mascaras and lip glosses. When I finished with her makeup, her eyes began to tear-up.

"No, don't," I fanned at her face. "This mascara isn't waterproof."

I took the towel off her head then turned her to face me. I used the blow dryer to make her hair straight. She actually had very pretty, long hair. I used my flat iron and straightened her hair even more to give it a style. I could tell her hair had a natural, nasty wave like mine.

When I was finished, I wanted to weep. I cursed myself for not taking a photo of her before the fix, so she could see just how bad she had looked. She was very pretty now. If I went to school with this girl, I wouldn't have recognized her after this fix.

"Everyone is going to think there's a hot new student in their school." I turned her to face the mirror. She screamed then started to cry fresh new tears. I fanned at her face again. "Michelle, you're going to have to stop that. You are ruining everything I've created."

She threw her arms around me and hugged me tight. "I know, and I'm sorry, but no one has ever cared enough to show me anything."

I wiped under her eyes with a tissue then powdered her up again. I pointed at her. "No more tears until after we're through with the shots."

She nodded and smiled shyly. I grabbed the other two outfits in one hand and pulled her to my studio with the other.

I got some really great shots of her. Those senior guys won't know what hit them when she walks through the door on the first day back to school from summer break.

When we were finished, Michelle put her old clothes back on. She looked a little depressed when she walked out of the bathroom holding a small wad of money.

"You don't have to pay the sitting fee. Go buy yourself a new outfit Michelle." her eyes lit up.

"Do you really mean it?" She began to tear-up again, but I was finished with her shots, so I didn't care if she cried a river.

I nodded and smiled back at her. "Only if you promise that you won't tell anybody about today. I want you to walk in that school with your head held high, and let everyone see how beautiful you are. I'm not taking credit for this, mainly because I don't want a bunch of teenagers at my door wanting beauty tips." I looked at my watch. 11:24 a.m.

"Go on now, I'm running late." Michelle hugged and thanked me again, then out the door she went, with me right behind her.

Chapter Nineteen

I drove like a bat out of hell, mainly because I knew that when I reached the outskirts of the city, I was going to be creeping with the noon rush hour traffic.

I arrived at Cavernous five minutes late. Maybe he hadn't given up on me. I opened the door of the little corner restaurant and walked in. It was packed, and there were people waiting to be seated, sitting on benches by the door. I scanned them for Adam, and when I didn't see him on the benches, I went up to the front of the line. A few people gave me dirty looks, but I wasn't cutting in front of them; well I guess I was, but I was hoping Adam was already seated at our table.

The hostess looked up and gave me a fake smile. "Party of one?"

"No, I'm meeting someone. Chamberlain, Adam Chamberlain."

The girl gave me a funny look, then said, "Right this way." What was that about?

I followed her through the main dining room, then into another room that was almost as big. She led me to a corner booth at the far end of the room. It was still crowded, but there was not as much noise. I spotted Adam, and he rose from his side of the booth to greet me.

"Sorry I'm late. My last appointment was a fixer-upper." He smiled as I sat, then he sat too.

"No worries. I took the liberty of ordering you a glass of Chardonnay. I didn't know what you would want, so I ordered what you had last night." Had he noticed that much about my date with Mason?

I really looked at him then. There was a dark shadow around his left eye. "What happened to your eye?"

He gave a nervous laugh. "I was hoping you wouldn't notice. One of the nurses went over it a little with some of her makeup. It looks a lot worse without it."

"I'd imagine it would. What happened?" Had Mason done this out of jealousy? If he had, I wouldn't be taking or returning any of his calls. He knew I had to see Adam this week.

"Sherri didn't take too kindly to the way I acted toward you last night. She got the impression that I was more interested in you than I was in her." He'd made the same impression on me, but I wasn't going to let him know that I had noticed.

I focused on the menu, because I didn't know what to say. The waitress walked up with my wine about that time, saving me from having to speak to Adam right away. I normally didn't drink alcoholic beverages during the day, but the waitress set a glass of water on the table beside my wine, maybe he wouldn't notice if I didn't drink what he ordered me.

"Are you ready to order, Ma'am, or do you need another minute?" I looked at Adam and he motioned for me to go ahead.

"I'll have the chicken salad sandwich with chips please," I said, and she jotted it down on her ticket book then turned to Adam.

"I'll have the same," He said to her, but he was looking at me.

When we were alone again, I felt awkward. What could I say to him? I knew I had more work to do with converting him to Christianity, but where the hell should I start? I didn't want to discuss the loss of his family. I knew the reason he didn't believe, but it wasn't making my task any easier.

"I want to apologize for the way I acted yesterday, Kendra." Did he mean at the cemetery, or last night? I was betting on the cemetery.

"You are forgiven. You already apologized to me on my machine. I got the message."

"Ask him why the sudden change of heart?" Rhyan said in my head, and I didn't question him; he was trying to help me. It was about time.

"Why the sudden change of heart?" I repeated aloud to Adam.

He turned his head to the side and stared at me a moment. He shook his head like he was clearing his thoughts. "I was a jerk, but I was only taking you out there so you would understand and then leave me alone. I didn't expect for you to not see it the way I do. You intrigue me."

"How so?" I asked.

"You are so dedicated to this task. Anyone else would think you are a crazy woman. I still haven't ruled that out."

So he did think I was crazy. "I'm not crazy. There are a lot of terrible things that happen in this world that no one can do anything about. I'm sorry that you lost your family, but you didn't lose your life. Look what you've made of yourself. You are an excellent surgeon. You have saved countless lives..."

"Two hundred and thirty-two, counting you." And I was very happy to be on that list of survivors.

"Fine, you have saved two hundred and thirty-two lives. Do you not think there is a reason for that?"

The waitress showed up with our food. She asked if we needed anything else, and Adam told her that we didn't.

He sighed. "I don't know what to do. I don't want to believe there is a God. I can't believe that if there was, he would make decisions to destroy so many innocent lives. I became a surgeon because...the lives that he decides to take; I make sure they stay here where they are supposed to be. I lost you twice on the O.R. table, but I didn't give up, and look where you are now."

"And you think if something happens to me Friday, that you will be able to keep me here...by operating?"

He shrugged his shoulders. "If your head is still attached, and your heart is in one piece, then the answer is yes."

I covered my face with my hands. *"Help me, Rhyan."*

"You aren't going to be able to talk God into his head, Kendra. You're going to have to show him. What did I tell you yesterday? He

needs to know love."

I sighed again. What did I have to lose by trying? My life and soul were already at stake. My problem was, I'd never been in love myself. How did I show him something I had never experienced for myself? I loved my family, my friends, and even Hercules, but from what I'd heard, the kind of L-O-V-E Rhyan was talking about was different. I'd never felt that kind of love. I think I was afraid to.

"You can do this. Get to know him. He's your soulmate... unfortunately."

I removed my hands from my face and looked at Adam. He was staring at me with squinted eyes, like he was trying to figure out what I was thinking. I didn't think I had said anything out loud. "What are you doing the rest of the day?"

He sat back in his seat and sighed. "You just don't give up, do you?" I shook my head. He stared at me another brief moment before responding. "I have a surgery at one-thirty. It shouldn't take over an hour and a half. I should be leaving the hospital by three, but I'm on call. Why?"

"Come to my house when you're finished." I grabbed my purse and retrieved my wallet out of it.

"I got the bill, Kendra. Where are you going? Aren't you going to eat?"

"We aren't settling anything here, and I have a few things to do before my next appointment." I said as I stood, then I put a ten on the table. "It wasn't a date, remember? If it isn't a date, then you don't get to pay for my meal."

"But…" He began to talk, but I cut him off.

"Call me when you get off and I'll give you directions to my house," I said over my shoulder as I walked away from him.

Chapter Twenty

I wished I'd gotten a to-go box. My sandwich and chips were still sitting on the table at the restaurant, and I was hungry. Damn.

I had lied to Adam. I didn't have anything to do before my appointments this afternoon, but I couldn't sit there and argue with him any longer. I'd thought the "not a date" would have went smoother. I was praying that it would go better when he got to my house. I sighed.

"Rhyan, I need some company, care to pop in?" I said out loud, and then I heard the loud pop. It was a lot louder in the confined space of the car than out in the open, or even in my house.

I stuck my finger in my ear and wiggled it, trying to get the ringing to stop. "I would do anything for you, Kendra." he said with a grin.

I smiled at him. Man, he was handsome. I think he got better looking every time I saw him.

His grin spread and I blushed. I had forgotten that he could read my mind.

"I think I'll visit you more often." he said.

"Stop," I said and glared at him.

"Why did you walk out on him at the restaurant?"

I shrugged. "We weren't getting anywhere, and I was getting frustrated. I can't get into his heart by sitting across a table from him in a crowded restaurant."

He gave me a puzzled look. "Sooo, how are you going to get into his heart later when he stops by?"

I smiled. "By getting into his pants."

His jaw dropped, and his grin was long gone. "I am definitely going to have to find something to distract myself later. I can't watch you be with him. I know it's meant to be but," he sighed and looked sad again. "I love you, Kendra. There have been many times that I would sit and fantasize about being with you...like that."

I pulled in my driveway, and killed the engine. "Come inside and keep me company. I have about an hour to kill before my next appointment, and I need help brainstorming about what to do about Adam."

We got out of the vehicle and he followed me into the house like a normal person, instead of popping from my vehicle to the inside of the house, like the angel he was.

Hercules ran straight to him, sniffed of his feet and then sat on his haunches and looked up at Rhyan. I shook my head as I looked at my dog. "You're turning into a traitor." I walked to the kitchen and tossed my keys on the counter where I always put them. Rhyan followed me; I could feel him behind me. I tried to keep my thoughts empty, but I knew what I wanted to do.

I turned around to face him, and pursed my lips together. "I want to ask you a question, Rhyan. You said that you fantasize about being with me, right?"

He was definitely more alert now. His eyes grew wide. I didn't know if he was embarrassed about telling me, or if he was trying to look in my head and see what I was thinking. I kept my thoughts blank.

He slowly nodded as if he were confused. "I do."

I sighed. "Well, I'm not offering to fulfill your fantasy, but do you think it would complicate things between us if I kissed you?"

He shook his head. "Not at all."

I lowered my head and could sense him slowly walking toward me, as if he was afraid that if he moved too fast, I would change my mind. "If I kiss you now, are you certain that you won't have resentment towards me later? You know I am meant to be with Adam, but you've watched over me my whole life and I want to give you something back, something you want. I don't love Adam, not yet, but if I do fall in love with him, I will be his, not yours. You understand that, right?"

He placed his hand gently on my cheek and stared at me with amazement shining in his eyes. I had never had anyone look at me like that, and at that moment, I wished that Rhyan was the one I was destined to be with. I wished the man in front of me was my soulmate.

He moved his hand to the back of my neck and pulled me to him. A small sound escaped my throat as our lips touched. I wrapped my arms around his waist, and then opened my mouth to him so we could explore further. I had never in my life been kissed like this. It felt like I was floating on a cloud somewhere alone with him. The kiss became hungrier. We were pressed together so close it was like we were trying to switch places with each other.

I wanted him, and he knew I did. I wanted to be with him like this, and more, forever. I could feel the love rushing through my veins, heading for my heart. I knew it had to be love. I had never felt anything so strong and wonderful in all my life.

Rhyan suddenly broke the kiss and pushed away from me. I stumbled a little and braced myself on the kitchen counter. Before I could even think, he started speaking.

"I'm sorry, Kendra. I am so sorry. I didn't mean for it to go that far…"

I reached for him, but he only shook his head and took a step away from me. "Those aren't your feelings. You don't love me, not really. Those are the feelings I have for you. The guardians are very powerful, or very weak. I am very powerful, because you have chosen me over your guardian demon. Patrick is very weak, and if he had kissed you the effect wouldn't have been the same. I was so strong that you were feeling my feelings for you. They were not your own, and I am sorry to have burdened you with this."

My chest was aching and I put my hand over my heart. A tear fell on my arm. He looked at it and cupped his hands over his mouth for a moment.

"You are now feeling my broken heart." he said after he let his hands fall away. "I have to go so it doesn't get worse for you." he lowered his head then, and I wanted to scream out, "How the hell could it get worse?" I felt like someone was trying to rip my heart out of my chest. "I will never touch you again. I'm sorry. I don't feel like I can apologize enough to make up for this." He popped out of my kitchen, and I stared at the blank place where he'd been.

My doorbell rang. I wiped at my eyes and tried to pull myself together. I'd found out how it felt to love, and moments later, was intensely aware of how a broken heart felt. I didn't like the second feeling at all.

Chapter Twenty-one

My first client was more than forty-five minutes early, but I didn't mind. I needed the distraction. I took my time with her and gave her more poses than I do for most clients. I was work focused now, so any thoughts of the new men in my life, including Rhyan, were pushed into the shadows.

I finished with her, and was able to work through two more clients in record time.

I was finishing up with my third client after lunch when my phone rang. I let the machine get it. If it was important, they would leave a message, and I could call them back.

It was Kobhye again. She was threatening my life if I didn't return her call today. She ended by saying that she was going to drive over and check on me later. Panic shot through me. Adam would be here later. I ran for the phone and got there just before she hung up.

"Hello! I'm here," I said a little breathless.

"What were you doing, Kendra? Is Aven over there?" Why did everyone think I was always having sex?

"No. He isn't. I'm working. I have a client. Senior shots all this week and next." I took a breath. "I'm fine. I've just been working really hard since I got out of the hospital. That's why I haven't returned anyone's calls. I'm sorry."

"Okay. Hey, what's the name of that sexy-ass doctor of yours? Can you get his number for me?"

Shit!

"Um, I'm sort of seeing that sexy-ass doctor. It isn't monogamous or anything, but I think it may be soon." There was silence on the line for a moment.

"Oh well, then how about that good looking nurse that was with you when you came into the waiting room."

Shit! I was seeing him too, but I knew it couldn't last with Mason. I had to cut him loose eventually, better sooner than later. "I'll see what I can do about Mason," I told her, then I said I had to get back to work and we said our good-byes.

I hung up the phone and laid it on the counter. It was good to know I didn't have to worry about her showing up. I turned and started for my studio when the phone shrieked again. I answered it. If I let the machine get it, and it was someone else threatening to drop by, I'd just have to come back and answer it anyway.

"Hello." I had a slight feeling of déjà vu.

"Kendra?"

"Adam…" My elbows had been propped on the edge of the counter, but the moment I heard his voice, my knees buckled and I went down. The cordless phone fell out of my hand, hit the floor and slid under the dining table. I crawled quickly to retrieve it and put it to my ear.

"Adam,"

"Kendra, are you all right?"

"Yeah, sorry I…I fell." I felt like such a klutz.

He laughed. He had such a good laugh, and I was sure he didn't do nearly enough of it. "Well, you're really one for accidents this week. Are you normally so clumsy?"

"No." I said as I rolled my eyes. "You need directions?"

"Actually, I don't. I got your address from your medical records, and I used my GPS to find your house. I'm standing at your front door." I looked at the phone then heard the knock at the door. Well, shit. I thought I was going to have at least thirty minutes to mentally prepare for his arrival.

I walked, phone in hand, to the door and opened it. Kobhye had been right; he was sexy. He didn't have to try to be, he just was. He was still wearing the smile I'd heard over the phone a second ago, and I felt myself start to swoon. I regained my composure enough to turn my head. I had to get better control over myself. I was going plain stupid over men lately.

I opened the door a little wider so he could enter. "Come on in, Adam. I'm just finishing up with a client." I looked at my watch. 4 p.m. Where had the time gone? "My next appointment should be here any minute." I glanced over his shoulder, and saw that my next appointment was indeed arriving now. "And there he is."

I could hear the girl I'd been shooting walking up behind me. "That was great, Ms. Larkin. I know those pictures are going to look awesome." She handed me some folded bills and walked past me. She slowed a little when she passed by Adam, no doubt trying to make eye contact with him, but he wasn't looking at her. His eyes were on me. She turned back to me and smiled. "Thanks again, bye."

The girl stopped to talk to the guy that was getting out of his truck. I wasn't going to wait on him. He could knock or come in when he was ready. I turned to head back into the house and asked Adam to shut the door behind him. He closed the door and joined me in the kitchen. I got down a glass from the cabinet. "Want something to drink, tea, coke, Mt. Dew, Dr. Pepper, Sprite, water..."

He laughed softly. "Dr. Pepper is fine." I grabbed two of those from the fridge and handed one of them and a glass with ice in it to him.

"What time does your on call shift end? I have a bottle of wine I was thinking of opening up after my last appointment leaves." I opened my soft drink and took a drink from the can. I noticed that Adam had set his glass on the counter and was drinking from the can as well.

"I actually got out of being on call tonight. Richardson is taking over for me." So, I was important enough for him to find a replacement. I must be making progress. "I don't have any objections to wine later."

I heard my front door open, then footsteps coming toward us.

My next client was Quarterback of the Cougars and class president. Alex Marks stood, in all of his splendor, at the edge of my kitchen. I could see why all the girls in school were in love with him. He definitely had the looks, but I knew Alex and his family, and he was really a down to earth nice guy. He also had a very large crush on me.

He had on that nervous smile he always wore around me. "Hi, Kendra." He eyed Adam a little suspiciously.

"Well hello, Alex. Are you ready to get your picture taken?" I said with a smile.

He nodded toward Adam. "He gonna be here the whole time?" It really wasn't like Alex to be rude, but like I said, he was crushing on me big time; had been ever since he was fifteen and hit puberty.

Adam gave a snicker. "I can leave if it's going to be a problem for you, man."

"No, you're not." I said, then gave Alex "the look".

He dropped his eyes, like a toddler who had just gotten in trouble for touching something he wasn't supposed to. "It isn't a problem."

"I don't think so either. Now, let's go take some kick ass photos of you so you can give them out to all those girls who dream of you at night."

He smiled shyly. "Can I give one to you?"

I gave him my best smile. "I would love a picture of you, Alex. I'll put it in a frame on my bedside table." I knew it was wrong to lead the boy on, but he would grow out of this nonsense sooner or later. I looked at Adam. He was watching the whole thing with silent laughter.

Alex assessed Adam again, then said, "You a nurse or something?" I took that as my cue to get my props set up for his first shots. I was listening to their conversation, but wasn't adding in any of my thoughts.

"Or something...I'm a doctor, a surgeon. I actually saved Kendra's life a couple of days ago." Adam said and I could feel Alex' stare when he looked at me. I cringed. As far as I knew, he hadn't heard anything about the accident, and I had wanted to keep it that way.

"That true, Kendra? Did you almost die? You didn't call me? I mean, you didn't call my mom?" The look of horror was real in his eyes. He was really smitten with me.

I shook my head. "It wasn't as bad as Adam is making out, but yes, he was there when I needed him." I gave Adam "the look" and he must have understood me, because he changed the subject.

"So, you play football...or something?" Adam nodded to the Nike duffle bag Alex was carrying. There was a helmet sitting atop it.

Alex nodded then went straight to talking football. Guys were so easily distracted. I finished setting up then gave a deafening whistle through my fingers. It would be the only way to get the guys' attention away from sports. They both shut up and turned to stare at me. Good, I still had it in me. I hadn't whistled like that in years.

"I'm ready for you. We'll take a few shots with what you're wearing then you can change behind that screen over there." I wanted to make it perfectly clear where he would need to change. I didn't want any misunderstandings like I'd had the other night with Mason. I was positive the boy had a nice body, but I was eleven years older than him, for Christ's sake, and I wasn't a cougar. It was sooo not going to happen with me and Alex, no matter what he dreamed would someday happen.

I walked to Adam with a big smile on my face. "What?" he said.

I took his hand in mine and led him to the props where Alex was standing. I let go and went to set Alex in his first pose. It was a pose that I used with every senior. He was leaning with his elbow propped on a pedestal, with his fist to his temple. "Class of 2012 was written in block letters running down the length of the wooden pedestal. I made sure he was perfect then went back to Adam.

I positioned my camera on the tripod and brought Alex into focus. I leaned back and then handed the clicker to Adam. He took it, but looked at it like it was a snake about to bite him. He could make a precision cut in human flesh with a scalpel, but he couldn't take a photo. I found that freaking hilarious.

I laughed then pointed at the camera and told him to look. "You have to wait for the perfect moment, then capture it. A person's features are constantly changing. You tell them to smile or not, and they do what you ask, but different parts of their body are moving in tiny fractions every second. I could have him stand like that, tell him not to move, take ten pictures, and every one of them would look different. That's why we take so many shots of the same pose. Then we choose the one that's the best. You're going to have some fun today, Adam."

"Wait, he's taking my pictures?" Alex said, aghast.

I laughed. "Not all of them. I'll take most of them, but Adam here is going to learn to have fun, and learn something new while doing it; something that doesn't require saving lives, but rather seeing the beauty in life."

Alex rolled his eyes, but he didn't say anything else. Adam was still looking at me with a horrified expression.

"When I tell you to click, push this in like this." I looked back at Alex and said, "Smile!" he complied, and I said, "Click," then pushed gently on Adam's finger. The camera came to life and made the familiar, comforting sound it did when it captured an image.

Adam's face lit up like a kid at a carnival. Had he never taken a picture before? It was good to see him smiling. I wanted to keep that smile planted there for the rest of his life. I realized then, that I wanted to be there to see it for the rest of his life…or the rest of mine, however long that may be.

Chapter Twenty-two

We worked with Alex through five different poses. Adam was really kind of a natural. There were a few times when I was about to say "click," that he went with his own instincts and took the shot before I could say anything. He smiled at me every time he did it. I would compliment him and smile each time. The majority of the time I had to tell him to click, when I would look at him, he would be watching me instead of Alex. I wanted him to have fun, and if watching me was fun for him, we were heading in the right direction.

While Alex changed from his football uniform back to his khaki shorts and t-shirt, I put my props away and began setting up for my next appointment. A girl named Amy was due here at five. I didn't know her, but then again, I didn't know most of the kid's names, only their faces.

Alex hugged me goodbye and paid me for the sitting fee. "Mom told me to tell you to call her sometime. I think she wants to catch you up on the town gossip or something."

I laughed. "That's probably exactly why she wants me to call her. Tell her I have a lot going on right now, but as soon as things slow down a bit, I will."

He nodded and eyed Adam again, but finally smiled and stuck out his hand. Adam grinned and shook it. "You got a great girl here. Treat her right, or someone else will be trying to save your life."

"Alex!" I exclaimed in disbelief.

Adam laughed. "I believe you, Alex. Maybe we will come to some of your games this year."

I was in shock. I had to be. Not only did he not deny that we were seeing each other, but he plainly stated that we were.

Alex nodded then grinned at me. "I'd like that."

I shook my head. "Have a good year," I said as he walked to the door.

After the door closed, I turned and stared at Adam.

"What?" he said with a smile.

"Maybe we will come to some of your games? Since when are we a couple? Today wasn't a date, remember?" I said as I crossed my arms over my chest and leaned on the kitchen counter.

He smiled sheepishly. "No, you're right, today wasn't a date." He moved closer to me and I straightened up a little. "Tell me why I can't stop looking at you." He stopped about five feet away from me and leaned against the counter opposite the one I was up against.

My heart began to race, and so did my mind. If I told him, he would bolt. I had to handle this very carefully. "You wouldn't believe me if I told you."

His eyes got a little wider, like he hadn't expected me to say that. "So you know why?"

I nodded and forced myself to breathe steadily.

"Try me." he said, and then the phone rang; saved by the bell. Hal-le-lu-jah!

I stared at him a moment then went to get the phone off the bar. "Hello."

"Kendra." It was Aven. Shit. I really needed to start checking my caller I.D.

"Hey, I'm sorry I didn't call you back. I've been really busy with senior pictures." I said.

"That's right. I forgot you were going to be so busy. Hey…I really need to talk to you. Do you mind if I come over in a little while?"

"Can we talk some other time? I really do have a lot on my plate for the next couple of weeks."

"It won't take long. How about I come over tonight around ten? Will you be done with your clients by then?" I was actually going to be done with my clients by eight. I looked up and Adam was watching me.

"I'll be up all night developing the photos I've taken today. Now just isn't a good time for me." I didn't want to tell him I had company, but he was really leaving me no choice.

"I can help you develop," he said. He had never volunteered to help me do anything. What the hell was up with him?

"Is what you have to say that important? You've never helped me do anything."

He was silent for a moment, and then he finally spoke. "I think what I have to say is pretty important."

My eyes grew wide as I realized what I thought he wanted to talk with me about. We had been friends since grade school and friends with benefits for a little over a year. He clearly wanted to take the next step. Double shit! I didn't want to hurt him, but there was absolutely no way around it. He was probably never going to speak to me again when I told him, but I already had Adam, Mason and Rhyan filling my schedule. I didn't need another man.

"I'm sure it is, but I have company tonight." I said, quickly.

He was silent again for a moment then said, "You mean your clients?" I could hear the suspicion in his voice. I knew he didn't think I had meant my clients. We had decided that when either of us told the other we had "company," it meant that we had a date with someone else. That had always been fine before, but I didn't think it would be this time. Come to think of it, I was the only one who had actually used it. Aven never seemed to have "company" when I called him.

I sighed. "No, I don't mean my clients."

"Why didn't you just say that then? Is this thing with him serious or something?" he said, sounding a little upset. I figured he would be.

"Yeah…I think it is a little serious. I didn't want to hurt you." I was pleading with him to understand. If I'd thought he would ever want to get serious with me, I wouldn't have allowed "the benefits" to go along with our friendship.

"Don't worry about me. Have a good night, Kendra," he said, then hung up. That was the second time that day he'd hung up on me. I growled.

I stared at the phone in my hand briefly before setting it on the counter. I looked up at Adam, and my doorbell rang; saved by the bell, again. We really did need to finish our conversation, but I didn't think I was prepared for it at the moment.

I went to the door and Adam stayed in the kitchen.

Chapter Twenty-three

It turned out I did remember Amy. She was a cheerleader, and I had done shots of all the girls only a few weeks ago. She was petite, thin, and I could tell right away that she was photogenic. This should be an easy one for Adam. She informed me when she walked in that she wanted something different than everyone else had. She wanted most of her pictures to be taken outside. That was fine with me, but it would take longer and be harder on Adam. He would have to hold the camera instead of clicking the clicker.

I decided to take the majority of the shots and then let him snap a few at the end of each pose. We would find out if he had any real talent.

We made our way through the house to the kitchen. I introduced her to Adam and told her that he would be helping. She seemed to be fine with the idea. She was so fine with the idea that I thought if I'd suggested that she take off her clothes for the shots, it would've only taken her about five seconds to get undressed.

I turned to look at Adam. He was smiling at me. Were my thoughts written somewhere on my forehead?

"Yes." Rhyan said.

"I don't need your input." I snapped back at him.

I could hear him snicker, but I ignored it. I told Amy that I needed at least one formal, and that it had to be taken inside. She was fine with that, too. I gave her a tube top and pointed to the screen. She went to change. When she came back out, the tube top was pulled down lower than it should have been. Her cleavage was impressive, and that means a lot coming from me.

When she sat on the stool for her formal, I took the material from the front and tugged it up. She gave me a sour look, but didn't say anything. I draped the black material around her shoulders then buttoned it on the inside where the camera couldn't see it.

I moved the tripod and focused in on her. "Click," I said, and the camera came to life. I repositioned her then told her to smile for the next two. She did, and my camera went off before I could say anything. I smiled, adjusted her clothing a bit then turned the soft box on. When I moved out of the way, I looked at Adam. He had a look of concentration on his face until he clicked again.

I told her she could change, and she slipped behind the screen.

I took my camera off the tripod so we could go outside. "When you want to zoom in or out, you use these two buttons," I said to Adam. He moved in a little closer to me to get a better look at the camera. "She wants the rest of her shots to be taken outside, so the tripod will be essentially useless. You need to have a very steady stance when the tripod can't be used." I sighed. "We could use it, but it would take too long." I noticed then that he was really close to me. He was still looking at the camera, but I didn't think that was where his attention was focused.

He opened his mouth to say something and Amy cleared her throat. We both looked up, and Adam took a step away from me.

"I think I want my first picture to be under the trees in your back yard. You can take some of me up-close and some from a distance." I really hated when the client tried to tell me how to do my job, but she was paying me, so I really couldn't say a lot. Most of the time, I gave the clients that were easy and nice a break, but I knew that the girl in front of me wasn't going to be either of those. Oh, she was easy all right, but by a totally different definition. I'd give her all the poses she wanted, and I'd make sure they were all damn good. When it was time for her to pick out the ones she wanted, I'd make a small fortune off her. It was evident she was in love with herself. She would get her daddy to buy every one of them.

She was dressed in a thin, long sleeve button-up that was tied in a knot under her boobs so she could show off her belly button ring. She had only bothered to button up one button, and her cleavage was spilling out over the top of the tight material. She had on cut off shorts that were so tight, I couldn't believe she could actually breathe, and they were so short that I was positive her ass had to be hanging out the backside. To top it all off, she was wearing cowboy boots. I always thought it ridiculous when anyone wore boots with shorts. She looked like an amateur who was about to pose for a playboy spread. Who dresses like this for senior pictures? Her parents had to be proud.

I smiled sweetly. "I will do whatever you want, Amy."

We walked out of the house into my back yard. I saw Adam analyzing the unique windows of my studio from the outside. He was studying the rods, water pipes and lighting fixtures hanging over them for creating effects. I could tell he was curious, but he never said anything.

I had an awkward tree in my back yard that forked low to the ground. It was low enough that a person could sit on the lowest branch with their feet still touching the ground. One of the big branches extended horizontally for a short distance, like a seat or immobile swing, and then curved up to meet its fellow branches. The tree was definitely different, and I had, on more than one occasion, taken shots of it alone. It provided a lot of shade and reminded me of peaceful evenings. It was my favorite tree, and it was the first place Amy chose to pose.

She sat on the low hanging branch then primped herself without a mirror. I rolled my eyes behind the camera and began shooting. I had to get going or Amy's session was going to run into my next appointment. After I'd gotten at least four good shots of that scene, I handed my camera to Adam. This time, he didn't look at it like it was a snake. He had apparently made peace with the device. I watched him as he concentrated on his breathing and then took his shot. He took two more before I suggested we move on to the next scene.

I'd told Amy that there would be no time for her to run in and change between each scene, so she brought her duffle bag with us. We turned around while she went behind a tree to change. Not that she would've minded if Adam had watched, or even helped her undress.

We were doing shots of the last pose when I heard an ear piercing whistle. I turned to see a guy walking toward us. Amy let out a squeal, took off running, and jumped on the boy. She locked her legs around his back and began showering him with kisses.

I looked at Adam and smiled. "I think you're off the hook now."

He sighed. "Thank God."

My eyes grew wide as I stared at him. I raised an eyebrow at him and smiled. "Really? Thank God?"

He rolled his eyes and frowned. "It's a figure of speech that everyone uses, Kendra."

"Oh, I wasn't aware. I thought only believers thanked God." I joked.

"I am having a really good time with you doing all of this." he shrugged. "It's fun. Please don't ruin it by bringing religion into the picture."

It was apparently still too early. I knew he would ask me again later about not being able to stop looking at me. If he wouldn't believe in God, then he damn sure wasn't going to believe in soulmates and destiny.

Chapter Twenty-four

My next appointment showed up while Amy was still making out with her boyfriend. The client was another girl, but she was dressed appropriately. She gave Amy a nasty look as she walked to Adam and me.

I held out my hand to the young girl. "You must be Ashley," I said, and she nodded as she shook my hand.

Amy laughed in a sinister way. "You better watch it, Ms. Larkin, Ashley's looks will break that nice camera of yours." her boyfriend joined in with the cruel laughter.

I started to speak, but Adam beat me to it. "If it made it through your shots, the camera will be just fine after Ashley's session." I stifled a laugh as I looked at him. I couldn't believe he'd said that out loud, but I had to admit that I was just about to say something a whole lot like it. Maybe we were soulmates.

"I wouldn't lie to you about that. You know I would change it if I could." Rhyan said, but I could hear the laughter in his voice. I knew he thought Adam's remark was funny.

Amy scowled at Adam. She handed me some bills then stormed away from us with her boyfriend in tow.

"Her guardian demon has more control than her guardian angel does." Rhyan said.

"I can't help her, Rhyan. Don't ask."

"I wasn't going to. There are a lot of cases in the world that you can't do anything about. They have to want to help themselves. It usually takes a major catastrophe in their life for them to actually look

into their soul and realize how far gone they really are. Adam was actually too far gone to save, but Coen risked his immortal soul by cheating. He lost his soul, but it doesn't mean Adam has to lose his. I know you can do this, Kendra. Have faith."

I nodded then went to work on Ashley. I couldn't stand there and have a conversation with my Guardian Angel any longer. Ashley and Adam were beginning to give me funny looks.

It didn't take us long to take Ashley's photos. She was easy, and she had a great sense of humor. She had us laughing the whole time. She also didn't have a problem with Adam taking some of the shots, but her reasons were different than Amy's had obviously been.

Ashley changed back into the clothes she'd arrived in, paid me and then she left after thanking us both for a great evening.

I looked at the clock on my kitchen stove. We had about ten minutes before my last appointment of the night was due to arrive. I went to the fridge and grabbed a couple more drinks, I handed one to Adam.

He took it but he didn't open it. He just played with the tab on the Dr. Pepper can as he spoke. "Are you going to tell me the reason I can't stop looking at you?"

I shook my head as the doorbell rang. "I don't think it would be a good idea to tell you tonight."

"Why?" he said, but I was already heading for the door.

It was a skinny little guy in glasses. He could be nice looking one day, after he completed puberty and grew out of his nerdy stage. Some guys never did grow out of looking like a nerd, but this guy had potential, and I had every intention of trying to bring that out in the shots I took of him tonight.

He was wearing a plaid, short sleeve shirt buttoned all the way to the top, and his hair was parted down the middle. Lord, help him.

"The lord is busy, Kendra. You'll have to do it." I rolled my eyes at Rhyan, but the little dork in front of me was the only one who saw it.

"Come to the bathroom," I said as I turned and walked back through the house. He followed me, and I handed him a towel. "Get in the shower and wash that stuff out of your hair. I'd feel better about your pictures if we could do a few things differently with your hair and clothes. I'll go find something for you to wear." I eyed his outfit and mentally shook my head. He also hadn't brought extra clothes to change into for different poses.

I shut the door behind me then headed for my studio. I had all kinds of clothes. The boy would have to wear his own blue jeans, but they weren't totally hopeless. Most blue jeans looked like what they were in a photo, blue jeans. I grabbed a knit polo shirt, a black long sleeve button up, and tried to remember what color his eyes were. I thought they were green, so I grabbed a grass green cashmere sweater.

When I turned around, Adam was standing in the doorway looking at me. "He's a fixer-upper," I said as I walked by him on my way back to the bathroom. I laid the shirts on the floor in front of the door. The shower was still running, so I knocked softly and said, "I laid a few shirts out here on the floor. You'll see them when you open the door. Put one of them on when you get finished."

I heard the water cut off. "Okay, Ms. Larkin." He sounded a little embarrassed, but hopefully he would thank me later.

Adam was leaning against the counter when I came back into the kitchen. I was going to have to style his hair for him; evidently he wasn't capable of such a task. "He'll be out in a minute."

He looked at me with a smirk. "Was he that bad?"

"You have no idea. He wasn't as bad as a girl I had earlier this morning. She was thankful for her makeover, maybe he will be too."

I heard footsteps coming from my bedroom, and we watched as the guy revealed himself. He'd chosen the knit polo. All three buttons were buttoned up, but he looked a lot better than he had.

"We need to do something with your hair, and then we can get to work," I said as I headed toward the bathroom. Adam followed us this time and sat on the toilet lid. I had the boy sit on the stool. His hair was cut neat and was a little longer on top. I thought a neat business style wouldn't scare him too much. I moved the part in his hair from the middle to the left side of his head and used my blow dryer to get rid of the dampness and make the part stay. It didn't take much to fix him up, and for that, I was grateful. I looked at the whole of him then unbuttoned two of the three buttons. "How is your eyesight? If you lose the glasses for the picture, will you be able to get around?"

He took the glasses off his face and blinked a few times. "I've never been able to see myself without glasses. It's blurry when I look in the mirror without them."

I smiled. "How would you feel if I took some of your pictures without them? When I get them developed, you'll be able to see what you look like. You're very good looking. I think you may want to switch to contacts after you see the pictures."

He smiled at me and nodded. "Yes, I'd like that. You can take all the pictures without me wearing them." He talked like no one had ever told him he was good looking before. I was sure his momma had.

He stood and looked in the mirror. He stared at himself without the glasses for a long while before I interrupted him. "We need to get to work. What's your name again?"

"Raymond." he said. Raymond was a typical nerd's name, no pun intended; I just haven't met a Raymond that wasn't a nerd. His dad was probably a Raymond, too.

I nodded. "It's nice to meet you, Raymond. Let's take some kick ass pictures of you."

He actually laughed, as if he'd never heard anyone cuss before. If he spent any time around me, that would change pretty quickly.

The guys followed me to the studio. Raymond was wearing his glasses so he wouldn't trip over anything, and Adam had a big grin on his face. It was so nice to see him smile.

I got out a tux top in Raymond's size and had him change behind the screen. I had to have at least one formal of every student to comply with school rules. The students had to be in formal wear for the school annual.

I was setting up the soft box when Adam walked up behind me. He put a hand on each side of my waist, and gently pulled me to fit the front of his body. He had dropped a couple of hints that he was interested, and I had caught him staring at me more times than I could count, but this was the first time he had made it obvious that he wanted to do things with me other than taking pictures. The feeling I was getting from his hands on my waist was more than most men could make me feel in a whole night. I was captivated.

I couldn't speak; he had taken my breath away. I was instantly hot for him, and there wasn't anything I could do about it. It was the most natural feeling I had ever experienced. I guess he sensed my emotion, because he pulled me tighter to him and kissed the bend of my neck.

I opened my lazy eyes to Raymond staring at us wide-eyed. I broke away from Adam and stumbled into a prop. He caught me, and then righted my body until I could stand on my own. I looked up to his eyes. They were lighter than they had been before. Was his eye color becoming lighter because his demon guardian was losing? I didn't know why his eyes were changing color, but I could only assume it was a good sign.

I stood on my own and motioned, with a little embarrassment, for Raymond to have a seat in the center of the prop. I knew that I needed to work on Adam becoming a believer, but this was my last client of the day, and I needed to get it done before I could worry about the end of my life. I know it sounds stupid, but it's what I do.

Raymond sat down in his tux top. I walked to him and smiled before removing his glasses. He smiled back at me shyly. He really was good looking. He looked a hundred percent better than when he'd shown up at my door. I was betting he would go buy contacts tomorrow.

I could feel Adam looking at me, and I was a little distracted by it, but I needed to concentrate on my subject. I cleared my throat, and I felt him look away. I repositioned the soft box and the lights. The sun had started to set, so the lighting wasn't as good in the house anymore.

I positioned Raymond as I wanted him for the first shot. He smiled and I shook my head. "No smile for the first two pictures. I'll tell you when." He nodded and his face became solemn. It was perfect. I straightened his shoulders, and turned his head so he wouldn't be looking directly at the camera. I moved out of the way and said, "Click." My camera came to life. I repositioned him and moved back. Adam took another shot.

"You can smile for me this time, Raymond." He did, but it was clearly a fake smile. Most people aren't able to really smile unless they are truly happy about something. I moved to the side so I was directly in his line of sight and pulled my ears out from my head and crossed my eyes. I got a genuine smile that time and Adam took the shot. Maybe I needed to keep him around to help me with my work. He was actually good at this.

I had him change into the black long sleeve button up and I began changing my props while he dressed. I looked up and just stared at him when he walked around the edge of the screen. He looked dashing. I led him to the new prop, because without his glasses on, I wasn't sure he could see to walk without tripping over something. My equipment was high tech and very expensive, and I didn't want him breaking anything if I could prevent it from happening.

"Very nice," Adam said as I moved the tripod to a new scene.

I smiled as I looked at him, but quickly realized it wasn't my work with Raymond he was referring to. His eyes were lust filled and hungry. My body flushed with heat, and I had to make myself look away from him. I had a job to do, and there was a seventeen year old kid staring at us. When I finally looked back at him, he was smiling.

He stood from his seat and walked to me. I stiffened. I didn't know what to expect. He bent close to my ear and whispered, "I just wanted to see if I affected you, the way you affect me." He exhaled, and even that got my blood boiling again. "We can get back to work now. Your client is waiting on you."

I took in several deep breaths before I opened my eyes. Adam was all calm and collected. There was no sign that he had seduced me with his eyes. I thought it was mean what he'd done to me, but I guess he'd only done it because I wouldn't tell him why he was so attracted to me. I took in another breath, then got back to work.

We took three different poses of Raymond in the black dress shirt, two in the cashmere sweater and four in the knit polo. It seemed like the polo was his favorite of the three, so I gave him more shots in it. He changed back into his nerdy shirt, but this time he left the top two buttons unfastened. Much better, I thought.

I walked him to the door and he gave me an awkward hug. He sighed when he stepped back. "Thank you for taking the time to help me, Ms. Larkin. A lot of photographers would have just taken the pictures."

His eyes glazed over, and he turned and walked out the door.

Chapter Twenty-five

Adam was pouring two glasses of wine when I got back to the kitchen. I really liked it when a person made themselves at home in my house. I didn't care for the nervous type that would say no if you asked them if they needed or wanted anything, when you knew they really did.

I noticed a skillet and a large pan on my stove. I thought I might be going plum wacko, but I knew they hadn't been there a few moments before. If I ignored them, maybe they'd go away.

I could hear Rhyan's laughter in my head, and decided to ignore him, too. It wasn't funny at all that I was turning into a crazy person. Then I heard meat sizzling, and caught a whiff of beef. My eyebrows drew together; I knew I wasn't imagining that.

Adam handed me a glass of wine and smiled. "Usually, when I cook for someone I'm at my place, but we're at your place, and there isn't enough time to get to my place before I starve to death."

I looked at him for a minute then burst out laughing. I sat on the barstool and enjoyed my first sip of White Zen. "So, Chef Adam, I have a question I would like to ask you, but first, what are we having for dinner?"

"Spaghetti, and I may or may not answer your question, but you can ask anything you like." He grabbed my cutting board, a knife out of my wooden knife block, and an onion out of the onion basket.

I smiled at him. He'd said that same thing the first time we ever tried to have a conversation. Of course the circumstances were totally different now. "Is this a date?"

He shook his head. "No, I was just hungry." I looked at him, aghast, and his eyes lit up as he chuckled. "Yes, Kendra, I am considering this a date, but it's hardly fair, I think."

My eyebrows drew together again. "Why isn't it fair?" I asked.

He shrugged. "Well, you were the one who paid for the food and the wine. Didn't you tell me that if it's considered a date, that I get to pay?"

I laughed again then wiped at my eyes from the onion fumes. "But you're doing the cooking. I think that makes it fair. I would pay a lot of money to have someone else cook for me. It isn't one of my best talents. I can make good dishes; I just don't enjoy making them."

He opened the freezer and grabbed a loaf of cheese bread. I know you're supposed to eat garlic bread with spaghetti, but I don't like it, so I buy cheese bread instead. He set the oven temperature, tossed the diced onions into the skillet and got a jar of spaghetti sauce and salt from my pantry. He was walking around my kitchen like he knew where everything was. It was a little puzzling, but maybe he kept everything at his place in the same place I kept all my things.

"I'm guiding him to where everything is, Kendra. He can't hear me like you can, but he's following his instincts, me. He wouldn't have listened to me two hours ago. You're making progress with him. Keep up the good work." Rhyan said through my mind.

"Is that why his eyes are getting lighter?" I said back to him.

"I'm not sure, but I believe so." He said back, and I left it at that.

The doorbell rang, and Adam turned to looked at me with a disappointing look on his face. "You expecting another client?"

I shook my head as I got off the barstool. "I'm done working for the day. I don't know who it could be." I walked down the hall toward the door. I knew that Kobhye or Aven wouldn't be stopping by, but that didn't rule out my parents or other friends.

"Kendra, get rid of him. He's only here to cause trouble for you." Rhyan said, and I froze before opening the door.

"Who wants to cause trouble for me?"

Then I heard him on the other side of the door. "Kendra, it's Mason.

I need to give Adam something."

I started to open the door, but Rhyan spoke again. *"He's lying. Tell him to go away."*

"Why would he be lying?"

"Okay, ask him what he needs to give him, or why couldn't he give it to him tomorrow morning at work."

I wasn't going to argue with him. I knew Mason didn't like me seeing his best friend, and him too. "What is it, and why couldn't you just give it to him in the morning?"

I heard him sigh. "He left his phone at work. I figured he'd need it before morning in case there's an emergency at the hospital. I know Richardson is on call for him, but if they need more hands, they'll need to get a hold of Adam."

I hadn't heard Adam's phone ring the whole time he'd been here, but he'd called me from my front porch when he got to my house. He was lying.

"Thank you. Now tell him to leave you alone." Rhyan said.

I was confused. Why would Mason lie about something like that? Why would he lie, to get in my house?

"I found out why I can't find Mason's guardian angel. He doesn't have one. He is Adam's guardian demon. I would've told you sooner, but I just found out right before he showed up at your door. He knows your motives, and I think he's here to kidnap you so you can't complete your mission and get any closer to Adam's soul. Lock the damn door!"

I was in shock, and instead of moving forward, I took a step back away from the door and stared at the handle. I watched in horror as it began to turn. I rushed to lock it, but I wasn't fast enough. He opened the door and grabbed me by the throat, raised me up off the floor a couple inches and slammed my back into the wall. I couldn't breathe. He was trying to collapse my windpipe.

"You may have gotten to him a little, but you won't get the chance to get to anymore of his soul."

I heard the loud pop through the pounding in my ears. I fell to the floor as Rhyan knocked Mason away from me. There were swirls of neon blue color, and the wind was blowing heavily around them as they fought in my foyer. Rhyan forced an arm around his neck, and placed his other hand on Mason's chest. The pop that followed was deafening, and then they were both gone.

Chapter Twenty-six

I was still shaking as I stumbled back into the kitchen.

"You have to get Adam and leave. I can't hold him much longer, and he'll kill you if he finds you. His real name is Murry. You have to get Adam to leave with you until all of this is over!"

I could tell he was still struggling with Mason/Murry; his voice was strained.

Then I heard Mason shouting at me. *"There's no where you can hide that I won't find you, Kendra!"*

I stopped in the hallway and tried to catch my breath. I could hear Hercules barking and growling from his pet carrier. I kept him in it when I had a lot of people coming in and out of the house, and had forgotten to let him out so he could meet Adam when Raymond left. What could I do? Where could I take Adam so we would be safe until Friday? He wouldn't go with me and leave work that long. I hadn't gotten close enough to him for that. He still wasn't so sure if I was crazy or not.

"Kendra, are you all right?" Adam said to me, as if he hadn't heard any noise at all. I was looking at the floor, and I could feel him coming toward me, I looked up. He was looking at the open door with a puzzled look on his face. "Who was at the door?"

I made eye contact with him. I really didn't have a choice but to do this now. If he didn't believe me, then I was screwed. "It was Mason, Adam."

"Mason? Well, where is he? And why is your door still open?" He took my shoulders in his hands and looked me in the eyes. "And tell me why you look like the world is about to end."

I dropped my head. "Because mine is," I whispered around the large sore lump in my throat.

Adam looked back to the door, then back to me. He huffed. "Look, you're going to have to do a little more explaining than that. I don't have a clue what you are talking about."

When I looked back up at him, my tears brimmed over and slid down my cheeks. "You won't believe me."

His eyes grew wide at the sight of my distressed state, and he hugged me tight to his body. I knew he was scared and confused and maybe thinking about admitting me into an insane asylum, but he stood there and held on to me. "Does this have anything to do with me?"

I nodded.

He sighed. "Okay, does this have anything to do with me being so attracted to you?"

I nodded again.

"And does this have anything to do with me not being able to stop looking at you?"

I nodded, yet again.

"So what does Mason have to do with any of this?" he asked.

I ignored his question. "If you believed in God, this would all just go away."

He let go of me and held out his arms. "I don't know what "THIS" is, Kendra. Try telling me, and I will listen, and try to understand."

I took a deep breath in, and then exhaled slowly. "Mason isn't good, Adam. He wants to kill me."

His eyes grew wide and he backed up a step. He shook his head slowly. "Mason wouldn't try to kill you, Kendra. He isn't a murderer. He may be upset because he took you out on a date, and I moved in on his game, but he wouldn't hurt you because of it. I swear, Kendra," he said as he took my hands in his. "You have to believe me. Mason wouldn't hurt you."

I clucked my tongue twice on the roof of my mouth. "Well, he just tried to." I tilted my head back so he could see my neck where Mason had tried to choke me to death. He hesitantly ran his finger lightly over the red finger markings on my neck. "And he isn't mad because you are trying to steal me. He's pissed because I'm trying to steal your soul away from him. He's your guardian demon. He always has been, and he has more control over you than your guardian angel does. He is pissed at me because I was making progress in winning your soul back."

He saw the red marks. He couldn't deny that someone had tried to hurt me, but he still looked skeptical.

"And where is Mason now?" he said as he looked to the open door, like he wanted to run outside and kick Mason's ass for hurting me.

"He's gone for now. My guardian angel knocked him off me and took him somewhere. He can't hold him for long, and there will be nothing to stop him when he gets loose from Rhyan. Rhyan thinks I should take you and go hide somewhere until Saturday. But I don't know where to go that he won't be able to find us. He's really strong, and he is tapped into you like a GPS tracker. He hears your every thought."

Adam let out a long breath and ran his fingers through his hair. He shook his head again. "So, what happens if he doesn't find us, but I still don't believe in God by Friday?"

"I will die, and both of our souls will belong to him."

He walked away from me and went back into the kitchen. When he came back a few moments later, he looked like he was still thinking. "I've been around Mason for six years. He was working at that hospital when I started there. He can't be my guardian demon, or whatever you say he is. He's always had my back. He's a good person, Kendra."

I shook my head. "He influenced you to take that job. He has the power to make people think things that don't really happen. I bet he started there the same time you did, and only made the people at the hospital think that they knew him and that he had been there a long time.

This is some really unusual shit, and I know it's a lot to comprehend, but I wouldn't lie to you. My life and soul, as well as yours, is at stake."

"I don't really know you, Kendra. I know Mason, and he isn't some demon. What exactly is he trying to stop from happening? How are you gaining better control over my soul? I don't believe in God anymore than I did three days ago."

I shook my head.

"Tell me, Kendra, or I'm walking out that door and you will never see me again!" he shouted as he pointed at the open door.

I started crying again. "Because I'm your soulmate!" I shouted back.

He stared at me, clearly astounded. "I don't know what to believe, but it isn't going to be this. I turned everything off on the stove. Enjoy your dinner, Kendra, and leave me alone." He turned away from me and walked out of the house, leaving the door open. I heard his car start and then heard it quickly leaving my drive.

Chapter Twenty-seven

I leaned against the wall and slid to the floor as I cried. I sat in that same spot and cried for what seemed like an eternity, but was probably only about twenty minutes or so.

"I'm sorry, Rhyan. I have failed, and all is lost."

I heard the pop, and I quickly raised my head thinking that it was Mason, or rather Murry, coming back to kill me. It was Rhyan and he was wearing a sad look on his face.

"It isn't over yet. We won't give up until your soul is lost."

I had a thought. "If Murry kills me before my time is up, does he still get to keep my soul?"

He shook his head. "No, your soul will go to Heaven if he kills you before your time is up. I know it may sound selfish, but if we can't win, then I would prefer it happen that way."

I nodded as I stared at the wall in front of me. "Are there many good souls in Hell?"

He shook his head. "There aren't many guardian angels that would have made a deal like that. Coen was an exception, and he has been given the maximum punishment for it. His soul has fallen into Hell. He can never return."

Good, it served him right. "Where is Murry now?" I had to catch myself, I almost said Mason. That was what I knew him by. Then again, I really didn't know Mason either, did I?

Rhyan shrugged and slid down the wall to sit beside me. "I don't know. He got away from me. I came straight here so I could protect you if he came back." He inhaled deeply, and then let it all out at once through puffed out cheeks. "I can't protect Adam though, and I'm sure Mason will dig his claws into him even deeper if you're not around. There wasn't any other way you could have handled that, Kendra. It isn't your fault that Adam chooses not to believe."

I started crying again, and he looked at me with a helpless expression. I knew he wanted to put his arms around me and comfort me, but he'd promised to never touch me again. "Will you stay with me tonight, Rhyan? I don't think I can be alone."

He nodded. "You're never alone. I'm always with you, but I'll stay here with you like this if it will make you feel better. He won't hurt you if I can help it."

I took his hand in mine and laced my fingers with his. He stiffened. I didn't care if my emotions got taken over by his. I needed to feel the love that I had felt when we'd kissed earlier. I felt like I was slipping away from myself and he was the only thing that could keep me together. I loved him. I had to admit that I was starting to have feelings for Adam as well. I even believed he was my soulmate, but Rhyan made me feel safe, secure, and in control. I needed him like I needed air. Was it possible to love more than one man at the same time?

"They aren't your feelings, Kendra."

I met his eyes. "Yes, they are."

He looked at me, and his breathing shuttered. "They can't be. You've met your soulmate now."

"Is it possible that a soul can be split into three pieces instead of only two?"

He shook his head. "No. Adam is here and I am not. You can't be in two places at once."

"Then I choose to be with you, Rhyan. I've never been in love before, but I feel like my heart would explode if I couldn't see you and talk to you now. I want to touch you, and I want you to touch me. I want to kiss you, and I want you to kiss me back. I feel like if I am denied this that my heart will burst and I will die."

He held up our joined hands. "This is why you feel this way. You are experiencing my feelings, not yours."

I jumped to my feet and let go of him. I backed away from him all the way to the door. I closed and locked it while I was still looking at him. "You aren't touching me now, and I still love you. I still need you to touch me. If I'm not your soulmate, then who is? You should feel this way about someone other than me." I pointed to my chest.

He averted his eyes from mine. "I never met my soulmate. She was lost to her guardian demon over three centuries ago. I only felt true love for the first time when you were born and they assigned me to you. I thought that was the happiest day of my life, but every day since then has gotten better. When we kissed earlier," He ran his fingers through his hair, and a look of pure joy covered his face. "That was the best moment of my existence." then his smile faltered, and was replaced with a frown. "We cannot be together, Kendra, unless Murry kills you before Friday. I would never be able to forgive myself if I stood by and let him slay you, when I know you are meant to be with Adam." His voice trailed off in a kind of sad anguish.

I stared at him for a moment then realized that I was walking back to him. I didn't stop, and he didn't back up any. He stood his ground and let me come to him. His eyes were nervous, because he could see in my head what I was planning to do. I didn't try to block my thoughts from him. If he didn't want it to happen, he could pop out of my house and leave me there to face Murry on my own. He had an ultimatum on his hands. Either he could leave me alone, and Murry would kill me, sending my soul to be with him in heaven, or he could stay here with me now and get the fantasy he had always dreamed of.

I put my hand on the back of his neck. He closed his eyes and his breathing shuttered nervously again. I rose up on my toes and pulled his mouth down to mine. He didn't pop anywhere.

Chapter Twenty-eight

Rhyan backed me up to the wall in my hall. The pictures shook on their nails as my back slammed against the sheetrock. He grabbed my butt with both his hands, pulling me up further until I could wrap my legs around his waist. The kiss was even more intense than it had been earlier. I wanted to breathe him in. I wanted him to touch me as he had always wanted to. I wanted him inside me, and I wanted to be with him forever.

Our tongues tangled together in a wild dance, and I knew for a fact that I loved him. I had to let Murry win in order for me to also win. I wouldn't be saving Adam, but he didn't want to be saved anyway. You couldn't save someone who just clearly didn't want it to happen. Rhyan loved me and I loved him. It was the best feeling I had ever experienced.

My body tingled all over with desire. I had to have him soon. "Bedroom," I said when I pulled my lips away enough to catch a breath.

"Good idea." He breathed back before he crushed his lips to mine again and carried me to my room. He shut the bedroom door with his foot. Light from the quarter moon illuminated my bedroom furniture. I could see his silhouette as the dim light fell on his back. I wanted to see his face. I wanted to see who I was making love to.

As if he picked the thought right out of my mind, my bedside lamp came on all by itself. He broke the kiss long enough to smile down at me. I smiled back then found his lips again. They were so soft, so perfect for kissing and whispering promises to me that he would never break.

I tugged on his knit polo shirt, and he stopped kissing me long enough to yank it free of his khaki shorts, then over his head. I ran my fingers along the well defined muscles of his abdomen then looked up to meet his eyes. There was so much love for me there; those baby blues were so serious. This wasn't a friends-with-benefits sort of experience. I had never felt this way with Aven or anyone I had ever had sex with. This was tender, and he was so attentive to my needs. This was real.

He unbuttoned the top two buttons of my shirt, then bent and kissed my neck softly. He ran a trail with his tongue from my collarbone up my neck. He captured my earlobe between his teeth and sucked gently. He exhaled slowly in my ear, bringing a soft moan out of me.

I moved my hands to his back and pulled him closer to me. I needed to hold him closer still, but his body was already formed to mine, so he couldn't possibly get any closer without shedding the rest of the material we were wearing. Suddenly, that seemed like a brilliant idea. I pushed him gently enough so I could devour his mouth again while I finished the job he had started in unbuttoning my shirt.

His kissing slowed, and he pushed firmly against my core with his sex. My mind was screaming for more as my body flushed hot. He pressed firmly against me again; it sent me over the edge, and I fell onto a cloud of bliss as I screamed his name. It felt right, everything about this felt right. I swiftly unbuttoned my shirt. He lowered his mouth to my left breast and tugged my white lace bra down with his teeth, only pausing briefly before consuming my hardened nipple between his lips. A series of mini climaxes had me gasping for air. He was doing incredible things with his tongue that I never would have thought possible. He massaged my other breast softly with his hand as he began to unbutton his shorts with his other.

I was in the middle of a moan when his head shot up. "What?" he said in a panicked voice, but he looked like he was talking to someone other than me.

"What, Rhyan. What's wrong?" I said frantically.

"No, you can't do this. It was her decision; she chose me." His eyes filled with rage, but I didn't know why. He wouldn't talk to me.

I grabbed his face in my palms and made him look at me, but it wasn't me he was seeing. "What is it? Talk to me."

"I will not leave her alone! She needs me to protect her from Murry." He waited a moment then he reluctantly moved off me, then leaped from the bed to the floor. He was pacing and running his hands through his hair. I wasn't aware angels could have panic attacks, but I thought I was witnessing one.

"Rhyan, talk to me. Please. You're scaring me," I pleaded. He stopped pacing and looked over at me. His eyes were wild and filled with unshed tears.

"I'm not allowed to touch you anymore. They will not allow it until you have done everything you can to save Adam. If I touch you again, they will take me away from you and assign you to someone else. I can't let that happen, Kendra. I'm sorry. I had no idea they would do this or I would've never let you touch me."

I pulled the duvet up to my shoulders and just looked at him.

"I can stay here to protect you as long as I don't touch you. You can't touch me either, or they will force me to leave you here alone."

"But I choose you, Rhyan," I said.

He shook his head and laughed, but it wasn't a good laugh. "It doesn't matter to them what either of us want. I'm not allowed to mess with your free will. The way they see it, I messed with it the first time we met. We aren't supposed to show ourselves to humans. They've turned a blind eye and a deaf ear to me helping you, because they want you to save Adam's soul, as well as your own. If you can't do it, they are willing to risk both of you."

I was furious. "How does that make any damn sense?"

He shook his head. "I never said it made any sense."

I sighed then patted the spot beside me. "I won't touch you. Come and lay down until I fall asleep. We can come up with a solution in the morning."

He nodded, then put his shirt back on and stretched out beside me. I lay facing him on the Queen sized bed. We didn't say anything more; we just stared into each other's eyes until I couldn't hold mine open any longer.

Chapter Twenty-nine

I opened my eyes in a dream, and not a good one from the looks of things. Murry was standing in front of me, his face filled with rage. This was so not going to be a good dream.

"I hope you're happy, Kendra. I had to confine your precious Adam. You won't be seeing him again. I went to his place and tried to convince him that you were crazy, but for some reason, he believed you. While he didn't believe everything you said, the marks on your neck were difficult to explain."

"What have you done with him?" I shouted at him.

He moved his finger back and forth. "Uh-uh, I looked in on you after I got away from your angel. Seems he isn't much of an angel with all the sexual fantasies he has of you in his pretty little head. You've been a busy girl this week, Kendra. Adam wasn't very happy when I told him that you were in love with your guardian angel. He didn't want to believe any of it, but I convinced him in my own way. You, and even your precious Rhyan, couldn't sense us; you were so hot and heavy with each other. I should have fucked you. You seem to have a lot of experience. It makes me hot just thinking about it."

I turned my head away from him. I was so angry that I couldn't think straight.

"It was I who sent word to the guardians about what Rhyan was doing." He leered. "They didn't approve, but I guess you've already found that out." His face lit up. "I do have some rather good news for you. You succeeded in making Adam fall in love with you. That was fast, especially for someone I thought would never be able to love again.

I guess when you find your soulmate it's almost an instant thing, huh?" He scowled again. "Unfortunately, I have some bad news as well. When he saw you with Rhyan, he was beside himself with anger and grief. You made him fall in love with you, then he saw you with another man. How do you think he feels having lost the only person he's loved since he was thirteen?"

I clenched my teeth. "You are a bastard!"

He smiled a mischievous grin. "Why yes, yes I am."

"Where did you take him?"

He shook his head. "Even if you found him, you're the last person he wants to see. He may not be willing to give his soul over to me right now, but he'll never give it to you."

"Where is he, dammit?!" I screamed it at him.

"Happy hunting, Kendra," He held up three fingers. "Three days down," He added another finger. "Four days to go, babe."

I woke up in a cold sweat. Rhyan was trying everything he could do to help me without actually touching me.

He sighed. "Oh, thank God. I thought he had you. I couldn't get into your dream; he was blocking me. I couldn't touch you, but I was shouting at you to wake up. What did he do to you?"

I told him the whole dream, including the part about Murry bringing Adam into my room and what they saw upon arriving.

The sun was pouring through the window. I had to call all of my clients and cancel. I didn't have a choice. Murry was holding Adam somewhere, and I had to find him or I was doomed for sure. Murry didn't intend to kill me now. He knew if I found Adam, he would never forgive me anyway. I was staring at my fate, and it wasn't a good one, unless you considered Hell a place to have a nice long vacation. I know I didn't.

Rhyan was rubbing his temples as if he had a headache. I was getting one myself. "What am I going to do?"

He shook his head. "I don't know what we're going to do when we find him, but we have to find him, Kendra. If we don't, your soul will be lost come Friday. We have to try."

"I know we have to try, but after Adam saw us together," I shook my head. "He hates me now."

"He doesn't hate you. He's hurting, but he doesn't hate you." His eyes met mine. "Do you love him?" he asked me very quietly.

"Rhyan," I said, but he didn't let me finish.

He closed his eyes and spoke. "Don't worry about hurting me. I know you love me." He inhaled then slowly exhaled. "Do you love your soulmate?"

I couldn't deny it. It had broken my heart when Adam refused to believe me about Mason. It felt like something was actually ripping my heart out of my chest when he told me to leave him alone. It still hurt to even think about the look on his face as he said he didn't believe he was my soulmate. I loved Rhyan, I really and truly did, but I knew that I loved Adam more, and I'd do anything to get him away from Murry, even if he never loved me again. I had chosen Rhyan, but it had been because it was the easiest path to take.

He closed his eyes and nodded. "I'm so sorry, Rhyan. I didn't mean to hurt you." My eyes misted over.

"You gave me more than I could ever hope for. Don't be sorry that you love Adam more. At least you love me. You are meant to be with Adam. I know that. Don't feel bad about loving him. Loving him is what is going to keep you alive, and that is what I want for you more than anything, for you to be alive and happy."

I nodded with tears threatening to fall. I didn't know what to say. "I would kiss you right now if I could."

"I know you would, but only because you know that's what I want."

I shook my head and he held up his hand to stop me from speaking. "We need to find your soulmate. I don't think we have to worry about Murry trying to kill you until Friday. We have four days. I'm going to leave you for a while. I'll see if the guardians know where he's holding him. Are you going to be all right here by yourself?"

"I'll be fine." He looked at me a moment longer, maybe to see if I was lying, then he popped out of my room.

I got out of bed and headed for the shower. I needed hot water to clear my head. I didn't have the first clue where a guardian demon would hold a human captive. It couldn't be in Hell unless he was already dead, so where could he be?

Seemed to me that I should be able to tell where he was. He was my soulmate, right? Soulmates were put on the earth to find each other. I could find him, I knew I could, but how would I make him believe I was in love with him after he'd seen me and Rhyan together? I don't think I would be able to trust him with my heart again if the roles were reversed.

I closed my eyes and sighed as the hot water ran down my back. How did I get myself into this shit? More importantly, how could I get myself out of it?

Chapter Thirty

I dressed in comfortable clothes, jeans, a tee-shirt and tennis shoes. I didn't know what I would be doing, so it seemed more sensible to be comfortable than cute. Rhyan still hadn't made it back yet, so I dried my hair and just threw it in a ponytail. I did make an effort with a little makeup. I couldn't go out of the house totally revolting.

I heard the pop, but it sounded like it was further away than usual. I glanced in my bedroom and Rhyan wasn't there. I suddenly had a sinking feeling that Murry had changed his mind about killing me.

"I'm in the kitchen, Kendra. I didn't know if you would be dressed. I don't know what I would do if I saw you naked. I don't really trust myself right now."

I put my makeup bag away then hurried toward the kitchen. On the way, I wondered if he'd found out where Murry had taken Adam. When I saw his face, I knew he still didn't have a clue.

He shook his head. "I asked the guardians if they knew where he was. I think they really would tell me if they knew, because Murry isn't playing by the rules…but they don't know anything either."

"Do you think he would keep him at Mason's apartment?" I asked.

"It isn't likely he would be that obvious, but it's worth looking into. We can start there. Maybe we'll find a clue. Murry is playing a game with you, and he's having fun watching. I think he wants you to find Adam eventually, so he can watch Adam tell you to go to Hell."

I winced. "That was really harsh, Rhyan."

He shrugged his shoulders. "I'm only trying to prepare you. Do you expect him to hand you chocolates and flowers then tell you everything is all right?" He shook his head at me. "Murry knows what he's doing. This is what he does, and he's good at it. It will take a miracle for you to get Adam back."

"So, you don't think I have a chance?" I was getting irritated at his negativity.

He raised hands, palms out, and closed his eyes as he sighed. "I didn't say that. You've already experienced one miracle this week."

I crossed my arms over my chest. "That wasn't a miracle. That was Coen, and you know it. I would hardly say that was a miracle. He was the one who caused the accident in the first place."

"I wasn't trying to upset you. It's just that I know Murry's kind, and he won't give up, so neither should you."

I grabbed my purse and my keys. "I wasn't planning on it."

"That's why Coen chose you," he said as he followed me out the door.

We got in my vehicle and I started the engine. "No, Rhyan. Coen picked me because he knew that Adam and I were soulmates. He knew I wouldn't give up until I got him back or lost my own soul."

He nodded a little sadly.

I watched him as I drove. I know you're supposed to keep your eyes on the road, and I did look often enough to be relatively safe. "I really wanted last night to happen, Rhyan. I can't change that it didn't."

He looked out the window. "I'm not upset with you, Kendra. I'm just upset."

"Well, could you try to keep your pissy attitude in check until Saturday? I've got to find Adam, and I could sure use your help about right now." He looked at me and gave me a small grin. "That's better. Now, do you know where Mason's apartment is located?"

"On the other side of town, two blocks from Adam's apartment." Great. At least it wasn't rush hour.

"Well, we can go to Adam's apartment if we don't find anything helpful at Mason's place. I think Murry came to Adam's apartment to kidnap him, so there may be a clue there as well." He nodded his head in agreement. "Who is Adam's Guardian Angel now that Coen's soul was sent to Hell?"

He looked at me nervously for a moment then said, "He doesn't have one. They won't give him another one unless you succeed."

I hit the steering wheel with my palm. "Shit! Are you kidding me? I'm all on my own in this. Don't they care about my soul?"

"They're punishing you for making that deal."

"He tricked me! Don't they take that into consideration?"

He nodded again. "They are allowing me to help you."

I leaned my elbow on the door then let my forehead fall on my palm. "Sweet Mary, mother of Jesus." I took a few breaths. "How the hell are we going to defeat this son of a bitch when we find Adam? I know he'll be there waiting to attack us. He isn't going to let me win without a fight. I can't fight a demon. Look at me, Rhyan."

He turned his gaze back to me and let his eyes sweep slowly down then back up my body again. He wet his lips then smiled at me when his eyes met mine. I scowled at him. "He can't make you do anything you don't want to. If he kills you before Friday, then he loses in a way, so I don't think he will go that route. He will most likely wait until Friday."

My eyes grew wide. "So how can I beat him?"

"Find Adam and make him choose you, but the only way you can truly win is for Adam to believe God is his savior. Just getting Adam back isn't good enough; he will still have to choose good over evil."

"Why isn't my guardian demon interfering?" I asked.

"Patrick isn't strong enough to come to earth. I am able to because you chose to be on the side of good, and Murry is strong enough because Adam turned his back on God. Unless you fail in this mission, you'll never have to meet Patrick. He's in the pits of Hell, and your decisions keep him there."

I nodded. "Good...good, because I don't think I can stand anything else working against me this week."

We drove through the city and Rhyan directed me to Mason's apartment. The building was equipped with a security system that required residents to buzz in visitors who didn't have a key. I didn't have a key and I wasn't a cop, so I'd pretty much run into a brick wall.

We stood in front of the apartment complex, and I noticed Rhyan looking around. "I'll go up and take a look around. When I return, you will be the only one who can see me, so be careful about talking out loud. You don't want someone hauling you off to a psych ward." he smiled then popped out of sight.

I didn't know when people could see him and when they couldn't. I could see him; shouldn't everyone else be able to?

"He isn't here, Kendra." Rhyan said.

"Well, buzz me up so I can look for clues." The buzzer went off, the door unlocked, and the brick wall tumbled down. Woot-Woot! *"What apartment is his?"*

"5B," he said, and I made my way to the fifth floor. I could hear heavy metal music playing, but under that was a softer, classical sound. Well, he hadn't been lying about his neighbors. I tried the knob on 5B, and it turned freely in my hand. Rhyan was waiting for me in the living room of the small apartment.

"Did you find anything?" I asked, and he shook his head. I looked all around, then huffed. The apartment was neat and free of clutter. I sifted through some mail on his kitchen counter. "This looks like the apartment of a normal guy, not a demon."

"Looks can be deceiving, Kendra." he said.

"Tell me about it." I looked around for a few more minutes and came up with absolutely nothing. "Let's go to Adam's place. Maybe we'll find something there." I walked out of the apartment by myself. Rhyan was already sitting in my Land Rover when I got there. "Where to now?" I said as I buckled up and started the engine.

"Two blocks up; same side of the street." I nodded and we were off.

Chapter Thirty-one

The apartment complexes were much nicer on Adam's block. Mason's hadn't been a shit-hole, but these were clearly expensive. I would have been surprised to find anyone making less than a hundred grand a year living here. I had a feeling that was not a problem for Adam.

Rhyan popped out of sight again. *"There's nobody here, Kendra."* I started to say, "Buzz me in," but the buzzer sounded.

"Thank you," I said.

"No problem, his apartment is 12A."

All the way to the top, huh? I took the elevator instead of the stairs. I'd missed my run, but I didn't have time for exercise right now. It wouldn't do me any good to be in shape if I was just going to die on Friday.

The doors slid open on the top floor. Besides the elevator doors, there were only three others on the floor. Yeah, he definitely spent some money to live in this place. I turned left and made my way to the end of the hall. I turned the knob and walked into Adam's apartment. It was extravagant. Everything was glass, black or stainless, and screamed expensive. There was a five-foot by two-foot gas fireplace inserted into the only white wall in the whole apartment.

A huge black, white, and gray painting was hung high above the fireplace. It looked as though a first grader could have painted it, but then again, I wasn't big on contemporary art. I like to be able to see something real.

The floors were all done in shiny black marble, with little sparkly silver specks in it that looked like diamonds; hell, they may have been. He had glass coffee and end tables with stainless pedestals. I glanced at the kitchen; it was roomy with more stainless and black. Did the guy have a color theme going on here or what? I wanted to bring in a red vase and put it in the center of the room. It was nice, and clearly expensive, but it needed a little color.

I walked to his bedroom and Rhyan followed me. The bed was made, which seemed unusual for a man, let alone one living by himself. There were a few photos of his family on his nightstand. Something caught my attention beside one of the photos. It was a magazine opened and folded back to one of the articles that had featured me. I looked at the photo; I was smiling back at the camera. I didn't think he had bought the magazine after he left my house last night, so he must have bought it sometime before he went to work yesterday. He'd come to my house straight from work, or I thought he had. I shrugged my shoulders and laid it back on the nightstand.

"You didn't think I was going to make it this easy, did you, Kendra?" I jumped and let out a squeak. Murry was talking in my head, and by the look on Rhyan's face, he could hear him also.

"Where is he, you son of a bitch?" I said back to him.

"Awe, Kendra, how did you know my mother was a bitch?"

"Because if she hadn't been, you wouldn't have turned out as rotten as you are. Where is Adam, Murry?"

"I just knew you would address me as Mason," he said, faking a hurt ego.

I was getting nowhere with him, then I wondered something. Rhyan read my mind, and shrugged his shoulders with a blank look on his face. He didn't know either. Great. *"How are you in my head? You aren't connected to me."*

"On the contrary, Kendra, I am very much connected to you. You are Adam's soulmate, so I have access to your thoughts, as well as his."

"That's why you were angry at the restaurant. You knew all along I

was trying to make Adam fall in love with me, and you got angry when he reacted to me. You were mad at yourself for not having a stronger hold on him. Am I right?" I said.

He laughed. *"You catch on quickly, Kendra."*

"Why didn't you just kill me that night?"

"What, and let you be with your precious Rhyan in Heaven? I don't think so. If I wait until Friday to kill you, I will have both of your souls."

"WHERE IS HE?! Give me a clue, damn you!" I shouted out loud.

"Hmm, let's see. You want a clue? How about...try looking where you would play."

And just like that, he was gone. I didn't feel the presence in my mind that I sometimes felt when Rhyan was talking to me through my mind. He was gone, but I had no doubt that he could still hear me.

Rhyan nodded. "I can't hear him anymore either."

"He said he could hear me because I was Adam's soulmate. Why can't you hear Adam?"

He shrugged. "I've never tried to hear him. I didn't know it was possible. I've only ever been able to hear your thoughts because you are my charge."

I put my hands on my hips and stared at him. "Well, can you try now, please?"

He jumped like I had poked him. "All right, all right, I'll try. Give me a minute." He closed his eyes for what seemed like an eternity. His mouth moved every so often like he was silently talking to someone, and then he opened his eyes and gave me a smile.

"You talked to him?" I said enthusiastically.

He nodded then his smile faded.

"What is it, Rhyan?"

"I asked him where he was. I told him that I was in his mind to help him. He kept asking me who I was. I finally got out of him where he thought he was located, but he kept asking me...so I told him. I told him that I was your guardian angel, and he became very angry. He told me to tell you to just leave him alone, that he would rather die there than ever see you again."

My smile faded. "I can't let that stop me. We knew he would be angry at me."

His eyebrows rose and he scratched his temple. "Well, you aren't the only one. He had a few choice words for me as well. I think he really loves you, but he is so hurt about seeing us…"

"Don't give up, Rhyan."

"I'm not, but I think Adam has," he said.

"Where is he?" I asked as I left Adam's room and started for the door.

"He said he was in a cave somewhere. He didn't know where exactly. He said he was there when he woke up."

I nodded as we got in the elevator. He rode down with me this time without popping to my Land Rover. "Murry gave me the hint to look where I play. I bet he means where I climb. There are a lot of caves outside of the city where my friends and I go sometimes, but there are so many of them. We'll never find him before Friday."

"Call your friends and ask them to help you. You don't have to tell them what happened, just that there is a man trapped in one of them, but you don't know which one."

My face lit up. "You're a genius, Rhyan. I would kiss you right now if I could."

He smiled. "I know you would."

Chapter Thirty-two

I pulled out my phone and started calling all of my friends. Most of them would be at work, but they would answer and help me when they got off. My dad would even help me and call a bunch of his buddies to help as well. A man lost down in one of the caves was a serious deal around here. I would tell everyone that he was the surgeon who had saved me, and I'd caught wind that he'd gone caving last night by himself and hadn't shown up for work today.

I dreaded calling Aven. He wouldn't want to help me because he was mad at me, but I thought he would in the end. I just dreaded the conversation. I decided to call him first to get it out of the way. He had a lot of friends that were into extreme hobbies as well.

The phone began to ring as I headed out of town. I had flashlights and my hiking boots in the back of my Land Rover, so I didn't have to worry about stopping off at home. Aven picked up on the fifth ring. "What do you want, Kendra?" he sounded grumpy. Oh well.

"Aven, I need your help. The surgeon that saved me went caving last night by himself. I don't know which cave, but he's missing now."

"He the guy you're seeing?" he said.

Shit! I couldn't lie to him; he would see right through it, and he was one of my closest friends. I didn't want to lie to him, but I didn't want to tell him the truth either. "Sort of,"

"What kind of dumbass would go caving alone, Kendra? You sure can pick 'em. I thought you said he was at your place last night. Did you piss him off, too?"

I huffed. "He was...yes, I mean sort of I guess...Aven, can you be mad at me later? My, I mean his, life is at stake here. Can you call your friends and help me or not?" I was getting flustered, and I hated being flustered.

I heard him sigh. "All right, but I ain't doing this for you. I just don't want some stupid motherfucker dying, knowing that I could have done something about it."

I smiled and closed my eyes briefly. "Thank you, Aven. You have a good guardian angel."

"Yeah, whatever that means. My group will take the west caves. Make sure you look somewhere else. I don't want to see you right now. I'll call you if we find anything."

I sighed into the phone. I hated that he was mad at me, but there was hardly anything I could do about it. "Okay. Aven…I'm truly sorry that I hurt you."

The line went dead, and I looked at my phone. He'd hung up on me again. I didn't have time to worry about our friendship falling apart right now; I had a lot of calls to make.

I really wished I had another phone so Rhyan could help me, but how would that go if I did, "Uh, hello, I'm Kendra's guardian angel, and we need help finding her soulmate, who is being held in a cave by his guardian demon. Will you help us find him?" Uh, no, that wasn't going to happen.

I saw Rhyan smile out of the corner of my eye as I dialed Kobhye's number. "Do you think it would work?"

He shook his head as he laughed. "No, I don't think it would work."

Kobhye picked up on the second ring. She wasn't mad at me. "Hey, do you remember the sexy ass surgeon who saved my life?" She did remember; I had no doubt she would. I told her what I had told Aven, and she agreed to call everyone she knew that would help. She didn't have any problem being in the same cave as me, so I told her I was going to the north caves. She even said she was leaving work right away, what a friend.

I hung up with Kobhye and called my dad. He was on board with helping, but it would be after four before he could get off work. He told me that he would ask all of his co-workers and friends to help, and that he would call me to see where I needed them when he got off. I told him that was fine and we hung up.

I had reached eight other people before Rhyan and I got to the cave. I put my vehicle in park and shut off the engine. Some of the people I'd called couldn't make it until four or five, but several were already on their way to help. Aven said he was taking the west caves. I was taking the north with Rhyan and some of my friends. I sent my friends that lived or worked closer to the south side of town to the south caves, and there weren't any caves east of town that I knew of. We would search the cave from top to bottom, and if there was no Adam, we'd move on to the next.

There were about five caves to the west, but they were big. The north had about ten mostly small caves, but one of them was the biggest of all the caves around the city. There were only three that I knew of to the south. We hardly ever went south, but Murry may have, so I didn't want to exclude them.

I had called Kobhye a few minutes before I arrived at the first cave to tell her which cave we were searching first. She had figured as much, and was only a few minutes away. She'd gotten a hold of six people who were meeting us, including two friends who had been there Saturday when I'd fallen. Marc was leading his crew through the south caves.

I hoped Murry wouldn't hurt anyone who was looking for Adam. It was hard for me to think of him as evil. He'd been so nice when we'd first met. I guess the old saying, "don't judge a book by its cover" was true. It's hard to tell who you can trust in this crazy world. Adam had thought that Mason was his best friend for the last six years. In a way, I hated to be the one to break the bad news to him. He'd lost his family, then his best friend, and now he didn't want a damn thing to do with me;

though his rejection wasn't going to stop me from trying to save our souls. I had to try.

I saw a cloud of dust billowing up behind Kobhye's truck as she sped up the gravel road toward us. There were two other vehicles following a little ways behind her. She was dusting them out, but they all knew their way.

Rhyan didn't have to ask who it was; he was picking it right out of my brain.

Kobhye jumped out of her four-wheel drive Ford. Her family owned a ranch a few miles out of the city, and fancy cars just weren't her thing. They showed horses, and even had a couple racing horses. I'd gone on a few trail rides with her, but it wasn't interesting enough for me. I needed more risk. Although, I'd rather go trail riding than go up against Murry any day.

I wasn't looking forward to the look in Adam's eyes when he saw me. If he had stayed another minute or two last night, he would've seen the same look in mine. He'd broken my heart last night, but I had already forgiven him for it. Considering the circumstances, I wasn't so sure he would be as forgiving.

Chapter Thirty-three

We turned on our flashlights before entering the cave. There were bats and other creepy animals that weren't so nice that lurked behind the sharp twists and turns of the cave walls. Some of the caves around the city went deep underground; you could actually drive a big truck through some of them. This one was a little of both. It was the largest cave in the area and it went on for a mile or two, with many different paths to take. If you didn't know where you were going, you could slip right off into a deep ravine; some of them were twenty or more feet deep. It wouldn't surprise any of us if an inexperienced caver got lost. I had, on more than one occasion. It really sucks when you drop your last water bottle in one of those ravines six hours before you smell fresh air. I wondered if Murry had been cruel enough to have not given Adam any water.

"Would I do that to my friend, Kendra?" Murry said in my head.

I gritted my teeth. *"You aren't his friend. Don't pretend to be. He knows the truth about you now. Do you actually think he will choose you?"*

He laughed. *"I only have to keep him from choosing you until Friday."*

"Get out of my head, asshole."

"What?" Kobhye said then shined her light in my eyes.

I shook my head. "Nothing." With Murry laughing and talking so calmly to me, I had a feeling that I was in the wrong cave. He may know that there were more friends of mine in the other caves looking for Adam, but I didn't think he could read their minds. I looked at Rhyan.

He'd stayed visible so everyone could see him. I'd told them that he was a friend of Adam's. Now, wasn't that a big ass lie?

We searched for hours. I knew everyone was tired and hungry, but mostly everyone just needed water. Kobhye had brought along three bottles, but with nine of us sharing them, they hadn't lasted long. I knew we were going to have to take a break, and we were close to the mouth of the cave. We had taken so many twists and turns and tunnels that we'd ended up back near our starting point.

I had a feeling that Adam wasn't in this cave, but we could return to this one after we went through the others if he didn't turn up. My phone was about dead, and it needed to be charged soon. Anyone who found Adam was to notify me immediately, no matter what Adam said. I was pretty sure, if anyone mentioned my name, he would give them an ear full about just what he thought of me.

I could picture Aven finding him. Both of them were hating on me right now. Maybe they would start a Hater's Club and have my picture in the center of the dart board.

"Stop it, Kendra," Rhyan whispered so low that I was the only one who understood what he'd said. I sighed, then I caught sight of the dim light from the mouth of the cave. I felt helpless and broken. I felt like I had already failed. "It isn't over until Friday. You can be angry at yourself then if you want, but I need you to keep yourself together right now."

I nodded, and knew that no one but Rhyan had noticed.

We all exited the cave then made a circle of standing bodies beside my Land Rover to discuss what direction we needed to go next. I suggested that we get fast food and a case of water because I knew everyone wanted to, but no one was going to say it. I had a backpack in my vehicle and I knew Kobhye did as well. I could carry half the water and she could carry the other half. Our load would get lighter the longer we walked and the more we drank. Everyone agreed, and we all headed out for the closest fast food and convenience stores.

We pulled through a Burger King drive thru; Rhyan even ordered food. I shot him a questioning glance, and he had responded with, "I miss food. I can eat while I'm in this form." I had nodded then gone back to paying the pimpled-faced teenager in the window, and then we were on our way to the Exxon station at the edge of town.

I went in and bought a case of water and four packages of "D" batteries. I didn't want any of the flashlights going dead on us. When I walked out, Kobhye was waiting at my Land Rover with her backpack open. We were at the back of my rig where she thought Rhyan couldn't hear. "He's hot, Kendra. Hook me up." She nodded toward the back of Rhyan's head.

Dammit! "Ah, I would, but he's seeing someone." I knew what was coming next; that kind of thing didn't bother her. It didn't bother her conscience at all to sleep with a guy who was dating someone else or even married, for that matter. It made me wonder how in control her guardian angel was. "Yeah, so, he can tell his girlfriend that he was here looking for Adam the whole time. I only need an hour of his time, not a marriage."

Kobhye was just as opposed to a serious relationship as I was. I shook my head. "I think he loves her or something, Kobhye. You can try, but I don't think his interests are the same as yours."

She grinned. "A challenge...perfect." I turned my head to put some water bottles in my backpack and closed my eyes. I was so not going to enjoy watching this.

I heard Rhyan laughing in my head. *"Now you know how I feel."* His voice turned softer. *"I promise not to do anything with her."*

"Do what you want, Rhyan. You aren't my soulmate." I said as I shoved the last water bottle that would fit into my backpack. He didn't say anymore to me about it, so I didn't know if he would change his mind or not about Kobhye.

She loaded her pack and as she walked by Rhyan's side of the vehicle, she winked at him. I rolled my eyes and climbed into the driver's seat. We were off to the next cave. My phone was plugged into the car charger, and I planned to leave it there until we got to the next cave. It needed the juice. I checked it and realized I had three text messages. Marc and his crew were moving on to the second cave to the south. The second was from my dad. He was off work and was headed to the western caves to help Aven. Was it already after four? I looked at my clock radio; it read 4:13. The last one was from Aven; they had finished two caves. They were getting a bite to eat and fueling up with water before tackling "The Devil's Den." "The Devil's Den" was the most dangerous cave. It wasn't as big as some of the others, but there were steep drop-offs that wouldn't just land you in the hospital. I whipped the Land Rover to the shoulder of the road and slammed on the brakes. I glanced in my rear view mirror just in time to notice that Kobhye had done the same.

Suddenly, I knew for certain that's where Murry was holding Adam. The name of the cave alone would peak his interest. It would be very bad if I pulled out of the north caves to head to The Devil's Den, and it turned out my instincts were wrong. I just had such a strong feeling that he was there.

"Stick with the north caves, Kendra. If they find him, they will call you."

I nodded. "You're right. We'll stay here and search the next north cave." I stepped on the gas and we were off again.

Chapter Thirty-four

I stalled outside the cave as long as I could. I just knew that as soon as we were deep into the cave, my phone would ring, letting me know that they'd found him.

Rhyan started for the cave and Kobhye walked up beside him to start her notorious flirting. *"C'mon, Kendra, what if you are wrong, and he's in this cave? He may need water. They will call you if they find him; you know they will."*

I huffed then followed my crew into the cave. This wasn't a very big one, and it wouldn't take more than thirty minutes to cover the whole thing, so getting out quick wouldn't be that big of a deal.

We were no more than five minutes in when my phone beeped. I pulled it from my pocket and checked the text. It was from Lennie. He thought they had found him, but he was behind a rock wall that Aven, my dad, and everyone else were trying to get through.

"Stop!" I said, and could hear the excitement in everyone's voices, but I tuned it out as I tried to call Lennie. The call rang once then failed. I looked at my phone; it was jumping in and out of service. I turned and ran for the mouth of the cave without stumbling once.

When the sun hit my face I tried again. It went through this time. "Kendra, there is definitely someone in here. We were shouting through the rocks and he shouted back that he was okay, but we should hurry the hell up and get him out of there."

I closed my eyes and sighed as I hit my knees. "Thank God. We're on our way, Lennie. Has anyone called for an ambulance?"

"Yeah, I did that right before you called. I don't have any reception in the cave."

"Okay, how long do you think it will take everyone to get to him?"

"I don't know. I don't know how thick the rock wall is, but we can hear him through it, so it shouldn't take long with so many people digging. We can't figure out how the hell he got back there. It doesn't look like the ceiling caved in; it looks like the rocks were placed there to keep him in." I rolled my eyes; I knew they were placed there to keep him in.

"All right…" I sighed. "I'm on my way, if you get him out before I get there, call me and let me know where the ambulance is taking him. He will probably request the trauma center, even if he doesn't have many injuries; it's where he works."

"I'll call you. Bye, Kendra."

I hit the end button on my phone and turned to my crew. "They found him. They're digging him out now and he sounds fine." There were cheers all around, but Rhyan just stood there looking at me. We both knew that rock wall wasn't the final obstacle we would have to circumvent this week.

We loaded up again and hauled ass west to The Devil's Den. I turned my emergency lights on and prayed that I wouldn't pass a cop, because the gas pedal was on the floor. I decided to go around the city because it was a little after five. Traffic would be at a standstill in the city. It was a longer route, but it would get me to my destination sooner.

I looked in my rear view mirror; Kobhye and Kevin were keeping up with me, sort of. Kobhye was right behind me, but Kevin's car couldn't go as fast as ours. He was slowly slipping back, but he knew where The Devil's Den was, so I wasn't worried about him getting lost. The only thing I was worried about right now was Adam, and if Murry had any more surprises in store for me.

"Of course I have more surprises, Kendra." Just then my left front tire blew, and there was no way to stop what happened next; I was going too fast. My Land Rover swerved out of control then began to flip. The

air bags deployed, and that was the last thing I remembered before blacking out.

"Kendra, can you hear me?" It was Rhyan's voice, and he sounded strangely calm. I didn't know if I was dead or if I was going to make it through yet another miracle this week. *"Another miracle, but I couldn't get you to wake up, and it's Wednesday night. It's been twenty-eight hours. There's nothing wrong with you, but Murry has done something to keep you knocked out and me out of your mind. I just now regained access."*

"Where is Adam?" I said. *"I only have about forty hours left to help him."*

Rhyan sighed. *"He left the city. Murry isn't holding him hostage this time. Adam left for his lake house yesterday morning."*

"Did he know that I was in a wreck on my way to save him?" I asked.

"Yes," he said, but didn't elaborate further.

"Did he care?" I asked, aghast.

"If you open your eyes, we can go to him." He seemed to ignore my question and it pissed me off.

"Did he care?" I asked more firmly.

He was silent for a moment then he finally finished shattering my heart. *"The ambulance brought you in a few minutes before Adam got here. I'm not allowed to interfere, but I had to do something. I told him who I was and tried to tell him what happened to you on our way here, but he wouldn't listen to me. He asked me if you needed surgery. When I told him that you didn't, he turned away from me and left the hospital."*

I opened my eyes and realized I couldn't see anything; they were blurry with tears. I sat up in bed, but Rhyan wasn't in the room with me, he was only in my head. My parents, Kobhye and Aven were sitting in chairs around my bed. They were all asleep in the uncomfortable-looking chairs, judging by their awkward postures. I wasn't hooked up to a lot of machines this time; there was only an I.V. in my arm. I removed the tape holding it against my arm with some difficulty. Man, they really wanted this thing to stay in my arm, I thought. I could hear Rhyan laughing. I held my breath, then pulled it out slowly and grabbed some tissue to put over the blood from the needle hole. My mom opened her eyes as though she'd heard, or sensed that I was awake.

"Kendra?" She rushed to me and hugged me hard. "Oh, baby, you have got to stop scaring me like this."

I looked over at the table beside my bed. I had a change of clean clothes and shoes there. I was betting Rhyan had brought them for me so we could leave as soon as possible.

"You would be betting right. Now come on, let's get out of here."

I pulled away from my mother and got out of bed. "I have to go, guys." The rest of my friends and family had woken up, and they were all looking at me like I was crazy as I grabbed my clothes and headed for the bathroom. Kobhye walked in behind me. I expected as much.

"You wanna tell me what's going on?" she said.

I quickly got out of the hospital gown and began to put my clothes on. Rhyan had chosen clothes for comfort. *"Thank you, Rhyan."*

He snickered. *"You're welcome, now either tell her, or leave; we don't have any time to waste. Adam's lake house is a three hour drive."*

Shit! My Land Rover had to be totaled. *"Yeah, it is, borrow Kobhye's."*

"I need your truck." I said as I tied my shoe.

"Oh no," she shook her head. "You aren't leaving here without me. There is some major shit going on with you, and I'm not letting you out of my sight. So, if you want my truck, you're going to have to take me with you."

I stared at her for a moment. She was my best friend and had been since the sixth grade. I had never kept anything from her, including Aven. We'd only had two fights, and neither of them was caused by her not believing or trusting in me. Maybe she would believe me now as well. "Would you believe anything I told you if I swore it were true?"

"You know I would," she replied.

"Good, then come on. You're about to get an earful." We walked out of the bathroom and turned to leave. Aven was blocking the door, so I stopped and scowled at him.

"Where are you going?"

I couldn't tell Aven; he wouldn't understand. "I need to be somewhere."

My dad spoke up. "You've almost died twice now, Kendra. The only place you need to be is in that bed."

"Look, I don't expect any of you to understand, but I have to go; I have to." I pleaded with them.

I walked over to my dad. "Daddy, I have to go. Please understand."

He met my eyes. "Help me understand, Kendra."

I sighed and my eyes misted over. "I'm in love, Daddy, and if I don't get to him now, I'll lose him forever." It was the truth, and it surprised me at how easy it was to admit that I was in love.

He looked at my mom then I turned to her. She nodded with tears in her eyes. "Let her go, Robert. I want grandchildren."

"Haley has two children, Diane. You already have grandchildren," he said.

She shook her head. "Not from Kendra." My mother was getting angry with him, and she never got mad about anything.

He seemed to realize that too, but he glanced at Aven. I looked over at him too. He had a pissed off look on his face, but he shrugged at my father then looked away from us. My dad looked back at me and nodded as he took my hands in his. "If this boy hurts you or gets you killed, I will personally knock his head off his shoulders." My dad was tall and muscular from years of hard labor, so I believed him. It surprised me that he was talking to me like I was sixteen and about to go on my first date though.

I nodded, and he let me go. I turned around. Aven was still blocking the door with his arms crossed over his chest. He shook his head. "You aren't leaving without me."

"Fine. You can come, but if you start calling me crazy, I'll slam on the brakes and kick your ass out. It's a three hour drive. You feel like walking?" I crossed my arms, imitating him.

He looked nervous, like he hadn't expected me to just let him come along. He must have thought I would give in and stay because he said so. He sighed in defeat and moved out of my way. I guess he realized we'd just spend the entire trip arguing with each other. I walked out of the room and left him standing there.

We made it to the ground floor and the same receptionist was sitting behind the desk when I walked up. She looked up in horror. I nodded, and she handed me the form I needed without taking her eyes off of me. I signed and dated it, then handed it back to her before heading to the parking lot. Kobhye followed me, trying to keep up with my long strides. I stopped on the drivers' side and looked at her. She rolled her eyes and tossed me the keys. "Keep it under eighty will ya? You seem to be a little accident prone this week."

She got in and I was pulling out of the garage before she even got buckled-up. I was trying to figure out how to start the whole conversation when I heard the pop. I rolled my eyes. I guess I could start there.

"Holy, Shit!" Kobhye screamed and I drove on, waiting patiently for her hysterics to calm. "Kendra, tell me what the fuck is going on!"

"Kobhye, meet Rhyan...my guardian angel." She had thought Rhyan was Adam's best friend; boy was she about to find out otherwise. Rhyan was sitting in the backseat of the crew cab truck smiling at her with his fingers laced together behind his head. I guess he thought this would be the best way to handle this.

When she didn't look like she was going to faint anymore, I started at the beginning with Saturday when I had died and made the deal with Adam's guardian angel. Then I told her everything in between about Mason/Murry and Adam not believing me about the soulmate thing, and how he'd left me. I told her about also loving Rhyan, and Murry letting Adam watch me and Rhyan getting all hot and heavy with each other, and then about Murry putting Adam in the cave. She'd been along for the ride, but she hadn't been aware of the why. I told her that I would die for real on Friday if I couldn't get Adam to trust me and believe in God.

She took in a deep breath, then let it out slowly and looked at me. "You do know this is some really fucked up shit, right?"

I nodded. "Rhyan, where are we going?"

"North to the lake," he said.

I was confident he would give me more detailed directions when we got closer to the lake.

Kobhye looked at me. "So, I guess this means that Rhyan is off limits too, huh?"

I laughed. "Yeah, I guess you don't get any of the men I've met this week." Then I had a thought. "Aven is available."

She rolled her eyes and shook her head. "That will so never happen," she said, and I laughed.

Chapter Thirty-five

We headed north to the lake and only stopped once to pee. Rhyan gave that typical male eye-roll that guys do when a girl needs to make a pit-stop on a trip. Whatever. I needed to pee; I'd been in a hospital bed for twenty-eight hours.

I grabbed a package of peanuts and a coke while I was in the store. I knew Kobhye would roll her eyes. She always thought it was gross that I put my peanuts in my coke. I got behind the wheel and opened the package. I looked at her and she shook her head then looked out the window. I could see her roll her eyes in the reflection. I smiled then drank a little of the coke before adding my peanuts.

I got back on the highway and looked at the clock on the radio. It was a little after eleven, and we were making great time. We only had about fifteen miles to go before we got to the first of the camping areas. It was still hot, and there was a little more than three weeks of summer vacation left for the kiddos, so I assumed the lake would be one big party spot.

I drank my salty coke and chewed on the peanuts. I'd been trying to decide what to say to Adam when we got to his house the whole damn trip, and I'd come up with nothing.

"Make a left turn in a quarter mile," Rhyan said. It surprised me. I was expecting to drive another ten miles then have to drive through town before Rhyan had to start giving me directions. I saw the paved road and turned left onto it.

"How much further?" Kobhye asked. I think she was just as anxious as I was. She hadn't offered any advice on how to get Adam back, but then again, we'd never tried to hang on to men; we were usually trying to get rid of them.

"The lake stretches this far out from town; they just built the town closer to the dam. Adam's lake house is about a mile straight ahead. His is the only house on this road."

Kobhye turned and looked at him. "You seem to know him pretty well."

He shrugged. "When I tapped into his brain to find him in the cave, I got his memories as well." He was silent for a moment then said, "There aren't many good ones."

I looked in my rear view mirror at him. *"Am I a fool for doing this?"*

He looked at me and shook his head. *"He's the fool. I would give anything to be your soulmate. Anything."*

That made me feel good, but it didn't make me anymore confident about the task in front of me, literally in front of me. Adam's lake house came into view and my jaw dropped. How the hell could he afford all of this and the apartment in the city? I knew the answer. He worked all the time and he got paid very well.

I parked behind a blue mustang that was parked behind his car in the circular drive. I cut the engine to Kobhye's truck. She looked at me and I shrugged. "The Shelby is his, but I don't have a clue who drives the other one."

We both turned and looked at Rhyan. He leaned his head back and looked at the ceiling of the cab, as though he didn't want to tell me.

The motion lights lit up on the front of the big house. I glanced at them then looked back at Rhyan. "Tell me who's in there with him."

He chewed on his lower lip for a moment. If he stalled much longer, I was going to find out anyway, because Adam and who-ever-else were going to walk out to greet us. He met my eyes, and there was desperation in them. "I figured they would fight, and she would leave before we got here. I didn't know they would make up...and be having sex right now." He shook his head. "I'm so sorry. I don't know how to fix this or I would."

I was stunned. "Sherri," I said, and pressed my lips together. I made it a statement rather than a question, because I already knew.

He nodded and I got out of the truck. I heard two other doors open to the truck, then they closed. I didn't know what I was going to do, but I had to interfere. He was my soulmate, not hers.

I walked up on the front porch and paused only a moment before ringing the doorbell. I looked back at Kobhye and Rhyan then the door opened to Sherri standing there in nothing but Adam's button-up shirt. I averted my gaze from hers and cleared my throat. Blood was racing through my veins and I was visibly shaking. I was mad. I was really, really mad, but it wasn't her fault. She'd been with him before I even came into the picture. I was actually stepping on her toes, but he was mine. He was meant to be mine.

I cleared my throat again, and forced myself to look at her. "May I speak with Adam?" She gave me a dirty look then glanced at Kobhye and Rhyan. Evidently she didn't think we were here to have a big orgy with Adam because she let us all in.

"He's getting dressed. You can make yourselves comfortable in the living room," she said.

My eyes shot to Rhyan. *"She did that shit on purpose, didn't she?"*

He nodded. *"She's jealous of you. She doesn't catch Adam's attention the way you do, and she knows it."*

That made me feel better, but it didn't change the fact that I just walked into the house of the man I loved to find he'd just finished having sex with another woman.

"He's coming," Rhyan said as he sat down on the couch.

"Can't we tell him that you and Kobhye are together, and what Mason showed him was all made up; that it wasn't real?" I said pleadingly.

He looked at me. *"You want to lie to him?"*

"I wouldn't exactly be breaking one of the Ten Commandments," I

said, then crossed my arms over my chest.

"No, but would you be able to sleep beside him at night knowing that he believed a lie you told him?"

My shoulders slumped in defeat. He had me there. My conscience always ate at me until I told the truth. I actually lost sleep over little white lies.

I heard footsteps coming toward us, and I looked up just in time to meet Adam's eyes. He was upset, but other than that, he looked fine, really fine. My heart gave a little flutter and I pressed my lips together. What was I supposed to say to him?

"Ask him if Murry hurt him. He'll remember that he didn't believe you."

"You look all right. I guess Murry didn't hurt you too bad," I said in a shaky voice. It was obvious I was nervous, but I couldn't help it.

"Why are you here, and who told you where my lake house was located?" he said. He didn't come any further into the room. He just stood there and scowled at me.

I was losing the nervousness, and it was being replaced by anger. "Do you not even care that I almost died again? I told you about Mason and you didn't believe me. Do you believe me now?" I didn't know where Sherri had gone. I assume he had told her to stay in the bedroom until I left. She probably hadn't liked it, but he was mad at me, so that would make it a little better for her.

"When I heard that you were brought in, I made sure your injuries weren't life threatening, then I left. I told Mason to stay away from me, and I told your boyfriend here to tell you the same thing." He pointed at the door. "Get out of my house or I will call the police."

"Do you love her, Adam?" I whispered.

"I don't love anyone," he said, but a muscle twitched above his eye as he said it.

"You're lying," I challenged, and began walking toward him.

He didn't back up, I knew he wasn't afraid of me. "What are you doing? I told you to leave."

I didn't stop walking and I kept eye contact with him the whole time. "Yeah, you did, but ask my friends how well I mind when someone tells me to do something."

He looked a little nervous now that I was so close. I was standing only a few inches from him, and he didn't have a clue what I was going to do. I looked up at him. "If you don't believe that we're soulmates, then kiss me; prove me wrong." I had to admit that I was doing this on a hunch, but surely something had to happen when soulmates found each other and kissed for the first time.

His eyes grew wide and he stepped back from me. "You're insane. You need psychiatric help, Kendra."

"Tell me, with me standing here now, that you don't want to look at me, that you don't want to touch me. Tell me that you don't want to kiss me, Adam. I know you still feel that way, because I still feel that way about you. I'm in love with you, Adam. We were meant to be together, and you know I'm telling the truth. You just don't want to believe it. I'm not crazy, because if I am, that means that you are too. You've seen your guardian demon and my guardian angel, just like I have. You feel the same emotions I feel for you. So, if I'm crazy, then so are you."

"I can't love you, Kendra," he whispered, and I could tell he was scared shitless.

"You already do," I said back to him; he shook his head and backed away from me. "What are you afraid of?"

"If I love something," he pointed to the ceiling. "*He* will take it away from me!" he shouted, then turned his head away from all of us in the living room. I was betting his eyes had misted over.

I flinched, but I didn't back away from him. "Just kiss me. I know that you..."

He turned to look into my eyes and I had been right, his were gleaming with tears. "I've tried to hate you since Monday night. I've never felt so strongly about anyone before, but when Mason brought me to your room…" His eyes shot daggers at Rhyan. "And I saw the two of you like that; I didn't have the will to live any longer. I realized when I was sitting alone in the cave that you may have turned to him because of the way I acted. I can't hate you. I still want to hate you, but I can't." He shook his head. "No, I don't love Sherri."

I took in a deep breath in and let it out. "Kiss me, Adam."

"I don't have to kiss you, Kendra!" he shouted. "I know that I love you. I already fucking know that! Kissing you will only make it harder on me when you die Friday."

I felt like he'd slapped me. I was stunned and I couldn't breathe. He admitted that he loved me, but he also admitted that he wasn't even going to try to save my soul. I got my breathing regulated and squared my shoulders. "Do it for me then."

"Do what?" he said a little more calmly.

"If I'm going to die Friday, I would like to know what it's like to kiss my soulmate at least once. Kiss me and you will never have to see me again. I promise to leave you alone."

He huffed. "Dammit…fine," he said, but made no move to come any closer to me. That was fine, I could go to him; no big deal.

I was nervous as I closed the space between us, like I was about to have my very first kiss.

His muscles tensed up when I touched him, then he let out a breath soon after and relaxed, as though my touch was the best feeling in the world. I had to agree; it felt really good to touch him. I didn't want to ever let go of him, and the rush was almost too much. I hadn't even touched his bare skin yet. I moved my hand up his chest and touched his neck. It felt like there was a magnet in my body pulling me closer to him. I slowly slid my hand behind his neck and waited. I wanted him to look at me, but he wasn't. I waited until he finally opened his eyes to look at me. They were a considerably lighter shade of brown than they'd been the last time I'd looked into them. I could see that he was afraid of me, but I could also see love in his eyes. I stretched up on my toes and gently touched my lips to his. The magnet became much stronger. Adam wrapped his arms around me and pulled me close to his body, taking the kiss to a whole other level. He devoured my mouth with his and kissed me like I was his last breath that he wasn't going to let go of without a fight.

If I had any doubts about loving him, or that he was my soulmate, they were all gone. If I had ever been in love with anyone else, I wasn't any longer. I belonged to the man in my arms, and I was never letting him go.

Adam abruptly shoved me away, and Kobhye caught me before I fell over the coffee table.

"I can't do this. I...I can't, please leave." He turned and walked out of the room.

He was gone. I had promised to leave him alone if he kissed me. He had done his part, and I had to let him go.

Chapter Thirty-six

Rhyan had to carry me out of the house. I was in shock and I couldn't move. The only thing I felt was my heart shattered in a million pieces. I'd done everything I could do to help Adam, and my best wasn't good enough. I guess the guardians didn't mind Rhyan touching me now, because he climbed in the back seat of Kobhye's crew cab and made me comfortable on his lap. I could feel his soft breathing against my body, and every once in a while, I felt his body shudder as if he were sobbing silently. All was really lost. I was going to die and Rhyan would lose my soul. I would belong to Patrick in Hell. It was too much to comprehend, so I didn't try anymore. I closed my eyes and drifted off to sleep.

The moment I opened my eyes, I knew I was dreaming. Murry was sitting in a chair across the room from me, and he was laughing. I jumped to my feet from my own chair. "Kill me you bastard, kill me now!" I shouted at him.

He stopped laughing, and turned his head to the side. "No," he said.

"You have him; you don't need my soul too," I sobbed.

"You know, I really thought you had a chance back there. I thought you were going to steal his soul away from me. It was like watching a really suspenseful movie. I was biting my nails the whole time. The ending was perfect. I would sell my soul to watch it again. Oh wait...I don't have one," he grinned. "But I will have yours soon."

"Kill me, please," I pleaded.

"I will...in about thirty-five hours," he said as he looked at his watch. "Give or take a few, I don't want you to know exactly what time you will die. That would drive a person crazy, wouldn't it?"

I sat back in the chair and cried. If he wasn't going to kill me so my soul could go to heaven, I wasn't about to sit here and chit-chat with him.

"Oh, now, Kendra…don't cry." I looked up then rushed him with every ounce of energy I had left. I knew I couldn't hurt him, but maybe I could make him kill me. I wouldn't stop till he did.

He grabbed my arms when I got to him, then spun me around and held my hands in place with one of his hands at the small of my back. His other arm was around my neck. I was pressed firmly up against his body, and could feel his heavy breathing by my ear.

"You don't have to worry about Patrick, Kendra. I'm going to keep you as my own. I won your soul fair and square. Therefore, you belong to me." He placed a big smacking kiss on my cheek. "We are going to have lots of fun, don't you worry your pretty little head about that."

"I couldn't take your photo because you're dead right?"

He laughed. "No, sweetheart, you couldn't take my photo because I don't have a soul. Your precious Rhyan's photos would probably turn out just fine. Tell me, how's he taking the good news?"

"He hasn't given up, Murry."

He smiled. "Have you?"

"Not until I take my last breath," I said, then turned and bit myself on my arm.

I woke up in my bed, with Rhyan lying beside me. He wasn't touching me, but he was staring at me intently. "Did he visit your dreams again? You were struggling."

I nodded. "He said he's keeping my soul for himself when he takes my life. He said I will be his, that he will own me because he won my soul."

Rhyan closed his eyes and sighed as I sobbed. "I'm going to talk to the guardians again. I didn't want you to be alone when you woke up. Kobhye is in the guest bedroom, but she's out cold."

"All right, but if it isn't good news, I don't want to know about it."

He nodded again.

"I tried to get him to kill me now, but he wouldn't do it. Will you do it? Will you cause something to happen so I can keep my soul?"

"If I thought you would be able to keep it and go to Heaven, I would do it for you. Even though it would mean my soul would be sent to Hell. If they know it happened intentionally, they would send your soul to Hell anyway; and mine too for helping you."

"Well, shit," I said. "Go talk to the guardians. I'll be fine." He looked at me like he wasn't sure I would be, then he popped out of my sight.

I wouldn't be fine, though. Some people wonder, and actually think they want to know when they are going to die, the year, the day, and even the exact time they will perish and leave this world. If you are one of those people, stop. I promise you don't want to know.

Chapter Thirty-seven

It was almost dawn when I was awakened by a sound. I looked at the clock on my bedside table. It was 5:15 a.m. I'd gotten less than four hours of sleep all together, but then again, I'd slept for twenty-eight straight hours before that. It wasn't a pop that woke me up; the sound had come from outside, so I knew it wasn't Rhyan.

I heard a car door shut. My head shot up from the pillow and I held still so I could hear better. Who the hell was at my house so early? Everyone I knew would let me sleep in until at least eight. I was suddenly afraid of whom it might be, but I didn't know why. I wanted Murry to kill me today so I could go to Heaven. If it didn't happen before tomorrow, my soul would be gone.

I swallowed my fear and crawled out of bed just in time for the doorbell to ring. Hercules looked up from the foot of my bed and began to bark. I was pretty sure that whoever was at the door didn't want to hurt me or they wouldn't have rang my bell. Then again, Murry rang the bell Monday night. I walked barefoot to the door, then realized what I was wearing. Kobhye or Rhyan had dressed me in my nicest black lingerie. Hardly anything was covered. I was betting it was Kobhye. She slept in crap like this. I asked her why once, and she replied: "You never know who is going to show up at midnight." This coming from a girl who fixes her hair and wears makeup to bed for the same exact reason.

I quickly ran back to my room to get something to put over it with Hercules at my feet. He was undecided whether to follow me or eat the monster at the door. He came with me. My black satin robe was lying on the bed. It went with what I was wearing; Kobhye had thought of everything. I wondered if she dressed me like this then called Aven to come over for me. Maybe she thought it would cheer me up.

I shrugged my shoulders and put on the robe. The doorbell rang again and I ran out of my room and to the front door before it could ring a third time and wake her up.

I did not, at all, expect what I saw when I opened the door. Adam was standing on my porch with his back to me. He was looking toward his car, but he turned to look at me when I stepped on the porch. There were tears in his eyes and he looked like hell warmed over. Had Kobhye known he would stop by?

Hercules growled and I cleared my throat, because I didn't know if my voice would be steady or not. "Why are you here?" I didn't say it in a rude way like he had earlier. I was merely curious as to why he was at my house after the way he'd reacted to me visiting his.

"Your, uh...guardian angel," he frowned. "He stopped by my house again a few hours after you left." That must have been when Kobhye was dressing me, but when I'd talked to Rhyan earlier, he hadn't mentioned anything about it.

Had he driven all the way here to complain to me about Rhyan. Didn't he have my phone number? "I didn't know that, I'm sorry. I'll talk to Rhyan and tell him to stay away from you," I said then turned to go inside.

"No, wait," he said in a panicked tone. He started to grab my arm, but I turned back around to face him and he froze. "He didn't wake me up or anything. After you left, I made Sherri leave. I told her to leave me alone, that I didn't love her and that I never would. I told her...that I was in love with you. She left without much of a fight. I couldn't stop replaying the scene in my living room, and the more I played it, the more I hated myself for hurting you. I was scared, Kendra." He looked away from me. "I am still scared. Everyone I've ever loved has been ripped away from me." He turned back to me. "I don't think loving you or not is a choice I have. I've tried not to, but I love you anyway." He turned and looked out across the yard. "I was struggling with what to do, then Rhyan stopped by." he laughed lightly. "Well I guess I should say that he popped into my bedroom."

I chuckled at the thought; Hercules lay on the porch at my feet and whined. "He's good at that."

"He told me I was a fool, and that he would give anything to be your soulmate. He told me that he had always loved you, and that it was his fault you had feelings for him. I just wanted to tell you that I'm sorry, and to thank you for saving my life."

"Was...so you aren't a fool anymore?" I asked. My heart was pounding in my chest; I was surprised he couldn't hear it beating against my ribcage.

"I don't want to be." He bowed his head. "Look, this may sound selfish of me, but if I only have a day left with my soulmate, I'd like to savor every minute of it. I'm not making you any promises, but I want to be with you now, next Saturday, and fifty years from now. It may not happen, but I need every second you can give me."

I went to him and took his hand in mine. He let out a great shuttering breath of relief, like he had when I we'd touched at his house. If a day was all I could have, I was going to take it.

Chapter Thirty-eight

I let go of his hand and nodded toward the door. "Would you like to come in? I canceled all of my appointments for the week when we started looking for you Tuesday morning."

He nodded like he really hadn't expected me to let him in. He must have thought I might reject him the way he'd been rejecting me since the day we met. He looked beat and dead on his feet.

"Come on, Hercules," I said. I thought I heard Adam snicker, but it may have been the wind.

"Have you slept at all?" I asked. He simply shook his head, then he bent and picked up my dog. I shook my head. He was really turning into quiet the little traitor. "Well, you can sleep now. You look like you're about to pass out. Aven left a pair of pajama bottoms you can wear, and I'll go to your house and get you some of your clothes to wear while you're asleep if you want."

His eyes became frantic; he set Hercules down and grabbed my shoulders, shaking his head. "I don't want you going anywhere without me. Something is going to try and end your life, and I'm going to be with you when it happens so I can bring you back."

He still thought he could save my life by sewing me up, but if it comforted him to think that, I was willing to suffer in silence. I nodded. "All right, I won't go anywhere without you. Kobhye is in the guest bedroom; I'll send her when she wakes up, or we can go together when you wake up. Will that work?"

He grabbed me and held me tight. I could tell he was struggling with his emotions, and he overcame them enough to pull me back so he could look at my face. "Do you mind if I take a shower?"

Hell yes, he should take a shower. I wanted him to scrub off any remnants of having sex with Sherri last night, but what I said was, "You know where the bathroom is. I'll get you something clean to wear."

I went to the kitchen and started coffee. He may not need it, but I did. I heard the shower turn on, and a hunger rose inside of me. He was naked in my shower. I shook my head to clear the mental picture and went to my bedroom to get Aven's pajama bottoms out of my dresser. He'd left the door open a crack, so I opened it far enough to lay them on the table that was right inside, then I pulled the door shut.

I went back to the kitchen to start breakfast. He probably hadn't eaten since yesterday, and I was starving. He'd need something in his stomach to help him rest, so I got out bacon and eggs from the fridge and a loaf of bread from the bread box for toast.

My mother always told me, "The way to a man's heart is through his stomach." That had to be true because my dad was a big man, and he loved my mother unconditionally. I smiled as I set the bacon to fry. I didn't really believe that was why he loved her, but she was a hell of a cook.

I folded a load of towels then went back to turn my bacon. I preferred my eggs over easy, but I didn't have a clue how he liked his, or even if he liked eggs and bacon at all. It seems totally un-American to not like eggs and bacon, but who am I to judge?

I heard footsteps coming from my bedroom, and could hear Adam and Hercules sniffing their way to the kitchen. I smiled as he rounded the corner, but when he came into view, my heart began to beat faster and I almost lost every thread of composure I had in me. The spatula slipped from my hand and fell to the floor.

He hurried over to help me pick it up, and he was too close to me. I couldn't think clearly. He wore Aven's pajamas a lot better than Aven ever had. Who knew flannel could look so good on a guy, and he wasn't wearing a shirt. Dear God, help me, I wanted to touch him so bad my hands were shaking.

He handed me the spatula with a smile on his face, and I quickly took it to the sink to wash it. I was trying to put some distance between us so I could think straight again, but he followed me. Damn. "You like eggs and bacon right?"

"Wouldn't it be un-American if I didn't? You need any help?" he asked.

Was he reading my mind?

I shook my head as I got the bacon out of the pan. I knew our souls were mated, but our brains seemed to be on the same wavelength as well. "No, I got it. How do you like your eggs? I don't eat mine scrambled, but Kobhye does. I was going to scramble some for her, so she'll have something to eat when she wakes up."

"Over easy," he said as he got two coffee mugs down from the cabinet.

I ignored the fact that we like our eggs the same, and focused on the two cups of coffee he was adding cream and sugar to. "You're going to drink coffee, and then try to sleep?"

He nodded with a grin then handed me mine. I took a sip. He'd put just the right amount of cream and sugar in it. "I do it all the time." Then he looked at my cup and gave me an "oh shit" face. "I'm sorry; I didn't even ask how you like your coffee."

I sipped it again then laughed. "No, it's fine. It's just the way I like it." I wondered if Rhyan was directing him again the way he had the other night.

"No, he's all on his own, I'm just watching until the clothes start coming off."

I blushed and Adam saw it. "What?" he said.

I shook my head. "Nothing." I set my coffee down and put four slices of bread in the toaster then put the eggs in the skillet to fry. He watched me work without pressing for any more details.

"If he doesn't stop playing that kissing scene in his head, I'm going

to have to find something to distract myself." I laughed out loud. I hadn't meant to, but it happened and I couldn't take it back.

"What?" Adam asked me with a confused look on his face. "Tell me."

"Rhyan is a little distracted by your thoughts," I said, but I couldn't look up at him, my face was already red enough.

I felt him move closer. He softly touched the small of my back with his fingers, then slowly guided them up until he could move my hair away from my neck. He leaned in closer to me and I froze. I could feel his sweet breath on my skin as he whispered, "Maybe Rhyan should stick with your thoughts if he's getting distracted. I can't control what I think when I'm around you." He didn't know it, but Rhyan wouldn't be any more comfortable in my head. The eggs were not going to be over easy if he kept touching me; they'd end up more like chewy egg-flavored plastic, and I didn't even want to think about what my house would smell like. He seemed to sense it, and took his hand away just before I dropped the spatula again. I took a deep breath then flipped the eggs. I got three plates down from the cabinet and divided the eggs between two plates.

I never thought I would have to concentrate so hard on cooking breakfast, but I could feel him looking at me, and I was almost positive what he was thinking.

"Uh-huh," Rhyan said.

"I think I can take it from here, Rhyan. You can go find something else to do. I'm not dying until tomorrow, remember?"

"All right. Yell if you need me."

"Will do," I said as I fixed Kobhye's scrambled eggs then put them on another plate. I put three slices of bacon beside her eggs, and put the plate in the microwave so she could heat it when she got up, which would probably be noon.

Adam and I ate at the bar. I hardly ever used the dining table unless there were more than three people eating. I had three barstools, and that was where I usually sat to eat. I watched Adam as he prepared his food. He used the flat side of the fork and smashed his eggs until they were nothing but jumbled bits on his plate, then he sprinkled salt and pepper lightly over them, more pepper than salt. Then he mixed the seasonings together throughout his eggs. He looked up like he knew I was watching him.

"What?" he said, and I shook my head.

"I was only wondering how many other things we do the exact same way." Then I began smashing and seasoning my eggs.

Chapter Thirty-nine

When we finished eating, Adam helped me clean up, even though I told him three times to go get in bed. He didn't say no, he just didn't go. I put the last dish in the dishwasher; I even had to dump the food Adam had cooked on Monday night that was still on the stove. The three-day-old spaghetti that had sat out didn't smell so good. It didn't look so good either.

I set the dishwasher to wash then Adam took my hand in his. I looked at him questioningly when he began to lead me to the bedroom. He gave me a nervous little smile. "I would like it very much if you would lie down with me until I fall asleep. I promise I won't try anything."

I could do that, but I wasn't really worried about him "trying anything." I was more worried about me trying something on him. If I only had one more day to live, sex was at the top of my "Top 10 things to do before I die" list. I wasn't sure what the other nine were, I couldn't stop thinking about getting my hands on him long enough to think of anything else. Maybe sex ten times would be the top ten things to do. I smiled to myself then pulled the comforter back so I could crawl in between the sheets. He got in on the other side. I turned my back to him, because he really needed sleep, and I'd never been able to sleep if I knew someone was watching me.

I felt him turn away from me. Then, a few moments later, he turned back toward me. He remained that way for a few minutes then turned over again. No more than ten seconds passed before he turned back to face me again. I heard him huff, and I stifled a laugh. I knew the bed was comfortable, so that wouldn't be why he couldn't get to sleep.

I felt him move closer to me, then he put his arm around my waist. I let out a shriek when he pulled me close to his body. He didn't try to do anymore than that. He relaxed with me in his arms then sighed and fell fast asleep.

I didn't know if he was a light sleeper or not. I didn't want to move and wake him up, but I didn't want to lay here awake for the next five to eight hours while he snored lightly in my ear. It was a comforting sound, and soon I was drifting off to my own dreamland.

I opened my eyes to Murry, and boy was he mad. I was so not looking forward to this conversation.

"You're more clever than I gave you credit for, but just because you got him to love you, doesn't mean you've won."

"Do you think I don't know that?" I said.

He was shaking with rage. I wasn't afraid he would kill me, but I was afraid he would hit me. "He will try to save your life when I kill you tomorrow, but he won't be able to."

I squared my shoulders. "I'm aware of that also."

"So, why are you torturing yourself by keeping him near you?" His anger had calmed, and he was really curious about my motives. Maybe he thought I had something up my sleeve that he didn't know about, even though I didn't.

"I don't see it as torture. He loves me, and I love him. If I'm going to die tomorrow, I want to spend my few remaining hours with my soulmate. Is that so hard for you to understand?"

He shrugged. "It doesn't matter to me how you spend the next few hours or so. Tomorrow, you'll be mine."

I lowered my head. "I know."

"And you're okay with that?" He was getting angry again. I didn't know why, and I really didn't care.

"No, but what choice do I have? I've done all I can do, and it wasn't good enough. So if you would be so kind as to leave me and Adam alone, I'll see you tomorrow."

He turned his head to the side and looked at me through squinted eyes. I think he still thought I was hiding something that I would use at the last minute to win Adam's soul and save my own. It was all up to Adam how this turned out, and I knew that no matter how much he loved me or how great his surgical skills were, it wouldn't be enough to save me. I wondered how Adam's sanity would fare when he couldn't bring me back. I knew it wouldn't be good. I was the first person he'd loved in almost twenty years. Coen had been right; his soul would totally be lost. Murry finally nodded. "I'll leave you and Adam alone until tomorrow. I have no problem with that."

"Would you consider giving me another week?"

He laughed. "I would not," he replied with an evil leer.

"Could you not make it too gruesome? I'd like an open casket for my family."

He smiled as he nodded. "Your body will stay intact, and it won't be too painful. I'll grant you that wish. After tomorrow, you will never feel pain again. I promise."

I lowered my gaze. "Yes I will. I will always feel the pain of my broken heart. You can't take that away from me, and I wouldn't want you to. I'll savor every moment of the pain because then I will never forget how it felt to love."

He looked up to the ceiling like he was watching something, or listening to something I couldn't hear. He stood and growled. The room began to shake and then the dream shattered all around me.

I woke to Adam softly kissing my lips. I didn't open my eyes, I just responded back by opening to him and kissing him back. I didn't know if it was because we were meant to be with each other or if he was just a really good kisser, but the butterflies in my stomach fluttered their little wings every time our lips met.

He pulled back, and when I opened my eyes he was smiling. He propped himself up on his elbow and looked at me. "You were crying in your sleep. I thought I could make your tears go away with a kiss. I was right." His smile broadened, making me smile back at him. Smiles are contagious. If you don't believe me, try smiling at someone and see what happens.

"Why were you crying?" he asked.

I looked away from him and he immediately took my chin with his finger and brought my eyes back to his. "Tell me, please. I want to know what's made you so unhappy."

I frowned at him. "Your guardian demon likes to visit my dreams to rub it in that he's going to win. He's keeping my soul for himself after I die, and I'm not too happy about that. That was the reason for the tears."

He lost any hint of a smile. His expression became frantic. "What?"

I rolled my eyes. "Do you think I would be happy about belonging to Mason for all eternity? We won't exactly be living here on Earth." The realization clearly showed on his face. "You really didn't believe me when I told you that I was losing my soul tomorrow, did you?"

He shook his head as his eyes grew wide. "If he's taking your soul tomorrow, does that mean he'll kill me too?"

I shook my head and thought for a moment. "I don't think so. That was in the deal I made with your guardian angel. I had a week to regain your soul, or I would die again." I shrugged. "I took the deal because I didn't have anything to lose. I got to live another seven days even if I failed, but if I succeeded, I'd get to go on living my life. I didn't find out until later that I would lose my soul to Murry if I failed. I raised hell about it. Believe me, I did. Your guardian angel was the one who caused my first accident to happen. He figured if our souls met, that would be the only way to get you back." I lowered my gaze. "Coen's soul was sent into Hell for what he did to me. And believe me when I say that I'm going to kick his ass when I get there tomorrow."

"You aren't going to Hell, Kendra. I promise to bring you back if you die." He said it so sincerely that I almost believed it myself.

I smiled through unshed tears and placed my hand on his cheek. "I know you think you'll be able to."

He put his hand on top of mine and turned his head into my palm, kissing it lightly. "He knows how good a surgeon I am. I won't let him take you. You have to believe me." He was pleading with me.

"I believe you, Adam," I lied then kissed his lips before he could see the truth in my eyes.

Chapter Forty

Adam took to the kiss and I forgot about my losing my soul. We had this time together. I knew it wouldn't last, but Adam still seemed to have faith in his surgical skills, if nothing else. I would let him believe that, if it meant we could be happy until it happened. I didn't want to fight with him. I wanted his last memories of us together to be the best memories of his life, and I wanted good memories of us together that I could look back on when forced to become Murry's puppet.

Adam kissed me tenderly; it was nothing like the kiss from last night. It was still hungry with eagerness, but there was a softness there that hadn't been there before. I had never experienced anything so pleasurable. He seemed to explore every part of my mouth with care and utter preciseness; pulling and sucking my lips with his, then sliding his tongue in to tangle with my own. His hands only touched my face, and only so he could change the angle of the kiss. I had never had a kiss this intense without touching, and I wanted more from him. I wanted to explore for myself, but every time I tried to touch him, he would take my hands away and place them gently on the bed.

He moved from my mouth and ran a trail of delicate kisses down my neck and over my collarbone, then untied my black satin robe so he could open up more of the package that lay before him. I wanted to touch him, and I knew that he would eventually let me. The urge was almost too strong now. I was about to burst from my need to have him.

He looked up at me in surprise. "You sleep alone in this kind of stuff?"

I let out a little gasp and covered my mouth with my hand in embarrassment. It took me a few moments to regain my composure enough to speak without bursting into tears or fits of laughter. I wasn't completely sure what would happen when I opened my mouth, but he was looking at me now like he wanted to rip the thin sheer material off instead of laugh at me. I removed my hand and took a deep breath. "Kobhye dressed me for bed. I wasn't able. I suppose she thought I'd have a midnight rendezvous with someone. You should see how she preps herself for sleeping alone."

He smiled. "Remind me to thank Kobhye later."

I blushed, and he resumed the task at hand. He slipped the slim strap of my lingerie down and didn't waste any time baring my breast. I ran my fingers through his short black hair and he either let me do it, or was too enthralled with his discoveries beneath my lingerie. He captured my hardened nipple between his lips and suckled gently. I gave a soft moan which he echoed. My entire body quivered under his experienced touch. He became more determined to get rid of my top.

I ran my hands over his shoulders and he didn't object. I assumed I was getting total access to him. I took advantage of the free pass with an overwhelming sense of anticipation, and ran my hands further down his unyielding but soft back. Then I relocated them to the front of his upper body so I could feel the thumping of his heartbeat with my fingers.

Passion doesn't come close to explaining what I was experiencing; desire couldn't touch it either. It was unlike anything I had ever heard defined, let alone experienced. I had been with men before, but this was different. I can't explain how it was different, because the way he was touching me had my head reeling. The only thought I could wrap my mind around was, I Needed Him Now!

He was still trying to be gentle when he moved to take off the panties, but his self-control was slipping away quickly. I heard him grunt in frustration, and then the soft material ripped. He looked up like I might be angry with him, and I laughed. He smiled and continued to remove the fabric. "The sexy sleepwear was nice, but I prefer you without it," he said with a mischievous smirk.

The bottom half of his body was under the comforter, but I knew he was still wearing the flannel pajama bottoms. I wanted him out of them. I placed my hand on his stomach, and he closed his eyes and sighed. I slowly moved my hand down to run along his waistband. His breath caught in his throat and he shivered. I smiled, then moved my body in alignment with his. I began to place kisses down his neck when I was close enough. He pulled me closer, and my hand slipped beneath the soft flannel to find him hard, aroused, and very ready for me. I wrapped my fingers around him and he gasped. He scrambled to remove the material from his body.

He finally got them kicked off his feet, and in one swift motion, he had me on my back, was in between my legs, and sliding into my hot core. I screamed out his name, and he screamed out mine as I hit my climax and fell into oblivion. I couldn't think about anything but the intense feeling his body was giving mine. We fit together perfectly, and why shouldn't we? We were made for each other.

"Again, Kendra...do it again." He crushed his lips to mine and rolled us over so I was straddling him. I moved forward and back, slowly at first, but he quickly took control, grabbing my hips and moving me faster and faster while watching my face with extreme concentration.

I could feel the orgasm building, like a rubber band that was stretched to its max. He pushed and pulled my body faster still until it broke free. I screamed. It wasn't a sigh or a moan, but a full-blown scream. I didn't have a choice in the matter. The excessive pleasure radiating through my body brought a sound from my throat so violent I thought I might have trouble speaking later. I couldn't move. My muscles had gone limp, but that didn't stop Adam. He grabbed me and scooted off the bed, still carefully cradling my body in front of him.

He laid me on the edge of the bed and I looked up at him with a lazy smile. "We aren't finished, Kendra. I'm nowhere near finished with you."

An hour and a half later, we were both collapsed in a tangled, sweaty mess and breathing hard. The comforter must have found better comfort on the floor, because that was where it ended up. The pillows were there as well, and the fitted sheet wasn't exactly fitted to the mattress any longer. I opened my eyes. That was the only movement I could manage at the moment, and I looked out my bedroom window. The sun was only about thirty minutes from setting. How long had we slept earlier?

Murry had promised to leave us alone so we could enjoy our last few hours together. Even without him interfering, I knew I was running out of precious time. It made me sad to think I couldn't be with Adam everyday like this. It didn't need to be this intense all the time; just waking up to him every morning for the rest of my life would be enough. That was the problem; I only had one more morning left of my life.

If I'd have known he wouldn't believe what he needed to at the end of the week, I would have just seduced him that first day so I could have had more days with him. With Adam, my soulmate.

Chapter Forty-one

Adam regained movement in his limbs before I did, but he didn't look a hundred percent as he stumbled to the bathroom.

"Would you like to shower with me?" he shouted from the bathroom, and I heard the water come on.

I found my voice and managed to get out, "I would love to, but I have this little problem of not being able to move my legs."

I didn't hear him coming, and I let out a girlie squeal as he picked me up in his arms. I started laughing as he carried me to the shower. "That problem can be remedied. No worries." he said, with a broad smile plastered across his face.

He stood me under the hot spray then steadied me until I could stand on my own. It wasn't as bad as I'd thought, so I didn't have much trouble with my balance. "I thought we could go out for a bite to eat. You feel up to it, or would you rather go back to doing other things?" He gave me a sexy seductive look. Sex with him was definitely in my immediate future, but I needed a little break. Food sounded good.

"We can eat and save the other things for dessert." He grinned at me as he lathered up my shower puff with body wash. I thought he was doing it for him, so it surprised me when he began to wash my body. He washed every inch of me, quite thoroughly in some places, I might add. I blushed, and he just smiled.

I realized he was aroused. How could he be, after what we'd just done? He bent and kissed my lips tenderly, and I became conscious that I wanted him just as ardently. My eyes were still closed when his lips left mine. He didn't touch me anymore, so I opened them to find him soaping his own body. He made slow, circular movements with the shower puff over his shoulders, pecs, and his stomach. I had to look away when he went lower; he was driving me crazy. He had that sexy smirk plastered on his face the whole time. How could anyone get so aroused from only watching someone wash their own body? I didn't know, but it was driving me insane.

I huffed.

"What?" he said, his grin spreading. He shrugged those perfect shoulders. "You said you wanted food." He stepped into my personal space and looked down into my eyes. The smile was replaced by a sense of seriousness. "Let's go eat, then we can come back, and I'll finish what I started. I promise."

"I don't take too well to broken promises." I said, meeting his stare.

"I'll try not to disappoint you then." He smiled and kissed my forehead. "And I'll try to behave until we get back, but no promises there. I only said I would try."

I smiled and got out of the shower so he could rinse off. "Where are we going so I can dress appropriately?"

"The Villa if you like Italian. If you don't, then you can choose where we go," he said.

"The Villa is fine with me," I said, and went into my room to find some clothes and change.

After I got dressed, I went to the kitchen to see if Kobhye had found the breakfast that I'd left in the microwave for her. The empty plate and fork were in the sink. I heard the shower cut off, and I went back to the bathroom. I had to dry my hair, and I couldn't flat iron it with the humidity from the shower, so I had waited for Adam to finish up.

He had the towel wrapped around his waist, and I had a sudden urge to grab it and bare that beautiful ass of his. Damn, it was hard to behave with a half naked man around that was so sexy.

"You look great," he said.

"With this towel on my head? Yeah, I'm sure great isn't the word for it." I laughed and then went to finish getting ready.

I had already fixed my hair and was applying the last of my makeup when Adam came in and sat on the stool. "You don't really need that stuff, you know. I think you're gorgeous without it."

"I can't go out in public and let my date look better than I do." I smiled then searched for my mascara.

"I got the impression that I was more than a date to you," he said. I didn't want for him to get all defensive about me living through tomorrow again. I wanted to have a good night with him.

I finished applying my mascara and then put it back in my makeup bag before responding. I looked at him and shrugged. "This is all new to me. I've never let myself get tied to only one guy. So, forgive me if I don't know the first thing about relationships. I do consider you more than a date. I just don't know how all of this works." I made a back and forth motion with my hand in between us. "Tell me how it works."

He shrugged and smiled back at me. "I don't know, but we'll figure it out together."

I nodded then looked down at what he was wearing. He had on the white button-up he'd been wearing when he got to my house this morning, but he was wearing the pajama bottoms with black dress shoes. I giggled. "Are you going to The Villa dressed like that?"

He gave me a hurt look. "You don't like what I'm wearing?"

"I would prefer you out of what you're wearing, but I'll behave myself, as well, until we get back."

His eyes danced with laughter as he looked at me. "I need to run by my apartment to change and get a few things. I'm not leaving you alone for even a second until all of this shit with Mason is over."

I only nodded then looked away from him to apply my lip gloss. I couldn't look him in the eye with him being in such denial. I knew what was going to happen, and he still thought he could fix it his way.

"I need to call my parents and let them know I'm all right. The only way I convinced my dad to let me leave the hospital last night was to tell him that I was in love and going after you. He said if you hurt me that he would personally knock your head off your shoulders."

Adam laughed nervously. "Is he a big man?"

"Very," I said with fake horror in my eyes.

"Well, I guess he needs to see that his baby girl is unharmed in person. I would like to meet your parents if that's okay with you."

My jaw dropped, and he laughed. "You want to meet my parents? I've never taken a guy to meet my parents."

He shrugged. "How else am I going to get permission to marry their daughter?"

My jaw went ahead and fell to the floor, and I stared at him with wide, frightened eyes. Did he just say what I thought he said?

"Yeah...he did," Rhyan said unhappily in my mind.

Adam stood up from the stool, walked to me, kissed my forehead and said, "I'll wait for you at the door, honey."

Chapter Forty-two

I braced myself on the vanity then maneuvered my way to the stool to sit down. I felt lightheaded all of a sudden, and I couldn't get enough air into my lungs. Married? I couldn't get married.

"Are you coming, Kendra?" Adam shouted from the living room.

Was I coming? I thought as I tried to stifle a panic attack.

"Yes, you are going. Just get up and start moving. Typically, when two people fall in love, they get married," Rhyan said.

"He's only been in love with me since last night, Rhyan. How can he already be thinking marriage?"

"Maybe because he knows he wants to be with you forever," he said.

"Yeah? Well, there is a little problem with that. My forever ends tomorrow," I said rudely.

He sighed. *"You don't know that yet. You still have four to twenty-eight hours left to change his mind."*

"Yeah, hours; I only have hours, not years, not months, not even days. I have hours, and soon it will be minutes. Adam loves me, but that won't be enough, will it?"

He sighed again. *"Just have a good night, will you? Don't ruin this for him, Kendra. If he's in denial, you saying anything about dying in a few hours will just piss him off. Just tell him you will marry him. You don't have to set a date tonight. If you end up pulling through this thing, the two of you can set a date later after you've calmed down."* He paused for a moment. *"He's coming back to the bathroom to make sure that you're all right. Stand up and make yourself be all right."*

I listened to Rhyan without responding to him. I stood up and had on a bright smiling face when Adam rounded the corner. "I'm ready," I said a little too cheerfully.

He gave me a suspicious look then nodded. "All right, let's go then."

I started walking then suddenly stopped. "Wait...do we have to go see my parents?"

He smiled. "I think that would be best, don't you? Like you said, we need to show your dad that my intentions are to never hurt you."

"We don't have to get married for them to see that, Adam."

He grinned. "That isn't the reason I want to marry you. I just can't imagine my life without you in it anymore. I want to go to sleep beside you every night and wake up beside you every morning."

"And what happens if my last morning is tomorrow?" I asked, and my eyes began to tear up.

He walked to me and wrapped me in his arms. "Then I will go through Hell to find you and bring you back. I promise."

I began to sob. "That's impossible."

He tilted my chin up so I didn't have a choice but to look at him. "I thought it would be impossible for me to ever love anyone again. You made that possible for me, Kendra. If that's possible, then anything is possible."

I nodded. I didn't believe he could do anything about it when it happened, but I nodded anyway. "Let's go eat, and then I'll introduce you to my parents."

He wiped my tears away and smiled. "I need to go change first, or would you rather me go to The Villa with you looking like this?"

I laughed. "No. You most definitely need to change."

We left my house and went to his apartment. I was still nervous all the way there, not about being around Adam. I was worried about how my dad would react about a guy he didn't know, and I barely knew, asking for my hand in marriage. It was not going to be a good night.

We were only a few miles from his apartment when he touched my hand. I jumped. "Jeez. Relax, will ya. Your dad isn't going to hurt me or yell at you."

"You don't know him, Adam," I said, and he smiled.

"You're right, I don't, but don't you think he just wants his daughter to be happy?" He said this as he pulled into the parking garage of his apartment complex. He cut the engine then turned and looked at me.

I slumped in my seat and huffed. "I guess you're right. I'm just not looking forward to it." I looked at him. "You know, you haven't asked me if I would marry you yet."

He smiled. "I need to get permission from your father first, don't I?"

I sulked in my seat and looked out the window at the Chevy we'd parked beside. "I guess he would appreciate it."

"Okay then, let's go up so I can get changed, then we will go see if your parents want to eat with us."

My head shot around so fast, I was sure to have whiplash. "What? No…we can go eat then go talk to my parents. I want to be able to leave if things get too hairy."

He laughed. "Okay, what are your parents' names?"

"Mr. and Mrs. Larkin," I said with a smirk. He rolled his eyes. "Okay, their names are Diane and Robert. My dad's friends call him Bobby, but he's Robert to you until he tells you otherwise."

"Aven called him Bobby when they found me in the cave. Did you take Aven home to meet your folks?"

"Yeah, when I was five. He's been one of my best friends since we were kids. Aven and my dad are pretty close, but it isn't because of me." He gave me a quick kiss then got out of the car.

We got in the elevator and I turned to look at him. "What?" he asked. *"Don't do it, Kendra."*

"When did you pick up the magazine that has the article about me in it?" I ignored Rhyan and watched Adam's face closely.

He shrugged. "After you left me at the restaurant Monday. Why?"

"When did you read it and lay it on your nightstand?" I asked.

"I was reading it when Mason popped into my room. That's when he took me to your room where you and Rhyan were…"

"So, you believe you have a guardian demon, and you believe I have a guardian angel, but you don't believe there is a God?"

"Kendra, can we not do this tonight?" he said, and I could tell he was getting agitated, but I didn't care, so was I.

"When can we do it? After I'm dead?" My voice was louder than I'd intended, but I couldn't help it.

He spoke calmly, but there was a hint of anger behind it. "I believe there is a God, Kendra. I always have. I just refuse to follow him."

"You won't even do it to keep me! You say you love me, but do you really? You may not believe me, but I really will die in a few hours if you can't do this for me. You are the only one who can prevent that from happening. They aren't trying to trick you. This is a done deal; a deal I made with your ignorant-ass guardian angel!" I'd been shouting at him, but I made myself stop and take a few breaths before I said anything else. When I spoke again, I was considerably calmer. "I love you, and I believe that we are soulmates. I would do anything to save you. If you love me the way you say you do, then why can't you do what's necessary to save me?"

He gave me a stern look as the elevator doors opened to his floor. "I will save you, just not that way."

"I told you that you should have kept your mouth shut."

"Shut up, Rhyan," I said, then hung my head.

Adam stepped out and I followed him to his apartment. He opened the door and just left it wide open so I could enter on my own. He was angry. I got that. I didn't like it, but I got it.

I walked back to his room where he had disappeared to, and sat on his bed as he rummaged through his closet. He was pushing the hangers excessively hard while he looked for something to wear.

"I'm sorry," I said in a cracked whisper.

He froze and dropped his head with his back still to me. "I know if something happens to you…and I can't save you for some reason, that it will be my fault. But I've built up so much hatred for your God that I can't do it." When he turned to me, he had tears in his eyes; he didn't turn away from me this time. "I want to...for you, but I can't. How does a God, that's supposedly so good, hold you to a deal like that when you were tricked? Answer me that."

"It wasn't made through God. I made the deal with your guardian angel. The main guardians are holding me to that deal. They aren't so lenient."

"And God is? I was thirteen, Kendra...thirteen when I lost my whole...damn...family." He crumbled to his knees in front of me. My hand went to my mouth and I touched his shoulder with my other one. He didn't pull away from me, so I dropped to the floor and hugged him tight. He grabbed a hold of me and sobbed.

"I'm sorry, Adam. I'm just trying to figure this out. I won't bring it up again. Can we still have a good night?"

He pulled back and blew a big gush of air out through his lips. He wasn't looking at me, but I hadn't expected him to. He pursed his lips and nodded. "Yeah...we can have a good night." I regretted ever bring it up, and I would give anything to wipe that sad look off his face.

Chapter Forty-three

We arrived at The Villa. I'd suffered most of the ride in silence. Adam didn't look angry anymore, but I could still see the sadness in his features. It looked like he was finally realizing that he might not be able to save me when the time came. I hated that I'd even brought it up, because I didn't know how to make him smile again. I didn't know what to say to make things better between us.

We got right in, but I wasn't surprised, Friday and Saturday nights were the busiest nights for The Villa, and it was only Thursday. The hostess seated us, then Adam ordered my favorite White Zen.

He surprised me when he spoke, but any conversation was good conversation right now. "Do you have any siblings?"

I nodded. "Haley is thirty-three. She's married to Mike Lebrowski. He's an architect here in town and he's considered to be one of the best. They have two children, Shelby and Brenden." His facial features relaxed a bit. Good.

"I know Mike. One of his employees took a nasty fall last year. Mike was at the trauma center with him the whole time. He's a good guy." I wanted to say that he'd said the same thing about Mason, but I didn't. I knew Mike was a good guy.

"Yeah, he is. He treats my sister and those kids like they're his whole world," I said, then took my glass of wine from the waitress. I ordered the lasagna with meat sauce, and fettuccini alfredo. Adam ordered the same. I didn't know if that was what he would have ordered if I hadn't gone first. If we ate anywhere else before I died, I would insist he order first. I shook my head. I didn't know why I was fixated on the coincidences in our tastes and preferences, but I just thought it was neat that we did everything the same way.

"That's how I feel about you. You are my world now, Kendra. I know how Mike feels and I can relate to that," he said then took a sip of wine.

If anyone had said that to me only a week ago, I would have bolted from the room. But sitting across the table from Adam, I found that I could relate to that as well. Adam was my world now, and that made me happy; I wanted to make him happy.

We got our meals, but we were actually doing more talking than eating. He wanted to know all about photography and my life. I could talk about photography, but when it came to talking about me, I drew a blank. Have you ever tried talking about yourself? He asked a few questions and we fell into a natural conversation.

I asked him about the worst cases he'd encountered in surgery. His eyes lit up as he spoke about some of them. I realized he actually loved what he did. It was a good thing I didn't have a weak stomach, because he didn't spare any of the bloody details.

When I talked, I noticed that he looked at me with a sort of fascination. I had succeeded in wiping that sad look off his face. Hal-le-lu-jah.

"Can you try to avoid making him sad again? His thoughts are really dispirited when he's like that. It's easier for Murry to gain control of him that way," Rhyan said, and I smiled.

"I won't bring it up again. You knew I had to learn my lesson the hard way,"

When Adam asked for the check I got nervous again. I closed my eyes as my stomach did a little roll.

"Cheer up, Kendra. If your dad kills you, it means you get to come to heaven with me." I laughed, despite the nervous bugs in my tummy.

Adam raised an eyebrow at me. "I miss something?"

I shook my head. "Rhyan was trying to help by making me less nervous about you meeting my parents."

His other eyebrow went up and did a high-five with the one that was already raised. "And how does Rhyan feel about me proposing?" Adam's head shot up instantly, like he was listening to something in his head, and was surprised to hear it. I saw him nod then shake his head like he was clearing his mind.

He wasn't upset so I asked. "What did he say?"

He shook his head and laughed lightly. "It freaks me out when he does that." He cleared his throat. "He said, as long as I'm treating you right and keeping you happy, he's fine with it," he frowned. "Does he do that to you all the time?"

I rolled my eyes and nodded. "All the time."

"Awe, Kendra, you act as if you don't like my company."

I laughed. *"You know I do. I was only trying to keep Adam from getting jealous."*

"Understood," he said, then he was silent after that.

Adam was still frowning when he stood up, but he didn't say anything more about Rhyan talking to me. I was sure it bothered him because he had seen, with his own eyes, Rhyan and I going at it all hot and heavy. I assumed he and Murry left before Rhyan got the good news that we weren't allowed to touch each other. Would telling him that we didn't have sex make him feel better, or would he think I was lying to him?

"I already told him that we didn't have sex, Kendra. Let it go." I nodded, then stood when Adam offered me his hand.

I was physically shaking when we got in the car. He looked at me with concern in his brown eyes. I did notice that they were a whole lot lighter than they had been only this morning. They were sort of a caramel color and very beautiful. He took my wrist in his hand and checked my pulse. "Are you going to be sick? I won't make you do this if it's not what you want to do."

"I'll be fine." I had a thought. "What if you meet my family a few times before you ask to marry me, let them get to know you first? I know they will love you, and my mom would be ecstatic with you asking permission tonight. She wants me married with children so bad she can hardly see straight. My sister will think I'm jumping into things and that our marriage won't last. My dad...my dad is another story all together. He doesn't care if I ever get married. He isn't against it, but he thinks I should be with Aven. He hasn't ever said it outright, but I know how close the two of them are. Aven goes fishing and hunting with my dad, they talk cars and baseball. It will take a while to convince him that you're the right man for me. That won't happen tonight; I can promise you that."

Adam sighed as he started the engine. "All right, I'll only introduce myself tonight." He looked at me and I was smiling at him. "Do you feel better?"

"Much better."

Chapter Forty-four

When we pulled up at my parent's house, my heart jumped up in my throat. "Adam, I think we need to do this some other time."

The car came to a stop in front of the house and he turned and looked at me. "What's wrong now?" he asked, with confusion written all over that beautiful face of his.

I couldn't think of a good enough lie to tell him so I huffed and settled for the truth. "Aven is here."

He shrugged. "So…I never got a chance to thank him for getting me out of that cave."

How did I explain this to him? "Aven was to me like Sherri was to you. We have been seeing each other intimately for a little over a year now, but it was casual, nothing serious." I took a breath. "It was Aven who called me Monday when you were at my house. He wanted to make things more than casual with me. When I almost died the other day, it made him realize that he wanted us to be more than friends with benefits."

Adam closed his eyes and rubbed his temples with his fingers. He looked at me and shook his head. "You want to hide our relationship?"

I thought about it a moment. I didn't want to. I wanted to let the whole world know that I was in love with the man beside me, but a little at a time. I wasn't sure how two very important people in my life would react. If I didn't do it tonight, and I died tomorrow, then I wouldn't have to do it at all. I'm a coward, I know.

I looked at him. He had told Sherri that he was in love with me, and I had told him that I would do anything for him. Yet, here he sat, looking like he was being rejected, like I was too embarrassed to introduce him to my family, like he wasn't good enough for me. "No, we can do this now. I'm acting like a coward, and I'm sorry for that."

He smiled a little. "A coward is someone who runs from a challenge, Kendra. You are far from being a coward."

If he only knew how bad I wanted to run that moment, he wouldn't think so highly of me. He pulled in the drive and cut off the engine. I could see there was a ball game on my parent's big screen through the picture window. I'd grown up in that house and could remember very clearly breaking that window with a baseball when I was ten. It was the same year that Adam lost his whole family. Back then, I didn't even know Adam and was only worried that my dad would be mad when he saw that broken window. He hadn't been angry. I sighed and got out of the car.

Adam took my hand and led me to the door. I was shaking again, and he squeezed my hand for reassurance. I gave him my best fake smile then walked in the door.

"Mom?" I shouted.

"In here, honey!" she shouted from the kitchen. I glanced in the living room. My dad and Aven were watching a baseball game on T.V. It was probably a rerun, or we were losing, because they weren't all excited like they usually were when a game was on. Aven looked back at me with a grim look then glanced at Adam. His expression didn't change before he looked back at the screen. I sighed and walked to the kitchen where my mother was.

She met me with a big hug then looked at Adam. Her face lit up like a Christmas tree. "Oh..." She glanced back at me, her face about to split in two with extreme happiness.

"Mama, this is Adam Chamberlain. He's the surgeon who saved my life a week ago." I looked at Adam. "This is my mother, Diane Larkin."

He shook her hand with a genuine smile on his face. "It's very nice to meet you, Mrs. Larkin."

She was flustered, and I could tell instantly that she liked him. "Oh, call me Diane. Kendra hasn't ever brought anyone home to meet us before. I was beginning to think she was embarrassed by us."

"No, only dad," I said as I munched on one of the chocolate chip cookies my mother had just taken from the oven. She smiled.

"Well, I'm very happy she decided to bring you to meet us," she looked at me a little nervously. "Your dad and Aven are in the living room. Shall we introduce Adam?"

I knew what she was thinking. I think my mother suspected Aven's feelings for me long before I had. Why hadn't anyone told me? I nodded. "If we must."

We passed Aven in the hallway. He was going to the kitchen to get my dad and himself another beer, no doubt. He gave me a cold look but I ignored it and walked into the living room.

"Dad."

"You sorry son of a bitch! I could have hit that damn ball, and I'm half blind," my dad said to the t.v.

I rolled my eyes. "Daddy," I said a little louder and he looked around at me, startled. Then he caught sight of Adam.

He got to his feet and extended his hand. "I'm sorry," he said as he shook Adam's hand. "You check out fine at the hospital the other day?"

Adam nodded and smiled at my father. "Everything was fine." He looked around as Aven walked back into the room. "I'd like to thank you both for getting me out of that cave."

Aven handed the second beer to my dad, then went to the couch and sat down. He spoke to Adam without looking at him. "Kendra was the one who said you were in a cave. You should be thanking her."

"I have," Adam said.

Aven mumbled something, and it sounded a whole lot like, "I'm sure you have."

"This was a bad idea, Adam. Can we go now?" I said.

He looked back at Aven where he was planted on the couch ignoring us. "No…no, I think Aven here has something he needs to get off his chest. Am I right, Aven?"

Aven tensed then looked back at Adam with fury in his eyes. Oh God, please don't let them fight. Aven was notorious for starting shit, and my dad had seemed friendly enough, but I didn't know whose side he would take.

Aven picked up a cup and spit in it. He'd been dipping since we were in Junior High. It was a nasty habit, but it was his nasty habit, not mine, so I left it alone. He was just never allowed to kiss me until he'd brushed his teeth. He glanced at me. "Do you have time to talk to me now?"

I so did not want to do this tonight, but if talking to him would keep him from fighting with Adam, then I was all for it. "Sure, why not?" I looked at Adam. "Will you be all right for a few minutes?" he nodded, and I looked at my dad. "Try not to scare him too bad, will ya, Dad?"

He shrugged. "Gotta see if he's man enough to date my baby girl, don't I?"

"No, really you don't. C'mon Aven, let's go out back." He stood and kept eye contact with Adam the whole time as he walked slowly by him.

"What the hell was all that about?" I asked, in a firm tone, after he'd closed the back door and we were alone.

He spit his dip out into one of my mother's flowerbeds then took a big drink of beer before looking at me. "Like your dad said, just trying to see if he's man enough to date you."

"It isn't your place or my dad's to make that decision, it's mine. I thought you were better than this, but you're acting like a sixteen year old boy whose girlfriend was taken away from him by another guy."

"You were!" he shouted at me. "I may not be sixteen, but I figured that I'd be the one you eventually got serious with, Kendra."

"You were just like me. You never wanted anything serious, so don't give me that bullshit."

"I did with you, but I knew it would scare you away if I said anything about it. Now you get serious with some guy you've known for less than a week? You bring him home to meet your folks? We've known each other since grade school; I've loved you since Junior High."

My eyes got wide. That was a shocker. "You never acted like you were jealous of me dating anyone else."

"Because I knew you didn't want anything serious. I had to wait for you to change your mind before I could make my move. I picked your limp body up off the ground and I knew I couldn't wait any longer to let you know how I feel about you. Don't do this to me." He stepped forward, and I took a step back. He stopped and stared at me. "You're really in love with him, aren't you?"

"It isn't that simple, Aven."

"Either you are, or you aren't. How complicated is that?" he said.

I didn't say anything for a long while. I knew this night was going to turn out rotten. I finally looked back at him. "I love him, Aven." There, I'd said it. It was going to come out sooner or later. I'd said it last night at the hospital, but I was betting Aven thought I only said it so my parents would let me leave.

His face fell as he stared at me. "Please tell me it's not true."

I nodded. "It is...I didn't plan for it to happen. It was already planned for me." I pleaded with him to understand, but there was no way that he could. He was not going to understand anything right now.

"WHAT THE FUCK EVER!" he shouted as he kicked one of my mother's flower pots off the back porch then stormed through the back door.

I stood there for a moment, shocked by his outburst. Then, I thought he might try to start something with Adam, so I went through the back door after him. I heard his truck start outside, then his tires peeled out on the street as he drove off.

My mother came rushing to me. "I'm all right, Mom; I'm all right."

She wrapped me in a big hug and rubbed my back.

"I can't believe you didn't know how he felt about you, honey. He didn't try to hide it."

I shook my head. "I guess I just didn't want to see it."

She pulled back and gave me a smile. "Is this guy special?"

I rolled my eyes. "Yeah, he's special."

"Well, he is very nice, and really, really good looking. The two of you will make very beautiful children."

"Mom, please…you wouldn't have a problem with me marrying him tomorrow, would you?"

"Of course not, dear. I only want you to be happy, and I want you to have children before I'm too old to play with them." Her smile faltered a little. "Are you getting married tomorrow?"

I rolled my eyes. "If it were up to Adam we would be, but it isn't, so no."

She frowned and followed me back to the living room. I walked in, but Adam and my dad weren't there.

"They're outside. Your father wanted to look at Adam's car." I should have known.

Chapter Forty-five

My mother and I walked outside to join the men. I shot a questioning look at Adam, but he was too busy talking Car and Driver with my dad to notice. The hood was raised and my dad was looking at the engine like a kid in a candy store. I swear there was drool at the corners of his mouth. I knew how he felt, because I'd looked at that car the same way when I'd first seen it. Adam hadn't been as enthusiastic then as he was now. I could tell he loved this car with a mad passion. I smiled to myself, because I had seen an even more passionate look in those eyes earlier today.

My dad was taking this a lot better than I thought he would. I even heard Adam mention fishing and hunting. I didn't know if he did any of those things, but he knew my dad did, and I was sure he would buy a gun and a fishing pole if he thought it would help get in my dad's good graces.

I tried to get Adam's attention a few times, but it was like they were in their own little world; neither of them could hear me. I looked at my mom. "Welcome to my world, Kendra. I never thought you would find someone exactly like your father…but I guess you have," she said with a smile.

"Adam." He looked up at me like he just realized I was there. I pointed at my watch. "It's eleven o'clock." I tried to tell him with my eyes, that we only had an hour before we had to start keeping a watch out for bad shit to happen. He seemed to get my meaning, because the excitement drained away from his expression.

He looked at my mom. "It was really nice meeting you, Diane." He shook my mother's hand then looked at my dad. "Robert."

My dad shook his hand. "Call me Bobby, Adam. You make her bring you back, all right?"

Adam smiled. "Will do, Sir."

I gave my parents each a hug and we said our goodbyes.

Adam was smiling when he got in the car. "Your folks are great. And you were worried your dad and I wouldn't play nice," he joked.

I smiled. "I am very happy with the outcome. They both like you very much. Now, you'll only have to be around them another fifteen times or so before you can ask permission to marry me."

His jaw dropped, and I laughed. "You're kidding, right?"

I laughed. "Yes, I am kidding. My mother would have us married tomorrow if it was up to her, but you may need to see my dad a couple more times to be on the safe side."

He nodded. I guessed he was okay with that. "How did things go with Aven?"

I frowned. "They didn't."

"You don't want to talk about it?" he asked.

I shrugged. "I'm sure you saw him leave. He confessed to me that he's been in love with me since Junior High. It was news to me. The only reason he doesn't like you is because I love you, and not him. He said he's been waiting for the perfect moment to tell me. I guess he missed that perfect moment. Not that it would have mattered."

I saw him glance at the clock again. It was the third time in five minutes. It was 11:17 p.m., and I was praying Murry didn't jump the gun. Or maybe I was hoping he would so I wouldn't lose my soul, but then I wouldn't have Adam. I knew one thing for sure; I wouldn't be able to sleep tonight.

I turned the radio on and he immediately turned it off. "What if I just drove off a cliff right now? Would that save your soul?"

The questions stunned me. I really hadn't thought he would suggest such a thing. I took in a deep breath then let it out. I shook my head.

"If my death is intentional, my soul still belongs to Mason. I mean Murry. I already thought of that and asked Rhyan to do something, but he couldn't."

He looked as though he were thinking again. He had a far off look in his eye with his fist up to his mouth. "Adam?"

He shook his head. "We'll go to my apartment then. It's closer to the Trauma Center, so if something happens, we won't be far away." He looked at the clock again; 11:20. "We have time to go by your place so you can get a few things if you need them. You can bring Hercules if you want."

I didn't respond; I only looked out my window. Adam had no intention of letting me be alone. I couldn't argue that his apartment would be the best place for me to be.

We drove to my place so I could get some of my own things and Hercules; I wasn't leaving without him. When we got there, I looked at the clock as I ran through the door. It read 11:28. Hercules was barking, and his short legs were trying to keep up with me as I ran through the house. "Outside, Hercules, outside!" He looked up at me and turned his head sideways. He knew there was something wrong and he didn't want to leave me to go out in the yard to pee.

"Adam, will you take him outside to do his business before we go so I can get some stuff together?" I said as he walked through my bedroom door. He didn't hesitate; he just picked up the little dog and left the room.

I grabbed a backpack from under the bed then went to the bathroom for my hair dryer, flat iron, toothbrush and deodorant. I threw them in the pack and went for underwear and clothes. After I had them in the pack and had it zipped up, I grabbed Hercules' food and water bowl and his pet carrier. Maybe Adam would take care of him if something happened to me. I was counting on it.

I locked my front door then looked up at Adam's car. Adam was sitting in the drivers' side, and Hercules had his paws up on the passenger door, looking out the window at me. I really wanted a photo of that, but who would develop it after I was gone?

I heard thunder and looked up at the sky. Streaks of lightening danced across the western horizon. I didn't know if it was really a storm or evil coming to get me. I didn't care if it was only a storm. Even a bad one I would welcome, but I was leery of the evil that was lurking in the windy darkness. I knew it was coming for me, and there was nothing I could do about it. Adam didn't seem like he was going to do anything to stop it, so I was up shit creek without a paddle, so to speak.

I didn't hold it against him. I knew he was scared to death that he wouldn't be able to save me. There was another, louder thunderclap as I got into Adam's car. The first drop of rain hit my arm as I shut the door.

He didn't waste any time waiting for me to secure myself with the seatbelt. He already had it in first gear before I even shut the door. I looked at him. "I have a dying wish."

"You're not dying, Kendra." He said sharply, then looked at me and calmed down. I had asked for something and he was curious now. "What do you want? I will give you anything you ask for."

I smiled and said, "I want to drive this car."

His eyes got a little bigger. "Can you drive a stick?"

I gave him a look. "Does a bear shit in the woods?"

He smiled. "Can you get us to my apartment before midnight?"

"Faster than you can," I said with a smirk.

He smiled and slammed on the brakes. "I doubt that, but if you can get us there before midnight, then you can drive my car." He opened his door and got out. I climbed over the console and sat behind the wheel. I had to scoot the seat up a little, then I buckled myself in. I put my foot on the clutch then shoved it in first. I was spinning tires before Adam even shut his door.

The rain was coming down harder and I searched quickly for the wiper switch. I found it and put them on high. I wasn't trying to get us killed, but I had limited time and the rain was pouring so hard. If it happened, well, it would just happen. I wondered if I'd go to heaven if I truly died by accident?

"Try to get there safely, Kendra," Rhyan said.

I took that as a no, or that he really didn't know. I floored it, knowing I was a better driver than most; I was comfortable with speed. I'd only had four speeding tickets in the last year. I guess my profession should have been NASCAR. I smiled as I took a sharp curve at sixty, the back end of the car slid around and I got it under control in impeccable timing.

"I'm impressed," he said. I looked at him and he was smiling.

"Glad I can make you happy," I said with a smile.

"Oh you do, Kendra, you do." He had that seductive look in his eyes again, and I prayed Murry would give me enough time to let him fulfill his promise to me. My heart sped up, but I didn't have time to think about playing with Adam with the storm bearing down on us.

"You would have really run this sweet ass car off a cliff to save my soul?" I was smiling, but when I looked at him, he wasn't, so I lost mine.

"Do you really have to ask me if I would?"

"I was joking. I know you would if you knew it would help."

He looked back out the windshield. "Just get us to my apartment."

I pursed my lips. I'd only been trying to make light of a bad situation. I knew he was on edge, but so was I. Arguing wouldn't get us anywhere. I didn't say anything more. I just drove as hard and fast as the car would allow me on the wet pavement.

Chapter Forty-six

We had two minutes to spare when I pulled into the parking garage. Adam had lost the smug look, and was clearly back in panic mode. I started for the elevator, but he grabbed my hand and led me to the stairwell.

"The stairs will be safer." I nodded in agreement. If I was going to die, I didn't want it to be in an elevator. I was guessing that wouldn't allow me to have an open casket; maybe, but probably not.

I glanced at my watch then looked at Adam. It was 12:02, and I was no longer safe from losing my soul to Murry. He squeezed my hand a little tighter and took the steps a little faster.

We were almost to the fourth floor when I looked up and saw a lone figure in a black hoodie. I came to a halt and almost yanked Adam back down the stairs. The guy was just leaning up against the fourth floor stairwell door.

Adam blocked my view of the man with his body, and the figure laughed creepily. I knew it was Murry. I looked around Adam as Murry pulled his hood off, revealing his face. I'd been right. Damn!

Adam was trying to keep me hidden, but I needed to confront this asshole.

He spoke before I could say anything. "I think it would be stylish to kill the woman you love in the same way I killed your family. Don't you agree, Adam?" Murry pulled out a small black gun from the hands pocket of his hoodie.

Adam went very still. I had to admit, so did I. "You killed my family?" Adam asked in a disbelieving voice.

Mason laughed. "I'm a little disappointed you haven't already figured that out. Now...Kendra will come with me and we can do this the easy way, or I'll have to break my promise to her. It really doesn't matter to me either way. I'm usually not one for keeping promises." He pointed the gun at my head, but Adam grabbed my arm a pulled me behind him again.

"What promise?!" Adam shouted.

"I promised her that she could have an open casket for her family's benefit."

"You bastard! I thought you were my friend!"

Mason made a fake surprised face. "Oh...you didn't get the memo?" His face turned sober again. "You see, Adam, you were my friend; I was your mentor. Coen was beginning to gain complete control of your soul when you were thirteen." He shook his head. "I couldn't let that happen. Now look at what Coen has gone and done. He's introduced you to your soulmate, and you've fallen in love." He shrugged. "It looks as though I have to take matters into my own hands again."

He began to move toward us and I heard the famous pop. Rhyan grabbed Murry by the shirt collar then slung him up against the wall. "Get her out of here, Adam!" Rhyan shouted as he punched the demon in the mouth then body slammed him on the concrete steps. Murry's foot came within inches of knocking Adam in the head.

We turned and scrambled down the flights of steps and out into the garage.

"There is nowhere we can go that he won't find us!" I shouted.

He started to get in the car, but I shouted at him, "Wait, we need to think of something to do. If we get in that car, he'll just cause us to have an accident, and I will die. If you're injured, how are you going to fix me?"

He hit the hood of his car with the palm of his hand, then ran both his hands through his hair as he growled and paced. Hercules was barking like crazy in his pet porter, so I set it on the concrete by Adam's car. If something happened to me, I didn't want my dog to get hurt too.

He stopped and looked at me with tears in his eyes. "Tell me what to do. Where can we go so you'll be safe?"

I shook my head slowly and my own tears fell. "There is no safe place for me."

There was a loud pop, and Murry appeared fifty feet from us. He ignored Adam and started for me. Adam ran and threw himself in front of me. There was another loud pop and Rhyan was suddenly in front of Murry. He grabbed the running demon around the neck and placed his palm over the demon's chest. There was a great pop and they were both gone.

"I don't know what to tell you to do, but I can't hold him much longer. Get to a church. He can't enter there."

Adam must have heard him too, because he picked Hercules' pet porter up, took my hand with his other, and we ran on foot out of the garage.

"Where are we going?" My voice was a little winded, I was able to speak at a full out sprint because I ran every day.

"There's a church about a block from here." Adam's voice, on the other hand, had major windage. Apparently he didn't run every day. It was actually nice to find something about us that wasn't alike, well, except for our professions and religion. I didn't ask him anything else. He needed to save his breath for running.

I grabbed the pet porter from him. He shot me a questioning glance, then he must have realized that he was slowing me down. I kicked it up a notch and Adam hung in there with me. I could see the great church up ahead of us. Only fifty yards left…now forty…and thirty…twenty left to go. I smiled and kicked it into overdrive, leaving Adam yards behind me. Ten yards from the church, I heard the pop. Murry was directly in front of me and I was going too fast to stop in time. I screamed as I slammed into him. He grabbed me and spun me around. He brought us to a halt and looked up as Adam screamed, "NOOO!" Murry put his hand on my chest and we were gone.

Chapter Forty-seven

When I came to, I was lying on a small bed or cot. I could feel something running down my face and I tried to wipe it off with my hand. I realized I couldn't, because I was tied at all four points to the cot. I quickly scanned the room. It was the same room from my first nightmare I'd had about Murry. I glanced over my body, but the blood wasn't there like it had been in my dream, or it wasn't there yet.

The room was damp and dim. I assumed I was somewhere underground, like in a basement or cellar of some sort. I could hear Hercules whining in his pet porter, and I sent up a silent prayer of thanks; maybe my dog had a guardian angel too.

What puzzled me was that I was still alive. Murry had been rambling all week that he was going to kill me on Friday; it was Friday, so what was the hold up, not that I was complaining or anything.

"Rhyan! Rhyan, can you hear me?" He didn't respond. Dammit!

I heard a door open and my head shot around to Murry walking through a rusty metal door. "Where am I?" I asked with a shaky voice. He didn't answer me so I asked another question. "Why am I still alive?"

He stopped by my head and looked down at me. "I wanted to take my time killing you. Adam was rushing me." He pulled out a scalpel from the pocket in his scrubs. I immediately tensed. He took my hand and flipped it over so he could see my wrist. I started fighting to get it away from him, but he only laughed then slashed at my flesh. I didn't feel it at first, then I felt the burning and the blood as it ran over my skin. I screamed and kicked as much as the ties would let me.

He moved to the other side of the bed. I screamed even louder. He grabbed my other hand, and before I could jerk it away, he slit my other wrist. So, this was how I was going to die. I was going to bleed to death in a damp basement, and then I was going to hell. I had to calm down. I did know that the faster my heart raced, the quicker I would bleed out and die.

I could hear him laughing to himself. "It won't be long now, Kendra. Your precious Adam is not here to save your life. He could still save your soul from where he is right now though, but we both know he won't do it. He's going out of his mind with worry. Rhyan is trying to find you, but I've blocked you from him and he can't hear you. Therefore, he can't find you. When they manage to find your body, you will have been dead far too long to be brought back. Would you like to come back and watch when Adam and Rhyan find your remains? They won't be able to see or hear you, but you will get to see the two men you love one last time." Murry kissed my forehead and tears began to flow out of the corners of my eyes, forming small puddles in my ears.

I knew this was the end. I could feel my body growing cold from blood loss. I could feel my blood soaking through the back of the dress I'd worn to my final meal.

"Please...please, Mason, don't do this." My teeth chattered as I pleaded with him. He didn't respond. I cried. I wailed in anguish and jerked at my bindings. I screamed for help. I shouted for Adam and I screamed for Rhyan. No one could hear me.

My sobbing slowed and my screaming stopped completely. I was going into shock. I had only one thing left to do. Through it all, I had never given up, and I wouldn't give up until I took my last breath. "God...if you can hear me, I'm sorry for making that deal, and I'm sorry for not being able to save Adam's soul. Forgive me Father, for I have many sins."

Murry rushed over to the bed from the chair he was sitting in. "Shut up, Kendra! He won't help you. He didn't help Adam's family nineteen years ago, and he's not going to help you now." He leaned down to my ear and whispered, "They prayed, Kendra. Oh, how they prayed for me to spare their lives. As evil as I am, I couldn't bring myself to kill that baby. I'm not so squeamish anymore." He kissed my cheek then stood up straight. "When I shot Adam's mother in the head, she fell forward with the baby in her arms. It never made a sound."

I ignored Murry and resumed staring at the ceiling as I prayed. My voice was low and sluggish, and I only remembered two prayers my mother had taught me, and I began to say them. They may not help, I would know that I died praying to God. "Now I lay me down to sleep, I pray the Lord my soul to keep. If I die before I wake, I pray the Lord my soul to take."

"Shut the fuck up, Kendra!" Murry shouted as he threw the scalpel across the room.

I ignored him and spoke as quickly as I could, because I was getting very cold and it was getting harder to keep my eyes open. "Our Father who art in heaven, Hallowed be thy name. Thy kingdom come. Thy will be done on earth, as it is in heaven. Give us this day our daily bread. And forgive us our debts, as we forgive our debtors..."

My voice was trailing off and the chattering of my teeth began to override my words. My eyes closed; I was so sleepy. I could barely feel my body, but I made myself say one last verse, "And lead us not into temptation, but deliver us from evil. For thine is the kingdom, and the power, and the glory, for ever. Amen."

I faintly heard Murry whisper something; it sounded like, "No...it fuckin' can't be." I heard a pop then I blacked out.

Chapter Forty-eight

"Kendra! Kendra can you hear me?!" Rhyan's voice sounded panic stricken in my head.

I was groggy and my brain wasn't working right, but of course I could hear him. *"Of course I can hear you. You're in my head, aren't you?"*

"Are you all right?" Was I all right? I thought I was. Then I remembered Murry taking me and draining me of my blood.

"Rhyan, I need help now! Murry slit my wrists and I think I'm dying or maybe I'm already dead. He's not here. He said something and then he left."

"I'm coming. Now that I can hear you, I can find you."

"How is Adam?"

"We may be able to talk about it later. I'm coming to get you. Sit tight."

Well what else was I going to do? It was like after my rappelling accident when I was on the operating table all over again. I couldn't hear anything except my own thoughts. What had happened to Murry? Was praying really all I had to do all along?

I was physically and emotionally exhausted. I knew I had to remain conscious, even if I had to talk to myself, but sleep seemed so much easier, so much simpler.

I started to hear things again; voices of men and women and metal clanging together. Were they about to take me to Hell? "Kendra, stay with me, honey. Don't you dare leave me after what I've done for you," Adam said, and I became more alert. I couldn't open my eyes. It was the same as last week; I couldn't feel my body, or see, or smell, but I could hear just fine.

"She can hear you, Adam," Rhyan said, and he wasn't speaking in my head, but directly to Adam.

There was no talking from my two men for a moment, but the voices of the other people were more distinct. I could hear that Debbie woman and Sherri talking. Surely Adam wouldn't let his ex-girlfriend in here to help; she had to hate me. I could hear the heart monitoring machine and my heartbeat was really slow. "I love you, Kendra. I don't want to disappoint you, so I am trying to keep my promise…and my sanity," He tacked on at the end.

I laughed a little in my head then heard Rhyan laugh. "She thought that was funny."

"Glad I can amuse you, honey," Adam said, then started talking to a nurse or someone. He was telling them to get more blood and fluids, STAT. His tone became almost violent as I heard him shouting at someone to get the hell out of the room, or else.

"Kendra, do you want me to leave these scars or make them disappear?" Rhyan said to me, as if he hadn't heard Adam threatening to harm someone.

I thought for a moment. *"I'd like to keep them if you don't mind."*

"No problem. They're going to get some blood and fluids in you, and I'll take care of the rest of the healing. You should be able to wake up soon."

"What happened with Murry?"

"We can talk about it when you wake up."

It may have been childish, but I wanted to throw a fit. I was anxious to know what happened to the demon who was trying to steal my soul. Was he still out there waiting for me to heal so he could try it again? Or was he in the pits of Hell, never able to surface again?

"Tell me now, Rhyan."

"No, Kendra, I won't tell you now. Go to sleep or just relax, and let us get you fixed up," Rhyan said.

He didn't have to be so rude about it.

"Yes I do, or you would never shut up about it. Go to sleep. I'll wake you up when we're finished." I could hear Adam snickering softly. I rolled my eyes to myself and drifted off to sleep.

Chapter Forty-nine

I woke up to the sound of a heart monitoring machine. The beeps indicated a normal heartbeat. I took in a deep breath then let it out. It was good to be alive and pain free. I opened my eyes to a small private room. It was just as it had been Wednesday night. My parents and Kobhye were sleeping in the uncomfortable chairs. The only one missing was Aven. I guess he really was mad at me. Where were Rhyan and Adam?

"We'll be there in a few minutes, Kendra. We're talking to the police," Rhyan said. I gasped, and everyone in the room woke up. *"The police! Why would you need to talk to the police?"*

"Well, for one, they think you're suicidal. You've had three major accidents in a week. They could all have been accidentally on purpose, if you know what I mean, falling off a cliff, flipping your vehicle, and now slitting your wrists. The last one, well, people don't really go around slitting both of their wrists by accident. Murry made sure it would make you look bad if you lived through this. I can make the police believe what I want them to. However, you should know your parents are thinking the same thing."

I nodded to myself. Everyone thinks I'm suicidal. A tear escaped my eye and I tried to reach up to wipe it away, but my arms were secured. I looked at them in sheer horror. "What is this? Mom, get me out of these things!"

She rushed to my bed and wrapped her arms around me, holding me tight. "Shhh, baby…calm down. The doctor will be in to talk with you in a moment.

Just then, the door opened and a black man in his mid-fifties walked in. He was wearing a white lab coat and scrubs. He must be the doctor. "Hello, Kendra, my name is Dr. Richardson. On a scale of one to ten, ten being the most painful, how much pain are you experiencing?"

I shook my head and stared at him in confusion. "I feel fine. Where is my doctor?" I asked, feeling a little frantic. My mom shushed me and rubbed my back.

"I am your doctor, Kendra."

I shook my head. "Get me out of here, Mom. Please." My tears were flowing, but I couldn't stop them or even wipe them away.

The doctor looked at my chart he was holding. "That was a pretty nasty fall you had last week. It almost killed you, didn't it?"

I gave him my best pissed-off look. "Miracles do happen, Doctor."

His eyebrows went up at that. Maybe he didn't believe in God either, but I wasn't going to be the girl to help him. "Well, yes, miracles do tend to happen from time to time, but it looks to me like you've had three in a week." He sighed. "That...does not happen."

I was still wearing my pissed-off face. I didn't like this man at all. "What are you implying?"

He shrugged. "Have you ever caused yourself harm before?"

"I have never hurt myself," I said calmly, but in my most menacing voice.

"Who hurt you, Kendra? I can understand falling while rappelling, and even losing control of your vehicle, but I can't understand those right there." He pointed to my wrists. There was a three-inch scar running up both of my wrists. The wounds were already healed, and my skin only held a trace of a pink line. Rhyan had done an excellent job of healing them. But if I explained to this doctor about my miracle guardian angel and explained to him why all of the accidents had occurred, he'd put me in a nut house. Looking at him now, I wondered if he was thinking of doing that anyway.

I told him the only thing I knew to tell him. The truth. "Mason

Carter has been trying to kill me."

The doctor's eyebrows rose again. "Mason Carter? The Mason Carter that works here?"

I nodded.

"Mason Carter was here in the hospital working during all three of your accidents Kendra. You are mistaken." He glanced at my father and mother, then back to me.

Oh God. I was sure that Mason could make himself appear to be two places at once. What could I say to make him believe me? "Yes, the first accident last week was an accident, but Mason became obsessed with me. When Dr. Chamberlain and I started dating, he didn't take it very well. He may have been here, but I am positive he caused my accident, just as I'm positive he slit my wrists with a scalpel."

He looked back at my parents. "May I speak with the two of you outside?"

"I'm not crazy, Dr. Richardson. I'm the least suicidal person I know. I love my life," I said and the tears began to flow again.

He nodded, and waited for my parents to walk out the door. I looked at Kobhye. "I know you believe me."

She nodded. "You know I do, but I don't know how to help you with this." She took a shuttering breath. "I overheard the doctor talking earlier about putting you in that mental hospital outside of town. That is why the cops are here. Rhyan and Adam are trying to talk them into leaving you here for a few days until they can get some concrete evidence one way or the other."

"I'm not fucking crazy! Why isn't Adam my doctor? He's the one who operated on me."

"They won't let him because the two of you are dating. Sherri told everyone a bunch of lies. She is the one who got all of this started about your elevator not going all the way to the top. She's telling everyone that you are suicidal, Kendra. I'm sorry. I saw her earlier and gave her a piece of my mind. Security told me to stay in your room or I would have to leave the hospital."

"Well, giving her a piece of my mind is not all I'm going to do to her. I'm going to kick her fucking ass!"

"Easy there, Kendra. I took care of her for you. We're on our way. Sit-tight," Rhyan said in my head.

I huffed. I was really getting tired of him telling me to sit tight. What else was I going to do; I was tied up for Christ's sake. I heard Adam and Rhyan outside the door talking with my parents and Dr. Richardson. Adam's voice grew loud, but I couldn't hear what he was saying, then the door opened and he came in alone.

God, the sight of him took my breath away. I needed answers. I started to speak, but he shook his head like he knew what I was going to say. "Let's get you out of here, then we can talk. I promise." He took the bindings off of my wrists and ankles, and I got out of the bed instantly. I didn't want anyone to be able to catch me and tie me up again.

"Get me the hell out of here," I said as I grabbed my dress. It had blood all over it. I closed my eyes and sighed before throwing it in the trash. It looked like I was going to be walking out of there with my ass showing.

"I brought you some clothes. They're in the bathroom," Kobhye said.

"Thank you," I said and made a bee-line for the bathroom. Adam followed me.

He shut us in the bathroom together. I started to take off the hospital gown, and he grabbed me in a big bear hug before I could undo the tie on my side. "I'm so sorry, Kendra. I thought I'd lost you. If I had only listened to you last week, you would not have had to go through all of this. Please forgive me."

I pulled back out of his hold. There were tears in his eyes. "Everything happens for a reason, Adam. I'm not mad at you. But you are going to explain everything to me, in detail, when we get out of here."

"We won't have any problem leaving. Rhyan did something to everyone's brains. They think you're just here for a check-up concerning your accident Wednesday. I changed your chart myself." He snickered a little. "Sherri is having a longer bit of amnesia. She doesn't remember dating me at all."

I sighed. "Thank you." I glanced at my wrists. "I don't guess it was such a good idea to keep these. I wanted to keep them as a reminder not to trust people so easily in the future."

Adam smiled. "I guess I need a few scars of my own, but Rhyan can still take them away if you want him to."

I quickly dressed and we walked out of the bathroom. Rhyan was talking with Kobhye, and they both looked up when they heard us. "I told your parents to go home. I said everything checked out fine. No one knows anything about what happened today except for us."

I went to Rhyan and gave him a hard hug. I didn't know what I would do without him.

"I will always be here for you. All you have to do is pray."

I pulled away and looked at his face with sadness. *"We'll still be able to talk to each other, right?"* I asked.

He shook his head, and looked a little sad himself. *"I will hear you, but you will only be able to feel me through your instincts."*

I covered my mouth with my hand and let the tears fall. "No, Rhyan. I need to be able to hear you. Make them let me hear you, please." He grabbed me and held on tight while he ran his hand over my back.

"Shhh. You'll be just fine. I'll see you again someday; you and Adam both." He let me go enough to shake Adam's hand. "I'll make it very hard on you if you don't treat her right."

Adam smiled. "I should have a very easy life then."

Rhyan nodded then turned back to me. "I'll miss spending time with you, but I'll always be here with you." He hugged me again, and I couldn't stop crying. I was going to miss him so much. He pulled back and looked at me. "See you later?"

I nodded and managed to get out through my sobs, "See you later."

We all heard the loud pop, and Rhyan was gone. I closed my eyes and Adam wrapped me in his arms.

Chapter Fifty

Adam took me to my house and Kobhye went back to her place. We were finally alone. Adam fixed me a glass of wine while I sat watching him from a barstool. He was so at home with me, so comfortable. I was still waiting for him to explain everything, but he didn't seem to be in any hurry.

He crossed the kitchen with two glasses in his hands and handed one of them to me. He held his up. "Here's to a new beginning."

We clinked our glasses and took a sip. "To a new beginning," I said, then cleared my throat. "Are you going to tell me what happened?"

He looked a little nervous for a moment then gave me a shy smile. "I have something I want to do first, if you don't mind."

I furrowed my brow in confusion, then he set his glass on the counter and bent down on one knee. He put his hand in his pocket and pulled out a little black velvet box.

I gasped and my hand went to my mouth. "I thought you were going to ask my father for permission first?"

He smiled. "I did. I asked him last night when we were looking at my car. It was before you came outside. When we brought you into the hospital, he told me if I couldn't find a way to get you out of that mess with the doctor thinking you were suicidal, then I couldn't marry you. He didn't believe that you were crazy for a second."

My eyes instantly went misty, and I couldn't help but smile at him. I assumed, since he was on his knee before me, that my daddy said he could propose.

Adam opened the box and revealed a very large, very beautiful...did I mention it was very large...diamond ring. I couldn't speak, but I didn't have to. "Kendra Larkin, I've been a lost soul for most of my life. You helped me find it again, and you've captured my heart. I will be a very miserable man if you don't agree to spend the rest of eternity with me. If I die first, I'll wait patiently for you in Heaven. Will you be my wife?" He shrugged and smiled nervously. "I went ring shopping the moment that your dad gave me permission and I knew you were going to be okay. When I got back, Rhyan was about to do some kind of karate moves on those cops. I had a better plan and I guess he liked it." He took my hand in his shaking hand and smiled nervously up at me. "Kendra, are you going to keep me waiting forever?"

I nodded and couldn't stop smiling. I wiped at my tears and threw myself off the stool and into his arms. "Forever sounds great, but you don't have to wait any longer. Yes, I'll be your wife, Adam. I will marry you."

He hugged me back fiercely, and I could feel him sobbing softly. We held each other like that for a long while before he let me go. His face was wet, but he was wearing a smile a mile wide, just like the one I had to be wearing. He stood, then helped me up.

"You were right, Kendra. I couldn't keep you without God in my life. I'm sorry I was almost too late in realizing it. Rhyan couldn't hear you for the longest and we thought you were gone...until he heard you praying. He grabbed my head and put my forehead to his; I could hear you too. Without even thinking, I began reciting the prayers along with you."

I stared at him with a sort of fascination as he told me for the first time that he believed in God. He really believed.

His smile faltered. "When we found you in that room...I thought we were already too late. Rhyan couldn't do anything until I got some blood into your body. I was going crazy, but I knew I had a job to do. I have never been so scared in all my life. Not even when I found my family dead. I knew that I had to do everything in my power to keep you here with me."

I kissed him hard on the mouth, then he pulled back with an even bigger smile than before. I hadn't thought that was possible. "I have a brand new guardian angel."

I know my expression was a mixture of excitement and shock. "Have you met him or her?"

He nodded with that big smile still in place. "She's my mother, and she likes you a whole lot. She told me to thank you, for saving her son."

I was speechless. What could I say to that? "Tell her I said you're welcome." Somehow, that didn't seem good enough. I shrugged. "I'd do anything for my soulmate."

He smiled and pulled me tight against his firm body. I could tell he had "other things" on his mind. "And I would do anything for mine," he said, then he kissed me softly.

Epilogue

"Welp, folks, I guess you already know what happened next. Adam and I got married, of course, and we're expecting our first child early next summer. We found out today that it's a boy. I haven't told Adam yet, but I want to name him Benjamin Lee. It was the name of his baby brother. He may not want to, but I'm adding it to our list of potential baby names.

I forgot to ask Rhyan to take away my scars before he left. I was looking at them a few weeks ago, remembering that I'd forgotten to ask him. They began to disappear before my eyes. Of course, I began to tear up. I knew I wouldn't hear a response, but I knew he was listening when I thanked him for being my guardian angel and told him that I really did love him very much. Suddenly, I felt a presence nearby. I looked all around me. My eyes focused on a blurry object standing in the center of the living room. It never became solid, but I could tell it was Rhyan. He winked at me and then he was gone. A light gust of wind blew through the house, but there were no windows open. A single photo floated on the wind toward me. It landed in my lap and the wind disappeared. I looked down at the photo and instantly began to cry. Rhyan was staring back at me with a big smile on his face. I looked at it for a long time then finally flipped it over. He had written these words: I am with you always, Kendra, and I will love you forevermore. Congratulations on the baby. The guardians have already chosen his guardian angel. I made sure the one they chose is just as good as me. I know you will make a wonderful mother. Love Always, Rhyan. I smiled and clutched the picture to my chest. It was definitely possible to love more than one person at a time.

Adam was my soulmate, and I loved him unconditionally. I couldn't live without him now that I'd found him, but Rhyan would always have a special place in my heart, and Adam knew that. It doesn't bother him. He knows how much I love him.

My parents love Adam too, and they're always asking me to bring him over. They don't realize how busy we are. Oh, by the way, Adam took a leave of absence from the hospital. He hasn't decided when, or even if, he'll go back. He's been helping me with my photography. My work interests him, and I'm thrilled that we get to spend so much time together.

And lastly, Kobhye has finally decided to settle down. I bet you wouldn't have guessed she'd choose Aven. They're happy, and Aven has forgiven me for not loving him back. They aren't talking marriage yet, but she stays at his place more than she stays at her own home. I'm cooking supper for the four of us tonight. Well, Adam will be doing the cooking. I'll be supervising.

I hope you've enjoyed reading about this most important chapter of my life. If I could give you any advice at all it would be: "Love conquers all evil. Don't judge a book by its cover. Everything happens for a reason and...If you haven't found your soulmate yet, don't ever, ever give up hope; he or she is out there somewhere. I only hope you don't have to die to find yours."

Meet the Author

Forbidden Touch Fanpage http://www.facebook.com/forbiddentouch

Save My Soul Fanpage

http://www.facebook.com/kshaigwood

Blog

http://www.kshaigwood.blogspot.com

Twitter

http://www.twitter.com/kshaigwood

Goodreads - http://www.goodreads.com/author/show/5779135.K_S_Haigwood

Facebook

http://www.facebook.com/kristie.haigwood

Author page

http://www.amazon.com/author/kshaigwood

Other books by this author:

Forbidden Touch

http://www.amazon.com/dp/B008DKORNU

Books coming soon from this author:

Eternal Island

Eternal Immortality

Eternal Inception

The Last Assignment

Biography:

Kristie Haigwood started writing her first novel June, 2010. Two years later, after finishing her sixth book, she finally decided to start her self-publishing career as a novelist. She lives in the south U.S. with her daughter, husband and two dogs.

Made in the USA
San Bernardino, CA
04 December 2014

DEDICATION

For Joseph whose belief lives in me…
For Kathy whose belief I live by…
For Abigail whose belief becomes my air…
And for Stephan,
Whose belief was my salvation.

ACKNOWLEDGEMENTS

Writing this book has been a long and sometimes daunting task. This second edition gave me as much joy as the first and revealed those who are essential to a writer's journey. Writing a multi-faceted character as Leroux's Erik required a great deal of research, but more importantly the enthusiasm of many.

Endless thanks to author Nina Pierce who stood by me through thick and thin when the first edition came out, and went above and beyond as friend and critique partner while on this journey. You encouraged me with honesty and the humor necessary to hone my skills. I can never thank you enough and can't think of a better friend to have as a fellow author.

To Stephan, whether it's been my career as a writer or my journey as a person, I thank you for the honesty you shared and belief you had in me. Through good, bad, and ugly, you did much without a thought of yourself. May the Lord continue to bless and guide you in every way, through fire and blood. *Toujours dans mon Coeur.*

And lastly to my daughter Abigail, my greatest joy. You will forever be my source of complete happiness my life's inspiration. You know exactly what I need to keep my spirits up and my imagination flowing. Someday I will see you realize *your* dreams with the same love and support you always offer me.

~Jennifer Deschanel

There is no past that we can bring back by longing for it. There is only an eternally new now that builds and creates itself out of the best as the past withdraws—

Johann Wolfgang von Goethe

PROLOGUE

Paris—1885

Paper. Ink. Figs.

The contents were nothing if not consistent. He never asked for any of it, but who was he to refuse them? The package was always there, the first of every month, consistent in every way—a small bundle painstakingly wrapped in plain brown paper and tied with twine. Sighing, he picked it up. The paper had turned moist from humidity. He rotated it several times and found what he always found. No markings, no card, no indications whatsoever of where it had come from or who had left it. It was a package, and like him, wrapped in complete anonymity.

He wouldn't open it this time, as there was no real need. He had enough paper to last for some time, and the packaging kept the pages from getting too soiled. The ink would dry if the seal were cracked. He could wait. But the figs couldn't. Those blasted, wretched figs.

Long fingers nimbly unwrapped a corner. The figs were always in the same spot. The whole thing was maddening in its consistency. Removing an inner brown bag tied with another piece

1

of twine, he paid no regard to the other contents nestled neatly inside. He fumbled slightly with the knot. Even the string was damp.

Water seeped through the walls around him. Paris had been unusually rainy this spring. It invaded everything in his labyrinthine home, making the floors slick, moss grow thick on the rock, and the waters of the lake deepen. No matter to him. He was used to the water, the damp, and the darkness. What he wasn't used to was charity.

He was perfectly capable of tending to his own needs. The packages had been arriving now for months and for whom else could they be left? Some other hunted man living below Paris? Some other misunderstood outcast? No. They were for him. The paper gave it away long ago—being immaculately lined for a Maestro's notes.

Lengthening his strides, he was propelled past the steps that curved upward toward the opera house. He no longer stopped there to listen to the music.

The stairs he followed led deeper into the labyrinth, further from the place he wanted to be and closer to the place fate forced him to. One angry twitch snapped the string around the figs. He threw the tiny parcel into a murky corner. The rats would eat them, as they always did.

He hated figs.

ONE

"More treats for him, Anna? Has a month gone by already?"

Anna tripped over her feet, nearly plowing headfirst into an abandoned pushcart. She glanced left to right, scanning the fog covered street and spotted the elderly woman hugging the wall of an alleyway. Anna's wind-burned cheeks stung as she smiled. "Yes, Madame." She tapped her parcel. "Paper, ink and figs."

"Who is he? Lover?"

Anna laughed as she scampered across the road to share the dark alley. Mud splashed from the streets and splattered the hem of her dress. No cobblestones in this area of Paris. Nothing noteworthy existed in this quarter. Nevertheless, before darting into the alley, she checked to make certain no one took note. Unlikely they would. In this neighborhood on the opposite side of the green-hued Seine, the poor were in limbo. They didn't rule like in the heart of the Saint-Antione, rather darted like bedraggled rats out of sight of wary eyes. Anna fished in her coat for the remains of her morning bread and gave it to the old woman.

"I've no idea who he is," she replied. "You're well aware of that. Stop making him into some fancy gentleman." Her smile grew at the woman's toothless grin and her eagerness to steal the package. Anna kept her steps and laughter as lively as the old hag's, lifting the package high above her head. They'd played this game every month and still the woman never learned that Anna wouldn't give

3

in.

"How many does this one make?"

Anna skipped backward avoiding the weathered hands swiping at her head. "I've lost count."

Their laughter tumbled around them. How many years had she entertained the hag in this way? Anna was well known around the streets of Paris, among the rejected and lonely. Most outcasts regarded her as one of their own. While not rich, Anna had a roof over her and her basic needs attended. What she didn't need she gave to others.

The thought of that roof filled her mouth with a bitter taste. Contempt bound her chest as she glared in the direction of the Académie Nationale. The place was more prison than home. Anna knew nothing about music, nor did she fit in with the bourgeoisie that seemed attracted to the arts. The debt her family owed is what bound her there. Every day her routine followed the same unrelenting pattern. She slaved for the administration, bonded to them with barely anything in return with the exception of the few meager coins permitted her. And even that money she spent on others. What Anna most desired couldn't be purchased anyway.

"What does he look like?" The woman hopped, both hands swatting for the parcel in-between nips at bread. "Handsome, I bet."

"You think so?"

"Handsome, handsome, handsome!"

A wind gust knocked Anna's unruly hair across her eyes making the world turn auburn. She placed the parcel on the ground, careful not to set it in mud, and gingerly put her foot atop it. Grabbing hair by the fistfuls, she tamed her runaway locks into a long braid and paused for a second, frowning at her frayed ends. Only twenty-three years old and lightning would strike her before she caught the eye of a handsome man.

What does *he look like?* Anna wondered as she studied the old woman who crouched low waiting for any chance to swipe the parcel. From one fleeting glance she knew he was tall and hidden behind an expressionless mask. She had seen firsthand the prejudices forcing the infirm and imbecilic into hiding. His living arrangement didn't shock her. She had seen the desolate live in many places—under bridges, on rooftops, or in crates on the street.

Anna picked up her parcel and hugged it to her chest. She stared off into the distance as she recalled the night she followed him into the cellars of the opera house. Though she'd quickly lost sight of him, she'd uncovered enough to know his genius. Anna glanced at her arm. The music had been as chilling as the sight of him in that mask and recalling it made her flesh pebble.

She shivered at the memory, or perhaps it was the chill to the air. Either way, both were hard to escape.

For whatever his reason, he didn't want to be known. She knew that feeling well enough. Anna stood in the alleyway, watching a cluster of clearly lost people huddle close together. They avoided the shadows as if giant rats were going to leap out and devour them alive. They blurred the streets in colorful dresses and fine suits as they hustled to find their way out of the derelict side of town. For a second she was glad she had nothing to fear from the filthy or the poor. It kept her life moving at an even pace, until that hot lump of envy clogged her throat.

Anna yearned to taste the life of a lady and have a gentleman upon her arm. To live in a world where worry didn't hang overhead like a loose guillotine would be bliss.

"Not a chance of that happening," she groused, staring at a young couple hastening down the street.

"Anna's sad again." The old woman clawed at a corner of the package.

Anna swatted her away, and nodded toward the couple. "Can you see me upon his arm? Thank-you for your company, Monsieur, but I must tell you—before you charm me further by your affections—I'm desired not only by you, but by the English authorities, the German authorities, the Belgian authorities…" She groaned. "*Definitely* the Belgian authorities."

"Anna's been bad."

Anna sheepishly smiled. That expression was no stranger to her face. She was used to covering up her shame and remorse in anyway she could. Her past was not her doing. Her life of crime was forced upon her. *Maybe my strange Maestro is a criminal too. His hiding would make more sense.* Hiding was the last thing Anna wanted to do. Envy rose, brining the sting of tears. Crying never solved anything. She swallowed the lump of emotion burning in her throat and took a deep breath. It was getting late, so she patted the elderly woman upon the hand and assured her she would be passing by the first of next month as usual.

Stepping into the street, Anna pulled her threadbare coat close around her, intent on heading toward the Garnier. What a contrast between Anna's two Paris'—the cold and desolate outskirts, and the prosperous inner city.

Such distinctions made her shuck her coat and drape it around the woman's shoulders before she left in earnest.

The early Spring air blasted her skin with needle-like tingles that stung to her bones. Using the package as a shield against the biting wind she tried not to breathe too deeply—the air was cold in her nose and mouth. Anna hastened carefully across and dew slickened streets. Dodging and weaving her way in and out of the hustle of carriages and crowds, she didn't stop until she reached the Rue Scribe. Winded, her breath fogged in front of her as she squatted. At a small stone archway at the entrance of a sewer, she pretended to fumble with a muddy bootlace.

She smiled slyly at the parcel. She confessed to not understanding music, but the music she'd heard him play spoke to every unwanted soul and uplifted the spirit. If she couldn't walk equal among the women she passed, maybe such a great Maestro as he could walk equal among the men. Perhaps her parcels would help.

Once certain she was undetected, she shoved the package between the grates of the archway. If not for the mushrooming gas of rot and mildew, she would wait to see if her parcel was delivered. The stench jerked her upright for a fresher breath of air.

"You can't wait for him. Stop being ridiculous," she scolded to herself. Her curiosity would get her in trouble one day. *Help who I can and move on. Attachments mean trouble and I'm far too versed in that!*

"You must know."

A mantel clock started to clang out the hour. The lateness of the night and weary droop to the box keeper's shoulders didn't deter Erik's questioning.

Folding his arms, he leveled a stone-hard stare at Madame Giry and watched with gathering dismay as the older woman tried to focus on anything but him. Erik knew the office was dark enough that his eyes shone like two lit candles through the depths of his mask. It wasn't the first time their unusual trait made the floor beneath Madame Giry turn to hot coals. Her jig annoyed him.

"I don't know, Monsieur. Please leave."

"You are the concierge, Madame Giry. It is your duty to know everything that goes on in this opera house."

"Monsieur, I know no more than you. A stranger is reaching out and thinking of you in kindness. It's a random act. Leave it be."

He unfolded his arms. Not many in the opera house knew the intimate details of his life. Appalled at how blasé Madame Giry seemed, considering the circumstance, he changed tactics. "It would be wise if you told me what you know, Madame Giry. A stranger taking interest in what lurks in this opera house could arouse suspicion. Would you rather another investigation?"

The old woman's wrinkles drained of color making her face stand out remarkably against her faded black dress.

"I don't wish another investigation," she quavered.

"Nor do I. What makes you think I want to see my peace disturbed?"

The clip to Erik's voice jolted the woman backward. He instantly regretted his sharp tone, but a part of him was unable to apologize. Far too long he'd been labeled a monster and a madman. Kindness was a confounding luxury rarely extended his way.

"The investigations into the Phantom of the Opera are over." Saying that out loud made his emotions swing like a pendulum. Erik shoved them all aside. The only emotion he knew perfectly was anger. To him nothing existed underneath it, certainly not *pain*. "But if you know something to the contrary—"

"I told you, Monsieur, I know nothing!"

"Then *why* is this occurring? Why would anyone pay attention to me?"

He was a condemned man—fate had seen to that. The atrocities Paris suffered under the grip of the Phantom four years ago were firmly stacked upon his shoulders. Erik faded away into the great, unsolved mystery of the Paris Opera House. After the investigations into his former crimes closed, no one had bothered to look for him. He blocked off all entrances to his house on the underground lake beneath the theater and sealed himself away to live in a tomb. His only contact was Madame Giry, theater concierge and box keeper.

"You are every bit as entangled in this as I," he continued. "The very nature of you keeping my anonymity makes you an accomplice. I know nothing of this stranger's intent. I…"

Oh, what was the point? She had no say in the events that

condemned him to wallow in the cellars of the Opera Garnier. Threatening her would be a waste of time.

"My apologies, Madame, you are not deserving of my rants. I will bid you good-night." He was almost at the door when her whisper stopped him.

"Why can't I deny you? I damn fate for bringing you into my life."

"Fate had nothing to do with it. You serve me because it is what you wish."

"You're mistaken, Monsieur."

"I am not mistaken," Erik snipped, intending to drive his point home. "You have been kindly compensated for tending to my eccentricity. Have I not rewarded you for serving my necessity to live as a recluse? A franc here, a box of English sweets there? And do not forget all I have done to promote the dancing career of your daughter."

The feathers of her hat swayed as she nodded. "Very well."

Her air of bravery fell short of being well performed. Her squared shoulders and lifted chin were ineffective under the way she trembled, branding Erik with an unsettling sense of responsibility. He'd given her control of too many of his secrets, and it pained him to see her as vulnerable to them as himself. In an unconventional move, he knelt in front of her. One by one his long, slender fingers came to rest on the back of her hand. As intimate a gesture as he could display.

"Madame Giry, who?"

Erik followed her gaze to the back of her hand. Her aged eyes scanned his fingers, moving as if she couldn't rest. Even Erik could feel the difference between the perpetual iciness of his skin and the warmth of hers. Uncertain what her look meant, he lifted his fingers and coiled them into his palm. Rarely touched in his life, what right had he to intimacy? He heard her indecisiveness as she took a breath, and he found he held his as well.

"There's a woman. Her name is Anna. She's worked for Messieurs Laroque and Wischard for two years now. Not many pay mind to her unless something is needed. When she's not here, she spends her time administering to the homeless. I believe you're one of her charges."

So it was charity or pity. Those were two things in life he neither needed nor wanted. Erik was on his feet in seconds. "Good-night, Madame."

He hastened to the door in a race to escape the feelings intensifying inside him. Whoever this Anna was he didn't ask for her kindness. The world was an uncompassionate place that was wrapped first in the swaddling clothes of his infancy, and then later disguised as the dark vaults of an opera house. Quickening his pace, Erik moved deeper into the familiar sanctuary of the darkness. Mankind was better off not knowing he existed and this Anna posed a risk. Something had to be done.

The answer was simple, but the consequence of such haunted him.

Anna had to be stopped—by whatever means necessary.

Little could distract Erik from his thoughts when they were dark and they had been since he learned he was a charity case. Nothing he had done thus far had freed him from that horrifying thought of potentially having to kill again.

Murder, he vowed, would remain in his past. The idea of it knotted the back of his neck making his eyes throb so much he couldn't enjoy the festivities around him.

Years ago, gala evenings were a source of entertainment. A welcome distraction when he needed them to be. Carefully cloaked, he would study the patrons as they filled his theater. He'd glared at nobles and the feeble-minded members of the bourgeois as they jostled for rank and prestige; he'd listened as they made pompous attempts at besting one another on the subjects of music and kings. Erik loathed them, knowing the airs they painted were self-inflicted masks. In the past he might have desired a sword upon his hip to partake in the air of forced fraternity, but such frivolity had waned through the years.

Back then, Erik had controlled everything in the Opera Garnier and had done so in complete anonymity. He'd had no need to cajole himself to the classes.

This evening's gala was different. War and revolution had long ago stunted the crowds and squelched the groveling he used to enjoy. This republic was a confused beast, a paradoxical political regime he found oddly still monarchial. So few were the patrons, it seemed unnecessary for him to wander in shadow. Caution, however, was a necessary evil, thanks to his past.

Angry over being some stranger's cause for pity and charity, and ripped apart over thinking about killing again, Erik had been launched him into a morose mood. To calm himself, Erik attempted to do what he'd avoided for years—view the evening's opera from his box.

Only to find it rented.

That he couldn't indulge himself in the pathetic rendition of *La Traviata* angered him further. A man of peculiar habits, he expected, despite the passing of time, for things to remain the same, so he held no remorse when he kicked open the door to Madame Giry's office with such force she shrieked in pitches usually reserved for the reigning diva.

"Why is my box rented?" Erik panted like a bellows.

"Your box, Monsieur?"

"Yes, my box." Within two strides, Erik had Madame Giry backing away from the door and collapsing into a chair. He gestured behind him. "Someone is in Box Five and Box Five is to be kept empty. I thought myself clear, Madame."

"Even if you're dead?"

That statement hit Erik directly between the eyes. He wiggled his head and rapped his fingers against his temple. "Ah, yes. Erik is dead. Forgive me for momentarily forgetting." Sarcasm curdled at his feet like day-old milk.

"Knowing you faked your death and printed your obituary, I didn't think it would be wise to leave the box empty."

Erik made a wide arc with one arm and let it slap against his thigh. He conceded to the old woman's wisdom.

"Death at birth would have been easier." He chuckled morosely. His voice bounced from wall to wall like an invisible acrobat. It entertained him, but obviously didn't amuse Madame Giry. She rushed to the door and scanned the hall before shutting it.

"Do you fear Death, Madame, or just me? To quote Bacon: 'Even at our birth Death does but stand aside a little. And every day he looks toward us and muses somewhat to himself whether that day or the next he will draw nigh.'"

"I don't like to speak of such things, Monsieur."

She twisted the skeleton key and locked the door. She may not fear Death, but she feared him. To her credit, he had a habit of startling her.

Fanning his cloak out of the way, he took a seat on the divan.

With a flick of his finger, he motioned for her to sit in the chair across from him.

"Speaking of death is nothing compared to being imprisoned by it." He waved his hand over his face.

The full-face mask was a second skin, shielding the world from the revulsion of his deformity. He was a hostage to an ebony prison, its fake nose and perpetual lack of expression kept him caged beneath a false sense of dignity. His thin lips were the only part of his inhuman ugliness, a death's head on a living body, vulnerable to the leering eyes of man.

"Why are you here, Monsieur?"

"I am everywhere, and Death is always nigh, Madame. And I am tired of having only Death when I could have so much more."

Erik let his breath seep out the nose he lacked instead of sighing at her lack of response. His life was a frustrating contradiction. He had a voice more angelic than the heavens, more seductive than any libertine, but a fate that wouldn't allow him any pleasure. What the good Lord did by giving him such a face and condemning him to such a vexing life, He compensated with the genius He birthed into him. It was a shame the Lord didn't realize man would judge by appearance alone.

Leaning back in his chair, he pressed his fingertips together to study the way Madame Giry couldn't sit still. Her nerves proved why he never bothered to permit the gentleman in him to surface.

"I'm not certain what you expect of me, Monsieur. Did you come here because of your box? What is it you wish?"

"To live like anybody else."

"Don't do that Monsieur! You're supposed to be *dead*!"

Erik gnashed his teeth and stuck a finger in his ear. The pitches the old woman could achieve at times bested him. He didn't like being reminded of his faked death and Madame Giry bouncing her knees over it annoyed him.

"It would be bad, very bad for you to return!" She wrung her hands. "You're are a wanted criminal."

"You do not need to remind me of such, Madame. Though I did nothing more than merely love her."

Erik refused to say *that* name.

"You *kidnapped* Christine Daaé. You tried to *kill* the Vicomte de Chagny!"

"I let her go, and I spared his life. I am sure the lovers are living happily ever after," he rumbled. The woman should learn not to mention the unmentionable.

Erik sat back and folded his arms like a wounded child. Looking away from the old woman's reprimand, he knew the crux of his melancholy and his desire for company tonight. It didn't lie in lecturing Madame Giry. That confounded girl and her blasted packages pounded in his head like a kettledrum. A far cry from ecstasy he used to have when thinking of Christine.

"Please, Monsieur. I don't know what it is you wish of me tonight, but I beg you: don't make trouble. What's the point in pining for love unrequited?"

Madame Giry sometimes surprised him with the wisdom he found behind her words. Erik made a note to give her more credit.

"There is no point." He didn't bother keeping resentment from his voice. "That wretched vicomte with all his aristocratic glory could never love as wholly or as ardently as I."

"The past is done, Monsieur. You've been forgotten. Don't change that."

"And what makes you think I am trying to change that?" A flick of his wrist indicated that the world beyond her cluttered office could go to hell. "I hate men and the world they walk so freely in." He rethought and shrugged one shoulder. "Perhaps not hate. Envy."

"How ironic," Madame Giry whispered.

Erik coiled a fist to his mouth, unappreciative of her reply. Certainly irony, given there was nothing he couldn't achieve, not a man he couldn't overpower, nothing in this world outside his realm of comprehension or mastery. Men should envy *him*, but they never would. So long as the human race refused to look beyond his face, all the genius and beauty buried in his soul would never matter.

"I never should have told you about those packages," she regretted. "I knew it would stir something in you."

Erik lowered his fist and snapped his head in her direction. "You have no need to worry over my actions, Madame. That meddling little Samaritan is very much alive—for now! But, be forewarned. I will do what I need to do. I do not require your counsel, nor do I need your pity in addition to hers. I have far too much of that already."

He stood, shoving the chair backward across the stones, creating a shrill scream that made Giry cringe. At the door, he twisted the key and threw it at her feet.

"My box is to remain empty. And rest assured, I will take up no more of your company. Erik is, and always will be, dead!"

Even with her vivid imagination, Anna could never have conjured such a fantastic realm as the backstage of the Opera Garnier. The atmosphere buzzed like a hive of honey-drunk bees. Everyone fed off the excitement whether they wanted to be in the limelight or a part of the company making the magic happen.

Anna wanted nothing to do with any of it—especially on gala evenings. Distracted by her want to leave, she plowed head first into a patron.

"Mademoiselle, watch yourself!"

"Pardon, Monsieur, my mistake." Scooping up his top hat and brushing it clean, she sheepishly handed it back to him.

He swiped it out of her hand and continued in the opposite direction. Anna always moved against the flow. The gentlemen she passed this evening had one destination in mind. The salons. Elegantly appointed rooms well suited for aristocracy's comfort, filled each night with gentlemen enjoying the company of dancers. Anna often fantasized about being a part of the parties she only heard about in stories. It was just as well that she stayed away. She didn't really like the aristocracy—or more precisely *they* had her reasons for disliking *her*.

But it wasn't out of need to escape the wealthy that hastened Anna through the crowd.

The familiar tap of Jacob Wischard's walking stick clawed over her nerves and tensed her shoulders. What she wouldn't give to grab it and plunge it through the man's heart.

"Anna, I know you hear me." Wischard's rebuke stopped her. "Where are you going?" he demanded, reaching her side.

"Any place you are not."

"Watch your tone, Mademoiselle," Jacob snapped. He lifted his cane and rested the tip against her bosom. Using it, he backed her toward a secluded area of the hall.

Anna knocked the offending stick away. "What do you want, Monsieur?"

"Stay out of the way of my patrons. You're to be worked, not seen. Why are you roaming about on a gala evening?"

Gala evenings meant mindless work. She'd had enough of that

for one day.

"No reason," she lied. She hated this man slightly more than his partner Edward Laroque.

"You best watch your behavior, Anna. You're here out of the kindness of my heart."

"You've a heart?"

He snatched her arm and hauled her in close so the stench of cigars and scotch overwhelmed her nose. "Listen to me you meddling little wench. You're only here as payment until your bloody father gets me the money he owes. Were it Edward's choice, you'd still be living on the streets."

"Much preferred, Monsieur." She gritted her teeth against the pain when Jacob shoved her against the wall.

"Spare me your tongue. I know you long to be a part of these parties."

Anna followed Jacob's hand as it wiped imaginary dirt from her shoulders.

"You're small and ordinary. You've no chance of ever receiving such attention. Your rightful place is astride me, or cowering from Edward."

Anna's heart throbbed forcefully in her throat. The muscles in her back seized as the cane rapped against her breast. "I suggest you be in your bed this evening. I might call on you. You wouldn't want your father to find you were naughty and not there for Jacob, now would you?"

Anna froze watching him leave from the corner of her eyes. The thought of nightfall and the sound of Jacob's walking stick moistened her brow. She waited until she saw his back before spitting at him. Tonight, she'd spend away from her meager blanket and bed.

Sleeping on the floor was better than waiting for Satan to arrive.

Anna was more than happy to do as Jacob desired. She made herself scarce. The cellars of the Garnier were as tremendous as the opera itself. Totaling five, they supported the layout of the stage with a network of traps, hatches, winches, counterweights and revolving doors.

Anna often found respite among the wheels and pulleys of the sub-stage level. She enjoyed wandering among the giant machinery. When lucky, she could watch the teams of horses as they rotated the wheels, which operated the hatches that moved scenery. Sometimes, she even sneaked a pat of a muzzle or two. No horses were employed this evening, so Anna contented herself with roaming free from the demands of the managers.

Tonight, however, it appeared she wasn't alone, having spent the last several minutes watching the figure of a man move along the far wall. One could easily make a wrong turn in the maze and get lost in the cellars. Certain this was the case, she called out.

"Lost, Monsieur?" Anna moved around a huge wheel. "The way from the first cellar toward the salons is around that corner. You should take care and travel with caution; it's easy to get disoriented."

The gentleman kept his back to her and refused to answer.

"I beg your pardon, Monsieur." She squinted trying to discern shapes in the shadows but it was near impossible sometimes to tell fantasy from reality in the Garnier. A sudden breeze chilled her but nothing moved around but her. Anna scowled and turned in a small circle.

"Monsieur?"

An arm came from the shadows behind her. It wrapped her shoulders keeping her locked against a male's chest. Her body flashed cold as her scream got lodged behind her fear. Two seconds tore by before anger ignited her senses. Anna bucked and thrashed, dislodging her voice and renting the air with curses as her assailant caged her against his length in an iron tight grip.

His hand slapped against her lips, stifling her cries. So cold were the thin and bony fingers pressed to her upper lip, that pain shot from her mouth into her brain. The more she wrestled, the harder her assailant held her—and the angrier Anna became.

Too many times in her life she'd experienced the darker side of men and their lustful needs. Her life of crime made her a tasteful lady for those of malicious minds. It honed her instinct to fight. Anna drew her knees to her chest and squirmed with every ounce of strength she had. She whipped her head from side to side, managing a breath to scream.

"Get your filthy needs over with already, you bloody bastar— doh!"

Anna hit the floor so hard her breath punched out of her lungs.

Rolling to her feet, she scrambled out of the way, frantically searching every corner. The man had evaporated into the darkness.

"Be done with it I say. Have no mercy on me if you must, but let it be a scar on your heart of how you repay a lady who was merely concerned."

The shadows rumbled to life around her.

"I have done many things in my deplorable, wretched life, Mademoiselle, but I will not even address the filthy assumption you just passed. I assure you, *that liberty* I will not take unless it is freely given. You stand warned. This is my kingdom in which you so boldly trespass."

Her heart battered her ribcage. "I *do* beg your pardon then, Monsieur." Anna scrubbed her mouth. Her lips were still cold.

The cellars would offer her no relief tonight and unwilling to return to her bed, Anna bolted.

It took only a matter of seconds until she was out of sight and Erik was left alone to ponder what had just happened.

He squinted at the girl as she ran off, trying to ignore the twitch in his stomach. He only had that unnerving sensation when he thought he'd have to kill again. And he only killed when he found it necessary to protect his secrets. Each time plunged him into a gloomy pit of self-abhorrence. Too many years traversing Europe as a highly skilled assassin had seeped self-loathing into his soul. The genius in him contorted to a darker being as he was forced to do the bidding of wicked men. The power deflected a world that abused him as a degraded and repugnant freak. He spread his fingers across his mask and slammed his head backward against a wheel.

That was too close.

He never asked for the blood upon his hands! It had become a necessary means of survival.

Music and noise rose in his mind forcing a low growl from deep in his throat. The blessing and curse worked against each other to create chaos of his thoughts.

Damn!

He despised being associated with the vermin who'd force themselves upon a woman. Manipulation served as his only means to communicate his deepest desires, until her comment made him drop her. He banged his head again, ignoring the pain that raced up his neck.

This woman couldn't wander freely about his cellars. His

secrets were his only sanctuary and solitude the vice that draped a veil over his demons. To safeguard his life, all he need do was follow and finish the deed. Yet something fixed Erik to his spot. All he desired was peace.

Wasn't it?

⇢•••——————•••——————•••⇠

Erik had no idea how long he remained on the sub-stage level, staring off in the direction Anna had ran. But by the time he had moved and made it to his house on the artificial lake below the opera, Erik was in a foul mood. He stared at the music in front of him until it blurred. The same stanza stayed trapped in his head, the same word pounding with every beat.

"Pity, pity, pity!" He arched his arm out and sent papers flying from the organ. The inkbottle shattered against the stone floor, making a small pool before it seeped away into a crack.

The word pity tangoed with shame. He wallowed in them for so long they were second shadows. Erik tired of their unrelenting duet. He poked and pulled a stop knob on the organ making it pop with a satisfying rhythmic snap.

"I want to live like anybody else. Why is that so difficult?" He glowered at the stop-knob; aware he spoke to an inanimate instrument adding to the mark he was irrefutably insane.

Somehow he allowed his genius to be buried beneath his madness. Remorse consumed his life like a spider glutting on a meal. He didn't even know how to take the simple company of Madame Giry, an old harmless woman, without getting angry any longer.

Plunking his hand on the keys, he drew a moan from the organ.

Such lack of social skills was not his fault. He'd dismissed humankind long ago. Interaction with man he found unendurable and preferred to stay as far away from others as possible. Or so he tried to convince himself. His genius and solitude, matched with a lifetime of emotional and physical scars from a realm reacting to his face alone, had made him a miserable and unpredictable fellow.

He kicked his organ bench backward and rose. He tried not to dwell on the past. He'd plenty of luxuries to share, excellent wines, teas, not to mention his genius talent. Erik could be gentlemanly, if he could figure out a way to have company without being so morose.

Movement from the corner of his eye caught his attention. "But I *do* have company!" Clapping, Erik bowed before his guest. "What is it you would like? Ribbons, bows, a day at the Tuleries or perhaps a row upon the Seine? Name what you wish of Erik and any desire would be yours. I will make you a queen for a day—or a king?" He raised an eyebrow.

The rat didn't respond with its gender or to Erik's offer.

Pacing the nap of his Persian carpet did nothing to help and speaking to a rat made him seem ridiculous, so he returned to the organ.

Before he took a seat, he ran his fingers across his bookcase. He had no interest in the titles there, only the sketch lying across a vacant part of the shelf. A simple drawing of a Sunday spent in the park where men locked arms with the women who loved them and their children frolicked at their feet. He caressed each figure, tracing the lines. Over time, loneliness had worn away the charcoal.

To taste a life like that was all Erik desired; instead he was a faceless man in the lowest cellar of an opera house. Forget about bringing his genius to the world. No one would ever be able to accept him. Music was his only friend. It would never betray him, pity him, or shame him.

It would never fault him his madness.

The spilled ink had all but disappeared. He mindlessly kicked at the broken glass. Until the arrival of these packages, Erik never questioned his existence. It was and had been since investigations into The Phantom of the Opera ended, ever since he published his own death. Yet…he stared into the shards looking for something.

The packages, aside from the abhorred figs, were so specific to his music. This Anna had to know of it, but how? When he sang, he gazed upon no one except his shadow cast upon walls by the candlelight. The music belonged to him alone. It reflected his haunted memories, his profound loneliness, and his most ardent desires. No one had been near his inner sanctum, of *that* he made certain.

Erik mastered the art of solitude, forcing a comfort in loneliness, only making human contact when absolutely necessary. Then what drew him to these packages? Why had he spared the girl?

He stooped and picked up the shattered vial, remnants of ink coating his hand. Man wasn't designed to live in solitude and despite what men had made him to be, he remained one of them.

A stranger is reaching out, thinking of you in kindness. It's a random act. Leave it be. Madame Giry's wisdom echoed in his mind.

"I will not leave it be." The shard glinted in the candlelight.

Someone knew. Someone heard. Someone saw, and didn't run.

Energy surged through him in a strange new way, making his fingers pulse greedily with an unexplored need. He rose and walked to the table by the organ. Taking the brown package, he ripped the paper off.

It seemed he would need that ink after all.

TWO

If she stared long enough into the flame and relaxed her eyes, it appeared to divide and hover in midair. Blinking abruptly, Anna pulled the oil lamp closer and attempted to focus on the task at hand.

Polishing opera glasses proved more daunting than anticipated. Such tasks were thrown in her lap so the management could keep her occupied in every way imaginable. The previous night, Anna had scrubbed the already immaculate floor of the Escalier. She couldn't complain—afterward she had had a lively late night conversation with the rat catcher. Tonight, she polished opera glasses; tomorrow she would tackle bird excrement on the front steps. Anna's nose crinkled in anticipation of anticipating the stench. She plunked her forehead down on the desk, her groan echoing against the wood. That task took forever for each glob she scraped up, another bird would drop more.

Anything but bird droppings...

Aggravated, Anna scooped the opera glasses into a basket, not caring if she chipped the lenses. They were rarely used anyway. One thing the management excelled at was running the theater into the ground. It made no sense as to why anyone would patronize the Opera Garnier. The music was awful and the acting abysmal. From what she knew, the opera used to be the gem of Paris.

Anna turned the key on the lamp, gradually fading the room to black. She glanced at the clock as the room dimmed. The hands pushed past midnight. No wonder she hardly had any friends. Keeping such hours, how could she?

Though loneliness and exhaustion tugged at her, and too fearful of Jacob to go to bed, she wandered the darkened theater. The halls were blessedly silent. During the day the theater was unfamiliar, filled with wealth and talent and filled with constant reminders of what she'd never have. While she slaved, with nowhere to go escape the hell of Jacob, other women came and went. They were either students eager and thrilled to be at the opera, or other employees, like Madame Giry, free to come and go as they pleased.

Tired, Anna rubbed her eyes as she wandered onto the stage. The theater was silent. A few gaslights were lit, enough to fill the space with a warm light. It made the reds and golds of the seats appear warm and inviting.

As if I will ever be invited to sit in any of them.

Envy ached in her again as Anna ambled the stage. Arms clasped behind her and her head tilted so far back in study of the catwalks above her, she nearly stumbled twice. She pictured herself entering the theater on the arm of a handsome man, pointing out to him how the flies worked and the scenery moved. She marveled at the catwalks and the maze of ropes that suspended them from the darkened heights. She stared until her vision swam then turned to focus her attention on the trapdoors under her feet.

Engineering genius.

Opera could be intriguing after all.

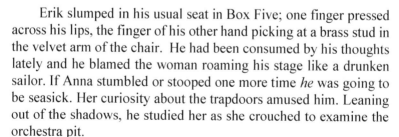

Erik slumped in his usual seat in Box Five; one finger pressed across his lips, the finger of his other hand picking at a brass stud in the velvet arm of the chair. He had been consumed by his thoughts lately and he blamed the woman roaming his stage like a drunken sailor. If Anna stumbled or stooped one more time *he* was going to be seasick. Her curiosity about the trapdoors amused him. Leaning out of the shadows, he studied her as she crouched to examine the orchestra pit.

The girl had come close in her innocent meddling to meeting his madness at an intimate level. His gut seized, making his face twist. He hated his murderous past. And though that way of life had been a necessity, the remorse it caused feasted on his conscious.

It was absolutely wrong to think of killing another. The concierge he'd dispatched years ago was more than enough, not to mention the stream of political assassinations he left behind during his years in Persia.

Erik rubbed the mask, trying hard not to ruminate over that. He had tortured himself enough as is about it. The kidnapping of his young music student, Christine Daaé, however, had been entirely different. Erik had long ago released his feelings for and her and her lover. He had no desire to think on them any more. But still, the echo of Christine's angelic voice was the tip of an addict's needle pushing the monstrous obsessions deeper into his mind.

Erik yanked a brass stud free and flicked it toward the stage. The girl was humming.

Pour l'amour de Dieu, kill me now. It would be better to listen to a rusty hinge. Nonetheless, her curiosity fascinated him. He had a nagging urge to know more.

Perhaps she actually enjoys *music?* His finger thumped across his lips. *Intriguing idea.* But he'd rip his ears off before he ever finished the process of polishing her voice.

"No!" Erik rammed his fist into the arm of the chair. He would not revisit the past.

His shout sent Anna peering into the darkness. Shouting had turned her curiosity into a cautious examination of every shadow.

"Damn it all," Erik muttered.

He leaned forward more intrigued than ever. What an odd sort of woman. The stage belonged to the beautiful and elegant and she was ordinary. The dress she wore, probably at one point a vibrant blue, had faded to a washed-out gray. It resembled the mist that swirled on his lake. She wore no accessories except a kerchief around her neck and an inquisitive expression.

That braid she wore was nearly as long as she was tall, which wasn't saying much. Anna was tiny in comparison to most that graced his stage.

He huffed. Based on her hair, the shape of her face, and the style of dress, he would label her Germanic. Just his luck.

He hated Germans. They barged into his city during the war, caused riots and ruin and left behind his deep-rooted distaste for the country and culture.

He folded his arms against the memories and summed her up like any healthy man would. He may live like an eccentric and have

22

an inexcusable face, but he was at least in acceptable physical condition. He had his theater to thank.

He contended with six thousand steps, a lake, traps, and a network of ropes and flies on which he was used to twirling himself around as he studied everything that went on in his opera. Not that he needed the exercise to remain trim. No fat stuck to his lanky frame. Thinner than most would deem comfortable, Erik was of impressive height, agile and knew the theater inside and out.

Anna climbed off the stage and lowered herself into the pit, her dress catching on a foot-lamp and inching up in the process. Erik quirked a brow and glanced away lest he see parts of a lady a man should not. Music stands clanged together as she hit the floor, shooting Erik to his feet.

The minx would destroy his blasted theater if left to her own devices.

Abandoning his box, he was in his auditorium in a matter of seconds, walking the center aisle. Completely oblivious to him, his target rushed to fix the mess she'd made of the music stands. Anna thoroughly enraged him, yet he couldn't help but be entertained. She had the stealth and agility of a cat, but the nerves of the mouse it chased.

Casually maneuvering around the carelessly reorganized pit, she stopped every now and then to fondle a discarded sheet of music. Eventually, she climbed the steps to the Maestro's stand, quite unaware of her audience. Erik kept his impatience in check as she faced the stage.

Smiling, he indulged in his voyeurism. Too taken by this odd woman to turn away.

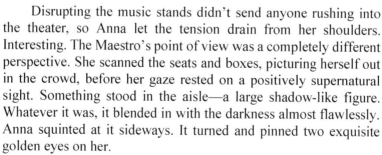

Disrupting the music stands didn't send anyone rushing into the theater, so Anna let the tension drain from her shoulders. Interesting. The Maestro's point of view was a completely different perspective. She scanned the seats and boxes, picturing herself out in the crowd, before her gaze rested on a positively supernatural sight. Something stood in the aisle—a large shadow-like figure. Whatever it was, it blended in with the darkness almost flawlessly. Anna squinted at it sideways. It turned and pinned two exquisite golden eyes on her.

"Holy Mother!"

Anna reeled off the back of the Maestro's stand and tumbled back into the pit. Her elbow collided with the arm of a chair setting off a second chain reaction around her. Ducking stands that went clanging in every direction again, sheets of music rained around her.

Scrambling to her feet and clutching her throbbing elbow, she anxiously searched the theater. Not a sound stirred in the auditorium but her laborious breathing and the grating sound of metal against metal as she tripped over scattered stands. First finding her balance, Anna centered herself with a deep breath.

"That was a stray cat. A very... tall... cat... " Anna stared at her feet for a moment, getting a hold on her runaway nerves, before struggling out of the pit. Rubbing at the pain in her arm that was likely to bruise, she searched the theater, but this time saw nothing. Maybe she should find her bed. She was tired and seeing things. "It's just a stray cat playing in the light and shadows. That's all. Mere light and shadows."

She shook her head at her ridiculousness. Anna glanced to her arm and stopped rubbing it. When she looked up two yellow eyes stared back at her grabbing the breath out of her body.

"Light and shadow make for excellent illusions, do they not?" the man said.

Anna blinked rapidly. Slow knots of apprehension froze muscles, and tied her to her spot, but her mind was wailing at her to run.

"Are you hurt?" he asked, coming closer into what light existed.

She fought against her paralyzed tongue to respond. The man's physique, his dress, and his eyes held such intensity. But it was the black, foreboding mask covering all but his mouth, which held her spellbound. With no way to read the face it hid, the only thing Anna could do was stare. He walked down the aisle and stopped before her, as she stood rooted in her spot. In all her days of wondering on the mystery man in the cellars, she never thought she would see him face to face. Not that she actually could. The tip of her head barely reached his mid chest. Anna backed away, trepidation starting to creep up her spine.

"Are you hurt?" he questioned again.

Anna tried to speak but couldn't force out a sound. His voice carried an allure that made her bones soften, but at the same time squeezed her stomach.

He circled her, forcing Anna to rotate as well. By doing so, she engaged him in a bizarre yet eloquent dance. Their eyes remained locked. Anna skipped backward as he boldly moved closer. He lifted a gaunt hand toward her face.

Him!

Anna leaned away, her breath quickening at the sight of those fingers. It was that lunatic in the cellars! The man who grabbed her was her masked stranger? She followed his unusually long fingers beyond his wrist and arm to stare at his face.

She gasped as he reached out and snatched a strand of her hair untamed by her braid. Its length slid across his palm.

"Amusing," he observed, cocking his head. "Do I frighten you?"

A silky intoxication poured off that whisper instantly making Anna's spine melt. It's tone taking the edge off her fear. Warm, gentle pulses seduced every part of her body. She wanted to drift away on the lilt of his voice. It captivated her in a way she couldn't attempt to describe, perched somewhere between the beauty of heaven and all the power of hell. He rotated her strand of hair under and over his fingers, until he let it slip away.

Locking her gaze on his black mask, she answered his question with a quick shake of her head.

"Good." His heady voice drifted directly into her ear sending shivers marching across her body. "There are packages to deliver."

The last sentence knocked any composure Anna had right out of her. He knew it was she who delivered the packages? But…how?

Before she could react, he evaporated into the darkness. Anna whirled right to left, then back again being chased by nothing more than her own breathing. Each rotation quickened her blood when the disembodied voice of a master ventriloquist echoed across the vast auditorium.

"Red ink—Anna."

Her name floated on a lonesome beauty, yet she was certain she heard sinister laughter following the mention of it. Sinking into a seat, her legs shook like she had run for miles. Nothing made sense.

All she knew was he'd discovered her secret, he needed *red* ink—*and* he knew her name.

Thin streams of afternoon light diminished as Erik moved from the archway toward the depths of the sewer. Once again the package was not in its usual spot. Erik had checked on multiple occasions over a span of several days since his encounter with Anna and each time met with disappointment. He found it pathetic to be waiting like a cat expecting to be scratched. He'd become accustomed to their arrival. He didn't expect his emotions to be so disorganized.

What did you expect that poor girl to do? Go scampering off, gathering provisions like she was invited to a Sunday picnic at the Bois? You pitiful fool.

Rejection had become a reliable emotion.

Exhaling loudly, he pulled on his gloves. Erik moved deeper into the labyrinth, desperate for distance from the hustling sounds of the streets above. Waving his hand over a random stone, he set off a chain reaction among the gas torches on the wall. Row after row of torches obeyed his whim and ignited the passageways ahead of him, bathing the corridors in soft, warm light. Darkness disappeared like an invisible lover running from the idea of his embrace.

He only walked a few paces when he stopped short. Something was off. Erik knew his labyrinth like a second skin and the scuffling setting his teeth on edge was too heavy to be attributed to a rat.

Erik quickened his pace, the silk rope he was rarely without already coiled in his hand. In a matter of seconds, he could strangle the interloper and feed his body to the rats.

As he rounded the corner he slammed right into the girl.

He swallowed a curse as she bounced backward off his chest. Anna slipped and stumbled over moss-covered stones, for several seconds as she fought not to fall. A sudden burst of adrenaline coursed through his body. Erik clamped down on his teeth and brushed past her, tucking the silk rope out of sight.

Damn fool girl! I could have killed you!

Striding forward, putting distance between him and the infernal woman, until several paces away he finally gained enough composure to turn. He spun so sharply his cloak split the air, the sound ricocheting against the endless amount of stone. He pierced her with his glare.

Now what? Instinct told him to defend his territory, but his mind beat against him. *You curious thing. You actually came down into this Godforsaken pit?* She either had to be a fool or one audacious little hoyden. *Who are you?*

It would be unwise to leave her standing in his sewer like a startled deer. Annoyed, Erik yanked on his cloak.

"If you are simply going to stand there, then I suggest you give me my package so I can be on my way."

She squared her shoulders in reply but didn't relinquish her parcel.

"Fine." He waved her off and continued down the corridor without it. "You have two choices, Mademoiselle: follow or remain as you are."

Upon hearing her cautious footfalls break into a jog to catch up to him, he pondered whether she'd made the correct decision.

Erik glanced over his shoulder. He expected to be met with a cowering, mess of a woman, but each time he turned her intense stare seemed to record every move he made.

They didn't stop until they came to the shores of his lake. The confounded girl crept toward it, her jaw slacking open. Not many knew a tributary of the Seine was discovered when the Opera Garnier was built, forcing the creation of the lake. Anna glanced from whence they came, then side to side.

Erik sneered at her reaction. They were *meters* below ground—not merely in a cellar. She should have considered that before following him and upending his life. He bent to untie a small boat, jerking the rope so sharply small droplets of water fell at his feet.

No going back now. I initiated this contact. Now what do I do with....

Her boots appeared right next to his making Erik spring to attention. He bared his teeth only to prevent himself from shouting out his stupidity, but it backed the girl off fast enough.

You irrational, lonely, stupid old... How desperate must I be to risk bringing another into my realm?

"Get in!" he roared.

He didn't move out of her way or assist her into the boat and within minutes they were rowing across the lake. Each time he plunged an oar into the water, he might as well have been stabbing his last grain of sanity.

The farther they rowed from the banks and torches, the deeper they became engulfed in a thick darkness. He chanced a glance at his passenger before it became too dark to discern much. She cocked her head at an awkward angle and stared at him, her eyes open wide. Erik rowed with powerful strokes, forcing the boat deeper into the embrace of ear-numbing silence. Pushing farther into darkness he stared at Anna's slowly moving lips, pondering if she were cursing herself or him.

Either that or she's praying.

When the boat hit the opposite shore, Erik leapt from it, missing landing in the water entirely. The need for distance drummed against his gut making him take the steps to his drawing room two at a time. He made his way through the entry of his home, removed his cloak and gloves, and gradually turned to face her.

Anna had stepped from the boat unfazed by standing knee-deep in water. Her skirts floated around her and she batted them down, still wearing that stupid expression. They'd moored at a small shore, leading into a drawing room. Baskets of flowers gave the place a bit of life. The room overflowed with bouquets, like the ones sold on the Paris streets. Their silk ribbons dangled stupidly from their stems. Erik surveyed it along with her. It actually looked quite ridiculous, for nothing truly alive could thrive in such a place.

He lifted a brow at her slack-jawed study of his home. She swayed like a piece of jetsam, in an attempt to peer beyond the drawing room and into the house itself. Aggravated, Erik pounded down the steps again and sloshed into the water. He gestured toward his parcel.

"My package, if you please."

Anna looked at the crumpled brown parcel she hugged and pressed it into his hands. She scowled when he snatched it. Erik held her gaze a bit longer than comfortable. He rushed toward his inner sanctum, noting his guest hastened to follow.

She stopped in her tracks in the middle of his living room before, upon seeing the water dripping from her skirts; she raced backward to stone shore. Equally as wet, and leaving as much a mess, Erik glanced from the puddle she left on his carpet to the embarrassed expression on her face.

Anna shook her foot free of water then the next as she craned her neck to see beyond him.

He too glanced toward his bedchamber and suppressed a rumble. The keyboard of his pipe organ, which lined the wall between his chambers and the rest of his home, had her undivided attention. Ignoring the curious warp to her face, as she wrung water out of her skirts, keeping clear of his expensive Persian rugs, he stopped to unwrap her parcel. He first removed the paper, pressed out the creases, and placed it on the stack with the others.

Next, he found the ink. He raised the vial to the candlelight and rolled the liquid around. Carefully, he arranged it into a neat row among countless vials of black ink.

He addressed the figs by flipping the pouch into a pile of similar looking bags.

"This is my home," he abruptly announced. "You are not a prisoner here. You may come and go as you please, provided you can continue to find your way. The routes down here are many and the labyrinths appear to shift. An... unfortunate and rather deadly adjustment I made years ago."

Erik rammed his hands on his hips at the thought. He had safeguarded his life by any means possible after the investigations into the Phantom closed. He couldn't risk any... unwanted guests

"The lake is the easiest route," he continued, "but rest assured you will not find it again. You may explore what you like, but you will touch nothing. Do you understand?"

She nodded.

"Good. You may ask what questions of me you like within reason, and I will determine if they are worth answering. One final rule." His voice cracked like thunder. "You will speak of this to no one. Is that understood?"

The girl took a deep breath and nodded again.

"You are a woman of many words," he rumbled.

Turning from her, he took a seat at his organ and, resting his chin in his hand, he silently brooded over the situation. Anna's voice broke the silence.

"I have a question."

"And what might that be?" His hand muffled his voice. He didn't bother to turn and address her like a proper gentleman should.

"What's your name?"

That knocked Erik in the gut, leaving him breathless. He scanned the worn manuals on the organ, hunching deeply over them, hoping it would ebb the loneliness sucking on him, before studying the ceiling. He couldn't recall when last asked his name, and worse, when anyone last used it.

"Erik," he quietly replied, his name sticking a knife in the loneliness in his throat.

Turning, he met her eyes. A few moments of judgment passed

between them before Anna turned her back and headed down the closest corridor.

It would figure she'd dare not stay. Though he pondered following her, the thought disappeared as quickly as it came. She chose her corridor wisely and would find her way back to the theater. With dozens of ways into his underworld, he had to trust she was clever enough to figure them out and smart enough not to breathe a word about them to anyone. His concern lay not in if Anna would want to find her way back to the theater, but if she would find her way back to him.

What would he do if she did?

THREE

The interior of his house glowed in a warm bath of candlelight, its essence tranquil and inviting. Erik sat on a small divan, re-stringing a violin. He swayed, leaning in and out of invisible notes, as they possessed his body. Moving to the music in his mind served to calm his unsettled thoughts.

It had been days since he'd given that girl the key to his kingdom. Nightly he waited to see if she'd return, but was always met with detestable silence and deepening disappointment. The music he composed in his mind served as the only barrier keeping him from going insane over it all. Everything in his mind orchestrated precisely to the solos he was destined to perform, everything, that is, except for the footsteps that brought his music to a screeching halt.

"So you do return after all." Erik laid the violin down, stroking its veneered surface as though it were a precious child, and stood. "I somehow suspected you would not be too eager to do so."

The fact she did sent an odd quiver through his stomach. *This* sensation confounded him and an overwhelming unease drilled those shivers into his core. He approached, his hand fisted at his sides as he tried to hide their trembling.

"Why *did* you return?" he clipped, eyeing her sideways.

Anna didn't reply with words. Reaching into the folds of her dress, she produced a tiny bundle and held it out to him. Grimacing, he snatched it.

"Figs?"

A sweeter odor seeped from the package, though. Erik held the bag to his mask, inhaling deeply. He locked gazes with her and, curious, he opened the parcel. The rich scent of strawberry spiraled out of the bag and filled the air. He grabbed one of the ruby gems like a greedy child plucking a toy from its box.

"You don't like figs." Anna pointed toward the discarded bundles of fruit near the table.

Erik nodded—struck silent. He glowered at her smugly folded arms and her jutting chin. Looming over her petite frame, he was utterly baffled by her seemingly unflappable demeanor. Anna stared at his mask and glowered.

He stopped his inspection. A proper gentleman would have thanked her by now.

Erik was, however, not exactly proper.

He extended one hand to her, the other sweeping with the strawberry toward his home. Bowing, he bid her welcome in a voice as rich as he could make it.

"Mademoiselle, welcome."

———

Erik was not content. Rarely did he admit to making bad decisions, but as weeks passed, he was beginning to think he had.

Endless nights of wrestling with his confounded emotions since inviting Anna into his world was starting to gnaw on his nerves. The girl, however, seemed comfortable in the labyrinth, at peace with the hesitant bonds of friendship building between them.

"What—are you making *now*?" Erik lifted a wine glass to his lips and scowled over its rim.

Anna's reply to his irritable rumble was to grin and lift a tattered scarf, its stains halfway embroidered over with an intricate design.

Erik rolled his eyes. *Just like the child to attempt to make something ugly beautiful.* "I take it that is for one of your *other* charity cases—out there?" He flipped his hand toward the ceiling in the direction of Paris.

She nodded and resumed her stitching.

His scowl deepened. "A woman of many words, as usual."

Anna had been arriving nightly for weeks. She usually did

nothing more than quietly sit on his divan–a maddening trait in itself—sewing or knitting something for the world above. *When* they spoke, it mostly focused on common subjects—rarely about music. He'd discovered little about her beyond her age.

"Who is that for?" he asked.

Anna peeked at him. "An old woman."

Erik leaned forward waiting on an elaboration, but he got none. Sighing, he gestured at her with the glass. "I hear a sloppier German accent to your French. Where are you from?" Trying to get the girl to converse was near impossible.

"Austria."

He took a larger sip and waited for her to reciprocate and ask about him. Never did she question his existence beneath the opera house, and not once did she mention the mask. This stupefied him. All Erik's life he'd been pursued by unrelenting inquiries as to who he was, where he came from, and why such a creature was allowed to live.

Erik swirled the Tokay around his glass, watching the reddish-brown wine ebb and roll. Though a connoisseur of fine wines, he rarely drank. It was bad for his vocal chords and he found drink tended to make men stupid.

Erik didn't take kindly to stupidity.

This particular evening he felt the need to indulge. It took the edge off just trying to talk to the girl. Slumping in his chair, he studied the way her hand wove in and out of her stitching. It was hypnotic.

Or was it the wine?

Erik took another sip and gestured about his cavernous home. "Why do you not run, Anna?"

Her sewing fell into her lap. "That's an odd subject for the evening, Erik."

"Ah! Now you speak." He jabbed an accusing finger at her. "You come here night by night asking nothing of me. Why?"

"You... invited me. You said I could come and go as I pleased. Are you now rescinding that invitation?"

He was aghast at the way Anna assumed she could make herself comfortable, despite his invitation. To make matters worse, that blasted flutter in his core kept him awake at night. Anna kept him guessing, and guessing games were not his favorite pastime. Erik glared at her quirked brow through the wine glass, the liquid dividing and discoloring her face. He found wry humor in that.

"You should be afraid," he mumbled sullenly.

"Of you?" Her head snapped back as the words slapped her. "Surely, you've had too much to drink! You may be peculiar, but I rather enjoy that about you. You always seem perched on the edge of some sort of thought or emotion." She resumed her stitching.

Erik launched to his feet, knocking his chair aside. He pitched the glass through the air crashing it into the far wall, making it bleed wine. The shattered crystal echoed like an explosion, raining shards and wine in every direction. Across the room Anna jerked, the sewing crumpling in her hand.

"Yes!" he shouted a dangerous undercurrent in his clipped tones. "You should be afraid, yet you do not run. You keep coming back yet know nothing of me. Why, Anna? Why do you keep returning? Why not run?"

He lunged across the room, driven by the questions pounding in his mind and the aftereffects of too much wine. Erik reached the divan and fell awkwardly onto the seat beside her.

"You sit next to a demon, Anna. Erik has burned in hell so many times he no longer feels the pain. Why are you here?"

"*Erik* has burned in hell? That's a bizarre way to refer to yourself."

"Answer me!"

Anna leaned away. "I like it down here. I thought *we* enjoyed the company."

He pounded his fists into the divan like a frustrated child. "No! That is not the answer."

She leapt to her feet. "If you have something to say kindly do so without the tantrum!"

Tantrum? How dare she! Erik blinked then studied her eyes as she gathered her sewing with sloth like speed. She had a nagging way of testing his patience. Clutching her sewing like she used to his packages she approached his organ, spun around and purposefully plunked herself on the bench. How dare she. The instrument was forbidden to her, yet there she sat in outright defiance. He took a deep breath and let it hiss out through clenched teeth. He had a feeling if he picked her up and hung her on the wall, she'd still find a way to defy him. Although drunk and angered at Anna's chosen perch, he leaned back in his chair and relaxed.

"You are unlike the others I have dared call friend," he drew out the last word with supreme caution

Anna reeled back. Erik scowled. Was he not allowed call her that, sarcastic tone or not? Her reaction pulled him back to that vat of pooling bitterness he held toward the human race.

"You do not need to know about me, child, but I need to know something about you." He leaned across the divan and pointed at her, emphasizing each word with a stab of his finger. "Why. Are. You. At. My. Opera. House?"

Anna stared at him out of the corner of her eye, obviously suspicious, but not intimidated. "Everyone has a story, Erik. Why are you asking for mine now, in this state?"

"Because you do not want to know my *other* states." The heat of her insubordination was angering him as much as the drink.

"You want to know? Fine. I'm a pawn. A piece in my father's twisted games of manipulation and deceit. I've spent my life being shuffled around as payment for his debts."

Erik noted a different, icy tone to her voice that made her accent even more grating to the ears.

"I wasn't a wanted child, rather a drunken mistake," she continued. "My parents were forced to marry into a loveless relationship because of me, and I became the object of their bitterness and resentment. My mother tried to be kind; she at least acknowledged my existence was not my fault."

"How fortunate for you." A finger rested on his upper lip, pressed there to keep his opinions from coming out his mouth. Mothers were despicable beings.

"But my father saw in me everything wrong in his life. He's a liar, thief, a compulsive gambler, a con artist, and... a drunk."

The words stuck to Erik given his current state. He dismissed them with wave of a hand.

Anna slapped the sewing aside and shielded herself with her arms. "Any living my family made was gambled away by him. If a con went bad, or the debt exceeded what money we had—he pawned me. Men, he learned, viewed me as an acceptable form of payment. Collectors would readily accept a young girl in exchange for a purse. My mother couldn't stop him, she... died when I was young." Anna swiped an eye before glaring at him again. "I wish I had."

"You know nothing of wishing for death," Erik rumbled.

Her face reddened. "I learned many trades in my years of

servitude to his debts. I slaved for blacksmiths and cobblers, seamstresses and cooks. I was bonded to doctors and merchants. I was also a thief, a liar and, my personal hell, a whore."

Erik slumped back in the divan and wiped his lips with the back of his hand. He looked away in revulsion, unwilling to meet her eyes.

"When I was sixteen, I ran as far away as I could get. I found myself in Paris at the faubourg Saint-Antoine. I fit perfectly with the vagabonds and thieves of the Cours de Miracles. It may be the filthiest and poorest of neighborhoods, but there I saw many others whose lives were far worse than mine."

Erik lowered his finger from his mouth as her voice softened and grew distant. Empathy dulled any irritability he had.

"They took me in," Anna recalled, gratitude and compassion obvious in her tone. "I repaid those who cared enough to look beyond the thieving and begging by teaching them the trades I knew.

"Two years ago, my father found me. He was in debt deeper than he'd ever been to Edward Laroque and Jacob Wischard, this opera's management. My father tried to control me, but I was too old for his whip and too wise for his manipulations."

"Then why are you here?" Erik said flatly. He sat straighter now that the full impact of her story had sunk in.

"In my absence, he remarried and had a little girl. He threatened if I didn't do as he demanded, he would force her to do so. I do this to save her. I thought about leaving many times, but the managers are always threatening to contact him if I act out, using the fate of a sister I've never met to keep me chained." Anna picked aimlessly at the sewing to her side. "Sometimes I wonder if she even exists. But it's not worth condemning another child to this life. I can manage this. It's a life I know how to lead."

"Where is this man now?"

Anna shrugged. "When he dumped me here I told him I never wanted to see him again. It doesn't matter. My family lies in the streets of Paris."

Anna jerked her hands down the front of her dress when she stood. The move did little to brush away the tension swirling in the air around them.

"You ask why I don't fear you, and why I don't run. I see nothing in you *to* fear. If you have a story you feel will do so, then tell it and let me understand you. I won't judge. But I'll not ask you for it. Your history is your business, not mine. I've nothing to fear of the past, yours or mine. What is done is done. I'm through running. I too have burned in the far reaches of hell, Erik. You're an ignorant man to think you hold that distinction on your own."

Sewing held against her chest like a shield, Anna started toward the corridor that would lead her to the dormitories. However, even in his drunken state, Erik's reflexes were swifter than hers. Leaping up, he blocked her path. Placing his hand on her shoulder, he marched her backward onto the organ bench.

"Sit."

A storm brewed that would be too swift for either of them to stop.

Despite knowing the wine had made him unrecognizable, Erik found a fresh glass and continued to pour himself a drink. She saw nothing in him to fear? He chuckled morosely at that as he studied the ceiling. Perhaps he should ruin her illusions the easy way, rip off the mask and begin his tale with life as the sideshow freak, The Living Corpse. Destroying her beliefs sickened him, but he had to.

He was starting to trust her.

"My story? I am a murderer. A murderer and a Maestro, a magician and a mastermind. There is nothing in this world I have not mastered, nothing unattainable beyond my grasp. I am a wealthy, powerful genius, with the voice of an angel and the soul of a madman…"

FOUR

Anna jolted awake. She bolted upright not fully knowing her whereabouts. Her eyes were gummed up and blurry making her blink until the house on the lake came into focus. Groaning, every muscle rusty and stiff, she wrestled with her limbs to move. A wool blanket left her arms itching as it slid to the floor. She stared dully at it, rubbing one eye. She never recalled having one on her.

Erik.

Memories of the previous night and the stories he spun flooded her mind. The kind token of a warm blanket when she must have dozed off sharply contrasted the stories he'd woven for her.

Anna searched, but Erik was nowhere to be found. There was only one room where he could be. She draped the blanket over her arm and breathed deeply. Limping as her legs limbered up, she walked past the organ to the chamber beyond. She never dared previously to approach the room. By the way Erik fiercely guarded it, she'd learned to never cross the threshold. If she were a cat, she would have expended her nine lives already trying to get close enough to see within.

Anna hesitated and chewed her bottom lip. Within that room was a man whose history made her toss and turn all night. Sideshow freak? Political assassin in countries she never heard of? Anna swiped one palm down the length of her dress waiting for her stomach to settle. Her hands were just as dirty ... though never by choice. Nerves aside, who was she to judge?

Her curiosity over Erik's rabid possessiveness over that room was amplified now by the stories he told. She hesitated before taking a deep breath and walking to the doorway. Anna stepped inside.

When she did, she dropped the blanket and with it her composure.

Anna gripped the sides of her dress to keep her hands from shaking. Erik's bedchamber was morbidly depressing. Black cloth hung from the walls, and an unfamiliar stave of music repeated across them. The coffin centered in the room sent goose bumps across her arms, and made her swipe down the hair at the nape of her neck.

She couldn't tear her gaze off it. It wasn't a closed box, like the ones she'd seen piled on the roadsides near vagabond camps. Those were natural and commonplace in her life, nothing that would send shock waves through her. But this... this was unnatural.

Anna's mouth ran dry. It took a few moments of her fighting to swallow for the image to sink in before Anna found herself staring at Erik.

He sat below a canopy of red brocade fabric on the edge of a small platform, his back to the offending box. At least he wasn't *in* it. Anna took some comfort in that. Barefooted, his cravat discarded and his collar unbuttoned, he leaned forward with his elbows on his knees and his head bowed low enough to shield his face from her view.

Erik nursed a hangover.

The mask lay on the bedside table. She tore her gaze away from him and his coffin and stared intently at it. It had been casually tossed aside as if it were a perfectly normal piece of clothing. *Nothing about this is normal.* "Erik?" she whispered.

He stiffened and swung his back to her, his hands crushing hard against his face. Anna hung her head feeling her heart drop to her stomach, regretting her sudden intrusion upon his privacy.

Refusing to turn around, he snatched his mask from the table and molded it to his face in one fluid motion.

"Mademoiselle." He turned and flicked her back toward his living room, refastening his collar then fumbling with the crumpled silk of his cravat with his opposite hand. "I do not wish you in here."

That made two of them. Anna pointed at the coffin finally

getting rid of her cotton-mouth. Her voice scratched. "What…who…why?"

Erik gave up on the cravat. He sighed and pinched the bridge of the nose on his mask. "Yes, I sleep in a coffin." He gave the offending box a dismissive flip of his hand and brushed past her toward the living room. He flatly pointed backward to the stave of music on the wall. "The Dies Irae, you know. One must prepare for eternity, after all."

How he could be so indifferent to all of this? Anna nodded though she didn't agree… not with any of this. She picked up the blanket and made her way around him tossing it on a divan beyond his macabre bed. Giving wide berth to his coffin, she hastened back toward the living room. Last night he made a point of omitting what lay beneath his mask, and she dared not ask.

"Come. I'll make tea before I go," she offered.

Barely nodding his thanks, he rubbed at his temples. It wasn't until she was far from his room and at his tea tray that she realized her breathing had finally slowed. Anna lifted her eyes every so often to study him. He'd folded his arms and leaned against the wall watching as she lit a samovar. Fishing around a small basket of pinecones set near the urn, she added a few to the charcoal then lit it with one of the scraps of birch bark rolled in a tin nearby.

"Are you wondering if I'll rummage around your life like I do your tea tray?" Anna grinned, trying to break the stress she sensed around him and knock aside her own unease. "The fact I even know the proper way to brew tea in a samovar should prove many of your assumptions of me are wrong."

He jerked off the wall. If she could see his face, Anna would have been certain his brow furrowed.

"The past is the past Erik," she announced, wiping clean a cup and walking it over to him. "I didn't know the man you spoke of last night, so I can't condemn him. You were kind enough to let me sleep, to give me a blanket. That is more than any man I know would have done. I'd like to continue to know more of you… if you would help me understand the man you are now." She nodded toward his room and her abrupt discovery.

Erik took the cup. He scrutinized it, his bottom lip curling like he saw something vile inside, before inching his gold eyes from the china to her face. Anna smiled, but it faded as he looked away.

She gathered her things and hurried off to begin her day,

leaving Erik to finish brewing his tea. Heaviness spread throughout her body as she dragged herself away. Understanding Erik would be harder than she thought and she had a feeling he would never allow her that honor. Anna looked back to see him slink toward his bedchamber. The teacup shattered against the floor as he tossed it aside. She huffed, about to voice her protest, when Erik abruptly stopped. Not acknowledging whether he knew she was still there, he slowly knelt. Taking a piece of the broken cup between two long fingers, he twisted it in the wedge of candlelight. He had stared at that cup with such contempt when it was whole and beautiful and now, broken in pieces, he studied it looking for something entirely different.

Rising to his full height, the omniscient air he left behind him feathered against her skin as he palmed the china into his hand and walked into the open arms of darkness.

-->-•-------- ---------•-<-

Wet spring faded into summer. Life in the opera house mimicked life on the Paris streets. The halls buzzed with activities and the dormitories filled to capacity with talent old and new. Rehearsals were loud and lively events, an energetic rivalry of sound between the orchestra and the chorus. The opera preened and prepped for the upcoming season in a flurry of activity.

Erik made certain over time that the opera wove its spell across Anna. He enlightened her to the music and allowed the magic to work its charms.

Though curious over how she accepted him, he grew, at long last, to be comfortable with Anna's companionship. Trusting another was usually difficult, if not impossible, for Erik. The trembles in his stomach kept growing each time he saw her. Over time he waited, eagerly to feel them… to see her.

Months had passed since their confrontation. After that night, he entirely opened his realm to her. He lowered his defenses to enjoy her presence. They took company together for minutes to hours. One moment her fiery attitude was ablaze around him, but the next had her wearing caution.

Tonight, he leaned against the strings on his violin with his bow. Alone in his thoughts, his body wove in and out of the images in his mind. He coaxed an intoxicating, beautiful voice from his violin. It was the first instrument he chose to speak for his soul and it would be the last. He paused mid-sway when he saw Anna arrive and lean against the far wall. Erik resumed playing, sending rich notes to greet her. Rocking slightly, she kept in time with the rising and falling song of an unseen bird. Usually, Erik stopped playing when she arrived and often scolded her for being late or sneaking up on him. This time he didn't, but greeted her with a smile and played on.

She slid a strand of hair from her face, her fingers momentarily touching the ridges in her brow. So it would be caution she would wear tonight?

Erik painted notes on the air with waves of music that were sheer seduction. In several minutes time, her brow smoothed, and her back arched. Erik wanted that. He wanted each note and chord to reach into the very depths of her and tug at some undisturbed thought or emotion. Every move he made was hypnotic. He allowed her to discover the two sides of him: a mysterious, dark man with a deeply disturbed mind, and the quiet gentleman hidden below the surface of his closely guarded emotions.

The music lured her into a trancelike calm.

He didn't mind the silence. The notes lulled his demons asleep. Watching her listen so intently was like a drug for him. He drew out one soulful note to give him time to weigh the idea her fascination created. Music only calmed the noise in his mind. Anna silenced it altogether.

Like a flash of lightning, he made his decision.

Erik tucked his violin and bow under one arm. In a move dripping with well-practiced allure, he curled one finger at a time into his palm, inviting Anna to join him. As she drew near, his lips parted at the blush blooming across her face.

Anna began to speak, but he placed a finger upon her lips. She stiffened. Inside, Erik's stomach trembled more.

"Erik?" she whispered, her brow furrowing.

"Shh."

Setting the bow and violin aside, he placed a hand under her chin, lifting it.

"What are you doing?" she asked.

"Shh," he commanded again, walking behind her. Lightly, he moved his fingers back and forth across her shoulders then down her arms. His primary objective was to place her in the perfect position. His hands progressed down below her ribs pushing a gasp of surprise from her lips. Before she could dart away, he pressed slightly on her lower back causing her spine to straighten. The contact made her jolt, but Erik's resolve didn't waver. A glance to her face confirmed the pink on her cheeks had turned an all-out crimson. Easing his hands slowly up her bodice to her arms, he readjusted the chin she kept moving. His focus was absolute.

Sliding her braid from the drape over her shoulder, he smoothed it down her back. He moved to stand closely behind her, hesitantly pressing his body against hers. He'd never come so near her. Her shudder rippled against his chest. The nerves made him smile. Turning, she gave him a quizzical look, one eyebrow raised, her bottom lip jutting out in a pout he found rather appealing. Nevertheless, he once more forced her back into position.

He reached for his violin and bow, then around her waist. With the violin in front of her, its back to her breasts, he lifted her left arm. Her dress sleeve slipped aside, allowing his fingers to slide across her exposed flesh. He pressed the violin into her arms, forcing her to hug it tightly. In his eyes, there was no more intimate way to know the instrument than to feel its every curve pressed firmly against the body. Leisurely, he removed his violin from her embrace and tucked it under her chin. Anna tried to step aside, but he caged her in his grip.

"Erik, this is daft."

"Shh," he cooed into her ear, waiting patiently for her to stop fidgeting.

Placing the bow in her other hand and positioning her fingers correctly, Erik wove his hand around hers. He guided her fingers in harmony with his along the delicate neck of the instrument. He lifted her hand, touching the bow to the bridge, and coaxed music from the strings.

Shallow breaths fell from her lips, while his stayed calm and focused. The flush on her cheeks warmed her face. What he wouldn't give to feel such warmth on his bare skin instead of through his cold and artificial mask...

When her breath caught in a sigh, a smile grew across his face. For the first time, the noise in his tormented mind faded. He heard nothing but music.

Blissful, intoxicating music. He had no idea how she managed to silence the noise, but she did, and he could live off that sensation all his days.

Erik swayed as notes floated across the labyrinth. Any woman who could silence his hell was truly worthy understanding what sort of man... and madman... he was. Erik took a deep breath, his every thought centered on the woman in his arms. An unearthly beauty embraced them as he whispered the words he knew Anna had been waiting to hear and the words he never imagined any moment would demand.

"To understand me, is to understand music..."

✦•••———•••———•••✦

It had only been a week since Erik helped her play the violin, but the intimate gesture had opened something between them. Though still not comfortable with the corpse-like perception he had of himself, Anna had seen people think a lot worse of themselves.

Erik and Anna rarely chanced a walk in the Tuileries together, let alone the streets beyond, but when they did, it was with the utmost caution. Cloaked in his blackest eveningwear, Erik reluctantly agreed to accompany Anna on her rounds. He was resistant, at first, to learning what she did. Erik had confessed to having issues with being one of her "charity" cases. But to Anna the people she helped were not cases to pity, but family to care for. Erik was simply another member. She glanced up as he tugged on the brim of his hat, again.

"Why do you keep doing that?" she asked.

"The people you help do not even notice me, Anna. How can they ignore the mask?"

She sighed, tired of having to remind him again. "The desolate pay no mind to differences, Erik, only indifference."

Their evening walk ended at a silent opera house. They calmly fell in step together, moving down the halls, each absorbed in their own world.

"Anna?" A woman called out

As Anna turned to the sound of Madame Giry's voice, Erik immediately vanished into a shadow.

"It's very late," Madame Giry remarked. "Have you been out?"

Anna groaned in Erik's direction, wishing for the thousandth time he wouldn't hide. "Good evening, Madame Giry," she greeted. "I hope I didn't startle you."

"Not at all, but you shouldn't be out at this hour."

"With all due respect, Madame Giry, I'm not a student at this

44

opera."

"I understand, Anna, but I've sound reason for being protective of those beneath the Garnier's roof." The plump concierge folded her arms in a comical attempt to make herself look formidable. "Though I may be merely an old concierge, I see all the employees in my opera as *my* responsibility!"

"*Your* opera, Madame? You are well aware it is *my* opera." Erik artfully stepped into view to stand beside Anna. "I assure you the Mademoiselle is perfectly capable of tending to her own needs."

Anna scowled. What the devil was going on? Erik *knew* her?

"Monsieur, what have you done?" Madame Giry asked, her voice trembling.

Anna slid a suspicious gaze over to Erik. Madame Giry knew *him*? Anna cursed her tendency to assume. She thought he had opened himself to her entirely, but clearly he hadn't told her everything.

"Done? Why I have done nothing. Cease acting like a frightened rabbit. It is not becoming on a woman your age."

Anna refused to budge when Erik took her elbow in an attempt to lead her away.

"I'll not have this Monsieur, not again," Madame Giry begged. "Please."

Erik released Anna's arm and spun toward the woman.

"You will not have this? You are a feeble-minded box keeper, Madame. Need I remind you it is not your place to tell me what I can and cannot have?" Erik snatched Anna's elbow again. "Come, Anna, we must be going."

She clawed at his fingers and wrestled for her arm. Prying free, she yanked down hard on her sleeve.

"What's going on? Erik, do you know this woman?" Turning toward Madame Giry, she was met with the same unreadable emotions she saw on Erik. "You know of him? How?"

"You will tell her nothing!" Erik's voice shifted like an angry wind. It took on a fantastic resonance that buzzed in her ear. "Anna, come to me."

Anna touched her hand to her ear to silence the odd echo of Erik's voice. Whatever tricks he played with his voice, they wouldn't work on her.

"No!" Madame Giry rubbed furiously at her lobes. "This won't begin again, please." She reached for Anna's hand and held on tightly.

"Child, now!" Erik's tone dripped with authority.

"No," Anna clipped, breaking free from Madame Giry's grasp. She marched up to Erik; planted herself head to chest with him and looked him directly in the eye. "You lied to me Erik! You know how I despise that. You told me no-one knew you lived below this theater. You. Lied."

Erik's hands flexed and curled, his thin lips twitched. "We will not discuss this here. You are mine and you will come with me now."

"I'm *yours*? Spare me your anger, Erik, it's *my* turn." Fury snaked off her tongue with one word. "Leave."

She stood her ground as Madame Giry shrunk. Erik's stare darted between the two women.

He pointed at the old woman, directing his annoyance where it had obvious impact. "You will tell her nothing." He punctuated the warning with a swirl of his cloak and evaporated into the shadows.

Anna didn't turn to see where he went. Instead she waited for the tension to drain out her shoulders, but it was useless. Her body wound tight. She turned to Madame Giry, her back stiff.

"Whatever trance he has cast over you, you must break it," the box keeper blurted. "He's a very dangerous man."

"Dangerous?" Anna scoffed. "Ridiculous. Erik's not dangerous." *A liar, yes, dangerous, no.*

"Anna, listen to me. Please understand. I've spent years serving that man. You don't know with whom you are dealing."

"In all the years I've been at this opera house, you've never so much as had a bit of concern about me. I'm to believe that you do now?"

"You don't understand him. You don't know who he is or of his past. Oh, this is all my fault! I told him about you and after all these years, he's still a madman."

"His past? What of his past, Madame? That he is a fugitive? A murderer?" Anna gestured toward whatever random shadow Erik had disappeared into. "I know all about his past."

Madame Giry's face blanched. "Anna, please! I'll not have this happen again."

Anna stomped her foot to smash the impatience billowing inside of her. "Have *what* happen again?"

"I dread what might happen for betraying his trust, but I can't keep silent any longer. Not if he is going to entrap another in his twisted web."

Twisted web? Anna barely knew this woman, but she had an uneasy feeling their lives were about to be irreversibly entwined. Anna held her breath as Madame Giry asked:

"What has he told you of The Phantom of the Opera?"

Erik was so furious over the idea of Madame Giry and Anna speaking about him that he had no concept of time. For all he knew it could have been morning.

In the past such fury would have easily transpired into murder, but Erik made a point of staying deep underground. Every pound of his feet against the stone, each splash his boots made in the puddles matched a savage rhythm in his mind. He hadn't wanted Anna to learn of the secrets Madame Giry kept. Punching the air, Erik shouted to the stone around him. How arrogant he was to step from that shadow.

You damn fool.

His fist pounded against his thigh as he walked. Madame Giry only thought about *her* needs. Like everyone else. People like that exposed his fragile scar tissue to the world and clamped the manacles that came with his prison tighter around his wrists.

Erik's attempts at convincing himself that he didn't need companionship, be it Anna or the vagrants he stepped over in the streets, was useless. Something inside twisted with longing when he thought of her. He actually hated that feeling. It was far too different from the way his gut would flip when obsessed over Christine. Erik tripped over his thoughts, fisting his hands until the pain reached his elbows.

Rounding the corner into his drawing room, leading with his anger after pacing for hours through his vaults, he stopped short. His fists sprung open upon seeing Anna. He straightened his hunched posture and tugged on the sleeves of his jacket, prepared to meet Anna's smoldering gaze.

Her chest heaved as she sat on his organ bench. The corners of her eyes were alive with small, tense lines. Leaping up, she toppled the seat with enough force to send it cracking into the footboard. It slammed against the pedals shooting deep echoing notes around the room before it hopped off and rested on the floor.

"How dare you!" she shouted.

Once the echo subsided both of the notes and her voice, Erik removed his cloak and gloves and laid them neatly over a chair, arrogantly ignoring the formidable opponent in his living room. He came in close to her.

"I have nothing to say to you, Mademoiselle. I refuse to explain myself so you might as well leave."

"You refuse to explain yourself?"

"You are the one who said you had no fear of the past—mine or yours, so this conversation is over." Erik bent low, paying more attention to the insult to his organ bench than to Anna. He dusted it with this hand before trying to right it.

"It's not over! You lied!" Anna reeled her fist backward.

At an angle to get in a good jab, she aimed for his face. Erik barely saw the fist flying toward his leather-encased cheek. Off balance to begin with, he turned his head to a punch coming at him with surprising speed. Cursing as he scrambled upright, he blocked the fist shooting out at him. The room flashed crimson before his eyes. The noise of his madness roared in his mind and, adrenaline coursing; he instinctually defended himself, bending her wrist back with one fluid snap of his hand. The sickening crunch of her bone rippled his fingers.

Anna dropped under the pain, the sound of her knees hitting stone only slightly less heartbreaking than seeing her lips open, a cry of anguish locked in her throat.

Horrified, he released her fist like dropping a handful of fire. Erik stumbled backward dazed then sickened as Anna slowly hid her head in her knees. The move seemed far too habitual. Sobs racked her body so hard that *his* hands shook.

"*Mon Dieu.*" He dropped to the floor beside her, the consequences of his ungoverned anger ripening before him. "Anna, look at me."

She did, cradling her wrist as her eyes glistened with tears. "Was… was that the Phantom?"

His cry of remorse choked him and all he could do was gasp for a breath. Her question pierced the armor around his heart.

Erik rolled off his knees and sat before her, blanketing his face with this hands. "No, Mademoiselle, no! Forgive me. Please forgive me. I am not that man." He blanketed her face with his hands. "I did not want you to know. Not this way."

He parted his trembling fingers enough to see the tears drip off her chin.

"I don't ca… care about that man, Erik. Who… who am I to ju…judge you or anyone by their past?"

Erik leaned away. The burden of her tears too heavy for him to bear.

"I know the man *now*. I accepted *him*. Why did you lie to me?"

The piercing look she gave him wracked him with guilt. He stood and circled her frantically as he tried to compose himself. There was no escaping the guilt, no escaping the madness rising in soul. Noise and music were clashing in his mind making his skull pound. From every corner the madness attacked him; the only sound worse were the tears of the woman at his feet.

"To protect you from this!" A great cry of grief escaped his lips as he shoved a finger at his face. Falling, to his knees he crawled toward her. "What did she tell you, Anna? Did she tell you I am made up of Death? That my wretched mother would not allow me to kiss or touch her? That my father never saw me, and my mother made me the present of my first mask so not to look on me? Did she tell you my cursed ugliness has condemned me to wallow in madness?" He clutched his face. "Every waking minute I exist, I fight him…The Phantom."

That word sliced through him sending a blinding pain through his brain. To dig the noise out of his mind with his bare hands! The madness of the Phantom starved him of his sanity. It came out of him in rounds of wild, agonizing laughter. Anna started at the maniacal sound.

"I try!" He wailed over the hum in his mind. "Oh yes, I try to be like other men! All I want is to be a normal man. When I did try to have what other men have, I was rejected. I was condemned. I was forgotten!" Growling, he shook his head, trying to dislodge the rising racket. "I could have hurt an unheard of number of the human race when Christine refused me."

Erik's breath left his lungs, leaving him contorting into his remorse. The sickened look upon Anna's face only deepened his agony.

"You are surprised Erik could have a woman? I did, you know—Christine Daaé belonged to me." Taking a hold of the pinky of his left hand, he caressed the small gold band that circled it. "She was to be my bride. She once wore my ring. But no! *She* lied!"

Laughter tore from his lips. It was a whisper compared to the acidic sounds in his mind.

"A simple request, you see. All she had to do was accept my proposal, and I would not blow a quarter of Paris sky high. I would not kill that blasted vicomte lover of hers. Are you looking at me, Mademoiselle? Are you looking? Consent to be wed and no one would be dead."

"You… you would be wed?"

"Wed or dead!"

Anna jerked backward as Erik leaned into her. He teetered in his spot, overcome with dementia. Giving into the mania would provide a blissful relief, but he knew that soon after would come the darkness that led him down dangerous paths. The temptation though! The temptation was insane and powerful. It had every nerve in his body on high alert. "Do you have any idea how close my madness came to destroying an ungodly number of people?"

When she didn't respond, Erik came eerily in command of all his senses.

"You grow pale? Why? I could have made all of Paris hop like a grasshopper by lighting the powder kegs stored beneath this opera house. Remnants of the war, you know. But I did not. I did not hurt any more people. I *wanted* her to marry that boy. I *wanted* her to be happy… in the end. But such noble intentions do not matter in a life such as mine. I am plunged into an abyss of loathsome hatred when all I want is to love and taste life like a normal man."

He clawed at the sounds scratching in his brain. "Madness, Mademoiselle, madness—in here—condemns me to Don Giovanni's fate. Yet unlike he, I repent, yes, Erik can repent. But I am still sentenced to burn in Hades. Is that warranted? Can my desires make me like anybody? Does that make me normal?"

He searched the cooling blue depths of Anna's eyes for some sign he wasn't completely insane.

"Can a man like me ever be normal? Behind this…" Erik gestured to his face. "…there is no beauty."

Silence closed around him like a lid on a coffin.

Anna struggled to her feet, no easy task with one arm cradled against her stomach. She leaned sideways, gripping her wrist and curling into the pain he'd caused. Erik winced as shame folded him in two.

"Normal? N...no you can't be normal! You wear a mask!" Anna shook as her eyes darted across it. "That aside, do normal men carry their height as well as you? Do normal men move with such authority? Do normal men have your indescribably beautiful voice? Do you even *know* your pure and utter genius?"

"What does all that matter? Madame Giry told you what lies beneath the mask. I can see it in your eyes. You had to search for those words."

The raw intensity of her gaze made him pray to retain his one small scrap of self-esteem. His gut seized as he stared at her, fear of what she may ask of him running his throat dry. Erik buried his face in the crook of his arm.

"Please," he said in quiet agony, "do not rape my dignity. Do not ask me to remove it."

"The mask doesn't make the man, Erik. You're not sentenced to be the Phantom because of it."

With two sentences his shoulders lifted of a burden worthy of Atlas. He remained caged by his arm as his breath left his lungs. The sigh only warmed his flesh momentarily before the cold sensation returned to his skin.

"Erik and The Phantom...are they not bonded, one and the same?" He stared at his warped reflection in the organ pipes.

"Madame Giry mentioned the investigations closed long ago. The authorities were unable to prove any man existed. You're the one chasing a Phantom."

"Am I? Tell me then, why does she fear this ghost so deeply if his life is nothing more than myth?"

"Because she's known no other man. You're angry, Erik, and anger is unresolved pain. Madame Giry and I are two very different people."

His lids lowered. "I have been battling the monster and the man for too long. I cannot keep up with their duet."

"Then choose one to be and play it out."

He looked back at her for a long moment before turning away. The way she cradled her hand, only reminded him of how hard that would be. "And the others who know? Are you so sure they will ignore the past and accept it as you do? My crimes cannot be denied."

"Christine?"

The memories and rejection associated with that name

weighed heavy on his shoulders and tied knots in his stomach. He nodded, sadly. "Christine Daaé, Anna. The Vicomtess de Chagny."

The name tasted bitter. Not wanting to continue, he carried the bench back to the organ and sat. Erik stared sadly at the worn manuals and the dull stops, testimony to many nights pounding out his loneliness through music. Anna followed and sat beside him. Her body heat hovered over the organ, cloaking it with warmth. Erik lightly touched a key. It was cold beneath his fingers.

"Do you still love her?" she asked.

"No." His voice lifted in pitch, betraying him.

"I'm your friend, Erik. Don't lie to me."

He chose not to answer. Silence settled between them before he hesitantly reached to take her hand. Anna winced and he pulled away. Never hearing a drop of music again, would be better than bearing the agony of what he'd done.

"Forgive me, Anna."

"You didn't mean it. It's just a wrist. I've endured worse."

She tried to be brave, and it was his fault. Erik reached for her again, grimacing when Anna bit her lip. "Oh, Anna," he grieved, "I broke it."

"I'm aware." Anna sniffed away her tears, scrubbing her nose with her opposite wrist.

He would have to hurt her further in order to splint and set the bone. He cursed the demon inside of him. Erik lowered his head and squeezed his eyes shut. The injury could have been much worse than a broken wrist.

His thoughts were wrenched back to the present when a strange pair of hands cupped his chin. Flying his lids open, panic ripped across him until the unexpected warm from Anna's touch warmed his entire face.

"Will I play again, Monsieur?" A glint appeared behind the pain in her eyes.

His breath leapt from his mouth. Despite his anguish he chanced a smile.

"Anna," he gently insulted, "you are a terrible violinist."

FIVE

The brougham clipped along at a steady pace, the horses' hooves drumming a cheerful rhythm matching Raoul's mood.

On many levels it was good to be back in France. Native soil beckoned to a noble son. The vicomte shook his head, scolding himself for leaving. Though he enjoyed the simpler delights of his Norwegian estate, a nobleman's place was with his fatherland. Staring at the invitation in his hand he pondered if it had become habitual of him to stay away.

They didn't have much to do with the city he'd adored as a boy. He hid his regret from his wife by rubbing a finger across his small, blond moustache. Christine had stopped performing for the Garnier after her abduction by the Phantom of the Opera four years prior. Whisking her away from all her troubles, Raoul divided their time between their stately home in Norway and their estate in France. Judging by Christine's pout, he could tell she wished they hadn't cut their northern visit so short.

Chuckling under his breath, he dismissed the thought.

He admired the lean muscle of the champion stallion trotting alongside his brougham. What jealous rumblings would spring from the lips of his peers when he partook in a hunt astride that beast! The mounted groom gave a tip of his hat, seeking approval to break from the caravan and ride on to the opera stables. Raoul granted it with a wave of his hand.

He stopped studying his horse to look to the building beyond.

His mood faded. As the brougham whisked past the theater, he could have sworn people stopped and pointed at the crest adorning his carriage. He hoped it was his imagination.

Raoul Jean-Paul Marie, Vicomte de Chagny stared out the window toward the Acadèmie Nationale, still as majestic as when he'd left it as a stoic keeper of many secrets.

He glanced at his pocket watch. Nine o'clock. They would have plenty of time to relax at the hôtel de Chagny in the faubourg Saint-Germain before their afternoon meeting with the managers.

Tucking his watch away, the exquisite woman seated across from him caught his attention. Even the sun would dim in jealousy over Christine's beauty. Her eyes usually sparkled like the sapphires encircling her neck, but now seemed dull. Raoul enjoyed the rolling hint of Swedish still present in her French, but all he heard now was the occasional sniffle.

Raoul reached for her. His fingers slid effortlessly through golden waves of hair and cascaded over his knuckles. He rotated his fingers for a second pass, enjoying the cool silk of her tresses against his flesh.

"I know what you're thinking. It was a foolish idea to come." He settled back in his seat.

It took some time for her to pull her regard away from the carriage window. "Don't be ridiculous. This was our home."

"Then why the tears?" Raoul indicated the kerchief she drew from her sleeve.

"I'm happy." The short flip of her shoulder spoke otherwise and he made note of it with a quirked brow. "Very well…it's nerves, but nothing more. I assure you."

"You've nothing to be nervous about. If you're thinking of *him* you needn't. He's dead. The Phantom is nothing more than a closed chapter in your life."

"I can't help but think of him."

The way her voice cracked set his jaw.

"My life has moved on, Raoul, to a blessed one, but I can't help but wonder about Erik and dwell on the past. It's only been four years but…sometimes it seems like yesterday."

Raoul's nostrils flared at how casually Christine mentioned that demon's name. "He was a madman, Christine. You shouldn't connect your life with his." He shifted, forcing a smile. "You needn't trouble yourself with these concerns. Didn't I promise to keep you safe? Give you the world and more?" When she nodded his grin broadened. "We can return to Norway this Fall, sooner should you wish."

"Chagny is your home, Raoul. We should remain here. The viscounties need your attention."

Reaching across the carriage, he stroked his fingers against the back of her palm. He admired her strength and devotion to his duties. "My brother will return from Spain soon enough. We've no need to rush to Chagny." She opened her mouth to protest, but a well-practiced raise of his brow felled her silent. "Let's enjoy the reason we were asked to return to the Garnier." He raised the letter in his hand. "Promise you will tell me if you ever feel uncomfortable doing this?"

He relaxed when Christine reached for his hand and gave it a little squeeze.

"Yes, I promise."

⇥ •————— ••• —————•• ⇤

"People are stupid."

"Good morning to you too, Edward." Jacob Wischard entered the office sensing already by his partner's quip and the glass of scotch in his hand that he should take cover. It was far too early in the bloody morning for this. He shoved the door closed behind him with his foot.

Edward Laroque lifted his glass in a toast, laughing aloud at some good fortune. Jacob groaned. Edward considered himself quite brilliant in comparison to the rest of the human race. A view not shared by Jacob. Far be it for him to voice an opinion to the contrary.

"You're in an uncommonly chipper mood," he rumbled.

Edward's laugh shook the walls.

Jacob removed his hat and shrugged off the waistcoat swallowing his frame. Laying his outerwear across his desk and tossing his walking stick aside, he took a seat on the desk's corner and poured himself a drink. He, like Edward, paid no mind to time of day when a fresh carafe of scotch was present. Jacob scrutinized the devilish gleam to Edward's eyes and the rosy color to the tip of his nose. When his partner was this gleeful it usually meant he had something up his sleeve.

"To what do I owe this occasion?" he interrogated.

Edward clapped once and rubbed his hands. "Because, my dear friend, we're about to become extraordinarily wealthy."

"We're already extraordinarily wealthy."

Edward leaned across the desk to clink his glass in cheers. Jacob winced against his laughter.

"What is it this time, Edward? You haven't cut the company's salary again have you? If you have there will be mutiny on our hands."

For years they'd been milking the opera. They were masters at skimming the books and stealing money with bogus reasons for cutting the staff's salary. They overcharged patrons, underpaid players, and no one was the wiser. Three years ago they'd stumbled upon a starving opera and saw a gold mine.

"You underestimate me, Jacob." He reached into a drawer and threw an old playbill across the desk.

Jacob held it at arm's length. He was blind without his reading glasses. "Gounod's *Faust*. What's this?"

"Our ticket to greatness."

Jacob tossed the playbill aside. "It's *Faust*. That's hardly a ticket to greatness." Before Edward exploded with delight, Jacob conceded defeat. "Will you get to the point? I've a pressing engagement with a rather attractive chorus girl."

Edward rose and strutted like a peacock. "Do you know who performed that opera?"

Jacob scanned the program. "Margarita was Christine Daaé. So?"

"So? So?" Edward croaked, scotch flying from his mouth "Do you know who Christine Daaé is?"

Spreading his hands, Jacob stressed his annoyance.

"Christine Daaé is now the Vicomtess de Chagny! Really, Jacob, you need to get your head out of your ass sometimes."

"Ah. Chagny, the former patron?"

"*Oui!*" The floorboards groaned in pain as Edward's bulky frame skipped excitedly.

"So?" Jacob yanked on his watch fob. This was already taking too much of his time.

"Forget about your tryst. Today we plan the con of a lifetime."

Edward's enthusiasm was contagious and Jacob's curiosity grew. He traced the rim of his glass with one finger.

"Go on," he encouraged.

"Picture this: *Faust* the original opera which brought down this opera house was sung by Christine Daaé. Now, who better to return in honor of this opera's upcoming anniversary than the diva herself? She left Paris shortly after the performance ended, fleeing from a Phantom of the Opera."

Jacob's brows rushed up then down as Edward waved his hands around, moaning like a ghost. "A what?"

"He's some sort of legend that was never fully explained. If you would spend more time reading and less time shagging you would know this. This Phantom apparently stole her off the stage before a theater full of people on the night she was to elope with the Vicomte de Chagny. It was a scandal Paris spoke of for years. If you ask me, the woman was slightly insane." Edward shook his glass in emphasis, making scotch splash over the rim.

"Edward, I think *you* are slightly ill in the head."

"She had all of Paris searching for some horrifically deformed demon, a man legend says was nothing short of Satan himself. Now… people love a good mystery and gossip," Edward touched his glass with Jacob's again, "brings in patrons. Patrons bring in money and…"

Jacob's hollow cheeks grew in bulk with his smile. "And we pad our pockets. Brilliant Edward! You are the master. One small problem. You may have the Diva, but there's no Phantom of the Opera."

"Don't be so simple minded. It's a minor detail. We'll find out what the legend holds and rebuild it."

"Re-create a man who never existed and a scandal between a nobleman and his wife?" He slurped the scotch. "Edward, you're insane. What makes you so sure anyone will play into the notion this Phantom ever existed?"

"Something clearly went on at this opera house. Something made them all run. Murders happened."

Jacob spit his drink into his glass and rubbed the scotch off his vest. "Murders?"

"A chandelier crashed killing the concierge. An investigation was launched for Lord's-sake! The authorities crawled all over this theater for months. They found nothing, but the foundation was laid. People are afraid of ghosts and have morbid fascination with fear." Edward returned to his chair. It complained as loudly as the floorboards.

"What's the first step? *We* haunt the opera house?"

"No, for Christ's sake, don't be daft! I've a plan. Starting with that the vicomtess believes she's here for the anniversary celebration, which she legitimately is. We announce her surprise arrival during a masquerade ball—an event I specifically chose because of how it plays into the history of the Garnier. I figure gossip will do the rest. We merely sit back and watch the show."

"And exactly how did you manage to persuade her?"

"Didn't have to. I wrote to the Vicomte de Chagny inviting him here. His acceptance letter included something about revisiting old friends, love of the Paris Opera, putting to bed old wounds. Bah... I told him the opera had been suffering in the past years, and it deserved a moment of grandeur. Damn fool."

Jacob pushed off the desk, and reached for his outerwear. He first adjusted his hat, which fell close around his eyes then reached for his coat and stick. "Edward, you may not know a damn thing about opera, but when it comes to running a con, you're a genius."

"I know," he gloated, seeing Jacob out.

They paused in the doorway, leering at the girl who walked past. Anna shot them a look that had them dodging the daggers coming from her eyes.

Edward flashed a wet and toothy grin. "I learned from a master."

⧉•••————•••————••⧉

Figures below moved like puppets on a string Erik didn't control. Perched high above the stage, he nestled like a spider in the web of ropes and catwalks. He left the sanctuary of his cellar home, choosing instead to keep a silent presence in and around the empire he'd built. Content for the moment to only observe, he hadn't made his presence known. Breathing deeply, he filled himself with the earthy fiber of the ropes, the dusty folds of rolled scenery, and the alcohol lingering from the breath of fly men.

The dress rehearsal was in full swing. His opera had come alive in the last few weeks. A group of ballet students stood straight and proper before their teacher, leaning on her instruction and copying her every movement. Skinny legs wobbled under their costumes and their arms were sloppy. They were as coordinated as drunken foals. He glared at the Maîtresse du corps de ballet. She could do much better.

Bored with them, he pondered the orchestra. He shouldn't be too hard on the ballet mistress, for the ballet could only dance as well as the music commanded. The rats in his cellar sounded better than the musicians warming up. Not a single one had a sense of pitch. The orchestra's display was as terrible as well. Erik drummed his fingers against his cheek. He should introduce the concertmaster to the meaning of the word 'bow-mark'. He huffed. What good would that do? The concertmaster could only follow as well as he was led.

Crossing his arms and anchoring himself by his feet, he looked at the current Maestro. Fontane was practically tone deaf and had no concept that an audience not only watched the stage but the pit as well. As he studied the scurrying stagehands, he critiqued the chorus lining up. The opera had moved on and had done so poorly. Erik blamed the two blithering idiots wandering the stage directly below him—Edward Laroque and Jacob Wischard.

Everything about them was detestable. They gestured madly, quite like the drunken foals. Leaning out of his nest, he strained to listen to what had them so excited. The managers were buzzing about something, that much was certain.

"We'll spare no expense in this, Maestro Fontane. Your every focus must be on making this event a success."

The fat one strutted about the stage like an overly pompous stock dove.

Laroque and Wischard seemed pleased at how the opera leapt at their every command. The ballerina's appeared eager to impress. Stagehands hurried to organize scenery and the orchestra tuned their instruments loudly. Everyone seemed starved for the attention.

Almost everyone.

A satchel soared through the air and hit the floor between the managers with an ungraceful thump. It belched hundreds upon hundreds of envelopes at their feet. Anna strode toward them. She gestured to the sack.

"They're done. And I'll not do anything else. I'm not your slave."

Erik swallowed a laugh. She did have a little spirit of shrew in her. Perhaps his afternoon would not be dull after all. Erik twirled himself to a lower fly. She had not shown up in his labyrinth since that dreadful night when he hurt her. Her visits had waned over the last several weeks and now he knew why. Each time he thought of that night the burning warning of nausea coated his throat.

The unusual quiver in his stomach made him scowl, however. Did he actually miss her friendship? She was a curious toy to him, a tiny puzzle he had yet to figure out and one that made emotions stir in him that he thought he had dismissed long ago. He dared not seek her out for worry his emotions might cause him to become clumsy or—even worse—be seen. The managers had hijacked her, keeping her busy on whatever project they were so enthused about.

She is a slave indeed. Erik's fingers drummed against his cheek again. He pondered teaching them a lesson for interrupting the current status quo of his life. *That would be entertaining.*

He heard Wischard growl: "Have you no manners, girl?"

Erik bridled.

"Pardon, Monsieur," Anna said, with a roll of her eyes to the Maestro.

Edward Laroque gestured to the invitations overflowing at their feet. "They're doing us no good scattered here. Get them to the post."

"Get them there yourself," she spat.

"Don't test us, girl." Jacob warned.

Anna scrubbed her hands on her dress. She was itching for a fight, Erik could tell. Instead she capitulated and squatted to retrieve the invitations. Erik squinted as she slammed them into the satchel by the handfuls. In an instant he noted her un-splinted wrist and the ripple of pain on her face.

Blast you child!

Despite the time since their encounter, there was no way that wrist could have healed enough for her to remove his splint. A seething glare landed on the managers. He made her swear for the sake of her comfort to tend to *her* needs first, something Anna rarely did. He suspected her reluctance to wear it had something to do with the buffoons below him. Anna rarely spoke of them but when she did it was with a mix of hatred, and fear. It set his teeth on edge.

"See to it this one to the post as well." Laroque pulled a letter from his waistcoat and let it flutter to the ground.

Anna stared at the envelope then at the overweight slob leering at her.

"And I'll know if it doesn't get delivered. Jacob, shall we?"

He indicated his partner and stepped around her.

Anna spit on the envelope before shoving it in the bag. Slinging the satchel across her shoulder she stood, its weight pulling her to one side and into Jacob Wischard.

"Come now, Anna where's your pretty smile?" He stroked her cheek and leaned in for a kiss, but she turned away.

Wischard laughed.

Erik ignited.

He dared touched her! Outright murder would entertain him right then *and* teach that blithering idiot that Anna was his and his alone! If Erik watched any longer, he'd have had a lasso around that man's neck quicker than he could compose. He couldn't decipher why he was so possessive of Anna, he just was. Having seen enough, he left, determined to get her back one way or another.

Madame Giry stepped out of the way as Anna came off the stage and lumbered past her up the center aisle. She stared in pity at the girl as she made her way out of the theater. The satchel bowed her forward under its weight, slowing Anna's pace, but the girl's expression appeared heavier than the load over her shoulder.

"Madame Giry, a word please."

It wasn't the fact that the managers waved at her that made Madame Giry perplexed; it was the nagging sense something was about to change. She paused and shifted the stacks of playbills to her opposite arm, as they came from the stage to her side. Neither one of them paid Anna any mind any longer. Madame Giry sighed and tore her gaze off Anna's back to the managers. True, she had little contact with the girl but it seemed so wrong to her that she was worked to the bone like that.

"We beg your pardon for the interruption," the managers announced as they arrived, "but we have some rather exciting news we are certain you'd like to hear."

Madame Giry lifted a brow. Something was definitely afoot if they were paying special regard. She darted her gaze from the skinny manager to the portly one.

"Messieurs?"

"As you know, we're planning a much needed overhaul of this opera for its upcoming anniversary," Edward explained. "We're staging a grand masquerade, and we've put out a call for new composers to showcase their work during a fantastic concert series."

Madame Giry slowly nodded, her suspicion on the rise.

Knowing of the masquerade and concert series was unavoidable if you worked in the opera, so why were they seeking her out, a lowly box-keeper, to mention it directly to her? Something wasn't right…

"We'll need you to be involved," Jacob added.

"Involved, Monsieur?" She looked behind her toward the box to which Edward gestured.

"You're aware whose box that was?"

"Is," she corrected, puffing out her chest. "That box belongs to Chagny. I make sure it is kept in tip-top order."

"We've taken the liberty to make this a truly splendid event by inviting a certain… diva to attend." Edward leaned in toward her, drawing out the word diva.

She drew back not liking the sound of this at all. "Diva?"

"The Vicomtess de Chagny. I've been informed you know her personally."

She worked to keep her hands steady. Madame Giry brushed hair from her face and straightened her tiny hat. That news was nothing for her to be worried about…so they invited Christine Daaé. Nothing to worry about at all…

She fought the tightness in the throat to speak again. "I don't know her personally, monsieur, but, yes, I am acquainted."

"Excellent," Edward cheered. "She and the vicomte will be here shortly. I trust you'll see to their comfort. Now please don't let us keep you from your duties."

Madame Giry shot a glance over the managers' shoulder to the Chagny box and the equally empty Box Five on the grand tier. Before she could utter a protest, the two headed off stage.

Every nerve prickled in her body at the thought of the vicomte and his wife arriving in the opera house. If she didn't sit she would swoon. The vicomte and vicomtess had no idea of Erik's location. All assumed he'd died. None knew of her continued servitude to him. She brushed a hand across her forehead and fanned the rising heat on her face. She'd already seen Erik begin to lure another into his lair. If he discovered Christine Daaé was returning… The thought made a trickle of sweat slide down her neck.

Madame Giry turned in her spot, senseless whimpers eking out her mouth. Gulping down her panic, she made a choice. If the past had to be confronted, then she would warn them. She would only keep Erik's secret until then.

The box keeper's chest tightened as she turned in time to see

Anna disappear through the far door at the end of the theater. History was repeating itself in the girl and Erik, but this time something was different, and she feared there was little time to find out what. Bit by bit, Madame Giry's neck pulled back like being tugged by the invisible string of a marionette. She searched the catwalks for Erik. They swayed above her.

Six

Madame Giry shuffled around her tiny office. A raging headache cinched her temples and she cleaned in a frantic effort to distract herself. She picked up a program here, stacked it there, and moved a pile of opera glasses from one side of the room to the other. Nothing relieved the pounding. Her chin sagged against her chest when a knock at the door mocked her headache. With her hand on the doorknob, she thought seriously on the benefits of retirement before twisting it open.

"Good day, Madame Giry!"

"Monsieur le Vicomte!" She curtseyed so quickly she felt the feathers in her hat flutter.

He bowed slightly, stepping aside to allow the woman with him to enter first. His smile was genuine, the kind that shone first from the eyes then from the lips. He entered after her, removing his hat and gloves and setting them aside.

"I've known you since I was a little boy and still you're so formal with me."

Her cheeks heated and she hoped her blush wasn't too obvious. He smiled and indicated his wife.

"Mademoiselle," Madame Giry erased her mistake by waving her hands, "Forgive me, I mean vicomtess. Welcome back."

She smiled as Christine's face reddened. Clearly such a title still took her by surprise.

"It's good to be back and to see you are still an institution at this opera," she replied.

Ushering them to sit, Madame Giry began busying herself with a pot of tea.

"Are you well, Madame?" Vicomte de Chagny asked.

She studied herself in the polish of the teakettle. There were lines around her eyes and a droop to one side of her mouth. Erik had aged her. "I'm fine, fine. Everything is fine. Your box especially."

"The opera is bustling with energy," the vicomtess observed.

Madame Giry set the tea tray on the table between them. "A good deal of work is going into this opera house."

"No doubt," he agreed. "We were eager to be a part of the upcoming celebrations."

"Eager, Monsieur le Vicomte?" She handed the vicomtess a teacup and addressed him but kept her attention on her. Christine Daaé was still as lovely as ever. Secretly the box keeper prayed Erik would not notice a thing about her...about any of this.

"Quite eager. Messieurs Laroque and Wischard mentioned the opera's financial difficulty. We had to come to do what we could. We know how much this place means to Paris, you, and the effort you have put into it over the—"

"Raoul, please." The vicomtess tensed even though she smiled Madame Giry's way. Unlike her husband, it didn't shine from behind the eyes. "We came to see you and the friends we have here, not out of concern for his opera."

Madame Giry stopped fussing as the air in the room stilled.

His opera?

The past hung like a lead curtain threatening to crash down, silencing each of them.

Electing to ignore the comment, Madame Giry held her apprehension behind carefully chosen words. "The opera's been quiet, I assure you. Your concerns are unfounded."

Erik had been too quiet. She'd never known him to be so resigned. Comfort was found in the familiar and change was a frightening force. Erik was changing in ways unknown to her. If she had any grace toward him, she would have accepted the differences she saw in Erik, but fear made her set grace aside. It was a hard pill of guilt she swallowed. In all the years of ministering to his whims and genius while cowering before his madness and authority, she'd barely known the man. Comprehending growth in a man such as

Erik seemed impossible, but Madame Giry couldn't ignore the truth.

Guilt was a powerful emotion and history threatened to repeat itself. With the vicomtess here, guilt made the old woman wish she'd never been a part of the past.

Anna rubbed at her eye with the back of one hand as she dragged herself through the halls. It was taking all her effort to keep her eyelids open, let alone keep her balance. Anna stumbled into another chorus member. If she did that one more time she might as well fall down. She mumbled a half-felt apology.

Laroque and Wischard had been particularly demanding, and she'd grown weary of the Opera Garnier—in mind and body. Many times she thought of leaving, flee from the debt her father owed, but she couldn't bring herself to do it. The memories of her father's threats if she ever disobeyed himhis soaked her sheets in sweat nightly.

"Watch it," a stagehand warned, rumbling past with a cart bogged down with decorations.

Anna waved him off indifferently. All was being readied for the masquerade. The invitations were written and now delivered thanks to her aching hands and neck. With that monumental task behind her, Anna hoped to find a little respite in the secrecy of the cellars. She scoffed. Who was she kidding? Whatever scheme Laroque and Wischard were planning didn't involve pause for her. Apathetically moving through the hallways, standing clear of passing dancers and demanding divas, Anna wished she could simply disappear from this life and wake, totally in another. One that didn't involve her entire messed up life.

A troupe of young ballerinas pranced by prompting Anna to give them an exhausted, contemptuous glare. She'd give anything for their boundless energy. Resigned that such was not her course, Anna stepped out of their way and directly into the hand that snaked from behind her. Her scream caught in her throat.

More artfully than a ballerina, Anna was pirouetted clear of the hall and tumbled into an empty classroom. The door shut with an ear-splitting bang and the momentum of spinning out of her captor's grasp kept her stumbling forward. A surge of adrenaline forced her every nerve on high alert, her body wide-awake, as she whirled around to stare at the man reflected on the mirrored wall.

"Holy Mother of God!" Anna tore the satchel from her shoulders and heaved it at her assailant. "You scared me half to death!"

Erik wasn't quite fast enough to miss its collision. It smacked against his chest and tumbled to the floor. He gestured to himself, head to toe. "Forgive me, Mademoiselle, Death is to seduce a maiden. I did not mean to frighten."

Too late, she thought. Anna breathed deeply, trying to slow her pounding heart. Somewhere in the last few seconds it had nearly burst out of her chest. His humor was often macabre, seldom arrogant. "Then change your tactic." Wincing, Anna grabbed her wrist with her opposite hand. Throwing the satchel was not the wisest idea.

He sheepishly approached. "Are you all right? Erik did not hurt you again—did he?"

"No, I'm fine."

"That should still be treated." He reached for her hand. "Why have you undone my splint?"

"How would I explain it? I've no funds for something like that. If the managers saw me with an injury, any injury *tended* that is, it would arouse suspicions. They'd think I was skimming the books." A wave of her wrist insisted he put his concern and remorse aside. A newly healed wrist was merely an annoyance to her. The slump to his shoulders hurt her more. "I'm fine, Erik. Let it go. What are you doing here?"

He shrugged like a bored child. "Looking for you."

"Well, I'm found." She regarded him as he paced. He tilted his head back in an innocent study of the ceiling. She glanced at their reflection in a mirror and smiled. They were an odd couple, but Anna liked being accepted by a gentleman such as Erik. He didn't mind her history.

"Wischard touched you."

Her breath hitched. Obviously, he'd watched that display on stage. Anna had yet to find a time when she was in the mood to deal with Erik's possessive streak. He'd become fiercely defensive of her honor like some sort of demented round table knight, sheltering her from leering eyes on her rounds, or crossly questioning bums if they were brazen enough to ask for her attention. *Here we go again.* She was too tired to deal with Erik's over-protective streak.

"Wischard always touches me. Do we have to discuss this again?"

"Killing that lying gambler would be so easy." Erik plucked the bag from the floor and rummaged through it. He spun out of Anna's reach when she snatched for it.

An overlooked envelope rewarded his meddling. Anna wagged her fingers impatiently insisting he hand it over.

"No. I am not about to be challenged on my sources of entertainment, Anna. I am curious to see what is so precious to my managers that you have to remain indisposed and away from my cellars." Erik ripped open the envelope. *"La Fête d'Anniversaire pour l'Opera Garnier?"*

Anna inched her way toward the door knowing enough of Erik's twitches to get out of the line of fire. He covered the length of the rehearsal room with a few strides as he read on; pivoting sharply on his heel each time he reached the end of the room. The mirror mocked his fury.

"If you do not wish your neck to meet the end of silk rope, I suggest you speak!"

Anna crossed her arms, waiting out his fury. Erik yelled, driving each word into her like a nail: a masquerade ball, an open call for composers and a final concert to showcase the world's finest Maestros. She clicked her tongue waiting on his tirade to end, but inwardly she cringed. She knew she should have told him.

"I was going to tell you weeks ago when I had the chance, but you've been getting difficult to find and the managers kept me busy," she shrugged.

He crumpled the invitation tightly in his hand. "Some of the finest music in the world will be played under the acoustics of *my* roof, and I can have no hand in the composition."

"You're still very much a part of this opera house."

Erik stared at the paper in his fist and laughed bitterly.

"This theater wouldn't exist without you," Anna encouraged.

"Nor would it have fallen," he snapped back.

"You can still partake."

"No. I will have no part in this."

"You might as well because you... ah.... already do."

His lip twitched. Erik stared at her sideways. "What did you do, child?"

Anna shrugged, absently biting her thumbnail as she peered at him. "The violin concerto. I submitted it."

Erik's squinted, her confession stuck in an awkward spot in his ear. Taking advantage of the alarming difference in their heights, he hunched over her, forcing her to splutter quickly in her defense.

"Some of the finest composers in the world will be here, Erik! Your music deserves to be heard."

Anna swore somewhere a mountain leveled when Erik roared: *"You went through my music?"*

"Um. Yes?" The concerto, only second to his magnum opus opera, *Don Juan Triumphant,* was the accumulation of years of his work. It sang of his love of beauty, his heartbreak, shame, anger and his revelations on love.

"You meddling, infuriating little minx!" Erik yelled, making Anna flinch "You had no right!"

"I know."

"There are times, child, when you are chipping away at your own epitaph!"

Anna swallowed a smug smile and ignored his sarcastic wrath.

His tone changed. "Anna, there is no musician in this world with the talent capable of giving voice to that concerto but me."

She sauntered around him much like a rat catcher proudly parading his tailed minions. She placed her hands on his forearms and balanced so to get close to his ear. Anna ignored the tension in his arm as he jerked, a fraction, away.

Standing on the tips of her toes she whispered mischievously, "I know."

Before Erik could utter a word more, she snatched her satchel and scampered out the door suddenly filled with the energy of a troupe of ballerinas.

⋆⋅•──••─••⋅⋆

Madame Giry spent the better half of her time trying to convince the vicomte and his wife their concerns were unfounded. After all, she'd almost convinced herself. She toured them through the theater reliving the better days, speaking of changes and introducing them to eager and star-struck young pupils.

Weary, she was glad to see them safely off. The quiet isolation of the concierge office beckoned and she locked the door with a relieved click.

Her peace was short-lived.

In total exasperation, her head fell forward, knocking against the wood with a light thud. She didn't have to turn to know he was there. His presence filled the dark space, the air around her icy.

"Monsieur," she moaned into the woodwork, turning to lean against the door for support. "I've nothing for you. Why do you keep pressing me?"

"Madame, what do you know of this?" Erik tossed the crumpled invitation on her cluttered desk.

Looking at the ceiling through the feathers hanging over her hat, Madame Giry was utterly trapped, caught between the owners and Erik. She sighed in resignation. She always would be. "There's to be a masquerade and concert to benefit the opera's anniversary. Surely, you were aware this day would come."

"To whom were they sent?"

"The affluent, anyone who could pull this opera out of its disrepair. The managers are doing what they can to save this opera house, though it will never have the respect it once had. But they're at least trying, which is more than I can say about you." The confession popped out her mouth so fast, for a moment she was not sure it was out loud. Madame Giry quickly held her tongue.

"Those are the patrons," Erik snapped. "What of the players?"

"There was an open call for composers. Our diva and the opera company will perform what music the Maestro deems appropriate."

"Our diva and the opera company," Erik echoed. "What pitiful choices for redemption. Only I could restore grandeur to this house."

The underlying tone of remorse in his voice rubbed against her like sandpaper. She hadn't expected it. "The management assures us they have a way of filling the theater, Monsieur."

"And what way is that?"

"I've no idea." Not a complete fib… She rubbed her upper arms and shrunk from the chill wrapping around her.

"What is it you are so afraid of, Madame Giry?"

She pulled her arms tighter around herself and studied the floor. So abrupt was his question, it struck her dumb. She could choose to confront him about Christine Daaé, tell him she'd returned and urge Erik not to pursue her again, or, she could remain a victim to the entire farce all over again. Minutes dragged before she had the presence to speak. Their moment of confrontation was at its apex.

A considerable look of challenge unfolded in his eyes. "Madame Giry, *what* are you so concerned of?"

She glanced at the invitation with weary resignation, met his stare. "Did you go looking for..." Christine Daaé's name caught in her throat and no matter how she tried she couldn't push it past her lips. "...her?"

"Of course."

She couldn't understand why he shrugged so casually. "Why are you doing this?"

"I had my reasons."

She didn't trust his frankness. Erik retrieved the invitation and slid uncomfortably close to her, unlocking the door as he did. He momentarily caged her against it. Her breathing shallow, she moved enough to avoid his yellow stare. His whisper tickled her ear as warm breath touched her cheek.

"Your fear is groundless, Madame Giry; however, not without reason. I admit that. I will no more harm her than I would you."

Madame Giry chanced a sideways look at him, her lungs tight with her breath. The door slipped open and he moved like a liquid shadow, bleeding into the walls of his opera house and out of sight.

The breath rushed out of her lungs, as the pressure of holding lifted from her chest. Erik was trying to find Christine Daaé again! Folding her hands in prayer, she begged to God to understand Erik's motives and sought strength to act when it was her moment to take charge.

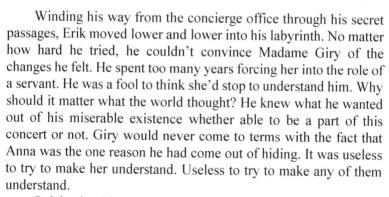

Winding his way from the concierge office through his secret passages, Erik moved lower and lower into his labyrinth. No matter how hard he tried, he couldn't convince Madame Giry of the changes he felt. He spent too many years forcing her into the role of a servant. He was a fool to think she'd stop to understand him. Why should it matter what the world thought? He knew what he wanted out of his miserable existence whether able to be a part of this concert or not. Giry would never come to terms with the fact that Anna was the one reason he had come out of hiding. It was useless to try to make her understand. Useless to try to make any of them understand.

Quickening his pace, a new and exciting emotion blossomed untamed to tear through the veil covering his existence. One person understood and one person was all he needed. With her, he could be a monster or Phantom. Erik could live with his madness and his genius and be accepted. It sent a white-hot energy through him. He knew what he had to face. Although it terrified him, it was such a welcomed emotion for what he viewed himself to be—a man.

No longer would he be ruled by an opera house and imprisoned by his fears. He'd navigated the hottest parts of hell and Anna had doused the flames.

SEVEN

Ghosts and ghouls, clowns and fools were all in equal standing tonight.

The masquerade took control of the Escalier of the Académie Nationale, filling it with fantastic costumes. Anna stood politely away from the center floor, so as not to interfere with the merriment of the invited guests. Clueless as she found the managers to be, it surprised her that they pulled something like this off. What amazed her even more was that she was permitted to attend. The invitation extended to her last minute came as quite a shock. A rare token of gratitude on their behalf...

Spinning in an awe-struck circle, she delighted in the costumes and the air of make-believe. One lady walked past and Anna couldn't resist reaching out to caress the silk of her gown, though she snatched her hand back before she was caught. The scratchy wool of her skirts might as well have been made of lead for all they flowed. She stood out like a weed among the garden of fancy ball gowns.

The gowns, however, paled in comparison to the elaborate costumes of the more daring guests. Anna was proud, at least, that she'd managed to make her own mask for the occasion. Swiping scraps from the costume department and borrowing a few from Madame Giry, Anna smoothed the feathers around her eyes. She had likened her face to that of a lark.

She stumbled to the side as a troupe of ballet students crowded in next to her. The girls giggled and flirted with the throngs of handsome single patrons. Anna self-consciously straightened her dress and mimicked their movements. She batted her lashes, glanced coyly over her shoulder, and laughed.

Tucking a stray strand behind her ear, she tossed her hair. Rarely did she wear it unbraided, but, fancying it her finest attribute, she did this evening. Perhaps it would turn a head. *Ridiculous notions again, Anna.* Her pathological inner-critic was notorious for making her out to be a fool. Her stomach knotted with disappointment when the last girl was whisked onto the dance floor.

She shook the gentlemen's dismissals off with a toss of her shoulders. No matter. She found herself moving to the music anyway. How could someone not get caught up in a masquerade? One particular couple caught her attention. They were a perfect match of grace and elegance. A flare of jealousy sparked inside of her.

The woman's face had the flawlessness of ivory dusted with rose powder, her eyes brighter than sun on an ocean. Anna's lips pursed into a small bow as she craned her neck to watch the gown sparkle as the woman twirled. Anna touched her own hair, taking a clump of the roughened edges into her hand while admiring the smooth blonde tresses waving behind the dancing woman. Twisting a lock between her fingers, she admired the lady's partner. Strong and tall, yet somehow gently effeminate, he seemed a handsome balance between man and gentleman. She swallowed a sigh, acknowledging she wouldn't mind taking a turn around the floor with him.

Watching them with a dreamy smile, she stayed neatly tucked away like an afterthought as the whirlpool of guests enjoyed the festivities around her.

The music swirled through the air, the lively beat matching the spinning colors of the ball gowns and the gay expressions on the faces of the dancers.

From a dark corner, Erik watched so intensely he blinked away the spasms in his eyes. Shadows dressed his shoulders in a cloak of black. He hadn't bothered to find a mirror to check his costume. Mirrors were implements of pleasure for the vain, instruments of pain for the ugly. He didn't take kindly to gazing upon himself. He endured enough knowing what he was. Seeing himself reflected in all his repugnant glory was to stab his eyes with the well-worn poniard of suffering.

He hadn't been out in a public spectacle such as this since the Bal Masque before Shrovetide some years ago. This time it was different. He didn't attend this affair to stalk sniveling little vicomtes like he had back then. His lips curled into a snarl. How dare that boy trespass upon his kingdom and steal the woman he loved.

A deep breath governed his emotions. The Vicomte de Chagny was out of his life as was Christine Daaé. Erik didn't don his costume and venture out in public to reclaim the past.

He lurked in the background, watching the upper crust of society flit about the Escalier. Everyone in Paris put on a mask of some sort it seemed. How many of these players were here to flaunt on stage and how many were genuine in their intent to be a part of the production?

A couple raced into his dark corridor. The youths fell together, hands and lips groping for any possible reward of flesh, forcing Erik out of his comfort zone. The voyeur in him took control. He studied the sway of their bodies as they pressed against their kiss. Watched their hands roam in exploration of each other. Did they really understand love and pleasure or were they caught in the air of drink and merriment?

He tore his gaze from them to scrutinize the ball. He came to this affair to understand exactly what love and pleasure could be. With a devilish smile toward the couple in the throes of passion, he stepped out of the shadows and joined the crowds.

The music changed and a new dance began. Some couples left the floor while others quickly took their place. Not a moment of color or joy was lost in the shift.

The tune sent images of secret rendezvous and heated embraces racing through Anna's mind. Staying far from the floor, knowing the wallflower she was, Anna swayed with the music's seduction. A ripple traced across her lower back and her scalp tickled when a breeze caressed her hair. An arm slowly encircled her waist making her stomach turn ice cold. Anna's breath hitched as a long arm stretched across her shoulder. She clamped down on her teeth so hard, pain shot to her ears. *You knew it was too good to be true, Anna you dolt! Why did you come?* Bracing herself for what she thought would come next, she waited to be pushed into the shadows by Jacob Wischard.

"Shh," the sound shivered in her ear. The rich voice made that single tone remarkably pure and warm. Her mouth slipped open to a silken voice far different from Jacob's. Relief flashed through her.

"Erik?" she whispered.

His arm slid from around her waist, as Erik stepped in front of her. Anna muffled a shriek of delight. The short coat of scarlet and long cape slung over one shoulder only punctuated his extraordinary height. Silent stammers of disbelief mimicked her rapid blinks. His vest and ascot boasted embroidery that rivaled her skilled stitching. Gold thread gleamed in the light. She laughed at the black felt hat perched rakishly on his head and the long plume draping from it. Erik usually dressed like a funeral was about to happen, so she couldn't stop marveling at how he looked wearing colors. Heat from her blush flashed across her cheeks and spiraled to her toes.

Erik's cold fingers brushed down the feathers around her face before he claimed her hand. Without a word, he coaxed her to the center of the dance floor.

At first he barely held her in his grasp, leading her delicately by the tips of her fingers. With warmth only experienced in fever, Anna's flush deepened. She tried to back away, but he reacted quickly, firming his grip. Their fingers tangled together in a union of fire and ice.

When he walked backward, she held his gaze. His look radiated such possessive intensity she nearly lost the strength in her knees. Around her, the space exploded in sound the closer she came to the center of the Escalier. Her nerves raced as fast as the couples twirling around them. Her blush spread in panic while the muscles between her shoulders clenched into a knot. She was not worthy of this. Her free hand frantically clawed at her dress. She'd be less vulnerable naked!

Fanning his cloak out of the way and catching it in the crook of his arm, he raised her hand to the level of his chest. Anna blinked. He was bowing to *her*? *Here*? If she didn't know the absurdity of it, she would have burst into flame. With a quick and expert movement, he lifted her hand, took her fully in his arms, and danced.

Erik was music personified, his body an extension of the Maestro's baton conducting her across the floor with ease, agility and beauty. Unmatched, their movements were seductive, playful, and exquisite.

Anna, too shy to look her partner in the eye, noticed the dance floor had cleared. Guests, hovering in tight circles muttered and pointed. Could it be *they* envied *her*? Marveling at the sea of masks swirling past her, she thanked her years of dancing around the communal campfires of fellow wanderers. At least she knew she didn't look like a complete fool. Her face must have matched the color of Erik's jacket for even her eyes warmed...

The dancers around them backed away giving Erik and Anna room to take the floor.

Erik cared not for the crowds or the stares. He took notice of no one but Anna. At long last nothing else held control of his mind. The freedom was liberating and addicting.

To him, nothing existed but music, his opera house, and Anna.

The music stopped, but for Erik, it had only begun. He stared at her, trying to regain his breath. Emotions in him he long forgot he had started to billow inside. Exhilaration, excitement... even joy. The effects were too much to take. They were strangling his lungs.

"I must go," he quipped. Far too many eyes weighed on him. He hastened away; hoping Anna would follow but fearing his vulnerability too much. The lights of the Escalier dimmed and the sounds faded as he escaped down the vestibule toward the street.

"Erik, wait!"

Stopping mid-stride, he stared at the doors. It would be easy for him to continue and slip out of sight. Pass through the doors and rescue himself from all his emotions, but instead he turned. He looked beyond Anna, to the crowds gathering around the marble steps in the Escalier.

"Don't go," Anna pleaded breathlessly.

Feathers fluttered against the rosy hue of her cheeks. Such a face should not be masked. Stepping to him, she took his hand and squeezed it slightly.

"Thank you for the dance. It was kind of you to notice me."

He caressed her with his gaze. The last several months of debating his emotion and torment came forward in his mind.

"*Ladies and Gentlemen...*" the sounds of the ball drifted around them.

Around her he was a man and a Maestro, part of the *human* race that had compassion and dignity.

"May we have your attention, please..."

He partook in this charade for one purpose alone. His heart slammed against his ribcage.

"Our esteemed and honored guests of this evening..."

Her fingers remained entwined in his, and he watched her eye twinkle as he covered her hand with his free one.

"...will now lead us in the grand tradition..."

She looked up at him curiously, but spoke nothing. He stepped toward her. How could someone so small fit with him so perfectly? The noise in his mind, his warning of madness, faded. Not even the din of the crowd beyond could replace the music.

"...of the Midnight Reveal."

Unsure of himself and his inexperience, he brushed a finger across Anna's forehead with the inquisitiveness of a child. He'd only kissed a woman once...on her forehead. In this instance the sordid memories of his past at the opera house disappeared from his mind.

His hand trailed down Anna's face, tracing the wrinkle to her brow, the small creases on the side of her eye, her mouth plumped in a slight pout. One finger came to rest against her lips, finding them as fascinating as any sculpture he'd ever seen. Breathing deeply, he closed his eyes. He couldn't resist the pull of having a woman's lips against his nor could he deny the powerful urges such a thought sent racing through his body.

"Let the countdown begin."

Twisting his hand, he angled her chin. Lifting the purse of her mouth higher, he bent deeply to meet them. For the first time in his life his cold lips brushed against the warm allure of a woman's. Nerves reached out and clutched him with invisible hands. His muscles seized at the thought of her pulling away. But he felt her shoulders melt into his grip.

Tangling a hand in the waves of her hair, Erik began to drown in emotion. His body took over and he lost himself in the haze of their kiss. All the passion he had found in their friendship moved across silken lips. When he pulled back, she covered her lips with her fingers and looked away.

He studied the rotunda again.

"Ten...nine...eight..."

Desires only ever present in his fantasies blossomed into vivid reality. His chest tightened. The earthy scent of her hair centered on a deeper need. His tingling lips recalled her sweet taste. And the passion? It surged from the depths of his soul—foreign, urgent and welcomed. Treasuring their friendship he discovered he loved the woman, and if she were to love the man—

"*...seven... six...*"

—she had to know all of him. Staring intently at the rotunda, he forced the shallow demand from his mouth.

"Anna, take off the mask."

Trembling, she pulled the feathered costume from her face.

"*...five ...four...*"

"No," Erik's voice pulsed. "Take off the *mask.*"

Anna gasped and dropped the one she held. Erik crushed a fist to his mouth. He would not cry out.

"Erik, I..."

"*...three... two...*"

"Do it!" Grabbing her shoulders, he braced himself for her inevitable reaction.

Erik's attention never left the scene over her shoulder. It had to be done. He couldn't bear to look directly into her eyes. He heard her crying. He hadn't meant to frighten her, but he had no choice. She teetered on the tips of her toes before lifting her hands to his mask. Hitching a breath, he jerked his head backward. He could feel the heat of her as they reached for his most intimate part. They trembled as the mask slipped away.

"*One!*" The rotunda exploded in jubilation.

Laughter and applause clogged the air but between Erik and Anna, the air stilled.

The deed was done. The distant light from the ball beyond cast odd, contorted, shapes across his deformity. Anna didn't move; she didn't take her gaze off Erik for a second. She closed her eyes and then slowly opened them; hearing his raspy breathing and feeling his hands shake on her shoulders. She knew what lay beneath the mask. She'd always known.

But nothing prepared her for Erik's face.

The blood rushed from her face and down her body. She fretted she would find scarlet pooling at her feet. Swallowing against her pulse, the pain she saw twisting Erik's face made the awesome unjustness of his curse more bewildering to behold. Taking a deep breath, she closed her eyes again. She'd allow herself one minute to stand paralyzed by the cruel irony of his face before reaching out to embrace the exquisite image she'd created of him instead.

When next she opened her eyes, she'd never seen a face that could hold more emotion than his. But now, with his lowered head and sad frown, the mask he wore —was shame.

The sounds of the ball continued to taunt them.

"And now ladies and gentlemen..."

Anna searched his face. She expected it to be hard and harsh, knowing what loathing toward the world he kept caged beneath the leather prison. She assumed it would be devoid of emotion. But the smallest of wrinkles decorated his brow. They deepened when he frowned. Anna stared at the unmistakable anguish of rejection etched permanently upon his face.

Her tears flowed as the revelry of the ball behind her mocked Erik's tension.

"Paris is truly honored..."

His back rounded, pulling his face deeper toward the pit of his stomach. He searched around them looking for a means of escape. Caging his face beneath his hands, he staggered away, the agony in those steps made Anna weep harder. Her tears strangled her ability to speak. She felt his pain. The ball moved forward as time stood still.

"...and the Opera Garnier is deeply blessed..."

His hands slid to the back of his skull and his elbows shielded his cruel deformity. A gargled word clawed past his lips, catching on the moisture of his sob: Monster. Anna tried to control the tears he attempted to drown out.

"Let me see your eyes," she begged.

Erik shrunk away like a reprimanded child at first, but lowered his hands enough to look at her.

"...to have here with us tonight..."

The beauty of the ball paled to what she saw. Anna could see Erik's eyes clearly, now that they were uninhibited by his mask. She'd met their frighteningly inhuman hue by night before. Witnessed them in anger, in pain, in madness, and now... in insecurity. They were paler than she ever thought, like the shard of glass she'd once found that had been softened by the waters of the Seine. Suspicion and suffering shone at her from them. Unless she was extremely close, his eyes could barely be seen at all. They were so pale a yellow they were almost empty of color.

Anna gasped when he moved deeper into the sanctuary of the

shadows. She didn't understand what odd twist of fate the Lord intended when He gave Erik's eyes that ability to intensify in hue in darkness, but knew beauty when she saw it.

Those eyes held so many stories, lessons, and feelings; all completely visible to her. He could never fully understand their seductive beauty, but she could. Joy tugged at her, as if birds fluttered around her heart. She bit her lip, swallowing a sob.

"I can see your eyes!" Laughing through her tears, she let them run down her cheeks, paying no thought to wiping them away. The only masks between them existed in a masquerade.

"I can finally see your eyes!"

"...a woman unmatched in talent and grace..."

Snatching her cheeks with his hands he yanked her him, setting his jaw as though expecting a fight. She didn't yell or turn away. If he sought rejection, he wouldn't find it.

"...the pride of the Paris Opera..."

She gasped as he relaxed his grip and sought her lips again. Anna closed her eyes anticipating, for the first time, a kiss of pure desire. Curling into the crook of his embrace, she lost herself in his lips. Taking the lead, she moaned as Erik followed her, moving against her lips, tasting her with long, deep pulls.

Her breath floated away when they gently parted. His fingers raked through her hair, pulling a breath from her lips before he spread his hand against her cheek and wept. Anna reached up, laying her hands on his forearms. She smiled. He found his voice and in it she found his beauty.

"Anna, I love—"

"...the Vicomtess de Chagny!" The rotunda exploded in applause.

An icy wind churned around them, lifting that name and spinning it through the air. Erik's hands dropped numbly to her shoulders as he lifted his gaze to the figures on the rotunda. Anna stiffened.

She followed where he stared. His gaze had locked on the woman being led down the steps by the arm of a dashing vicomte. His grip tightened. Anna beat against his forearms, but he ignored her attempts to gain his attention. The tension in the back of his hands could cause them to split in two. Veins beat with a grotesque rhythm against his temple.

"Erik? Erik?" She hammered at his hands.

His grip tightened more, digging into her shoulders. She buckled under the force.

"Erik!"

An awesome transformation took place before her. Malevolence poured from his gaze, stealing the gentleman that seconds ago held her transfixed. Now he looked on her with savage intensity.

"Did you know about this?" The heat of his passion burned away the cold wind.

"Know about what? That...that woman?"

He focused on the rotunda and the nobility that held the opera in the palm of their hands. Lip twitching and eyes flaring open in a sinister manner, he shoved her away.

"Damn you," he spat.

Anna's head moved in staccato jerks as she glanced over her shoulder to the woman in the Escalier. "Who? Damn who?"

He didn't reply. Her face rearranged in silent shock as she clutched Erik's mask to her breast.

He ripped it from her grip.

His whole body, absorbed by a perverse insensitivity, made no move to comfort as Anna covered her face with her hands and cried.

Leaving her, he stormed from the corridor, his livid strides forcing the cloak to sway behind him.

EIGHT

Anna held her breath as she stepped through Erik's home. Last night she was at a magical ball and now she walked through a war zone. The serenity of being held by Erik, the rush of desire when he kissed her, was now cowering in a corner of her mind.

Tables were overturned and chairs strewn at odd, broken angles. Reams of music coated the floor. Not a single fragile item was left intact. Wine dripped down the far wall, further emphasis of a blind rage. Pools of the scarlet liquid formed among bits of broken glass. The pungent aroma of well aged wine mixed with the oil-puddles from shattered lamps. Had he been drunk, or out of his mind with a rage she feared understanding?

She wove her way through the debris of the place she thought of as a second home, her throat tight. Never would she have imagined Erik would allow himself to drink to such oblivion, so she feared her other thoughts.

Anna found him, sitting in a heap on the floor beneath his coffin, obscured by its shadow. He barely acknowledged her.

"Leave," his voice poured past his lips, that one syllable overly annunciated.

"No."

"Do not test me, child, you are not welcome here."

"You don't mean that. Last night upset you. You're drunk and not thinking straight."

He stood, solid in his stature and stepped from his dismal perch. One boot hit the floor then the other, both grinding against a remnant of a destroyed token. He turned to her and the light.

Anna forced herself to breathe, suddenly aware she still held it. She closed her eyes for a second, his unmasked face still sending a stab of shock through her stomach. Blinking herself to her senses, she shoved the nerves aside. This was Erik, and his face didn't make the man.

With the exception of removing his blood red jacket, he hadn't changed from the night before. Sweat beaded his brow. His cravat lay limp around his neck. Wrinkles carved around his hollow eyes. Caution rocked her nerves. She searched for his mask, noticing it lying on a satin pillow in his coffin.

He cradled his violin beneath one arm, the bow a mess of snapped hairs.

Anna cursed her assumptions. Erik wasn't drunk. She knew enough to know he never would insult his music by playing that way.

"What… what happened down here, Erik?"

It looked like he'd torn apart his home in poisonous fury before escaping in the antidote of his music. Anna bit her lip as he gently laid the instrument in his coffin. His eyes darkened when he turned to her but he didn't respond.

"Can we speak?" she persisted.

"Leave."

"Erik, we need to speak."

"Leave, me!"

Anna flinched, his shout sending a sharp cramp racing across the muscles of her neck. "No."

"You will not disrespect me!" He grabbed the sides of the coffin so tightly she saw his hands pale. Best he does that, she figured, than crush them against anything more fragile.

"Erik—,"

He whirled toward her, the coffin rocking when he released it. "Leave!"

"No! We must speak. You're hurting."

"I am not hurting. Since the day I sprung forth from my mother's womb, I have never *hurt*." Striding past, he knocked her aside with his shoulder.

Anna grunted and clenched her teeth to govern her temper.

"Fine then! You're in denial."

He deflected that word with a shove of his arm. "I deny nothing."

"You're denying everything. You're denying me now."

Erik twisted his way through the house, knocking objects out of his path. He acted as though his entire life was in his way. Anna followed, stumbling over the aftermath.

"Look at this place," she indicated. "Do you mean to tell me you deny this disaster is because you saw her?" She fondled her once broken wrist recalling that dreadful night when he revealed all to her. "You told me all about the Vicomtess de Chagny, Erik. You can't deny she's returned here."

He stopped in his tracks, before turning to look at her. Spreading his arms wide, he indicated the room around him.

"Why would I ever deny Christine?"

Anna swallowed as his arms closed in around him, his fingers pressing into his upper arms. She knew the feeling of having to block words from reaching the heart. Who was this woman whose name tore apart his soul? What power did she have over him?

Anna resisted hugging herself as well, ignoring the jealousy tapping on her shoulder.

Erik dropped his arms and pulled himself up tall. He paced circles around his organ and her. "All I ever lived for was Christine. So tell me, why would all this destruction be a result of *Christine*?"

Anna rocked from one foot to the other. His tone made her hair stand on end. She scowled. "Because clearly you are upset she's returned!"

"This is not because of Christine's return, child. Think again!" Erik's finger sliced the air around him, making Anna flinch. "This is because of *your* invasion! I do not want you here. I curse the moment you arrived. I curse every last sensation you ever aroused in me!"

Anna jumped. His voice cut the air and with it the hope in her heart.

"What are you talking about? What invasion? I never invaded anything! You invited me here. And what… sensations?" His words kicked her in the gut. The sensations she knew were obvious last night in the way he kissed her. Dread of them being gone now made her head spin.

"Child I swear—Leave!"

85

Grabbing her dress, she twisted the wool, trying hard not to cry. "No! All those nights when we sat here and took each other's company… when… when you let me into your past is no reason to blow into some—rage!"

Anna's lip trembled as he touched his face above the empty cavity of his nose. His shoulders were heaving. Never had she seen him wear such controlled fury. Nothing made sense! She'd shown him compassion. Showed that even he—a murderer and madman— was allowed the feelings he denied.

"Wait." Anna gasped. "You think you've betrayed your feelings for her! Be... because of me?"

Moving faster than an uncontrolled tide, he shot out from behind the organ and pointed an accusatory finger in her face. Anna scurried backward out of his way.

"Leave, leave now. You will *not* assume my feelings. How dare you think you can understand a mind as complex as Erik's. You are no longer welcome in this house, my mind or my life! Leave my theater!"

"No!"

His inhuman voice reached levels she didn't think possible.

"Goddamn you, you maddening little Pandora! *Do you have a death wish?* I said leave!"

With a violent thrust he cleared the top of his organ of vials and papers. Anna ducked, vials and nibs, raced past her. The lid of an inkbottle flew off, dappling her forearm with blood red ink.

"Erik! I can't be Christine. She was your world, but she made her choice, she doesn't love you like you want her to! You didn't betray her."

"Erik said leave!"

Anna gripped her hair; maddened by his use of third person. "Stop it and slow down! You've been afraid of letting go because you were fearful of betraying her. You're not a prisoner. She will always be a tangible part of you, but why stay faithful to a love she never truly expressed? Infatuation is a fool's love."

When she took a bold step toward him, he backed away, his lips curling in a sneer.

"Come to terms with this, Erik. You've suffered long enough! Allowing yourself to love someone, anyone, is not betraying *her*, it is empowering *you*."

"Erik. Does. Not. Love."

Anna fought to keep the strength in her knees. This was not happening! Last night she finally felt loved by someone and now….

"I want you to leave this opera house," he demanded sharply.

Anna touched her fingers to her lips, her mouth slipping open. Her eyes heated as they filled. He'd made her cry in pain. He'd made her cry in what she thought was love. There was no reason for him to do so now.

"Why?" she asked as tears spilled down her cheeks. "So you can try to win her back? So you can be that… that Angel of Music again? So you can become a Phantom?" He didn't move. He didn't flinch. Her words had no impact on him. "I am just as worthy as she despite who I am! Erik, last night—"

"Was a mistake."

Anna gasped. Her hand dropped lifelessly against her thigh, his words cutting her off and slamming a guillotine between them.

"So… this is how you deal with anger and pain? Deny me and your feelings along with the rest of the world?" Anna bit the inside of her lip tasting her tears as she did. "It's sad… it is so sad that you won't allow yourself the honor to live like a real man. You don't know how."

She backed away from him, the echo of his words stinging like salt in an open wound. She'd spent her life being a mistake, wandering day in and day out, vividly awake in a living nightmare because of her family's transgressions. And he knew it.

"Last night was not a mistake."

"It was. Leave my theater."

His rejection hit its mark. "You know I can't! That's the only mistake!"

She turned and ran from his labyrinth, dodging splintered furniture as her footsteps pounded in time with the beat of her broken heart. She didn't look back.

She didn't ever want to look back.

It took a while but eventually all that was left of her was the sound of her tears falling around him, useless as desert rain. Turning in a slow circle, Erik studied the aftermath of last night. Pulling a hand down his face, he dropped to his organ bench. All night long the sensation of Anna's lips had lingered on his mouth, while visions of Christine floated in and out of the borders of his madness. Erik leaned forward and pressed his forearms to his thighs.

He glanced in the direction Anna had left.

It was too soon for him to come to terms with a love not grounded in infatuation or desperation.

It was too soon, too—hard—to love.

"Christine…"

He curled his hands against his chest and withered into the pain of his old obsessions. He squeezed his eyes tight against the rising noise in his mind and the pounding of his impenetrable heart.

NINE

Jacob breezed into the office. Last night's affair had put a spring in his step and brought a lively air to the opera around him. He enjoyed a good party when it involved throngs of feeble-minded members of the upper crust. Edward already sat at his desk, elbows on the arm of his chair, his fingers peaked in front of him.

"Edward! Brilliant affair last night." Jacob tossed his hat and stick onto a chair. "I feel a renewed interest in the opera coming. That diva of yours really turned them out. We may not need your scandal."

Edward leaned back in his chair, the springs squealing in protest. "Jacob, don't be so simple-minded. A bigger purse is at stake. A mere diva won't bring it in."

Arrogant bloke. Always thinking *he* oversimplified things while Edward's pompous ass was the brain behind their schemes. That man couldn't think his way out of a paper sack. The chair groaned as Edward shifted. Repulsed, Jacob leaned against his desk and thumbed through the morning's post.

"Drawing people in to see a pretty face is one thing, pulling off your scheme is quite another," Jacob muttered. A note landed in the wastebasket. "I honestly don't think you have it in you." Holding another to the lamp he discarded it as well. "You think these Parisians are stupid. They're not going to fall for your scam. I say we let your diva sing and steal from the opera like usual. The crowds will be large enough to satisfy our greed."

Edward cleared his throat. Jacob looked up in time for his curt nod to draw his attention to the windowsill. Jacob's wrist went slack. The mail floated to the floor.

"God in heaven…"

The man on the windowsill twisted his lips in a wicked sneer. Jacob inhaled a shallow breath, and then fought for another, unable to believe what he stared at. The man's boots were polished with the utmost care and he dressed in the finest black and ominous clothing. His jacket and vest were precisely tailored and molded perfectly to his extraordinary frame. Across the back of a chair in front of him lay a satin-lined cloak. Jacob followed his eyes from that, to thin fingers, which fondled a black mask in his hand.

"The devil take…" Jacob wiped sweat on his brow and chanced a look at Edward.

"Jacob, may I introduce you to The Phantom of the Opera."

The figure moved to stand behind Edward, mask still resting in one hand. Edward didn't move a muscle or so much as take a breath.

"Son-of-a-Bitch," Jacob gulped, fighting not to faint.

The man stalked him, his mere presence demanded fear, and Jacob provided it.

"Ed… Edward," he backed away, slipped over the bills littering the floor.

Edward spread his hands and linked them behind his head, his grin reaching from ear-to-ear. Seeing no help in his partner, Jacob's attention shot to address the man hovering before him. He backed against his desk and leaned as far away from him as he could–then the man winked.

Instantly to his senses, Jacob bucked off the desk. Summoning his courage he bellowed, *"You*! Where's my money?"

The man broke out in a hearty laugh and took a seat on the desk's corner. Tossing his mask aside, he entwined his fingers.

"You have my daughter. What more do you want?"

"Gentlemen, please," Edward intervened. He rose and pulled three glasses and a carafe from the cabinet. "We must be civil."

Jacob leaned against the opposite corner of the desk and snapped his neck from side to side making it crack. He straightened his collar and cuffs and sniffed loudly.

"Richard Barret, so you're what the letter we gave to mail

Anna was all about." He glanced at Edward who extended him a glass. Jacob grabbed it and knocked whiskey back before speaking. "Look at you. Christ. I hardly recognized you."

"Impressive isn't it? Edward said it would be the role of a lifetime."

Richard Barret could never resist roles. A master of manipulation and deceit, he lived for the thrill of a con and the promise of money and drink. He was a true criminal mastermind. Jacob hated admitting it, seeing as it only added to Richard's arrogance. The man raised his glass to Edward in toast and he eagerly accepted. With well-respected caution, and an empty glass, Jacob followed suit.

"Edward, how did you pull this off?" Jacob circled, marveling at the transformation. Richard Barret was an imposing, rather crude man, who barely could carry off what soap did to him. Yet, to his credit, he managed to wear this illusion flawlessly.

Edward shrugged. "I heard tales, snuck a peek at some police sketches, used a bit of creative genius, and voilà!"

Richard snatched for the mask and held it to his face. "Boo!" He extended his hand once Jacob climbed down from the ceiling and caught his breath. "Come now, Jacob, shake it. I'm a pussy-cat, really."

Jacob shook it, but fast. Putting aside reservations and fears of Richard Barret was worse than putting hornets down his pants.

"Ah…like old times, eh?" Edward raised his glass. "A toast."

"What's the next step?" Jacob poured another glass of scotch and took a greedy slurp. Nothing would be the same now that Richard was involved.

Edward stared at his cuticles. "We take our cues from our diva. You've seen the poor thing's nerves. She's bound to let something slip." He slapped his Phantom on the knee. "Do you wish to see your seed?"

Richard studied the scotch. Jacob watched his eyes harden.

"Keep her away from me."

Jacob snorted. He figured as much. Anna embodied everything that went wrong with Richard Barret's life. She'd ruined one too many cons as he'd dragged her across Europe. Richard's own stupid conscience prevented him from killing her years ago. Jacob was not about to soil his hands with the deed. Richard was the murderer in the trio.

"I trust she's serving you well?" Richard asked.

"She's rebellious and disobedient," Edward spit.

"Lower your standards and shag her every once in a while and she won't be," Jacob replied, lifting his glass toward Richard. "Her attitude *is* a bit annoying, but she has been a worthy payment. However, my bloody money is much preferred. Are you certain you don't wish to see her? She's at our beck and call."

"Not unless her *head* is on a spit." Twirling the remaining scotch, Richard downed it in one gulp.

"Ladies and Gentlemen, Father of the Year!" Edward toasted.

Richard threw his empty glass at him.

"Really, Richard," Jacob remarked. "You should be castrated."

The excited atmosphere of the night before hadn't worn off. Christine could feel the air hum with anticipation of the upcoming events. She and Raoul arrived that morning amidst the whispers. Young aspiring divas took to shadowing her every move, hoping to bask in her glory, steal glances at the unsurpassed looks of her vicomte and wishing for a tale of The Phantom of the Opera.

She worried her reputation would precede her. The past linked around her ankle like a chain, following her wherever she went, no matter how much the actual events had faded into fable. Christine was resigned and polite; assuring her young troupe such stories weren't true. She might be able to convince them, but never herself.

Erik's presence traveled like an unbidden ghost through her memories. She buried the images of him deep in its recesses, willing him never to surface. But he would. Too many times when she slept, his skeletal face would appear, taunting her, threatening to tear apart the life she'd made. But when she sang, her soul was tormented because the face that floated before her was that of her masked angel: patient, protective, and loving. She loathed Erik's deranged face and deeply respected the illusion that gave it life.

"I'll take leave of you here, Christine, and meet with you later."

Raoul yanked her thoughts to the present. "Where are you going?"

He kissed the wrinkle of worry upon her forehead. "You don't need me to select the music for the series. Maestro Fontaine and Laroque are expecting you."

She swallowed her protest when Raoul held his hands before

her.

"Christine, I only wish to have a look around, nothing more."
He ran his hand through her hair. "For your peace of mind."

Christine nodded as she watched him leave. How could his
resolve be so solid? He seemed certain the past no longer existed.
His self-assured strides spoke of a man who would not allow the
Paris Opera House to put him on edge. He knew the Phantom
couldn't be trusted. Erik's alleged death never did sit well with her
husband. What little they spoke of the past told her the darkest parts
of Raoul's mind didn't battle with a Phantom and an angel like she,
but instead dueled against a madman. Raoul would stop at nothing
to protect her.

She kept that thought close to her breast as she turned to face
the day.

"This one is lovely." Christine slid a sheet of music across the
table.

"Yes, indeed." The Maestro scrutinized the aria. "But it
perhaps is better suited to the range of our reigning diva?" He
handed the sheet to Edward.

Christine nodded in encouragement. Edward scrubbed his chin
in what appeared feigned interest. Swallowing a knowing chuckle,
she politely removed the music from his hand. Managers, it seemed,
knew nothing of opera and everything of money.

She continued to sift through the compositions, selecting
pieces for herself and the rest of the company. A leather bound work
set off to one side caught her eye. Sliding it toward her, she untied
its satin ribbon.

"An amazing violin concerto, Madame," the Maestro
remarked, having removed the tip of his baton from his lips and
jabbing it at the portfolio. "I have never seen an instrumental of its
quality."

The notes fell and climbed on the stanzas at a frenzied pace,
and then slowed, hovered and repeated. If paper were given voice,
this work would have all the angels in Heaven weeping on bended
knee. She shifted one page behind the other as the concerto wore
on, growing in beauty and drama with each sheet. In all her life
she'd never seen such a curious combination of maddening and
delicate notes. Her fingertips stroked her lips as she lost herself in

the piece… until she bit sharply on a finger.

Red ink.

Black to red, red to black, the colors shifted with the music. As she flipped the pages back and forth, her panic started to steal her breath.

"Who submitted this?" Her throat ran dry.

"I wish I knew, Madame. It came in anonymously," Maestro Fontaine lamented. "We want to showcase the piece, however, we are finding it difficult to locate a violinist capable of playing it. Our concertmaster is up to the task but even he will have a hard time."

Christine stared at the dizzying notes. It was his. It had to be. No one could write such music. No composer but him used red ink…

"When was this written? There's no date. Is this an older piece?"

"I'm unaware. It appeared mysteriously in my office."

She fanned the heat around her neck, the edges of her vision going black.

"He's here." The announcement floated from her lips against her will.

The Maestro tore his gaze from the aria he scrutinized. "Who's here, Madame? Do you know who wrote it?"

Maestro Fontaine leaned forward rapt with interest, as was Edward. The pages slipped from her grip and slid across the table. Feeling the blood drain from her face, she bid herself not to swoon.

"The Phan—" Taking a deep breath, she forced herself to her feet. "I'm sorry, Maestro. I thought it looked familiar, but I'm afraid I'm mistaken. I can't imagine who wrote this work. If you'll excuse me?"

Christine crushed a hand against her stomach and hastened to the door. She flung it open and gasped for a breath once in the hallway. Her morning meal threatened to reappear on her boots. Pushing off the wall and clamping a hand to her mouth she rushed down the corridor. She'd almost set the whole Phantom of the Opera fiasco in motion with her words.

She sent praise to God they hadn't sprung fully from her lips.

TEN

Richard Barret wore the air of self-righteousness like the scotch on his breath. The Opera Garnier was his realm and he its reigning king. After all, he was The Phantom of the Opera.

He snorted and wiped the spittle off his lips. This really was the role of a lifetime. Weeks had passed since the masquerade, giving Richard the time he needed to perfect his role as the famous opera ghost. Already a criminal, Richard took great delight in playing the role of an allegedly insane Phantom.

That would make me criminally insane. He laughed in earnest, leaning over the rope railing of the fly above the stage.

He liked the sound of that. In the few short days he'd been there, Richard haunted the opera house whole-heartedly; only enough to make certain the impressionable minds of the younger ballerinas believed something could be present. He did the usual things—noises in the night, stealing objects, fleeting glances of a swirling cloak. It was child's play and the opera was eating it up.

When not portraying the Phantom, the master con artist took to the streets telling tall tales about a diva and her ghost, encouraging all he could impress upon not to miss out on the concert event of a lifetime. Edward was right, people had a morbid fascination with gossip and ghosts, and their curiosity filled would fill their pockets.

Currently propped on the catwalk, he took large swigs from his flask and leered at the pretty heads of the ballerinas below him. The ballerinas gathered in tight circles of ribbon and tulle as they headed across the stage. He smiled broadly at the tales he heard while pulling at the neck of his costume.

"Madame said it has been years since the theater has been booked so tightly."

"I heard the music is going to be fantastic and it's all because of the vicomtess de Chagny. If only I could sing like her."

"I heard it's because of the Phantom." A wave of giggles burst from their lips.

Richard smirked and enjoyed the scotch rolling down his throat. His power burned in his veins as much as the liquor did.

"Do you believe the stories?" One ballerina asked.

"Eloise saw him."

"She did not!"

"She did. She saw a man in a swirling cloak outside the dormitories!" The ballerinas giggled again.

"He's killed people you know," another divulged. "With a dagger he hides up his sleeve." The ballerina made the sign of the evil eye to ward off spirits.

"Not a dagger you dolt. He kills with a lasso, the *Punjab* lasso."

"What's a Punjab lasso?"

"*I've* heard his violin," one girl bragged as the rest stood enraptured.

Richard took another swig. Their stupidity made him larger than life. Edward's suggestion that he learn the instrument was brilliant. He was getting quite good if he did say so himself.

"He uses the music to cast spells. I heard if you listen to the violin for more than a minute it will seduce you, then the Phantom will sweep you away to his dungeon lair."

A few girls broke out in frenzied hormone-induced laughter and covered their ears. Richard settled back in his perch, enjoying the scotch rolling down his throat and the tightness in his pants. He closed his eyes to rest for a spell, thinking how satisfying it would be to sweep away the fair, untouched womanhood of a ballerina.

⚬◦———— ·–·– ——··◦⚬

"Enough!" Christine commanded, entering from stage right.

Anna turned her attention from the broom she pushed and the giggling ballerinas to the diva. Christine stared at the cluster of girls while Anna stared at her. Judging from the pout upon her lips, the vicomtess' feelings had been viciously offended. Anna despised the stories circulating of the Phantom too. They had been flying around the opera house since the moment the vicomtess arrived at the ball. They held no weight, but they did make her think of Erik. Weeks had gone by without seeing or speaking to him. She figured he was hiding away in his underground prison, but she forced herself to stay away. His words had watermarked her heart and there was no escaping the scars they left.

The girls scampered off, issuing embarrassed apologies between their laughter.

"Don't be too hard on them, Madame," Anna urged, forgetting any manners and not waiting for the vicomtess to address her first. She leaned the broom against the wall. "Children will tell tales."

Her frank address caused the woman before her to go wide-eyed in shock. Anna's curiosity rose as she regarded the one who commanded Erik's heart.

So you're the famous Christine...

It didn't take much to understand why so many envied her and why she captivated Erik. Anna realized she was staring, and looked away.

"Have we met?" the diva asked.

Anna flicked her eyes back to the vicomtess, her gaze landing on the woman's delicate hand, which absently toyed with the fine lace around her neckline.

"No, vicomtess." No wonder Erik called her a 'simple child'. Standing before this woman, it was obvious why he would cast her aside. The vicomtess' dress highlighted a figure any woman would envy. The light from the stage became trapped in the blonde waves of her hair making it shimmer. Everything about her made Anna feel dull and harsh. Even the vicomtess' French, accented with hints of Swedish was fluid and lovely making Anna want never to speak again.

"Yes," the vicomtess nodded. "You danced at the masquerade with that *remarkable* gentleman. You're Messieurs Laroque and Wischard's assistant. Mademoiselle...?"

Anna was not about to provide her surname. It was a deplorable part of her character.

"If you want to call me that, then, yes, I'm their... assistant." Her lips puckered from the disgusting taste in her mouth the mere thought of them created. She forced herself to curtsey. Damn aristocracy. She regretted having stopped. Thankfully another group of students hurried past, this bunch swirling pieces of fabric behind them like waving opera cloaks. Anna noticed the wrinkles creeping onto the vicomtess' perfect skin.

"Pay them no mind, Madame. They embellish what stories they hear. There's always another side."

The vicomtess clasped her delicate hands together and pulled herself a bit straighter. Anna scowled under her examination. She knew judgment when she saw it.

"I beg your pardon. Exactly what other side have you heard?" she asked politely.

Anna studied the floor, chewing on her inner lip. Part of her wanted to answer, but she was uncertain of the vicomtess' reaction. If she took offense to the silliness of little girls, how would she react to what she knew? Her pulse quickened standing beside her. Anna needed this confrontation. Perhaps it would soothe the sting of the unexpected love she'd discovered and lost in Erik.

"I heard you had a great tutor who trained your voice into the instrument it is today. It was said he loved you deeply, and his passion for you clouded his judgment. When his love was unrequited, he hid from the world never to be seen again."

The vicomtess took a step back, blinking at her rapidly.

"You see," Anna continued, "children tell ghost stories, but what they should tell, is a love story. That's what his was all about. Ignore the tales you hear. There is no Phantom of the Opera."

Anna shook her head, sadly. She missed that curious gentleman that would occasionally sneak out from behind Erik's cynical exterior. But standing before Christine Daaé and knowing Erik as she did, it was best to set her needs aside. Erik's heart mattered. It was his happiness she wanted to thrive.

"Now if you'll excuse me," Anna quipped, quickly leaving the stage. She searched Box Five expecting to catch a glimpse of Erik, and believing with a heavy heart exactly what he wanted her to.

He would be looking for Christine.

⊰•———••———••⊱

That voice! That unmistakable, accursed voice!

Richard bolted upright. His eyes flew open, his lewd daydream irreversibly ruined.

Anna! You little wench. He tucked the flask in his vest pocket so violently he sent the fly swaying. *So, the Opera Garnier is not so big our paths wouldn't cross.* One eye narrowed to a thin slit as his cheek jumped. Not much of his precious little girl had changed. She was still a meddling little strumpet.

There's no Phantom of the Opera? Ruin one more con for me, Anna, and I swear... That girl was once again going to wreck his chances at fame and fortune. The mere sight of her made him either want to drink to a black oblivion or make her life as miserable as possible. He chose the latter. It would be more fun. Richard rushed out of the flies.

Time to play this game—his way.

-≫•••————••••————•••≪•-

Erik lurked in Box Five. He stared down at the horseshoe auditorium, locking his sights on Christine and trying his best to ignore Anna entirely.

He'd been holed up in his cellars now for weeks, trying to ignore the fact he had a conscious. At that cursed masquerade he wanted to hand Anna his love, but then Christine arrived at his opera house and roared his past back to the forefront of his mind. He'd broken Anna's heart that night and shoved his guilt and feelings for her in a box. He stopped thinking of her weeks ago.

All he could focus on was Christine and the memories that drifted in his mind.

Below him the ballerinas giggled over rumors of The Phantom of the Opera, punching him right in the gut. While hidden away in his house on the lake, he'd been oblivious to it all. It disgusted him to have the opera house humming with such gossip of him, but then again, hearing the rumors only feed his obsession for Christine.

His fixation over her made everything he touched feel fragile, every scent more pungent and everything he saw sharper. His mind hadn't quieted since the moment he'd seen her standing at the masquerade. His madness was on the rise. It was calling to him like opium to an addict, begging him to give in to it and ride on a wave of false euphoria.

And how euphoric it had been when Christine was his! Need for her tingled across his body. Christine's shock years ago when she discovered her Angel of Music was nothing more than mere man, was still a vivid memory. He could only imagine what it would be like for her to discover he wasn't dead.

His thumb stroked the fingertips on one hand as he watched the women below him. How should he make his presence to Christine known? He didn't want to frighten her. No…he longed to hold her again…he could almost feel her skin on his fingertips.

"Mademoiselle, wait," Christine called. "Where did you hear such?"

"It's a part of the mystique around this theater. Why? Is it true?"

The delicate feeling on Erik's fingertips evaporated. He balled his hand into a fist. The distance between him and Christine was narrowing, and now Anna had entered into his act uninvited.

I told you to leave my theater and yet you do not obey, Anna! Why, when I need you to leave my mind, do you continue to cling?

His glare could have melted iron.

"Yes, it's is true," Christine replied. "The Angel of Music was a great teacher and he did love me. He inspired my voice. He all but gave me this opera house."

Erik's body heated so much his head spun. He caught himself before he leaned too far out of his shadow. Caressing the arm of his chair, he imagined stroking Christine's sensuous form, whispering his adoration into her ear, and proclaiming his love for her in ways he had only dreamed.

Yes, I gave you it all, Christine. I would have gathered all the stars in heaven for you.

"And you gave nothing in return? He loved you."

The memory of how he'd shunned Anna wrapped around his body like a rope of thorns. The raw passion of needing her tightened those binds until he swore his heart would puncture. He forced such feelings away. He didn't want them. Not now. He clamped his teeth in an attempt to govern the thoughts tumbling drunkenly in his mind. The velvet armrest shredded beneath his fingers.

Damn it, you little minx. Stay out of my mind.

Christine wandered the empty stage, staring out across the seats. "There was nothing I could give. Least of all love."

Anna scowled. "Why?"

"He was dreadfully deformed. I was put through so much horror."

"Then why not tell the truth? Why continue with the lessons?" Anna demanded. "If you knew he loved you and you couldn't give that in return, why torment him?"

"I wanted the music for I had never experienced anything like it. I respected the Angel of Music and cared for him, but I could never truly *love* him. Not in the way he wanted. His affections were so powerful—they frightened me." Christine sputtered as she looked around. "Forgive me, but a woman such as you could never understand the situation. He was a distorted soul, a madman. I couldn't be expected to look on that with love. No one could."

No one could? That? Respected? Rejected!

Erik tensed as he shook from head to toe. Curse his ugliness! Anna had called him confused…damnable woman! He was that *and* more! With all his being, he tried to control his demons. His inability to do so was not *his* fault. Man made him this way.

He turned his attention to the woman beside her. Erik leaned forward, avoiding the urge to fold himself over the railing and scream to the women below.

Anna, make her understand me.

"A woman such as me? Did you even know him?" Anna shouted, fists clenching at her side. Her face reddened so fast as she stepped toward Christine, even from his distant box Erik could tell. Anna shook her head so forcefully her braid moved. "Perhaps fright made you *believe* you cared? You had so much invested in the Angel of Music you didn't want to see if you could love the *man*!"

"I beg your pardon," Christine admonished, taking a step backward as Anna leaned toward her. "You have no right. He was a violent person!"

"Of *course* he would react with violence! What other life did he know?" Anna swept her arm quickly out to the side as she plowed past Christine. "No one offered him compassion. Don't you know underneath anger and violence could be *pain*?" Though Anna thumped hard on her chest, Erik felt its vibration all the way in his box. "Regardless if you felt threatened, you took his love and still used it. You believed you could never escape him, and *pretended* to understand him for the sake of first, your career, then your freedom."

"I insist you stop speaking right now!"

Anna's voice rose. "Taking what he wanted was the only way he knew how to love. Outcasts are easy to fear, you know. They're often misunderstood because no one gives them a chance to *be* understood. When he professed his love, could it be you were ashamed to think you could love him back because of his deformity? Could it be you were too crippled by your own self-righteousness to discover the depths of your heart? He was a deviant and you a woman of society." Anna gestured at Christine. "What would that do to your status? To your vicomte? Perhaps you couldn't love someone for themselves because you were too *immature* to see beyond yourself." She stomped her foot, the sound ricocheting across the stage with her angry words. "Maybe you were too immature to see if he was a human being."

"You know nothing!" Christine sputtered, stepping a good distance away and clutching at a cameo around her neck. "Nothing of that man or what he put me through. Why am I even speaking to you? A complete stranger and a common peasant? You don't understand my roles in society. How dare you speak of them!"

"A common peasant, Madame? Were you not a peasant before you came here?"

"You hold your tongue," Christine leaned into Anna with one well-placed step.

Anna didn't budge. Erik watched as she walked toward Christine instead, and calmly recited every last detail of Christine's life as told to her by him. "Raised by your father, travelling faire to faire where he played his violin and you sang. Discovered by a humble professor and sent here for a musical education where you met a tutor you *never* expected…"

Christine was pale by the time Anna stopped talking.

"You could never separate man from father or Angel from Phantom so long as you refused to first know yourself," Anna said.

Lifting a shaking hand, Christine batted her lips with her fingers. "How could you speak of such things?"

"Because Guardian Angels do not exist for me, and I've stared phantoms of many kinds in the eye." Anna lowered her face. "Please accept my apology. I suppose I simply don't know the life you lead. It's difficult, you see, to be cast aside indifferently when all you wish is to give unconditional love."

Erik sat back in his seat and half turned away from the stage.

"Unconditional love? That man manipulated me. He deceived and used *me*. Why did I ever return to this opera house? Don't speak to me again, Mademoiselle. You know nothing but the opinion you've constructed from ruthless rumors. Don't tell me what I do and don't understand. It's *you* who doesn't understand."

Christine hastened away. Erik rose, moving enough to make his presence known to Anna. His all-knowing air flowed between them, as their eyes locked. She glanced over her shoulders only once before rushing out of his theater.

He sank to the seat, indifferent to being spotted. He watched until Anna's back was out of sight.

The years tumbled into each other as he sat in silence. Christine had been young, impressionable and her mind too easily molded to the whims of his voice. Naturally she would have been frightened. She could never have seen beyond the spell his music had cast over her, he had never allowed his guard down enough.

Beneath anger and violence could be pain? Yes... I know pain...

Pain was suffocating and senseless, like drowning in a puddle. No matter how he fought, he couldn't break the surface for air. There were profound differences between Anna and Christine, he saw now with glaring clarity, but he was sinking far too fast. With Anna he chanced vulnerability.

He'd given her a glimpse at the man.

He'd tried so hard to give Christine the world, filling her nights with intricate dreams through his music. Never had he attempted to awaken the woman within and present her an opportunity to meet the man. It wouldn't have mattered. Did he even know the man in him then? Anyway, he never would have been able to pay her such regard.

Then he'd never known how, because until one is looked upon in love, the soul remains in slumber.

ELEVEN

Three knocks stopped her dead in her tracks.

Madame Giry paused in her efforts to close down the boxes for the night. Over the years, and with due cause, she had developed a mistrust of the Opera Garnier when knocking came out of nowhere. Usually this time of night it was as silent as the dead.

And the dead after all, did walk and talk.

Certain she'd heard three taps, she glanced in front of her and then behind before hesitantly pushing the door to Box Five open. The Opera Ghost would always tap three times if he needed her, but why would Erik be in Box Five with an empty theater? She stuck her head in before entering.

Cautiously, she leaned her plump frame against one of the pillars in the box and pressed an ear against it. Knowing the hollow pillar to be one of Erik's hiding spots; she strained to hear any evidence of its retired occupant. Upon hearing nothing her knees nearly gave up on her, she was so relieved. Waving her hands, she shook off her silly paranoia and turned toward the hall, about to drag the door closed behind her. The loveliest male voice whisked away her relief and prevented her escape.

"Where are you going?" it asked.

That voice tickled the back of her neck like a spider dangling from a web. It had been hanging there for years.

"I didn't realize you were here, Monsieur."

"I am everywhere and nowhere, Madame, of that you are quite aware."

"You've not requested my services for a while. What is it you need?"

"Letters." An exhausted sigh floated like a feather caught on a breeze. "Deliver my letters."

Madame Giry snapped to attention, recalling the promises she'd made to herself. She would not be a part of his charade again, even if it meant flirting with Erik's unpredictability. She couldn't and wouldn't hold her tongue.

"No!" she barked with a shake of her head. "I'll not! I'll not cater—"

"One letter will be given to my managers in the usual manner. The other is addressed to you and your two most honored guests."

"I'll not be a part of your attempts to—"

"See to it you read the letter in their presence."

"I refuse to—"

"Madame Giry!" Erik's voice boomed like cannon fire, then suddenly softened. "Forgive my tone, Madame. I am weary. I mean no ill will. I only wish a brief audience with the vicomtess to put to rest her concerns."

That tone was so unlike him. Madame Giry scanned the box. Erik did seem everywhere and nowhere, but all she saw was only darkness. It made the invisible spider creep again.

"Don't you think discovering you're alive will add to her nerves instead of calming them?" she quavered.

Madame Giry cringed at the sound of fabric sliding across velvet. A dark silhouette rose in front of her. Erik turned. He draped his cloak across the crook of his arm and rubbed his thumb across this temple. The reprimand she assumed she would get, never came. Deep sadness over took her. Erik seemed tired.

He seemed…human.

"She dwells on the past, Madame, and with it me. If I am meddling with anyone's emotions, it is my own fool heart."

"Monsieur, you can't win her love."

"I do not need to win it, Madame."

A cold rush of air poured across her skin as Erik brushed past her and out of sight. Madame Giry sat for many long minutes as she tried to rotate herself out of Erik's request. Resigned Erik was a man never meant for her to understand, she rose. Placing a hand on the small shelf in the box, like she had done for years serving him, she searched for Erik's notes. Tears pulled at the corner of her eyes when she touched a parcel as well. Madame Giry smiled as pity flowed down her cheek. She placed the notes in the pocket of her dress, hugged the tiny package of English sweets and closed the door.

She had letters to deliver.

⟶••———•••———••⟵

Gentlemen,

Fondest greetings. Welcome to my opera house. You have my regrets for not greeting you earlier, but I have been unavoidably detained. I admire your Herculean efforts to take over the reins from your predecessors. They left my theater in a state of disarray and I am most certain did not leave you with any expressed knowledge of my existence. Now that I appear to have my affairs in order, I have a few simple instructions.

It has come to my attention you have acquired diva Christine Daaé, the Vicomtess de Chagny, to perform during the anniversary events. My congratulations on arranging such a feat, however, I respectfully command you put a stop to the ridiculous rumors regarding her and a certain 'Phantom of the Opera.' What is past is done.

I expect you to treat the diva with respect. Mark my words; I will expose you as liars and frauds if these rumors continue. If need be, I will take back control of my theater. Make no attempt to contact the vicomtess regarding my demands. I will see to it she is contacted personally. I strongly urge you to follow my orders. I am watching.

Your most humble and obedient servant,
Ph. of the O.

P.T.O: Monsieur Wischard, if you lay your hands on Mademoiselle Anna one more time, I will be forced to act.

"What in bloody hell are you trying to pull?" Edward burst into his office, the door smashing against the wall. The bewildered expressions on Richard and Jacob's faces angered Edward even more.

"Good morning to you too, Edward, what the devil—"

Edward cut Jacob short, roughly shoving a letter into his chest. The scrawny manager stumbled as Edward made his way toward Richard, who was reclining in his chair with his feet propped up on the desk.

"You son-of-a-bitch! You think to write me a letter as a veiled threat to make me do whatever you want? I run my cons my way," Edward growled.

He grabbed Richard's feet and flung them to the side, sending him toppling to the ground. No easy achievement for a man of Edward's unhealthy physique. Richard reacted to the insult in a split second's time. Springing to his feet, he slammed the portly manager backward and pinned his throat against the wall with his forearm.

"Gentlemen," Jacob shouted. "Richard, let him go."

Edward regained his composure; straightening out his collar as he took back the letter Jacob had read.

"Richard, what is the meaning of this?" Jacob interrogated, gesturing to the note.

"What is the meaning of what?" Richard bit back.

Edward flung the letter in Richard's face. "The letter you wrote me, you ass! No one tells me how to run my cons."

"Calm down. There must be an explanation," Jacob reasoned. He indicated the letter Richard held. "Unique choice of red ink, Richard. And nice touch with the P.T.O. Very affective."

Richard read, his nostrils flaring open. "That bitch. That meddling little blower! I didn't write this you idiots."

"You didn't write it?" Edward controlled his shout by pounding his fists in the air.

"Anna must have," Richard snarled, tossing the letter on the desk.

"Oh dear God, you're paranoid. Jacob, I need a drink! Screw the hour."

"Richard, what are you talking about?" Jacob asked.

"Not what. Who. Anna. It wouldn't be the first time that bloody girl has tried to ruin a con." Richard stalked to Edward and snatched the carafe from his hand. "I saw her yesterday speaking with your diva, trying to convince her there is no Phantom of the Opera. She's not an idiot. Anna has to know the money this petty rumor is pulling in. She's out to cheat you, and if you've been anything like the others I've dumped her with, I can promise she despises you." Richard swigged directly from the scotch carafe.

"Anna knows nothing of this," Edward replied. "She's as clueless as the day she was born."

"You think so, Edward?" Richard challenged. "I've seen that girl's intuition ruin far too many of my games. Why do you think I got rid of her?"

Jacob intervened. "I side with Edward. The girl is mindless. Anna is absolutely under our thumb. You're obsessing."

Richard sank on the couch and spoke over the rim of the carafe. "You only say that because without her, all you would ever be is piss proud and frustrated."

"I dab it up with plenty of women. Your daughter is simply convenient." He reconsidered. "Did she see you?"

"Of course not." Richard's knuckles turned white around the carafe. "Believe what you will, I don't trust her."

Edward raised his hands in defeat. "Fine then, what do you propose we do?"

He scowled at the two men and at the empty carafe. "I'll figure something out. I always have."

⇒•••———•••———•••⇐

Mesdames et Monsieur,

I recognize the shock you must be experiencing upon reading a letter from me, but I thought it best to address this matter with the utmost haste. I dislike scandal and realize what may arise from this. While I may appear to have risen from the dead, I have yet to die.

You have my apology for the state of the opera house. My neglect of the facility has been most reprehensible.

Please accept this note as a token of my esteemed appreciation on your return to Paris. I hope your stay has been comfortable. Since you have been so kind as to patronize my theater, I would like to address you each in turn and with regret for the time that has passed since our last contact. This letter is long overdue.

To the noblest Vicomte de Chagny I say this: Well done. You have proven a worthy opponent. I trust you have treated her well and with the admiration she deserves. Do not scorn her. If I had understood, as I do now, you would be in a very different position.

To Madame Jules Giry: You have my deepest and most respectful thanks. You have been a faithful and obedient servant through the years. I owe you a formidable debt of gratitude. I will see you are not held in contempt for your years of servitude; most people do not understand the circumstances.

As for the Vicomtess de Chagny, I will address her in person. See to it she meets with me tomorrow evening. Madame Giry will know of the appointed spot. I ask Christine to bring a certain violin concerto. It has come to my attention this work has been submitted for the anniversary celebrations without my expressed consent. I would like it returned. No harm will come to her. I only wish the briefest of audiences.

I remain in your kindest regard,
Ph. of the O.

P.T.O: Madame Giry, deliver my humblest and most heartfelt apologies. Tell her it was no mistake.

Raoul solemnly folded the letter. A remarkable calm draped over him as he ran a finger across the crease. The sudden comfort they had in his Paris had been eliminated with one piece of mail mysteriously delivered to their townhome. Out of the corner of his eyes, Madame Giry's fingers tapped repeatedly against her teacup. Her toes bounced in time. Raoul couldn't fault her nerves.

He turned to his wife. "Are you well?"

Christine sat stiffly in an overstuffed armchair, staring blankly into the morning fire. A short hour ago, they'd finished a lovely meal. She'd commented on the delightful morning and had looked forward to the day, but now their world had come to a standstill. Raoul knelt in front of her and reached to stroke her cheek.

"Christine, you need to share your thoughts."

Her body shook in unison with the dancing flames. A sickly hue colored her normally flawless skin.

"He's dead," she muttered. "He's supposed to be dead."

Raoul sighed. Rising, he turned to Madame Giry.

"We were informed he was exactly that, Madame—dead. His former lackey, known as the Persian, told us himself. We have a copy of his obituary."

"It took weeks for the information to reach us," Christine interrupted breathlessly. "Erik made me swear, at the time he kidnapped me years ago, that I'd return to put him to rest when he died. When I did…who…what did I bur…bury?"

Madame Giry rubbed her neck several times. The teacup rattled as she set it down. "You buried remains of a common beggar pulled from the Seine. The body was so decom—"

Raoul cut Madame Giry off with a sharp shake of his head as Christine turned greener.

"Who would know the difference between what he was in life and any other poor soul in death?" Madame Giry said instead. "He knew the length of time that would have passed until you returned. Combine that with the wet conditions in the vaults… faking his death in such way was simple."

The pools of Christine's tears magnified her blue eyes into a sea of emotion. Seeing her in pain made it hard for Raoul to hear over the pulse in his ears. The note crumbled in his grip. "This is sick. This is some sort of cheap jest focused on making a mockery of the torment my family went through."

Madame Giry hung her head. "Monsieur, I may be many things, but I'm not a liar. He's alive. He has caged himself away in those vaults as if he *were* entombed."

Raoul turned his back to the old woman and braced himself against the mantel. This was not happening again. He wouldn't allow that monster to have power over Christine again. He spent years getting her back on solid ground after Erik had kidnapped her.

And now, The Phantom lurked at the Opera Garnier once more. All these years, Erik had dodged the authorities and ignored the debt he owed society for the murders, for the chandelier, for Christine's abduction—for the murders…

"Years of servitude? Madame Giry, *why?*" Raoul pounded a fist against the mantel. A candlestick wobbled in its spot. "With all the patronage my family has given to the Garnier, why would you do this to us?"

"You don't understand, Monsieur. You can't possibly understand." She moaned. "I should have torn that letter to pieces and gone against his wishes. I tried to go to the authorities many times, but my life and his are so intertwined—more than you could ever know."

"Madame Giry, he's a demon!" Christine's color had not changed and now her voice shook. "He tried to kill my husband! How could you?"

"Please forgive me. You of all people should know the power of the Opera Ghost. But you must understand they were crimes of passion. Despicable, heinous crimes, but deep inside, he meant no harm. You have to believe me. He would never harm you. Especially now… he's different."

Raoul pushed off from the mantel and kept his eye on the old woman for a second. It was as long as his disgust allowed. If Erik had changed, then why did she look so guilty? "Different? You speak of him as a long lost friend. It doesn't appear to me he's changed, Madame."

"I didn't tell because I was frightened. You and the vicomtess fled, but my life was here. No matter how much I try to deny it, he's a part of it. I'm a simple woman, and he has a way of involving one in his affairs."

Raoul turned away from her plea, not willing to allow her to see the flicker of recognition pass across his face.

"I learned, like the other box keepers before me, if we allowed him his opera house, he was harmless."

"Harmless?" Outrage jutted his body backward. The fisted hand at his side, which held the crumpled note was ready to strike, but at what? "Is that how you view him? His blatant disrespect for life is harmless? His madness, harmless? Attempting to blow up a quarter of Paris, harmless? Is this letter to be considered such as well? Are we to believe what happened in the cellars won't happen again?"

"Why are you placing blame on me?" Madame Giry sat straighter as her voice raised. "When you ran, you knew he still lived. When you learned of his obituary, you knew that body was not solid proof. He is a trickster. Why didn't *you* pursue him?"

Raoul's tension diminished as his responsibility grew. Defeated, he dropped to the chair next to her. "You're right. Forgive me, Madame Giry. We mustn't divide ourselves. We all own a burden of responsibility, but we end this now. I'll not have my family chased by him any longer. Where is he?"

Christine's head shot up. "Raoul, what—"

He calmed her by laying a finger to his lips and turning a stern gaze on the older woman.

Madame Giry squirmed. "I don't know. He comes to me and very rarely if at all anymore. Something is very different about him. I can't quite understand it."

"The difference is Christine is within his grasp. He's likely in the labyrinths and cellars." Raoul said.

"They were sealed off after the investigations, Monsieur le vicomte. You know as well as I the efforts of Prefect of Police and his investigators. The passages lead to dead ends." Madame Giry sighed.

Something about the tilt of her head and the way she fiddled with her fingers made Raoul question her sincerity.

"Then what do we do?" Christine asked.

Raoul pulsed the crumpled note still in his fist and contemplated what it said again. "Tell her it was no mistake. What is he talking about? What was no mistake?"

"That he let me go. No mistake that he gave me my freedom so he could always haunt me." Christine lifted a handkerchief to her lips and attempted to stifle her tears.

Raoul threw the note into the fire and came to his wife. He buried his fingers in the cool silkiness of his her. Christine's sigh only confirmed how desperately Raoul needed to protect her. This was the one woman he could not live without. With one hand, he wiped a stray tear from her cheek.

"Abide by his wishes," Madame Giry encouraged. "Madame, meet with him and deliver his concerto." She produced a second note from beneath her sleeve and extended it.

Raoul took it and read, nodding once. "He asks the vicomtess meet him in her former dressing room tomorrow evening at six sharp." He crumpled the note and tossed it into the fire as well. "She will do no such thing. I'll not allow her to fall prey to his traps again.

I'll contact Inspector Legard. I'm certain he'll be willing to work with us."

"Work with us?" Christine gasped.

"I'm not going to let this go, Christine. If Erik is alive, this ends here. I can't have him tormenting you. He needs to be found." She opened her mouth, but he silenced her with a gentle thumb across her lips "He's a killer. I can't believe he means you no harm. There are crimes he's committed for which he has not answered. He was a fool to ever let it be known he was alive. This is his undoing. Now Erik will play by *my* rules, and this time I'll be waiting."

TWELVE

The mantel clock chimed thirty past one in the morning. Christine had been lying awake listening to the clock tick away the minutes and chip at her nerves since she went to bed.

She gingerly slipped out of bed, careful not to disturb her husband. She glanced around the stylishly appointed room Raoul insisted upon sharing with her, comparing it in her mind to where she was headed. Upon seeing her husband resting so peacefully, instantly her belly trembled. Unlike times previous, it wasn't out of desire, but raw nerves. Raoul wouldn't hear of separate bedchambers when they wed. The thought of how he wanted her near all the time warmed her at night, but now she could feel nothing but the rocks tumbling over and over in her stomach. She sat on the edge of the bed, watching him breathe. He was such a beautiful man in body, mind and soul, and she such a tormented woman.

Christine brushed her lips against his, careful not to wake him. She slipped out the door to her chamber, dressed, and checked one last time to be certain Raoul still slept. Positive he was, she snuck away, her feet padding softly through dimly lit halls. Swinging on a cloak, she took one last look at the hour and escaped through the front door.

Nerves swirled inside of her like the mist coating the fog-filled streets. What she was about to do crushed brutally against her, and she laid a hand against the pain in her chest. The brougham approached on time, the driver having done as instructed by covering the Chagny coat of arms on either side of the doors. Rumor was richer than an emperor's coffers in Paris. She didn't need prying eyes staring at their crest at this hour. Christine looked over her shoulder toward the window where Raoul slept. She didn't wish to deceive him, but an irresistible longing pulled at her.

A footman opened the door and helped her inside. He stifled a yawn as he tried to smile.

"To the opera," Christine directed. The snap of the driver's whip and the jerk of the carriage pulled her away from the security and love of her husband and toward potentially unknown machination of a madman.

Paris stilled this time of night with the exception of the farmers wearily pushing their carts through the streets to market. Occasionally a turgotine whizzed past on its way out of the city. The clip of the horses' hooves lulled Christine into a trance as they mockingly beat, *why, why, why...*

Why was she drawn to Erik was a question she couldn't answer. Trying to ignore his request would be like ignoring she had a heartbeat. She mustn't keep the Angel of Music waiting and she had long enough.

The city sped past her, moving almost as fast as the relief surging inside of her.

Erik is alive! Even as that euphoria whirled around her, Christine chewed her lip, picturing herself standing in front of him yelling out every bit her of frustration. Blaming him for the secret anguish she kept locked away, beating him over making her suffer through his death. Crying over him abandoning her...

Glancing at her wedding ring, Christine wondered if her hands shook out of relief, excitement, or anxiety.

The confrontation on stage with that girl kept her awake at night and made a wreck of her emotions. Christine knew her fear of Erik must be outgrown if she was going to take this second chance to redress her choice of lover. As much as she loved Raoul, part of her still slavishly wished to be chosen by the Angel of Music.

The empty streets faded away, until there only her reflection in the carriage window. She took a deep, determined breath. She was no longer too immature to address her need to choose again. Still, she studied her slight squint and wondered why it was there. So many nights she had dreamed about this moment and now that it was upon her, she was near paralyzed with nerves.

Christine closed her eyes knowing she may see his face again. The memory rose to the back of her mind and she shook her head trying to force it away. With it came the stark reality she kept trying to deny. If Erik was alive, then so was his madness. He could, and would, do any number of unthinkable things to Raoul. Re-dressing fool-hearty choices could ruin Chagny and her life that came with it.

Christine's apprehension rose as the opera house grew in the distance. A thick feeling gathered in the center of her chest—rock heavy. Raoul loved her. He gave her anything she wanted. He was the safe choice; the easy, comfortable choice. Making that choice had been easy years ago, but living with that choice still haunted her at night. That heavy feeling made it hard to breath. She didn't want to lose all she had in life with Raoul, but she couldn't ignore her aching when she thought of Erik. All of her life with Raoul could be gone. Erik was unpredictable and what could he offer her beyond love? The opera house loomed and with it—her guilt. Was love enough?

Christine banged on the roof to catch the driver's attention. "No. Return!"

The carriage swung around in a slow circle before heading in the direction it had come. Christine shut her eyes again in an attempt to make Paris disappear. The walls of a maze closed in around her and she was caught in the middle between the love of the devoted, handsome man sharing the bed she'd abandoned and the mysterious adoration of a dark, sensual angel roaming the deserted halls of the opera house.

She would not choose between the two tonight.

She didn't know how.

⋄•••————•••————•••⋄

Erik stared unblinking into the bleak emptiness of Christine's former dressing room. Many mornings years ago he'd stood in the false chamber behind her two-way mirror waiting to spring it free and coach her. Many times more he stood there, unknown, watching her brush her hair, read a script, or daydream like a silly child. Once upon a time it had completely filled his life.

The silence on the other side of the mirror taunted him now. The stillness of the room reflected his mood. The clock had long ago chimed six, then seven, eight and on. He thought she'd come—he needed her to come. Spreading his hands against the mirror, his mind argued against his heart.

Damn this fate!

"Christine, why?" Erik smashed his fist against the mirror. Tiny cracks spread like a spider's web across its glass surface. Erik mindlessly traced the progress with his finger. "Why did you come back? Why now?"

His forehead fell forward to meet the unfeeling glass.

Torment in his mind exploded with intensity and drove the memories of her raw rejection through him. His body joined his forehead, pressing his weight against the glass. It was a familiar move having embraced the mirror so many times trying to have Christine fill his arms. Erik yanked his face from the glass and braced his hands against the frame. His heartbeat pulsed in his fingertips.

Raoul de Chagny, how I despise you....

He had everything: freedom, unsurpassed charm, respect, and Christine's love. Curling his fingers together, Erik took a deep breath, controlling his need to smash the mirror. Madness tugged on his brain.

The boy is the reason Christine didn't come! The reason why I am unable to speak with her! I allowed Christine the freedom to choose whom she would love. Didn't I? Should I not be afforded that same scrap of respect? I spared your wretched life, Chagny! Should I not be spared my own pitiful existence?

Erik pushed his forehead backward with two fingers until his neck cramped. The noise and frustration in his mind rolled savagely with music. The name of one woman battled against the next. He had to profess to Christine no matter what came to pass, part him would remain hers for eternity. In the past he'd lived for Christine's happiness.

Now, he wanted his.

Loveless Hell was not where he wanted to be imprisoned. Long ago he'd wished for a wife to take out on Sundays. He thought he'd purged all need to live like a normal man, but as he stared into a broken mirror in a damp and narrow hallway, he found buried beneath his bitterness that he still longed for those Sunday walks.

Staring into an empty room did nothing but make him feel pitiful. He had a message for Christine and he was being ignored like a common mongrel. He traced the cracked mirror again.

The Phantom's voice will be heard. This is my kingdom, vicomte, beware how you walk through it.

Even mongrels had rights and Erik would get his message to Christine in the only other way he knew how.

He backed away from the mirror and turned to slink into the pitch-blackness of his labyrinth. For a change he didn't think of how he was built of the macabre. He pondered the sun upon his skin and the shimmer of the Seine by day instead of the mist of his lake by darkness. Picturing what joys would come from wrapping her feminine frame in the warmth of his cloak.

She had stowed into his dreams like an unfinished strain of music begging to be finished. Completely alone in his maze of catacombs, he envisioned her hand curl around his offered arm. He touched the unseen weave of her braid, swearing when next they met he would stab fate with the same dagger it had placed in his back and wander freely with a woman to love upon his arm.

Through his scorned resentment one sound calmed the rising noise in his mind. The shroud of his madness frayed when he whispered Anna's name.

Anna's foot sank in the pile of horse dung with a sickening slurp. Her nose curled at the stench.

Serves you right, you fool. Think twice before opening your mouth and screaming at a nobleman's wife next time.

Anna jigged and attempted to shake the manure off her boot. As expected, her insubordination to the Vicomtess de Chagny hadn't gone unnoticed by Laroque and Wischard. She paid the price by an added workload in the stables. Any daylight long ago faded from the windows, leaving the lanterns, and the stench, to highlight the piles of horse manure. The dance made no progress, so Anna used a point of the pitchfork to dig out the clump.

Remorse was probably called for. The disrespect she'd shown *had* been blatant. She laughed, however, for it had been worth it. She'd needed to see for herself what the allure was behind the famous diva. The pitchfork stabbed into the muck shooting a dull pain from her wrist to her forearm.

Yet another reminder of Erik.

She dug the prongs of the pitchfork into a steamy mess of hay and threw it into a wheelbarrow behind her. Anna completely understood how he could have fallen in love with the vicomtess.

He still is, she sighed.

Anna poked at the hay, trying to pick through her thoughts. Erik seemed to horde every emotion and need with such deep passion and act on them with abandon.

How could that woman not return his love? Not want to know Erik as I've come to understand him? Anna leaned on the pitchfork fighting the sting behind her eyes. *He's an intriguing—albeit it inexcusably insane—mysterious, childlike, utterly insatiable man.*

She tossed her feelings aside like the hay she flung around. Above all else, she wanted Erik to be happy, and if he wished to pursue the vicomtess' affection, then she'd not deter him.

Love will find me someday. I'd be dumber than horse dung to think otherwise. Anna told herself that so many times the lie was automatic. It would be selfish to stand in the way of anyone else's quest for it.

Still, she thought she'd found a hand to fill hers. Anna had never been in love and despite Erik's unpredictability; he filled her in a way she never knew possible. Her heart fell to her feet when she realized she would never explore love with him.

Anna twisted her back left to right. Every muscle ached, but the work kept her from being found by Erik, not that she thought he'd be looking for her. It was best to leave him be. Perhaps it was senseless to keep dwelling on it, but she didn't quite know what to make of their confrontation after the masquerade. The sound of his betrayal still beat in her head. *She was a mistake.*

Leaning the pitchfork against the stall, she dusted off her hands. A horse whinnied softly.

"I know how you feel," she muttered to the stallion, reaching out to draw a finger across the Chagny coat of arms decorating the horse's blanket. She swallowed the jealousy bubbling inside of her. The vicomtess already had a respectable man, why did she need Erik's love as well?

"Anna?"

She spun. The lanterns around her did nothing to penetrate the dark.

"Who's there?" She stepped from the stall. "I can't see very well, my eyes are stinging." The horse nickered nervously.

"Anna?

"Who's calling—?"

A bright flash of light flared in her peripheral vision seconds before the lantern crashed against the side of her face. Anna cried out, hands clawing at her head as hot metal and glass seared her temple. Losing her footing, she hit the floor. Rolling to her side, gagging on the stench of dust and hay, her heart beat in panic.

Shaking her head, she tried to stop the ringing in her ears, but it only made it worse. Her vision was blurring and blurring fast. Anna began to roll again, when a kick sent a stabbing pain across her lower back. She fought to obey the adrenaline coursing the command through her body.

Flee!

It came too late. Her feet wouldn't move. Prone on the ground, her vision growing dimmer, she lifted her head enough to make out black boots and the edge of a long cloak. A man stooped beside her. What she couldn't see, she could hear and feel. Breath tapped against her cheek and a male voice poured hatred into her ears.

"Stay out of my way."

The far reaches of Anna's mind registered a glimpse of her assailant. The image plunged her into the grip of unimaginable terror before her head thudded against the floor. The man rose, the hem of his cloak sweeping her aside, as he stepped over her and into the shadows.

Mercifully, Anna disappeared into a shadow of a different kind.

THIRTEEN

"To what do I owe this audience, Madame Giry? Are you not busy entertaining your precious little guests?" Erik flicked the music room door closed behind him curious as to why she summoned him here and not in her office as usual. "I believe your bothersome need to call me this morning is because the vicomte is ill-pleased with my note? It is, after all, quite unusual for *you* to come looking for *me*."

Erik strolled through the room, less than thrilled to have his time devoured by trivial requests. Madame Giry's trademark twitching didn't help his already perturbed mood.

"I imagine he does not rejoice that I live. And I am certain Christine is a bit... disenchanted." He clicked his tongue. "I only need to speak with her for a moment. Pity, the boy has not learned to mind my demands."

If Madame Giry patrolled the room any more, she would shred the already worn rug. It was as annoying as the rats constantly scurrying under his feet. Upon her fifth pass in front of him he whisked his arm out, nearly knocking her throat on his forearm.

"Madame Giry, why did you summon me?"

"There's been an accident involving the theater." She ducked under his arm and backed against the far wall.

"An accident? How unfortunate in its timing with your old patron and his wife visiting." He leaned against the door and gestured around the room in condescending concern. "Shall I ask what *kind* of accident?"

"It was horrible, simply horrible!"

Bored, Erik rolled his shoulder. "And why should this concern me? I no longer manage this facility. This opera has been faltering for years. Unfortunate events seem... attracted to it."

Erik projected his laughter making Madame Giry spin toward a snickering music stand.

"Anna's been assaulted!" she blurted spinning back toward him.

The laughter disappeared like water on a hot rock. Erik jerked off the door. He moved toward a chair, carefully stepping around the implication. He gripped the edge of the nearby desk for support as he sat.

"Assaulted?"

The word stung his tongue and rendered speech near impossible. Around him the room swelled in cadence with his mounting breaths. Erik's hand curled around the edge of the table, his calm fraying like a strand of silk.

"Was she..." Erik contorted his neck as those words twisted, knifelike, in his ear. "Was she... violated?"

"I don't think so, Monsieur."

The edge of the table cracked under the intensity of his control. Splinters dug into his fingers. The news was of little comfort.

"She's resting now, but is battered. The theater doctor tended her earlier."

Erik relaxed and breathed deeply to cleanse his mind. He had honed the technique through the years when the urge to give into the noise was far too great.

"Why did you not summon me immediately?" he barked.

A puff of air broke through her lips as her small bubbling steps turned into long strides. "Why didn't I summon you? Suspicion is running wild! The Phantom's name has already been uttered since the vicomtess arrived. And you added to the fire with your letters. That's why!"

She moved a chair and plunked it directly in front of him not waiting until it settled into place before she sat. Startled, Erik glared. Madame Giry was growing bold.

"No one knew you were still here or for how long," she stressed. "It's been peaceful. *You've* been peaceful. I knew if I told, you would immediately jeopardize that. I agonized over what this may stir in you. I didn't want to see anyone hurt."

Silence stretched the delicate strand of tension between them before Erik found his tongue. "What this stirs in me is of no concern to you, Madame Giry. If you also dread the presence of the Opera Ghost, then so be it. He has been buried so *I* can live. I was under the impression there were perhaps two who believed that, but apparently there is only one. You will take me to her... now!"

His fist slammed the splintered edge of the desk cracking the last grain of wood. The chair beneath him toppled as he rose. He stood aside to allow her to pass, noting she now dared not meet his eyes.

"You mustn't be seen," she urged.

They didn't say a word to each other as they moved through the halls. Erik couldn't, his mind was too gripped with the idea of any man laying a hand on his Anna.

Madame Giry opened the door to the concierge office where Anna lay sleeping on the divan. Erik paused in the doorway. A foreign sensation had a stranglehold on him, making it difficult to breathe.

This was what it was like to fear.

Madame Giry turned up the lamp by Anna's side. "No one has any idea how this happened. The stable master found her early this morning."

He fought for a deep breath, unaccustomed to the emotion swirling in his pit. Anna's breathing was shallow, one temple swollen from the brunt of her assault. A jagged cut ran from the corner of her eye to her ear and across a swath of brilliant red skin.

Cocking his head like a curious child looking upon a wounded bird, he pulled a chair close to her side. Erik lifted one finger to her temple. Her clammy skin prompted him to remove his cloak. Fingers tangled and tripped over the clasp. He never knew he could tremble.

"I will keep vigil over her. You may leave." As he draped his cloak around her, a treacherous sigh of grief escaped his lips. This was not how he envisioned his cloak wrapping her small frame.

"Monsieur, you must not get involved. The vicomte will arrive and with him half of Paris. Look at the circumstances. They'll be suspicious."

"Damn, the circumstances. Damn their suspicions. Leave us

be."

"Monsieur I beg you to go. I'll take care of her. I promise."

"*I'll* take care of her!"

"Lower your voice, Monsieur!" Madame Giry's fingers fluttered at the base of her neck.

Erik turned his back to her not convinced his mask would hide the grief tearing apart his face. How could he lower his voice when every last sensation in him was on the rise? Anna's hair spilled loose around the divan, so he focused on it lest the old woman realize how weak he was. Erik reached out and hesitantly ran his fingers down the length Anna's hair fearful if he did anything more, he would break her. With his hands hovering over her, he paused, not entirely sure of himself.

Over his shoulder he heard Madame Giry's breath hitch as he gathered Anna's hair together. He tried to ignore the tingling on the back of his neck as he sensed her stare drilling him. It took a few tries, but eventually he laid a perfect braid across Anna's breast and sat back, silent and watchful.

From across the room he could see Madame Giry reflected in a distant mirror. Her mouth gaped open and she covered it with her wrinkled hand. When her head tipped to her shoulder, Erik turned around.

"Leave," he muttered.

He didn't wait to see if she obeyed. If his humanity wasn't noticeable in that moment then the world could be damned. All he focused on was Anna.

Erik reached out and adjusted her braid while he sang, the room filling with the haunting notes of his concern. He wrapped the tendrils of his voice around Anna like the poignant embrace he was too afraid to do with his arms. Eventually he heard the rustle of Madame Giry's skirts as they brushed through the door and then, finally, the sound of it latching shut.

Erik slumped in the chair, relieved to shed the vulnerability Madame Giry witnessed. He kept singing, for it was the only thing he understood in that moment. For its intended recipient, the song would fall on deaf ears. It would do nothing but fill the silence.

Music rained down upon Anna, as if Death himself stood nearby weeping strains of pure grief.

Jolting awake, it took Erik a moment to register where he was; the understanding of it rushed over him in sickening waves. He rubbed a kink in his neck. He laid his hand on Anna's cheek. She had pinked, her flesh now warm.

"Anna?"

"She still sleeps, Monsieur."

Madame Giry emerged from a far corner of the room. When she returned or how long she had been there, he knew not. She approached, extending a cup of hot tea. He stared quizzically at it before accepting it. Nimble fingers wound around the knot at his neck until the silk of his cravat loosened.

"Why should you look so uncomfortable, Madame Giry? Have you not seen a man undo his neckwear before?" Bitterness fell around him like the unraveled bow. "How long did I rest?"

"Not long enough. You look worn."

"I assure you, Madame, I could look worse." Erik gestured toward his face, permitting his off-sense of humor to give Madame Giry a glimpse of the man he kept hidden.

"Anna looks better," she encouraged. "Rest and time will do her well. You had best be gone. The authorities will speak with her when the laudanum wears off. You shouldn't be seen here."

Erik kept silent. Placing the untouched cup on the side table, he tenderly brushed a lock of hair from Anna's swollen eye.

"Why do you stare so, Madame Giry? I find it disagreeable."

"Monsieur, what are you looking to gain from this? What is it you expect of her?"

Erik's brows pinched beneath his mask. "You have the serpent's tongue. I find I do not like your line of questioning."

"And I find I don't like your stubbornness!"

Erik rocked back in surprise. "It seems you have found a backbone."

Madame Giry's lips tightened. Giving an indignant bob of her head, she gestured toward Anna. "You can say I take my cues from her."

"You should not," Erik snapped. "Her tenacious spirit is not becoming on you. Do not play such dangerous hands with me. I am in no mood."

"What is this friendship you have forged with her?"

The box keeper's sudden audacity was a sword severing their well-constructed roles. Erik rose.

"You stare again, Madame Giry." Erik tossed the cravat aside. "Does such an action seem too normal for you? Braiding hair or singing a song too ordinary? Of course it would. Even friends instantly regard anything normal when applied to me as repugnant. You are shocked I use that word? I suppose that term could be applied toward us. You have been a faithful minister. If not afraid of me." He wandered the room, fondling objects he came in contact with.

He lifted a photo of her only child, and stroked the glass, catching the heavy lidded look behind her eyes.

"Did you give me a choice?" she softly asked.

He lifted a brow she couldn't see. She was growing frank in her old age as well.

"I have given you much over the years, have I not?" he replied. "My manipulation of the management advanced your child to the front of the ballet line. Your daughter's dancing was much improved. Shall we discuss the marriage I arranged for her? Is she happy as a baroness?"

The square to Madame Giry's shoulders had dropped and with it her attitude.

"Meg is fortunate and quite content," she replied gratefully.

"Would you have served me had you not received something in return?" Erik nudged the picture back in its spot making certain it was exactly as he found it. "You did me a great service years ago ministering to the Opera Ghost's needs, but it ceased there. Where your compassion ended, your ill ease began. You see, our arrangement did not evolve. I bribed you for it. You received what you desired and I the same. I did not have to do that with Anna."

Erik sat on the divan watching Anna's breasts rise and fall in her sedated slumber. "The years that have passed have seen some of my darkest moments. I was a pathetic shell of a man who thought faking my death would silence the madness of my sins. I was too cowardly to give in to death when Death appeared at my doorstep. I tricked myself into thinking I was worthy of love instead.

"I deserved nothing other than death. Even in that, I could not find peace until it found me. I am not deserving of her friendship." He nodded at Anna. "I did not trick her into coming to me by masquerading as a man for whom she yearned, like I did to Christine. I did not come bleating like lost sheep for love and adoration. I did not weave some spell across her." He pinned

Madame Giry with his eyes. "That is what you believe, is it not? That she is another Christine Daaé and I the dog that would lie at her feet?"

Madame Giry made no sound, but the subtle shift in her posture was loud enough.

"You can be certain, Madame, she is no Christine Daaé. I am no longer a fool."

"Fool? Your love for the vicomtess brought the opera house to its state today."

"Yes, an arrogant, unspeakable fool. I want to love Christine. I have always wanted to love only her. But, as Anna told me, infatuation is not love. I do not know how to love a woman such as Christine. She wanted the illusions of the Angel of Music—not the man. She would never have accepted my past, my fate, and my *face*." His expressionless mask met the confusion furrowing Madame Giry's brow. He clutched a fistful of the fabric on his shirt, desperately trying to reach his heart.

"I know what I am. How this mind works. Tell me, could Christine ever accept the man that lies beneath? Would I ever have allowed that monster to shatter her soul? I could not make her look on me in love no matter how much I wished."

He turned from Madame Giry to resume his silent vigil, thankful Anna was completely unaware of the revelations of love crumbling the walls he'd erected around himself.

"But Anna has accepted that man? I was at the ball. During the midnight reveal—I saw."

Tension drew across the room tighter than a bowstring. His hands scrunched the fabric of his trousers. Madame Giry stared at his mask with such scrutiny; he nearly drew blood on his thighs.

"What did you see?" Even a voice as perfect as his was capable of cracking...

"You kissed her. It startled me. I fled."

The room sighed when he sank back into the chair. Profound sadness edged into his voice. "A kiss made you flee? I try to taste life on the lips of a woman and even that is feared? Every part of me is to be repulsed then? I repent my sins, Madam. I know to pay for my crimes means I will be put to death. I do not have much time to be a man before my past catches up to me."

Erik's eyes heated beneath his mask. It was just as well that she couldn't see his growing tears.

"I exist, Madame Giry. Will no one let me live?"

"Does she love you?"

Erik shrugged. "Anna gave more to me than a lifetime on this earth. She never passed judgment and never questioned my reasons. She did nothing but accept me. One who has been judged dares not judge, you see. Yet my obsession for Christine destroyed my chances for love and with it any belief Anna had in me. I am left with only the memory of her kiss."

Exhaustion edged across him like a dull knife. A clock chimed the lateness of the morning. Madame Giry leapt to her feet.

"The authorities will be here soon," she cautioned. "You must heed my warnings and head back to your labyrinth. Time is the only thing that will help Anna now. You can do no more."

She swept her hands toward the door trying to usher him out. Erik rose, his legs feeling like lead. The situation was grave and he too weary to pose any argument... but how could he leave her? She was so small. So broken and unaware... and even like this, he was completely under her spell.

"I understand what you're saying... what you feel for her." Madame Giry assured. "Go now, I'll find you when she wakes."

She followed him to the door while sounds of the approaching police filled the halls. He veered off to one of his many secret passages. Turning to glance at Madame Giry, he caught the saddened pinch in the corner of her eyes.

Her look abraded him like desert wind.

FOURTEEN

The lamp burned, innocently doing its job, but its light sliced straight into the back of Anna's head. She groped for the lamp's key but stopped, the pain too intense to move. The steady rain tapping against the windowpane drummed unrelentingly loud making her temples pulse.

Anna touched the throbbing gash across her temple. A groan moved in her throat as an ache ran down her face. Everything was foggy and it hurt far too much to try to decipher why.

Hissing from the sting her probing caused, she slowly lowered her hand and squinted at the rain as it slithered its way down the window. She had no idea where she was and the pain made it hard for her to care. Her memory was a muddled mess of a brilliant flash of light followed by blackness. In a stubborn effort to collect her thoughts, she struggled upright. Anna squinted in the light and fought the nausea. She took a few deep breaths before swinging her feet to the floor.

"Be still. You mustn't move so soon."

She moaned. "Madame Giry?"

"Anna, rest." A glass of water found its way into her hand. "Drink this, I'll be back to explain as soon as I can."

Before Anna could blink, Madame Giry disappeared. She stared at her cup. The idea of anything in her stomach made it lurch again. Not wanting to vomit, she placed the cup on the table. Anna was forcing herself to her feet as the door swung open.

"Good Heavens, Mademoiselle, no!"

Anna teetered before falling forward. The man's reaction was swift as he caught her mid swoon. As he eased her onto the divan, swirls of color ebbed and flowed in and out of her vision. The smell of expensive soap filled her nose as his silk cravat brushed her cheek. The diamond stick-pin in in it flared brilliantly in the lamplight. She blinked to clear her vision and to get a good look at her stranger relieved to have not hit the floor.

"Who are you?" she asked, the words scratching out her throat, sounding like sandpaper to her ears.

"Mademoiselle, I am the Vicomte de Chagny."

"de Chagny?" Anna echoed. The name sounded familiar but she couldn't place it. She blinked away the fog in her head in enough time to see a graceful woman floating through the door behind him. Anna stared dumbstruck as what appeared to be an angel glided forward.

Anna peered at her in hesitant recognition as she reached for the blanket that had been on top of her before she stood. "Vicomtess de Chagny?"

"We came as soon as the authorities sent us word. Are you well?" the vicomtess asked, delicate notes of pity to her voice.

Anna jolted as memories of the previous night flashed through her mind. Her fingers found their way to her temple once again, pain racing down her cheek when they made contact. No doubt the confusion and fear pinching her face were adding to the pain muddling her thoughts. She looked to the vicomte for answers to questions she couldn't verbalize.

"You were assaulted last night," he said pointedly.

"Vicomte, some compassion!" his wife gasped.

Anna winced at the sound of chair legs on wood as the vicomte pulled a seat directly in front to her, wife standing at his side. He leaned in toward Anna with a gentleness reflecting behind his eyes that contradicted his curt words.

"We need to know what she remembers so we can help the authorities," he insisted.

"Authorities?" Anna's pulse quickened her temple throbbing now in panic.

"For Mercy's sake," the vicomtess begged, "the girl has been through enough."

The tone of her voice split Anna's already aching head in two. She raised a hand to silence them.

"I remember nothing," she mused, working to make sense of the fragmented images flashing through her memory. She caressed the black fabric in her lap, finding comfort in the feel of it in her hand. There was something familiar to the way is slid under her palms.

"Mademoiselle, anything you can remember will help the authorities. Your assailant's size, his shape, anything at all."

Her gaze bounced from the vicomte's frustration and his wife's concern. What had happened? The horrible images of masks and capes shadowed in darkness and wrapped around the pain throbbing at her temples. She gripped the drape in her lap in an effort to remain grounded in the present. "I can't." The words rasped over her, even as panic chilled her to her core.

Confusion had her tightly wrapped with no way to loosen the binds. Remarkably drowsy, she didn't notice the door had opened until Madame Giry was standing next to the vicomtess.

"Vicomte, vicomtess," Madame Giry said, quickly glancing over her shoulder.

Anna swallowed around the rock in her throat and leaned to one side, trying to see who else she should expect to arrive.

"Are you safe, Madame Giry?" the vicomte asked. "I was informed of this assault shortly after breakfast and told my meeting with Inspector Legard would need to be here. We were worried about you."

"I'm fine, Monsieur, your worry should be for Anna."

Anna flashed ice cold. What had happened to send the authorities down on the opera house? She didn't want any authorities anywhere near her! The room spun as her breath came all too fast.

"Relax, Mademoiselle," the vicomtess calmed. "We'll see you safe from this injustice."

Questions plagued Anna, but she couldn't find her voice. Her glance wandered toward the vicomte looking for any answer she could discern in his face.

"I'm concerned for her I assure you, Madame Giry," he stressed, his tone low and serious. "However, a note mysteriously appeared in my drawing room this morning. It was rather blunt, its author making it clear he despised the fact certain—arrangements—

were not met last night. He said he had a message for my wife he was forced to deliver 'by other means'. I intend to help the authorities locate the Mademoiselle's assailant, but she doesn't know what implications this holds."

"Im… implications? " Anna groggily forced out the words.

She clung to her makeshift blanket; drew it closer around her body. Its scent touched something distant in her mind even if through her fear it did nothing to warm her. Next to her, the vicomtess shot to her feet, snatching it from her lap.

"Where did this come from?" she blurted. "Did he wear this cloak?"

"Mademoiselle, do you recognize this?" the vicomte asked.

It was a cloak? Anna stared at the fabric. Somewhere in her memories she saw fluid waves of black as that cloak rolled elegantly against the air as an extension of… someone's body, but through her pain and confusion she couldn't place who's.

"You do know! He wore this cloak and a black mask. Didn't he?" The vicomtess swung around toward her husband, outright fright replacing concern. "It's him. This was his message. He meant this for me!"

The assault came flooding back like a tidal wave: the swirl of a cape, the flash of a mask, and the impact of the lantern. Silent screams unhinged Anna's mouth. She grasped frantically at the air around her. He wore a mask!

"The Phantom," the vicomte spat. "I've heard enough."

Anna looked from him to the vicomtess. Her gaze fell on Madame Giry. Anna shook her head whimpering 'no'.

Madame Giry froze in shock. "I can't fathom he would—that he could…"

Anna's mind replayed what she saw; the pain of it clubbing her over and over again. She couldn't take the sudden betrayal and bolted for the door.

"Mademoiselle, no," the vicomte grabbed for her.

The final thing Anna saw before a cocoon of darkness enveloped her was the face of the vicomte as he swept her into his arms.

FIFTEEN

Raoul found the inspector, cheek to floorboards staring intently at oil-slicked hay. When he rose, it was with such slow deliberateness that the weight on his shoulders could almost be seen. He moved with caution, pausing every now and then to look around, measure something, or kneel once more.

"Inspector?" Raoul called out.

Inspector Jules Legard stood quickly at the mention of his name, brushing hay from his meticulously groomed uniform. He kept his focus locked on the task at hand and replied without bothering to see who addressed him. He raised one finger toward the sound of the voice.

"Move no further lest you destroy my evidence." He stabbed at his notebook with a lead before jamming it into his jacket pocket. "Why I must tolerate interruptions when in the middle of an investigation is beyond me!"

Raoul clasped his hands behind his back and respectfully waited for him to realize whom he addressed. Legard turned. Raoul hid his laughter at the embarrassment he saw flash across Legard's face behind a well-placed cough.

"Vicomte de Chagny!" Legard exclaimed.

"Greetings old friend."

Legard, moving toward him, extended his hand and Raoul shook it. "Forgive my disrespect. The Prefect mentioned your return. He told me you wanted to speak with me but didn't say why." Legard indicated the burned hay. "I regret this has fallen in the path of our contact. What brings you to the middle of my crime scene?"

"Did you find anything?" Raoul gestured to the broken glass and fire scarred floor.

"No. We're fortunate the whole building didn't burn. I've not questioned the poor girl yet. I'm still gathering evidence here." He resumed his pacing of the scene. "The doors weren't locked. I've told the management to do so at night. The city has been riddled with muggings and rape. I blame it on absinthe and loose attitudes. I only hope the girl was not violated in such a vulgar manner. There's no evidence as to the identity of her assailant here."

Inspector Legard was a tall, proud man, several years Raoul's senior. He was the best in his field, working tirelessly until the crimes he was involved in were solved and taking personal blame if they weren't.

Raoul reached into his jacket pocket, produced the note, and handed it to Legard. "I've all the evidence you need."

The Inspector's lips pursed. "Perhaps I don't want to know why you're back in Paris and wanted to meet with me after all, especially while being armed." He lifted a disapproving eyebrow.

Raoul hastened to cover the pistol previously concealed by his coattails. Legard unfolded the note. As he read, Raoul stared at the charred hay counting down from ten as he waited for the reaction he knew was going to come.

"*Merde!*" Legard's pacing reminded Raoul of a caged animal impatient, or crazed. "Why didn't you tell me you were coming to Paris? Is this for certain?"

"I'm afraid it is, Jules."

Legard stopped in his tracks. "The man is *dead.*" Raoul's expression spoke all the truth Legard needed. "Where is your wife? Is she safe?"

Raoul nodded toward the far end of the stable where Christine fed his stallion.

"So this assault?" Legard gestured to the hay with the note.

"Him."

"Christ!" Legard plowed his hand through his hair.

Raoul filled him in on the details they'd discovered when speaking with Anna, all the while Legard kept pacing, his strides growing longer with each sentence. Without warning the Inspector spun, releasing his disbelief by kicking a hole in the nearest stall door. Raoul shot a glance in Christine's direction, but luckily she was far enough away not to be startled. He couldn't blame Legard for any of his reactions. If it were within his upbringing to do so, Raoul would have done much more than merely kick a stall door.

"He's alive?" Legard spit. "That son-of-a-bitch is still here? I breathed that investigation night and day, uncovering nothing. I ate, drank, and slept that case and got nowhere. We couldn't even prove he existed, and now you're telling me he's alive? *And still in my city?*"

"Jules, lower your voice, please."

"Vicomte, I'll have every last one of my men in this opera house. I'll tear it apart until I find him. I—"

"Your voice, Legard." Raoul held a hand up, knowing his authority would not be argued against. "I want this kept quiet. I don't need any vendettas. My wife endured enough with the last incident of the Phantom. I don't want this tormenting her again."

"Then what are you proposing?" Legard asked restlessly. He stood like a matador ready to wave red. "I want this man's head mounted on my wall."

"You will have to fight me for it. Walk with me, Jules."

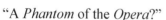

"A *Phantom* of the *Opera?*"

Edward snorted. He leaned back in his chair, making the leather upholstery squeak under the substantial girth of his thighs. He pondered the pretty aristocrat before him. The Vicomte de Chagny appeared the type more comfortable with sipping fine champagne from a fancy glass than making heads or tails of his con. The fool had confirmed for Edward that nobles were indeed a dim-witted bunch of ninnies.

"A Phantom of the Opera?" Edward repeated for good measure. "My dear vicomte, I assure you this assault was random. I've no specters in my opera house."

Edward smiled politely then quickly let it dropped it. This meeting grated against his last available nerves, and he did his best to keep that from showing. While he expected the rumors to bring the vicomte groveling into his office, Edward didn't anticipate any assaults. The new development made him clench his teeth so hard his ears rang. Behind him Jacob sprung his pocket watch open and shut, making a distinct clicking sound that was driving nails into the back of Edward's head. He was inches away from swinging around and shoving Jacob's unease down his throat.

"Gentlemen," the vicomte replied, "I know this is difficult to comprehend, but the Phantom is very much a man. You've most likely heard about the stigma marring my name. I'm telling you truthfully, there's a man in this theater who will stop at nothing to claim my wife."

The vicomte leaned forward, his forearms upon his knees, his head bowed in servant-like respect of the situation.

Edward cleared his throat, wanting to laugh at the man's obvious frustration. The vicomte had no idea how he was being played, but tipping his hand wasn't part of their plan. He forced his back straighter, folding his arms in an attempt to lend more weight to his words. "Vicomte, I'm well aware of the rumors, but what you're describing is unbelievable. The attack on that poor child was a message meant for you and the vicomtess because you shafted a Phantom?"

Whoever was responsible, and Edward had a fairly good idea who was, it complicated matters, while at the same time adding to the illusion he had built. It was infuriatingly brilliant.

"It runs much deeper than that, Monsieur," the vicomte cautioned.

Edward nodded slowly and rose, and turning his back to the vicomte, he faced Jacob. "Where the hell is Richard?" he hissed into his ear before turning to address the vicomte again. "Forgive me, but what more is it you want me to do? The authorities were notified."

Edward nearly choked on that word. Damn inspectors. Luckily France had no clue about their rather disagreeable life across Europe or else this con could get difficult. "They'll be treating this as the heinous crime it is, but to ask me to pursue a Phantom?"

The vicomte held up his hand forcing Edward to swallow the air he rolled over his tongue. What a sad attempt on the vicomte's behalf to strengthen his pathetic view of the situation. "Gentlemen, I'm am not asking you to get involved in any pursuits; you clearly underestimate what I'm telling you. I merely ask you to do everything you can to make certain this opera house is secure. I'll spare no expense in keeping the vicomtess safe."

Edward's ears pricked up like a hungry dog. "You'll spare no expense?" He thought on his feet, weaving together another component to fill his pockets. He did his best to feign concern. "Vicomte, perhaps it is best we cancel the celebration and you take your wife home where it's safe."

He heard the snap of Jacob's pocket watch again and before it could give one more click, Edward shot him a look. He'd baited a hook and if Jacob's anxiety blew it for him, he'd dump him in the Seine.

"Monsieur, that's precisely what we don't wish," the vicomte said. "The opera needs this event. Too much ill air is associated with this place and this event could turn it all around. We'll not allow this man to drive us away. I want this manhunt kept quiet. Worry not about the finances, gentlemen, name your price and you have my money."

The pocket watch suddenly fell silent. Glancing behind him, Edward smirked at Jacob whose brows had shot up. He too could hear the vicomte's coins rattle into his greedy hands.

"I've arranged security for my wife," he added. "It's imperative she be kept safe."

Edward covered his grimace by scrubbing the heat that blasted the back of his neck. He flared his nostrils as anger centered in his gut. He wouldn't have to deal with security or police if that bloody thorn in his side named Anna hadn't had her face rearranged and he was certain he knew who did it. The entire thing reeked of Richard's temper. Richard, the unpredictable ass, had been certain Anna was out to destroy this con; it would be like him to destroy her first. Now Edward had to contend with the authorities creeping around his theater.

"Very well, Vicomte, do as you wish." Edward encouraged, though his voice tightened.

"Thank you, Monsieur. We'll stay in contact, and please take care."

Edward and Jacob nodded emphatically as they escorted the vicomte to the door. Edward didn't waste any time in shoving Jacob out the door after him.

"Find Richard," he growled.

❋❖•••———•••———•••❖❋

Anna sat in the windowsill tracing a writhing line of water down the length of the glass. Glass, like happiness, was easily destroyed. She'd had one moment of bliss at a ball, but even that was a well-constructed con—just like her life.

Through the reflection in the window she saw Madame Giry poke her head in and out of the door ever few moments, pace the room, then start all over again.

Anna's life had roared back at her as she had relived what she could recall of her attack to an Inspector Legard. Sitting near him, replaying what she knew, made her wish to crawl away to the nearest hole and hide. Anna hated the authorities and their fear inducing judgments against her character. Now she had a new man to hate in Inspector Legard—and all he was to her was a blurry image of a man in uniform in her mind.

The years of abuse closed in around her slowly shredding her spirit and pushing her deeper into a claustrophobic world of her own. She leaned her temple hard against the pane; trying to splinter the image of the one man she had trusted betraying her in the worst possible way.

Beyond her reflection, Madame Giry had poked her head out of the door one final time. Focusing on the sound of the rain, Anna all but drowned out the stunted conversation going on behind her.

"Please, Monsieur, you must go."

"You summoned me to your office. Now, let me see her, Madame Giry."

"Monsieur, things have changed! You must go!"

A blurry figure pushed past Madame Giry's reflection, and into the room, but Anna looked beyond it. She studied the rain, wishing she could drown in the drops.

"They're all here, Monsieur—the vicomte, vicomtess, the authorities. You must leave until this is figured out."

"This is my opera house, Madame. I will deal with their suspicions later. Anna?"

Anna lifted her head from the window. She stared deeply at her reflection and that of Madame Giry's, watching the rain warp their images.

"Anna?" the voice called again.

The mirror image grew in size, a distorted black mask taking shape in the pane. Like a raven coming in to perch on her shoulder, it grew larger and made a distant memory surface in her mind. Anna fought the panic threatening to overtake her.

Leaping from her seat, she slammed her back against the wall pressing herself as far away from the man, and the memories, in front of her as she could. Anna's vision spun at the sight of him. She was a stupid, love-struck fool to ever trust a man! If she could, she would have yanked her heart out and destroyed the last remnants of it herself. She never should have allowed herself to believe that Erik could care for her.

"Anna, it is me. You are safe. I promise you…"

She didn't care if his voice was gentle and his posture passive. She wanted to climb the walls and over the ceiling to avoid being anywhere near him. What was coming to light in her mind was leaving her legs numb beneath her.

"I know it's you, you lying, betraying son-of-a-bitch! And don't you dare act like you care! I can care for myself!" she cried, desperately trying to make her way toward the door. "I've done nothing to you! Nothing! But you…. you did this," she jerked a finger at her face, "The man who hit me wore *that* mask and I swear as long as I live I never want you near me again!"

"He *what!*" Erik's head snapped like the crack of a whip in Madame Giry's direction.

"Monsieur, I tried to tell you!"

Anna moved closer to the door.

Rounding on her, Erik grabbed her shoulders and kept her pinned to the wall. Anna shrieked.

"Anna, it is me, Erik!"

Digging her nails into his forearms, she jerked her knee into his groin as hard as she could. The instant she heard him cry out, Anna ducked under his arm. Erik was too swift and hooked her arm, whirling her back into his embrace.

"Anna!"

The power of his voice rattled her so violently she froze until she saw those eyes she thought had loved her. "Let. Go Of. Me."

Like the strike of a match, the fear inside of her blazed to life. With every ounce of strength she had, Anna rounded herself against him and broke free.

As she flung the door open, her haste caused her to trip over the threshold and tumble to the floor.

Erik leapt for her the instant she landed. In such a state she would run herself into God knows what trouble.

Anna propelled herself backward with frantic swimming motions of her arms and legs. Catching her by the ankle, he dragged her, kicking and screaming obscenities back toward him. A dark mask of dread covered her face as her skirts shuffled up in the scuffle.

"Anna, stop." Erik dodged her fist. "Please, listen to me!"

A primal need to fight replaced any sort of reason in her. He ducked kicks and swings and a string of curses unlike he had ever heard. Had he any sort of sense of how to handle himself like a gentleman under such circumstances, the situation would not have been nearly as traumatic for her or as confounding to him.

"Stop!" he snapped again, artfully deflecting the small foot that flailed at him as it made several vicious passes at his mask. With a feral growl, Erik lunged, succeeding in pinning Anna's arms. "Listen to me!" he growled, subduing her with all his weight.

She turned her head. Her breath came in shallow pants. "Be done with it," she mumbled, defeat smothering her will to fight. "Do what you need and be done with it."

"*Anna, mon Dieu, no!*"

"Monsieur, they are coming," Madame Giry harshly whispered. "You must go!"

"I will not leave, Madame Giry!" Erik spat over his shoulder to her. "She is not thinking straight. I will not have her believing I would ever touch—"

A voice interrupted his confessions.

"Madame Giry? Mademoiselle?"

In tandem with the box keeper's, Erik's head spun toward the far end of the hall. For a fleeting moment his eyes locked with Raoul's. The sniveling boy went pale while Erik's face heated beneath the mask. He struggled to his feet. Legs straddling the woman beneath him, he loomed to his full height.

"You!" Raoul shouted, spinning Christine away from the sight. When the vicomte shoved her aside and began to race down the hall, Erik threw the gauntlet at his feet.

"Pass no judgment on what you see here."

Racing against Raoul's approach, Erik spun and knelt before Anna. Turning her face to his, he forced her to look him directly in the eye.

"Listen to me, Anna."

She tried to turn away. "Don't hurt me again, please..."

Erik's grip tightened. Raoul's shouts were louder and his approach quickening. Erik caught a glimpse of the pistol in his hand.

"Anna?" Erik bent in close and pressed his lips to her ear, whispering with a light and daring pressure against its lobe, "Listen to my voice—I am not the Phantom."

He quickly glanced at the vicomte and then into Anna's eyes, frantically searching for a glimmer of recognition.

Anna focused on his face as her gaze traced his mask. "Your voice. It's... it's not that of the man who hit me. Er... Erik?"

With one quick leap he vanished, disappearing into the walls of his opera house.

SIXTEEN

Madame Giry's eyes widened, fear buckling her knees under her as Erik and Anna fought. She reached to her side, one arm groping for the doorframe as the vicomte slid to a stop before them. She didn't start breathing again until he shoved the pistol out of sight. Though he buttoned his waistcoat to conceal the weapon, he made no effort to act apologetic.

"Are you both unharmed?" He extended a hand to Anna and helped her up.

"Yes, Monsieur," Anna replied, though her voice quaked enough to warrant his additional inquiry.

"Are you certain? Did he harm you further? Did he put his hands on you in *any* manner?"

"Vicomte, please." Madame Giry softly called to him worried Anna may faint. The subtle shake of her head respectfully asked for silence. Anna seemed shocked enough; now was not the time to add to her confusion. Taking Anna from the vicomte, Madame Giry kept her close as he frantically conducted a search of the shadows.

"How did he get near you? Was the door locked as I instructed?"

"Yes, Monsieur," Madame Giry replied, the blatant fib sliding easily off her tongue. A perplexed squint squeezed the corners of Anna's eyes. Before Anna could contradict her, Madame Giry wrapped an iron tight grip around her shoulders.

"Mademoiselle, is there anyplace you can go?" the vicomte asked. "That man, your assailant, he'll be looking to harm you again."

Madame Giry bit her tongue at the confusion distorting Anna's face.

"That couldn't be the man," Anna stammered.

"That *was* the Phantom," the vicomtess insisted, joining them. Her hand, too, hovered over her chest. "Forgive me and my words the other day, Mademoiselle. I never would have wished the Phantom on you."

As the vicomtess lowered her head and empathy filled her stance, and Anna's bewilderment deepened, Madame Giry's resolve coiled like a cobra constricting the last ounce of life from its meal. A fierce urge to protect Erik sliced through her chest so sharply she nearly lost her breath. Erik was a man, a mere man, not a Phantom! She had witnessed it herself. The need to usher Anna away was imperative. Madame Giry didn't know what was going on, but she knew she had to get Anna safely away from any assumptions the vicomte and his wife had regarding Erik and the situation.

They, after all, didn't know the same man.

"Vicomte, Vicomtess, she should rest. Anna can return to the dormitories. She'll not be alone for a moment. You can station what security you wish, but speak of this no more. For Anna's sake."

Madame Giry hustled Anna away and chanced a look behind her. The vicomte held his wife as tightly as she gripped Anna.

"Madame Giry," Anna asked softly, the notes of profound sadness painting her voice. "Did Erik do this to me?"

Swallowing down her nerves. Madame Giry quickened her pace. "Hush, he'll tell you himself."

⟡ ⸻ ⸻ ⟡

Richard Barret sauntered into the office, followed by Jacob Wischard. He kicked the door shut, as Edward wasted no words.

"Richard, are you insane?"

"Of course I am Edward; it's one of my more endearing traits."

Richard casually took a seat on the couch and crossed his legs. He straightened out his vest and brushed nonexistent lint off his costume. Satisfied he was as gentlemanly as he should be, he bit at a loose piece of flesh on his pinky as Edward turned various shades of purple.

"You beat the bloody hell out of your daughter?" Edward barked. "What were you thinking?"

Winking, Richard slung his arm over the back of the couch. "I didn't do it. Rumor has it, it was a Phantom."

"This is doing nothing for my constitution, Edward." Jacob bemoaned.

"Oh please. If you were there, you would have gladly taken advantage of her position." Richard swallowed a lewd laugh. "She's lucky I was only in the mood to knock her senseless. I told you I'd take care of her meddling. This is no different from when she was a child."

"Richard, the authorities were here. I've a vicomte who wants a bloody private security force running around this damn opera house. We're already wanted men, you Goddamn fool! This was a simple con, what the devil were you thinking?"

"No con is simple, Edward. Have you learned nothing? Jacob tells me the vicomte will spare no expense to keep his wife safely out of the clutches of this Phantom."

Edward shrugged as Richard rolled his head against the back of the couch. Seriously, how stupid could his partners be? "How much will he pay if she were *in* the clutches of a Phantom?" He stunned Edward and Jacob into silence, like he'd hoped. "I've done you a favor gentlemen. The stakes just got higher. This is *my* con now."

The reins of control were firmly in his grip. The hierarchy had been reestablished and Edward and Jacob could do nothing other than stoop to his whims. Richard headed for the door, roughly smacking Edward and Jacob on their backs as he passed. They stumbled out of his way. It wasn't a bow but would suffice.

"If you'll excuse me, gentlemen, I need to play the violin." Richard pantomimed playing his imaginary instrument and slammed the door behind him.

The two snifters clinked together in an apathetic attempt at cheers. The morning had been filled with activity, but the image of Erik escaping into the shadows was the only thing replaying endlessly in on Raoul's brain. He leaned on the mantel watching Legard stare across his townhome's library, seemingly uninterested in the volumes of books he inspected.

"You can be rest assured, I'll see she's protected," Legard promised. He seemed ready to have every army in Europe protecting Christine. "Tomorrow, I'll ask that some of the finest gendarmes work with the theater and Paris police. We'll keep this silent until we find him."

Raoul nodded his appreciation as he stared into his drink. "What of the mademoiselle, Anna?"

"A watchful eye will be on her as well."

The vicomte studied his friend. Legard paced first left to right, then forward and back, before repeating the sequence. A clear indication he was sorting through his evidence.

"He has to be in those vaults," Legard said decidedly. "Where else could he have been hiding?"

"You know, as well as I, that all the entrances are sealed. At least the ones of which we knew. Madame Giry assured me she knows of no way into them."

"What of the gate on the Rue Scribe side?"

"I never found that entrance to the underground lake. You know that, I know that, the Prefect of Police knows that. It's useless."

Legard's steps became more agitated. He tapped his fingers against his glass splashing his drink around the tumbler. Raoul quirked a brow at him. Was that another way for Legard to sort his thoughts, or a nervous tick? Either way, Raoul would allow neither to get in the way of this investigation.

"I don't want this to cause the upheaval of innocent people," Raoul demanded. "I want nobody involved but my family and those in service to you. Do I make myself clear?"

Legard stopped pacing. Either he didn't agree or he knew what Raoul asked was impossible.

The tension snapped when a servant arrived with a note on a silver platter. Raoul accepted it, dismissing the servant immediately. Raoul took one look at the scarlet writing, cussed and handed it off to Legard. He walked to the window, bracing himself against the sill as Legard read aloud.

Monsieur le Vicomte:

> *Your suspicions disgust me. I assure you, I am the most hospitable of gentlemen and have nothing to do with this heinous crime. While I acknowledge*

your need to increase security about my facility, I implore you; your concerns involving me are unfounded. I will personally be looking into this assault and suggest you do not make it difficult for me to move about my theater. I would like to attend to my affairs unhindered.

In addition, I beseech you again for a moment of Christine's time. Fret not her safety; there is absolutely no need. Any yet— my fondest greetings to Inspector Legard. I trust you scampered off for his assistance again. I hope he is well.

I remain your most humble and obedient servant, Ph. of the O.

P.T.O. Nevertheless, Monsieur le Vicomte, if you pull your pistol on me one more time, you will truly make me angry.

Raoul laughed in horrified unease at Legard being bid welcome personally in the letter; the blasted Phantom really did know everything.

"You pulled a pistol on him?" Legard asked, clearly incredulous at such a show of stupidity and bravado.

"Yes. Next time I'll fire."

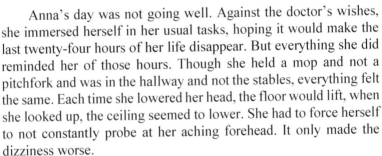

Anna's day was not going well. Against the doctor's wishes, she immersed herself in her usual tasks, hoping it would make the last twenty-four hours of her life disappear. But everything she did reminded her of those hours. Though she held a mop and not a pitchfork and was in the hallway and not the stables, everything felt the same. Each time she lowered her head, the floor would lift, when she looked up, the ceiling seemed to lower. She had to force herself to not constantly probe at her aching forehead. It only made the dizziness worse.

Like the peasants she passed on the streets asking for handouts, reminders seemed to lurk everywhere. People stared at the bruises on her face as she walked by and the burn near her eye stung with every blink. The vicomte had reopened the investigations into the Phantom of the Opera and Inspector Jules Legard had security at every spot. The gendarmes wore plain clothes so as not

146

to arouse suspicion, but Anna saw through their façade. She no longer had to run from the authorities, but old habits died hard and their presence put her on edge.

It was Erik that lurked in her thoughts the most. His final admission haunted her: *I am no Phantom.*

If only she could believe those words.

She didn't think she'd ever believe those words not after—

"Anna. There you are." Madame Giry plucked the mop from her and leaned it against the wall. "He's left something for you." She pulled a parchment note from the folds of her dress, pressing it into Anna's hand.

Anna turned the note over. The unfamiliar seal in deep black wax and the scarlet ink addressing it to her attention leapt off the page. A note? From Erik? A childish scrawl of shaky and misconnected letters hovered haphazardly across the page. She scowled at Madame Giry.

"Go on," she coaxed.

Anna broke the seal and squinted as she read:

My dearest Anna:

> *You have my deepest and most heartfelt apologies for this tangled web in which you have become involved. I write this letter with the humblest of hearts in the hopes you will understand.*

> *I will do everything in my power to find the individual responsible for the crimes committed against you. This assault was not at my hand. Do not believe anything told to you by the vicomte or his wife. Their judgment of the situation is clouded. Believe only that I meant to meet with Christine to speak with her in person. Though that has yet to occur, I assure you I mean her no harm. I only wish to deliver the message that you were right.*

> *Christine was my world. She was the essence of my art and the voice of my soul. But I built the most triumphant illusions and could not see beyond my pitiful existence to embrace reality. But you saw beyond it and you were right. She could not and she will not ever wholly love the man behind the mask.*

If there is a way for a scarred and jaded heart to beat again, I have found it. There was no mistake. Your benevolence, empathy, and friendship ignited a passion in my soul that lies far beyond my realm of mastery.

While Christine was once my world, you have become my air. If you will have me, I remain yours, in love.

I have the honor to be, your most sincere and devoted admirer,
E.

Anna pressed her trembling fingers to her lips. Such eloquence exuded from the pages, bringing back to her the image of that shy gentleman she knew in Erik. The tears running down her face stung the corners of her burn.

"Forgive me, Anna, for taking so long to understand him as you do."

Anna controlled her tears, though she could weep rivers. "Madame Giry, can I trust you?"

"Implicitly."

"I need to find him, but the guards…"

"We'll find a way. " Madame Giry's voice held the determination of an army of thousands.

SEVENTEEN

Anna's fingers glided along the hedgerow, coaxing awake the heady aroma of the roses. The beautiful blooms rambled along the garden wall drinking in the last moments of the afternoon. Twilight would soon fall and night would tuck them safely into bed. Anna envied the roses. They would spend the night safe under the stars and wake in the morning with not a care in the world.

The paths she roamed led away from the street and iron gates that exposed her to the stares of the citizens on the opposite side. Anna cocked her head and dragged her feet along the soft soil beneath her boot. She wondered on the kings who'd meditated on these paths and the traitors who'd plotted on them. But it was the lovers who'd strolled on their evening trysts that she dwelled upon. Her heart quickened thinking that she may be among them. Anna never had a suitor. The thought of being in love was both intoxicating and frightening. Such hope filled her at the idea she swore she would burst, until a plunging sank through her. What if the gendarmes found Erik out here? What if he wasn't sincere and it was him who attacked her? So many things spun in her mind it was a wonder she could walk straight at all.

The massive cypress trees guarded her from any curious eyes as she waited. The gnarled trunks contrasted the flat and pristine paths they decorated while large branches divided the isolated part of the Tuileries into a garden of light and shadow.

Anna sat on a stone bench and pulled the note from her pocket. She stared at the scarlet writing, willing it to replace the awful images in her mind. Anna puzzled through all she felt over the last week she'd last had any true contact with Erik.

The idea that she'd someday find love seemed ridiculous. She'd never received a letter before, let alone a love letter. Perhaps she'd been wrong to dismiss the idea that her someone could be Erik. Neatly creasing the note, she tucked it into the folds of her dress.

Anna was assured it would be safer for Erik to find her outside of the opera house than for her to attempt to slip unnoticed into his labyrinth. It was a fitting rendezvous, knowing he often chanced wandering these gardens, spying on young couples and pondering his fate. Here, among the falling twilight and shelter of the trees, she waited for the unlikely man she may call a lover.

Movement caught her eye. Erik appeared in the distance, cautiously rounding a massive trunk. She rose, feeling like a flower waiting to bloom in his presence but fearing she'd wither if he rejected her. Erik's impeccable manner of dress was gone. Beneath the jacket he wore, his shirt was smudged with dirt and he neglected a cravat. His sleeves were rolled to his elbows exposing pale forearms, and his boots and pants were wet.

Erik edged around the garden. His eyes turned a brilliant gold as he passed from shadow to shadow. Perhaps he moved in such a way to be wary of the bounty on his head, or like she, his guarded steps echoed a man worried over rejection as well.

Keeping his chin tucked and the collar of his jacket around his mask, his gaze rested on the ground between them until he looked upon her face. The world stilled when he looked at her, and Anna knew behind his eyes was her strength.

Step by step, she closed the distance between them. If she were going to speak, she figured it best to do so quickly before her nerves caused her to run away.

"Erik, while I've been led to believe it was you using me to get at the vicomtess, I know no part of you capable of doing that to me or to her." She walked closer to him, shame dipping her head. Once near him she reached out and placed a hand on his arm. "Forgive me for even thinking it."

Erik's gaze dropped to her hand. His arm stiffened for a second. She wanted nothing more than to make him believe that

150

being touched and loved by another wasn't a forbidden desire.

"You have nothing for which to apologize, Anna."

The flowing tones of his voice poured over her. "Erik, your note..." her voice cracked, forcing his stare from her hand to her face. Anna chastised her weakness and, gathering all her emotions, she took a deep breath. "I will... have you."

They stood motionless, held bound to one another, in the fading light of day as if her words had been more than he could bear. Looking on her he saw her bruises and the evidence of all she had already endured, and to love him, she'd have to endure far worse.

"Do not say such things, woman, unless you understand where my mind can lead you." Though he wanted to cherish the words she'd uttered, he realized the wicked deception of his madness could tarnish them in an instant. "By having me, you belong to me and all that I am. And I am not a normal man. This world you have lived in exists for me as a different plane of reality. I do not fit into the world's standards. I am the very embodiment of all that men fear and hate."

"Erik, I know—"

"Oh, but you do not know. I can strive to live and taste of your world, but you can never live in mine." He stared at the heavens, knowing she had more to understand of him than there were stars in the sky. A chasm had split between them and he feared she might not have the strength to take the leap across. He lowered his eyes. "Unless... you dare to trust me."

"Dare to?"

"Trust I know and understand my mind, and that I can control the battles being waged beneath the beauty and music I constantly hear."

"What battles, Erik?" she asked, dropping her hand from his arm.

He reached for her hoping to help her bridge across the divide between their worlds but nerves got a hold of him and his hand brushed the air instead of her cheek. "The battles between my dementia and genius, the past and present, anger and joy, right from wrong... good from evil."

He circled her, stressing each painful word with a fist to his chest.

"Between my passion to live like a normal man and my want to act on all the desires and sensations normal men have, and the stark reality that so long as I live there will be scorn, ridicule, prejudice and fear. So do not say you will have me unless you understand the precipice upon which you stand. Unless you recognize the prison to which you sentence yourself. Unless you truly understand *me*."

Dreadful silence stood between them like an invisible sentry.

"To understand you, is to understand music," she recited, slowly like a woman determined to pass a test. "To view the world in layers with all its harmony and counterpoint, understanding that one gives birth to the other. They are two sides of the same thing. They look at things differently, each sound barren and meaningless if played separately. One can exalt and support while the other can equalize yet create discord. But somehow they entwine in richness and join music. The harmonist in you moves from chord to chord with each being finished in its beauty. While the contrapuntist is never at peace, unpredictable, and achieves nothing until the music is made totally complete."

Her eyes locked on his and he was certain she could see into his very soul. Erik slowed in the circle he carved around her. The woman before him understood more than he could have hoped... Erik hung on her every word barely wanting to breathe lest he miss any indication he may be truly loved.

"Music can be soothing and full of beauty." Eyes still pinned, she moved her head following him with each calculated rotation he made around her. "Yet it can switch in a blink to be painful and full of dissonance. You are made of madness and Death just as you are full of passion and life. It's my choice to run or listen. And if you are giving me the choice that you denied the vicomtess, then I choose to listen."

His chest collapsed as he released the air trapped in his lungs. Could she really have said that? A lump filled his throat as he listened to words. He'd be her breath for the rest of his days if she would only say what he hoped....

"I know your demons," she continued, "but I can feel the need of a willing gentleman repressed for too long by judgment. I understand your music and I will have you—but more than that I wish you."

Her words lingered in the air before trailing away like a puff of smoke. Erik shut his eyes as the declaration he'd waited a lifetime to hear caressed his ears.

"I love you."

He rocked backward with the impact of those words. Not a composition in his soul could match them. He approached, intoxicated by three words easily taken for granted by those who'd heard them from birth. He dared not speak lest anything chase away their lilting sound.

Air trapped in his lungs as she stood on the tips of her toes and reached to his face. She teetered as she entwined her hands around his neck. With gentle pressure to the base of his skull and an amazing strength that belied her petite size, she pulled him toward her. Her lips closed over his.

His entire body deflated the moment she stole his control. Like a sailor drawn to the depths of the ocean and drowned by the beauty of a Siren, he stood bewitched by her affection and transfixed by her seduction. His mouth fell open to greet hers, and he slipped away into the gentleness of her kiss. He could do nothing other than be a pupil as Anna taught him to be a man. She parted her lips and invited him in, this kiss more daring than the one before. He hesitantly followed her lead, exploring her with his tongue—seeking, learning, and understanding.

The crescendo of sensations rose and rocked him with waves of deeper and more urgent needs. Her scent, her taste, and their union in such a simple gesture he would not live without again. The instant she confessed her love and offered her lips, his murky existence faded and he swam toward the music.

He curled his arms around her tiny waist, lifting her level with him. For the first time nothing seemed to exist but the present. He drove his kiss deeper, seeking to make it match the profound pulsing of his heart.

Erik touched his tongue to his lips, savoring a second taste of her when she gently broke the kiss. He lowered her and grabbed her hands to lay them against his mask wanting to feel the warmth of her flesh flow through it. In her hands it was beauty. Gazing on her for a long time, his mind searched for the words to reply—words for the moment he knew only how to express in music. Instead, silence said all he needed. The only things he wanted to hear echoing in his mind were the three words she'd just said. Awestruck, he wrapped her hand around the crook of his arm, and walked.

"You're wet," Anna noticed, wiping her hand on her dress.

"I had to make some adjustments to the labyrinth—again."

Anna stared remorsefully at her feet. "Erik, I'll fix this. I'll go to the vicomte and tell him it wasn't you. I'll get him to end the investigation. He'll have to understand. They're hunting you for no reason. This is unjust. It's my fault."

He forced his lips to curve into the semblance of a smile. "Your naivety is most endearing. What is just does not matter. In this case, only the past does. Do not worry about the vicomte; he is the least of my concerns. You are to bear no burden in this. None of this is your fault, nor is it without cause. They have their reasons for suspecting me."

Anna couldn't meet his gaze. "As much as I accept your past, it has become evident how hunted you truly are. Yet they're looking for a Phantom, not you."

"I told you before, for many they are one and the same. I am not about to ignore my past; it has defined who I am." His defensive tone carried with it an edge of warning. "Nor will I allow it to catch up with me. Let them hunt. They will not be able to hold me. My only concern is to find the man who did this to you." He turned her to look at her face in the fading light. "That may scar," he sighed with painful familiarity.

"Should scars matter?"

"To me they do not." Erik brushed her cheek with his knuckle silently vowing she'd never see another scar as long as he lived. "Anna, do not let this investigation weigh on you. I want you to be safe. My only concern is for you."

"And what it will do to the vicomtess?"

That name was a hot iron to his heart. He nodded. The truth had no place hiding from Anna. She was like the violin he prized, in tune with his every emotion.

"Oh, Anna, I love her." Erik turned his head to peer at her from the corner of his eye. "It is wrong of me now, but I do not know how to stop loving her."

She spoke to her feet. "I'm not one to look to for answers in that, Erik. I, unlike you, have never loved before until now. I suppose you'll always love her. If I must, I can live in her shadow."

That saddened him, for Anna deserved nothing but the warmth of the sun. "You live in my heart, Anna, not in another's shadow." He sighed, wrestling with his emotions. "I love her, and you must understand Erik always will. But my mind wrestles with

disorganized notes when I think of her. I want my mind to be still."
He slid his arm to untangle their embrace and turned her to face him.
"You make it so. You complete the counterpoint." He lifted her
hand to his lips and kissed her palm. His fingers caressed where his
lips had been. "I cannot live like anybody else without speaking
with her, without seeing her one more time. I must let Christine
know I meant her no harm. I cannot completely rid myself of her
until I see her and explain everything."

"What will you do?"

Before he could answer, footsteps approached. Pressing his
fingers to her mouth, he gave a quick nod toward the direction of
the garden's center.

"Are you seriously going to let him get away with this,
Edward? I'm telling you the man is insane."

"The man is a genius, Jacob. If he wants to run this con, let him
run it."

"Edward, you saw what he did to the girl. This is madness."

Erik twirled Anna against the trunk of a tree, rounding them
out of sight. He leaned on their every word, watching Anna intently.

"Jacob, since when are you so concerned about Anna? Do you
think with all the police about you won't be able to force her into
your bed at night? You're as bad as him."

A soft cry escaped her lips. Erik reached for her arm to calm
her, his anger toward the two men raging. His flesh became an
inferno beneath his mask. No man would touch her again.

"I'm concerned about his intent toward the diva. We have no
idea what his con is going to involve."

"*We* have no idea, Jacob? Perhaps *you* don't know his intent
because of your damn nerves."

"We need to take back our control!"

"When have we ever been able to take back control from
Richard Barret?"

Anna quaked in his arms, her breath falling in rapid pants

"He's here? I'm going to kill—"

Instead of finishing her sentence she bolted like a bullet
speeding from a pistol in the direction of the managers. Grabbing
her around the waist, Erik whirled her to the ground, rolling so to
take the brunt of the fall. They landed roughly as a tangled mess of
arms and legs. She struggled atop him for a moment, but his stern
look silenced her tongue as forcefully as he held her in her spot. The

voices drifted into the distance and disappeared. Against his chest, she shook with a savage anger he'd only witnessed in himself.

"Anna?"

"Richard Barret is my father!

EIGHTEEN

Richard's fame had swept Paris the days following Anna's attack. Or rather—the phantom's fame. He *owned* this con and these feeble-minded people. Every time he overheard mention of the young girl who'd fallen prey to the monster, he mentally patted himself on the back. It seemed that strumpet of his still had some usefulness in his cons after all.

He was alive with the excitement of the havoc he was to unleash, or perhaps the woman he stalked caused such. The vicomtess walked a few paces ahead of him, as ignorant as the rest of the opera company.

"Vicomtess de Chagny?"

It took a few seconds for her to turn. *Meek little thing.* He cleared his throat and straightened the cuffs of his well-tailored suit. Every part needed the right costume. He'd tucked away the Phantom for a new role.

"Beg pardon, Vicomtess, my tardiness is most inexcusable."

A flicker of recognition flash across her face. And what a pretty face it was...

"You're to be my escort?"

Richard tipped his head and moved his coat aside to expose the pistol on his hip. She nearly melted in a pool of relief.

This was going to be a savage delight.

"My name is Richard, Madame. I'll see to your safety."

The vicomtess smiled. He returned the gesture. *Meek, dependent, stunning* and *rich*. He gestured for her to continue walking.

"Thank you for agreeing to my husband's wishes. It isn't our intent to put you in danger."

"Put your concerns to rest. I've years of experience. The vicomte can breathe easy when you're with me." Richard hid his chuckle by looking around.

Christine smiled and stopped before a classroom and indicated the door. "I need to warm my voice before rehearsals."

"I understand, Madame, by all means." Richard bowed and placed a hand on the door. "Please allow me to look first?"

He stuck his head into the room, giving her a reassuring nod. "I'll remain right outside the door." When she laid a trusting hand on his arm, he barely contained the cackle that nearly blew his ruse.

"I feel safer already. I'll do whatever you wish of me."

"Oh, I have no doubt you will… "

Once Christine cleared her mind and let the music take over, her soul relaxed and the world was once again peaceful and perfect around her. Calm and confident, she could greet the remainder of the day's rehearsals with her best foot forward. She'd ignore the guards and rumors and focus on the music. That's why she'd returned to begin with. Most of all she would ignore any suggestion that the past was rearing its ugly head and trust that Raoul had the situation firmly in hand. Opening the door, she smiled politely at her escort.

"Finished, Madame?"

She nodded at the man with a kind smile.

"Might I be so forward as to say you sing like an angel?" he complimented. Taking her elbow, he led her down the hallway.

Such flattery never failed to bring warmth to her face. "Thank you, Monsieur," she said, though her words left her hollow.

They weaved through the hustle of the hallways. If Christine didn't know any better, she'd never have thought anything was amiss at the Opera Garnier. With the exception of the plainclothes police, who nodded their acknowledgements to her and Richard as they passed, the opera continued as it always had. It saddened her to know that behind the excited exterior beat the heart of a man she was forced to consider a Phantom. She turned down the corridor that would take her backstage, but a sharp tug on her arm prevented her.

"Do you always travel backstage this way, Madame?"

Christine nodded.

"Might I suggest a different way? If the man pursuing you is as crafty as I'm told, he will know your habits."

Christine hesitated for a moment, and then nodded her compliance. Her warm blush rose to a nervous heat as she hastened down long hallways, twisting more times than a mouse in a maze. She glanced at her escort, whose sudden stoic exterior only heightened her nerves. They sped through progressively darker corners of the opera house, winding farther and farther from the upper levels. Instinct told her something was amiss, but she reminded herself that Raoul hired this man for her safety. Cool air swirled and chilled her with an impending sense of dread. It reminded her of cellars.

She didn't like cellars.

"Are such tactics necessary? The vicomte has this opera house well secured. I'm sure it would be safe for us to use a less involved route."

"Of course it's necessary, Madame. You wouldn't want to cross your Phantom."

His hand slid possessively around her waist. He yanked her close and smiled eerily.

"Unhand me!" Christine's heart kicked into a wild rhythm. She swallowed hard trying to clear the roar of fear that raced into her ears as she twisted to pry herself free.

The cold metal of a pistol rammed into her side so harshly the flesh bruised beneath her corset.

"Who are you? What do you want?" she stammered.

He opened a door.

"Inside," he growled.

A jarring pain traveled up her wrists as he threw her to the floor. The stench of mildew and rot filled her nose. The door slammed shut with an earsplitting crack sealing them both in the murky darkness.

Her eyes adjusted to the dim light. Staring down at her were twisted horse's heads, birds arched back in silent calls, and distorted masks of every shape and size forever frozen in painful, angry emotions. Discarded and gruesome objects from long forgotten operas crammed every available space in the waste prop room. This was as far away from the theater as one could get before venturing into the cellars that led to the lake.

To the Phantom.

Chills, like millions of icy fingers, raced around her body. No one came down to this room. The amount of rat feces stinging her was testimony to that. Her hands slipped on the dust-coated floor. Her legs tangled in her petticoats as she scrambled away from the man looming over her.

Richard knelt before her, tucking his pistol into his waistband. "Let us—"

"Release me!" she shrieked, swinging her hand toward his face.

He ducked so her slap only batted away cobwebs. His maniacal laugh booming through the small space froze every limb in her body. His laughter stopped as quickly as it began when he dragged her toward him, giving her no room to resist.

The blow from his hand stung viciously on her cheek. The demon gripped her upper arms so hard her flesh bruised beneath his fingers. Christine tried to arch away so desperately as he jerked her toward him, her back and shoulder ached. He was so close she could feel the heat from his face and see his pores.

The room was filled with her fear. It bounced off everything as her breathing quickened, filling the room with tiny, panicked pants.

"Now," he yanked her to her knees, "let's have a little talk— *Christine*. I can call you Christine, can't I?" Richard twisted his hands in her hair, liking how strands of the golden locks broke free in his grasp. "You can scream all you want—no one will hear you. I made certain to keep you as far away from them as I could. I apologize for the state of your room." He laughed. "It was either here or the communard dungeon and I figure that would be the first place they'd look; here, the last." He gave a quick click of his tongue. "People are stupid."

He produced a rope from an inner pocket of his jacket, still keeping a tight grip on her opposite arm. Slapping that to the ground, he twisted her arms behind her back, grabbing both wrists with one hand. With her arms bound, her position provided him with a view of her décolletage and her heaving bosom. The way she struggled made him hard. What a delight it would be to ruin her then and there.

A second rope secured to the first tethered her to an exposed beam against a dark corner barely giving her enough slack to sit comfortably.

"Forgive me for binding you, but I can't have you running. You're going to be safely tucked away for a while."

The scream she finally pushed past her fear pierced the small room. Though he didn't worry she'd be heard, he backhanded her, just to remind her who was in control.

"You would make a lovely little mollisher now wouldn't you?" He usually forced Anna to serve as mistress to him and his various partners in crime, but it would be a sweet change of pace to have a beauty do so instead.

Hot pants of horror fell from her mouth, fueling his need to have her.

"You vile man! Get away from me!"

"Come now, dear, you can't possibly find pleasure night after night dallying away your ladycocks in the bed of a pretty, rich boy?" He stroked his pistol, briefly considering all the things he could do to her. Tempting though they may be, he had more pressing matters than his libido. "If your husband is wise, he'll abide by our demands and deliver the ransom we desire. Or rather the ransom the *Phantom* desires."

"What?" she croaked.

"You really are a lovely woman," Richard brushed his lips lightly against hers, laughing as she yanked her head away. "Sit tight, Madame, we shall return."

Without further regard Richard slipped out, locking the door behind him. He sniffed loudly and grinned at the man waiting in the hall.

"Is she settled and comfortable?" Edward asked.

Richard chuckled. Is any woman comfortable when he was in control? "About as much as Anna is in a brothel."

"Jacob is questioning your motives."

"Jacob's a fool." He shoved Edward down the corridor. "Stick to your job of keeping him in the dark and all will be fine. Trust me."

Trusting Richard Barret was like relying on a coiled cobra not to strike. He smiled as cordially as possible when Edward turned to meet the stare penetrating into his back. Richard raised an eyebrow, challenging Edward's next move. His look had the desired effect. Edward gulped, stepping aside to allow Richard to pass.

It was Edward's place to follow.

———————

Christine had never experienced such helplessness. She shrieked as the bony tail of a rat whipped across her ankle. Her voice echoed in the room before being swallowed by silence.

What ransom the Phantom desires? This can't be real. Erik wouldn't do this to me. He's an Angel. He loves me! The ropes chafed her skin raw as she jerked to free herself.

Fear gripped her soul. History was repeating itself and she was once again its limelight.

She cried again and kicked violently at another rat.

"Please! Somebody! Help me! Erik, help me!"

The Phantom's name bounced off the walls, taunting her. It fell lifelessly at her feet but sank daggers of shock right into her bones.

"Lord, forgive me." She forced the correct name from her lips… "Raoul, help me!"

———————

"Monsieur?"

As if Jacob didn't already have a heaping dose of madness to deal with, a second helping of it was served up with the sound of that voice. He glanced sideways to the clock and the empty carafe in front of him. Resigned he could do nothing about the hour and his lack of scotch; he removed his reading glasses and tore himself away from scrutinizing the books.

Anna stood in his doorway, her head cocked in the defiant little way that always got under his skin. She was going to be difficult, he could feel it. Jacob shrugged and sank back in his chair determined to at least get some pleasure out of her arrival.

"What do you want? I didn't summon you." Aggravated, he tossed his glasses on his desk.

"A word, Monsieur."

"A word." He snorted. "Anna, you never have just a word."

He laced his fingers and tilted his head, mocking her posture. She stared at him with a tiny, insolent air about her—her bottom lip out, wrinkles in the corner of her eyes as she glowered.

"Have your say then and get out of my office."

"What con are you running with Richard Barret? What does he want with the Vicomtess de Chagny?"

This was an interesting development. He was not prepared for those words to tumble from her.

"That was a mouthful." He rose, moving to the corner of his desk.

"I know he's here running a con."

"Running a con?" Jacob sighed theatrically. "Anna, we're respectable and retired gentlemen. If you think Richard Barret is here, it has nothing to do with any cons. If he's here, it's probably your fault."

"It damn well isn't and you know it!"

Jacob fanned the phony heat on his neck. "My, what vulgar language from a lady."

Anna's face scrunched and he knew it was best not to incite her. She'd only launch into a tantrum and what was the point? Richard was clearly insane, running a con under the noses of the police.

"Do all Barrets have such attitudes?" He pushed his lip out to match her face. "Yes, Anna, Papa is here. Did you come running to Jacob to protect you?" A scuffling sound behind her cut him off. He studied the room but saw nothing.

"The rumors around Paris, the ghost sightings, the haunting—it is all him, isn't it?"

"Your father was right. You are an intuitive little wench. Yes, Papa is the mythical Phantom of the Opera. He's rather good at it don't you think?" Jacob winked and touched the corner of his eye indicating her inflamed flesh. "Edward's idea this time. Re-create the scandal to bring in the patrons." He slid the leather bound book across the desk toward her. "See for yourself. Works rather well, too."

Anna shoved the ledger away. Jacob smiled. He liked her feisty.

"I heard you in the garden. What does he want with the vicomtess?"

"Even if I knew, I wouldn't tell you. Your father has turned a harmless little con into an opera."

"Don't think for a minute I won't expose him. I have before."

Jacob, irritated, rose. Walking, he came next to her and hitched a hip upon the desk. "Look where that got you. What do you plan on doing? Are you going to run to the vicomte and tell him a phony Phantom is playing him the fool? That some petty country con artists have turned them into the laughing stock of Paris? Please, they hardly had cause to notice you until your Papa made you cry."

She snapped. He knew she would. Anna wheeled her fist back to strike. One hand was all it took to block her blow. Grabbing her, he wrestled her between his legs. She growled a string of rather inappropriate expletives, arms and legs flailing in protest. He gripped her tightly and laughed. Finding an exposed spot on her neck, he nipped, prompting more thrashing and louder cursing. His lips bit her earlobe while one hand dove between her legs, hiking the lengths of her skirts.

"Really, Anna," he crooned, crushing her against his arousal, "this sudden bravado is quite alluring."

A shadow erupted and was on Jacob before he had a second to blink.

Grabbing Anna, Erik spun her a safe distance away as murderous vengeance began to eddy around any sense of reason. He pinned Jacob against the desk. The incomprehensible ferocity of his possessiveness unleashed itself against the man's miserable little throat.

"Two rules," Erik spat, knocking Jacob's head roughly into the wood. "You do not molest her and you do not mock me."

The swell of Jacob's cowardly eyes and his stammering tongue only fed Erik's disgust. He dug his thumbs deeper into Jacob's windpipe, his lips curling into a menacing smile.

"Who...who...are you?" Jacob sputtered between gargled breaths.

"The Phantom of the Opera. Now answer the lady's question!"

Moments later, Anna had to jog to keep pace as Erik fled through the opera house, passing from shadow to shadow like a man possessed. She didn't know what to make of the situation, but she knew as she followed him through the winding passages that he could have killed Jacob Wischard. The restraint it took for him not to do so was terrifying to witness. Erik left the office so abruptly he had no idea that Anna followed. Any attempt she made at calling for him to stop fell on deaf ears.

As he rounded a corner, he pulled up short, causing Anna to jump back in surprise. She panted, thankful for a second to catch her breath until he shifted his weight and tripped a door below him.

"Good God!" Anna leapt back as the floor swallowed him whole. Her last rational sense had been blasted away in all this madness. Looking around her to make sure no one was about, she had no choice but to hasten through the floor after him.

Pain shot through her ankles when she hit the floor. She caught her breath and squinted in the darkness.

"Erik? Where are you?"

In a split second's time the answer rounded on her from a shadow. Erik was hunched over, a wild look blazing from his eyes.

"Erik, it's me!" she shouted, before he lost his mind and reacted with any sort of blind rage. "You ran from the office so suddenly. I've been trying to catch up to you."

Eerie silence hung between them for a second. "Erik?" she asked apprehensively.

The breath slipped out of his lips. A rising furor began to lift his voice.

"You will be wise to note how close you came to meeting a man you do not want to know. Not much can restrain Erik when he does not wish restraint! You will learn not to follow Erik when you are not invited." His roar bounced from wall to wall.

He was speaking in third person again. He only did that when something unthinkable was in that mind of his. But Anna knew that, given a moment, the disastrous degree of his anger would fade and she would see a calmer man before her. She was not about to back down and bend to his requests. He paced like a jungle predator searching for the scent of its prey.

"Where would Barret take Christine? What does he want with her? What will he do to her? Of what is he capable? Answer me, Anna!" His questions tumbled out on top of each other, his eyes glowing a brighter gold as his anger rose.

"Slow down! I don't know. He's capable of anything. I've seen him do it all. He's clever and calculated and a man you don't want to cross."

"It is me he does not want to cross. I will not have Christine harmed, do you understand me? Erik will not allow harm to come to her. Not now, not ever." Erik paced circles around her each word coming urgently louder.

"You don't have to tell *me* that!" Anna jabbed her finger at the ceiling. "But you can't fly around this opera house like some raving lunatic."

"Forgive me, Mademoiselle, but I *am* a raving lunatic and you and your rebelliousness are inches away from meeting the end of a silk rope."

"Blast my rebelliousness and deal with it! If the vicomtess is missing, you can be certain they think you took her. You can be positive they'll be looking for you tenfold now."

"They should be looking for Christine! Erik must find her himself." He pivoted and headed down the hallway, his fists balled against his sides.

Anna tapped the heel of her palms against her temples wanting to scream. Trying to get through to him when he launched into that detached third-person madness of his was like trying to squeeze water in her palm—a fruitless effort. Erik charged back and forth on the lines of a dangerous battleground, and she had no idea which side of the man she attempted to love would win. Sinking into dismay, she called his name.

"Erik, stop. Please just stop and slow down…"

He kept pacing, his hands pulsing until, in time, he relaxed and turned. Without looking, he extended his hand her. She entwined the tips of her fingers in his. He guided her to him.

"I warned you, Anna. You stand on a precipice and face life imprisonment to attempt to understand this mind. I know control, but I will not rest while Christine is in harm's way. She needs me."

"I'm not asking you to rest. I know you could never do that. But I need you to slow down and think."

He pointed down the hallway, showing Anna a passage that would lead her from the cellar, issuing one gentle warning. "Do not involve yourself in this. You were not a part of my past."

Erik teetered imperceptibly. Anna winced, understanding the signs of his madness when it reared its ugly head. He turned to leave but she flung herself into his embrace, keeping a firm, possessive grip around him. The tension threatening to crack his spine relaxed as she hugged his waist. Snuggling against him, she heard his deep breath as the tip of his mask bent to her hair.

"I wasn't a part of your past, but I think you want me in your future. Don't deny me my choice, Erik. Just promise me you'll slow down."

"Go," he replied, backing away from her. "I cannot be near you now. I need to... think."

In a flash, he evaporated very much like the Phantom he was.

His neck purple, throat raw, Jacob Wischard tore apart his office at a frenzied pace, gathering what items he could and shoving them into his briefcase. He kept checking the door, the walls, the windows... That madman had come out of nowhere and evaporated into nowhere as soon as he gave up the information Anna wanted. No con was worth being hunted by the actual Phantom.

The authorities would be onto them soon anyway. But that was the least of his worries. He only cared about that black masked madman who poured terror down his gullet. The door behind him blew open, making Jacob jump sky high. He didn't acknowledge Richard except by packing more frantically.

"Going somewhere, Jacob?"

"To the devil with you, Richard. I'm leaving."

He'd barely moved his fingers out of the way before Richard shoved his briefcase closed.

"Leaving?" He leaned on the case. "You can't *leave* in the middle of a con."

Jacob yanked the briefcase from Richard's grip. "Blast your con. A madman is running loose in this opera and I'll have no part of it."

Richard's question tumbled around his laughter. "What kind of madman?"

"A bloody masked maniac! He was here with your damn daughter. She was ranting about cons and divas and *you*. Then *he* came from nowhere. The man is a living shadow, and I'll not be caught in its path again."

He grabbed his coat and walking stick and started for the door. Richard blocked his path.

"What did you tell Anna?"

"Everything! I would have told them about your intent toward the diva, but thankfully I have been kept in the dark on that." Jacob stabbed his walking stick against Richard's chest and pressed him backward. "You would have told as well if you found your neck on the wrong side of that demon!"

Richard grabbed the walking stick and threw it across the

room. Jacob stumbled backward as Richard came toward him.

"You betraying son-of-a-bitch," Richard spit. "Let's see how you fear the wrong side of me.

NINETEEN

Seven hundred and fifty people, three acres, seventeen stories, seven of them underground.

Sitting behind the desk in the concierge office, with the reality of the situation marching though his mind, Raoul stared in dismay at the dusty copy of the Garnier's architectural plans. No wonder no one ever knew the Phantom lived in the bowels of the opera house, save a select few. His lair could stretch in endless directions.

Raoul took a break, rubbed his bleary eyes and swiped his hair out of his face. Madame Giry was correct; all the ways to penetrate the lower cellars that Raoul knew existed were sealed off to prevent anyone from going in or coming out.

A puff of breath broke through his lips as he leaned over the designs. His palms wrinkled the paper. If he had to, he'd tear the place apart brick by brick in order to keep Christine safe. A knock reluctantly pulled his attention from the plans.

"Enter," he called wearily, then straightening up as soon as he saw who entered. He knew Inspector Legard well enough to have learned a lot about his body language. "What's wrong?"

"There's been an incident."

Those words, and the controlled caution that made Legard's tone slow and deliberate knotted the back of Raoul's neck. He matched the tone with one of his own. "Christine?"

"Safe. I saw her with a member of the theater police."

No doubt Legard heard his relief escaping on a shaky breath.

"Jacob Wischard is dead." Legard clipped. "A maid found him in his office about an hour ago. His neck was broken. I've no doubt he was murdered."

Raoul ran dusty hands through his hair trying to unhear what he just heard. *Merde. Let this demon be caught already.* "This is a coincidence, Jules, merely a coincidence."

"I doubt that." Legard produced a note. "This was addressed to you and found with the body."

The letter snapped as Raoul snatched it. He tore the envelope open, painfully conscious of how his chest heaved. Fury or fear? The note was one bone-chilling sentence:

Vicomte, abide by my demands or I spill more blood.

A numbing silence filled the room until Raoul had the presence to speak. When he did, his words were like sand in his mouth. "Locate my wife. I want her by my side. Then find Edward Laroque and bring Madame Giry and the Mademoiselle to me."

Hatred, years in the making, began deep in his gut and rolled until Raoul saw the room turn red.

With a shout of boiling rage he upended the desk vowing to do the same to the Opera Garnier.

The hem of Anna's dress blurred as she stared at her boots. Shaking her thoughts and vision clear, she quizzically glanced at the man who walked beside her. It was the same man, that Inspector Legard, who had questioned her earlier about her assault. It came as no surprise the theater police were looking for her. Anna figured it had something to do with her confrontation with Jacob.

Stupid snitch.

Erik's explosion with Jacob was not a good sign. His temper was shortening as the entire affair wore on. He'd lost control of the opera house he'd taken steps to regain, and losing it to unfounded rumors. Erik was on a warpath to locate her father before he laid his hands on Christine and Anna's best judgment told her none of it was good. She might not have been a part of his past, for which she found herself more and more thankful, but she was tangled in the present and hoped Erik knew what he was getting himself into.

As Inspector Legard led her through the halls she studied the solemn expression on his face.

Maybe Jacob, the old weasel, had a heart attack.

Choking on a laugh, she recalled the look on his face when Erik went mad on him. Her laughter stopped as Inspector Legard took her gently by the arm and opened the door before them. He indicated Anna to enter; Madame Giry and the vicomte were already present.

"Where's Christine?" the vicomte asked as Anna was escorted in.

"Officers are en route to fetch her," the inspector responded.

"Find them," he snapped, dismissing Inspector Legard.

Confusion creased her brow. A reprimand by theater police or gendarmes she could handle, but to be scolded by a nobleman was insulting. A long and calming breath helped silence her while he spoke.

"Are you all right, Mademoiselle?"

The vicomte emphasized his concern by laying a hand upon her upper arm. Anna glanced at his hand and sneered. She may not be viewed as a proper lady, but she still had her boundaries, especially with noblemen. Rolling her shoulder away from his touch, Anna swore she heard the walls of the room hiss in response to his touching her.

"I'm fine, Monsieur le Vicomte." She scanned the room for hidden serpents. Certain it was only in her mind, she took a step out of the vicomte's reach nonetheless and glanced to Madame Giry who stood still as marble in her spot.

He turned to comfort the box keeper. "The situation here has escalated. I worry for your safety as well as Christine's." Next, he turned to Anna. "You as well Mademoiselle, as you've already been the Phantom's target. There is no easy way to say this. Jacob Wischard has been murdered."

Madame Giry withered into a chair, her wrinkled hand clutching at her collar. Though their eyes met, neither woman spoke.

"He was found with this," the vicomte continued. A note landed on a nearby table. "Another little warning from our friend."

"That's impossible!" Anna grabbed it. She turned it over recognizing the neat hand was unlike Erik's matchstick scrawl. "Vicomte, this is a mistake. You don't know with whom you are dealing."

"Mademoiselle, I'm certain I know with whom I am dealing.

You and Madame Giry are to leave with the vicomtess. I've made arrangements to take you to our chateau in Chagny."

Anna's temples pounded. This entire farce grew more complicated by the minute. Leaving the opera house to sit around pampered in some nobleman's estate she wouldn't tolerate. Not with her father running one of his notorious schemes. Innocent people were in danger and she wasn't about to back down. Madame Giry was another matter, Anna noted, seeing the pallor upon her face.

"I'm sorry, Madame Giry," he apologized. "I know how much this theater means to you, but I'll not have your life endangered. Like Christine, you need to recognize the Phantom for what he is. I'll not allow him to hold you captive any longer. Until arrangements have been made, I want a gendarme with you at all times."

Anna gasped. Of all the ridiculous demands! The blinders upon the nobleman were unbelievable.

"Monsieur, I'm begging you to listen to me. I know far more than you think and I'm telling you the man you call a Phantom has nothing to do with this."

She obviously had overstepped her boundaries, or the vicomte wasn't used to being addressed in such a manner. His expression had hardened. As he rose, Anna followed the path of his eyes to the tip of the scarlet note peeking out from the corner of her dress pocket.

The vicomte snatched the letter.

"Exactly what is it you claim so ardently to know?" he asked.

Anna pressed a hand to her belly. She stared at Erik's note wanting to see his handwriting and relive every sensation words seeped into her. "Please. Give it back."

The vicomte's expression darkened.

"What is this, Mademoiselle?"

His eyes shot to Madame Giry, but she averted her gaze. Anna swallowed hard as the vicomte read every word. The invasion of her privacy made her burn. Taking a step closer to Anna, he waved the letter in her face

"What kind of sick joke are you playing? How do you know the Phantom by *name*?"

Anna's breath hitched as the door swung open. Her letter fluttered in the air as Raoul waved Legard and another man in.

"I'm afraid we've another situation on our hands," Legard informed. He indicated the man to his side. "This Lieutenant was to be assigned as the vicomtess' personal guard."

"*Was* to be assigned?"

"Yes, Monsieur le Vicomte," the lieutenant replied. "We're unable to locate the vicomtess."

"You told me she was with her guard!" he shouted at Legard.

He nodded. "She was seen with a member of the theater police."

Anna bit her tongue to keep it from whipping both men. This was all another signature move by the great Richard Barret— murder *and* kidnapping. She tried to contain her disgust. Judging by the color on the vicomte's face and the twist to his upper lip, any suggestions she'd make at the moment wouldn't be well received.

"What did he look like?" he demanded of Legard

"His face wasn't seen, but he was tall, thin and incredibly well-dressed."

"That's all the information needed. Inspector, find the vicomtess. Lock this opera house if you must. You, Lieutenant! Escort Madame Giry wherever she needs to be until the arrangements are made at Chagny. See to it she remains safe."

The vicomte nodded at Madame Giry as she left with Legard and the lieutenant, but when Anna tried to follow, he put a hand up to stop her.

"You're going nowhere, Mademoiselle." He waved the letter again and indicated an empty chair.

Anna caught the subtle nod Madame Giry made toward a shadow before disappearing through the door. That explained the old woman's silence and the hiss Anna heard.

Erik, whatever you do, think first then slow down. What I would not give to be a snake charmer right now. Anna refused the vicomte's request she sit.

"How do you know of Erik, and why does he speak of Christine in this letter?" he asked.

Anna dodged the question. "The man you're looking for is Richard Barret. The man who attacked me is Richard Barret. And the man masquerading as the Phantom you chase is Richard Barret. Find him and you find your wife."

"Answer my question."

The vicomte stood too close to her judging by the low growl

that vibrated the room.

Lion taming would be good as well...

"How do you know Erik and why does he write of Christine?"

Anna chose not to reply. She didn't have to. The room did instead.

"Vicomte."

The silence that followed penetrated the room. A shape took form in the doorway. It blocked the light and cast long, dark shadows across the floor. The vicomte turned toward the address, startled out of his interrogation, and came face to face with his Phantom.

Erik moved with strong, deliberate steps and with unfathomable calm. "I am rather disillusioned I was not invited to your little meeting." He reached out with one finger and shoved the vicomte away from Anna.

The man stumbled to the side. Anna folded her arms and watched the vicomte's lips subtly move. If she were him, she'd be praying too. With nerves like that, he wouldn't last a second on the streets of Paris. The vicomte moved with caution, once again taking the position he had and placing himself between the Erik and her.

Erik paused, studying him like a hunter pondering if such a meager prize was worth his appetite. He smiled at the paltry show of bravado.

"Protecting the lady? Ever the gentleman, vicomte."

"You live," he said.

"So it would appear." Erik passed a hand over his mask. "Looks can be deceiving you know."

He leaned against the desk and folded his arms comfortably, waiting for the vicomte to make his next move. He stood as king while the vicomte was merely pawn.

Erik chuckled. "You've not changed. Somehow I suspected you to be different. You are still a bit feminine in feature."

Erik's smile grew as wide as Anna knew her eyes to be. He was baiting the vicomte and judging by the way the man struggled to maintain calm, Anna thought it not a good idea. Erik shrugged; ignoring the incredulous glare she shot him.

"So the sniveling, spoiled boy has nothing to say in my presence? Perchance a man has replaced him? Impressive. How long did it take for you to grow a spine?"

The vicomte didn't react to Erik's taunts, except to reach out and gently put a hand on the small of Anna's back. Anna arched forward despising any touch but Erik's.

That single move made Erik bolt off the desk. Even if the vicomte's gesture was a feeble means to protect her, Erik didn't view it that way. Possessiveness rallied around him. His lip began to twitch. A faint tremor shook his shoulders. A rumble came from the bottom of his soul as he took one step forward.

"Do. Not. Touch. Her."

Reaching beneath his coat, the vicomte drew his pistol and aimed the barrel at Erik's face in one seamless motion.

"Don't think I'll allow her to fall prey to you as well."

Erik glanced at the pistol before he leaned back against the desk. "Put down your weapon, vicomte. I am unarmed."

"You're never unarmed."

"Where are your manners? Would you strike me down in front of a woman?"

Anna stumbled as the vicomte backed her toward the door, his aim never leaving Erik's face.

"Mademoiselle, run," he urged.

Anna stood her ground.

"What a wonderfully outrageous display of valor." Erik laughed. "Anna is a feisty little mongoose. I dare say she tends not to *obey*."

Erik took a step forward, which only served to make the vicomte hold the pistol higher.

"Vicomte, you are beginning to make me angry, and I do not have the time to be angry." Erik spread his arms. The posture made him appear larger than life. "I suggest you listen to what the girl has to say if you intend to find Christine."

The nobleman's shoulders stiffened. In a flash, he lowered his weapon. With a sudden burst of energy, he lunged. Anna yelped as he knocked Erik off balance and pressed the pistol against his mask.

The vicomte pinned him against the wall with a strength that must have stored years of anger. "Where is she?"

The pistol shook. The air flowed like an untamed river, poisoned with disgust. The scales balanced in the vicomte's favor for only a moment.

"Vicomte," Erik spat, "you are trying my patience. If you wish to find Christine—,"

"Her name will not come from your foul mouth!"

The trigger cocked.

"Erik!" Anna screamed, diving toward the vicomte.

He pivoted as she flew at him, giving Erik the opening he needed. With an enraged shout he backhanded the vicomte, reeling him into the opposite wall, crumpling him to a heap. The pistol flew into the air and crashed against the floor.

Anna rushed to Erik's side. "This has turned to madness!"

"You never would have made him understand." Erik panted, heat of his passion coming out in great puffs. "I tried reason, Anna. For your sake I tried. But sometimes the past simply cannot be ignored."

"Well try again!" Anna shook the vicomte, but he didn't move. *Come around, come around...* "More violence is not going to solve this!"

Erik laughed. "Look at you trying to wake him. My madness seeps to your mind now. He has already had my trial and cast my sentence, Anna. You may shake all you wish, but you will never make him understand. Help me find Christine *my* way."

"*What?*"

Erik softened his voice. "Help me find Christine."

This was all unbelievably out of control. She didn't have some invisible crutch for him to lean on and unfortunately for all of them—she didn't have any answers.

"Erik…"

"Please, Anna…."

Never in what she knew of Erik's history did he ever ask another for help. Christine Daaé was his one weakness in life. The desperation dressing him tore at her, but Anna knew what she had to do.

She'd done many difficult things, made choices that tainted her soul, but nothing was as soul-ripping as refusing Erik.

The vicomte moaned, tearing Anna's gaze from the mantle clock. Though only minutes had passed since she'd sent Erik backing out of the room with a look on his face she never wanted to witness again…it seemed like a lifetime.

"That's the second time I have had that murderous soul within my grasp and the second time he's slipped away," the vicomte moaned.

Anna wanted grab the ledger from the desk and smack him

back unconscious. She resented everything about him right now. Anna couldn't have left him helpless on the floor to follow where Erik went. Lord knows what would happen to the vicomte if her father showed up. No doubt the vicomte had a headache judging by the way he slumped on the couch. Struggling to sit upright, he rubbed lightly at his bruised jaw. It would most assuredly make his face shades of purple within the next few hours.

Good.

Anna couldn't blame him for his defeated posture or the ill look upon his face. If the vicomte felt he was failing his wife, she understood. Her heart beat nothing but agony since betraying Erik. The look of rejection behind Erik's eyes held more misery than she ever believed possible.

Convinced the vicomte functioned with the same stubborn inability to listen to reason as before, Anna started for the door.

"Where are you going?" he asked.

"To find Edward Laroque. What is with your lifted brow? You were perhaps hoping I'd say to find the Phantom? One thing I'm not, Monsieur le Vicomte, is stupid. You'll never understand him as I do. He slips from your grasp because it invigorates him. If you were not so obsessed by the past, perhaps you'd realize Edward Laroque is nowhere to be found. Didn't you summon him as well?" He hesitantly nodded. "And did he come?" She took satisfaction in the hesitant shake of his head. "Richard Barret is here for a reason— because Edward Laroque asked him to be. It's Barret you want."

"I don't trust anything you say. You've been seduced by a madman as my wife was until she saw him for the monster he is."

"Monster, Monsieur? I see nothing but a man."

The door burst open making the vicomte leap instantly to his feet.

"Monsieur le Vicomte," Inspector Legard called as he swung through the door.

"What is it? Did you find my wife?"

"Not yet, but I'm sure she will be located soon. A man is in the theater asking to speak with you… urgently."

TWENTY

The rehearsal came to a standstill. With one bellow demanding silence on behalf of the Phantom, Richard had made puppets of them all. Below him, clusters of frightened chorus girls gathered in tulle circles, hovering close to the safety they found in their ballet mistress. Richard laughed as stagehands and fly men emerged from every angle possible and the Maestro and his orchestra stood, baton and instruments frozen in shocked silence.

Richard leaned back in a lush seat to watch a plump old lady bounce on her tip-toes. She looked around as if searching for impending doom.

Impending doom. Excellent choice of words.

He basked in the limelight and counted the number of people eyeing him expectantly. All eyes shifted to Legard, the vicomte, and Anna as they rushed on stage.

"Ah, Monsieur le Vicomte, glad you could make it," Richard shouted, moving to lean over the railing. He sniffed loudly and cleared his throat. "Now we can conduct business."

The small crowd swung their attention, looking in anticipation at the Vicomte de Chagny then back to him. This con was entirely too easy, judging by the stance of the nobleman. The buffoon stood so stiff it seemed a pole replaced his spine.

"What business? Who are you?" the vicomte demanded.

"Begging your pardon, Monsieur, I forgot that not everyone

knows who I am."

Richard pounced upon the railing like an agile alley cat. The crowd gasped but one unmistakable voice lifted through the din.

"You bastard," Anna spat, shouldering her way forward from behind the two men.

Richard laughed. He would have fun toying with her. He caught the puzzled look the vicomte gave her. Oh, how he fed off looks like that! Fear in the eyes of men… it was better than a bed full of harlots!

He seems suspicious of her too. A most excellent development…

Anna's hands twisted her dress. She still did that when uncomfortable? He snorted. Her discomfort made Richard positively gleeful. Life was a delight when hers was miserable. Still standing on the narrow railing, he leaned against a column close to the wall. Richard folded his arms and crossed one foot casually over the other. "My name is Richard Barret. And I believe I have something you want."

"My wife?" the vicomte shouted, signaling to Inspector Legard with a high hand. Instantly pistols were drawn.

"Vicomte! I suggest they lower their weapons if you want me to continue." Richard smiled smugly as the nobleman bent to his whim.

"Good," he said. "Your wife is fine, currently unharmed." He padded along the rail like a tightrope walker and gave a mock teeter to elicit gasps from below. "Quite the lovely lady I might add. She smells so good."

The deadly glint in the vicomte's eyes telegraphed his murderous thoughts as he stormed across the stage. Only the body of the inspector and a few whispered words kept the man from doing something foolish. The pathetic little rat of a noble was no more frightening than a dog on a leash.

"Where is she!" The vicomte yanked his arm free from the Inspector's grip.

"She'll remain unharmed so long as you meet our demands." Richard leaned back into position.

"*Our* demands? Who are you working for? What do you want?"

Impressive the way the vicomte could yell so forcefully, Richard mused. "Oh, yes, didn't I mention? Do forgive me. I'm merely the messenger you know, my associate is somewhat of a Phantom."

"You lying snake!" Anna stomped across the stage.

He looked at her, his nostrils flaring open. "Don't tell me, you meddlesome little tramp, let me guess. You want to climb into this box and rip my throat out if not for that nagging dread in the pit of your stomach?"

"More like your heart!" she spat.

He flicked her away with a wave of his hand. Bothersome little flea. He turned his attention back to the vicomte who was giving her a granite stare. Richard smirked when he finally glanced back at him.

"Your *associate*? You work *with* the Phantom?" the vicomte said, incredulously.

"Seems that way. Your Phantom fellow is not one to be crossed," Richard remarked. "I know it. You know it. And certainly by now your wife knows it." He let loose a deep, pleasurable moan. "Oh, but the way it seems the Phantom can make her tremble. The things he does to her are sinful."

Richard wouldn't be at all surprised if the vein in the vicomte's temple ruptured.

"If that creature so much as touches her..." the vicomte shouted. *"Where is he?"*

"He couldn't make this particular meeting." Richard jumped back into Box Five. "The Phantom will be in further contact with the conditions of his demands. His first is that you call off your private army. It makes moving about rather difficult. I strongly suggest you follow his instructions if you want your wife to remain unharmed. You wouldn't want her to end up like Wischard... *or* Laroque."

"What of Laroque?" The vicomte took a few cautious steps forward.

Pathetic. Even Anna's bravado was better than that. Richard crossed his arms and smirked. "What of him?"

The vicomte strode across the stage. "If you lay one hand on my wife..."

Richard tugged hard on his ear. "You're not listening. Not *me,* the Phantom. Good day gentlemen. We'll be in touch. Oh, and Anna?" Richard folded himself far over the railing and kissed the air. "Nice to see you again."

He'd feast on the way she blanched for hours to come. Richard laughed his way out of Box Five and the auditorium slamming the door behind him.

⟶⟫•▬▬▬▬ ▬••▬ ▬▬▬▬▬••⟪⟵

"*Mesdames et Messieurs*, Maestro Fontaine, I urge calm," Raoul addressed, attempting to get his voice to lift above the mayhem of the theater company. "As you all undoubtedly witnessed, there's a situation at hand. As of this moment, Jacob Wischard and… apparently Edward Laroque have been removed from their positions and no longer manage the Opera Garnier. I'll be acting in their stead until suitable replacements can be found."

Below him, the rehearsal was nothing more than chaos, as dancers, stagehands, the fly men and orchestra all spoke at once.

Erik paced an empty fly, glad at least for the moment, of the physical distance placed between him and Barret. If not for his concern over finding Christine, Erik surely would have killed again. The urge mushroomed inside; building and roiling like a black plague. Hatred conducted toward Richard like lightning to a rod. Erik wanted to kill for the abuse he'd perpetrated upon Anna. He would make Richard suffer for laying his filthy hands on Christine. And now—most fervently—he wanted to kill for the ridicule. For a phony Phantom to be abusing the power Erik had carefully crafted disgusted him. The respectable life he'd tried to build was crumbling around him.

The letters he'd sent upon Raoul and Christine's arrival were written with utmost respect. Shouldn't that have been testimony to his reform? He'd tried to project his intent as an honorable man, not a Phantom, but clearly the expectations of him lay elsewhere, thanks to disgraceful gossip. He couldn't separate himself from the past now, not with another investigation, not with another *Phantom*.

Erik twirled himself from rope to rope, up and down the flies as he worked out his thoughts. He wouldn't have Christine within such a contemptible man's grasp. The thought of Richard Barret being near her turned everything crimson. Barret couldn't have what was not his…

If those below so vehemently believed the Phantom had been instilling this terror, let them have their ghost. No one in the theater, save Madame Giry and Anna, cared that a man lay behind the mask.

Erik swung himself around one final rope before taking a

moment to catch his breath. He wanted to feel his renewed power course through him. He surveyed those on stage like a puppeteer, deciding which string to yank next.

He listened as excited whispers floated upward.

"This matter will be addressed quickly and with swift justice. I implore you to continue with your usual routines." Raoul nodded at Maestro Fontaine, urging him to continue as he took Anna securely by the arm.

Erik set his sites on Raoul, his madness pulled to a dangerous level. If Chagny wanted to become a marked man, this was the way to do it.

"You, Mademoiselle, will stay with me," Raoul declared. "A bargaining chip if you will."

"You're being played a fool, vicomte," Anna snapped.

Erik had reached his boiling point. He damned the fate that sucked on his veins, pulling blood and madness through him. With his gaze locked on Anna, he leapt to his decision. His choice to relive the past plummeted him into a bleak misery faster than gravity to the stage.

Erik landed on his feet with a crack that shook the stage, his cloak briefly engulfing him. The girls of the corps de ballet shrieked. Their pitch sent Raoul's and Anna's heads whipping in their direction. With a magnificent swirl, Erik fanned his cloak out of his way and surveyed the crowd cowering before his grand entrance. He laughed arrogantly as the police started toward him. It only took him one well-practiced glare toward Raoul and the Inspector to get them to stand down.

"Bonjour, Messieurs," Erik greeted. "Were you not expecting me? Perhaps you thought I was myth?" He sighed. "Ah yes, I recall now—that famous obituary 'Erik is dead'."

His voice amplified like he leaned on an invisible sustaining pedal and pulled screams from the mouth of the youngest ballerinas.

"Erik is alive!" he exploded. "I have a message for my new manager. It is regrettable our reunions could not have been more civil. I truly did not wish for our paths to cross in such a manner." He circled Raoul and Anna. "Heed my warning. Do whatever is asked of you without question or pause."

He sensed Raoul's tension for it left finger marks upon Anna's arm. If he acted on his impulses, he would have wrenched Anna free from the vicomte's haughty grip. But he knew the self-important little aristocrat didn't have the presence of mind to help Christine. Erik relied on his belief that Anna's ever-defiant spirit would be able to deal with the vicomte and would prompt her to believe none of what she was about to see.

"Do not underestimate the situation if you intend for Christine to remain unharmed. You will never understand me, Vicomte de Chagny, so do not even try. It will only lead you down the path of madness. There are those around you who know dimensions of me you could never possibly comprehend."

As he passed behind Anna, he grazed the small of her back with his hand. Did fear of him or something else cause her to tremble? Erik's lips didn't move as he slipped by her, yet the whisper of his apology floated to her ear.

He backed from Raoul, holding his gaze steady. "Obey the demands for Christine's sake." With a sudden earsplitting noise he disappeared, swallowed by a trap door.

TWENTY-ONE

The stagnant props surrounding Christine poisoned her memories from her years at the opera. Silent horses, circus clowns, and mythological beasts turned happy memories into nightmares.

She'd stopped struggling to free herself hours ago. Her writhing gave her bracelets of red skin and every time she swallowed, her throat scratched. It was no use. No one could hear her.

She was a prisoner to the Phantom's needs, yet her mind twirled wildly in denial. Her memories were egging her apprehension on, but she refused to believe Erik would live only to treat her so cruelly. Nothing made sense. Not even her choices or her heart. Horror and love remained locked together in an endless cyclone of emotion. The harder she tried to separate herself from Erik, the farther she was dragged away from the peaceful eye of the storm.

Blinded when the door opened and the light of the lantern flooded the room, she squinted sharply, and crawled farther into her corner. He was back! That demon of a man doing Erik's bidding.

"Let me go!" she yelled, Richard's frame filling the doorway.

"You really should stop screaming. A pretty voice such as yours shouldn't sound so hoarse."

"What do you want with me?"

"Oh, Madame, that's a question a woman of your beauty

shouldn't ask a man like me. Beyond the ransom your vicomte will pay, you're of no use."

She bit her quivering lip as Richard knelt in front of her. The light from the lantern made strange shadows over his face. She looked down and fought the fear pebbling her flesh.

"Do you mean for such a pout to seduce me? You should know I think you're an excellent temptress. I do enjoy it when women tremble for me." She tried to wrestle her chin from his grip, but his fingers were so strong. "Come now, I'm giving you a choice. Usually I don't ask."

He leaned in for a kiss. Christine jerked away, freeing herself from his grip. His fetid breath nearly made her wretch.

"What does the Phantom want with me?" she asked breathlessly.

"Well, little lady, the Phantom wants you."

His fingers crawled through her hair like a million lice as he toyed with a stray lock. It churned her stomach even more.

"I get the money; he gets you," he continued. "That was our arrangement. Ah well," He slapped his hands on his knees and stood. "I suppose I should save you for him."

"I don't believe you." As she spoke she could taste acid in her throat.

"It would be best you did. The Phantom doesn't take well to folks who think him a fool."

Christine followed the thin beam of light arching across the room as Richard gestured with the lantern to the doorway beyond. Her mouth opened and then closed as she tried to gather breath to scream. The light illuminated the lifeless body of Edward Laroque strewn across the floor.

"Poor old chap got in his way. The *Phantom* regretted having to kill him, but he prefers to work alone and Edward would have become difficult to deal with once he found out about dearly departed Jacob Wischard." Richard laughed into his fist.

The sight of the dead man's bulging eyes and grotesque expression launched an uncontrolled horror in her. Christine started to scream only to have her stomach seize and her ears ring. She shot her face away from the dead man, spilling vomit across the floor. Through her tears she hoped against hope itself that some angel would deliver her from hell.

→≫•••———•••———•••≪←

Erik thought it best not to ignore or suppress his anger.

He found his display on the stage invigorating and wanted to feel power course through him like it once did. Too long he'd kept his emotions in check while he did battle with his inner demons. Not this time. Not with someone holding Christine in the balance and playing with Anna's mind. The power gave him renewed determination to put an end to this abomination. Erik used that strength to drive him through the opera house as he stalked Richard Barret. The drum of his boots against the floor matched the throbbing in his temples. His cloak whipped around his ankles mocking his anger as he pivoted through dark corners of the opera house... and his mind.

Night fell quickly. He moved uninhibited, driven by the stories he replayed in his mind. He was a genius, not a mind reader, so in order to find Christine he had to think like Richard Barret.

Unfortunately, he knew enough of the man to do just that. Richard acted on his threats, with no regard to woman or child. Too much was at risk to take this opponent lightly. The man was a drunk; Anna had suffered great misfortunes as a result. Erik knew precisely where Barret would likely end up. It would only be a matter of time before Richard went to the opera's wine stores. He'd corner him there.

Erik didn't bother to let his thoughts settle when he reached the stores. He simply waited, enjoying the heat rising from the back of his neck and the tension tightening his hands.

A figure, arms laden with wine, shuffled out of the stores, prompting Erik to sink farther into his hiding spot. He breathed deeply, a familiar sensation awakening his body. The feeling was a great relief of energy, a surging tension of mind and body, building before releasing in one long and glorified explosion. He'd always equated such ecstasy to what it must feel like to bed a woman.

Erik waited for his prey to pass, forcing himself to prolong his agony and wait for his release until the right moment. Barret walked past him, studying a bottle of wine. Erik held back, coiling his need, focusing his desire.

Barret stopped.

Erik rounded.

The thin, silk rope snaked from his hand and hit its mark around Richard's neck. The bottles crashed to the floor spraying alcohol everywhere as Barret clawed at the rope.

Erik snapped back on the silk. He held it taut, satisfied that the vermin on the other end could do nothing in defense. The man gargled for air, jerking from side to side, and fighting to keep his feet from sliding out from beneath him. Moving from behind his victim, Erik smiled when he saw the bone-white color of Richard's face. The man twitched as the elegant lasso bit into his neck. Erik enjoyed that expression. It was one of the glories of killing by silk. No need to soil the hands and no blood was spilt. Years ago the Punjab provided a detached method of dispatching those Erik deemed not worthy of further efforts.

Holding the silk in one hand, he slightly released the tension with his other, still keeping the rope securely around Barret's neck. Erik moved into what light the wall lamps emitted. Controlling his prize like a dog on a leash, Erik cast an evil look deep into the eyes of Richard Barret.

"Bonsoir, Monsieur. I believe you wanted to meet me."

Richard blinked hard. Erik blinked as well, deliberately knowing the eerie quality of his eyes would drive those not used to it near mad. He chuckled as what sounded like curses tried to rip from Richard's throat. The vermin tried desperately to loosen the cord around his neck. Erik took pity and gave him enough slack to allow him to respond.

"You're real!" Richard cracked.

"Quite."

"What do you want with me?"

Erik jerked on the rope again and reeled his captive closer by the neck, closing the breadth between them. Richard stumbled forward.

"I want the vicomtess. Where is she?"

Richard stopped struggling as his breath came out in rasping, shallow pants. "I won't tell you." He fought to smile which incited from Erik another violent tug on the lasso. Richard cried out and clawed at the rope, but still curled his lip in a sneer. "And you can't kill me because then you'd never find her."

That was the wrong answer.

Erik yanked the Punjab and pulled Richard into his grasp. Dropping the rope Erik gripped him by the collar, swinging him hard against a wine rack. The bottles crashed, sending glass and wine everywhere. Erik kept him pinned against broken bottles, suppressing his taste to murder him right then.

Richard winced arching his back away from the broken bottles. "I see you get my point."

"What do you want with her?" Erik shoved him backward fighting the urge to ram the bottles through his spleen.

"Why would I tell you? If you so desperately want her, you can have her when I'm through!" Richard popped his shoulder free enough to dive under and around Erik.

Erik jumped toward him, but Richard dodged the oncoming attack. Rolling out of the way, Richard grabbed the shattered remains of a broken bottle. Erik twirled out of reach as Richard lunged at him with his makeshift dagger. Erik jumped backward out of reach as Richard slid his jacket aside and drew his pistol.

Erik froze as the steel of the gun glinted in the dim light.

"You're a worthy opponent," Richard panted, yanking on the rope and freeing it from his neck. "That's an unusual choice of weapon, but quite effective." He thrust it toward Erik. The cock of the pistol echoed in the silence around them.

Erik caught his rope, his lip twitching as he fought for control. Eyes on the gun, his mind devising a plan as fast as he could, he slowly coiled the rope around his hands.

"What are your demands?" Erik snapped, watching every move Barret made. The worm may think he had the upper hand, but he underestimated Erik's cunning. Barret wanted something. If he didn't he simply would have shot.

"I've only demands with the vicomte. I'm under the impression he doesn't like you very much."

Erik held the silk strand tighter feeling it cut the circulation in his hands.

"You could actually be of use to me," Richard mused.

Erik's jaw stiffened as he clamped on his teeth. His rage wanted to claw its way out and feast on Barret's heart.

"I might get more out of this con by running it with an *actual* Phantom."

Erik weighed the options. He had no idea of Christine's whereabouts and no time to conduct a search of his opera house or the streets of Paris. Being a wanted criminal would make doing so difficult.

The only hope to find Christine lay in working with the despicable man and not against him. If any Phantoms were going to be running around his opera house, Erik would rather it be he anyway. The fluttering in his stomach became increasingly persistent the more he stared at Barret's despicable face. He'd rather do thing his own way, but he couldn't have Christine harmed. Barret was the only one who knew where Christine was... and in what condition. Erik couldn't rely on the incompetence of Raoul or the Inspector to find her. The idea of Christine lying somewhere injured in anyway twisted a knife-like pain in his gut. Killing Barret now could put her life at risk and that was a gamble Erik was not willing to take.

"Go on," Erik urged.

"Excellent. You help me get what I seek, do whatever it is you Phantoms do, and I'll give you the girl." Richard raised the pistol higher. "The game is played my way, however, lest you want me to kill her."

Erik hated playing second fiddle. He would play Richard's game only until he had a chance to turn the tables.

"Very well," he rumbled irritably.

"Perfect. I need you to write a letter. I understand that is an area in which you excel; beyond that, when I need you I'll contact you. Ahh... how exactly does one contact a Phantom?"

"*You* do not."

"Fine." He shrugged. "I dare say you're better at being a ghost than I am anyway." He gestured toward the door. "After you."

Erik locked eye with Barret as he passed, taking a brief glance at the pistol still aimed at him.

"So, you have a soft spot for the diva? Does she love you?" Richard laughed as he fell into step behind Erik.

Erik quickened his stride. If he stayed, he might change his mind and kill Richard now.

"I've heard the tales you know," Richard called after him. Erik glanced over his shoulder prompting Barret to wave the pistol so he kept moving. "Scorned and rejected by the beauty because you're a monstrous beast. You don't think the diva ever loved you?"

Erik's loathing churned like a ravening hunger. It mingled with a longing he dare not tame. Centering his thoughts on that sensation willed away the need to give in to his madness. He glanced at the rope he held with a perverse want for the relief it would bring and a grim recollection of a past he was trying to forget.

Slow down. Anna's sweet voice echoed through the anger in his mind. *Focus on her, find Christine and then end this ridiculous cheat.* Barret should consider himself lucky. The thought of Anna was the only thing keeping Erik in check.

Barret's laughter punctuated the air. "You don't honestly think there's a woman alive who could love you, do you?"

Erik stopped short. He turned. "Actually, there is."

"I dare say I would like to meet her!"

Erik turned from Barret, for the first time feeling fortunate he was condemned to the vaults of the theater. For if anyone had crossed him at that particular moment they would have witnessed Richard Barret meet a violent and unforgivable end.

TWENTY-TWO

The minutes ticked off one by one, each moment another second Christine was in danger. Worse than the time, which seemed to laugh at him, was Raoul's self-loathing. What an incomprehensible weakling of a man he found himself to be, sitting there, unable to save his wife from the monster that had haunted their lives. Unable to even keep her safe from common street thugs. To make matters worse, was Anna's silent contemplation of everything around her. It scorched Raoul's last nerve. The dimly lit manager's office was the perfect setting as he replayed the horrific nightmare in his mind.

Raoul tapped a pencil on the desk in tune with the ticking clock. Each strike of the lead on the blotter was another strike against his honor and another dosage of fear. That Phantom would pay! He'd pay with his life if it were the last thing he did.

The pencil rapped against the desk so hard, Raoul snapped it in two.

Caving to Barret and the Phantom's first demand and ridding the opera house of its security may have been the death knell for his wife. The thought turned the back of his neck ice-cold as fear pumped through him. Forced to dismiss Legard as well, Raoul had to go it alone as a one-man army. Damn that he was not in command!

Raoul tried to ignore Anna, who sat at the opposite desk, but he sensed her eyes on him. He squeezed his shut, cursing the entire situation. He was alone and un-chaperoned with a young lady in an office of two murdered opera managers—everything about this blasted road to hell was *not* good. Normally in the presence of a lady, any lady, he would have carried himself with more dignity. But at the moment, he damned propriety and stuck a finger into the bow of his neckwear and ripped the thing open in frustration. It was a noose around his neck.

"How do you know Richard Barret?" Raoul rubbed the back of his neck upon seeing her steely gaze. "Fine, say nothing then. How do you know the Phantom? Do you still expect me to believe what this letter implies?" He pulled her note from his jacket pocket and waved it before her. Naturally she didn't reply immediately. Raoul slapped it down on the desk, loud enough to make her jump. A flush rushed across her cheeks.

"Believe what you want," she murmured.

Raoul shoved the desk chair backward. The legs screeched against the wood floor. "I will!" he snapped. "I hope what you witnessed on that stage proves the man who wrote this is incapable of mercy, let alone love."

He spat out that last word as if the association of it with the Phantom was a sour milk in his mouth.

"What I witnessed, Monsieur, is the desperation of a man who is still deeply devoted to a woman who was once the light of his world and whose shadow I'll always be in."

Raoul jabbed a finger toward Anna as he paced, not giving a care to the twist on her face. "Don't ever... *ever*... associate my wife with the Phantom again!" He paused and whirled toward her. "You know what I believe? I believe you play into this somehow and will be useful in helping me find my wife."

Anna's faced hardened this time, not just her gaze. "So I'm a pawn? *That's* never happened before." The sarcasm clogged the air. "I tried to reason with you. I told you about Richard Barret, but did you believe me?"

Raoul schooled his impatience. "What do they want with my wife? What are the Phantom's demands going to be?" What he wouldn't give not to be a gentleman and shake her until she broke and spilled their plan. Staring at the Phantom's sure-fire accomplice, he stroked his mustache to keep from punching a hole in the wall behind her. "Answer, Mademoiselle."

"Erik has nothing to do with this. He only wished to respectfully speak with the vicomtess. He's told you that countless times, but you choose not to listen."

Raoul paced farther from the desks, but even that was not enough distance between him and this entire situation. "I wish you wouldn't call him that."

"Erik? Why not? It's his name. Does it make *Erik* too human to you?"

"No," Raoul came forward and rapped two fingers against the desk in front of her. "Because it only draws you deeper into the spell he has cast over you!" Damnation, the woman was thick! Thick and love struck with a demon. Raoul took a deep breath, the air burning in his lungs as he fought for control. "Mademoiselle, I'm not keeping you as a pawn. I wish to protect you from him. Clearly I was unable do so for my wife, and I'll not have another woman fall victim to his twisted mind." He glanced over the red and angry burn on her temple. "You've suffered enough already."

"I'm quite capable of taking care of myself. I don't need to be protected from Erik, nor do I—,"

Anna and Raoul both turned as the door opened interrupting her mid sentence.

"Vicomte?"

"Madame Giry!" Raoul exclaimed. "Why are you here? My *maître d' hôtel* should have sent someone for you by now. I shall call for a carriage to bring you to my estate. And this time, you are to leave."

"No, Monsieur," she pleaded. "I've been a part of this longer than you. I'll not leave this opera house. I… I was resting in my office until your coach was to come." She extended a note. "I found this on my desk."

Raoul ground his teeth; he was growing weary of notes. "What does it say?"

"Box Five."

Raoul raced for the door, Anna close behind.

The newly installed electric globes on the stage were lit and a few were left to illuminate Box Five. The rest of the theater remained shrouded and emotionless as a tomb. Erik kept himself tucked out of sight while Richard reclined in his usual pose, feet propped on the balcony railing. The mongrel's disrespect of his box was testing Erik's temper.

"My apologies for the lateness of the hour," Richard shouted as Anna, Raoul and Madame Giry flooded the stage. "But we'd rather not have an audience."

Erik swung his glare from Richard to Anna. For the first time the thrumming in his mind, building and building as each second of this hellacious cheat wore one deflated slightly upon seeing her. It lasted only until Raoul shouted out.

"Get to the point," Raoul demanded.

"As you wish." Richard reached into his jacket and jerked a weighted envelope forcefully toward the stage. It spun and sliced through the air to the stage below. "Those are our demands and some additional conditions from The Phantom."

Additional what? Erik's jaw hardened.

Seething, he moved from the shadows and glanced at the letter as it hurdled to the stage. Though Barret had asked him to—Erik never wrote any note for Barret. The dog never told him what he wanted him to write. Erik, chest swelling with anger, his face heating beneath his mask shifted his glare from the note now bouncing across stage to the man next to him.

"What did you send in that note?" he growled to Barret while below them Madame Giry crossed the stage to retrieve it.

"Just our demands."

Barret was smug and lucky Erik didn't rip his face off then and there. "What demands?"

The smile creeping across the lecherous rat's face oozed mockery. Turning from the insipid man, Erik found Raoul staring at him.

Incompetent fool, that vicomte. Erik stared as intently back at him but the boy refused to look away. Raoul remained fixed in his spot. Impressive resolve, though one of Raoul's hands quivered next to his hip, betraying his nerves. The way Raoul flexed his hand screamed of a hidden pistol beneath that jacket. Erik sneered. Go ahead; draw that hidden pistol and aim. Aim right between his golden eyes and extinguish them forever, if he be so bold.

Erik stared at the vicomte with calm indifference before focusing his attention on Anna. The anger ticking away in his mind dulled a fraction at the sight of her, but flared as Richard looked at him. His gaze went from Erik, to Anna.

"It's not polite to stare, Anna," Richard snipped.

"You won't succeed with this con," she warned.

"Oh! Oh! The strumpet finds her voice!" Richard clapped before striking the arm of the chair with his fist. "I *always* win, Anna. Haven't you learned that yet? Tell me, how's that sister of yours?"

That one sentence pinned Anna to her spot. Even in the low light of the theater Erik saw her face blanch.

"Poor little strumpet. You never had one did you?"

A gasp escaped Anna's lips as if the spirit Erik had grown to admire had shattered. He shot a look of pure hatred on Barret as he recalled the entire reason why Anna spent her life living as she did—to protect the sister she thought she had from suffering Barret's evil. Erik wanted to swing down to the stage, gather the pieces of Anna's broken soul, take her in his arms and make her whole again. But Christine's life hung on his letting the retched man beside him believe he was in control.

Erik clenched and unclenched his fists as Anna's mouth opened and closed as she tried to reply. He suppressed any reaction as she choked back a cry and crushed her hands to her ears, unable to do anything to force out the sounds of her father's laughter. That laughter combined with her quiet tears made Erik snap.

"Some respect in my theater!" He grabbed Richard's feet and shoved them off the balcony railing. It did little to satisfy him. Erik paced in front of the railing trying very hard not to rip him apart limb by limb.

Richard glowered. "You really do have a temper."

"And a wise man knows not to tempt it!"

Erik forced himself to stare intently at the Vicomte de Chagny when Madame Giry returned with the note. Raoul read it then looked to Box Five, he too turned white.

"What kind of deviant madman are you?" he shouted at Erik.

"We expect you to obey the demands, vicomte," Richard replied, staring at his cuticles.

"This... this is unjust." Raoul looked from the note to Anna and back again.

"You know the options," Richard warned. "Don't scorn the Phantom for you wife's sake."

Erik took a step toward Richard, but spun his back to the stage at the last second. What the hell was in that note! He wouldn't be seen crushing his fist to his mouth to keep his roar of rage inside. Every minute he permitted Richard to have control was a minute longer than he could stand. He could lift Richard Barret, demand the conditions of that note then throw him to his death right now, but Erik forced himself to think of Christine.

"I want to see my wife," Raoul shouted making Erik turn. "I'll do none of this until I see her—until I know she's safe."

"You'll see her, Monsieur," Richard interjected again, this time biting around his thumb.

Erik, frustrated beyond reason, and very close to snapping Barret in two, watched contemptuously as the vulgar man spit the nail on the seat. When he started to stand, Erik shoved him back down, his mind racing faster than the notes he composed. He had to find a way to get Christine out of the reach of Richard Barret and safely into his hands.

"She will sing in the concert series tomorrow as her public expects," Richard announced. "I'll see to it she takes the stage. You'd dare not risk her life by doing anything rash in front of hundreds of people. Be forewarned, I'm an excellent shot. One false move and we kill her."

We?

Hatred like he'd never known churned inside of Erik as Barret brazenly tapped his finger between his eyes to emphasize his point. Barret would find a bullet in his brain rammed there by Erik's bare hands. No-one would ever suggest that he would harm Christine.

"Agreed," Raoul conceded. "Allow her to sing, and I'll meet all these demands."

The vicomte glanced at Anna, scrubbing a hand down his face before he waved the note at Erik. Suspicion filled Erik's gut.

"When do I deliver this?" Raoul added. "When will you bring me Christine?"

Erik's thoughts raced. What had Barret asked of the man? It was just like that coward Raoul to abide. This was insanity. If not for Christine, he'd wrap his hands around the dog's neck and be done with this whole charade. He had to think quickly—and like the phantom "When retribution is paid!" he bellowed.

"*Erik! What?*"

Anna's tone made his stomach writhe like a nest of snakes. He stood stone still trying to maintain his control, while the man beside him turned his attention toward Anna. Erik hated the lewd and curious way Richard leered at her. Though he wanted to rip the expression off his face, the deadly silence that had descended upon Erik's mind after Anna's shout was awesome.

Richard's lustful gaze bounced from Erik to Anna and back again. The man's smug expression of understanding was nearly his undoing. He clenched his fist tightly to keep from throwing the rat to his death.

"I'll accept the delivery, Monsieur," Richard chimed in. "When we're certain everything is in order we'll deal with your wife. Follow through with the demands as—"

"She will sing the Madrigal." Erik's voice thundered across the theater, booming from wall to wall. He locked his gaze with Madame Giry's. If anyone could tell he had a plan brewing, it would be her. "I will provide instructions. When she sings it, see to it all demands are adhered to *exactly* as written. Make no mistakes as to how it is carried out."

Madame Giry nodded emphatically. She took Anna's hand and gave it a light squeeze.

"Madrigal?" Anna mouthed to Erik.

Erik looked at Anna, his expression hardening like granite beneath its leather prison. His mind taunted him, accused him for not controlling the situation. The scratchy sounds of madness tuned out all sense of reason. If he stayed one second longer, blood would shed and all would be lost. Erik couldn't hold back the growl of frustration escaping through clenched teeth. The hem of his cloak balled tight in his fist was all that kept him from laying his hands on Barret. Clinging desperately to the last threads of his self-control, he turned on his heel and left Box Five.

The Madrigal was the only composition Erik had taught Anna on his violin. It was the first intimate gift he'd ever given a woman, but he'd not been brave enough to share with her its mournful lyrics. It was a sentimental piece to him—the key he handed Anna to unlock his mind the instant she grasped his violin. A tune that had Erik's heart and mind arguing against each other and questioning exactly whom she had freed with that key—man or Phantom?

Richard sauntered out of Box Five not caring a whit as to where his 'partner' wandered off. He skipped down the Grand Escalier humming a merry tune about fame and riches, certain he was about to have life feasting out of his palm. His spring lost some of its step when he saw his Phantom fellow pacing the base of the stairs like a rabid animal.

"I don't like being interrupted like that," Richard warned, slowing his steps on the last few stairs. "My con, my way. Remember?" Nothing was more empowering than when he had the upper hand.

He barely saw Erik's fist split the air between them. One swift crack flattened Richard to the floor.

"Son-of-a-bitch!" Richard growled to the marble. Before he could scramble to his feet, Erik had him by the collar, yanking him off the floor.

Air shot out of Richard's lungs, his back nearly snapping in two as Erik slammed him against the marble banister. He grunted hard, but covered his pain with a laugh. "I didn't think you were the type of man to resort to throwing punches."

"I prefer techniques that use a bit more finesse and calculated thought, but flesh contacting flesh just feels good."

The room lurched again as Richard was yanked forward.

"What was in that note?" Erik growled.

Swiping his lip, Richard stared at the blood on the back of his hand before spitting what was on his lip onto Erik's mask. Richard rounded his shoulder into Erik, forcing him backward and breaking his grip. "Don't do that again for your diva's sake."

"The note," Erik snarled.

Richard rubbed at his jaw. "Ransom. And don't think you're getting any of it. The vicomte delivers the money to Box Five and once everything's in order, you can have your way with the diva."

Richard brushed past Erik and jogged down the remaining steps.

"You are lying." Erik's voice thundered across the Escalier, reverberating through Vestibule de Contrôle.

"Am I now? That's the mystery that makes Richard Barret, Richard Barret. It's a simple con." He swaggered toward the Grand Vestibule. "You're the one trying to complicate it." Turning, Richard snorted. "You really want to kill me, don't you? Or perhaps hunt me down, find the girl and whisk her away like a knight on a white stallion? You see, that's the beauty of it all. Your reputation precedes you, mine doesn't. Ultimately, they want you, not me. I'm merely the messenger. Or perhaps you already know that—*Erik*."

Man didn't need to see a face to understand the body. Richard sneered when Erik wavered. He parted his jacket, his pistol adding power to his warning. "Come now, I dare you to follow, kill me and save the girl. Easy, isn't it? But let me remind you, I'm a damn good shot and will level you before you even drew another breath!"

Richard's shout echoed around them. Damn Phantom was suppose to make the con easier, not ruin his fun. He unhooked this pistol and drew it slightly.

"I'm sure Anna has told you how many I've killed." The Phantom didn't move, driving Richard's arrogance higher. He wasn't wanted across Europe for little reason. "Try anything to stop me and you won't like the results. Recall, I'm the only one who knows where she is. We're much alike, you and I, except you may indeed have the brawn, but I, the brains."

Shit. That only angered the crazy bastard more. Erik came at him ravenous in his approach, like a tiger stalking his prey. Jaw already throbbing, Richard thought quickly to reply.

"And the girl..."

Erik stopped.

That was too easy. Richard smiled greedily. "You really are lovesick aren't you? Tell me, does your sweetheart know?" He backed away and spread his arms triumphantly. "Now, who could that sweetheart be I wonder: the diva, the strumpet, or perhaps both? Oh the irony that a man such as you would have two women!"

Richard stopped before the mirrored wall in the huge main foyer. He kept his hand above his pistol and gesturing around him at Erik's reflections.

"But do *you* have them? Or does he? Or he?" He pointed first to one reflection and then across the hall to the next. "I'll share with you something, Monsieur, since I pity you so deeply. Taking command of a woman's body, thrusting unrelentingly into her is sheer delight!"

Erik raced down the vestibule toward him quickening Richard's pulse. It was quite possible that Erik would kill him right there, so Richard made certain to bring him to a standstill. He drew the pistol at his hip and aimed.

"I've already tasted of one in that manner multiple times. Who do you think that is, the diva or my daughter?"

Erik stopped. Richard chuckled. What made his masked freak do so? The imagery or pistol aimed at his chest?

"Christine will sing the Madrigal," Erik growled. "You will bring what I give you to her."

Richard laughed. "What makes you think I'll deliver anything to her?"

His laugh fell away. Richard cocked the pistol, an arm's length away from a black mask. The heat of Erik's breath, met his own in the space between them as Erik slowly backed them into the shadow of massive column. Richard gripped the pistol tighter to hide his tremble as the shadow lit the monster's eyes a blazing gold.

"Do not parry me when the well of my hatred is deepest, Monsieur." Erik spat. "My music, *my* way."

Erik stood in the silence of the Grand Foyer, a space big enough to hold two hundred people as Richard Barret stumbled away.

The worm of a man was lucky to be living. Erik's breath heaved, his shoulders hunching with each pulse. He got Barret to agree to bring Christine what she needed for the Madrigal, and though Erik had come out the victor, the mirrors around him reflected a fool.

The ten chandeliers that lit the foyer's length had been dimmed long ago, so barely a glimmer of light illuminated the space. His teeth clenched so hard his ears rang.

Erik stormed the center of the foyer; a huge raven of death watched by the busts of famous Maestro's long gone. He wanted to kill the Vicomte de Chagny as well for caving to the whims of Barret and standing down the theater police. This foyer might not be empty if Raoul wasn't a coward. More people might be looking for Christine if Raoul wasn't so weak.

Erik blamed the boy for all this.

If he'd been allowed the freedom to speak with Christine when he'd asked, perhaps this grim farce wouldn't have been created and she wouldn't be locked away somewhere cowering in terror. And, he assumed, in terror of him.

Richard Barret had indeed succeeded in resurrecting a Phantom, but the Phantom wouldn't be played the fool.

Erik stopped in the middle of the foyer squinting against the unorganized noise in his mind. A sharp pain sliced through the back of his head. Try as he may, Erik could lie to himself all he wanted, but Christine loved the boy and misunderstood him.

The reason stared at Erik out of the corner of his eye.

He whirled. With a vehement shout, he sent his fist and forearm colliding into his reflection. Relief kicked him in the gut when the mirror crumbled to the floor. If only he could shatter this con in the same fashion.

He stared at the hall he'd fled down days ago when he first kissed Anna. When he tried to outrun the emotions he'd discovered still existed inside of him. In the past he'd forced Christine to choose whom she would love. He had threatened her with violence, forced her to choose him by holding Raoul's life in his hands. Now Barret was threatening him by holding Christine's life and honor in one hand and Anna's fragile psyche in the other. Barret didn't know it, but he was forcing Erik to choose.

He had to choose Christine.

He'd see to it she was found safe. Erik would tell her what he needed, kill Richard Barret and then deliver Christine to the arms of her vicomte.

Wretched boy. Let her love him. It matters not.

He would not relive the past. Erik only wanted the life he was yet to have.

A new and unfamiliar emotion shook him: insecurity. Though he chose to aid Christine, he loved another and was uncertain if he was ready to face that.

Erik paused before retreating to the bleakness of his underworld. Kneeling, he fanned his cloak out of his way and picked up a piece of the shattered mirror. Its sharp edges bit into his flesh and made a small trickle of blood coat his fingers.

The present only echoed the past, urging the company to take the stage in unchallenged performances.

The part of leading man was a role the Opera Ghost was hesitant to play.

TWENTY-THREE

Christine faded in and out of a restless sleep. Her dreams were a combination of the gentle affections of her husband and the dark, alluring mystery of her masked Angel of Music. Her shoulders ached, her wrists burned, and her spirit was breaking. She only wanted someone to rescue her—anyone.

She gasped, hope fleeing from her soul when the door swung inward and in sauntered Richard. Lord deliver her, she was going to die!

"Hello, diva dear. It's dreadfully late. Were you waiting up for me?"

Christine tried to crawl away from him but the ropes kept her bound to her spot. She struggled as Richard dragged several small bundles into the already cluttered cellar.

"Now," he began, "I'm going to untie you and you're going to listen to me. Understand?"

The pain around her wrists was sharp, robbing her of breath. She was going to be trapped in this horrible place forever! The only man she was ever going to see was the ghastly creature in front of her. Broken, Christine nodded. She stiffened as he crawled uncomfortably close and reached around her waist to fumble at the knot tethering her to the wall. She craned her neck as far from his face as she could get, the fear stiffening it, making it hard to move. Christine gasped as she was freed. Bracelets of raw and angry flesh marred her wrists. She thought to flee, but exhaustion had command of her legs.

Richard carried a basket to her. A fresh facille poked out of the linen cover and the pungent odor of a maroilles wafted around the warm loaf. Her stomach rumbled and her mouth watered instantly.

"The Phantom," he griped, "is a very demanding fellow. He insists you eat. He claims you'll need your strength." He shoved the basket toward her and held out a large flask. "You're instructed to drink this. Something about your voice."

The heat from the flask made her cold fingers tingle painfully.

"From him as well." A large box landed at her feet. "I'd much prefer you naked and writhing beneath me." His smile was toothy and wet, making Christine clutch the flask to her breast like armor. "The Phantom, however, seems to prefers his divas in pretty things."

Christine reached out and dragged the dress box toward her, the gift giving her a glimmer of a teacher she knew long ago. Confusion circled her mind making her dizzy.

"And… this." Richard produced his final parcel, slapping it down top of the box. The clap was so loud Christine jumped.

Her eyes welled with tears. A leather folder held the pages of an unfamiliar score. The beautiful silver hair comb and the freshly plucked rose woven between its teeth sent her tears falling over their brim.

"Oh spare me your bubbling tears. Learn it," he snapped, gesturing at the score. He kicked his lantern toward her. "It's nearly dawn and you sing tonight." Before she had time to react Richard swung out the door, locking it behind him.

None of this made any sense. Why would Erik send her these things? Why would he know such a wretched, terrifying man? She caressed the box. Opening the lid, she peeled away the tissue that protected its contents. Her body went suddenly weak, the confusion sagging her shoulders. The most exquisite dress she'd ever seen lay before her. She knew the fit would be perfect before ever trying it on. In the past Erik had sworn on bended knee that he'd pay attention to her every need and fancy.

The lantern made the old opera props around her glow grotesquely. Their shadows danced in the low light. The twisted faces of the figurines contradicted what lay in front of her. There was only one answer.

He loved her! Erik still loved her. Kidnapping her again was proof of that! As she fingered the pearl beading on the dress, nerves tickled the back of her neck.

Setting the dress aside, wincing at first at the pain in her wrists, she hesitantly reached for the score. She undid the ribbon that clasped the binder shut, careful not to damage the comb and rose. With a final tug on the ribbon, she lifted the comb to her nose. The floral scent of the rose chased away the dank mildew clogging her nose.

Her hands shook as she examined the next gift.

Across the top of the score in Erik's odd scrawl was written: *Madrigal du Rossignol.*

A sad melody, perfectly matched to her range, poured off the pages. The notes rose and fell like the song of the nightingale itself. Christine could almost hear the bird's mournful song in her ear.

When Nightingale falls scorned from favor of heart and flock; seeks his trial and alone bleeds against a thorn; He sings to deaf heaven a final dirge as he commits his sins against nature's sword...

The lyrics seized her with an agony so deep; she hugged herself against the aching. She read on, pitying the bird. The love pouring from the score gripped her hard and wouldn't let go. Christine covered her lips as she read, her tears dripping, salty, over her fingers.

The music shifted. A simpler tune followed and replaced the agony with such brilliant hope. For the first time since being locked in this dungeon the air in the room seemed fresh and light. Christine's heart beat faster with every stanza until it nearly spun from her chest.

But... wait. She stared at the message being conveyed to her in a combination of notes and words, barely able to breathe.

Denial cramped her stomach, curling her forward. She'd waivered over her feelings for Erik for years and hid them from the world and now it was too late. He... he didn't wait for her? The lie she'd been living roared to life inside of her but she was too exhausted to scream.

Christine rocked, fearing what her realization would mean for her husband, his title, and his life... yet thinking on the future of hers.

She shouldn't, couldn't, be in love with Erik, yet she was.

Reading and rereading the lyrics, the message screamed at her like a siren. She refused to believe them. She wouldn't! A tiny fire in her pit blazed wildly out of control, as Christine clutched the sheets to her breast and gave in to her jealous tears.

TWENTY-FOUR

Anna reluctantly accepted the vicomte's hand as he helped her from the carriage onto the grounds of the Opera Garnier. Thank heavens they were back here. Having spent the night at the vicomte's Paris home still kept a bitter taste in her mouth. It made her loathe the aristocracy even more, what with all their comforts but little common sense. The early dawn light barely glowed as they turned through the doors and into the near-deserted building. She didn't agree with the vicomte's decision to leave the grounds the previous night. It had been Inspector Legard's last request, before his services were severed. His reason for it was his concern over the vicomte becoming a victim of the Phantom as well. It was nothing short of ridiculous. The entire charade was as preposterous as her being paraded at a nobleman's side.

"You seem tired," the vicomte observed. "Didn't you sleep last night? I should have insisted upon you staying in the guest chambers instead of that chair you chose in my drawing room."

An overly plush chair by a warm fire was far superior to a muddy street or mildewed stack of rope. "My lack of sleep had nothing to do with the chair and everything to do with knowing your vicomtess was in the arms of Richard Barret. I doubt you can tell me any differently."

"I didn't rest knowing my wife is in the arms of the Phantom."

Anna suppressed clicking her tongue. "I'm telling you, Erik

means her no harm. That person we saw on the stage was not who he truly is."

The vicomte didn't say a word in response until they were inside. He twisted the knob on the office door and shoved it inward, gesturing her inside. He shut the door and shrugged off his waistcoat, recklessly tossing it on the divan. It exposed the pistol strapped close to his hip.

He turned the key on several lamps.

"You speak as if you intimately know the Phantom," he said.

"I know Erik."

"You know nothing." He pointed at her, a rude gesture on his behalf, but Anna had seen worse. "You know nothing of our history. That beast tried to kill me. Four years ago he trapped me in a room of mirrors, Mademoiselle, a torture chamber of his own creation, which blazed with heat and then tried to drown me while the woman I loved watched his every move. He then drugged and chained me in the Communard's dungeon." The vicomte slammed a fist on the desk so hard he sent the blotter teetering. "I managed to avoid being chained there by the commune, only to be imprisoned there by a deviant madman! My screams couldn't be heard, my wrists bled from the chains and my abhorrence of him hit levels I never knew possible. But worse—I couldn't reach my wife. I had to rely on others to act as the man I couldn't be. The Phantom is pure evil. I'll not be convinced otherwise."

Anna empathized with his suffering; she'd known such fear in her life as well. What she didn't empathize with was his stubbornness. If he'd only listen to her!

"The Phantom plays disgusting mind games." He rapped his knuckle against his temple. Anna wanted something stronger right about then to knock some sense into him, but she listened anyway. "My wife tried to kill herself once because of them. She spent a fortnight locked away with him while he terrorized her and forced his filthy mind on her. He tried to manipulate her into loving him. And now, he tries it again. The monster is obsessed. The man's mind is like an endless wheel churning up filth and there's no way he can or will ever love."

"Erik can love. I know because he loves the vicomtess more than anything." That truth was too much to bear but she spoke it anyway. She'd rather live with the truth than live in denial.

"Mademoiselle, I'm in no mood."

Even though she ached at the thought that Erik would never love her like he did the vicomtess, she needed the vicomte to understand he meant the diva no harm. "Erik wants the chance he gave you and the choices he gave her. He released you from that dungeon and presented you to your bride unharmed." Anna watched his brows shoot up. "Yes, that look upon your face is correct, Monsieur le Vicomte. I know more than you think. Erik wants to set things right and live like anyone else. Have you no mercy for second chances?"

Anna returned his blank stare. He sat behind Edward's desk, motioning to the chair behind the other desk. And though she was loathe to warm the spot where Jacob once sat, her knees no longer had the strength to keep her standing. Timidly, she twisted the inkwell on the blotter to and fro and spoke to it, instead of the vicomte.

"Monsieur, may I ask for the return of my letter?"

"Why? Trust me, he meant none of it. That note is another manipulative trick."

It wasn't a trick… she hoped. Though Anna knew with a sinking heart that she'd always be second best to Erik's one true love. No matter what, she thought as she stared into her warped reflection in the inkwell, she loved Erik and needed to keep his words close.

"Spare yourself the pain," the vicomte rumbled. "He has nothing but evil in his soul."

Anna yanked her face up, holding the inkwell still in her hand. "You don't know his soul. I felt no evil when he took me in his arms and lifted me to kiss—"

"Enough!" His face turned a sickly green.

"Enough for you maybe, and I'm not some servant you can order silent with a flick your hand! You only want to believe what the past dictates for you. Is that the only way a man should be judged?"

"You're naïve, Mademoiselle. I'm right to protect you. I'll not have your innocence scarred or ruined."

Anna spun the inkwell away. It slid off the desk and shattered against the floor. "Naïve? Innocent? How *dare you* assume anything about me! I spent the better half of my time on earth fighting to stay alive, whilst you pranced about upon your pony. I did things and saw things no woman should as you and your vicomtess lived the comfortable life your precious little noble indicator allows."

Outrage fanned her barely banked façade of calm, forcing her to her feet. She had no doubt the angry flush heating her face was visible to the vicomte. "I was forced to live a life that would send most people running to church begging for absolution, so the last thing to worry about in this, Monsieur, is my naivety or innocence! I can take care of myself, which is more than I can say about your wife. The only reason I'm permitting you to keep me as some bloody adornment on your arm is because I know and understand the man you should truly fear—*Richard Barret!*"

She swiped at her mouth with the back of her hand as if she could erase the foul taste of her father's name from her lips.

Wide-eyed, the vicomte leaned back in his chair. "Is that so? You're positive Barret is the man to fear? *There's* your naivety. I'm going to ask you one more time and I expect an answer. How do you know Richard Barret?"

The question shot arrows of hatred through her. "He killed my mother."

The rapping at the door startled them both and permitted a bit of color to return to the vicomte's face.

"Come in," he snapped though he glared at Anna.

"Monsieur?" Madame Giry called, forcing the vicomte to lose the stare down. "Pardon the interruption but—"

"But what, Madame?"

"The concert series is this evening and—"

"And?"

"We're without managers. You said you'd be acting in their place. Maestro Fontaine needs to speak with you."

"Madame Giry, please handle him, I've bigger problems to face."

Anna sneered when he looked right at her when he said that. Richard was his problem. Not Erik. Not her.

The box keeper puffed out her chest. "The *manager* deals with the Maestro. As well, the reporters of *Le Époque*, *Le Matin* and even *L'Echo* wish to speak with you. And Inspector Legard is on the grounds as well. I deal with the boxes."

"*L'Echo?*" The vicomte cursed under his breath. "The last thing I need is to tango with a reporter from Paris' primary gossip rag."

Anna folded her arms. "The last thing you need is Richard Barret."

The vicomte sent her an unappreciative glare.

"Word of murder travels quickly in the streets of Paris, Monsieur," Madame Giry replied.

He grabbed his waistcoat and swung it on. "I'll deal with the Maestro first. Have Inspector Legard handle the reporters. I don't want a word of this leaking out. And don't let the mademoiselle out of your sight."

Anna clenched her teeth, weighing whether she wanted to strangle that man or scream in in frustration. Once the vicomte was gone and she had her opening, she bolted for the door but stopped short as a stammering, Madame Giry blocked her path.

"Why does the vicomte want me to—"

"Let me pass, you bloated old ninny, lest I knock you senseless! I have to find Er—"

She didn't have a chance to finish her sentence as Erik blew into the room and kicked the door shut behind him. He shoved a bundle of scores into Madame Giry's arms.

"The vicomte will be busy for a while. Keep these safe," he demanded.

His smoldering gaze leveled on Anna. In three strides, he backed her against the far wall. Pinning her to it with one finger on the soft spot beneath her chin, he gestured back to the music.

"My concerto was not easy to finally get back from your meddling need to submit it for this concert! *Never touch my music again!*"

Anna glanced at the sheets Madame Giry held. That would explain Maestro Fontaine's fury. The concert tonight was without its final act. Laughter burst past Anna's lips but she coughed it back down it as soon as she saw Erik's lip twitch.

"Reprimand me all you want," she shrugged. "You don't intimidate me."

His low rumble shook her so hard that it took all her concentration to stay on her feet. Erik shifted his finger and cupped her cheek. Anna's breath hitched as his thumb caressed her cheek. Her pulse quickened the closer he came to her ear. Anna swore her knees were going to finally buckle when his thumb traced her lips. His voice shivered against her cheek.

"While I find it incredibly tempting to investigate the seductive nature of a woman's pout, you would be wise not to light fires in me I cannot address at the moment."

The touch of his ice fingers sent heat racing across her skin. Letting her go with one final pass of his thumb to her warm lips, he paced the room.

"Erik, what's going on?" Anna asked, briefly touching tingling spot his thumb had touched. "When you dropped from the flies and landed on the stage in front of the entire company and the vicomte? What on earth was that ridiculous display? And then in the box?" Anna gestured out the door before ramming her hand in her hair. "That was not like you. Would you prefer I call you Phantom?"

"Do not call me that!"

"Then tell me what's in your head! Seeing you with my father is not what I anticipated."

"Your father?" Madame Giry gasped.

"Not now, Madame Giry!" Erik and Anna yelled.

Her last nerve was about to die. Anna took a deep breath. This was getting to be so twisted there was no way to fix it. "I'm sorry, Erik, I didn't mean to call you that. It's not easy for me to see him. This investigation is…"

Giving up, she walked back across the room and sunk into Jacob's chair as the reality of the entire situation forced her down.

"Parents are disagreeable creatures." Erik grumbled walking toward her. He stooped and picked up the inkwell. "I can only speak for the monstrous woman that bore me. I cannot say I know what that despicable man you continue to refer to as a father put you through, but I know enough to believe the sooner Christine is safe, the better." He stared at the inkwell for a moment before placing it in on the desk in front of her.

She looked away not liking the sight of it. Perhaps all of this never would have happened if she never delivered ink to him in the first place. Erik would still be metaphorically dead and she wouldn't know how much love could hurt. Stupid packages. Anna hated the vicomtess' name coming out of his mouth. How she wished he didn't love that woman as much as he obviously did.

"I need your help, Anna."

Guilt raced through her. The vicomtess was in grave danger—that's what mattered most, not her breaking heart.

"Do you know where the vicomtess is?" She tried her best to hide the pain in her voice. Erik shook his head. "But you have a way of getting her?"

"I will be able to get Christine off the stage when she completes the Madrigal. She will not be thrilled to see me. I will need you to take her and assure her I mean no harm."

You mean assure her safety and that you love her. Anna put on a brave face and nodded.

Erik looked toward Madame Giry and back to Anna. "Once you have her, bring Christine to Madame Giry and keep her safe. I will then locate the vicomte and tell him where she is."

Madame Giry nodded, but Anna frowned, skeptical that it would work.

"Wait beneath the stage when the Madrigal ends," Erik instructed of Anna.

Anna slumped in the chair and rubbed the burn on her temple. This nonsense was making her head throb. "The vicomte won't let me out of his sight, Erik. How will I manage that? Why not bring the vicomtess to him yourself? Show him you are doing this to save her. Prove them all wrong."

Erik chuckled morosely. "I can see the image now—the Phantom escorting the vicomte's wife to him with an apology and polite bow?" He reached out and lowered her hand from her temple until it rested against the desk. He kept his on top of hers. "Anna, stop looking for my redemption."

"Someone has to."

"I cannot change the past!" he clipped, jerking his hand off of hers. It knifed her in the gut. "You will get away from the vicomte, somehow."

The bitter undercurrent to his voice carried the undeniable threat of a man who was dangerously close to embracing madness. Only a suicidal fool would ignore the folly of challenging him. It caused a shiver to crawl up her back.

"Just do as I ask and keep Christine safe. Paris hasn't truly known the horrors of the Phantom."

TWENTY-FIVE

Pacing the courtyard of the *Cour de l'Administration*, Raoul tugged at his jacket and pulled at his cravat. Evening fell and though he prided himself on being levelheaded, the longer Raoul catered to the Phantom, the likelier he was to act on the acid flowing through his blood.

Couples wandered arm-in-arm, decorating Paris with a carefree air. Hooves rapped on cobblestones as carriages rolled past the opera. The clang of plates and chairs scraping the ground rang out as nearby cafés prepared for what they expected to be a bustling evening.

Raoul glared at the marquee that proudly announced the concert series. He wondered if the star was his wife, or the Phantom. The opera was ready for this evening's performance and, thanks to his family's patronage of the opera for so many years, he had at least a working knowledge of how things should ebb and flow. His saving grace was his insistence that Maestro Fontaine find something to replace the second act. Raoul didn't bemoan the loss of the violin concerto. He knew who took it. Yet another way the Phantom thumbed his nose in Raoul's face.

He glanced over to Legard who stood a distance away from him on the far side of the *Cour de l'Administration*. Raoul made a point of keeping out of sight of the reporters he'd let Legard expertly address. Gossip traded like gold in Paris, and Raoul had no doubt he'd provided quite a bit of the currency for it in the past. He preferred to keep it in the past.

He waited while Legard thanked the reporters and turned them away.

Once safely out of prying eyes and ears, Raoul approached. Inspector Legard removed his hat and shook Raoul's extended hand.

"I can't thank you enough for this, Jules."

"My stories will satiate them for now. This evening is another matter. I'm glad you came to your senses and summoned me."

He forced his lips into the semblance of a smile, hoping the Inspector believed him happy about the situation. The fact was he had no choice. "As much as I think with my heart, at present I need to think logically." He extended the ransom note. "We had another late night meeting with the Phantom after I dismissed you. He delivered this. Christine is to take the stage tonight as scheduled. Barret assures me the Phantom will be watching and taking aim if we try anything. I'm to carry out those demands," Raoul jabbed a finger against the note, "as Christine sings."

Inspector Legard had a dark shadow upon his face. "Anna is the girl that was assaulted. Why would they want both her and your wife?"

"Isn't every man's fantasy to be with two women?" Raoul snapped.

"Vicomte!"

"Jules, forgive me, I've not slept. The Mademoiselle professes the Phantom loves her. Then why take Christine? Why demand Anna be delivered to Richard Barret if he is such a demon?"

"Do you think he'll act on his threats if we don't bring him the Mademoiselle?"

"Barret and her… they're connected somehow. She claims he killed her mother so I've I every reason to believe Christine will suffer if I don't."

"This is a substantial sum of money, Monsieur le Vicomte."

Raoul had already realized that and arranged for what money he could. Crossing his arms, Raoul tried not to think of the consequences of the choice he was forced to make. "I've the funds, but I don't make it a habit of traveling as a walking bank. I can only give him what I have in the accounts here in Paris. I've no time to get the rest. Hopefully he won't notice."

"When is the opening curtain?"

Raoul fished for his pocket watch. His stomach clenched. "Six o'clock."

The Inspector read the note closely. "And Barret is to meet you in Box Five to gather all of this before Madrigal's end?" Raoul's nod made the Inspector shrug. "I'll have my men there at the ready. We'll grab Barret then."

As if it could be so simple. Raoul shook his hands on either side of his face. "And the Phantom, have you forgotten? Think, Jules. We're working against a man and a demon. You must recognize he knows everything, he sees everything. The Phantom is everywhere. You make one move against Barret and he'll know. He'll harm Christine."

"So we let him take the girl?"

Hearing Legard's voice crack emphasized what Raoul was about to suggest was nothing short of incredulous.

"When the Madrigal ends, disperse your men and get them backstage. Let Barret and the Phantom think I have done their will. Let them have the Mademoiselle. As soon as Christine comes off that stage, I swear Legard—you get her!" Raoul's chest tightened as much as the fist did at his side. "Barret will not be able to get far with the mademoiselle—not with these crowds. We can get her back."

Raoul's forearm tightened as he clenched his fist. Legard was not reassuring.

"I certainly hope so, vicomte."

⇒•———•••———•⇐

"The crowds are gathering, diva dear," Richard proclaimed. Leaning against the doorframe of the prop room, he leered at Christine as she frantically struggled to clasp the final few buttons on her gown.

"Come here," Richard commanded, waving her forward eagerly. She moved like an automaton, clutching the silk of her dress close against her body. Her fingers shook against the bodice.

"Magnificent," Richard exclaimed. "Your Phantom has fine taste in women's clothing."

Dragging his fingers across her shoulder as he made his way behind her, he admired his prize. He stopped behind her, his fingers grazing the flesh of her back as she fumbled with the buttons she

215

couldn't reach. Christine arched away from his touch.

"What's the matter?" he cooed, leaning over her shoulder. "Have you been so pampered you've become used to a dresser to help you don your clothing? I could take them off…"

Hot breath caressed her cheek. One by one he purposefully undid the buttons she'd managed to close. He ran a finger down her exposed skin and tugged at the laces of her corset.

"Too bad there is not time to explore such flesh." He pulled her backward against him allowing only enough space to twist each pearl button closed. "Tell me, those tears you shed when your Phantom gave you this gown, they weren't of fright, were they? I know tears of fright. Those were tears of want." Richard drew out the last word and pressed his lips against the crook of her neck and shoulder, her skin like silk against his lips. Her tremble centered on his groin. He picked up the silver hair comb.

"I don't think a woman who so feared a man would shed such tender tears." Gathering the sides of her hair together, he groaned. "Marvelous how hair so soft could can make me so hard." Her shaky breath fueled his need. Richard hastily secured her tresses with the comb. Not wanting to behave a minute longer, he drew her backward against him so she wouldn't miss a word. The pistol wasn't the only thing hard against her hip.

"You must look ravishing when you confess to the Phantom your love for him. But… what if he loves another?" Richard licked her cheek. She tasted like honey.

Christine yanked her head away. Even the darkness of the cellar couldn't hide her surprise. Richard read the fragile emotions of this tender young thing like an open book. The chaos he was about to release on the Opera Garnier thrilled him beyond belief.

"Come." He laced her dainty hand around the crook of his arm regretting his need to behave. He had a delightfully painful throb between his legs. "We've a concert to give. Worry not; you've done nothing wrong. It's fine to love two men. Why, duels to the death have been fought over a pretty face."

Richard smiled. Her ruby lips stood out rich as blood against her porcelain face.

⟅⟆ ••——— •••———•••⟅⟆

The Opera Garnier basked in the glory of the evening. Splendor and majesty reigned again at the great opera as patrons flocked to witness the concert series. The salons sparkled with the finery of their guests and hummed with excited chatter. The first act had been met with thunderous applause and set the stage for the next act and anticipation of the diva's long awaited grand appearance.

Anna sat next to the vicomte in Box Five. She scanned the crowds below, nervously stroking the arms of her seat. The theater's dim light cast eerie shapes across the mouths of the ornately carved muses decorating the columns surrounding her. Whether the faces were forever frozen in a laugh or scream, Anna couldn't tell. She found it fitting that Erik, a man whose expressions couldn't be deciphered, would choose this box as his. The muses mocked any who dared come near. It seemed like Erik was everywhere and, even without him near, Anna sensed his presence. Staring down at the finely dressed men and women in the seats below and watching as they leaned together in excited prattle, Anna wondered who were they really here to see, the vicomtess or the Phantom?

Anna scowled. How would she get to Erik before the Madrigal ended? She turned her attention to the gentleman at her side. The vicomte blended in perfectly. Elegant in his evening dress, he projected the image of refined taste but the pose he struck spoke otherwise. Chin upon his hand, a frown strained his face.

Together, they waited for the top of Act Two. While Anna pitied the vicomte's plight, she admired his devotion to his wife.

"Monsieur le Vicomte," she implored, "Erik is doing everything he can to get your wife away from Richard Barret."

He straightened his sleeves and brushed them clear of imaginary lint, completely ignoring her. Anna followed his study of the patrons below. She saw several of them point to their box; several more whispering as they glanced their way. If he was concerned about the gossip in the theater over the reasons as to why a woman such as her was seated at his side, he should listen to her and let her go. Anna rose.

"You don't have to worry about the vicomtess or me."

The vicomte reached up and grabbed her forearm. She stifled a cuss when he forced her back into the chair.

"I'll not have any more of your delusions. Somewhere in this opera house the man who abducted my wife and who tried to kill me is attempting to haunt my family again. And this time, he has convinced others to do his bidding. Stop trying to persuade me that Erik is any semblance of an honorable man! It's fruitless. It disgusts me to even think about it."

Anna's eyes narrowed in disbelief as she gripped the arm of the chair. To think she thought to pity this man! She would have tossed her empathy aside if not for the way his fingers hovered over hers as if he needed to hold onto something solid and familiar. Instead, he sighed, curled his fingers into his palm and dropped them into his lap

In the past, an excited ripple would be energizing her. But instead, a cold chill rushed across Christine's body making it hard for her to breathe. She searched the seats and the flies above, wondering who would be listening—Angel or Phantom? For the entire first act she was trapped in the shadows backstage, out of sight of everyone but Richard Barret. The temptation to scream for help kept a burn in her lungs. Barret's grip made her skin crawl and his lips on her shoulder sickened her stomach.

Now ready for Act Two she stepped from the shadows numb to the excitement around her. The pistol Richard had pressed into her side was neatly concealed. Performers and stagehands hustled by wishing her good luck, none the wiser. She fought down the acid that burned her throat and prayed for Raoul, while the man beside her winked.

"All the world's a stage. And all the men and women merely players," he crooned.

She glanced at him, his lewd stare churning her stomach.

"Surprised I know Shakespeare?" he laughed. "Even a vulgar man can be cultured."

The pistol twisted, making her lean to one side.

"Don't do anything you'll regret. Sing your pretty song and all will be well. I've no problems killing you if you attempt anything. I'll be watching as will your Phantom lover. Now, your public awaits." He shoved her toward the stage.

Stumbling from the wings, she struggled to get her legs and breathing under control. The light stung her eyes and she jumped as the theater exploded with applause. Trembling, with nothing to hold on to for support, she did her best not to fall. Once securely in the limelight with no means of escape, she said a prayer and glanced to Box Five.

Who will be there, Lord, who will be there…

Raoul! Her pulse pounded in her neck, her heart battering her ribcage. With no regard to the thousands staring at her, she rushed across the stage. She wanted to be near him, she longed for the sense of safety and security he brought to her.

He discreetly held his hands up. "It will be alright. I love you," he mouthed.

Christine demurely nodded, comforted by his mere presence. Taking a deep breath, she turned to face her adoring public. She dipped her body gracefully into her curtsey—silently cueing the past into present.

Looking to her left, she acknowledged the man approaching her. The Madrigal had been written for her voice, the music to be performed by the concertmaster. He entered the stage in a fantastic cloak and hood in a bird motif, a violin and bow tucked under his arm. The hood of the cloak fanned out around his face, framing it in feathers and shrouding it in darkness.

Christine smiled at him, but frowned upon glancing in the pit. She pursed her lips and shook her head telling the Maestro she didn't understand the meaning of his frantic gestures. He jabbed his baton to the spot on his right.

The confused concertmaster had yet to leave his seat.

⟫•————•••————•⟪

Erik approached, stealing a glance across the sea of wealth that churned in the theater before looking into the pit. The concertmaster stood, sat, and then stood again as the confusion built around him. Maestro Fontaine looked between Erik and the concertmaster before glancing back at the audience. He'd have no choice but accept the change of performers. Erik studied his theater before looking at Box Five.

Resentment simmered at the sight of the vicomte sitting there openly with Anna at his side. It should be Erik in his box, free to sit in public with Anna at *his* side, like he had long dreamed. But the miserable past kept him bound from anything remotely normal. It took all his power to move his gaze and focus on the woman crossing the stage.

The past sucker punched him in the face. The onslaught of emotion as Christine walked toward him nearly rocked him off his feet. Nothing could have prepared him for being this close to her again. Seeing her from afar had been a buffer to the past but this...

this brought it all back. Christine's hair shone in the limelight like that majestic angel of his past dreams. Her beauty bound him to his spot.

Erik's heart seized with the memories of tutoring Christine and the sound of her voice as he coached it into a perfect instrument. The plans he'd woven for their future, and his lips upon her forehead.

Erik followed her gaze as she scanned the audience and boxes.

She glanced down toward the concertmaster, noting the man's bewildered expression. Erik's pulse rose. He didn't think Christine would catch on that it would not be the concertmaster leading her in the Madrigal, but he couldn't be sure.

Erik tightened his grip around his violin as he followed her eyes toward Box Five. Hiding his growl of hatred for Raoul, he bowed to her, forcing her attention back on him. Applause ripped through the theater when she curtseyed.

Rising, Erik's gaze twisted around Christine's body from the hem of her dress, to the small of her waist and to her neckline. The sight obliterated all else. How many nights had he imagined being this close to her again? His blood quickened with her scent: honey and lavender.

Why are you not mine, Christine?

She looked back to the box again. Erik's jaw muscles tightened as he dragged his gaze there with hers. The answer as to why stared at him, not from behind the despicable eyes of the vicomte, but from the eyes of Anna…

It was ice water to his face. He shivered briefly, before it snapped him to his senses. He flexed his neck, despising the site of Raoul with Anna. Every muscle in his body wanted to leap from the stage and claim that spot by her side, needing, desperately, to move on with his life, but instead he raised the violin and began to play.

The theater hushed. Intoxicating tones, painful in their beauty, stretched from the violin seducing all that listened. Erik moved with persuasive majesty as the introduction to the Madrigal wore on. Placing himself with his back to the audience, directly in front of Christine, he raised his face so only she was able to see who he really was.

A pent up breath leap from her mouth. Erik leaned into her shock, deeply bowing the violin as she leaned away from him. The fire and ice that filled his soul were played out upon the jarring notes of the violin. Erik circled her in such a way so that only she saw his face. Her dainty hand trembled. He laughed softly at her shock, sending those notes directly into her ear.

"Did you think you'd never see me again?" He whispered.

The hand against her chest had turned to a claw that dug against her breast.

"Is that longing, or shock that makes you twist your hand to your heart so, Christine? Sing."

"No," she whimpered.

"Your mind disobeys, but your soul demands willing participation. It always did…"

His voice trailed away as she missed her cue. No one knew. Erik disguised it perfectly.

"Sing, Christine," he prodded again.

"No," she begged. "Tell me what the Madrigal is supposed to mean."

Erik positioned himself in such a way she had no way to escape his eyes. Her cue approached again and his command hit her ears.

"Sing…"

Erik sighed as Christine, shrouded in obedience and wrapped in a curtain of seduction she couldn't shake off, lifted her voice and sang his Madrigal.

"When Nightingale falls, scorned from favor of heart and flock, seeks his trial and alone bleeds against a thorn; He sings to deaf heaven a final dirge, as he commits his sins against nature's sword."

In a blurring whorl of man and cloak, Erik swept in, commanding, making the violin wail out decades of remorse and shame. A surreal hand of music reached toward Christine, lifting her voice and soaring it throughout the theater. The air vibrated with painful, stabbing notes of a man wanting to die until the music gradually faded. Erik played on, coaxing Christine to continue.

"His final pleas, simply for love: wishing he your heart possessed; to be loved like the One with whom your affections rest; Looking even in Death to shroud his plumes with that of most men's fortune."

"Christine…" he moaned as her voice draped the lyrics with such deep sorrow and regret. She swayed as she sang, her movement mimicking the ache of a breaking heart.

Her voice sent tremors of desire spilling down his back as music coated the air with years of his profound longing and sadness over her.

"What music Nightingale once loved—he could love no more; And despising these thoughts he would wish to die…" Not a sound rippled through the theater but Christine's mournful voice, the beautiful nature of her tone holding everyone entranced "…singing plaintive anthems that peal forth his eternal bitter pain, he dead and cold, deems once more upon his rightful grave to die."

Drawing out long, grief-stricken notes, the drunken desperation in her gaze was all Erik allowed her to control. His voice and violin commanded her every move.

Erik moved closely behind her, so the bird he portrayed practically perched upon her delicate shoulder. He taunted Raoul with his pure and sensual motions, boasting his rule over Christine. Swaying, he lured her into a trance with the music. He leaned in toward her when she laid her head back on his shoulder. It sent a shudder of warmth rippling through him. Her body shivered and arched in protest.

Erik stepped away, and playing on, ordered her with a shift of his eyes to look to Box Five. Silently, she was forced to study the woman seated there.

Christine's lip quivered while Erik's drew into a thin tight line. Her eyes welled with tears.

"Sing, Christine," Erik insisted sharply, instead of melting the command past his lips. He spun, and looking to Box Five, he released a string of beautiful notes that rolled across the theater.

"Until by chance the Lark of day alights upon his sword and freedom in the dark didst rise anew! A breath, a song, not written, not heard, not felt before, perched life upon his soul."

The tears glistening down Christine's cheeks didn't deter the passion behind his playing. Erik shot her a threatening glance, urging control. His playing took over the next few stanzas—abandoning Christine entirely.

Erik knew she could do nothing as the Angel of Music commanded the stage and, unwillingly, her heart.

TWENTY-SIX

Raoul smelled Barret before he heard him.

"Lovely night for the opera," Barret commented as he slid into the darkened row of seats behind Anna.

Out of the corner of his eye, Raoul saw Anna arch away from the sound of Barret's voice. Raoul fisted his hand as Richard leaned forward and rested his chin upon her shoulder. Leave it to a creature such as Erik to find a despicable rat like Barret to do his dirty work for him. All Raoul had to do was round on the bastard fast enough to send his nose into his brain, but thousands of theatergoers would see… and he could do nothing to jeopardize Christine at this point. Sitting in his box with a woman such as Anna had already drawn attention and Raoul couldn't risk anything going wrong. If Erik had solicited the help of Richard Barret, how many others, among the theater were working for him too?

Raoul's stomach seized as Richard drew his tongue across his mouth, mocking the small speck of blood glistening on Anna's freshly bitten bottom lip. Raoul panted in anger. The vile rotter! Seeing how Barret acted around Anna, blacked his mind with horrific image of his wife alone in his clutches. His fingernails cut into his palm as frustration coiled tighter around his body.

"Are you ready, vicomte?" Richard asked.

Raoul reached into his jacket pocket. Were he able, he'd rip his own heart out. The thought of how he had let this happen to

Christine again would never make it beat correctly again. He'd let her down in an unforgiveable way. Raoul jerked his hand out, the tightness of failure coiling around his chest, and held a billfold up between him and Anna.

"Just go," Raoul whispered brokenly. He shot a look at Anna praying the girl was as strong as she seemed to be. If she was able to take care of herself, perhaps someday Raoul could forgive himself for sacrificing her to Barret. "That note you threw me on stage said if I gave you the money and Anna, the Phantom will deliver Christine to me. When?

Richard stood and grabbed the back of Anna's neck. The girl jerked forward.

"That's the Phantom's call," Barret declared as Anna writhed to break his grip. "He's watching and will be in contact. Enjoy your evening. Come, Anna. You're mine now."

"Wait!" Raoul launched to his feet. To hell with anyone who saw. "There has to be another way. Why take the girl, too? You have my money!"

Barret's reply was a sinister laugh as he dragged her around the seats. She bucked and fought the bastard all the way to the door in the depths of the box. Raoul braced himself as Anna whirled from Barret. She rushed several steps forward from the shadows of the box toward the railing. For a second Raoul swore she was aiming to leap. In less than a second though, Barret had snared her by the braid and had his pistol at the ready in his opposite hand. He yanked her back toward him like a dog on a leash, but not before her piercing scream toward the stage shredded across Raoul's nerves.

As the box door slammed shut and her cry of 'Erik' still reverberated in his ear, Raoul turned to the stage. Fear—like a black and unseen sickness—wound around his body.

"Son-of-a…" the breath left his body as it all dawned on him. Erik was on the stage! The monster had her again. That nefarious demon was touching his wife right under his nose! Christine's sweet voice soared throughout the theater but fury pumped hard in his ears.

"With such thought Lark's song can such blissful succor bring; that Nightingale would perchance lift his song with dawn. Guided by the Lark of day he chances to withdraw the sword; to wipe the breast of Death with love—and sing her ardent chords."

Christine and Erik moved like one body as she sang and he

played. She paused in front of him, facing the audience, her voice lifting higher and higher. Raoul's white-knuckled grip on the box's railing went whiter as Christine reached behind her and stroked Erik's feathered hood. Erik moved his head in unison with her caress as she turned in his arms and faced him to complete the Madrigal.

Raoul's heart hammered. Erik had her under some kind of spell! He had to have her under some twisted evil control like he did years ago!

Damnation Christine, fight him!

"In thought that Lark's song can such happy acceptance bring; if Nightingale would perchance in daylight sing."

Christine barely touched the hood when Erik grabbed her and tripped the door beneath their feet, plunging them below stage.

Raoul bolted from the box. If Christine was harmed…

Pain shot through Erik's ankles and buckled his spine as they hit the floor. Instinctually he rolled to his back, taking the brunt of the fall in order to protect Christine from any injury. Thunderous applause and the sound of the curtain dropping didn't drown out the footsteps running back and forth across the stage above them. Erik scanned the ceiling. No doubt his trick had caused chaos. He'd have to move fast. They'd be coming after him with an appetite for death.

Ignoring the stage, Erik locked his attention on Christine, who, breast heaving, was still lying tight against him. Her precious face was inches from his mask and filled with a wild confusion. Though his adrenaline was pumping hard, his hands gentled as he touched her hair. She was bone-white but thankfully seemed unharmed.

"Legard, Madame Giry! That was the Phantom." Though muffled, the panic in the vicomte's voice from the stage above them cut through the air.

Time was running out. Even a fool like the vicomte would figure out where he was. Erik rolled her to his side and shot to his feet, wincing but no worse for their fall.

Throwing off the feathered cloak, he scanned the area. He darted in and out of wheels and twirled his body around ropes.

"Madame Giry?" Legard's muted voice floated down from above this time. "All these traps lead to the sub-stage, correct?"

"Amongst the wheels and pulleys," Madame Giry replied.

"Then he's probably still down there," Legard interjected. That didn't take long. They had to move. Erik rounded on Christine. Her jaw lay slack and as she glanced rapidly back and forth between him and the stage above. Her breathing grew faster by the second. Even a man such as he knew what those signs indicated.

"Do not scream."

Christine's mouth dropped even wider as she stared at him and to the trap above. Her chest filled further. Erik leaned over her, both palms pressing the air between them.

"I am warning you, Christine. Do. Not. Scream."

Before her wail had a chance to break the air, Erik lunged. Yanking the cloth from his sleeve, he smothered her nose and mouth. Her arms pushed repeatedly against his chest as she flailed against the sedating effects of the Mazenderan scent. Her breath rattled in her throat. The fight left her as she fell lax in his arms. Damn this fate of his! His heart grew heavy. It didn't surprise him that he'd have to be prepared to sedate her. His life seemed destined to be in an endless loop of habits he thought he left behind.

"Erik will not harm you, Christine." Her eyes dropped shut and she fell helplessly into the cradle of his arms. Laying her gently at his feet, his remorse was heavy.

"Anna?" No reply. "Anna?"

Christine moaned. Time was wasting. They'd get to the sub stage level soon enough. Lucky for him, Erik had used the trapdoor only he knew about. Last thing he needed was a flood of crazed imbeciles dropping on him like spiders from the stage. He searched the darkened area again, listening closely as Legard's voice floated down from above

"Vicomte. Control the Opera House. I don't give a flying fig how you do it, but don't let anyone leave and for damn it all, don't let them panic. We need to get this man. If you shoot—shoot to kill."

Erik snarled at the stage.

"I want the vicomtess unharmed. Now go!"

His patience wore thin. Drugging Christine complicated matters for now she couldn't leave with Anna on her own accord. He didn't want to resort to such measures, but he couldn't have her screaming, letting them all know he was still on the sub-stage. The scent would wear off quickly. Erik dashed around another wheel.

Anna left Box Five, like instructed didn't she? She was to meet him here below stage and take Christine to Madame Giry while he tracked down Raoul. That was the only way to do this safely! Legard and the Raoul had already cast his sentence. If they saw him taking Christine anywhere else, he'd be burned at the stake. It was bad enough they probably already thought he'd kidnapped her.

Again.

"Anna?" he snapped. "Now is not the time for you to prove a point, child! I need *you* to take her!"

Silence.

The voices grew louder. In and out of wheels and pacing circles around Christine, Erik growled for her again. When she didn't reply, he had no other choice but to take Christine himself. His face burned so hot he swore he'd be ablaze any second. Either Anna was trying to force him to take her to Madame Giry himself, or something had gone horribly wrong.

Grabbing his violin and bow, Erik studied Christine's listless face. She lay like an injured bird at his feet. Tenderly he reached out and caressed one perfect cheek and ran his hand through her hair, sighing as her tresses spilled over his arm. Laying his violin and bow on her chest and folding her fragile arms across them, he cradled her as close as he dared.

At least Christine was safe from Barret. Erik's gaze swept across her face as he held her. In his arms, she'd always be safe. *Though you never knew that, did you?* Erik shook the thoughts loose from his mind and forced himself to focus on the present.

With a quick scan of the ceiling above him, he shoved down frustration that was gnawing on his bones. It was best he called his rising panic that, for if anything happened to Anna…

"Damn you! Where are you?"

—⟡•••———•••———••⟡—

"Make this easy for me, Anna. I'm not in the mood for your attitude right now."

That only made Anna squirm more, just to spite him. How she wished the loathing toward her father could leap at him like a hungry wolf right now. It couldn't though and the reason made her scan the crowds in the Grand Escalair.

She should have known better. Erik didn't know how tricky her father could be; *she* did. All along a nagging voice inside of her said getting away from the vicomte wouldn't be as easy as Erik had thought. She should have heeded it as a warning not to underestimate Richard Barret in all this!

The pistol rammed into her back didn't frighten her. He had pulled the thing on her more than once in her life and had yet to pull the trigger. Though she wanted to scream and draw attention their way, she knew better. The plan had been changed, for there was no way she would get to the sub-stage now, but Barret's focus was off the vicomtess and Erik, and for that, at least, Anna was willing to be the sacrificial lamb.

Erik hadn't heard her cry, though. She felt it in her gut. How could he, being as focused on the vicomtess as he was? Richard shoved his pistol into the small of her back, causing Anna to clamp down on her teeth and swallow her ill-timed heartache. The gun was a harsh reminder of the bigger picture.

The vicomtess had to stay safe and she had to help Erik. She could do no less. She wasn't certain he would have abandoned the vicomtess to save her anyway. Anna tried to swallow around the emotion clogging her throat, but gave up as Richard twisted the steel.

"Get me out of this Escalier, away from crowds, and do it without so much as a ripple of attention," he demanded. "I've twenty-three years of dealing with your attitude under my belt. Don't try anything."

Richard and Anna wove their way through the sea of silk and waistcoats crowding the Escalier. The gendarmes and police milling around were deterring his escape. For the first time in her life, Anna was glad to see so many authorities in one place. With a crowd this size no one noticed her struggling as she wound them toward the empty arena of ticket offices.

"You impress me, Anna. You really know this opera like the back of your hand. Remind me to buy you something pretty as a reward."

"And remind me to saw your bullocks off and throw them in the Seine."

Anna didn't stifle her cry as he snatched her by the scruff of her neck and yanked her into a secluded corner. The stench of his filthy hands clogged her nose as he muzzled her one-handed. Lifting the barrel of the pistol with his opposite hand, he jabbed it in her face warning her not to do anything stupid. Keeping her caged against a wall with his body, he holstered the pistol long enough to check his windfall. Greed coated his face as Richard's fingers rippled through the money. Faster and faster his fingers moved until he slapped the billfold shut. He shoved it into his waistcoat pocket.

"Only a fraction of what I asked for. Stupid move, vicomte. No one shafts Richard Barret."

"No one?" Anna smirked.

"Shut it, Anna. He'll get the point, and the rest of my money, when I use that little china doll of a diva of his as collateral."

Richard's eyes shifted like they were too loose in his sockets. That crazed look always happened when he was panicked and forming a plan.

"Well you don't have her now, do you?" she taunted.

Drawing his pistol again he rammed it into Anna's stomach making her gasp.

"This Phantom fellow of yours—Erik you called him? He was the one on that stage with the diva wasn't he? He tricked me. He has her, doesn't he?"

Anna winced at the pistol he twisted into her stomach and she replied by spitting in his face.

"Wrong answer!" Richard said through clenched teeth as he wiped his face clear. "I'm not about to be duped by the vicomte, and have my meal ticket stolen away by an insane apparition." His hand encased her neck.

Her lungs wanted to explode as her fury grew. Anna glanced to her feet. If she kneed him hard enough in the groin he'd be singing soprano and she'd have a chance to run. Blood roared in her ears as she tried to think as fast as possible. Breaking free from him and running now set her free, but it would also set *him* loose on the opera.

She had to keep him close.

"Where did he take her?" Richard growled.

"I don't know."

"For a Barret, you're a terrible liar." Grappling with her, he forced her forward, his hands like an iron manacle on the base of her skull. "I'd think you'd want to tell me. Are you so certain you want Erik alone with such a pretty prize? Because if I didn't know better I'd say my suspicions were correct and you were sweet on him."

Anna skipped a step. The very idea of her father thinking

anything about her and Erik was a shot of poison to her heart. Erik was the one precious thing in life Barret had not ruined for her.

Yet. Anna swallowed hard enough for him to hear.

"My little strumpet, you are! I knew it!" He spun her to face him. A sharp tug backward on her braid forced her face up to his. "What an interesting little boudoir scene that would be: his pretty little diva astride one hip and you perched on his other."

"Stop it."

"I can see it now. He pounds out his lust with one and has a spare in case the first faints dead away in repulsion."

"Stop."

Richard jerked down on her braid, wrapping it tight around his wrist. Anna hissed as the flesh around her face went tight.

"Take me to him, so I can reclaim my diva and what is due me. If you don't, mark my words, you'll not live long enough to find out which one of you he chooses to straddle."

He lost that crazed look and his face darkened in a way she'd never seen before.

TWENTY-SEVEN

Sequestered in the one place he didn't want to take Christine, Erik leaned his forearms against his coffin and railed against fate. He could only hope when his drug wore off that being back in his house under the lake would be a comfort to her.

Though his hope was slim at best.

He glanced toward the room Christine was in, but he focused on Anna. Anger and worry were moving in passes through his mind. Anna was bull-headed. If she'd wanted to prove a point, she'd do it. But then again, Erik had known no one as devoted to him as she was. Either she didn't show because she hadn't wanted to, and that thought made his blood boil, or she couldn't... and that chilled his bones.

Damn it all. Damn this life, love and everything about it. How easy it would be to slip into his coffin and drift into eternity like he had intended years ago. To give in to the comfort of insanity that had caressed him all his life and tell the life he led currently to go to hell. Trying to live and love like a normal man was too hard. Tucked in another room, Christine slept off the effects of the drug. If only it were that simple to sleep away the past.

He sighed as he reached into his pocket and pulled out his most prized possessions.

Two pieces of glass, one a broken inkbottle, the other a scrap of a teacup tumbled in his hand. They clinked together in a strangely musical way that had become oddly soothing for him. He'd picked up that shard of an inkbottle the first time he realized that he'd wanted to know more about the Samaritan who had been delivering him packages. Anna–his unexpected gift in life. That softened any anger in his mind. The inkbottle clicked against the piece of teacup he saved when he realized how much he loved her. Erik nodded as he stared at it. That had dawned on him only after he'd shattered that cup against a wall after she handed him tea. Anna had made a broken life whole again.

A third piece, a sliver of a broken mirror still wicked enough to reflect his hideous face, tumbled in his hand as well. He'd saved it when he'd realized how completely Anna had changed his conscious and his life.

Change was harder than he thought.

Erik twisted them faster and faster in tune to the noise wrestling the music in his mind. He wouldn't give in to his madness but it was oh, so, tempting.

Christine is here. I can have her. Love her. Touch her. But Anna…

Erik winced at the noise rising in his mind and fought to focus only on Anna. Thoughts of her dimmed the noise in his racket that he'd always associated with his madness. The shards slowed the more he concentrated on her until his mind fell completely silent. He looked toward Christine's room.

You never made my mind go silent like this. Only Anna has…

Erik held all three pieces in front of him before slipping them back into his pocket.

Then why do I still love you, Christine?

Reality was hard to swallow. No matter where he turned there was an ache over that truth centering in his chest, lingering, like his past. Christine was his infatuation; a dream, a vision of love that would never be more than a fantasy. But Anna … Anna offered him hope and the chance to leave behind the Phantom and become a man who loved and could be loved in return. Wasn't it what he wanted?

Pushing off the coffin, Erik rubbed the weariness kinking his neck. The weight of this nightmare was a yoke hanging always on his shoulders. He rolled his neck, but nothing undid the knot. Erik wanted a future, but, at this moment, that was impossible. Not until he buried the past and Christine was safe.

Ignoring the pain, Erik stood tall and turned his back on his coffin.

It was time to claim his future… no matter who it may hurt.

Christine curled deeper under the blanket. A lush, soft pillow cradled her head on a cloud and invited her to stay sleep, but the dank, musty scent clogging her nose made it impossible. Something about it all felt vaguely familiar, but the stabbing pain in her temples made it too hard decipher.

Her eyes opened and closed heavily as the room came into focus. She rubbed the heel of her palm against her eye trying to break apart the muddle in her head.

Where am I?

Wincing, she stopped and stared at the raw, red welts on her wrists.

Wave after wave of memories flooded her mind until she feared she would drown in fear. Christine's heart pounded in panic as she fought for breath. Where was she? The prop-room? Someplace else? Was that madman here?

She bolted upright on the bed, her breath coming in fast pants. No, this wasn't the prop room and she didn't see that horrible man anywhere. A mahogany desk was on the far wall as was an open door to a bath. Looking to her left, her eyes paused over a chest of drawers and a cluttered whatnot. She'd been in this room before…

Her memories ripped open as the night came rushing back so fiercely Christine gripped her head to stop it from pounding. That man, the stage. The Madrigal… Erik.

Christine gasped so suddenly she swore she lost all the air in her lungs.

I'm back in his house! I'm by that lake! How can I be back in his house?

Christine jumped as the door opened. Lord, no! It's him! The Phantom's black mask came into focus with each of his long strides.

"Don't touch me! Don't you come near me!" The words ripped from her tender throat before she could stop them. "Where's Raoul? What have you done with Raoul?"

"You must not yell, Christine. It will do your voice no service. Drink this, it will help."

Christine stared at the extended cup Erik held and then at him. His unthreatening stance did nothing to assuage her growing panic.

"I don't want any more of your potions!"

She knocked the cup aside sending it shattering against the far wall. Erik shook his wet hand, his mouth pulling into a tight line. Christine gripped the bed sheets as tight as she could, uncertain as to if he meant to yell or seize her.

"That was tea, Christine, and in rather fine china."

Christine grabbed at her temples, rubbing at the reverberating echo of Erik's voice. She didn't—couldn't—respond. He turned to a small table by the door where a tea tray was laid out that she hadn't noticed before. He poured a second cup and walked to her.

"Now drink all of this. It will help clear your mind."

The scent of tea cut through the damp air. Erik's lips had relaxed and he made no move to lunge at her or strike. He stood there, a floral patterned teacup and saucer extended in his thin and bony hands.

This couldn't be happening. This all had to be a dream still. Everything. From that madman who tied her up to being here at the underground lake… Christine couldn't focus on anything but the shock making her skin cold. She'll wake soon, next to Raoul, and this would all be some awful nightmare…

"Christine. I insist. Drink this and your head *will* clear."

It wasn't a dream for Erik was a real as can be. He was there—standing—staring at her with those eyes that could burn into the soul. He was as she remembered, not that she could forget. Unbelievably tall, with that odd presence around him that demanded obedience but could light awe deep in the belly.

Shaking, Christine took the cup as Erik sat at the foot of the bed. He folded his arms and watched as she hesitantly took a sip. It was strangely warm as she swallowed. She was cold, inside and out. Christine fought to free her voice from the tight bands of disbelief strangling her.

"You're… you're *truly* alive," she stammered. The teacup rattled against the saucer.

"Obviously. I thought that was patently clear on stage."

Christine placed her other hand over the cup to stop it from shaking. She stared at the tea through her opened fingers. "It was…. I mean… I knew it was you." It was no use. Her hands started to shake even more as her mind cleared by the second. "I…oh… nothing is clear in anything anymore! What's happening?"

Erik folded his hands in his lap.

"Christine, you need to calm yourself."

Calm herself? She didn't need to calm herself; she needed to know how she ended up back in his house and how he ended up... alive! Christine closed her eyes, the shock pebbling her skin.

With the audience gone and far from the entrancing sounds Erik could create on his violin, with the flare of the limelight not shining in her eyes and the fear of her nightmare trembling off to the side of her mind, Christine let it all sink in. The heat from the tea moved back and forth across her neck but did nothing for her disbelief. For years she longed for Erik to still be alive. For years she fought the guilt of making the wrong choice. Day in and day out she lived with a man who worshiped her, but with whom she couldn't love as much as she did her Angel of Music...

Erik...

Christine opened her eyes, the guilt nearly making it hard to see. "You... you let me believe you were dead all these years?"

"Again, obviously."

Her anger flared hot and hard, demanding to be released. She hurled the cup at him. "How could you? I mourned your death! I lived with the agony! How could you?"

Erik dodged the cup and swung himself to his feet as the second cup bounced off the bedpost and shattered against the floor as well.

"I've not all the tea cups in world, you know. One of us it going to have to start throwing pillows."

She took her anger out on the bed linens atop her, crumpling them into a ball and heaving them across her with a growl of frustration.

"Where's my husband?" She asked, swinging her feet to the floor. His presence wouldn't intimate her. "I know this room. You kept me here years ago. There's a secret door in here, isn't there?" She ran toward a wall, her palms searching the stones for a latch or knob. "You used to have a torture chamber behind this wall. Did you lock him back in it? Where? Where is he?"

"Calm down, Christine. You have been through an ordeal."

"Don't tell me to call down!" She barely felt one of her nails break. "Where's my husband? Is he in here, Erik? Is he in here?"

She whirled her back against the wall, her breath heaving. "I won't be your prisoner again and forced to choose to love him or you!"

"The boy is fine, Christine. I will bring you to him eventually."

Christine gasped. "The boy? *The boy*?" Flinging herself at Erik, she pounded her fists against his chest. "Say his name! The least you could do is say the name of the man you *left me with*! Don't *make* me choose *him* again!"

Oh mercy. Guilt dug its awful teeth into her and wouldn't let go. She didn't just betray her husband with such awful words! Stunned by her own admission, she backed away staring at the space between she and Erik.

"Raoul," Erik said. "His name is Raoul."

Christine stiffened as Erik came toward her and guided her toward the bed. The world seemed to move in slow motion as he settled her on its edge. She tried to see if her declaration registered anything in him but all she could see was his unemotional mask.

"Raoul is safe," he reassured. "And I will not make you choose, Christine, I promise you that. I will find your husband and bring you to him. I intend to keep you safe, not a prisoner. Richard Barret will not find you here. This will all be over soon."

The anger and panic seeped from her muscles, slowing her breath and leaving her feeling weak. Her heart sank. It seemed unaffected by his admission, yet his words had made her empty and sad. Going back to Raoul left her hollow. She pressed a palm to her stomach convinced her shock would be there forever. How could she have done this to Raoul? He loved her and her wicked soul betrayed him.

The shock deepened as Erik sat next to her. She dropped her gaze and noticed his left hand. A gold ring encircled his pinky. She pointed to it, her hand trembling.

"You're wearing the wedding band you gave me. You insisted I come back to bury you with it. But it wasn't you I buried." Mercy…she was going to be sick. The badly decomposed body, the sound of the shovel striking against the earth, the dim light that cast awful shadows across the makeshift grave… "Why? Why make me think you were dead?"

When Erik sighed her heart leapt. She swore she saw his shoulders drop. If she wasn't careful she'd start crying for she swore that was a sign of remorse. Perhaps Erik missed her. Perhaps he too wanted to choose a new life and start all over again. With her…

"I needed peace, Christine. I needed to forget you. Not that I ever could."

"Forget me?"

"When you returned upon my alleged death and buried that body with my ring, I had my answer. You truly did love the boy. You made your choice and it was not poor, unhappy Erik. You did not wish my love."

Christine swallowed her sorrow. How could he possibly believe that?

A tear of regret and confusion slipped down her cheek and Erik's skeleton finger brushed along her skin to capture it. She couldn't stifle the gasp of disgust as she recoiled from his icy touch. It was instinct that had her wiping the repugnant sensation from her cheek.

"Do forgive me," he said, his voice tight.

She shouldn't have recoiled. But he was so cold! He left the bedchamber, leaving her behind to calm her tears. Chilled by that one touch of his, she wrapped the blanket around herself before following. Her eyes never left him as he shrugged on an overcoat and concealed a slender rope in an inner pocket.

"I apologize for bringing you here," he remarked. "It was not my intent, but the plans were altered. There is more tea in the samovar and if you are hungry—I have figs."

He waved toward a table, but she ignored the gesture. The thought of Erik leaving her again wrapped iron bands around her body making it hard to breath.

"Please. Wait." Through the ever-present mist of his lake outside his doors and the glow of the candles, Erik truly looked angelic. He couldn't forget her, not ever. He had to be confused about it all. "Don't leave me. You know you want to stay. Look… your hands quiver. That's because you want to stay. Isn't it?"

"You will be fine alone, Christine."

"No. Don't leave again. Stay here. Stay with me."

The blanket slid off of her and onto the floor. Blasted by the cool air, Christine's hands fluttered over arms and breast. She straightened her appearance like a nervous schoolgirl before her first love. When she did, Erik snapped his attention off of her and stared at his organ. She saw his breathing increase in that same way of ravening desire she often saw in her husband. Erik shifted slightly, half turning to look at her before shooting his attention back to the organ. Christine's face heated.

"Do… do you desire to stay, Erik?" She couldn't know for certain what he thought, only what his body told her. His gaze occasionally skimmed past her only to land elsewhere. "Do you… desire me?" The heat on her face grew to spread across her bosom. "You couldn't forget me. That's ridiculous. You love me. Don't you?"

Christine dabbed away a tear rolling down her face. If she had only obeyed him years ago and never unmasked him, she never would have left him. So long as she never looked on him, she could have loved him. He knew that, didn't he?

She drew a breath and moved closer to him, cursing the leather that made his face always appear harsh and cold.

"Isn't that why you brought me here again? To love me?" she asked.

"Nothing could be further from the truth."

His words were a harsh, invisible slap right to her cheek.

"Then why have you done these horrible things?" Christine's face burned as her cry caught on her disbelief.

"I have done *none* of what you think. You have been a victim in a cruel con set out by a man with selfish intentions and it is my intent to prevent it from progressing."

Christine's temper flared. His voice was harsh and short. "If you profess to know what I think, then what am I thinking now?"

"It does not matter what you think."

Disbelief pushed out her mouth. "How can you say—"

"Years ago," Erik clipped, his voice rising and his eerie eyes flaring in front of her, "you chose to move on with Raoul along with the world you so easily command."

Christine stiffened as he gestured to the ceiling above. What did that have to do with anything?

"I stayed here," he continued, "where madness forces me to be. To you I am the Angel of Music, some... fairytale guardian you believed God created for you. To you, I am someone you could love—but only conditionally so long as the truth remained hidden."

"What truth?" she balked as Erik pinned her with his stare. "Do you mean your face?" Christine pulled herself as tall as she could while summoning the courage to mention his mask. If he were going to lecture her, he would see that she could be brave.

"No. The truth that I am a madman and madness doesn't go away if you tuck it into bed at night." He thrust a hand behind him toward his chambers. "Trust me, Christine, years of solitude has had a way of driving me even madder."

"You think a touch of madness will bother me?" She whisked the train of her gown out of her way and stepped around him. "Don't we all have a touch of madness in us?" Nerves popped her voice, betraying her.

"I am a wanted man, Christine."

"I can try to forget that."

"Love does not keep record of the wrongs, there is no *'can try'*! Because of the past, I am now a living, breathing legend. Do you know what that is like? Existing in body, yet questioning if you ever really existed in soul?"

Poor, unhappy Erik... Christine's eyes warmed.

"Oh spare me the look of pity!" he spat. "Once, perhaps, I needed it, but no longer. I have accepted all that has come to pass and who I am. I am not a legend or myth. I am not this Angel of Music and I am not a *Phantom*."

Christine's back stiffened as she looked away from him and the passion behind his voice. The more he shot truths at her, the higher she built her wall of denial. "Don't say such horrible things to me."

"I am merely a flawed man. It took a long time to recognize that. A long time—and a lot of packages."

Christine scowled, unable to decipher why his voice changed when he said that. "Didn't you kidnap me again because you want me to see you for this man?" she countered. Christine tried to keep her lip from quivering, but Erik's rejection of her was cutting her to the bone.

Erik pushed his palm at the air between them as if warning her lips not to tremble. "All I have wanted from the beginning of this mess was to speak with you. But that boy of yours never understood. His denial did nothing but put you in danger."

His words clung to her like a constricting mist, which no means of warmth or light could burn away. As Erik dropped his hand and stared at her, the lyrics of the Madrigal, and their implied meaning, hit her full force. Reaching for his hand, Christine braved his touch.

"Tell me the Madrigal's meaning."

Erik pulled from her grasp. "The meaning was clear. Lingering on the past does nothing but deny the present a chance to become the future. Now rest."

"No," she reached for his hand again. This wasn't happening! "No! If that's the answer then that song meant you're rejecting me, and for who? Who! I won't *lose* you again, Erik! You can't leave me. You love me."

"Christine—"

"No. You love *me*."

She loved Raoul but in the dark reaches of her mind she knew she would always be in love with poor, unhappy Erik, and he with her. It was the secret comfort she had run to all her life. Without a second thought, she brushed her lips against his. The kiss only lasted an instant.

Christine took a sharp breath and curled her lips into her mouth. Her lids fluttered in surprise. How soft his lips were! How sweet they tasted! The horrible curse hidden under his mask contradicted those beautiful lips. She reached to kiss him again to confirm it was not a jest, but he turned his face away.

"Erik?"

Grasping his cheeks she turned him back to her and fanned her fingers across his face to possess his lips—this time urgently. She boldly explored his mouth and slowly let her fingers glide beneath the mask.

To gaze on him, and all his repulsive ugliness, would be her final confirmation that this was the man she was meant to love.

All time and space seemed to fade away as they stood there, so close, pounding hearts could have moved the air.

Erik's hands flexed at his sides. Honey flooded his mouth, as he tasted her. Memories flared to life flashing and spinning around him. As Christine's fingers slid along the mask's edge and grazed his flesh beneath, his entire body blazed. Her body molded against his, her breasts pressed against his chest and her smooth, graceful fingers teased the length of his mask, threatening to expose him.

Yes, please, yes…

For a moment he desired her to remove the barrier that had stood between their love. For a second he had wanted Christine to gaze on him with unconditional adoration. He wanted her to accept his fate, his face, and his madness; to take him as he was in mind, body and soul. For so long he had needed her to love him and only him. Erik longed for her to make him whole.

Her kiss deepened and he responded forcing more passion behind it.

Yes, if there is a God, please!

Erik's heart found a rhythm that was greedy for her touch. Her lips moved like silk against his, her tongue stroked his need for her. Gently the mask lifted upward.

Yes. Take me! Want me. Look, upon my curse! Accept my madness! Heal my devastated soul. I have spent too long broken in pieces...make it whole again for me!

Broken? Like the pieces of an inkwell, a china cup and a mirror...

The thought banged against Erik's chest shaking the breath loose from his mouth. Raising his hands up, he seized Christine's wrists and lowered them from his face. Rattled back to his senses, his own words haunted him: *Lingering on the past does nothing but deny the present a chance at becoming the future.*

"No one looks upon my face but her." Erik stared into the storm brewing behind Christine's expression.

"Her? Who? Who is she?"

Her bottom lip trembled and he chose to offer her no words of comfort. He rubbed a finger across the taste of her on his own lips and turned to leave. "When I am able, I will bring you to your vicomte. Until then, rest."

"Wait. Then you actually meant what you wrote in that song? You've another woman? How... how could you betray me like that?"

Her wail slapped him against the back. He forced himself to turn, refusing to play into her guilt or her denial. There were other places he needed to be, others he needed to see and Christine's reddened face wouldn't sway him.

"I don't know you anymore!" she shouted.

"You never truly did." Erik gentled his voice when she staggered. "That is my fault. I had much to understand. The past is past, Christine; there is nothing in it that can be revived."

He left through the drawing room, leaving her sobs and cries behind him.

"Who are you?" Her shout bounced from wall to wall. "Angel or Phantom?"

Erik stopped, but didn't turn as he followed the echo of her desperate plea. She'd devoted her entire soul to believing he was either her Angel of Music or a Phantom, just as he'd devoted his entire life to being either a man or a madman.

"Rest, Christine." Erik disappeared down a corridor.

"Who are you?" Her distant sobs followed him and rang through the darkness. *"Angel or Phantom?"*

Erik paused long enough to project his voice backward toward her. The walls of his home repeated his exhausted and haunting whisper:

"I am Erik."

TWENTY-EIGHT

Raoul tossed his waistcoat and vest on the office couch and with them his gun. He didn't even feel the loss of its added weight. All night he had it within his reach and was he man enough to draw it? Power was at his fingertips and all he did was roll over like a dog. As he had made his way to the manager's office, the opera had slowed to a dull hum. He did as Legard asked. Took control of the throngs of people, directed them to various salons and parties to meet the composers, dancers and performers.

Oblivious! All of them were oblivious to the Phantom of the Opera and the fact that the monster had kidnapped his wife, again, and right out from under his nose. Raoul punched the air and spun in his place. How the hell could he have let that happen to Christine when he had a gun on his hip!

Raoul jerked the desk chair backward and sat, taking his anger out on it. Slumping behind the office desk, exhaustion suddenly dragged across every muscle except the fury tightening his jaw. He spied a carafe of scotch on the edge of the desk and snatched it, and a glass. He poured himself a glass and tipped half down his throat. It did little to take the edge off. Disgusted with himself, he tossed slammed the glass down on the desk.

"Raoul?"

Marvelous, now in addition to failing Christine, he was hearing things. Raoul strained to listen but the office was silent, like

Wischard and Laroque had left it before their demise. He rubbed his neck, feeling the chain of his religious medallions roll against his skin. Maybe he should start praying because he sure as hell wasn't doing enough to save his wife.

Christine I swear I will find you.

"Raoul?"

Now *that* he heard. He scanned the room in front of him, seeing nothing, until a hand reached over his shoulder and plucked his glass from the desk.

"*Merde!*" Raoul rocked back in his chair as his worst nightmare appeared in front of him.

"I am disappointed you would choose to drink at a moment such as this." Erik walked around the front of the desk, sniffing the drink before tossing the contents into a nearby plant.

Raoul's neck heated as he shot to his feet. The chair skidded backward as his fist came down hard on the desk. "You bastard! You inhuman, subterranean—"

Erik leaned casually against the other desk, crossing his arms. "Are those your words or the scotch talking, because I much prefer Erik."

"Where's Christine?" Raoul shot to his feet. The chair skidded backward.

"Christine is fine. She is safe and none too happy with me at the moment, which should please you immensely."

Raoul edged his way toward him like a man balanced on a thin blade in danger of falling off. His eyes moved from Erik to the pistol on the couch. "I did as you asked, now bring her to me."

"Not with Richard Barret running around. Christine is safe where she is. Anna can take you to her. She knows my ways into the—oh you spineless imbecile!" Reaching down, Erik snatched the pistol. "Is this what you want? Your vain attempts at creeping toward it are most annoying." He heaved the pistol through the air.

Raoul scrambled to catch it before it misfired. "You're insane! That's loaded!"

Erik shrugged. He gestured to it. "A coward's weapon by the way, no art or finesse involved. I did not intend to bring Christine into my house. I do like my privacy and I have had enough of women roaming about my home of late. My aim was to get Christine from Barret. Anna was to get off the ridiculously tight leash you had her on and meet me below stage and deliver her to

Madame Giry and then on to you. I figured since you have spent the last several days arrogantly ignoring my letters and casting my sentence, you would not trust me to do so. I assumed you would trust Anna. Clearly that did not happen. However, since Anna knows the labyrinth intimately, she can be your escort to Christine now."

"Where is she?" Raoul growled.

"Christine? How much of that scotch did you drink, vicomte? I just told you."

Raoul raised his weapon. "Anna, damn you! If she is to take me to her then *where is she*?" He cocked the trigger and blinked away sweat. Moving from behind the desk, Raoul aimed for Erik's face. "I did as you asked. I gathered your money and gave it and Anna to Barret. *You* were to deliver Christine to me once I did that, you lying snake, and now you say the plan was different! Where. Is. Anna? *Get me to my wife.*"

Erik scanned the floor while a deadly silence filled the room enough to punch fear into Raoul's gut. He swallowed hard and stared down the blue steel of the pistol's barrel.

"What?" Erik's voice was rough, dangerous.

In one long stride he was in Raoul's face. He slammed Raoul against the far wall, Erik's unworldly reflexes not allowing Raoul a chance to use the pistol. Erik wrenched it from his grip and tossed it to the desk, the red-hot fire of his voice searing the room.

"*You gave her to Barret?*"

Raoul grunted as Erik pinned him to the wall. "I did what I had to do to get my wife, and I plan on getting Anna out of your reach too. Two women will not fall prey to your filthy lusts! Now where is she?"

Raoul's accusation blasted out his mouth as Erik's fist landed a crushing blow into his stomach.

"I usually prefer more sophisticated ways to demonstrate my temper," Erik snarled, "but I am finding I rather enjoy this more masculine means of display."

The room whirled as Erik spun Raoul around and slammed his back into the desk. Blotters and books careened across the room. Fear and rage narrowed Raoul's focus. Groping for the closest thing within reach, he swung the carafe toward Erik's head but was out muscled. Erik grabbed his hand with an absurd strength until Raoul's grip weakened. The carafe dropped with a thunk to the table.

"Your damn attempts at honor are no help to this charade, Monsieur le Vicomte. I suggest you stay out of my way."

Pain sang through Raoul's skull as Erik shoved him down, cracking it on the desk. Groaning, he looked up in time to see Erik storm toward the door and jerk it open. If he got away he'd take Christine and Anna and use all his tricks so no-one would find them *ever* again...

Without a second thought Raoul rolled toward the discarded pistol taking careful aim. One well-placed shot arched Erik through the threshold of the door and sprawled his body to the floor.

Raoul lowered his shooting arm as the air cleared of the pistol's acrid smoke. He staggered, his gut still throbbing from Erik's punch. The pistol hung limply in one hand as Raoul stared at the man he cowardly shot in the back. Cautiously Raoul approached the doorway.

Erik attempted to rise, but his arms slipped from beneath him, slamming his body back to the ground. Rolling to his back, Erik stared at the ceiling, gasping for breath. Tracks of blood spread crimson across his coat and spilled on the floor.

Raoul heard the pain drag from Erik's lungs as he struggled to his feet. Erik clutched his shoulder and upper arm as disjointed steps pitched him back and forth. The blood snaking down Erik's arm dripped to his palm.

Stooping over him, heat blasted Raoul's neck as his chest heaved. He finally had Erik right where he needed him. He lifted pistol again when Erik reached beneath his overcoat. "Don't move or I'll shoot again."

"I will consider myself fortunate you are a horrible shot," Erik croaked, and faster than Raoul could pull the trigger, he whipped his hand from beneath his coat.

A thin lasso flew through the air.

The Punjab lasso! The Phantom's deadly weapon! Raoul knew it well and instinctually moved his opposite arm to the level of his eyes, to prevent the rope from wrapping around his neck but instead, it hit it's mark with exact precision, coiling neatly around Raoul's opposite wrist.

Heat hammering, Raoul sighted as faster than he ever had and squeezed the trigger as Erik yanked backward, jerking the pistol from his grasp. The stray bullet splintered the wood floor as the pistol spun across it. The air filled with Erik's hair-raising roar, as launched himself off the floor. Raoul swung his fist for Erik's face, but, even injured, the beast was faster and stronger. Raoul bucked against Erik's grip as he had him head-locked in a moment's time. Erik jerked on Raoul's wrist, freeing the rope.

"Once again, vicomte, you stand between me and the woman I love," Erik snarled. Raoul resisted, but Erik's lock tightened, his arm cutting the breath from Raoul's throat. "I had a plan all along to get Christine away from Barret and I was going to handle *him* once she was safely delivered to Madame Giry by Anna. Now your *stupidity* has put *Anna* in danger. If anything further happens to her as a result of your paranoia of me, I will kill you."

Before he could gain his footing, or his breath, Erik threw him to the floor, pain searing up his back, darkness creeping along the edge of his vision. By the time he rolled to his feet, and retrieved his pistol not a trace of Erik existed. Raoul dragged air into his lungs. As he did, Legard and his men skidded around the corner.

"I heard a gunshot!" Legard shouted, cursing at the pool of blood on the floor.

"And it hit its mark!" Raoul's voice rang out, clapping against the walls. He ignored Legard's incredulous expression. "Find the Mademoiselle Anna and Barret. I'm going after Christine and the Phantom myself."

"Now is not the time to be *more* irrational than you already have! You can't do this alone. Which way did he go?" Legard put his hands up, moving as if to seize Raoul by the shoulders and block him from charging forward.

Raoul twisted away. "I swear to God Legard, you get in my way right now and I will have your badge *and* your head!"

Legard reached out and seized his shoulder nonetheless. "Get *your* head on right before you kill yourself! What the hell were you shooting at?"

Raoul ripped his arm free. "Erik."

"*Merde!* Where is he?"

"You're the damn detective! Figure this all out!" Raoul rammed a hand through his hair as he paced, filling Legard in on the plan as he understood it, and the very *different* plan Erik had in store. Legard had best detect something before Raoul took Paris apart with his own hands, to hell with anyone who got in his way.

Legard nodded when he finished, far calmer than Raoul.

"Which way did Erik go?"

Raoul nodded toward a trail of blood on the floor. "I find myself most fortunate that living shadows bleed."

The pain pitched him from wall to wall, ripping his body in two as wild thoughts drove his staggering feet forward. Erik's vision blurred as he rocked side to side. He had to find Anna…find her and take Christine to that spineless, fool of a vicomte…

Perspiration trickled down his cheek as the corridor dimmed. The vicomte would pay if Anna were harmed. He'd pay; Erik swore he'd pay….

He slumped against the labyrinth wall as he feet began to buckle. Every sense was under siege. The air stung with the fresh metallic scent of his blood; each time he moved the world darkened and spun. Somewhere beyond the walls in which he hid, he heard Legard and Raoul shouting…

He had to move and find Anna… get Christine to Raoul…

Everything around him was whirring so fast he swore he'd be sick. Hot pain blasted the length of his arm while the remainder of his body was ice cold. Suppressing a cry, he shook off his overcoat and glanced at his scarlet sleeve. Warm, sticky sweat coated the inside of his mask. He laid his cheek against the wall, panting hard and hoping its cold surface would penetrate it and calm the heat burning down his arm. He tried commanding his hand to move, but his fingers scarcely moved. Erik sucked in air. Forcing his hand into a fist, he screamed against the scalding pain shooting up his arm.

Erik clenched his teeth to keep from shouting again. Fumbling with the silk around his neck, he yanked his cravat off. The pain arched his back off the wall and slammed him backward against it again. Shaking it off, he fought against the blackness threatening to make the world go dark. Clenching his teeth against the pain breaking his body apart, he bound his arm best he could.

He had to move or else he'd faint. Erik dragged his overcoat back on and shoved off the wall. His heart hammered, but was nothing compared to one agonizing thought.

Richard Barret had Anna.

Anna had no idea how long it had been since she was able to

break free from the iron grip of her father, only that she'd been running from him most her life. Her breath was hot in her lungs, like the first time she used that old trick of hers to slip from him. Taking a left, then a right, a sharp turn and a jump down through a trap, then a left again… she ran as fast as she could on the slick stone floors of Erik's underworld.

Anna's foot slid from under her as she rounded a corner. Stumbling but not falling, she quickly regained her pace. That vicomte had changed everything, and the thought of what to do next pumped her blood as fast as she ran. She knew she'd have to think fast the instant he handed her over to her father.

The halls twisted and turned at a blinding pace. That corner was a dead end, this one an illusion, a trick of Erik's strategically placed hidden mirrors. Anna spun herself through the dark labyrinth never pausing to look behind her. She knew better than to think twice when fleeing from her father.

Sweat dampened her brow by the time she burst into Erik's house. At least here her father would be far from the vicomtess. Surely by now Erik had taken her to Madame Giry and this disaster was at its end. A ripping pain doubled her over and Anna gripped at the stitch in her side. Her breath was fighting to find room in her lungs. Straightening did nothing to stop the cramp wrapping around her middle. It only worsened when a woman leapt from the divan.

"Mademoiselle!" the vicomtess cried.

Anna blinked, dumbfounded. She knew the plans clearly had changed when she didn't arrive under the stage to meet Erik, but she never thought he would bring the vicomtess back to his house. It was leading her directly into a hot bed of suspicion. What was Erik thinking! With Richard Barret tight on her heels, Anna's plan of keeping him away from the vicomtess just took a disastrous turn.

Thinking on her feet, Anna lunged at her.

"Get to the boat." Pulling on the vicomtess' sleeve, she dragged her toward the drawing room.

The vicomtess tripped over the layers of her gown. "What's going on?"

The harder Anna tugged her, the more the vicomtess leaned away.

"What? Why? Where are you taking me?" the vicomtess asked, looking toward the drawing room and the lake beyond it.

Anna swallowed and winced, her lungs burning too much for

details. "Not safe. Must go. In boat. Now!"

The woman stumbled out of the way as Anna rushed past her and back into Erik's living room. At any second Barret could show, so every move she made had to count. Take what she could find useful and do it fast! Any bag of tricks would come in handy against her father. Anna turned in circles whipping first one way then next. There! A satchel on the wall! Racing for it, Anna yanked it from its hook and threw anything she could find of use into it.

Anna slung it over her shoulder when she caught sight of Erik's violin and bow. They would be useless against Richard Barret, but Anna snatched them anyway. She had a gut feeling this was all not going to end well and her days at the Opera with Erik were numbered. If they would have to flee this nightmare, she wasn't about to leave Erik's music behind. Anna tried to catch her breath as she laid them in the satchel. She wasn't entirely sure Erik would be *hers* to flee with any longer.

"What are you doing? Why… why have you been running around here and like you know this place?" the vicomtess stammered.

The suspicion Anna heard in her voice grated on her quickly fraying nerves.

"What are you doing with that satchel and violin?" she demanded as Anna gave her a hard stare. "Those… those are Erik's. Put them back!"

Anna started to reply when the sound of shattering glass echoed around them. Her father's voice filled the air with curses.

"He's broken one of Erik's mirrors. He's figured it out." Anna raced across the room and shoved the vicomtess from behind. "Get in the boat."

"How dare you put your hands on me. Tell me what's going on!"

Frustration shot up Anna's spine and right out her mouth. "Vicomtess, get in the boat! Get in the boat! *Get in the God-dammed boat!*"

"I'm not going anywhere."

"I'm not giving you a choice," Anna grabbed her with one arm and pulled her in close. "Fight me and you'll lose. Now you'll do as I say and get in that boat, unless you are wise enough to survive this on your own. Richard Barret is on his way here and you've got to get in the boat!"

"Anna?"

Both women spun at the sound of a different voice, gruff, but not nearly as angry as Richard Barret's. Erik staggered from a hall slowly taking shape from the shadows. Anna didn't give anyone a chance to speak. She flung the satchel in his direction, barely noticing how he stumbled upon catching it.

"You've got to get out of here!" she shouted. "They're tearing the opera apart looking for you. I tried to get the vicomte to understand. I tried to get to *you*. The vicomte duped Barret, the con went bad and Barret still wants *her*." Anna gestured wildly toward the vicomtess. "He's figured out you and I have a connection and he forced me to take him to her. *Bloody holy hell*, I crossed Barret! Do you realize this is going to end in blood?" Anna gasped and grabbed her hair. "I diverted him here. She was supposed to be with Madame Giry! *Why of all places did you bring her here?*"

Erik swayed in his attempt to answer.

"You're bleeding." The vicomtess gasped, stepping toward him. A scream ripped from her mouth the closer she got, as the blood ran down his arm. "What happened?"

"Nothing of concern. Erik is fine," he grimaced.

"You're not fine," she exclaimed, hands flying to her mouth. "You've been shot!"

"I am fi… fine," he faltered seconds before his knees buckled, slamming them to the ground at her feet.

"Mother—of—God." Anna lurched forward as the air punched out her lungs. She shoved the vicomtess out of the way and grabbed him; forcing him from his knees and making him sit in a nearby chair. Her shaking hands fumbled with his makeshift bandage.

"Who did this?" Anna followed Erik's numb stare as he focused on the vicomtess.

"Raoul," he replied.

"You lie," the vicomtess gaped, ignoring Anna to kneel before Erik. "Don't say such dreadful things." She lifted Erik's hand to her lips, brushing the back of his knuckles against them. "Raoul would never do such a thing. He knows how much I—"

"Get me the wine," Anna snapped.

The vicomtess clutched Erik's hand closer to her breast, but didn't move.

"The wine," Anna hollered. "Other side of the room, in the stand next to the divan!"

The diva moved only when Erik slipped his hand from hers. Breath coming in short pants, Anna dug frantically through the satchel. She slipped Erik's hand from the woman's grasp, eyeing Christine with a look of disgust and sending her scrambling. *Don't you dare feign concern when your husband did this.*

Blood. There was so much blood.

Panic wrapped around her, making it harder to breathe. She searched frantically in the satchel, unable to make sense of the things she'd gathered in haste—not even sure what she needed to help the man she loved.

A knife…. she'd seen a knife in there somewhere…

Where is the damn knife! The gentle touch of Erik's hand caressing her cheek cut through her confusion and fear, instantly warming her blood and settling Anna's muddled thoughts. A weak smile trembled across his face, as his finger trailed across her lip, centering her and giving her strength.

"Take a deep breath," he urged. "You will be fine." He comforted her one-second, and then eyed the knife she pulled from the satchel the next. "Are you versed as a surgeon as well as a blacksmith, cobbler…?" Pain forced an end to his sarcasm.

"Don't start with me, Erik." Anna inspected his crimson arm.

The ball entered at a steeply awkward angle but it was close to the surface. As best she could tell, by means of a miracle, it missed bone. The lead slanted through the fleshy outer edge of his shoulder and upper arm leaving a gaping hole of raw and torn flesh in its wake.

"I… I think I can get it." She tried to take another deep breath. It would do no good if panic made her pass out. "I helped a doctor do this when I served him."

"I think you just leave it," Erik groaned.

Her fingers dug against the wound, ripping an agonizing cry from his mouth that sliced Anna in two. She'd seen plenty in her years to recognize the seriousness of the wound.

"This will hurt," she warned. "I have to make certain the bullet is out. I don't need you infected. You need to trust me."

Anna stood in front of him, meeting him eye to eye. He lifted his gaze at the foolishness of her demand. Erik rarely trusted anyone. Silence moved like a thin tendril of smoke between them. His lips barely moved as he mouthed 'only you' to her. Anna accepted the indiscernible nod that she proceed, but rejected how his gazed moved off of her to stare the vicomtess. She swallowed her ill-timed jealousy.

She twirled to face the vicomtess head on. "Stay out of my way."

Not willing to waste any time, she grabbed the bottle, used the knife to dig at the cork and poured the liquid across the blade. She offered Erik the bottle.

"Drink this. It will calm you—"

"Me? Why don't *you* take some breaths for the sake of my arm?"

"*I'll* calm him." The vicomtess stepped in and grabbed his opposite hand, clutching it like a bride holding the just wed hand of her groom to her breast.

Erik didn't protest and now was not the time for Anna to rip the vicomtess' arm off and throw it in the lake. It was a kind thought, considering how she stole Erik's heart. Anna shoved aside the thought and focused on the only one that mattered to her—Erik. "Keep him still," she spat at the vicomtess. "And don't faint!"

"Where… where is Barret now?" Erik panted.

"I lost him in the labyrinth. I made sure to lead him into the mirrors."

A shaky grin lifted his mouth. "My little phantom—"

His next breath was a torturous scream as Anna dug for the bullet.

TWENTY-NINE

Bits of cloth, sticky with blood, littered the floor—amid them, a small round lead. Erik's breath rattled out of his mouth as Anna wrapped his arm and packed moist cloth against the wounds. Though the bandages made his arm throb even more, it was his heart that pounded the hardest. Anna was safe, she'd broken free from Barret, but that didn't stop his mind from whirling with worry.

"Are you all right?" Anna used the hem of her dress to wipe the blade and her hands clean of blood. Her voice quieted as she slipped it into her dress pocket. "If this gets infected—"

Reaching forward he stilled her fussing, ignoring the heat burning down his arm. Such compassionate hands should never be soaked in blood. It tore at his soul. Whatever she relived in the time her father had her, had dulled her eyes. Anna's bravery made him proud, but she never should have suffered in any of this. The guilt ripped at him as she pulled from his touch and began to wipe the blade again. Anna's eyes hardened as Christine reached for him.

"Erik?" Christine stroked his mask. She'd gone bone-white. "You're going to be fine. I'll take care of you."

Erik twisted away, unable to bear her touch. The one woman he wanted touching him had gone quiet as she wiped away his blood. He grabbed Christine's hand, lowering it from his face.

"Anna! An-na!" Barret's voice grew closer and closer. A renewed energy dragged him to his feet.

"How did he get this far?" Erik heard Anna swallow.

"He's been shattering the mirrors. He's figured out your tricks that make the hallways seem to shift. He'll only get closer now."

He swung around with deadly purpose toward Barret's voice. "No, he won't."

"Erik, stop," Anna warned, blocking his path.

"Child, stand aside and let me do this." He'd never wanted to kill any man with such perverse intensity as he did Richard Barret. Raoul may have stolen Christine from him once, but no hatred compared to what he felt toward the man who had made Anna's life a living hell.

"Erik, you're hurt. You're underestimating him and..." When Anna paused, she looked hurt. "... the vicomtess is what matters now."

Anna stood her ground as usual, infuriating him. Erik balled his fists as he stepped around her. Even the desperation in Anna's voice didn't deter him.

"You must get her out of here," she insisted, hooking him by his good arm. "You can't go through the passages, the gendarmes are everywhere, and the place is thick with crowds. Barret is armed and angry and, trust me, you don't want him to find her. He can't follow you on the water and I don't know my way across the lake."

Erik lifted his eye from her fixed gaze and glanced toward the shoreline. Anna had never crossed the lake alone, and he pondered with slight remorse, the deadly traps he hid across its surface. She'd never navigate her way around them *and* the darkness. She'd be dead before she rowed a few feet.

Anna's determination bore into him and no matter how hard he wanted to fight her, she had a point. Growling in frustration, he moved to the boat.

"Christine, get in the boat," Erik rumbled as he picked up the satchel and grabbed for the oars.

"Anna, so help me God," Barret called out.

"Erik, go now," Anna yelled.

As Barret's voice grew closer, Christine stood paralyzed. Erik stood next to the boat and extended an arm to her.

"Christine, come to me," he commanded with immeasurable softness rolling his fingers into his palm. Like a trained canary alighting on a perch, she instantly obeyed. "Anna, get in the boat, I am not leaving you."

"No. If I go, Barret will know he's been deceived. If I stay I can stall him, divert his attention from her, and cover the direction you went."

"Anna Reneé Barret!" her father screamed.

"For once will you not defy me!" Erik roared, fear for her flashing across his body. "I am not leaving you with him."

"Erik, I can take care of myself."

"Anna, you will not disobey me." It was one thing to fear of any harm coming to Christine... but to Anna? The thought pounded his pulse in his ears so forcefully he swore he'd go deaf.

"Erik! She's *Christine*. You love her."

Anna's use of Christine's name shot through him. Why did she have to be so astute? Shouldn't the mask have hidden the anguish that pinched his eyes?

"Go," Anna insisted, bringing to him a lantern she'd lit. "Bring her to Madame Giry as planned—that will be safest. I'll find you later."

If there was one thing he knew it was that Anna would not be swayed once she set her will in motion. What he once admired in her he now cursed. Inside, his gut twisted with a worry he had never experienced before.

"Promise me you will run," he demanded, taking the lantern and hooking it on the boat. "If he breaks through that labyrinth, swear you will run again. Do not do anything rash."

Anna nodded and turned toward him.

"Anna—" when she turned around again, Erik abruptly fell silent. The words he wanted to say falling dead on his lips. He looked first at Christine, who stared at him from the boat with trust and a child-like awe and then at the woman slowly backing away, the one who had stolen his heart, only to grow tired of the absurdity of his life and the madness he couldn't seem to outrun.

Blackness pressed in on them like the dark thoughts swirling in Erik's mind. Only the feeble light from the lantern, cut through the murky mist of the lake. The rhythmic slapping of the oars was the only sound echoing through the eerie silence. He'd had no idea how long they rowed; only that pain was screaming up his injured arm every time he worked the oar, the weakened muscles no longer able to maintain a steady stroke. The only thing steady was the fear for Anna tightening like a noose around his neck. Erik could only see a foot in front of him, but the pictures of Anna on that shoreline were blazing in his mind. A bead of sweat snaked its way down his neck as he moved to drag the oars again, but pain had lit his arm on fire.

"Why are we stopping?" Christine asked timidly as the boat slowed and the rowing ceased.

"I need to rest."

"The pain is terrible?"

Erik nodded.

"That doesn't surprise me. That woman practically tore your arm off."

"The *bullet* is to blame," Erik corrected, straining to hear sounds from the direction they came. Nothing greeted him, but the dreadful silence he'd too many times called friend. "When we get to shore I will bring you to Madame Giry. You are to stay with her and lock the door until I can get you to... Raoul." He spat that name out like it was poison in his mouth. Erik rolled his shoulder and flexed his hand trying to get feeling into his fingertips. That blasted vicomte had shot him in the arm he held his violin with. Damn that boy to hell if Erik couldn't play again.

Christine winced. "Here, allow me."

Erik scowled as Christine reached for him. She gently took his hand, trying to massage feeling back into it, but she was only shooting a blinding pain up his arm. Erik grunted and clamped down on his teeth, but said nothing. He watched her intently as her slight fingers rubbed his palms and caressed the back of his hand. In the past Christine had never tried to touch him. Repulsion and fear were the looks usually on her face anytime he had reached for her. New feelings of confusion moved in on Erik that were far from the situation at hand.

"Raoul didn't mean to shoot, I know it. You're lucky he didn't kill you."

"Your husband is a lousy shot, my dear; however, I do wish he had not hit my primary arm." He took back his hand, the numbing sensation chased away by her touch. If only he could chase away the feelings he had for her and all the confusion that came with them. Erik reached for the oars.

"No," she insisted, "you must rest."

"There is no resting. There are people looking for you."

"Let them look and let them wait." Christine's voice took on a determined tone. She peered at him. "What's different about you? All those horrid things that occurred years ago seem like you were a man possessed compared to now. That monster was different from who I see before me." She reached for his hand again, choosing this time to gently stroke it. "One can't forget, but one can forgive."

The boat pitched dangerously as he leapt to his feet. "What do you mean by that?" He didn't want her forgiveness. Everything he'd done had been for her. He'd worshipped her soul, tended to her every need. He didn't need her forgiveness, for if he had to—if he wanted to—he'd do it all again to pave her a way to greatness.

"Exactly what are you saying?" he snapped.

"Seeing you again, hearing you reject me in the Madrigal made me realize so much. I'll never forget the fortnight I spent locked away with you. One can't forget your intent to destroy the theater and a quarter of Paris, nor can I forget how you tried to kill my husband."

She turned her eyes away from the mesmerizing dance of the blue smoke above the water to meet Erik's eyes.

"I can forgive you all that because time can change a person. I can't love two men, yet I do. I can't choose one over the other, but I suppose I must. I love Raoul, yet I selfishly give you my soul. How is that possible?"

Erik dropped to the seat making the boat lurch, and plunged the oars into the lake. How is that possible she asked? He jaw seized as he clamped his teeth together in frustration. Loving two people is entirely possible, and incredibly agonizing. Erik hauled the oars with long strokes, keeping his focus straight ahead and off the woman in front of him. The pain stabbing him in the arm was the same as the confusion stabbing him in the back.

Christine reached toward his cheek. He swung a glare on her that made her jerk her hand away and look at him like a wounded child. The more she reached for him the more his confusion ebbed.

"Love Raoul with all your heart and me with all your soul. It is possible." Her face twisted in confusion. He gripped the oars like a life ring against the overwhelming emotions threatening to drown him. "I love you in every way I know how. " As the boat gently rocked, beams of light from the lantern fell across her face, making her smile brighten the darkness. It only made Erik tighten his grip. "That is why I am risking everything to keep you from the danger you are in."

Christine's eyes began to glimmer with tears. Her smile grew as she reached to wrap her arms around him.

"Stop," his voice boomed, halting her gesture. "I may have just sacrificed my heart for you."

She glanced around in the inky blackness, her smile fading from sight. "The past says *I* am everything you ever sought after."

"Damn the past! You saw how I lived. What my life has become! Even in my fabled death I was condemned here like a mole in a burrow. I am tired of it. Tired, I tell you. Erik no longer wants secrets!"

"I don't understand."

"You do not have to!" He leapt to his feet not caring how the boat rocked again. "I do not care if you do not understand, Christine! I finally understand!" He pointed in her direction. "Before you arrived I was coming to terms that there could be life beyond these cursed vaults for me. I began to believe I could live like a normal man despite my despicable actions. That I could have all of that without *looking* like a normal man and without resorting to locking a woman away and forcing her to love me." Christine opened her mouth but Erik swiftly cut her off. "I began to believe I could think and act freely, whether as man or madman, *and* still have a woman to dote upon. I thought I had everything arranged, but seeing you again makes me see how much of a cheat my life is."

Still gripping the oars, he threw them down, the sound of the wood knocking against wood echoing around them in the silence.

"How is your fear, Christine? Can you tell me? I frighten you still, do I not? And do not lie to me for I know you can not and will not ever trust me."

She held her body stiffly. "Fear can be survived, Erik. I know my feelings."

"But do you know how you feel about Erik or only your Angel of Music? I have no doubt you love two men. Even broken hearts have room enough for two loves. But it is critical you trust whom you love!"

"Behind us is my life. Standing on the shore of a lake, holding back a man who has done nothing but abuse her, is a woman willing to do anything to prevent my heart from breaking again. *My heart* from breaking, Christine! Which she knows will happen if any harm ever came to *you*. I love you, Christine. How many ways and how many times must I tell you that? I love you, but I…"

Erik collapsed in his seat and leaned onto the top of the oars despite the pain in his arm. The awareness of what he had been trying to deny dawned on him in wild revelations.

"I love you," The words tasted bitter on his tongue. "But I have every intention of being *in love* with her, my heart, my soul—every ugly and damnable inch of me—is hers.

"You don't know what you're saying." Christine's voice shook in the darkness. "You know nothing of intentions or need, nothing of fear. Love is not as clear as you would think. You're making a foolish choice, choosing her. I know all about foolish choices. In her you're only choosing what you *think* is best."

"That is hypocritical of you, Christine. Years ago I asked you to choose who you would love, Raoul or me, and if you chose wrong, I would blow Paris sky high. You foolishly chose *me* when you knew it was not what you wished."

"What did you expect me to do? You terrified me! You were threatening Raoul. I accepted your proposal to save him *and* Paris. But these last few weeks have proven to me that I really accepted your proposal because I loved you!"

A laugh of disbelief leapt out his mouth. Love didn't mean picking and choosing what was best in the moment. It was not conditional.

"No, you cannot, for it is not me you love. You love yourself. You never tried to know my madness or who I am. You loved your Angel of Music. Tell me, what did I do for you because I loved you enough to keep your heart from breaking? Or have you forgotten?"

"Even though I said I would remain with you, you ultimately gave me my liberty and I married Raoul, but—"

"But nothing, Christine. Had you loved me unconditionally, you would have remained to love me into a better man. But you did not. You say Erik has made the fool's choice in what he chooses now?"

She knew so little about the woman he left behind on the shoreline. Anna loved *him* enough to keep *his* heart from breaking, for break it would—still—if anything happened to Christine. *That* loved selflessly.

He dragged a chill breath into his lung and took up the oars. An ache spread across his body at the though of losing Anna and hurt in a way nothing ever hurt before. He spoke more to the darkness than to Christine.

"I will always be imprisoned in some way. I have cried too many times at the mouth of hell to believe I can ever be free. I am what I am. And if I am made better because of true love then at least I will know there really can be a man in a madman."

Thirty

The water stared blankly back at Anna as she stared at it. The mist stopped its seductive tango, the ripples undulating until a calm washed over the water and the shore fell as still as the dead. She said a quick prayer for Erik and the vicomtess, begging God to keep him safe. Though she wanted to force the vicomtess out of her memory, she couldn't do it. *For Erik's sake.* The ache of loving him, the insanity of this mayhem was bound to wring her senseless.

She wanted to turn back time more. Back to a time and place where the vicomtess was still safe from the Opera Garnier. Back to a place where her warnings would be heeded. Back to when it was she, and Erik, and a tender kiss in a garden.

But her memories traveled farther. Back to a time and place that could have changed her life forever…

Standing there on the shoreline, Anna was sixteen again. Breast heaving at the end of a dark alley, facing a crowded Brussels street instead of an eerie lake, still not knowing which direction to turn before her father caught up to her. The difference now was she was alone and there was no crowd in which to hide.

"Anna!"

That voice smacked her on the back of her skull and snapped her to her senses. It was her verses her father now. Anna had faced this battle a thousand times in her life. She was never more exhausted over it all. Rubbing the lifted hair on the back of her neck she turned and faced him.

Richard Barret was red from more than the fury on his face. One hand was smeared with blood from a small cut. Too bad the piece of mirror he thrust aside didn't slice his throat. Anna pushed past him out of the drawing room, forcing him away from the lake.

"Didn't anyone ever teach you to come when Papa calls?" he growled as he wiped his hand on his trousers.

"I thought you were right behind me. Did you get lost?"

"Lose the sarcasm, Anna," he snapped as he followed her. "You know how I hate it when you make me angry."

Anna knew it far too well, which is why she stopped walking once she was far enough from the lake. The last thing she wanted was for him to know the direction Erik and the vicomtess went. Richard stopped short as he scrutinized the cavernous house. Having him down here, in the place that had been her sanctuary all these months, coiled her stomach.

"My, my, my… is this your little hideaway down here? Strumpet's been relaxing in the lap of luxury! Does all this belong to your Phantom fellow? Because if so, he certainly has fine taste, present company excluded of course."

Anna's jaw clenched at the sight of him touching Erik's things. He rummaged through piles of music, flicked books off of shelves and wandered into distant rooms. She followed, as he entered Erik's inner chambers, her neck heating as Richard roamed around. He stopped directly in front of the coffin.

Anna clenched her teeth as he reached into the box and caressed its lining. Richard pawing Erik's belonging made her vision film red. As he laughed at the divan in the corner, with its piles of overstuffed pillows and blankets, Anna battled her desire to haul him from the room and keep his vile hands from soiling Erik's sanctuary.

"A divan *and* a coffin. A choice for pleasure," he remarked. "How… macabre. Tell me, Strumpet, is this coffin nice to roll in with him?"

Anna stood her ground, refusing to cower under his lecherous gaze. He swaggered toward her, taking a final long stride until he was right in her face. Richard snatched her chin.

"When he lies with you in all his repugnant glory, his need stiff in want of such a fine lady as you, does he keep the mask on or take it off?"

"Let go of me!" Anna battled his hand, but he refused to let go, his fingers digging painfully into her jaw. "Let go, and leave me alone!"

Her father laughed, his foul breath smacking her in the face. "What? No curses? No spitting in my face?" He searched her expression and instantly he knew the truth. "Wait...you can't be serious? Don't tell me you two haven't...with all the men you've shagged? Hah! This gets better and better. Just as well. No man would ever bed you out of sheer love anyway. You're damaged goods."

Anna tumbled over her feet as he shoved her aside, her jaw burning. He sauntered out of the room and toward Erik's organ. It would feel good to plunge a knife in his back and watch the devil bleed like she'd wanted to in Brussels. Anna shook with tension and fury as her father sat at Erik's place behind the instrument. He shifted, wedging himself in the corner of the semi-circle of manuals and propped his feet upon them, his elbows resting on the keys behind him, his heels on the keys in front of him. A long, mournful note cut the air as if the organ also protested the indecency of his presence.

"So, where are Erik and my diva?"

Anna chewed on the hatred wanting to fly out her mouth, and shrugged instead. "I thought he would bring her here, but clearly he didn't."

Shifting his weight, the organ yelped again. "Then where are they?"

"I don't know."

In a flash he yanked his feet off the organ manuals and sat upright on the bench. He lunged, snaring Anna by her forearm. A sharp pain shot up her weakened wrist blurring her vision. The edge of the Persian rug caught her feet as he pulled her forward, slamming her knees into the ground at the organ bench. Anna stifled a cry as Richard stared at her. That look haunted her for too many years. Anna clawed his hand hard enough to color her nails red with his blood.

Richard snarled, but didn't flinch. "I suggest you figure that out, Anna. You're testing my patience and if you continue, I'll have no problem teaching you a delightful little lesson in that coffin he has yet to shag you in." He spread his legs and yanked her between them.

"Get off!" Anna launched her free fist right down on the bulge between his legs.

"You blasted bitch!" He yelled, snatching her neck and dragging her to her feet with him. Anna clawed at his grip. "If you can't find him and my diva, then we deal with the money due me in a very different way. Take me to the vicomte and no more tricks. Is that understood?"

Anna gasped as he let go. It took all in her power not to make matters worse by spitting in his face. She'll lead him somewhere, so long as it got him out of Erik's home. Her father was always easiest to deceive when he *though*t he was getting his way. Her stomach lurched as he roughly kissed her forehead.

"That's my girl."

Raoul stumbled down the hall fighting against the gendarme holding his arms behind his back. Even his anger and fear were no match to Inspector Legard and his men.

"In here, then leave us." the Inspector ordered, holding the manager's door open, following him in and then slamming it shut.

Once free, Raoul rounded on his friend. "If you ever disrespect me like that again, I will—"

"You'll what?" Legard got up to his face and locked their eyes. Raoul refused to be intimidated. "If you get in my way–,"

"Shove your title up your ass—*Raoul*! I'm giving the orders! Of all the stupid, impulsive, asinine things I have ever embarked upon!"

Raoul yelled in frustration, punching the air as he turned from his friend. Legard was right to pull him from the maze of dark passages beneath the Opera Garnier. All they'd been doing was wasting time feeding Raoul's anger. He'd seen only red, after losing the trail of Erik's blood. There was no way to track that monster on in his territory. Their search, and Raoul's hotheadedness had only gotten them hopelessly lost.

"He's down there, Legard, and I—"

Legard's voice fell like a guillotine, snapping Raoul's attention back on him "Shut up and listen to me! Living shadows bleed? Bleed they may, vicomte, but we're not bloodhounds. That is the last time I follow you half-cocked anywhere. We're lucky to have found our way out of that maze alive."

"He's there somewhere, Jules. What will you have me do? Sit here and wait him out while you and your men hunt him down?" Raoul covered his fist with his opposite hand tempted to ram it through the wall. "When I find him—I'll kill him."

"Wonderful. You do that and I'll arrange for an upscale cell for you in my prison. I'm well aware the Phantom is somewhere, but this opera house is obviously full of those secret passages. No wonder he's remained hidden all these years." Legard paced between the door and the desk. "If we can't track him, we'll have to wait him out."

"Wait him out? Hell no!" Raoul shouted. "I spent years waiting out the Phantom and I refuse to let history repeat itself. There'll be hell to pay before I allow anything to come between me and my pursuit of the demon haunting my marriage!"

Raoul's lungs hurt as the burn of his anger grew. Legard seemed unimpressed.

Calmly, the Inspector reached for the couch and grabbed the jacket Raoul discarded earlier before he shot Erik. Raoul stared at it, loathing that he hadn't aimed for Erik's heart at the time. Legard held the jacket out to him.

"You need to realize the difference between a man like me, trained to protect and serve, and a man like you. Put that jacket on, straighten your cravat and calm your ass down! I told you to stay calm through all of this and let me handle it, but instead you chose to fire pistols and chase down Phantoms. You're lucky no one heard you! Let me do my job. Right now you need to do yours. There are still patrons out there doing whatever it is you *gentlemen* do after these operas. Get out there and make sure none know a damn thing is amiss!"

Legard jerked open the door.

The Inspector's brows drew fiercely together as Raoul took his jacket and shrugged it on. A struggle went on behind the Inspector's eyes and Raoul hadn't liked how his rage got in the way of what this man was determined to do. Damn Erik for persecuting more than only *his* life. The Phantom had clearly been the cross Legard had to bear too.

"I'll not fail you this time, vicomte." Legard asserted as Raoul passed.

Raoul paused, taking note of the weight behind Legard's voice. "You never did, Jules. You never did."

The boat bumped against the opposite shore. Slinging the satchel over his shoulder, Erik stepped from it, first laying the oars aside before tying the boat to its mooring. He took a deep breath of the cold air to clear his mind before extending a hand to Christine.

Refusing his offer, she clambered to shore. Her lips were pursed in a sad attempt to appear defiant, though Erik knew he'd hurt her. Love, he was coming to learn, did just that sometimes. They'd crossed the remainder of lake in silence after he rejected her. He didn't expect any less now that they were on shore. He focused on her hemline as she brushed past him.

"Not that way, Christine."

"I know my way, thank you, Monsieur. It's not been so long since you guided me through these corridors for my lessons." She trudged up the road before turning on him with a self-assured air. "We've years of history between us. I can't simply dismiss them as you have."

"I have not dismissed it." Erik pointed with the hand of his uninjured arm. "We need to go this way."

"I spent years wondering if you were well, hoping against hope itself you still thought of me. I was so stupid!"

Erik let her fume. "Christine, please." He gestured toward the corridor again as she moved to storm off in the wrong direction.

Christine stepped toward him, scowling hard. "Don't toss this all aside like it's some outworn history. You were obsessed with me, and my husband the target of your jealousy! That's too significant for you to simply brush me aside. You've seeded yourself in my soul, and I've fought for space between your roots for too long."

"Then weed." Erik stepped aside so she had plenty of room to pass him. "This way."

Christine grabbed the side of her skirt as she plowed past. "This is how you repay all you put me through? By deceiving me and faking your death? To think of all those nights I lay awake, sharing my bed with Raoul whilst calling up *your* voice in my mind."

Erik didn't answer; thankful his mask hid his face. She'd turned to face him, her arms folded, fingers tapping. Shocked, Erik pushed past her ignoring her implication. A reply was far more than he could handle right then.

"I suggest you follow," he said. "I am not taking you through your dressing room back to the opera. I am bringing you to Madame Giry as promised. I am certain you do not know the way there."

"You're tired of living down here yet you speak of choosing a life with a woman such as her. She can bring you nothing." Her hand grabbed the back of his cloak. "Erik, listen to me. You're a man of exceptional talent and you choose to shamefully waste it. Your place is standing in a society where your genius can shine. That woman can't bring you into those circles. Only I can."

What audacity. Never had he heard Christine speak with such resolve or passion, but it would do her well to choose some other topic. She wouldn't have been great without his tutelage and she wouldn't have been a Lady without her husband's title. She couldn't take him under her wing if she was the wind itself.

"I can help you, Erik. You can't tell me that she understands you as I do."

Erik jerked to a stop, his patience worn thin. One thing he could say with absolute certainty was that Anna understood him. He schooled his temper. "Christine, please, I need to bring you to your vicomte, so I can deal with other matters."

"Nevermind the vicomte!"

Alarmed, he spun in time to see her cover her mouth. Rightfully so, she should be appalled at that comment. "Nevermind, the vicomte?" Disgraceful. "Love isn't something to set aside and visit only when you want it, my dear."

Disgusted, he turned his back to her and began walking again.

"I can give you so much," she said calmly. "Why can't I?"

Erik stopped. All he needed to do was turn around, extend his hand, and offer Christine that chance without any doubt she would foolishly accept it. The problem was, he wasn't convinced she'd follow her heart. Not unless she had something to gain. The way to love wasn't so the lover could shine. It was through loving, another shone brighter.

"Tell me one thing she has done for you that I did not," she said.

Only one thing? A thousand things that Anna did for him ran through Erik's mind and he'd love to proclaim them on the street corners to anyone who passed by, not just to Christine. Erik turned. Even in the dark corridor, Christine's radiant beauty rose from her posture. Her scent and her grace could easily drop any man to their knees. But instead his mind sought the refuge he found in the beauty of a very different woman.

Erik made certain the darkness played against his eyes. Christine instantly looked away, her gaze going over his shoulder instead. A glaze of discomfort coated her face, like a woman who'd rather look anywhere else but deep into his unusual eyes. Erik leaned forward hearing her gasp as he came close to her ear.

"She listened."

As he stepped back, that perfect bottom lip of hers began to shake. Erik stepped aside as she rushed past, not swayed by the tears he saw tracking down her cheeks.

Erik slowed as they wound their way out of the labyrinth sensing in the back of his mind that something was wrong. Faint sounds of the usual post performance bustle could be heard in distant corridors, but around Madame Giry's office was an unnerving stillness. The halls around this one spot had been cleared as if on purpose. He paused and stared toward her office door trying to make sense of the change. He'd expect to have to dodge numerous people in order to get Christine inside without being seen. Yet another reason this would have been far easier if only Anna could have done it. Erik squinted hard and forced aside the worry for her that eddied through him. He concentrated on the hall.

"This is madness." Christine attempted to push beyond him. Her patience was short, his shorter. "If you are going to take me to my husband then do it already. I'm not about to creep about with you any longer." She plowed past him.

Erik reacted with split-second reflexes. Despite his pain, he reached out with his good arm to brace her against the wall. Something was off, he could feel it. "Wait."

"For what?" Christine struggled and Erik released his pressure on her. "Wait for you to take me to Raoul so you can disappear out of my life again? With no explanations and no apologies? So you can race off with another woman utterly wrong for you?" Christine moved again swiping at her cheeks.

Erik forced her back against the wall and rounded, pinning her shoulders with both hands. A jarring pain shot up his arm and growled out his mouth. "What more do you wish from me, Christine?"

"The ability to make my own choice, not the ones you, or some impossible situation makes for me! I want the answers I'm worthy of! Is that possible?"

"So. The susceptible child disappears and the woman emerges? Make haste to recall, my dear, I still do not tolerate disobedience."

"Answers!"

"You vain woman," Erik criticized. "Whom are you going to question? Your Angel of Music or Erik? Who is it you wish to reply or have you still not figured that out?"

Christine's lip quivered, her display of strength knocked down. "Why did you bring me to the house on the lake tonight if you meant to bring me here, to Raoul, to begin with?"

Erik loosened his grip and took a step back. That's where he'd brought her in the past. Where he thought she had, for at least a portion of a fortnight, felt secure. Christine wouldn't understand the reasons he would instinctually flee there. She didn't understand him. He'd made a snap decision and obviously chosen poorly. He hadn't meant to confuse her.

"Well," she observed, arrogantly, not giving him a chance to explain. "Perhaps you took me there because you want to redress the choices you've made too? Maybe you don't love this other woman between us as completely as you profess?"

Erik grew weary of her persistent assumption that he didn't understand his heart. Any pity he had for her evaporated as tenderness softened his voice. "Do you recall when you first saw Anna?"

Christine shrugged. "At the masquerade. Dancing with a gentleman who was quite enamored by her, I might add. Everyone could see that. The Holy Ghost Himself couldn't have cut in on those two."

"No, and I would not have let Him."

Christine blanched. Her mouth opened and closed before any words came out. "What? How... how... could that have been you?"

Certain things he didn't think she'd ever understand in terms of how love could better a person. His fingers traced lightly down the hurt on her face. "Raoul loves you, Christine. Someday may you honestly learn that. Come now."

Erik turned his attention back to Madame Giry's door and ignored all else of Christine. He would see this charade through to its end and then address what he had been denying. He could look forward toward a future without his past poisoning it.

Taking Christine by the hand, Erik started for door. He twisted the knob and waited a second before pushing the door open. Spinning Christine in first, he came in behind her and paused, finding Madame Giry staring into the mirror. The room was darker than normal but that didn't bother him. He knew the old woman well enough to know something was wrong. Madame Giry's expression was vacant and she was paler than normal. Her voice shook when she spun around to greet them.

"Vicomtess, thank Heavens, you're safe!" She struggled to speak when her gaze landed on his blood-soaked shirt. "Mercy, what happened?"

Removing the satchel he still had slung over his shoulder, Erik lowered it to the floor. "Nothing of concern. Keep Christine here and do not leave this room. Barret is looking for her and he has my Anna. I must find her as well as Raoul." He turned to the door.

"Monsieur, wait!"

Her warning came too late. The door flew inward, knocking Erik off balance. Hands grabbed him, pushing him backward, slamming him into a table and knocking the breath from his lungs. Giry's collection of opera glasses shattered on the floor and programs scattered from their neat stacks as Erik wrestled to free himself from the Inspector's grasp. Screams erupted from the women, mixing with the frantic shouts of the gendarmes and Erik's feral growl of frustration.

Erik flung the Inspector off and fought the remaining guards with a raw, inhuman fury, but he was no match for the sharp blow of the rifle butt that rammed directly into his blood soaked arm. The room tinted black as pain ripped across his body, weakening his knees. A bellowing scream ripped from Erik's mouth as the gendarmes wrestled his arms behind him. Knees buckling, Erik fell to the floor, his shoulder and arm turning deeper and deeper shades of scarlet.

"Monsieur they came moments before you did! They were hiding in the shadows in the hall!" Madame Giry wailed. "They made me tell them all about you! All your plans! How long I've known you! Mercy, forgive me!"

Inspector Legard panted like a bellows as he wiped blood from his nose. "Are you ladies all right?"

Sweat stung Erik's eyes. Had he not been injured he would have done far worse than bloody the man. Neither woman answered. The color had drained from Christine's face and Madame Giry kept hers hidden in her palms. Near the door and out into the hall more guards stood at the ready.

"Out of my way! Let me through!"

Raoul cut through the crowd and into the office, his arms open when he saw Christine. Erik watched as she flung herself into his embrace. At least she was safe again…where he needed her to be.

Raoul let go of Christine, set her aside, and began to circle him. Each time he passed in front of him, a profound hatred surged inside of him. Erik coughed through the pain and fought the gendarmes like an animal not knowing he'd been trapped.

"The Phantom is at a loss for words?" Raoul asked.

"If you want to have words with me, Monsieur, might I suggest we do that alone, man to man?"

"Man to man?" Raoul stripped the mask from Erik's face and flung it aside. "Hardly!"

Erik roared as cold air blasted his exposed face. Legard muttered a string of curses and covered his mouth with the back of his hand. Several of the guards backed away, but the ones holding Erik were forced to remain where they were, gripping a man whose mask of Death held at bay a sovereign anger.

Erik's lungs were tight with such hatred; he thought they'd explode. His gaze locked with Madame Giry's. In all the years Erik had known her, she'd never seen him unmasked. The hands upon her cheeks trembled. Even her lips had blanched.

"Do forgive me, Madame Giry. I apologize for Monsieur le Vicomte's lack of manners. This should not occur before a lady."

Legard intervened, waving for his men to get Erik to his feet.

"Make this easy and tell us where Barret is," the Inspector demanded, his gaze looking anywhere but, Erik's face.

"I do not know. He has Anna. She was leading him from Christine."

"Or *to* me." Everyone turned to Christine. "He's lying. He… he's lying! She was leading him *to* me. That man called her Anna Reneè *Barret*."

"I *knew* they had a connection," Raoul rammed one fist into his opposite palm. "The woman told me he killed her mother. I never thought she could have been his kin." Raoul stepped up to Erik's face while others backed away. "How many more lies are we to be fed, Erik? Your twisted games of manipulation are over. Get him out of here."

The gendarmes wrenched his arms tighter behind, him pushing him forward, but Erik writhed like a reptile in their grip. He lunged toward Christine.

"You are the one who lies, Christine!" He wanted to wrap his hands around her and shake the truth out of her traitorous mouth. "Why is it you cannot look on me if you speak the truth? Is it because you speak only lies, lies as hideous as I?"

"Away with him!" Raoul shouted.

Erik's reply snaked from his lips, "Perhaps, Monsieur, it is not *my* mask you should remove." He jerked his head to Christine, and yelled at her as the gendarmes dragged him toward the door. "You know damn well of Anna's intent!"

"I don't know anyone's intent anymore." Her husband's body, curved protectively around her, muffled Christine's tearful response.

Erik spewed curses as he tried to pry free from the gendarmes grip. His face blazed hot, his screams so loud those not hauling him to the door, backed away.

"Barret and Anna are somewhere in the opera house," Legard directed his men. "If we're fortunate, we'll find them now that the Phantom is restrained. They're not to leave this theater." He gestured toward Erik. "Deal with him first, then join the others in the search. Get him to the wagon. Lock him in the cage."

Cage?

Paired with the raging pain shooting down his arm, his normal razor sharp focus disappeared. A brief paralysis washed over him with that one word before mindless panic set in. He was not about to be caged like a common mongrel or shut away in any prison not of his own doing…

THIRTY-ONE

If only Anna had obeyed Erik and run.

Anna wasn't sure where her common sense had gone. Surely she'd lost it somewhere in the cave when she was reasoning with the vicomtess. How else would she have allowed herself to be in her father's clutches once again?

"Keep your face down, Anna. Have you forgotten everything I taught you?" Barret snarled.

Anna clamped down hard on her teeth, the sound of his voice had been shredding her last nerve since she lead him out of Erik's home and in search of the vicomte.

The halls were still full of patrons enjoying after parties. Throngs of men in evening dress hurried back and forth from one dancers' lounge to the next. Foremen wound their way in the opposite direction, seeking respite from the evening's affair in local pubs. Mingled among them were gendarmes trying to look inconspicuous while they searched the Opera Garnier.

Barret's fingers clamped tight upon the base of her skull. She stared at her feet, looking up occasionally, only so to give her father the illusion that she was leading him somewhere. Anna had no concept of how much time has passed, but the longer she stalled Barret, the more time Erik had to get the vicomtess to Madame Giry and then the vicomte to his wife. So long as she kept her father's attention on her... it was off of everyone else. The thought of

274

preventing anyone else in the opera house from getting caught up in Barret's web was the only thing keeping her from being completely sick. The two walked in tandem, artful in the way they moved together. That they did so with such practiced fluidity nauseated her.

"See, like old times, isn't it strumpet?" He tickled the back of Anna's neck with his fingers. "Move away from the gendarmes— locate the vicomte. He owes me the rest of my money and you know how much I hate to be cheated from what I'm owed."

She knew too well how much he hated being cheated. Cheat Richard Barret and it meant certain death. Anna's skin pebbled at the thought as a new panic tossed her stomach. The vicomte had no idea how dangerous her father was. If she led Barret to him the fool would probably argue, or not comply and then he'd be dead. Anna's mind raced.

She'd have to get to the vicomte first. Knock sense into him. Warn him. Something! But that meant losing her father and risking his rage unleashing on the patrons of the opera as he went off searching for the vicomte himself. It was a risk she'd have to take. The vicomte had to be warned. Eventually her father would catch on that she was only leading him in circles. With luck, enough time had passed and it was a game of wits, she against her father now, and Erik had everyone safely reunited.

Holding her breath, she risked trying to make eye contact with one of the gendarmes searching the hall.

But Barret missed nothing. With the corridors of the Garnier packed with gentleman and the ladies, it was easy for her father to twirl her away from the gendarme's gaze. Before she knew his intention, he bent her backward, faking a lover's kiss that stopped the gendarme from investigating further.

"Don't even think of crossing me." Barret spoke the words through clenched teeth. "You're mine until I have my money." He righted her, his laughter clawing down her spine, adding to her resolve.

Until? Anna gave her father a hateful look, the liar. He wouldn't release her even if he got his money. She'd be right back at his side; his favorite little pawn and she'd never see Erik again.

No! She wasn't going to let that happen! She had to get to the vicomte first and warn him. If Erik successfully got the vicomtess to Madame Giry, then he was probably on his way in search of the vicomte too. With luck, they'd be together and if anyone could bring down Richard Barret, it was Erik.

Anna swallowed hard. If she ran Barret would simply follow. He always liked a game of cat and mouse. He wouldn't kill her though. Anna had called his bluff on that threat too many times in her life. She was all he had to bargain with in his life. She'd have to create a bigger diversion to give her a better lead.

They continued, moving like two cats gracefully perusing a hunting ground. Anna winced as each step brought thumping to her right thigh. Confused, her hand crept toward her dress pocket and dipped inside. As soon as she did she winced and yanked her hand out, staring at the pin-pick of blood on the tip of her finger.

Holy hell, the knife!

If only she had recalled having it sooner, when they were alone and using it against him would have been far easier. The recollection of that Brussels street flooded back to her as her memories replayed in her mind. She'd stabbed him once and ran. She could do it again.

Crowds were a good thing. Gendarmes, however, were not.

If she pulled out a knife and swung on her father, she'd be arrested in a flash. Her father would claim some story about being attacked unprovoked and she'd end up in a Paris prison. Anna's hand curled around the hilt as her pulse quickened. Praying for a distraction, one came as two drunken stagehands burst through a door and out into the hall. Gentlemen yelled and pulled ladies aside as a mad ruckus of fists and boozy curses rent the air, pitching the two men from one side of the hall to the next. Anna trembled against the frightened sixteen-year-old inside of her and inched the knife from her pocket, careful for it not to be seen.

If she could get a few paces farther down the hall, closer to the drunks... The nearer she and her father got the faster her breathing came. Anna willed for one of those drunks to miss a punch. Miss, and stumble in their direction…

"Watch where you're going, or I'll level you myself!" Barret yelled, as Anna's opportunity came.

As soon as the drunk bumped into her father, Anna swung backward with the knife, aiming to sink the steel into Barret's thigh. The momentum from the drunk was too much, however, and the tip of the blade snared in the fabric of Barret's trousers. His hands sprung off of her as he cursed and leapt backward out of the way of the blade and the drunk, the knife clanging to the ground between them.

The drunk wobbled between she and her father. "Pull a knife on me did you?" he slurred to Barret as he reached down to grab it.

Anna was never so glad to be in a drunk's way. Her eyes locked her father's before the drunk roared up into his face. Like a rat scurrying away from light and using the commotion to her advantage, she dodged and wove her way in and out of the fray that followed.

Crowds were a good thing.

Getting lost in an angry mob, even better.

⟶•••————•••⟵

The pungent aroma of stale hay filled his nose, nearly gagging him. So different from the sweet smell of fresh hay filling the stalls of the horses where the beasts had no choice but to be locked away, awaiting their freedom. This cage where they'd shoved Erik clawed at his sanity. The idea of relinquishing control to be thrown in a cage like a common animal sent blood pounding to his brain. He got to his knees and threw himself at the door only a moment after it closed and locked, slamming his face against the unforgiving wood.

Ahead, behind, and to the side of him—he was trapped. This is what he'd avoided all his life—a sentence not of his doing.

His vision narrowed on the door. Memories of his youth as gruesome entertainment as a sideshow freak burned through his mind. Even then, at the hands of showmen and his manager, and subjected to a public that freely viewed his unmasked face, Erik had a modicum of control. Here he did not. He was exposed and at the mercy of others.

Erik clawed at the lock like a cat trapped in a box. He kicked and threw himself at the wooden door. This humiliation he wouldn't tolerate. He didn't save Christine only to be stripped of all the power he had. He wouldn't be chained to rot in some dark and repulsive prison like a deviant of the underworld. Not when his bleak existence had found a way to the light.

Erik's black rage rose. The carriage door locked away all chances of fleeing his past and beyond them was Anna.

Any kind thoughts of Christine waned to resentment over her betrayal. Fury at the thought of his actions to save her causing Anna any harm, made his hands whiten as he gripped the bars on the window of the wagon door. The entire wagon rocked along with

277

Erik's rage.

Unspeakable dread took control. His mind closed in around him, locking out all facets of reason. The darkest parts of his memories fueled the panic roaring through him.

"Stop your ruckus!" a guard shouted.

Erik shook harder.

"Stay down, or we will keep you down."

Erik pounded harder.

"He'll rip himself to death at that rate." A gendarme laughed.

"What good it will do him," the second replied. "He is already a living corpse."

Vengeance swelled in his chest. His fists thrashed at the wooden barrier. The gendarme's cries transported him to a time and place where fairgoers shouted their demands too him: More tricks! More song! The crowds begged for the fantastic and back then, Erik didn't mind. Back then he humored them. In all that time, he'd had the race he so despised completely under his command.

That was until the voice of his manager rang louder than any of them. *Behold the Living Corpse...* Sweat blurred his vision; his breath ragged as Erik leaned his temple against the cold steel of the carriage bars and fought the memory of those words. *Behold the Living Corpse!* They had seeped into his soul and began to drown away whatever bit of humanity he thought he had. Erik's shoulders heaved as he panted, he heard the gendarmes laughing, squinted his eyes as they stung from the acrid scent of manure. The words had transformed man into Death and Death into an alluring ally.

A bead of sweat trickled down his cheek as he stared at his white knuckled grip on the bars.

Erik screamed.

Face blazing, fist pounding, his body thrashing against the door. If Erik had to revisit the madness of Death to save Anna—then so be it.

THIRTY-TWO

Memories for his last encounter with the Phantom years ago flooded Raoul fast and hard as he ushered his wife down the hallway safely away from Madame Giry's office and the chaos still going on back there. The image of Erik's heinous face burned in his mind, but he tried to push it aside. All he wanted was a safe and quiet place to gather his wife in his arms and do something, anything, to bring color back to her face.

Getting her to the manager's office as fast as he could, he shut the door, locking it behind him. Christine moved with unsteady steps and sank to the divan. Raoul passed a hand through his hair and took a deep, centering breath, before crouching in front of her and laying his palms upon her knees.

Her hand shook upon his lips as he kissed it, feeling for the first time his heartbeat a normal rhythm. "My world stopped when I thought you were gone. I'll order my carriage and have you returned to the flat. My *maître d'hôtel* will be contacted to see to it everything is ready for your return to Chagny. I'm staying here until we find Barret and Anna." He swept the hair from her face, aching over the sickly pallor of her skin. What he wouldn't do to take away every wretched moment of the last few days and turn the unshed tears in her eyes back to tears of joy.

"I'm sorry you had to see Erik taken like that. I know how—" he had to force the words from his mouth, "—deeply you once cared for him. But you need to trust in *my* love, Christine. Trust I'll keep my promise to you. I love you. I love you with everything that I am. Erik will be brought to justice and you will never have to go through anything like this again."

"What of Mademoiselle Barret?" Christine whispered.

Raoul scowled. "I don't exactly know what to make of her."

"What are you going to do?"

Raoul sighed. The youthful, uncertain sadness to her voice contradicted how strong he knew her to be. "Whatever I need to do to bring you justice and everything you wish in this."

"I'm not worthy of you and your love." She reached to brush a line of hair from his face.

Raoul lifted her hands to his lips and kissed each one. "You speak foolish things pooled from all you've suffered. This *will* end. Erik will no longer possess you. You became my life when I took you to my side. Whatever you need of me, I will make it so—my life, my name, is all for you. That's my choice. That's my love."

"What will happen to Erik?" she spoke so softly Raoul had to lean forward to hear her.

"He'll pay for what crimes he's committed. Erik condemned himself to Devil's Island. If not there, then execution. I can only imagine the latter to be more humane." A gasp leapt from her mouth as she paled even more. Raoul swept into the spot beside her, taking her hands and praying she would gather strength from his grip. "You know I will always offer you the truth, Christine. You see him now for what he has always been. The man is mad. You can't deny that. He'll pay for what he did to you."

Raoul brushed his thumb across her soft cheek, swiping away a tear. Finding her lips, he kissed the next salty one away, and then the next. He'd see her strong again if it was the last thing he ever did. He'd make every tear she shed tears of joy or ecstasy and never again would any man, or demon, lay a hand on her exquisite head. A sob caught in her throat as he tipped their foreheads together.

"Christine, I promise you I—" Raoul's attention shot to the door as it rattled in its jamb.

Heart thumping, Raoul rose, holding a hand out to his wife, signaling her to remain where she was. He held his finger to his lips. Raoul's hand twitched over his pistol, blood pressure rising, as the door rattled harder and harder. Hand hovering, ready to draw the pistol and shoot, Raoul unlocked the door.

It slammed inward, knocking him backward as Anna shouldered her way in.

"Thank God you're here!" she shouted. "You're wife is safe! Trust me, Erik has her! But Barret… when he finds me, no matter what he wants, do it! What he asks for, give it to him." Anna whirled to slam the door. Spinning back around, her eyes widened at the sight of Christine. "What are you doing *here*?" she yelled. "You should be with Madame Giry! Barret runs his cons his way and when everyone doesn't play nicely he tends to get unruly."

"You would know, wouldn't you Mademoiselle *Barret*?" Raoul spat.

Anna quieted. "How… how do you know my surname?"

Raoul followed her gaze to Christine. His wife's face turned stone hard.

"What happened? What went wrong? Where's Erik?" Anna demanded.

"I suspect halfway to a Paris prison by now," Raoul replied.

The flush on Anna's cheeks faded to white.

"Should you be in that prison along with him?" he asked. Her reply never came as the door crashed inward; whirling Raoul toward Richard Barret, his pistol drawn and a crazed look in his eye.

"Now you've made me angry, Anna." Richard leveled the pistol on Raoul. "Go ahead, vicomte, continue to reach beneath that waistcoat. Anna, get his weapon."

Anna didn't move. Richard, foam forming around his lips, waved his pistol wildly. Raoul didn't think twice as he threw himself between Barret and his wife.

"Anna this is not Brussels, get it now!" Barret bellowed, his face turning red. "Defiance might be worth the risk to your life, but I doubt you want to try my patience and see if it worth the risk to theirs. Now move!"

Raoul spread his arms keeping himself as a shield between Barret and his wife. The suspicions in his mind grew as Anna moved and encircled her hands around his waist. The lying vixen. To think he thought to fight for her honor.

"And here I felt guilty for handing you over you to him," he whispered. "You've played me the fool, Mademoiselle. Quite cunning."

With a sharp jerk, Anna freed his pistol. It rocked him closer into her. "You've lived a sheltered life, vicomte. In my pedigree," she nodded toward Barret, "you learn to do as you're told, when you're told." The pistol slipped free and she stepped away.

Richard grabbed it from her and tucked it into his waistband. "Now," he continued walking farther into the room, "it appears the vicomte owes me some money."

"I gave you what I could. I don't have the funds you demanded in Paris."

"Not my problem," Richard bit. "Before I begin, where is the Phantom fellow?"

"Caged like you'll be very soon." Raoul took a bold step forward until Richard swung his aim on Christine. "Alright! Alright!" Hands in the air, his entire body heating in fury at the fear on Christine's face, Raoul stepped back again.

"Strumpet, did you hear that? Your lover is caged. Isn't that just bestial? Thank you, vicomte, you've made my night. This will flow much easier now. Get me my money."

"It's the middle of the night, I can't. I'll do what you want. Just don't harm my wife!"

"Give him the evening's receipts," Anna instructed.

Raoul scowled. "What receipts?"

"The booth agents bring the money here before it can be couriered to the bank. It will be in the safe." She indicated a corner of the room.

"Ah, Anna, sometimes you are good for a thing or two." Richard gestured impatiently with the pistol. "Do as she says."

Do as she says? The last thing Raoul would do is listen to Anna Barret. "I don't know the combination."

Richard rolled his eyes. "Really, vicomte, I tried to do this politely."

Barret's arm blurred as it swung away from Christine's face long enough for him to fire off a shot into the safe in the corner. His arm bucked as burnt powder filled the air and the lock shattered. Raoul reached behind him, grabbing Christine and backing away from the blast as her scream shook the rafters.

"Vicomte, shut her up!" Barret shouted aiming between Raoul's eyes. "Anna. Get the money."

Raoul gave Anna a fleeting glance as she gathered the money before staring down Barret's pistol again.

"Take it and go," Anna slapped a billfold into Barret's outstretched hand.

As Barret's fingers closed around it, and he tucked it into his jacket pocket, the fool girl lunged, aiming for the pistol tucked in his waistband. Whipping his hand from his jacket, Barret's face turned red, as he backhanded her hard across the cheek. Raoul roared, leaping forward, launching all his momentum into Barret's chest. A foul blast of Barret's breath smacked Raoul in the face as they crashed to the floor.

Raoul had the mount on him, his fist ready to crash down hard and fast toward Barret's nose. Barret reached up. He grabbed hold of Raoul's collar and pulled Raoul hard down on him before the fist had a chance to break his face. Bridging up with his left foot and exploding as hard as he could upward, Barret rolled. Raoul didn't have a chance before the pistol came down upon his temple.

"Raoul!" Christine's scream cut the air.

Raoul barely felt the man's weight lift him as Barret stood, the room spinning too violently to make sense of anything.

"Guess that means you'll be coming with me, vicomtess." Barret's voice buzzed as warm blood trickled into Raoul's ear. His vision swam as Barret grabbed Christine's arm, hauling her toward the door.

Raoul reached for the hem of his wife's dress, his fist coming away empty. He fought the blackness creeping along the edges of his vision, working to stand and make his leg hold his weight.

"I don't think so, vicomte," Barret growled. His foot came down hard on Raoul's knee. The crunch of bone-against-bone shot a scream from his mouth. Coughing, as he tried hard to breathe through the pain, he barely heard Barret's next words.

"Now, this is the part where I leave. I expect safe passage out of Paris and to be certain that occurs, she," he indicated Christine, "will stay with me. Anna!"

Raoul lifted his head, the edges of his vision growing dim as Barret pointed the pistol at the girl and waved her forward.

"Come," Barret said. "You don't think I'm leaving you here as his nursemaid do you? You need to do what you do so well and steal me a horse."

"I'm not going anywhere with you," she spat, the back of her palm pressed against the bruise on her cheek.

Raoul struggled to get his legs to work under him, his ears to stop ringing as a shot whizzed past Anna's head, dangerously close to her face.

"Raoul!" Christine squirmed against Barret's grip as Anna drained of color.

Pain, anger and frustration warred in equal measure as Raoul fell to the floor. His last vision was that of his wife being hauled away by a true madman.

⟶ ••———— ••• ————•• ⟵

The horses kicked whenever he lunged, but the door to the prison transport didn't budge. Erik sank against the wall of his prison, out of breath, and out of will. The wound in his shoulder hurt with such intensity his entire body shook with the pain.

Erik clutched his arm and rocked the back of his head against the carriage wall. Pointless. The carriage door was stronger than he was.

I've lost her. I've lost it all. Closing his eyes, the familiar numbness of madness started to wash over him, and he let it. He saved Christine, only to be betrayed by her, and lost Anna to it all. All he wanted was to grab time by the neck and throw this entire chapter of his life away... save for the moment Anna arrived. Erik rubbed his temple, madness and rage having brought on a blinding headache.

"I'm only the messenger, sir. You can argue with me all you want but I'm telling you again the Inspector told me to fetch you. He needs you get the Phantom's accomplice and transport him here to the hold as well."

That voice sounded familiar. He opened his eyes and strained to listen to what the gendarmes rumbled over. Erik groaned as he struggled to his feet, his beaten body and stiff muscles making it hard to move.

Outside the carriage the gendarmes' voices dimmed and grew distant. Erik moved toward the door trying to see through the window. Surely they had not left... Erik reached for the iron bars when a flash of steel arched in front of the window followed by the ear-splitting crack of breaking metal and wood.

Erik cringed, adrenaline shooting through his body as the door swung open, the lock shattered to pieces. He'd no time to waste. Thoughts spinning in a thousand directions, each one aimed at finding Anna, Erik flew at his opportunity for escape. Leaping from the back of the carriage he caught his breath only long enough to see the stone-hard expression on Madame Giry's face.

"Go, quickly, before they find I out I lied and come for you!" She shook his mask insistently in his face. "Go! Find Anna."

Taking it, Erik placed it upon his face. Never would he have expected such a daring move from the woman he'd thought served him only out of fear. Madame Giry's eyes glistened as she scanned the area before they stopped and rested on his face. Those aged eyes held more motherly love than he'd seen in all his life. She'd risked her own innocence to save him and he found all he could say before darting for a shadow was a simple word:

"Merci."

⇥••————•••————••⇤

Anna chanced her first look sideways as they finally stopped in a darkened corner of the carriage house. All the while, as Barret kept the gun under her ribcage and the vicomtess tight in his other hand. Anna focused forward, her every sense on high alert now. Never had her father shot at her! He'd threatened her, hit her and done unthinkable things, but never had he come so close to killing her. The man had gone completely insane.

"Steal us a horse," he commanded, shoving her forward toward the stalls. Anna grabbed her side, clutching at the spot his pistol had been. "You do remember how to steal a horse?"

Some children learned nursery rhymes; Anna learned how to steal horses.

"I think I can recall," she replied.

"There's that sarcasm again, strumpet." Richard cocked the pistol and forced the barrel to the vicomtess' temple. Anna shot her eyes off of him to the fear spreading across the vicomtess' face. "Do anything stupid and I sink a bullet in her brain. I think you know I'm serious by now?"

Too serious.

Anna hadn't moved with such stealth since the last time she was employed by her father. The situation seemed remotely familiar. Lurking about, devious intentions, and gendarmes she couldn't do a damn thing about.

Anna eyed them as she bolted from the shadow and across the aisle to a row of stalls. They were too far away for Anna to get their attention. In the past when working under Richard Barret, getting the attention of the authorities was the *last* thing on her mind. Surprisingly, it would've been her last choice at this particular moment as well. It would be preferable to her to find Erik, save him, leaving Richard to his own devices, but she had to think of his captive.

With great care, Anna silently lifted tack from the wall and ducked into a distant stall. Her mind raced in a thousand different ways trying to figure out how to foil her father. She cursed the life that had returned full circle on her. Free, for a moment, from the grip her father had on her, Anna let tears fill her eyes.

"Easy boy." *Stay composed and talk calmly and the horse will be still*, she reminded herself as she gave the stallion the bit. It was her heart that couldn't remain still as the horse's lips tickled her hand. She was even subjecting an innocent creature to her father now.

"Let's go, Anna." Her father's harsh whisper pebbled her skin.

Anna wiped at her eyes. She fumbled as she untied the horse's tether from the wall and coiled it in her hand. All she wanted was a normal life. She just wanted—

Erik?

A pair of golden eyes dashed from one side of the stall to the next. Anna exploded with relief as Erik stepped from the shadows. A moan—deep and guttural came from the depths of his throat. Erik trapped her gasp as his lips crushed against hers. Backing her away from the horse and deep against the coarse wall of the stall, he devoured her with his kiss, holding her lips with an intensity she never thought possible.

Forehead against forehead he locked their gazes. A long slow sigh escaped her mouth.

Putting a finger to her lips, he slowly pried the rope away, forcing her to let go.

Anna didn't heed his request for silence. "I'm trying! I'm trying to stop him, but I've never seen him like this! You have to! You have to Erik, he has the vicomtess."

Erik peered from the stall. "Let the boy save her. It is your safety that worries me. Come. Let me get you out—"

"Erik! You have to get *her* out of here."

He leaned back into the stall, his gaze narrowing in on her cheek. Erik's mouth shook, the intensity of his eyes piercing the dim light in the stall. "He touched you."

Anna had seen him angry before, but this time his voice lifted the hair on the back of her neck. "He'll do worse to her."

Erik's fists pulsed at his side as his gaze moved off her cheek and back out the stall door. "He hit you."

"Erik—you're frightening me."

"It is about time."

His detached glare rattled her bones.

"She needs you."

Richard's voice broke their stare down. "Anna, my horse!"

"I'm working on it," she spat back. Her fingers dug into his arm, her gaze imploring him to help the diva. "What's happened to you? You have to help me save her. Erik—where did this sudden angst toward her come? What did she do to you? She's your Christine! Erik—"

"She *was* my Christine! She did nothing to *me*. It is how she betrayed *you*." Erik laid his hands over her fingers. "I am not about to discuss such matters now. I am getting you out of here."

"You're getting *her* out of here." Anna yanked her arm free. "I'm used to taking care of myself. I know you love that woman, and if you let anything happen to her you'll never forgive yourself. I'm used to being second best, Erik, it doesn't bother me."

He followed her gaze out of the stall. Anna looked from Erik, back to where her father hid, and then back to Erik again. The sound of Legard's voice got progressively louder as the insistent commands of her father got bolder.

Erik carved small circles in the hay around her. "As silent as you may make my mind, you also have a knack of gnawing your way into it. It drives me madder than I already am."

Anna eyed his hand, which pulled close to the hip where he always hid his silk rope. "No killing, Erik, please. Whatever you do, get her out of here, but—no killing."

"Does Erik kill?"

Third person. It was too late; his madness was on the rise. She held her breath. Erik's gaze sank deep into hers; a penetrating gaze that was so sudden, so sharp, Anna backed away. She'd never seen such a tremendous look before…

Erik stepped in close; so close she saw the pulse fluttering at the base of his throat. He leaned down to her ear; his voice perched precariously on the right side of danger. "You are not second best."

Anna slid her hand to his forearm, in a desperate bid to keep him calm. Erik's voice was warm as his whisper found her ear.

"Do you still claim to understand me?"

"Yes," Anna whispered back. The inches between them pulsated with her shallow breathing.

"Do you know me?"

"Yes."

Erik teased the nape of her neck with his silken tones. Her legs lacked the firmness his voice held. His voice had turned remarkably husky

"And you are not frightened now?"

Anna swallowed hard. "No."

Erik hunched over her, the cold fabric of his mask sliding over her flushed flesh. She wanted to grab his hand, run away, and spend as much time together in peace as they had in this madness. Instead, a shudder raced down her spine as she turned her face into his touch. Anna's breath shook with each stroke Erik made of temple against temple, chin against chin. Her breath quickened as she moved with him, constantly seeking, but being denied the lips that passed by hers.

"Do you... trust me?" his gruff voice was hot in her ear.

"Yes," she replied, her voice shuddering past her lips, her knees nearly losing their strength.

He enveloped her face in his hands, and drew her tightly against him. She came in as close as she could and stared up, breathlessly, into his golden eyes. Behind them she saw a longing that ached for years to be ended.

"Then never let your heart believe I am anything but the man you unmasked."

Erik tilted her face up more before—in an achingly slow movement—he slanted his mouth over hers. Anna's breath hitched as he ran his tongue against the seam of her lips, begging to be let in. When she opened for him, Erik showed her exactly what he meant as he drove every thought aside other than his kiss.

Her heart thumped as he leaned back. His eyes intensified like two just-fed fires.

"Now Erik will show the world the madman they expect."

THIRTY-THREE

Strong hands grabbed his shoulder as he limped, adding insult to injury.

"I'm alright. Damn it, Legard, I can walk on my own!"

Raoul rolled his shoulder out of Legard's way and picked up their pace despite the pain throbbing in his knee. He winced; hair sticking to dried blood as he pulled his cravat off his temple crammed the bloodied silk into his pocket. Nothing was more profound than the agony of watching his wife being hauled away as his world had faded to black.

"That's the last time I'm leaving you without protection," Legard growled. "Barret could have killed you."

I'll kill him first. Raoul would thank Legard later for discovering him in the office and getting him back on his feet. Right now, all he wanted was to find his wife.

"How long were you out?" Legard asked as they entered the carriage house.

Long enough, which was too long. "Tell me Barret is still here somewhere," he barked back. He'd find Christine if he had legs and half his head blown off. His wife was in the grips of a devious madman and his daughter. To hell with his current state…

As they entered the carriage house, Raoul stopped short, as did Legard, swallowing the ripping pain that raced up his thigh.

The door to the prison transport hung open. Thin slivers of

wood and the shattered remains of the lock were scattered in the hay on the ground. Erik was nowhere to be seen.

"What the deuces…" Legard shouted at the gendarme racing toward him. "Why are you not at your post!"

"We were sent to look for you!" the man blurted as he trotted forward, gaping at the sight of the carriage. "We were told you had Barret—"

"Who told you that?" Legard demanded.

"Nevermind who," Raoul roared. "Barret has my wife and now the Phantom is missing. All I can assume is that Anna Barret is their accomplice." Legard's brows drew down. Raoul jabbed a finger the direction they came wishing he was thrusting a knife through Barret. "She was with them in the office and logic would have them heading in this direction if they haven't already. I heard something about her stealing a horse before I blacked out."

Raoul punched the air with his fist and stormed away from the carriage. If only he hadn't blacked out. If only he had gotten to his feet. He turned as Legard shoved his incompetent man aside and signaled for the gendarmes at the far end of the stable.

"We'll start here first and work our way back to re-cover the opera house. Secure the exits!" Raoul followed Legard's glance to the destroyed carriage. "Monsieur le vicomte, the Phantom could be anywhere. I want— "

"That is right Messieurs, where could I be?"

Startled, Legard and Raoul both ducked as the carriage house reverberated with that thunderous voice. The sound punched Raoul right in the chest, heating his face with fury, but he wouldn't be cowed. Raoul straightened searching for any signs of the two golden eyes he should have extinguished years ago.…

"What the blazes was that?" Richard cursed, jerking the diva closer to him.

A sinister laughter followed that tremendous voice, sending the hair on the back of his neck standing on end. If this was another trick of Anna's, he'd kill her and leave her body for the first mongrel he found. What was taking that girl so long with his horse?

"Quit your whimpering!" he spat, ramming his pistol into the vicomtess' side. That shut her up. Pretty little thing she may be, but if she didn't keep quiet they'd be seen before Anna got him his horse.

Richard planned on leaving this opera house with his plans intact, and his pockets filled with cash, his sanity was another matter.

"Ready for me, Messieurs?"

Maniacal laughter engulfed everything. There was no telling where the owner of that voice was.

"Move. Move!" Richard hissed, dragging the diva deeper into a shadowy corner as the vicomte's voice filled the air next.

"Your tricks are useless!" the vicomte shouted back at the disembodied voice.

"Tricks, Monsieur?"

"Your mind games," the vicomte yelled. "You have no power over me!"

"Raou—"

Richard shoved his hand over the diva's mouth before her scream had a chance to split the air. He cocked the pistol and twisted it into the bone of her corset and gave her a look that drained her face to white.

"How bold, Monsieur."

"Where the hell is that coming from?" Richard rammed a finger in his ear, the buzzing louder each time that voice boomed forth.

Wherever it came from, he didn't have time to wait any longer. Anna was taking too long with his horse. Keeping the pistol tight into the diva's gut, Richard leaned out of his shadow. The vicomte and Inspector blocked the way out in front of him, and that eerily faceless voice permeated everything. He had to get out—and fast. His only means of escape would be through the vicomte and the path he blocked. Richard still had a very good reason for Raoul to let him pass. He grabbed Christine and darted from the shadow.

Erik peered around the corner where he hid and took everything in at once. The stable was dimly lit; the opera's snow white horses could be seen resting in their stalls, while in others were horses boarded there for one reason or another. Carriages at the far end were left to wait until needed. In all, it stood as it always had on the rare nights he left his labyrinth to take solace in the opera's horses. Only the distant prison carriage stood out as a reminder of what was to come. Across the aisle where he had left her, the tip of Anna's head could barely be seen peaking around the open stall door.

"Er... ik?" she whispered.

He didn't answer. Tempting as calling to her would be, he'd rather her not see this side of him. Even from a distance he could see worry wrinkling her face. It only worsened his need to give in to the anger, the outrage, and the madness pulling through his veins so this farce could end once and for all. Anna leaned out further and whispered for him again. Instead of replying Erik focused his attention down the length of the stable where the inspector, his men, and the vicomte turned in bewildered circles. Erik smiled. Precisely as he wanted them to be.

He checked on Anna again, wanting nothing more than for her to remember their kiss moments ago. It would be better for her to see him as that, instead of the monster he wrestled with inside of him. A scuffle in the opposite direction caught Anna's attention. Erik heard it too and looked behind him as Barret and Christine darted from a shadow and across the aisle.

"Vicomtess!" Anna shouted.

Her warning didn't go unnoticed.

"Christine?" Raoul's shout tore through the stable, whipping Erik's attention back in his direction.

Erik couldn't resist adding to the confusion. Enough of it had been rising in his soul since the moment he took Christine from the stage as is. She could lash out at him all she wanted, hate him, and blame him, whatever she needed, but for her to aim anything but gratitude toward Anna was unforgivable. Erik slowly projected his voice around the stable...

"Christine... why?"

The haunting whisper of her name made every one pause—except Barret. Erik smiled. Precisely what he wished to occur. Nothing could stop a roach scurrying from light, nor a man seeking escape. Who would know this better than Erik?

"Stop right there!" Legard shouted, spying Barret as well. He stood staunchly in his spot, aiming his pistol down the length of the stable.

"Such valiant words," Erik complimented, unseen from his shadow.

"Stay out of my way, Inspector, or I'll kill her." Richard yelled as he aimed his pistol at Christine's temple. He walked toward the inspector—giving him wide berth—while searching for the voice pursuing him.

"Such bold acts," Erik critiqued, his voice keeping the others unfocused.

He watched their heads swivel, confusion written on their furrowed brows. Their jerky movements were as unfocused as their eyes were, as they examined shadow-to-shadow. None were sure who posed the most threat. Legard and his men swung their pistols between Barret and the shadows, then to the rafters' in search of Erik and his disembodied voice. Barret's attention wheeled in all directions, his focus between the authorities and the voice bounding from wall to wall. Erik had complete control over total chaos. Pistols swung wildly in every direction, hands too shaky and minds too deluded to pull any triggers.

Erik laughed again. Was there no way for him to escape the arrogant stupidity of the feebleminded?

"Confused, Messieurs? I am right here. Who wants first try?" Erik stepped into view. Spreading his long arms he arrogantly swaggered down the center of the aisle, his sights set on Richard Barret.

"Nothing to say Monsieur?" Erik asked him. "Your Phantom has arrived."

"I intend to take what is mine and leave," Richard croaked, leveling his pistol on Erik. "Don't follow me."

Erik moved down the center of the aisle toward them all, aware his eyes glowed menacingly like the flames of hell. Knowing his voice was his supreme weapon; Erik changed the timbre, his words exploding through the building like deadly bolts of lightening, drawing the attention of everyone. "You cannot take what is not yours, Monsieur!"

Not even a beast as powerful as a stallion was saved from the awesome monstrosity of Erik's anger. A shrill neigh rent the air as a stall door exploded open, Erik whirling around toward the sound. Behind him, massive horseflesh thundered out of the stall, the force of the startled stallion dragging Anna with it. Reins yanking out of her hand, Erik's heart nearly stopped beating as she tumbled into the aisle. Curling into a ball was the only thing sparing her from the thrashing hooves. The horse bolted down the aisle.

"Erik!" Anna screamed, as the horse charged toward its

unsuspecting victims.

The horse raced past him. Erik followed, storming down the length of the stable, his long strides rapping out a drum beat on the wood floor drowned out only by the thunderous hoofs. He followed behind the charging horse as those in its path scattered out of the way. Richard spun to the side in time to dodge the frantic horse. His doing so momentarily separated him from Christine and tossed him to the ground, his pistol skidding across the slick hay and out of his reach. As the horse galloped past Raoul, he wasted no time, seizing on the distraction. He ran toward Christine, spinning her into his arms. Richard rolled to his feet and grabbed for the other pistol in his waistband, but came up empty. Slipping and sliding on the hay, Barret's head whipped from where that pistol landed. Erik watched him look to Raoul and Christine and Legard and his gendarmes before Barret's face turned a vicious shade of red and he took off running.

Erik dove for him as he bolted by, but Barret ducked passed him. Tucking into a roll before he hit the flood didn't spare him red-hot pain that raced up his injured arm. Scrambling to his feet, Erik's world filmed red as Barret ran past Anna, catching her arm as she turned to flee. Given no choice, she was dragged down the length of the carriage house tight at his side.

The edges of Erik's vision narrowed with wrath, as all he saw was Anna. A great rush of energy overcame any pain and all control as Erik gave in to the monster inside of him.

He would not have Anna harmed…

He would not have her in fear of her life…

He would not have Anna taken from him…

Consumed with fury, Erik took off in pursuit of Barret. The roar of emotion released from the depths of his soul trembled through Paris and shook the very bowels of the opera house. Though Legard's warning shot whizzed over his shoulder, it did nothing to slow Erik. He was consumed with one target and one alone.

Anna dug her heels into the ground, anything to slow her father. She fought his grip, clawing at his hands and kicking out at his legs. Her size hindered her efforts. Her father dragged her around the sharp corner at the far end of the stable, hurling both of them into the carriage bay. Unsure in the dim light of the unfamiliar stables, he stumbled to a stop.

As he slipped, Anna threw herself against him.

Ramming her shoulder into his side as hard as she could, she knocked him off balance offering her the opportunity to run. She turned up and down aisles of waiting carriages at a breakneck pace, increasing her distance between her and her father with every pivot. This was the only time Anna was ever glad to be in the carriage bay. They had made great hiding spots from Jacob in the past and now provided the perfect barrier between her and her father. Anna's vision blurred from the exertion. She leaned back against an old carriage, gasping for breath, working to cool fire in her lungs.

Footsteps slapping against the floor forced her up, but a sharp cramp knocked her sideways. She grabbed at the stitch in her side, stumbling forward when a hand came from behind, sliding around her waist. Her breath hitched as she was pulled tightly against a solid chest. A second hand emerged to slowly brush the hair from her neck.

"Anna, don't make a sound."

She did as the voice bid. Taking a deep and cleansing breath, she melted into her calm. The peace rushed over her like a steady rain, washing her free of any fear, before she bucked backward with every ounce of strength she had. Her fist made prime contact with Richard's groin.

"Bitch!" he growled.

Anna scrambled away, but he gained the upper hand as she lost her footing on the slick hay. The carriage rocked with the impact as Richard, gnashing his teeth, shoved her against the carriage wheel. Anna grunted as it jammed into her lower back.

"I've had enough of you, Anna. It's bad enough you've ruined my life, must you ruin my fun as well?"

She caught her breath enough to spit in his face. Anna's face whipped sideways, bright streams of light shooting in her vision as his backhand split her lip

"You always were a spirited one, so bold with everyone, yet so easy to manipulate when it comes to me. Move." Richard commanded.

Anna turned to look him in the eye as the salty taste of her blood coated her lips. Richard smiled. That possessive, belittling smile she always hated as a child. Over her dead body would she go anywhere with him again. Hatred welling, Anna struck out with a blow of her own, his skin catching under her nails as she raked his face.

A satisfying scream of pain flew out of his mouth seconds before he pinned her to the side of the carriage.

"Tell me, strumpet." Richard's mouth foamed with anger; spittle flew from his lips. "Where is your Phantom fellow now?"

"I hate you."

"No you don't. You adore me. Don't you feel it, Anna? The thrill of the con? The allure of days gone by?"

His hand wrapped around her neck. Anna shut her eyes at the proximity of his cruel grin.

"That's right, refuse to look at me. It only makes this more exciting. You know how I love a challenge. A secluded spot, the authorities hot in pursuit. It makes the need become great indeed."

Vomit filled her mouth making Anna cough and lurch to the side. Keeping her eyes closed was the closest thing she had to death, and any darkness was better than trying to block out her father and his arousal hard against her hip.

The impact of that fist across Anna's face rocked through him as Erik slid to a stop in time to see a trickle of blood slide down her mouth. He moved slowly, nary making a sound. His fury closed the distance between him and Barret. That familiar need to kill rolled in his gut, churning his blood with vengeance.

The man's hands touched places they shouldn't. His mouth uttering words no loving father would ever say to his daughter.

"I dare say," Richard crooned, "that Phantom's not your type."

Erik roared. Fueled by red-hot anger, he wrenched Richard off Anna, flinging him across the bay with superhuman strength. Richard flew into the far wall. The board cracked with his impact. Erik pinned him, one hand digging into his miserable neck.

A Punjab lasso would have been more efficient, elegant and impersonal. But Erik desired to watch this. He wanted to see the terror in Richard's eyes, hear him struggle for breath, his hands clawing at Erik's cold flesh. He wanted to see the bastard's draining flesh. Erik needed the satisfaction of choking every last contemptible piece of life out of him.

Richard flailed. Erik shook with the effort it took to crush his windpipe. The quiver in his stomach grew urgent. Richard thrashed and kicked, and it wasn't until his neck was purple did Erik have enough of seeing his face. He threw him to the floor and reached for his silk rope. With a quick stroke, Erik coiled it around Richard's neck.

"She is *precisely* my type."

And with two sharp twitches and a loud snap, Richard Barret went slack.

THIRTY-FOUR

"Stop! Murderer!"

The vicomte's voice buzzed in Anna's ear as she wrenched her gaze off the grotesque angle of her father's neck and down the length of the carriage house. She staggered from her spot as the carriage room filled with gendarmes, trailed by the vicomte and his wife.

Anna struggled to hear anything over the thumping of blood in her ears. Her face went ice cold, her hands heavy at her sides. People with furrowed brows and angry expressions were racing in their direction, but for Anna, time stood still.

She moved from her spot against the carriage wheel, around the crumpled body at her feet and collapsed against the wall. The rough wood of the wall pulled at her hair as her knees gave up their strength. Seated against the wall, her palms dampened with sweat as she grasped fistfuls of hay trying to hold onto something other than the shock racing through her body. Erik placidly coiled the rope out of sight and back on his hip. His mask showed no expression, but his mouth had drawn to a tight line. He straightened to his full height and walked toward her, his every move dripping with zero remorse. Anna looked up to stare into the unfeeling eyes of the Angel of Death.

They show like twin suns in the dim light. On a shaking breath she turned to the bloodshot eyes of Richard Barret. The burn of that devil's words still echoed in her ears. Her lips were still salty with blood from the crack of his backhand. Somewhere close she heard Legard barking orders and the vicomte voicing his rage, but Anna seemed trapped in a long tunnel where all she saw was Erik's hands on her father's neck. Her gaze moved up Erik's legs as he stooped in front of her until she met his mask and unemotional stare.

The man had killed. In front of her eyes, he'd taken her father's life as if it had meant nothing.

She'd understood now, the terror he'd brought to the Paris Opera House years ago. Witnessed that murderous vengeance he kept in constant check. Met the demon he battled with every waking moment.

Felt Erik's madness.

Glancing down, her father's eyes had grown redder. Coughing into the hay, Anna vomited as Erik moved and blocked the sight of her father with his body, his stance unrepentant.

Anna wiped her mouth and winced at the acid left burning in her mouth. Time seemed to stand still for her but she knew, as the sound of the drumming of feet grew closer, that the world was spinning fast around her.

Legard shouted this time, forcing Anna's shock away. Palm over palm, she slid her way up the wall. The blaze behind his eyes had dimmed back to that gentle glow she knew so well, his mouth no longer thin and hard but drooping in a frown.

An invisible metronome ticked between them. His voice filled with an age-old sadness.

"Make your choice," he said. "I am who I am."

Anna's hand crept along the wall, knocking against the lantern hanging there. There wasn't any choice to make. The answer was obvious and had been made a long time ago when he gave her, her first real kiss. She was no stranger to life on the run and had accepted a long time ago that there was nothing in the past that she could change. But she could always change the present.

Never taking her eyes from his soul-piercing stare, she lifted it from its hook. Erik watched her, the black of his mask lit orange as the lantern light reflected against his face. Lifting it back toward her shoulder, and launching it as hard as she could, Erik didn't flinch as it flew past him. The lantern whizzed past him. Oil and fire coated the floor as it shattered, igniting the hay and sending flames leaping into the carriages. A fast and furious heat blazed around them as dry hay went up in flames. The fiery wall grew high between them and those pursing them. The air vibrated with the heat as Anna, empowered by the sudden heat around her, extended her hand to Erik.

She would set herself on the same path as he. She let her heart choose. Whatever path he would travel, Anna would share it.

His lips slipped open. Erik reached for her hand, but paused to glance through the fire over his shoulder. She followed his gaze through the waving heat and saw, as he did, the vicomtess cradled protectively in the vicomte's embrace.

Erik's eyes never left the vicomtess as he entwined his fingers around the ones extended to him. Anna's breath shook with relief as she exhaled. She would never have survived his rejection if, with that one brief look backward at Christine, he changed his mind. But as frantic shouts rang out on the other side of the roaring fire Erik firmed up his grip.

Christine Daaé had made her choice. Seeing Erik's resolve to leave the past behind, she let him lead her into the shadows

⇒•————•••————••⇐

They stood in the shadows of the distant alley, his fingers still entwined in Anna's. The fire spread, making the primary need to get the horses to safety before the ceiling collapsed. A small army was enlisted: gendarmes, stable hands, men upon the street—it mattered not who, as long as they had a strong back and the courage to douse the flames. Sparks lit the night as the Paris streets filled with the acrid smoke swirling into the sky. A curious crowd converged on the site while horses neighed in terror, tethered a safe distance from the mayhem and men shouted among the confusion.

For a blissful moment, no one sought a Phantom.

When it was clear the chaos would keep him safely cloaked, Erik turned. "I will return." He started toward the flames.

"Are you out of your mind? You can't go back there."

"There is something I must do. I will be fine. Stay here."

"I don't have to stay here!"

"Anna, please," Erik pleaded. "There is something I need. Stay, and hold this." He shoved the bulging billfold he'd deftly lifted from her dead father's pocket at her. Anna's face contorted. Erik clenched his teeth. He'd rather see anything but that confusion on her face. The last thing he wanted was to make matters worse.

300

"And...I need you to steal a horse."

His words snapped her attention from the billfold to his face, but he could do nothing to stop her widening eyes.

The flames coiled in the night air as Legard paused to shuck his jacket. He might as well let it burn with the carriage house. The fabric was permeated with the scent of burnt wood and singed by falling ash. The carriage house would be a complete ruin, but thanks to the army of men dousing the surrounding area, the flames would mostly spare the stable portion and wouldn't touch the opera house.

Legard cursed the events leading to this mayhem. Every passing moment he lost was a moment lost in his pursuit of the Phantom. He tossed his jacket onto the footboard of a nearby landau. Every officer has that one elusive case that haunts him. He'd had a second shot at pursing the Phantom and it all went up in flames.

"Damn him!" Legard rammed his fist sideways into the carriage door. He bit back on his anger when the vicomte approached, his expression grim as he brushed ash from his jacket.

"It's over, vicomte." The words were sour in his mouth.

"For this evening it's over." Raoul replied.

Legard stared at the fire. "You're going to continue this... absurd pursuit? It's useless, can't you see that? We can never win."

"Jules, in all the years I've known you, your goal has been to see justice served. Are you admitting defeat against this madman?"

"It's easier." Legard had to chew on those words before he was able to get them out. He studied the night over Raoul's shoulder. A light dusting of ash had turned the young man's blond hair a premature gray and somewhere, out there, was the fugitive responsible for both their frustrations.

"I need you, Jules. I'll not rest until I see this creature pay for what he has done to my family."

Legard huffed out a laugh and paced. "You may *have* to let it go. It's not giving up. The man hasn't broken any laws! Show me the evidence of Erik's previous crimes. Show me *proof* of any crime he committed here tonight."

Raoul snatched Legard's arm and stopped his pacing. "I could see your commission stripped for that, Inspector. We all witnessed kidnapping tonight, another murder and, arson as well."

Legard jerked his arm free. "Arson, yes, and *that* was Anna Barret's doing. Kidnapping?" Legard backed up, inches from shaking sense into Raoul. "That could be argued as part of a stage performance. Murder, a court could prove as self-defense in coming to another's aide. You saw Mademoiselle Barret and how she was dragged away by Barret. We don't know the circumstance."

"Murder is murder. Have you forgotten Wischard and Laroque?"

Damn his stubbornness! "Were they by his hand?" Legard shouted.

The air between them was thick with tension.

"You know as well as I, there are crimes of which Erik is guilty," Raoul shouted back. "So long as he's out there, this opera house is some bizarre catalyst for him." Legard ground his teeth; there was no knocking sense into the vicomte. "I made the mistake of not seeing this through once and I've lived with the guilt of that for too long, not only because of Christine but because of all the others involved."

"That's not a distinction you hold on your own." Legard bit back.

"Then do something about it!" Raoul's brows drew together. "Now *more* murders have been committed. I'm not saddened Barret is dead, but murder is still murder. Tell me you don't think Erik is guilty."

Legard stared at the swirling smoke. What he believed didn't matter without proof. He winced. This was all making a meal of his skull. "I believe he is guilty."

Raoul grabbed him by the shoulder. "You're a genuine man, Jules. I can't see this through without you. Say you'll be there for me. Say you'll be there for Christine."

The plea for help and justice behind Raoul's eyes he'd seen before. In the eyes of every victim he ever helped. Turning that look into one of hope and gratitude for the law he swore to uphold was Legard's reason for living. He let out a long deep breath, his entire body heavy with exhaustion, but not about to abandon his beliefs. "I will."

"Then we continue at dawn and each dawn thereafter."

Raoul dropped his arm from Legard's shoulder and wove his way through the crowds, taking command of a cause Legard deemed lost. Grabbing his jacket, he dragged it on. He may think Erik guilty but the courts…the courts were another matter. Legard rubbed a hand down his face, but nothing wiped him clean of this mess. He'd seen pain and disappointment rise behind the eyes of countless victims who watched the accused go free.

As he followed where Raoul led, he prayed, when the time came, that he wouldn't see that look behind his old friend's eyes.

He'd already let Chagny down once. He couldn't do it again.

Madame Giry ignored the late hour, ignored the ache in her heart—ignored everything. She thought to go to the carriage house when word of the fire reached her, but she was exhausted. Rumor had spread fast enough. The vicomte and his wife were safe and Richard Barret was dead… at the hands of the Phantom.

The Phantom.

That name was once again being whispered in hushed undertones, trembling through the opera house halls and shivering through the streets. All the years of secrecy, evaporating like the shadow himself. Madame Giry stared into a mirror on her wall and touched her face. Her gaze moved across new wrinkles, her hand touching a strand of hair that was grayer than before. She stopped looking for signs of her exhaustion when a figure appeared in the mirror over her shoulder.

"You're safe," she said on a heavy sigh to Erik's reflection.

He nodded.

"You're leaving, aren't you?"

He nodded again.

"Where will you go?"

"I do not know," he remarked, his voice still holding that quiet authority. "But this time it is clear I cannot remain here. I need you to tend to my opera house."

"What of Anna?"

"She… she wishes to come with me."

Madame Giry nodded at the sudden insecurity she heard in his voice." Good. Good," she replied, as she rubbed her hands together. Even they had more wrinkles.

She followed Erik's reflection as it left the mirror and he came around to kneel in front of her. She stared down at him, her eyes wet. He'd knelt in front of her many times before, but never had she wanted hold him like one of her own.

"I owe you more than my gratitude, Madame."

Madame Giry moved to dab her cheeks with her hands, but Erik captured it in his. His long fingers contrasted vividly with her plump, stubby ones. The way he covered them was so gentle and kind, it made her heartbeat slow.

"I owe you my life and my deepest most ardent apology for everything I—"

"Erik, stop."

In all her years serving him, never had she addressed him by name. No reprimand followed, but a smile lifted his lips. Smiling back at him only caused his face to blur.

"Will you be in contact?" she asked tearfully.

"If you wish." Erik withdrew his hand and moved to where the satchel, violin and all, still lay before he had been hauled off.

"I'm glad you came back for it," she whispered.

"As am I, Madame."

He slung it over his shoulder. Madame Giry wondered if more than the bag made him heavy with sorrow.

"Monsieur, wait." Madame Giry rushed across the room and returned, draping Erik's opera cloak across his arms. "For when you reclaim your theater."

She cleared her throat on the crack of her voice and wiped a tear that fell free, Trying to fight the fountain of emotions the Opera Ghost commanded at his will was impossible.

"You have always been a faithful servant, Madame, and a silent friend even if it was my bitterness which prevented it from being pursued." Erik brushed away a tear with his thumb. "*Merci, mon ami.*"

With those words he disappeared as quickly as he'd appeared. For one final time, she marveled at how indistinguishable Erik was between the shadows and the opera house. Touching the chilled echo of his hand upon her cheek, for the first time, she'd felt the gentleman she'd always known him to be.

Anna wiped the cut on her lip from where her father had hit her and glanced down at her trembling hand. Wood smoke stung her nose as billows of steam wound their way into the air in the distance as the flames came under control. She'd caused such mayhem? She thought acts of destruction were behind her, but it seemed tonight proved the past couldn't be outrun. The stolen horse stood tethered out of sight. Stealing the beast was—to her at least—a much lesser offense.

"Anna?"

"Erik." Anna sighed in relief. "I was getting worried. Where did you go?"

"Saying goodbye to an old friend."

"The opera house or Madame Giry?"

He didn't answer, but the way he reached for her hand, as if his arms had been carrying too heavy of a burden for too long, spoke volumes. "Come, we need to make our way out of here."

Anna took one last look at the havoc they'd unleashed, thankful it at least let them go unnoticed. They were only a few paces out of the alleyway, when a backlit figure moved into their view.

"You can't leave," the vicomtess said.

Erik's grip on her hand tightened, making Anna skip a step.

"I do not see as I have much choice this time, Christine," he replied. "Do you intend to turn us in?"

"What good would that do? Either way you will find a means to leave."

"If you truly wish to help," Erik said, "then tell your vicomte the truth. Tell him what Anna did in that labyrinth to *save* you."

Erik was asking the impossible; Anna could see it behind the vicomtess' eyes. The woman refused to look at her.

"Tell him the truth?" the vicomtess stammered. "What is that, Erik? It has been twisted in me for so long I don't understand it anymore."

"The truth, Christine?" Erik parroted, dropping Anna's hand and moving toward the vicomtess. "The truth is that I kept my word, then and now. I let go of you. I allowed you to move on without my interference. I allowed you to choose your life. The fact that you cannot accept the choices you made, or that you now wish to choose differently is not my concern." When Erik turned and walked back toward Anna, she saw the vicomtess look away until Erik spun around. "There is one critical point you must remember." The strength behind his voice backed the vicomtess up a step. "*You* returned to *me*. *You* came back into *my* life. I did not return to yours."

"You came back into my life the instant you rose from the dead," the vicomtess retaliated.

"I did not do that to come back into your life. I did that to come back into *mine*. You will never be able to fully understand the man that lies behind this mask."

"Was I permitted the chance?" she asked boldly, shoving her way between Erik and Anna. Anna cocked her jaw and stepped around her back to Erik's side. "Don't abandon me to tread unrealized waters alone, Erik. I'm drowning in a whirl of affection I hold for *two* men, and I can't swim. You're responsible, in part, for this charade between us. You can't just walk away."

"Let me, Christine," Erik snapped. "You had your choice long ago."

Erik pressed his hand to the small of Anna's back and urged her to walk. He didn't move to follow, making Anna fear his reasons as to why. There was as much anger in his voice as there was sadness, and anger fueled by that could easily be swayed. She stopped a few paces away, dread welling from her stomach.

"All I asked you for was love." Erik's voice was passionate. "That is all I asked from anyone. All I desired was a chance—one chance—to be equal among men when it came to the simplest need. I wanted to be loved for *myself*, but no one allowed me to prove who I could be. I gave you the only thing in my life that loved me in return. That never denied or betrayed me. I gave you my *music*—my soul."

Anna turned in time to see Erik jab a finger toward his mask.

"I cannot take back this face!" he yelled. "I cannot exchange the atrocities of my past. Nor can I risk madness any longer by trying to rotate my life to make my imperfections fit with you."

The vicomtess jolted backward when he indicated her. All Anna saw was outrage and shock. She prayed insecurity didn't show on her own face.

"I cannot change to suit a world that will not have me. I am a product of what society has made me to be, what rejection caused me to be." Erik thumped at his chest with a fist. "I have lived too long in a dark and unhappy world, pouring everything I desired into music—hoping someone would unravel the melody and listen. I thought you had. But you only heard what you wished to hear."

The vicomtess stood paralyzed under Erik's impassioned plea. Anna held her breath, praying the woman wouldn't plea for Erik to return.

"When it came time to choose, Christine, you chose to love *your* ideal and *my* music," Erik continued. "That destroyed me. My music is the one thing that, once given, could never be taken back."

Anna heard the vicomtess swallow as Erik stopped talking, but the diva kept her stance stiff. He stared at the night sky, his eyes glowing in search of something Anna didn't think he found. When he studied the vicomtess again, his eyes had dimmed with a weighty sadness.

"The melodies I composed, the ones reflecting the man beneath the mask are complex. If you had truly listened, and if I had known how to allow you to do so back then, you would have heard the counterpoint." Erik's voice grew serious as he partially turned from the vicomtess. "I told you once, I will tell you again, so you can move on as I. I want to live like anybody else. I do not want to be left to weep alone."

Erik stormed down the alley, his hand shooting out behind him as he passed Anna. Anna reached for him, relief, at first, sagging out in her sigh but being dashed away when her hand grabbed empty air as Erik whirled around again.

"You can still my breath, Christine. But for all our carefully woven illusions and lies, we cannot find what we need to complete each other. Forget me." He swept the air in front of him with his arm. "Forgive me for the past and what I put you through. You will always hold a piece of my heart. I will *always* love you."

Anna wrapped her arms tight around her shoulders, shielding herself from Erik's heartbreaking confession as he kept speaking.

"But I am seeking the missing part of me. My *happiness*."

Anna's heart squeezed when he stormed by her this time without reaching for her hand.

"Erik," she called, but he refused look at her. She was certain the pain coiling his stance was not from the wound in his arm.

Anna glanced backward toward the opera house, where the vicomtess stood against the glowing embers and dying flames. A profound ambivalence shone behind the vicomtess eyes as she watched Erik mold himself into the night. Erik's strides grew longer with each step. The farther he moved away, the more Anna's world spun. Did he or did he not want her?

His pace quicken into a jog. Anna stopped breathing. Erik didn't turn around again but reached backward with his hand, his fingers outstretched behind him.

Anna couldn't make her feet move fast enough as she raced toward him. Taking one glance behind her, the vicomtess' eyes had leveled upon her and carried all the jealousy and hatred in the world.

THIRTY-FIVE

They stopped in a dusty vagabond's camp far on the outskirts of Paris. The jumble of misfits cluttered around campfires, their only goal for that night to look out for one another. For Erik, the camp had the faint echo of his years spent wandering from fair to fair.

The night they intruded upon was a lively affair of shared meals, music and dance. Vulgar music at that. Nothing like the opera or arias he'd spent his life crafting. It seemed in these outlets no one had a past. The idea of such was nothing more than an obsolete narration of days gone by.

The fire Anna built added to the winking lights of the camp. Off in the distance the fires of other travelers twinkled like fireflies. With the smell of ash and smoke on his clothing, it seemed like Paris was closer than it was.

In his lifetime, he'd committed a number of atrocities that caused him to live like a fugitive. But no horror seemed as unsettling as the final way he'd bid his beloved Paris goodbye. Every time he fled his sins, Erik managed to find some place to settle where his word became law. None was quite as comfortable as the Opera Garnier. No place was as steeped in music, as yielding to his creative genius, as safe from the persecuting and judging eyes of man—or as close to Christine.

And no place so foreign as where he was now.

A shower of sparks caught his eye. Anna had tossed another

log on the fire. She hadn't said a thing to him in an unbearably long time. Taking a deep breath, he faced her.

"You are cross with me."

Anna threw another log and bent to stoke the flames. "I'm not cross. Now take off your shirt."

"Mademoiselle!" Erik crossed his arms. That fire had burned away her senses. "I most certainly will not!"

Her face puckered unpleasantly, a clear indication he'd tipped her temper. That anger she claimed she didn't have vibrated the air between them.

"You're still bleeding. Unless you want every four-legged animal following us as well, you need to rinse that shirt."

Her curt nod directed his attention toward the brook. Blood seeped through both bandage and shirt. He'd managed to ignore the pain over the last few hours. Seeing the blood made it all too real again. Jaw tight, he winced as he peeled off his shirt. Flesh stuck to blood-soaked fabric.

Thankfully, Anna ignored him. He felt so self-conscious and vulnerable when his torso was exposed. The fact that she ignored the ugly scars and gruesome flesh eased his concerns. He stared toward Paris again, wringing the blood out of his sleeve. He swallowed a grunt of pain. Fresh blood broke through the barrier of Anna's bandage and seeped from the wound. The icy water he splashed on his shoulder and arm hit him like a thousand tiny stones. He forced the pain from his mind and picked at the areas of dry blood, fearing the water in the brook was turning crimson.

"Come here," Anna demanded.

If she wasn't mad, then her voice certainly didn't say so. He turned slightly. "Erik will not."

"Erik."

"Erik does not wish to."

"Get over here now!"

Lest he scorn her more, he moved to her, laying the shirt before the campfire to dry. Usually she wasn't this sullen. She stoked the fire with the blade of the knife and indicated he should sit.

He did, though hesitantly. "Why are you so angry?"

Anna sliced the blade she'd been tending through a coal.

"I'm not angry. I'm overwhelmed. Now sit still."

Erik followed the glowing knife as she removed it from the fire. Its fire lit the determination on her face.

"Why?" The red-hot blade quivered with heat.

"Why? *Why?* Over the last several days I have been thrust into a situation I still can't figure out. I'm a fugitive—again—having taken part in events beyond my comprehension. I've left behind the Paris streets, the only place I've ever called home, where there are people who will be wondering where I am." Anna glanced in the direction of Paris, her eyes hard agates when she looked back at him. "Good portions of the French authorities pursue me as an accomplice for kidnapping, robbery and murder over events that apparently span both past *and* present. I burned down a carriage house, stole a vicomte's prized stallion, and you ask me why?"

Anna's shout clipped the air as Erik took a good, hard look at the horse resting nearby. Erik's smile flashed, then dropped when he turned and saw her expression hadn't changed

"On top of all that," she continued, "I watched you kill my father, so please, *do* pardon me if the I'm a little overwhelmed! Not to mention, I'm traveling this path with a man who I'm fairly convinced loves another woman more than I initially estimated."

Erik couldn't meet her eyes as Anna positioned herself beside him. She had a way of always seeing the truth. He winced as she jerked off his bandage.

"Here. Bite on this. Hard." She shoved a stick in his face.

"No."

"Erik, do it!"

"I said no!"

The finality in his voice could have knocked the stars from the heavens. Whatever pain was to come…he deserved it. He had put her through far too much. She had every right to feel what she did. Anna didn't argue with him further and he didn't provoke her. He recognized a stalemate when he saw one. She snatched his bicep. He jolted, schooling any reaction.

"Are you ready?"

Erik swallowed. No, he wasn't ready and he regretted ever suggesting the idea. Anna grew deathly quiet as she sat there, knife in position. He glanced at it, fighting down a wave of panic. Under the circumstances it was the only way to treat his wound. Cauterization would clean and seal them—thus stanch the bleeding—but the pain…

"Just do it," he whispered, looking away.

He barely had a chance to compose himself before he arched

and screamed into a white-hot pain that ripped open every nerve in his body. The air hissed as metal scorched flesh. Two more times the knife moved. He bucked backward and shoved Anna to the ground.

The bottomless pit of agony radiated down his arm and shot fire out his fingers. The scent of burning flesh turned his stomach. Erik sucked in deep gulps of air as he rolled to his feet. His world spun out of control and if not for the tree he collapsed against, he would have hit the ground in peaceful blackness.

He clawed and punched at the bark of the tree until seared flesh waned to a tolerable level. He pushed off and jerked his arm several times, trying to throw off the burn.

"I'm sorry," Anna apologized. "I... I don't know if I did that right... but the bleeding had to stop. I'm sorry, Erik!"

Erik nodded through clenched teeth unable to offer much else of comfort through the pain. Anna sighed and cut a swath of cloth from the hem of her dress. Taking the long piece off and dabbing out her smoldering hemline, she indicated for Erik to sit once more. This time she bound his wound with greater care.

"We'll need to find some cleaner cloth," she mused. "The first house we come across I'll steal what clothing I can find for bandages and get you a new shirt. We'll bury the old one. They will probably come after us with dogs..."

She seemed so tired as her voice trailed off. "I did not want this, Anna. There are things that one cannot control. My past will always be a part of me. There is no escaping it. What would you have me do?"

Anna kept her focus on his arm.

"I do not love her like I once did." Erik hissed as she tightened his bandage. Perhaps it was purposeful. "Not in the same way," he added, though he recalled the moments in the labyrinth. He dared not confess the feelings he knew Christine held for him. He tossed a stray twig into the flames and watched it shrivel to ash.

She sighed weakly. "It has been a long journey, for all of us."

He'd rather not think about it.

The fire cracked, breaking the silence. No matter how far they'd run from Paris in one night, it was his final words to Christine that chased him. What was happiness? It was something he wove an intricate web to catch, but then never feasted upon the rewards. Christine had been his world. Anna was so very different.

Anna smoothed down his bandage making sure it was tight. Physically he'd heal, but what of the scars ripped open by the past? Wasn't he destined to be with Christine? That is what he'd thought for so many long and lonely years.

Long and lonely.

He was tired of lonely thoughts, lonely conversation, and a lonely bed. Christine had Raoul, the source of some form of happiness for her. Couldn't he have his? Could he be happy hunted by the Vicomte de Chagny and the woman they both loved?

Feeling disjointed and out of place in a world he couldn't control, he gave up figuring out how he came to be at a vagabond camp smelling of smoke, ash and blood. Instead, he concentrated on the woman beside him. Erik fidgeted. The more his feelings for Anna surfaced, the more foreign they seemed. He became self-conscious without his shirt.

"Stop fussing," she said. "You're making this difficult."

"Erik wants his shirt."

"It's wet, you'll catch the death. Erik, stop moving! What's the *matter* with you?"

"Anna, please." He pulled his arm away, and folded them protectively around his chest.

She opened her mouth to say something, but then fell silent. Through the orange glow the fire cast against her face, he saw her cheeks pink.

"Forgive me, Erik. I didn't mean to make you uncomfortable. I had to—"

"You had to do what you had to do." Vulnerability gnawed at his nerves as he drew his arms tighter. "Now you understand all the ugly reality as to why I live as I do."

Why wasn't she looking away? Damn her, she should be looking away!

"Go ahead." He indicated his arm. "Looking at me to tend my wound is one thing, looking on in morbid curiosity is another. But by all means continue if you must."

She continued.

Their eyes met briefly before she lowered her gaze. Erik knew the unjust ugliness he was built with extended beyond a mask. He'd hoped Anna would have reacted differently upon realizing this, but rest of the world was repulsed with him, why shouldn't she be?

"Erik." Anna looked down only long enough to reach for his

hand before looking him back in the eye. "I see nothing but a strong and capable man."

He stared at their intertwined fingers before looking into the campfire. He couldn't understand why she accepted him as she did, but as her small fingers wove so easily with his, Erik knew he wanted to spend the rest of his life finding out why. Silence settled between them as Anna prodded gently at the fire. Lifting an orange tipped stick, she gestured east.

"*Österreich*," she teased, her eye twinkling as they reflected the firelight.

"What about it?" If she was toying with him right now, he was not amused.

"You're not the only one with a colored past, Erik. Austria, remember?"

"I recall a distant conversation about you being…German." The word tasted bad in his mouth and had since the war.

"Austrian, there's a difference. You'll like it there."

Like it there? She'd gone madder than him! Erik shot his brows up, leaning away from her and those words. "Absolutely not! I cannot, and I will not speak German—"

"Austrian."

"—it is a boorish, horrid language. I dare say there is no music to it!"

Erik scowled as her laugher tumbled around him. "The language is beautiful, Erik. Besides, France is out at the moment."

She had a point. They couldn't roam France. He rubbed his arm trying to push the idea off of him.

Anna nudged him with her shoulder "We best get some rest. We'll need to move as soon as this camp breaks."

Erik nodded as she spread out the coals of the fire like she'd likely done a thousand times in her life. The woman was a complete marvel, confident and capable. Erik wondered if she knew her own strength. She spent her life on the run, just as he had for years. She recognized the madness in him, and wasn't repulsed by it. She could look on his hideous face and not turn away. She made him laugh, thrilled his mind and made him experience feeling he never knew existed. Most of all, she silenced the ever present noise in his mind and brought him peace.

Anna finished the fire and leaned down, giving him a peck on the soft leather of his mask. Erik couldn't contain his want to know more. He abruptly shifted, catching her in his arms and rolling her across his lap.

A small cry of shock escaped her lips, seconds before he captured them with his own. She relaxed the instant he held her close. The warmth of her body and the exquisite softness of her lips filled him with a blissful intoxication. Nothing else mattered but the feeling of her against him. Erik groaned as she slid a hand behind his neck. Her skin was hot against him; he'd never known anything as blazing as her touch. When Anna pulled him deeper into the kiss, Erik's pulse quickened. He wanted more. Wanted to lay her backward and explore every place his lips could find. He wanted her body against all of him and wanted her now....

"No," he gasped, jumping to his feet.

Anna rolled from his lap, bracing herself to keep from falling into the coals. "Erik?"

He circled the campfire, rubbing his temple, trying hard to stop the tingling in his lips and body. With Anna staring at him confused and never more beautiful to him, he had a hard time keeping his breath even.

"Anna, I cannot."

"You can't—what?"

Groaning, he pushed his palms to his eyes, trying to maintain control. He wanted nothing more than to show her exactly how much she had command of him, but the timing was all wrong. This was not how he'd envisioned such desire and passion to be roused in him. Not like this, not here, not in this way. How could he make her understand?

"I... you..."

It was no use; he couldn't find the words to explain. Anna studied him out of the corner of her eye, the confusion on her face slaying him a thousand times over.

Erik sighed and knelt next to her. Her cheek and lip were bruised. They'd most assuredly be purple by morning. The burn on her temple had turned a fiery shade of red and her untamed hair was sooty from ash.

You've been through so much for me.

Each bruise and scar defined a fit woman capable of taking care of herself. But her eyes drove Erik mad, for there was nothing simple in the way they questioned him; nothing simple in how they absorbed the details of every moment to lock them away as some memory to be recalled later. Desire tightened his stomach and staring at her like this made it hard to fight the urge to act on it. Anna raised an eyebrow. Her expression begged him to finish his sentence.

"Anna, you ignite in me a passion unlike any I have ever felt," he blurted. "There are certain desires..."

Erik balled his hands into fists to control the surging in his body. Why was this so hard to say?

"Desires that I have had before but... have never fully acted upon."

Anna reached for his hand, her touch putting him on fire. "Erik, I—"

"Anna, listen." He had to get this out, and damn it all she was not making it easy. "Never have I felt so complete of a man than when I am with you. I want nothing more than to love you with the ardor and intensity I have only dreamed of, but I cannot. I cannot put you through that."

He took a deep breath, as he glared into the dying fire. The flames blurred before him as he prayed hard she wouldn't reject him. He wasn't going to force her to endure him, not with how furiously he wanted her.

"What are you telling me?" she asked, rejection edging into her voice.

Erik spoke unblinking toward the fire. "Men have always taken whatever they want from you. They have used you to play out their lust." Those moments he knew of, though few, repulsed him. "Anna, I want you with every part of me, but I am afraid that I will do something wrong, that I will move too fast that I will..." Erik rubbed at the noise in his mind that grew at the mere thought. "I fear my inability to control all I feel; that I will be like them. I will not do that to you. I cannot make you revisit those places—not ever. Not after all you have been through and all I have witnessed."

Would she be willing to stay with him if he refused her in such a way? It was a sacrifice he would make for her honor a thousand times over. The crack of the fire was the only sound until Anna's tears joined the popping wood. She reached for his hands and lowered them from his temple.

"Erik, those men didn't want what you do. They wanted to hurt me. They did hurt me." Erik squeezed her hands. If he could take away that pain from her life he would. Anna squeezed him back.

"You want ...to love me. There is now way you can be like them."

"I am not a normal man. I do not wish to hurt you with my love. There are ways a gentleman should behave before a lady and as much as I try... I... I never know when..." Erik tapped his head, damning the madness inside of him. The words wouldn't come. As much as he tried—he knew he was different. "Do not make this seem so simple, Anna. Nothing between us is simple."

"We're both naïve, Erik. I've never experienced what you most desire either. I want to live like anybody else, too."

She reached to him and pulled the one pathetic strand of hair out of his face. Erik shuddered as her fingers skimmed his mask, her hands capable of sending pulses deep throughout his body.

"Everything is still so raw," she whispered. "When the time is right—and if you still wish me—I'll be here, waiting. I've waited my whole life for you."

Anna's eyes brimmed with tears as she lifted one shoulder. She glanced down to the fire briefly and it was long enough that Erik didn't want her to ever look away again. He was finally loved for himself, and he never wanted to see anything else but those beautiful tears that Anna batted away.

She had waited her whole life—for *him*.

"Anna." He wanted to say her name. To hear it on the air. To feel it on his lips. To see her reaction to it in her eyes. "I never had a reason for living beyond my music." Erik stripped the mask from his face and swiped at his eyes with his hand.

"I thought I had found my reason in Christine. But she was not my reason for living. She was my distraction from dying." Anna's sigh and her newly found tears reached deep into his soul as she laid a hand on his thigh. He gestured with the mask they both stared at. "My past filled me with such sorrow, my face with such bitter loathing. I buried all hope that joy existed. Instead I created a life filled with illusions and fantasy and tried so hard to make them fit together." Erik set the mask aside letting the silence between them wash a peace over him before continuing. "I never imagined the one perfect fit for my life would be the one illusion I did not create. I saved something from each time I knew you were the answer to my dreams."

Reaching into his pocket, he pulled out the shattered remnant of an inkbottle, a once perfect piece of china and a shard of a mirror. Anna's mouth slipped open, the slightest wrinkle on her brow.

When she reached out to touch them, Erik palmed them together, his slight of hand making them slip out of sight before her eyes.

Anna gasped.

"If I had known I could one day have the most exquisite dream and not fear waking, I would not have poisoned my life with regrets. Anna—" Erik slid his ring from his pinky, scarcely able to breath at the sight of her. She followed every move his hand made, each time she glanced into his unmasked face; she made another tear fall from his eyes. "In you I find my beauty. I am not afraid of living. The moment you hugged my violin and learned my Madrigal—you held *me*. And it is in those arms I wish to die. If you will have me... I will love you—ardently. When you fall asleep at night, it is my eyes that close. When you breath, my body fills. You are all in this world that is worth living for." Erik glanced from his ring to her tear filled eyes. "Be my reason, Anna. Complete me?"

The breeze carried her sigh of yes and swirled it around the camp. Erik didn't wait for the breeze to carry her sigh of 'yes' around the camp. He glided the ring onto her finger and dragged her into his arms, coating the nape of her neck with his tears.

"Je t'aime avec tout mon cœur. Je t'adore."

He cared not where their travels would lead; so long as he had his Anna he had music.

THIRTY-SIX

There are steps to acceptance, the first being an awareness of one's past. And though nothing can be brought back from it, through acceptance, the past can be transcended. Had I been the purveyor of such wisdom years ago I would not have lived sedated by an ethereal black pool of misbegotten desire. If I had known my past would be embraced, I would have been more aware of the possibility of a future—Erik

Dawn rose, as reliable as ever. As it struggled to wipe the sleep of night from the sky, Erik lifted Anna on the stallion then mounted behind her. He held her like blown glass, fearful if he didn't the previous night could be shattered and lost in an instant. Most of the wanderers headed west as the camp broke, Erik turned the stallion toward the sun. Like the rest of the indigents and vagrants, he followed only where the road would lead. Focusing straight ahead, he made no effort to glance toward Paris. With no possessions, their burdens were light even if their pasts were not. They had nothing to their names except their horse and a small satchel containing his exquisite violin, opera cloak, and an odd assortment of seemingly meaningless things.

As the day grew older, the warm sun and the rhythmic clip of the horse's hooves made Anna sleepy. Erik smiled, taking peace in the rise and fall of her breaths. He relished the feeling of his arms wrapped contentedly around her waist.

There was music filling his mind. Erik swayed to the symphony he heard. He sighed at the sensation of her body against his chest as the sway of the horse moved her in rhythm to the patter of the hooves.

A louder clip of a less elegant steed came up beside them bringing the music in Erik's mind to a grinding halt. Anna stiffened and turned toward the gray haired old man trotting beside them.

"Good day, little lady," he said to Anna tipping an imaginary hat. "Mind if an old traveler shares the road?"

"Quite, Monsieur," Erik snapped, turning to look at the man head on, none to happy to have had his music interrupted.

"Good God! What's with the mask?" the old man blurted.

Tension shot an arrow straight up Erik's spine. He clicked to the horse and urged him into a faster trot. The old man was not deterred.

"Oh, come on, old chap. I didn't mean anything by it. Everyone has a story. It defines who we are and makes the journey ahead more interesting."

Erik yanked the reins, jolting Anna and sharply wheeling the stallion around. The horse danced nervously with the sudden change in his master's temperament. Anna twisted around to look at him, her eyes urging calm. Erik took his cue. He lifted Anna's palm to his lips and let his kiss linger. Pressing her hand to his chest, he turned the stallion in a small circle. The horse's hooves drummed to the staccato beat of his voice.

"My story? I am a murderer: a murderer and a Maestro, a magician and a mastermind. I have slept in the far corners of hell with my face as my shackle and my voice my only respite. I have dreamed of beauties far beyond the reaches of earthly imagination only to be held hostage to the nightmares of my past by the restlessness of my deranged mind. I awoke from an inhuman world to defy my fate and embrace my past because of paper, ink and figs…"

Please Enjoy this excerpt from
the next story in the Phantom series:

PURSUED

BY THE

Phantom

Coming Winter 2017

What if a demon were to creep after you one night, in your loneliest loneliness and say, 'This life which you live must be lived by you once again and innumerable times more; and every pain and joy and thought and sigh must come again to you, all in the same sequence. The eternal hourglass will again and again be turned and you with it dust of the dust!' Would you throw yourself down and gnash your teeth and curse that demon? Or would you answer 'Never have I heard anything more divine'?

—Friedrich Nietzsche

PROLOGUE

Outskirts of Paris—1885

"Leave the camp. Leave the camp!"

Her shout pierced the dawn. The barely-there slumber that blurred the forest floor when Erik opened his eyes, evaporated to a razor sharp focus as Anna burst from the tree line. A stray branch tangled in her skirts, sending her tumbling into their makeshift hideaway. Her breath came fast, and he knew from one look into her wild eyes that the pursuit was on.

"How many?" he demanded.

"Ten… fifteen…" she said on a ragged breath. Fighting to fill her lungs, she grabbed her side and kicked dirt onto the still glowing embers of the fire. "Take the horse. I'll make it on foot."

Erik scrambled to his feet. How he made it to the stallion he had no idea for his mind was moving at lightning speed. Adrenaline sent his heart pounding against his ribcage. He jerked on the reins, breaking the branch they were tied to. "You are not staying here. On the horse!"

"Don't... argue. Go—now!"

"Anna, get on the horse!"

She moved frantically around the camp in an untamed state of panic, the sound of horses' hooves pummeling the ground in their direction. They'd be on them in any second. Left with no choice, Erik cursed and swung himself up on the stallion. Agony ripped up the gunshot wound in his upper arm, but he bit down the pain and yanked the horse towards her.

"Anna. Now!" He swiped at her, but she bolted out of the way. "Anna!"

"Head east then south," she commanded, breathlessly. "They're getting closer! Go!"

They could run him down for all he cared; he was *not* leaving her behind. Erik jerked the horse back around and made toward her again.

"Erik, go! I can draw them away from you! Go!"

"I am not leaving you!" The thought twisted a knife into his gut. He wouldn't see her sacrifice herself for his transgressions again.

"Yes... you... *are!*"

The stick she swung flashed through the air, smacking hard against the horse's flank. Erik barely had a chance to firm his grip on the reins as the beast jolted forward.

"You find me!" Erik shouted over his shoulder. "Are you listening to me? They have no right to hunt us. You find me!"

The forest and trees swallowed his last glimpse of her as Anna dove into the bushes.

A loud snort burst out the stallion's mouth when Erik yanked on the reins and forced the horse up the ridge in the opposite direction. Looking behind him, the orange glow of torches joined the graying light of dawn where their camp had been. Angry shouts and beating hooves rose from the ransacked area below him.

His heart pounded, fury swelling in his chest. Safe in the cloak of thick trees, Erik searched the mayhem below. He squinted to make out her form, but he couldn't tell if Anna had made it into the safety of the brush undetected. His eyes narrowed in on one man dismounting in the center of the confusion.

A trickle of sweat snaked down his cheek below Erik's mask. Killing that son-of-a-bitch would be easy; choosing not to was much, much harder. He made a promise never to lift a hand to another man and he'd already broken it once. He wouldn't break it again.

Heart tight in his chest, he searched for Anna before reluctantly turning the horse east. If any harm came to her, he swore he'd break that promise and never regret it. With one final look down at the camp, Erik spurred the horse into a gallop, trying to cool the hatred burning through his veins.

Raoul, the Vicomte de Chagny, should consider himself a very lucky man.

About the Author

If one is going to query a publisher, Jennifer suggests not doing so in pink ink. Her first, written when she was twelve, was nothing if not colorful. Her passion lies in writing historical romances from forgotten pieces of history. In addition to her series expanding Leroux's *The Phantom of the Opera*, she writes romances set in the Regency and Victorian eras.

Writing from a tiny French nook, Jennifer admits to being country mouse with city mouse tastes and is constantly fighting to keep the little critters in line. She firmly believes in OCD awareness and organizations that support mental health research, and her books often explore such challenges. She can't pronounce pistachio, hates lollipops with gooey centers, and thinks watermelon is the spawn of the devil. Most of all, she dearly loves to laugh. When not writing she enjoys spending spends time in the kitchen with her daughter, digging through antique stores for a quirky find, and entertaining the whim of her mischievous pug. Turns out, the pug has her well trained.

If asked for her motto, Jennifer points to the following quote upon her wall: *"Because I love you, Love, in fire and blood!"* ~ Pablo Neruda

Made in the USA
Middletown, DE
20 January 2019